$5.00 FEE PLUS FULL PRICE
FOR EACH ITEM LOST

S0-AWV-249

1000 09 056726 0 3

The Red and the Green

The Red
and the Green

IRIS MURDOCH

New York · The Viking Press

M

Copyright © 1965 by Iris Murdoch
All rights reserved
Published in 1965 by The Viking Press, Inc.
625 Madison Avenue, New York, N.Y. 10022
Library of Congress catalog card number: 65-20778
Printed in U.S.A. by The Colonial Press Inc.

To Philippa Foot

The Red and the Green

One

Ten more glorious days without horses! So thought Second Lieutenant Andrew Chase-White, recently commissioned in the distinguished regiment of King Edward's Horse, as he pottered contentedly in a garden on the outskirts of Dublin on a sunny Sunday afternoon in April nineteen-sixteen. The garden in question, secluded behind substantial walls of rough golden stone, was large, and contained two ailing but gallant palm trees. The house, a dignified villa called "Finglas," with big square windows and a shallow slate roof, was washed a light, slightly streaky blue. It was both neat and spacious, built in a style of confident "seaside Georgian" which in Ireland had felicitously continued until the beginning of the present century and after. The house and garden, the walls and palm trees, the property of the father of Andrew's fiancée, were situated in Sandycove Avenue, Sandycove, one of the bright little roads of multicoloured villas which run down to the sea from the main road which leads from Dublin out to Killiney and Bray. The road on which Finglas stood, or from which, conscious of a certain superiority over the other houses, it withdrew, was clean and very quiet, seeming always full of a grey, luminous light from the sea, which could be seen and indeed

3

heard at the foot of the hill where the road ended casually in the
water and the pavement turned into yellow rocks, folded and
wrinkled and shining with crystalline facets. The road partook,
indeed, of the hardness and cleanness of the rocks and the coldness and clearness of the water. Visible to the left, if one went
right down to the end, and visible, too, from the upper windows
of Finglas, was the bulky headland with the Martello tower upon
it, the Acropolis of the village. The headland concealed the view
of Kingstown, but from the sea's edge could be seen the folded
back arm of Kingstown pier, its terminal lighthouse rising in the
middle, seeming to end with the gaunt obelisk, happy commem-
oration of the departure from Ireland of George the Fourth.
Straight ahead, across the very light, dirty, grey-green waters of
Dublin Bay, lay the blue couchant silhouette of Howth Head, and
to its right the open sea horizon, a line of cold mauve above the
grey: whereon even now Andrew, pausing in his task, saw the
smudge on the skyline which was the approaching mail boat. In
spite of increasing activity from German submarines the mail
boats reached Kingstown with scarcely diminished regularity,
though an erratic course, adopted in the interests of safety,
brought the smudge of smoke into view at various and unpredictable points of the horizon.

The scene was, for Andrew, intensely familiar and yet dis-
turbingly alien. It was like a place revisited continually in dreams,
both portentous and fleeting, vivid to the point of necessity, but
not entirely real. Here, too, it was as if his senses worked at a half
pace, and smells of houses, rough feels of garden walls, echoes of
voices in conservatories, were spread out and enlarged into something weird, too big and too close for comfort. Andrew's family
were Anglo-Irish, but he had never lived in Ireland, although he
had spent most of his childhood holidays there. He had in fact, by
what he regarded as a somewhat tiresome accident, been born in
Canada, where his father, who had been in the insurance business,
had once spent two years. Andrew had grown up in England and
more especially in London, and felt himself unreflectively to be

English, although equally unreflectively he normally announced himself as Irish. Calling himself Irish was more of an act than a description, an assumption of a crest or picturesque cockade. Ireland remained for him a mystery, an unsolved problem: and a problem which was in some obscure way disagreeable. There was, of course, the religious question. A far from devout and, in England, .an uncontentious, uninterested, almost entirely non-practising Anglican, he felt, on arrival in Ireland, his Protestant hackles rise. There was an aggressive tingling, and something deeper which was unnervingly like fear. Today was Palm Sunday, and Andrew, together with his mother and his fiancée, Frances Bellman, had attended matins at the Mariners' Church in Kingstown, On emerging from the church they had found the streets filled with those others who, streaming in far greater numbers out of their chapels, were now parading about, more slowly, more confidently, carrying palms in their hands. For them it seemed, and for their sins, Christ was even now entering Jerusalem, and their demeanour exhibited already a satisfaction, even a possessiveness, which made the congregation of the Mariners' Church, trotting more soberly homeward with averted eyes, feel unreal and perfunctory, unconnected with the great events to honour which these arrogant strollers were almost casually decked. Andrew's personal apprehension of this difference, this contrast with something gaudier, more vital, and more primitive, was heightened by the fact that a number of his Irish relations had, to the extreme, almost incredulous, horror of his mother, become Roman Catholic converts.

Andrew's father, who had died just over two years ago, had been himself a scholar *manqué*, a gentle, bookish man who had passed thoughtfully and ineffectually through life, always a little diffident and puzzled. He had wanted Andrew to be a scholar, and had been overjoyed when his son effortlessly collected a history scholarship at Cambridge in the year before the war. This achievement, however, seemed to have exhausted Andrew's academic capacities and ambitions, and he had spent an idle though not particularly riotous year at the university when the war came. He left Cambridge with the intention of enlisting, taking with him a passion for Malory and a vague ambition to become a great poet, and very little else in the way of higher education. His desire to serve his country was checked, however, at the outset by a prolonged bout of asthma, an ailment from which he had suffered intermittently since childhood. Pronounced fit at last, he had joined up in the autumn of 1915 and had been rapidly commissioned.

Andrew detested and feared horses. It was therefore, to those who knew him well, a matter of some puzzlement that he had chosen to serve in a cavalry regiment. The key to this phenomenon lay in Andrew's Irish cousins. He was himself an only child, and as such had pondered long and with fascination upon the mysterious and frightening sibling-relationship of which he was deprived. His various cousins, all of whom lived in Ireland, had served him in those long, hated and yet loved holidays of childhood as sibling-substitutes, temporary trial brothers and sisters, for whom his uncertain affection took the form of an irritated rivalry. He felt himself indubitably superior to this heterogeneous and, it seemed to him, rather uncultivated and provincial gang of young persons, always noisier, gayer, and more athletic than himself. But his superiority was rarely recognized. More often he found himself forced to play the dull one, left out of the game, not understanding the joke. This had especially been so in the matter of horses. All his cousins were natural, casual riders. They were a race of young horsemen, passing him by with the insolence of the mounted. Indeed, his earliest memories of Frances, who was herself a remote relation and had belonged to the "gang," were of a swift mounted girl, a graceful side-saddle Amazon, outdistancing him, disappearing.

So it was that Andrew's now so distressingly close association with horses had come about through a simple desire to impress his cousins. There was in it, too, though Andrew recognized this less clearly, an element of masochism. It was like his irresistible desire always to dive off the highest board in the swimming baths, although he was terrified of heights. He had, for very fear, to press close to him the object of terror. He had established his relationship with King Edward's Horse long before, in peacetime, with no other idea than that of getting some inexpensive equestrian experience. Since he could count himself for these purposes as a Canadian, he had found it easy and convenient to attach himself to this eminent and predominantly Colonial regiment. The arrival of the war converted his game into a dreadful seriousness and hoisted him with his own petard. Pride forbode any contemplation of a change of unit. And now in his dreams he found himself pursued and cornered by enormous horses wearing German uniforms.

Andrew had had a brief but entirely uneventful glimpse of France. He had completed a strenuous training at the cavalry depot at Bishop's Stortford, where at that time hard-riding Australians were arriving weekly, and in February, shortly after receiving his commission, had been sent to join C squadron of the regiment which was then stationed in exceptional luxury at the Château of Vaudricourt. When he arrived the squadron, besides enthusiastically enjoying the amenities of the Château, were mainly engaged in felling trees and building stables, and the communal aims seemed distinctly domestic rather than military. It was only later that Andrew learnt that the desire to make one's surroundings convenient and comfortable is one of the more important motives in the economy of war. After a week or so of this, the divisional mounted troops were all moved to Marthes to spend some days in the First Army training area. Here they encountered not the Germans but a devastating snow-storm, and for some time Andrew's only concern was finding dry, unfrozen places for horses. The horses survived the experience with equanimity, but Andrew himself came down with severe pneumonia and had to be shipped back to England. Pleurisy followed the pneumonia, and he crawled out of hospital at the end of March, an exhausted convalescent, told to report to the Reserve Squadron of his regiment in a month's time. More than half of that month had now elapsed.

Andrew was a confused soldier. The role of soldier was perhaps the first role in life into which he had made a positive attempt to fit. He had played the part of an undergraduate casually and, somewhat to his own surprise, not very whole-heartedly. He did not entirely like the *mores* of those who set the tone at Cambridge, and, what was perhaps a more serious matter, he lacked the money to compete with them. So he had set himself up a little defiantly and yet not very confidently as a recluse. His work had benefited little. The idea of himself as a soldier, an idea which would have been entirely repugnant to him in peacetime, was now, of course, backed up by the enthusiasm of an entire community. Yet Andrew had still not been able to draw onto him the skin of soldiery or to swagger into the part with the ease which he envied in many of his contemporaries. His *persona* as a soldier was still disparate, composed partly of childish romanticism, partly of schoolboy conscientiousness, and partly of some yet veiled adult attitude of fear and resignation. Of these perhaps the first was at present the most active, though Andrew would have blushed to admit how much his zeal depended on early impressions of the more patriotic passages of Shakespeare and a boyish devotion to Sir Lancelot.

From the details of warfare his imagination still shuddered away. A knowledge of the facts of the war in the trenches had not destroyed his attempt to make sense of it all by means of romanticism, but it had increased the quite separate and veiled area of his fear. In the snowstorm at Marthes, as on training exercises at home, it was his plodding conscientiousness that he relied upon, and he hoped that in a situation of danger it might at least serve him in lieu of courage. Whether he possessed courage was an agonizing mystery. He despised himself for being glad that the routine concern for the welfare of the horses tended to keep the mounted troops behind the front line. He could not help being relieved rather than otherwise that the concept of the cavalry charge appeared to be outmoded. But he viewed these sentiments with alarm as deep symptoms of funk. He was intensely disappointed that he had not, during his short time in France, broken his duck in this respect.

It was an additional sorrow to him that, since he had to do a soldiering trade, he had not managed to get himself into some more modern and highly mechanized unit. He was a keen amateur of wireless telegraphy and of motor cars, and at Cambridge had been much in demand as a mechanic among his wealthier car-owning companions. He had even at one time privately decided, though he never told his father this, that he would go in for motor-car design when he was through with his degree. He would have been prepared now, though with his imagination strictly switched off, to interest himself in machine guns, and he had learnt what he could at Bishop's Stortford about the Vickers and Hotchkiss guns which were there in inadequate and intermittent supply. But during his training he had spent much more time with his rifle and even with his sword, an object which had given him initial pleasure and which he now detested. At Vaudricourt he gathered that little wireless work was to be hoped for and that C squadron had not yet been issued with machine guns. The most directly warlike regimental occupation, now popular in B squadron, was something known as "bombing from horseback," which involved galloping in single file past Boche gun emplacements and hurling in Mills bombs. Andrew, who did not like the sound of this, noticed that his senior officers approved of the Mills bomb and suspected the Hotchkiss because with the former a mounted detachment could still emulate the traditional behaviour of cavalry. There was a nostalgia, among the regulars especially, for a vanished superiority, a once useful expertise; and when, one evening in the mess, young Andrew had loudly remarked, "After all, a horse is only a means of conveyance," there had been a shocked and scandalized silence.

The Reserve Squadron of the regiment had moved to Ireland the previous year, and after being stationed at Curragh had just

now moved out to Longford. It was there that Andrew was to
report at the end of his leave. Meanwhile he was trying, with a
certain amount of success, to ignore the future and to live as fully
as possible within the little world of feminine claims and pam-
perings represented by Frances and his mother. He found himself
almost loving the complex, preoccupied trivialty of the lives of
these two near and dear beings, and he stayed close to them as if
to claim the protection of some small, forlorn, yet powerful innocence. It was not only that he grasped their little world as a
contrast to "out there"; it was also that it somehow represented a
necessary defence against all the other things that Ireland meant,
the men of Ireland, his male cousins. Andrew put it to himself: I
really cannot be bothered with Ireland just at the moment. And
he had in fact put off—now disgracefully long, his mother told
him—going to visit other members of his family.

Andrew's mother had lately and precipitately decided, very
much to Andrew's dismay, to sell her London flat and move to
Ireland. The efficient cause of this decision was the Zeppelin raids
on London, which Mrs. Chase-White represented to her eager and
credulous Dublin friends in vivid, even lurid terms. Her nerves,
she claimed, could not stand it, with those Zepps always coming
over. Andrew felt extreme irritation, not only at what he regarded
as a shameful lack of stamina on the part of his parent, but also at
what he suspected to be the formal cause of her decision, an
atavistic urge to return to the soil of Ireland. Hilda Chase-White,
née Drumm, was, like her husband, Anglo-Irish; but, whereas
Andrew's father had spent most of his childhood in Ireland, Hilda
and her younger brother Barnabas had been brought up in London. Andrew was vaguely aware that his mother and his uncle
had in some way not got on with their parents, but he had never
troubled to diagnose what was wrong, nor indeed been in a position to, since his grandparents both died when he was a small
child. His maternal grandfather had been a civil servant of small
means, but well-known in his circle as a gay social man and a
party-giver. He was also by way of being a famous practical

joker. It may have been that these antics offended Hilda's sense of dignity, or it may more simply have been that she compared the London ménage unfavourably with the bigger, grander, and altogether more ceremonious houses of her Irish relations. Andrew recalled from childhood the tone of slightly querulous envy with which she spoke of these establishments: a sentiment not shared by his father who, although he retained a strong, nervous interest in his family there, and especially in his half-sister Millie, seemed always thankful to have escaped from Ireland.

The purchase, therefore, just completed, of a house in Ireland no doubt represented for Hilda the fruition of a very long-term intention; and, especially since her head was turned by the extreme cheapness of Irish properties, it was with difficulty that Andrew had persuaded her not to acquire one of several available castles, each one damper and mouldier than the last though undeniably inexpensive, and had coaxed her at last into buying a pretty and reasonably sized house in Dalkey. His Uncle Barnabas, for some long time now settled in Ireland, had been of little assistance. But, as Hilda often said, not much now could be expected of Barney. Barnabas, who had figured as notable in Andrew's childhood because he was a crack shot rather than because he was a promising mediaeval scholar, had latterly, it was generally agreed, gone to the dogs. Barnabas, too, had felt the urge, as Hilda herself put it, "to escape from the parents," though Andrew could not understand what in this case was felt as menacing. His uncle was the reverse of snobbish. But he, too, had evidently felt some imperative need to return to Ireland, had married into another branch of the family there, and, to Hilda's and indeed to Andrew's intense horror, had become a Roman Catholic. He was even, so Hilda would sometimes report in a whisper, said to be writing a history of the Irish saints, an activity which his sister found for some reason highly improper. It was, in addition, said of him that he had at one time wanted to become a priest, but Hilda would never publicly countenance this rumour. The fact that Uncle Barnabas had also apparently taken to drink was almost welcomed as a more normal manifestation of black-sheepishness.

That some of the family were converts was something which Hilda felt as a continual affront to herself. It caused her real pain, and she spoke about it as little as possible, even to the point of keeping it dark. She had been deeply wounded by her brother's defection, for, although her conception of family ties in general struck Andrew as rather worldly, she was, or had been, extremely fond of Uncle Barnabas. "The family" was a great subject with Hilda, and Andrew had become a little reluctantly interested in the matter himself, especially as he somehow found it necessary always to explain that Frances was a distant relation. The situation was complicated. "We Anglo-Irish families are so complex," Hilda used often to exclaim with a kind of pride, as if complexity in families were a rare privilege. "We're practically incestuous," his Aunt Millicent had once added. "What does that mean?" the child Andrew had asked, but no one had enlightened him. He sometimes felt now that "the family" had indeed something of the fascination of the snake that eats its own tail. He was both interested and repelled, and the sense that the family occupied or pervaded Ireland, managing to inhabit most of its corners, largely composed for him the sinister power of that island.

In fact, Andrew had in recent years seen happily little of his remoter relations who owned farms in Clare and Donegal. Frances and her father, Christopher Bellman, who had at one time lived in Galway, had now moved to Sandycove, and Andrew felt no urge, though his mother sometimes suggested it, to go on a familial tour. Dublin and its neighbourhood contained quite enough of the cousinry, and those, indeed, with whom Andrew had always had most to do. The exploration even of this branch of the family, which was needed in order to make clear his relationship with Frances, was in fact complicated enough. His paternal grandmother, Janet Selborne-Doyle, "a great beauty," as his mother always said when she was referred to, had married twice. Her first husband was John Richard Dumay, from whom she had issue two children, Brian and Millicent. Of these Brian—it was always said, whether truly or not, as a result of a nervous breakdown—had become a convert to Catholicism when still a student at Trinity. The great beauty's second marriage, after the death of her first husband, had been to Arnold Chase-White, and the one offspring of this union had been Henry Chase-White, Andrew's father. Henry married Hilda Drumm, and Brian Dumay had married one Kathleen Kinnard who was, in fact, a connection of Hilda's mother's family, and who had caused pain and scandal by forthwith adopting the religious faith of her husband. Millicent Dumay then married Kathleen's brother, Sir Arthur Kinnard, and the third sister, Heather Kinnard, married Christopher Bellman, Frances' father. Both Mrs. Bellman and Sir Arthur Kinnard had died fairly young, and Andrew could not recall having met them. His Uncle Brian had produced two sons, Pat Dumay, who was a year older than Andrew, and Cathal Dumay, who must now, Andrew reflected, be about thirteen or fourteen. Uncle Brian had died when Andrew was about fifteen, and his Aunt Kathleen had caused some surprise and a good deal of adverse comment by subsequently marrying her co-religionist in the family, his Uncle Barnabas, who, it appeared, had been one of her early admirers. That marriage had been childless.

Andrew's mother had been impressed and continually preoccupied by the goings-on of her Irish relations, particularly the Kinnard family, possessors of an enviable mansion and an even more enviable title, who, especially in the days of Arthur's father, had set a standard both of grandeur and of social freedom which must have made Hilda discontented with her restricted London life and with the "mad" yet cosy society of her parents. There was no doubt that she coveted not only the traditional ease of the Kinnard household but also its Irish remoteness from the pettier aspects of the "bourgeois" world. Hilda had never been quite sure that her father and mother were blessed with good taste.

Although Hilda had talked about these things to Andrew all his life, he had only very recently begun, in relation to her, to understand them. He had much earlier, and with a kind of nervous distress, apprehended his father's quite different and strangely deep anxieties about Ireland. Some family demon haunted Henry Chase-White. He was fond of his relations, and especially fond of Aunt Millicent. But the source of the trouble, Andrew soon came to conjecture, was his half-brother Brian. Brian Dumay was older than Henry by several years and was a very different kind of man from Andrew's father. Uncle Brian had occupied some post in the Bank of Ireland which never seemed to provide matter for discussion, but in so far as he entered into the life of his nephew he did so in the guise of the perfect all-round out-of-doors uncle. Andrew recalled the scenes, always the same, on hills or beaches, with Uncle Brian leading the way, leaping from rock to rock, followed by the shouting children, while Andrew's father picked his way cautiously behind. And Andrew must have been about ten when he realized, with a tender protective pang which seemed to make him on the instant much older, that his father was a little jealous in case Andrew should compare him unfavourably with Uncle Brian. It was an occasion when they had all been swimming, except for Andrew's father, who had found the sea too cold and was sitting in the sandhills with a book. Andrew had run to him and been told almost roughly, "You don't want to be here with me. Go back to your uncle." Since then Andrew had liked Uncle Brian less. But it was not until his uncle died that he realized how extremely attached his father really was to his half-brother, who must have represented something robust, attractive, and puzzling, which produced in him a characteristic tremor of awkwardness. Andrew met with the same awkwardness, the same shy, disguised, puzzled fondness in his father's attitude to himself; this barrier was never removed, and Andrew felt a special pain when his father died to think that perhaps he had never known how much his son loved him.

Andrew had felt as a child an acute and uncomfortable interest in all his relations, but the magnetic centre of that field of forces had usually seemed to be his cousin Pat Dumay. It occurred to Andrew later that his own peculiar anxiety about Pat somewhat resembled his father's anxiety about Uncle Brian, only Andrew had never exactly felt any liking for his cousin. His interest in him was something more obscure and disturbing. He had spent a good deal of energy in earlier years in trying to impress Pat, and indeed it could scarcely be denied that the folly with the horses which had had such far-reaching results was an attempt to get even not so much with Frances as with Pat.

Pat, who was known in their childhood as "the iron man," and who effortlessly excelled in all their sports and games together, had never paid much attention to Andrew. Andrew, a slow-growing child, had often, with rage, been relegated to play with "the little boys," and he still felt that Pat casually took him to be younger than he was. There had never been any sort of confidence or friendship between them, although on a few occasions when they were older Andrew had made advances. Pat, who was not much given to talking, would then withdraw into a taciturn dignity, while at the same time seeming not to notice Andrew at all. He moved quietly, his eyes elsewhere, like someone avoiding a small obstacle in his path. In moments of revolt Andrew referred to his cousin as "pompous" and affected surprise that he was not more frequently ragged. Yet somehow Pat's formidable dignity seemed to impose itself on others less concerned than Andrew. Other children were usually a bit afraid of Pat, who was capable at times of a good deal of violence. Andrew was reluctant to admit that he had ever feared him. But he had, when younger, felt a sort of awe which had perhaps partaken of a childish horror at Pat's religion. With years of reason and tolerance the horror had diminished, but in the quality of his persisting interest in his cousin there was still a sort of shudder as at something primitive and dark.

The younger brother Cathal, though commonly said to be cleverer than Pat, was of course of less moment to Andrew. He had spent a good deal of time in the past avoiding Cathal, who, being so much younger, had usually figured in one way or another as an impediment. The relations between the two brothers seemed not of the happiest, and Andrew conjectured the existence of some ferocious jealousy. Pat had always, ever since Andrew could remember them together, enjoyed knocking his little brother about, sometimes with a brutality which was alarming to witness. Andrew most poignantly recalled a scene when he himself was about thirteen when he had intervened to save Cathal, then a small child, from a particularly vicious attack. Pat, who had retaliated by giving Andrew a black eye, was subsequently beaten, presumably for this misdemeanour, by Uncle Brian. This occurrence had somehow, for Andrew, defined and confirmed his unhappy sense of connection with his cousin; though he doubted very much whether the incident had had any significance for Pat.

Since he had become more or less grown up, and more especially since he had become a soldier, Andrew felt with some relief that his childhood obsessions about Ireland were beginning to fall away. The tradition of the annual holiday was discontinued, and the dark, wet island seemed less of the menace than it used to be. He had not been over there for some while, nor seen any of his relations, apart from Frances and Christopher, who were frequent visitors to England. During this period Pat Dumay had been studying law at the National University, and was now apparently working in a solicitor's office. Andrew, rather vaguely hearing news of him from time to time, was gratified to learn that he had not specially distinguished himself in his studies: and the notion that he was, after all, more talented than his cousin came as a salve to his, in any case diminishing, consciousness of that old rivalry. He was rather surprised that Pat had shown no sign of enlisting, a matter commented on adversely by Andrew's mother, who, vaguely conscious of him as a competitor with her own boy, rather disliked Pat. But this unexpected blemish in the heroic figure of his boyhood was in fact far from displeasing to Andrew, and although he publicly disowned his mother's scornful opinion he secretly shared it.

Andrew's satisfaction at being liberated from Ireland was a little checked by the excessive nervous disturbance which he now felt on visiting the place again, and especially on hearing that his mother proposed to settle there. He had reckoned on seeing very little of Ireland in the future. He had decided, though without announcing this to anyone, to remove Frances from it completely as soon as this could be arranged. The removal of Frances indeed represented for him a sort of final triumph over the past. He felt irritated, and in a curious way a little frightened, to find that the severance could not be quite so complete. He told himself rationally that he must really begin to behave about the whole thing in a more grown-up way. Yet when he thought of the visit which he was to pay the Dumay household on the following day, he was not only childishly pleased at the idea of showing off his uniform and his newly grown moustache; his heart beat faster, he did not know why.

This visit, and a subsequent visit to his Aunt Millicent, had been urged upon him as a duty by his mother, although as he well knew she felt no particular affection for any of the people concerned. Hilda regarded "the family" as having an importance which, while she might not have used this language, transcended affection. She would not have professed actually to *like* any of her relations, with the exception of Christopher Bellman, Frances, and her own brother; and even in these two latter cases there were cross-currents of a hostility very obvious in origin. Millicent Kinnard and Kathleen, as she now was, Drumm aroused in Hilda, whenever they were mentioned, a particular sort of almost physical jerky nervousness. These two very different persons were, Andrew knew, in different ways a disappointment and a scandal to his mother. Stationed at important points within the family machine, they simply failed to turn the right handles.

Andrew's father had been extremely though rather nervously fond of his half-sister, and this may not have endeared Millie to Hilda. He had also been devoted to Kathleen, though not in any way which could have caused rational annoyance to his wife, his gentle and complete devotion to whom had been a show-piece of the family. It was for Andrew felicitously axiomatic that his parents had been a happy united pair, and he was even now curiously conscious of his father's presence as a support to his mother and himself. Hilda's irritations with Aunt Millicent and Aunt Kathleen were more largely social in origin. Andrew was tolerantly aware that his mother was a fearful snob and that "keeping up with Millie," which was presented as a tiresome duty, was made considerably less disagreeable by the fact that Millie had a title. There was also the wealth, the splendour, and what was left of the ceremony. But it was just here that Aunt Millicent failed.

Andrew could remember when he was quite small hearing a side-whiskered gentleman at a garden party saying to another, "I say, Millie Kinnard is rather fast, isn't she?" The idea seemed to please the gentleman, but Andrew's mother, who was standing nearby, had indignantly hustled Andrew away in the course of the reply. There had never been, as far as he knew, any positive scandal connected with his aunt, but he was given to understand that she was a person who habitually "went too far," although whither it was she proceeded with unwonted celerity, overstepping what barriers, he never altogether discovered. Millie was, of course, known to hold rather progressive views on "the woman question," had taken a nurse's training—contrary to the family's wishes—during the South African war, and had managed to get herself briefly to the scene of action. She had, it was said, not mourned too long after her husband's death. She was rumoured to wear trousers and smoke cigars. She possessed and could fire a revolver. She had a great many gentlemen friends.

"Millie has style" was the sort of remark which people tended to make and which Hilda hated to hear. For her, Millie's style was bad style and Millie's undeniable form was bad form. Andrew's mother was anxiously conventional and indeed regarded convention, which she preferred to think of as ceremony, as a fortress against all that she most feared. Perhaps in the end it was a fortress against her father's practical jokes. Aunt Millicent represented, just where one might have expected an access of strength, a dangerous breach in the defences. Andrew had chanced not to see his aunt for some years, since she had been away on his last visit, and his memories of her went right back to a scene in some summer garden where what seemed a pretty girl in a white dress, under the dappled shade of a parasol, had laughed at him, but not unpleasantly, making him laugh too. He felt a certain interest in seeing her again.

Aunt Kathleen was quite another matter. While Aunt Millicent failed through frivolity, Aunt Kathleen, *née*, after all, Kinnard, failed through dullness. Millie's form might be regrettable, but Kathleen was formless; and it was this, even more than the monstrous fact of being a Roman Catholic, which Andrew's mother held against her. The Dumay house in Blessington Street was shabby, disorderly, even dirty; and in this Hilda deplored a sheer lack of inherited discipline. "When you think of Kathleen's opportunities," she would say as prologue to a denunciation. Nor could she forgive Kathleen for marrying Barnabas, and thereby confirming her benighted brother in a state of insanity from which he might otherwise have recovered. Hilda also resented, though for fear of giving it further publicity she never mentioned, the fact that Kathleen supported her husband financially. Barnabas, who had latterly been employed in the public service, gave up this work soon after his marriage to devote himself entirely to research. Hilda blamed his wife for what she regarded as his progressive demoralization, and when the drinking bouts began she would say, "It's all of a piece!"—meaning Catholicism, Kathleen, alcohol, and the Irish saints.

As Andrew meditated rather vaguely in the cool April sunshine of that Sunday afternoon concerning his forthcoming visit to the Dumays, he was engaged in the task of fixing Frances' red swing. The swing, its wooden seat painted with a sort of peasant design of white hearts upon a scarlet background, had been ever since long ago a feature of the Bellmans' much larger and wilder garden in Galway. That morning when he had been looking at a photograph album with Frances they had come upon a picture of her, a little girl with a big straw sunbonnet, sitting upon the swing, while Andrew in a sailor suit stood rather ungraciously by. As Andrew began reminiscing about the swing Frances had said that, in fact, they had brought it with them, it was somewhere around, and Andrew had said that of course he would fix it up forthwith. Then they had both fallen silent.

Andrew thought of and indeed referred to Frances Bellman as his fiancée, although nothing had yet been quite formally fixed between them. It was rather that an understanding, dating from somewhere very remote in their childhood, had gradually grown up, like a tall genie taking shape between them and joining their hands. They had been, on the many occasions when they had been able to be together, "inseparable" as children; and as soon as Andrew was ready to fall in love he fell in love with Frances, as if this were an inevitable and natural aspect of growing up. The frenzy of love had been calmed almost at once by the sense that he could not possibly lose her. There was already the security of a long attachment. He had felt no interest in any other woman, although he had had his share of opportunities and indeed of flattering attentions.

He was sometimes surprised at the ease with which he had been immediately conducted into this congenial haven, and attributed it somehow to the same kindly gods who had made him the only child of happily married parents. Frances, too, was an only child, and this made her seem quite especially of the same race as himself. Andrew adhered to no general theories of a romantic nature concerning the importance of a stormy initiation into love, and particularly now, with the prospect of a return to the war opening before him like a black hole, he was prepared to settle gladly for a security in his personal life which seemed likely to exist nowhere else. France, not Frances, would lay his soul naked.

Andrew had never formally proposed, though he assumed that some absolutely explicit suggestion, such as the naming of a day, would be necessary before the ceremony could be performed. In a way he would have preferred simply to wake up one morning and find that Frances was his wife; and he felt sure that she felt exactly as he did. She accepted and completed his half-voiced assumptions about the future, and their conversations were like a song sung in snatches by persons who know their parts so well that they need only by a note or two suggest them. He knew that Frances understood him perfectly. That was why they had both fallen silent suddenly together when they were speaking of the swing, since a swing suggested a child.

Andrew was still a virgin. Where Frances was concerned, two ideas were curiously enlaced in his mind, the idea of his first introduction to sexual intercourse and the idea of his death. The hours of both these events he pictured as flying towards him through the darkness like great scarlet darts; and although he did not doubt that the former would arrive before the latter, he sometimes, and especially in sleepless nights, thought that the latter might not come far behind. This returned his thoughts to what had made him and Frances suddenly silent.

The connection between the two ideas in fact went, for Andrew, deeper than anything suggested by the casualty lists. He profoundly feared the notion of the sexual act, and whenever he imagined himself doing *that* to Frances he felt appalled incredulity. This act, an act of terrible violence involving the destruction of both the aggressor and the victim, seemed something quite separate from his old deep love for Frances, and separate even from the uneasy excitement which he had felt during the last week at living in the same house with her and accompanying her as far as her bedroom door. It was as if the act in question would have to be committed in a clandestine manner, like a secret murder. He could not imagine it as a part of ordinary life, and as the scarlet dart flew nearer and nearer he had times of feeling most dreadfully afraid.

Another consideration which joined the two fearful ideas together and made him confused and frightened about what was to come was a vague sense that people surrounding him, his family, perhaps society, expected him to make Frances pregnant before he was sent to the Front. An old aunt had practically blurted out something like this in his presence; and he divined some such thought in the mind of his mother, who was in some ways ambivalent about his relationship to Frances. This sort of dubious "survival," offered as a kind of duty, made Andrew upset in a rather self-pitying way which he usually avoided. He wanted to live and be happy with Frances himself and to be under no obligations of that sort to the human race or even to her. He felt too, in these moods, hustled, and more inclined to procrastinate about the whole business. However, the moods soon passed, swept away by his sheer tenderness for the girl and his increasing sense that this was the moment to settle his destiny, or rather to confirm a settlement which seemed to have been so felicitously made long ago.

Andrew's mother was very fond of Frances, but had sudden little sharp bursts of hostility towards her, as he imagined she would towards any girl that Andrew proposed to marry. Frances let them pass, shaking her head like a pony, which she in many ways resembled, and Hilda would at the next moment be especially affectionate. Andrew was exceedingly fond of his mother, sometimes he felt alarmingly fond of her, although she exasperated him extremely almost all the time. He disagreed with her views on everything, and her ambitions made him shudder. He particularly disliked the social half-truths which she constantly told as a matter of instinct. She would imply that she had attended gatherings of which she had only heard, and when in Ireland would portray the glittering nature of her London social life in a way which amounted to serious misrepresentation. He flattered himself that he could observe with a sharp eye the world which so dazzled his mother; yet while he blushed for her vanity he could not see her as corrupted.

He had, in the past, felt a good deal of nervousness on the subject of whether his mother would think that Frances, an untitled, unfashionable girl, who had never even properly "come out," was good enough for him. He had gradually with relief become aware that Hilda regarded Frances as a rather special young person. He only subsequently realized that there was a particular reason for this. Christopher Bellman was extremely rich. Children are usually oblivious of any except the most evident differences in wealth, and Andrew had only lately acquired an adult awareness of how much, in that sense, particular men had "behind" them. He felt this awareness to be an onset of worldliness, especially when he noticed that such knowledge did in some way alter his view of people. But of course he had loved Frances and even wanted firmly to marry her long before he had apprehended her as an heiress. He was only thankful that this fact about her seemed to pacify his mother completely, who otherwise would certainly have been on the warpath in London in ways which would have greatly displeased him. He excused this covetousness in her, as he excused in himself a certain quiet satisfaction at the idea of marrying, quite accidentally, a rich girl; his parents had always been very poorly off and Andrew was just at an age to appreciate how inconvenient this was.

His prospective father-in-law, Christopher Bellman, was still a rather obscure and alarming figure to Andrew. He was constantly surprised to see how easily his mother managed to get on with Christopher. It was as if she simply failed to notice that he was a dangerous animal. It was indeed the spectacle of Hilda and Christopher gambolling together that most especially brought home to Andrew what seemed to him an adult insight: that someone can seem, and in fact be, quite different with one person from what he is with another. It was as if Hilda's mechanism was simply not designed to pick up a whole range of rays given off by Christopher, to which Andrew was sensitive and which led him to find Christopher "dangerous." Andrew thought that it was also very adult of him not instantly to dub his mother, for that reason, deficient. But neither did he, as he would when younger have done, regard her as daring. He searched rather for irrational features in his own attitude.

Christopher was, in fact, English, though Irish by adoption through his wife Heather, and an Irish "enthusiast" in a way which sufficiently marked him as an alien. When younger he had worked in the civil service, first in London and then in Dublin, but had retired in middle life to devote himself to scholarship, wherein, Andrew noticed, he concealed his systematic seriousness under an air of dilettante trifling. He was an expert on the antiquities of Ireland and possessed a large library on the subject, destined in his will for Trinity College, Dublin. He was familiar with Gaelic, although he had never joined the Gaelic League and was hostile to the wholesale cultivation of the Irish language which had come to be, for many of his acquaintances, such an important political end. He knew a good many of what he called "the Irish Ireland mob," but kept aloof from all politics and controversy. Andrew judged him, though not always confidently, to be a cold man. Yet his pursuits were harmless, he was obviously very attached to Frances, and had always encouraged Andrew.

Sometimes Andrew, forever making little of his fright, decided that it was simply Christopher's appearance that unnerved him. His future father-in-law was very tall and looked anything but English. He might have been southern French or even Basque. He had extremely black hair and large, dark eyes and a long, thin, very red mouth. He had always been clean-shaven, with a dulled, sallow complexion. His longish hair was looped back behind his markedly pointed ears and his bushy triangular eyebrows met and grew for a considerable way down the bridge of his narrow and slightly hooked nose. The brow was prominent, yellower than the rest of the face, and much scrawled over with fine wrinkles, so that it sometimes seemed that he was wearing a cap pulled down to eye level. This gave him a secretive air. Yet he managed to look handsome and even young, and his eyes, always rather cautious and watchful, were very often humorous. Perhaps it was simply that Andrew suspected that Christopher was frequently laughing at him. He felt however an immense respect for Christopher, for his learning and for his rather mysterious detachment. Exhorted for some time to call him by his Christian name instead of "Sir," he had found this difficult.

Andrew had by now almost finished dealing with the swing. It had not been a complicated operation, but he had dreamily prolonged it, simply glad to find himself mechanically occupied. The ropes were securely knotted onto a projecting bough of the big chestnut tree which stood beside the lawn, and as they chafed to and fro they dislodged a light dusting of bark which descended onto Andrew's blond head in a peppery rain, making him sneeze. The ropes slipped neatly through the slots in the seat and were knotted together below. Andrew had mended an incipient crack with a slat of wood and filled up a hole with putty. The red and white painted surface was as bright as he remembered it, the central spot of scarlet in those green childhood scenes, polished by many childish posteriors into a warm, soft glow. He was rubbing it over with his sleeve, almost as if for some magical evocation of the past, when he caught sight of Frances coming from the house to call him in to tea.

A number of blackbirds, who had been threatening each other upon the lawn, flew up at her approach. The garden was in that disturbing, expectant condition of the spring when everything is exuberantly leafy but nothing is in flower. All was green, that particularly pale vivid, damp-looking green which emanates from the Irish soil or is perhaps elicited by the dark brightness of the Irish light, a green washed over with silver. The slender spears of montbretia which fringed the house, the pallid waxy stripes of hemerocallis, the fuzzy, shifting masses of fuchsia gave to the scene something of the air of a lush, reedy water meadow. Against this dense vegetable harmony Frances advanced, wearing a full-skirted dress of white spotted voile and Irish lace with a wide sash of mauve satin. Andrew, who had been drooping lazily, sprang to attention, his glance darting involuntarily to her ankles, which the new fashion left clearly visible.

Frances was a small girl, inclined to plumpness, with something distinctly bouncy or frisky in her gait. Andrew had once punched another boy who called her "dumpy." There was, in fact, a brightness and vitality in her which forbade such a descrip-

Two

"What's on at the Abbey?"

"Some stuff by W. B. Yeats."

"The Countess Cathleen man? I don't think we feel strong enough for that, do we? What about the Gaiety?"

"D'Oyly Carte. I believe it's *The Yeomen of the Guard.*"

"Well, we might go there. Only don't forget my furniture is arriving at Claresville on Thursday."

It was about half an hour later and tea was nearly over. They were sitting round the low wickerwork table in the conservatory, while outside the garden was being caressed or playfully beaten by the light rain which drifted a little in the breeze from the sea. Rain in Ireland always seemed a different substance from English rain, its drops smaller and more numerous. It seemed now to materialize in the air rather than to fall through it, and, transformed into quicksilver, ran shimmering upon the surface of the trees and plants, to fall with a heavier plop from the dejected palms and the chestnut. This rain, this scene, the pattering on the glass, the smell of the porous concrete floor, never entirely dry, the restless sensation of slightly damp cushions—these things set up for Andrew a long arcade of memories. He shifted uneasily in his basket chair, wondering how long it took to develop rheumatism.

Christopher had lighted his pipe; Frances was sewing; Hilda, without occupation, was sitting very upright as if the organization of the party had suddenly fallen upon her. Her hair, a pale blond striped with grey, rather scanty and silky, pulled well away from the face and banded by a black velvet ribbon, looked like a neat cap, and she appeared older than her age. Her face, lightly wrinkled or rather perhaps crumpled, was a uniform colour of soft parchmenty gold, and often gave the impression of being weather-beaten or sunburnt, although Hilda in fact shunned the open air. The large straight nose and rather stern dark blue eyes completed the picture of a person of authority, although an inherent vagueness in Hilda's principles made her in practice a less commanding person than she seemed.

"I'm longing to see your house finished," said Frances.

"Thank God you didn't buy that crumbling pile at Dundrum," said Christopher. "I'd have had to help you keep it upright, and it would have been a full-time job."

What about me? thought Andrew, with a sudden pang, but then decided that he was being morbid.

"Kathleen said she'd find me a maid. I gather one has to pay ten shillings a week now."

"And most of them would steal the cross off an ass's back and can't be trusted to cook anything but rashers and eggs!"

"Oh, I'm good at training servants. I had a perfect little jewel in London. And of course I shall have the telephone installed."

"The telephone is fine here if you only want to talk to the exchange! Have I convinced you on the motor-car question?"

"Yes, Christopher. I think, after all, it would be foolish to buy a motor car just now. There are too many difficulties. I hear Millie has just bought a Panhard. She is so extravagant."

Andrew knew quite well that his mother was aware that she could not possibly afford a motor car.

"We might think in terms of a pony and trap, though. After all, one must get about. And when the war is over I shall certainly purchase a touring car. Andrew shall learn how to operate it."

A Vauxhall Prince Henry, thought Andrew dreamily to himself. When the war was over he would have money to spend. It was nice to think that he had a rendezvous in the future with a Vauxhall Prince Henry.

"I think I shall always stick to my bike," said Christopher. "The bicycle is the most civilized conveyance known to man. Other forms of transport grow daily more nightmarish. Only the bicycle remains pure in heart."

"I was very relieved Andrew didn't want to go into the Flying Corps," said Hilda, speaking as if her son were not present.

"What's on tomorrow, Aunt Hilda?" asked Frances, revealing a long straight row of white teeth as she bit a length of thread off from the spool. Andrew's mother had always been content with this formal mode of address, which increased Andrew's nomenclatural difficulties with Christopher, since to address him familiarly in Hilda's presence would seem a kind of disloyalty.

"*Tomorrow*, my dear," said Hilda, with the confiding eagerness she always evinced over any social plan, however trivial, "tomorrow Andrew goes to tea at Blessington Street. I can't manage it, I've *got* to be at Claresville then to see the builder. You'll go with him, won't you?"

"I don't mind," said Frances. "I like to watch Cathal growing up. He looks entirely different now every time I see him."

"He's such a big boy. It's hard to believe he's only fourteen. Children grow up so much more quickly nowadays. You'll go along too, Christopher?"

"Please not. That house depresses me. And Kathleen always makes me feel guilty!"

"I don't see why she should. But the house *is* gloomy, and there's always that curious smell on the stairs. Don't you think Kathleen has become awfully sour and self-absorbed just lately? And so dreadfully pious! Someone told me she goes to chapel every day."

"She does it to spite Barney," said Christopher, puffing his pipe, his gaze upon the quietly dripping palm trees.

Hilda, as usual, did not follow up a remark which made reference to her brother's religion. She went on. "And on *Tuesday*, I know it's a terrible bore, but we *must* go and see Millie, I did promise. She's back from Rathblane now, it's her time for being in town. How do you think Millie is these days, Christopher? Going downhill?"

"Not specially," said Christopher. "She's been hunting like a maniac all the winter."

"She certainly has plenty of energy," Hilda conceded. "I sometimes think she really might have been somebody if she'd been born a man."

"Can't one be somebody if one's born a woman?" asked Frances.

"Well, hardly in that way, dear. Though in plenty of other ways which are just as important," said Hilda vaguely.

"I think being a woman is like being Irish," said Frances, putting aside her work and sitting up. At such moments she had an unconscious gesture of pushing back her hair to reveal her large brow. "Everyone says you're important and nice, but you take second place all the same."

"Come, come, women have always had Home Rule!" Christopher always jestingly set aside his daughter's sometimes rather ferocious attempts to turn conversation into serious channels.

"The emancipation question is certainly a grave one," said Hilda. "I am not at all hostile to the idea myself. But there are so many values— And I'm afraid that your Aunt Millicent's idea of emancipation is wearing trousers and firing a revolver in her own house."

Christopher laughed. "That's about it. But one must start somewhere! Will you be coming to Millie's, Frances?"

"No, thanks."

Andrew had long been aware that Frances did not like Aunt Millicent, but he had never been able to make out why. Among the generalizations about women which passed freely around his regimental mess was one to the effect that women never like each other, since every woman regards every other woman as her rival. Andrew, while attending with interest to all such distillations of worldly wisdom on a subject which was still very mysterious to him, suspected that this one was over-simple. It was true that women, leading more isolated and emptier lives, were naturally, when opportunity offered, more frantically anxious to attract attention and more ruthless in their pursuit of the opposite sex, than were men, who had, after all, other interests, as well as more chances to know each other in an atmosphere of free fraternal co-operation. Or so it seemed to Andrew, who saw men as inherently dignified animals and women as inherently undignified animals. However, in his own experience, when he had noted a marked dislike of one woman for another there had usually been some reason for this other than the postulated general rivalry.

In the matter of dislike of Aunt Millicent, his mother, for instance, disliked her out of envy for her title and her money, and because she failed to further Hilda's social ambitions. While Aunt Kathleen disliked her because of Uncle Arthur. Kathleen had, it seems, been very attached to her brother Arthur and had, rightly or wrongly, felt him to be in some way slighted or belittled by Millie, who was in fact fairly universally said to have married Arthur for rather worldly reasons. Uncle Arthur's early death was also somehow vaguely felt to be Millie's fault. "Poor Arthur," Hilda used to say. "Millie simply ate him. Kathleen never forgave her." Frances' dislike, which could hardly be put down to loyalty to either Kathleen or Hilda, persons from whom to say the least she felt detached, could perhaps, after all, be more simply explained as the nervous envy felt by a young girl who, however much she might officially despise such values, recognized in an older person a kind of elegance and glitter which she could never hope to emulate. Or, more simply still, it might be that Frances had weighed Millie in some spiritual balance and found her wanting. Andrew noted, sometimes a little uneasily, that his the great man thus dismissed. He saw her draw breath to protest, decide not to, and half smile at him as if asking for approval, all in two seconds. He was pleased by the quick little exchange.

His mother was going on. "I can't understand why recruiting is going so slowly in Ireland. I saw an article about it this morning."

"I don't think it's going slowly. Irishmen are streaming into the British Army."

"Well, yes, but so many remain behind. And the *attitude* of people. Last week I heard a man singing a song in German in the public street. And in Clery's yesterday I heard a woman say to another that Germany might win the war. She said it casually, as if it were quite an ordinary thing to say!"

Christopher laughed. "Of course, the English never, ever for a second conceive that they can lose a war. It's one of their great strengths."

"Why do you say 'they,' Christopher, and not 'we'? You're English, after all."

"True, true. But having lived over here for so long I can't help seeing the dear old place a little bit from the outside."

"Well, I think it's very disloyal to talk in that way about the Germans, as if they could possibly win. After all, England and Ireland are really one country."

"So the English soldiers evidently think when they sing 'It's a long way to Tipperary.' But it's always easy for the top dog to extend his sense of identity over his inferiors. It's a different matter for the inferiors to accept the identification."

"I can't understand this talk about inferiority. No one regards the Irish as inferior. They are loved and welcomed all over the world! And I can't stand this jumped-up Irish patriotism, it's so artificial. English patriotism is another thing. We have Shakespeare and the Magna Carta and the Armada and so on. But Ireland hasn't really had any history to speak of."

"Your brother would hardly agree with this judgment."

"I am not impressed by a few moth-eaten saints," said Hilda with dignity.

"Ireland was a civilized country when Englnd was still barbarous," said Frances, tossing her hair back.

"My dear Frances, you are parroting your uncle Barnabas," said Hilda. "You know very little about it."

This, Andrew thought, was probably just. Frances was no scholar, and her views on politics, though often vehement, were extremely confused and discontinuous. Frances had always been very attached to Hilda's brother, and had never associated herself with the scandalized or mocking attitudes of the family towards the convert. Uncle Barnabas and her father between them had been her school and her university, and once for a short while she had helped her uncle with some aspect of his study of the early Irish church. It was something, she used vaguely to say, about the date of Easter, and more Andrew could not gather. Long aware of a friendship between Frances and "Barney," Andrew felt an undiminishing jealousy which he recognized to be both unworthy and irrational. He had never for a second been able to take his Uncle Barnabas seriously. While Christopher seemed to him, and rather formidably, a real scholar, he could not imagine Uncle Barnabas's toils as other than childish vanities, and Frances' muddled account of them seemed to confirm the view. "Barney" shambled on the outskirts of the family caravan, an irredeemable figure of fun.

"And all this nonsense about reviving the Irish language"—Hilda was going on—"with all due respect to you, Christopher. . . ."

"Oh, but I entirely agree with you. Gaelic should be left to us scholars. One should be content to be born to the language of Shakespeare. And in fact the Irish have always written the best English."

"The Anglo-Irish have."

"True for you! Those aristocrats who think themselves superior both to the English and to the Irish!"

"And when you think of all the money we've poured into this country . . . The Irish farmers have never been better off."

"Not everyone would agree with that," said Christopher. "I read an article in the *Irish Review* only yesterday saying that Alsace-Lorraine was far better off under German rule than Ireland under English rule."

"That couldn't possibly be true. It's just Irish spite. I wonder why people think the Irish have such sunny characters? Don't they realize there's a war on? Now they've been promised Home Rule and everything they want they ought to be grateful."

"Perhaps they don't feel they've got much to be grateful for," said Frances. "A million people died in the potato famine."

"My dear Frances, that was regrettable but has nothing whatever to do with the present situation. You argue like a street-corner orator. There may have been some unfortunate things in the past, but they're all long ago now, and I'm sure England never purposely hurt Ireland, it was just economics."

"There's something in what Hilda says," said Christopher. "Ireland had several bits of sheer historical bad luck, and one of them was that the potato famine coincided with the heyday of Manchester free trade. In the eighteenth century England would have relieved the famine."

"What were the other bits of bad luck, Sir?" asked Andrew.

"Eighteen hundred and one, and nineteen-fourteen. It was very unfortunate that this war started just before Home Rule went through. Remember Churchill saying that if Belfast wouldn't submit to Home Rule the British fleet would teach them to? The Liberals were really exasperated with the North. A year or two of enforced religious toleration and everything would have settled down. Whereas now we shall have endless trouble. But the Act of Union was the big Irish disaster. English government in the eighteenth century was the most civilized government in history. Fear of the French put an end to eighteenth-century civilization. Perhaps it put an end to civilization. It certainly put an end to the Irish Parliament. Ireland was really becoming an independent country; the great landowners thought of themselves as Irish.

And of course that began to scare the English stiff. Hence the Act of Union and all our tears."

"You think Ireland might have had a quite different history if it hadn't been for that?" said Andrew.

"I do. There was a real Irish culture at that time, a culture with its own brilliance and with international ties. Do you remember that monument I once showed you, Hilda, in Saint Patrick's cathedral, which talks about 'that exalted refinement which in the best period of our history characterized the Irish gentleman'? The date of that is twelve years after the Act of Union. Oh, they knew what had happened all right. If the Irish Parliament had survived, Ireland wouldn't be the provincial backwater it is today."

"Home Rule will make it even more provincial," said Hilda.

"I fear it may," said Christopher. "And idiots like Pearse don't help when they invent a romantic Irish tradition which just ignores the English ascendancy. Ireland's real past *is* the ascendancy. Ireland should turn back to the eighteenth century, not to the Middle Ages. Goldsmith and Sterne would turn in their graves to hear the nonsense about Holy Ireland that's talked nowadays."

"All that can't be quite right," said Frances. "I mean, you seem to be talking as if Ireland were just the grand people. You remember what Grattan said about *we* are not the people of Ireland. It's everyone having always been so poor that's awful. Compare the Irish countryside with the English countryside. There are no real towns and villages in Ireland. There are the same little featureless houses or hovels everywhere, and then nothing else till you come to the country mansions and the cathedrals of Christ the King."

"Catholicism is the curse of this country," said Hilda. "If only Ireland had followed England at the Reformation."

Christopher laughed. "You mean the Irish, having rejected the most civilized religion in the world, Anglicanism, deserved their fate? That's arguable! But they were just that much farther away, and the Fitzgeralds and the O'Neills went on being Catholics and being warlords in a quiet way. As for Ireland being the grand people, it's unfortunately true that until lately history has been made by the grand people. Frances is really right, though. What this country lacks is a yeomanry. The Irish peasant remained primitive and remained poor."

"Why?" asked Andrew.

"It's largely the same answer. No parliament. Think how important Parliament was in England from the very start. Ireland remained a country of overlords. The big estates were political prizes. Ireland was always a property being handed about. An insecure ruling class without a parliament is soon demoralized. And ever since the Irish princes sold out to Henry the Second there's been collusion between Irish gentry and English power. 'Her faithless sons betrayed her,' as the song says. Ireland's only hope of pulling herself out of feudalism was to develop a steady ruling class with its own culture and its own civilized organs of power, and that began to be possible in the eighteenth century, only the Act of Union wrecked it all just as it was becoming a reality. And by eighteen-fifteen, standards in English political life had declined so much, England was so gross with triumph, there was no help for Ireland there."

"So it looks as if the French are the villains of Europe," said Andrew. "A view I've long held!"

"Why do people in Ireland always talk about *history*?" said Hilda. "My head's always swimming with dates when I'm over here. English people don't talk about English history all the time."

"They don't have to ask the question, What went wrong?" said Christopher. "For them nothing went wrong."

"Well, I'm afraid Ireland is a thoroughly self-centred country."

"All countries are, my dear Hilda. Only selfishness shows more in the unfortunate."

"And now there's all this Trade Union nonsense and stopping the trams. It's so demoralizing. And all this playing at soldiers and marching about in green uniforms and so on. Even Barney got tied up with it at one time. Something ought to be done about it. People ought not to play at war when there's a real war on."

Christopher blew out a curl of blue smoke and watched it rise to where the rain was running steadily and now almost silently along the glass roof of the conservatory. A soft salty mist was filling the garden, penetrating the curtain of the rain. There was a raw smell of the sea. Christopher spoke now with a more deliberate slowness, like one who feels he has been too vehement or is afraid of becoming so. "After the Ulster Volunteers came into existence, and especially after they were armed, it was inevitable that there would be a similar movement down here. After all, it's the right of free men to prepare themselves to defend their freedom."

"The British Navy will defend their freedom. It always has done!"

Andrew, who sensed that both Christopher and Frances were getting a bit tired of hearing from his mother, interposed in his most objective and manly manner, "Wasn't it rather a mistake, Sir, for the British Army not to recognize the Volunteers in the South? I gather General Mahon recommended it to Kitchener. Especially after the Ulster Volunteers were formed into a division."

"Yes," said Christopher. "You'll find the Red Hand of Ulster in the British Army, but there's no sign of the Harp."

"Kitchener is afraid to arm the Irish," said Frances.

"I'm sure he's no such thing," said Hilda. "He told Mr. Redmond and Lord Carson that he'd like to knock their heads together."

"Do you agree," said Andrew, adopting Christopher's slow tempo, "with the people who say that Redmond ought to have demanded immediate Home Rule in exchange for Ireland's participation in the war?"

Christopher laughed. "Good heavens no. I'm not an extremist. Home Rule is a certainty after the war. Or else a hundred thousand men back from the army will know the reason why!"

"Is it conceivable that the Castle would be so insane as to try to disarm the Volunteers?"

"No, no. The English will behave correctly. After all, people are watching them."

"So you agree with Casement that the Irish question is an international question now, and not a local British matter any more?"

"Oh, no! The notion of 'joining Europe' is just another illusion. Poor old Ireland will always be a backwater. Imagine the most god-forsaken hole in the world and go on several hundred miles into the unknown and there you'll find Ireland!"

"I can't hear calmly about that man Casement," said Hilda. "To go over to the Germans and try to stab England in the back like that just when she's up against it . . ."

"It's the old story. 'England's difficulty is Ireland's opportunity.' Casement belongs to a classical tradition. And in a way I can't help admiring the fellow. It must be a lonely, bitter business out there in Germany. He's a brave man and a patriot. He does it purely for love of Ireland. To love Ireland so much, to love anything so much, even if he's wrong-headed, is somehow noble."

"He does it for love of gold, you may be sure," said Hilda. "It's the traitor mentality."

Christopher thought for a moment. "I think that word 'traitor' ought to be removed from the language. It's just a muddled term of abuse. Casement's crime, or mistake, if it is one, is much more complex than anything that blunted word could name."

"So you don't think there'll be any trouble in Ireland?" asked Andrew quickly before his mother could expostulate further.

"Trouble with the Sinn Feiners? No, I don't. And what could they make it with, hurley sticks? I was talking to Eoin MacNeill's brother about it all the other day. Eoin has quite returned to his Gaelic studies. He was never a firebrand leader, in any case. The Volunteers are really just like Boy Scouts, and James Connolly's lot, the Irish Citizen Army, are ten men and a dog. If the Germans actually invaded Ireland a few hotheads might help them, but with the blockade that's an impossibility. And anyway, as I say, what trouble could the Irish make, even if they wanted to? They've got no arms and they're not insane. I saw a squad of Volunteers drilling the other day with ten-foot pikes. It was pathetic!"

Andrew laughed. "Don't tell the Sinn Feiners, but our reserve squadron at Longford only has about a hundred rifles, and half of them are D.P., drill purposes only. They'd probably explode if you tried to fire them!"

"Your lot at Longford had better look out, then," said Christopher. "That place is a hot-bed of disaffection."

"You shouldn't say things like that, Andrew," said his mother. "You never know who's listening."

Andrew felt justly rebuked, and recalled suddenly to mind a rather unpleasant incident which had marked his arrival in Ireland. The one really constructive thing which he had managed to do when in France had been to get hold of a magnificent Italian rifle with telescopic sights. This extremely precious object had somehow or other disappeared at some point between the mail boat and Finglas. Christopher's gardener had sworn that the rifle had simply not been with the luggage when it arrived from the boat. Andrew now, of course, realized that it had been insane of him to take his eyes off it for a second in this gun-hungry country. Sometime later he overheard Christopher saying casually that his gardener was connected with the Citizen Army. Andrew thought he would probably never know the truth of the matter; but he felt the disappearance of the rifle as a hostile act, upsetting and menacing.

"No, no"—Christopher was going on. "I don't exactly see Ireland as explosive material. I agree with Bulmer Hobson. Ireland is a damp bog which will yet extinguish many a flaming torch and gunpowder barrel! The fact is the Irish are far more sentimental and emotional even than one imagines. It all ends in talk. This morning, for instance, when I was down in town I witnessed a curious little scene. I meant to tell you of it earlier. I was passing near Liberty Hall, you know, the Transport and General Workers' Union place, and I saw that some sort of ceremony was going on. There was a big crowd, and a girl in the Citizen Army uniform was climbing on the roof and unfurling a flag. It was a green flag with the Irish harp on it. And the I.C.A. men were all drawn up in ranks presenting arms and the bugles were blowing and the pipe bands were playing and then everyone started cheering, and do you know, quite a lot of people in the crowd had tears in their eyes."

Andrew was disturbed by this account; and he felt that Christopher had perhaps been more interested than he pretended to be. Frances had put down her sewing.

"But what did it mean?" said Andrew.

"Nothing. That's my point. The Irish are so used to personifying Ireland as a tragic female, any patriotic stimulus produces an overflow of sentiment at once."

" 'Did you see an old woman going down the path?' 'I did not, but I saw a young girl, and she had the walk of a queen.' "

"Precisely, Frances. Saint Teresa's Hall nearly fell down when Yeats first came out with that stuff. Though, in fact, if you recited the Dublin telephone directory in this town with enough feeling you'd have people shedding tears!"

"Well, I think it ought to be stopped," said Hilda. "I can't imagine how they can do it, with the town full of wounded soldiers, you'd think they'd be ashamed. And I'm very surprised indeed that Pat Dumay hasn't enlisted. I really must have a word about it with his mother. An able-bodied young fellow like that ought to be longing to get out to the front. I have the impression that he's becoming a rather disagreeable young man."

"I shouldn't say anything to Kathleen if I were you," said Christopher. "And I'd advise you not to show your opinion in any way to Pat himself." As he said this Christopher looked quickly at Andrew.

Andrew felt an immediate pang of annoyance and the familiar sense of a threat. As if he would be such a fool as to bait his cousin for not having enlisted.

"Well, you may be right," said Hilda, getting up. The sea mist now shrouded the garden and enveloped the house, curling damply in through the interstices of the conservatory. The rain had stopped, but water now hung on the interior of the glass in rows of glittering beads which would suddenly start rolling, coalesce, and fall with a small splash onto the stiff linen table cloth. Frances was packing up the tea things. As they began to drift in toward the drawing-room Andrew heard his mother saying to Christopher, "I've been meaning to ask you for such a long time. What *exactly* did Wolfe Tone do?"

Three

"Have you heard this one?

    'As a beauty I'm not a star.

    There are others more handsome by **far**.

    But my face I don't mind it,

    For I am behind it.

    It's the people in front get the jar.' "

"That's not very funny."

"It's not meant to be funny. It's philosophical. Well, and it is so, funny. And have you heard this one, 'There was an old man of Rathmines—' "

"Oh, shut up, Cathal."

"Don't be always telling your brother to shut up," said Kathleen, who was laying the table for tea. Her sons did not reply but waited with an air of abstracted politeness for her to leave the room, which she did a moment later.

"It's today the lily-white boy is coming."

"That's a fine way to be after talking about your cousin."

"I mean it complimentary," said Cathal.

"You do not."

"All right, I don't. And you don't like him either. Isn't he a sort of a bloody English chancer?"

"I don't mind him. I like him all right."

"Will he be in his uniform?"

"I expect so."

"Will he be wearing spurs?"

"How do I know? Yes, I suppose so."

"I shall laugh at his spurs. You'll hear me laughing and it'll be at his spurs."

"You'll behave yourself decently or I'll belt you."

"You will not."

"I will so."

"Yah! Yah! Patsie's not me da!" sang Cathal, waltzing the length of the drawing-room.

The Dumays' house stood at the upper end of Blessington Street, a wide, sad, dirty street due north of the Pillar, which crawled up the hill and ended at the railings of a melancholy little park. It had, under the pale bright sky, its own quiet air of dereliction, a street leading nowhere, always full of idling dogs and open doorways. Yet in form it closely resembled the other great Georgian arteries of Dublin, with its noble continuous façade of sombre, blackened red brick which seemed to absorb, rather than to be revealed by, the perpetual rainy light. Looked at closely, the bricks of these houses showed in fact a variety of colours, some purplish red, some yellowish grey, all glued together by a jelly of filth to form a uniform organic surface rather like the scales of a fish, the basic material of Dublin, a city conjured from the earth all in one piece by some tousled Dido. Iron railings guarded deep cave-like areas where dandelions and young saplings flourished, and a few steps led up to each front door, above which was a graceful semicircular fanlight. The ornate pillars which flanked the doors, battered and flattened by time, had the air of Grecian antiquities. The windows above were, the length of the street, handsome and elegant as upon their first day.

The doors varied. They were serious affairs, solid and many-panelled, and if well painted and provided with handsome knockers and a brass plate or two could sufficiently announce, even here, the residences of substantial citizens, well-bred reticent professional men. But by now many of the doors in the street were broken-down, their paint peeling off, chequered with mysterious holes, and lacking their knockers so that visitors had to shout through the letter box. Various strange activities had meanwhile developed in the basements, such as a bicycle shop in one, a carpenter's workshop in another, and in one area a man sat all day mending cane chairs. While through grimy glass the fanlights displayed, besides the usual gaudy little figure of Christ the King, the cards of hairdressers and of chimney sweeps. At the end of the street there was even a house which had a sweet shop on the ground floor.

Yet the street had a spirit above these matters, and in the evening when the lamp-lighter was just going his rounds, or on certain soft days when the sun shone through cloud, making everything vivid and exact as in a print, the street looked beautiful, with that particular sad, resigned, orderly beauty of Dublin. Those squared, cliff-like, blackened Dublin streets, stretching on and on, still had some inkling of perfection, even though the terraces sometimes looked more like warehouses, even had become warehouses, or in the poorer streets had gaping holes for windows and doors. Even then they seemed to know that they represented, they still in their darkened condition were, the most beautiful dwellings which the human race had ever invented.

The Dumays' house was not the finest in the street nor was it the shabbiest. The door had been painted dark green some six years ago. It had a large brass knocker in the form of a wreath which the servant Jinny, a single girl of advancing years, who was paid eight shillings a week and lived in some nearby tenements affectionately called "the little hell," occasionally polished when the matter came into her mind. On entering the house the first impression was of an ecclesiastical darkness and of the smell referred to by Mrs. Chase-White. The ecclesiastical air was contributed by a stained-glass window on the half landing which was, in fact, inside a lavatory the door of which, when untenanted, stood always open. This place may also have accounted for the smell. The upper landing, which was long and lit by a skylight, was divided into two, for no very clear reason, by a faintly jangling bead curtain, while along the walls stood a series of shrines or side-chapels containing stuffed birds, cairns of wax fruit, and cascades of disintegrating butterflies under glass domes.

The drawing-room in which Cathal was now prancing was a long brown room, dimmed by brownish-white lace curtains, and very full of bulbous mahogany furniture. There were a number of coloured pictures of flower gardens, a large pinkish print called "The Love Letter," and a prominent crucifix. Both Kathleen and Pat were indifferent to their surroundings and accepted the miscellany of brass bowls, ginger jars, embroidered clothlets, and photos in upholstered frames as a natural part of the daily scene, as little remarkable as the rocks upon the sea shore. Only Cathal displayed any concern with interior decoration, and his interests so far were limited to the collecting of model animals, which now jostled the other inhabitants of the tall and extremely complicated overmantel, causing Jinny, when the day for dusting them came round, to utter under her breath words which would have startled Father Ryan. In the midst of the overmantel, whose unsymmetrical undulations suggested a natural growth rather than the workings of the human mind, was a slim, extremely tall elliptical mirror, which showed in reflection an even more melancholy room filled with an atmosphere the colour of strong tea.

Kathleen had returned now and was placing upon the blue and white cross-stitch tablecloth the large silver milk jug and sugar bowl reserved for special occasions. Her sons fell silent. They never addressed each other now in her presence. They watched her with a faint detached curiosity as one might watch an animal which had wandered into view close by. She, for her part, was irritably aware of them. She was wearing an old-fashioned skirt of brown serge which reached almost to the ground and a high-necked white blouse over which she had drawn for the occasion a long knitted jacket of purple and orange stripes. Her hair was still fairish, though dulling now towards a peppery grey, and strained straight back into a large round bun. She had a small, straight nose and large, light-brown eyes. Her forehead was not so much wrinkled as pitted and crumpled with anxiety. She had been handsome and still looked strong, but in rather a haunted way.

The two boys had returned to their books. Pat was reading a novel by George Moore, and Cathal was studying O'Growney's *Simple Lessons in Irish*. Pat was fond of his mother, but there had always been much awkwardness between them. Pat had been nearly sixteen when his father died, and Kathleen, out of an anxious fear that the boys might now get completely out of hand, had attempted to impose a strict regime upon him. Pat had accepted his father as a force of nature to be endured, evaded, and in later years challenged, but never resented. His mother appeared as an arbitrary human will, and his struggle with her produced in him excitements and emotions which he found in some way loathsome. He punished her subsequently by his silence and had now got into the habit of speaking to her very little. He had found her second marriage entirely incomprehensible; and although he liked rather than disliked his stepfather he felt contemptuous of him and had never regarded him as a person with any sort of authority.

"They're here now," said Jinny, ushering Frances Bellman and Andrew Chase-White into the room. Kathleen kissed Frances and complimented her on her dress. There was a mumble of greetings and a rumble of heavy chairs as everybody settled down about the small low tea-table, knocking it a good deal with their knees.

Pat stared at Andrew Chase-White without troubling to conceal the fact that he was inspecting him. Andrew had grown up a good deal since their last meeting. He had, almost, the face of a man, and an imposing blond moustache which he plucked at affectedly. He looked well in uniform, seeming taller and broader, and Pat felt no inclination to laugh at the glittering spurs and highly polished boots. Even Cathal seemed rather impressed and silenced. There entered the room with this smartly turned-out young officer the strong atmosphere of a larger public world. He seemed almost too good-looking, too typical, as if he had been chosen as a special envoy, a role which he seemed almost consciously to be playing, as he twitched his moustache and talked gallantly in a loud voice to Mrs. Drumm, casting sidelong glances at Pat. He also spent a good deal of time examining the room as if to make sure that there had been no unauthorized alterations in his absence. His gaze returned uneasily to the crucifix.

Pat was surprised to find how much he was affected by seeing Andrew in uniform. He had no particular interest in his cousin, though, as he had said to Cathal, he "didn't mind him." As a boy he had only been concerned with children older than himself and Andrew had always been among the small fry. What struck him now was simply that whiff of the public world, that incarnate image of the soldier, official, stamped and approved. Actually to have this large topical object planted, as if by a practical joke, in his own drawing room affected him not so much with annoyance as with surprise. There was also a certain envy, though not of Andrew personally. The young officer was an emblem of power. But Pat had his own reasons for not joining up.

Pat, who was vaguely aware that he had been, at various childhood times, rather "hard on" Andrew, was conscious now of his cousin's almost frantic desire to impress him. There was an atmosphere of revenge in the air. Pat noticed it absently, casually, since he felt himself entirely invulnerable through being completely superior. He was prepared, even with a sort of amusement, to let his opponent enjoy what he took to be an advantage, easily inhibiting an assertion of personality which would have put young Andrew definitively in his place. As far as Pat was concerned, Andrew was still the little shouting boy who had followed him about, making a nuisance of himself on beaches all round the coast of Ireland. The present phenomenon was interesting not as an individual but as a type.

Kathleen was now talking to Frances, laying down certain principles for dealing with the servant problem which were to be passed on to Hilda. The conversation among the other three was staccato: Andrew condescendingly over-friendly, Pat distantly polite, Cathal, now recovering from his first discomfiture, definitely truculent. Andrew addressed his remarks to Pat, who offered minimal replies, while they both ignored provocative interjections from Cathal.

"I see you have an Irish grammar there. How interesting. Who's studying it?"

"Cathal is."

"Is Irish a difficult language?"

"I understand that it's not an easy language."

"It must be grand to know it."

"Why don't you learn it, then?"

"Do you think it important that the Irish people should learn it?"

"Sure, aren't you Irish yourself?"

"It has a certain symbolic value."

" 'A country without language is a country without a soul.' "

"Yes, I appreciate that it has a symbolic value. On the other hand, if one is born to the language of Shakespeare—"

"You mean the language of Cromwell."

"Don't keep interrupting, Cathal."

"Well, I know when I'm not wanted!"

Cathal turned his chair right round to face Frances and his mother. Pat felt, like a small electric shock, a change in the emotional temperature which he realized to be Andrew's apprehension of their being left as it were tête-à-tête. Pat began to feel extreme irritation. He hoped that the conversation would not start to come round to the question of the war. He thought he could feel, and that with even more annoyance, Andrew deliberately avoiding the subject. At the thought that the "lily-white boy" might see himself as tactfully sparing his interlocutor an embarrassment a jeering scowl invaded Pat's face. He composed his features with difficulty.

"You must come round and see my mother's new house."

"Oh, yes."

"She's always asking after you."

"I trust Aunt Hilda is well."

"She's fine now. She was awfully upset by the Zepps, you know."

"Was she?"

"And how is my Uncle Barnabas these days?"

"Very well, I believe."

"I'm so glad. You see I haven't had time to come and see him since I came over, actually."

"Really."

Calmly determined to let the conversation run if necessary to a stand-still, Pat fixed his eyes upon the crucifix above Andrew's head. He realized that this object somehow upset his cousin. Andrew squirmed in his seat. Pat thought he would try to force Andrew to look at the crucifix. But at that moment there was a little uproar from the other group.

"Our Lord said, 'I bring not peace but a sword.'" Cathal, who was incapable of tolerating a conventional conversation, had somehow steered the talk onto more general topics and was raising his voice.

"He meant the sword of the spirit," said Kathleen in a subdued way. Having spent so much of her life as a widow with two high-spirited boys she had cultivated a particularly soft rather dispiriting voice guaranteed to lower the temperature of any discussion.

"No, He didn't, and I tell you why, because He was a Socialist."

Frances laughed.

Pat, unable to resist contradicting his brother, turned round and said, "Even if that were true, which it isn't, it wouldn't be very relevant."

"How do you know if it's relevant since you don't know what we're talking about?"

Frances said, "We're discussing pacifism." She emulated Kathleen's slow, soft voice.

"I told you it wasn't relevant."

"It is so relevant. War is right when it's a fight for social justice."

"But you don't have to kill people fighting for social justice," said Kathleen. "I agree with Daniel O'Connell, 'No political reform is worth shedding one drop of blood.' "

"Are you a pacifist, Aunt Kathleen?" asked Andrew. His air of friendly condescension made Pat want to kick him.

"No, not really. I just feel about this awful trench warfare—it can't be right. War has changed its nature."

"It's all a matter of ends and means," said Cathal.

"But some means are so terrible they can't really *be* means any more because the end gets lost. And some means are wicked in themselves, like torturing people or murder."

"We call killing murder when we think it's means to a bad end," said Cathal. "Of course this war is senseless, but that's because it's an imperialist war, and not because—"

"You don't even know what 'imperialist' means," said Pat.

"You want to say," said Frances slowly and softly to Kathleen, "that it could be all right with bows and arrows, but *this* sort of thing couldn't possibly be all right. I think I agree with you. When you really look at what's happening the world seems to have gone mad."

"So you think Cousin Andrew's acting wrongly?" said Cathal, in a loud voice.

"Oh, no, no!" said Kathleen. "I was only speaking for myself."

"Something can't be right or wrong just for yourself. If it's right or wrong it must be right or wrong for everybody."

"Not at all," said Pat, "it depends what you mean—"

"Of course, in a way I agree with you, Aunt Kathleen," said Andrew. "It's all very well for people in places of safety to exhort us all to fight. But once one's been at close quarters with the business it's another matter."

There was a short silence. "How close quarters have you been at?" asked Pat, who very well knew the answer to his question.

Andrew flushed and frowned. "Well, I can't say I've seen any action yet. I wasn't long in France."

"It was smart of you to join the cavalry," said Cathal. "We all know the cavalry are kept miles behind the front line."

"That's not true, as it happens. And at least I've joined the Army. I'm not just sitting at home or playing at soldiers in the back garden like some people."

Cathal stood up, almost overthrowing the table. Frances and Kathleen started to speak in raised voices.

At that moment an extraordinary sound was heard just outside the room. It consisted of a series of loud resounding bumps accompanied by a tinkle of breaking glass and a human voice protesting in a traditional manner. Silence followed. Pat, interpreting the phenomenon, which was familiar to him in analogous forms, concluded that his stepfather, carrying some bottles of whiskey, must have fallen down the second flight of stairs, which, after creeping past the drawing-room door, he had been cautiously mounting. "Oh dear, oh dear, oh dear," said Kathleen. There was a general rush to the door.

Barnabas Drumm, wearing his hat, was sitting on the floor with his back against the newel post. A wide area of broken glass surrounded him, and from an extensive dark stain on the carpet there rose an overwhelming odour of whiskey. Barnabas looked sideways at the group in the doorway. Although he must have been perfectly aware that his predicament could amuse nobody and indeed must be causing a variety of different chagrins to all present, he could not help clowning it a little. He sat there with legs outstretched and began to whistle through his teeth.

Kathleen passed him by, stepping over him, and half ran along the landing. She returned in a moment with a dustpan and brush and, ignoring her husband, began to pick up the larger pieces of glass and put them into the pan. She worked slowly, in a resigned manner resembling the low voice she used to her sons, putting a quiet bitterness into the droop of her head.

Frances said, "Are you all right? Have you hurt yourself?"

Cathal retired back into the drawing-room and shut the door sharply behind him. He was always wounded and affronted by his stepfather's total lack of dignity.

Andrew put his hand on Frances' arm, as if to protect her from a rowdy scene.

Annoyed by all these reactions and infuriated by the author of the incident, Pat said, "For God's sake get up!" He pulled off his stepfather's hat and jammed it onto the post with a force which nearly split the crown.

With a good deal of dumb show, rubbing his bottom and his elbows, Barnabas began slowly to rise. He said, "Isn't it just the like of me to do a thing like that."

Barnabas Drumm was a short, round man with a mild, flabby face and a large golden moustache a little grizzled at the ends or soiled with Guinness. His brown hair fuzzed tonsure-fashion round a neat bald spot. The puzzled light blue of his eyes, invaded now by streaky reds and yellows, retained a childish quality. He still had a mouthful of good teeth and showed them often in a smile which though invariably gentle was also a reminder that he had once been better armed for the battle of life than he now seemed in general to be. Women, speculating about why level-headed Kathleen Dumay should have taken up with this muddle of a man, were divided between those who said that she had been pushed around by her first husband and now wanted someone she could push around, and those who voted Barney to be "really rather sweet."

"Hello, Andrew," said Barnabas. "We meet at last, though not in the happiest circumstances. Think of all that excellent whiskey gone bang. Oughtn't we all to go down on our knees and lick the carpet?"

"Barney, will you please see me to the tram?" said Frances

suddenly. Her voice sounded strained, as if she were about to burst into tears.

"Why, my dear, of course—"

Andrew said, "But, Frances—"

"No, don't you come, Andrew. You stay here. I've got something special I want to say to Barney. Thank you so much, Aunt Kathleen. I've so much enjoyed myself."

Frances had already seized her umbrella and her boa and was leading Barnabas away along the landing. Kathleen murmured something with her head still well down among the glass. Laboriously she was picking up tiny glittering splinters between her fingers.

Pat went back into the drawing-room and joined Cathal, who was standing stern-eyed at the window. Together, like a grim tribunal, they looked disapprovingly down upon their stepfather as he disappeared down the street arm-in-arm with Frances, sheltering under her umbrella in the light rain. He contrived to look jaunty. Pat detested jauntiness.

Andrew Chase-White, looking distracted, came running back into the room. The brothers ignored him. He seemed to run about for a little while like a dog. Then he returned to Kathleen and tried to help her with the glass, but the task appeared to be completed. He came back again and started to look for his raincoat. Pat wandered from the window and took up the George Moore novel. Andrew got as far as the door and then suddenly came back and stood before his cousin.

"Pat—"

"Yes?"

"Oh—sorry—nothing—"

"Good-bye, then."

Looking wretched, Andrew left the room, colliding with Kathleen, who was returning with the tea-tray. Murmuring thanks, he made for the stairs.

Kathleen, watched by her sons, began slowly to stack up the tea things. Pat noticed that she was crying. Big tears welled from her eyes and fell from her cheeks onto the tray. She always stooped double over any task she performed. Pat could not fathom his mother's frequent and unconcealed tears, but he felt them as an aggression upon himself and averted his eyes. These exhibitions displeased him without troubling him deeply. He found women obscure and mysterious but not interesting. Kathleen left the room.

"Ah well," said Cathal. " 'Up the long ladder and down the short rope, To hell with King Billy and long live the Pope.' What did he want, I wonder?"

"He wanted to apologize. He would have done so if you hadn't been here."

"Well, let him go. We don't mind him. He's nothing. Are you going to belt me?"

"I'll let you off this time."

"Pat—"

"Yes?"

Cathal came up behind his brother and gently put his arms round his waist. "When is it to be?"

"I don't know what you're talking about."

"You do so."

"I do not."

Four

"Over and over, like a mighty sea,
  Comes the love of *Jesus*, rolling over me!"

Several hundred youthful voices pealed it forth enthusiastically
as Andrew and his mother went with quickened step and stiffened
gait past the big marquee. A large red banner above it read *Children's Special Service Mission*, and *Saved by the Blood of the
Lamb*. Neither Andrew nor his mother referred to the phenomenon. They were on their way to visit Aunt Millicent.

  "You really must fix things up properly with Frances. After all,
it's up to you," said Hilda, as they began to pass out of range.

  "Once I was blind, now I can see,
    Once I was bound, but now I am free,
    And that's how I *know* there's a Saviour for me—
    Oh, such a Saviour!"

Andrew reflected, as the horrible sounds died away, that in
Ireland religion was a matter of choosing between one appalling
vulgarity and another. Wondering which he would vote for if he
had to choose, he concluded sadly that of course he would have

to be with the young people in the marquee and their boisterous mentors. "Yes," he said absently.

At the moment Andrew could think of nothing else but Pat Dumay. He regretted everything about yesterday's scene. He felt he had cut a rotten figure. He had failed to protect Frances from a sort of grossness in the atmosphere. He had construed her rushing off with Uncle Barnabas as a reproach to himself. He had helplessly witnessed his uncle playing the buffoon. And worst of all he had allowed himself to be provoked into taunting Pat. He had scarcely troubled to formulate any intention or resolution about this beforehand, so impossible had it seemed that he should affront his cousin. It had been for Andrew an axiom that Pat was a little larger than life and far too dignified and authoritative to be in any way goaded or jeered at. Such behaviour would only belittle the jeerer; as he now felt himself belittled. More than this, he felt an acute regret, almost a sentimental pain, to think that he had probably ruined his chances of becoming Pat's friend. He now realized, inordinately, surprisingly upset by the incident, that so far from being "liberated" from his uncomfortable interest in his cousin, he had returned to Ireland with the ardent hope of being treated as his equal, of winning his respect and even his affection. Yesterday's encounter had been very important to him, and now that it had misfired he was left with an emotional problem. He had hardly been able to bring himself to leave the house, he could not remember whether he had said good-bye to Aunt Kathleen, and he would certainly have attempted some reconciliation scene then and there, had not the maddening Cathal been standing by.

"After all, Frances wants a formal proposal, any girl does"— Hilda was going on. "It's a great moment in one's life. She'll want to be able to remember it later on. It is really time there was an announcement. And you must do something about a ring. It isn't fair to other young men, and now that Frances is going more into society you don't want to land her in difficulties."

With an effort Andrew switched his attention to Frances. Yes, he really must get Frances fixed up. And of course, yes, a great moment. My dearest Frances, I have something of very great importance to ask you. I wonder if you can at all guess what it is? Indeed, dear Andrew, I cannot conjecture. You will have to tell me. I wish you to do me the honour of becoming my wife. "You are quite right, Mama," he said.

"I do hope Christopher will be on time. I saw him this morning at Bewley's in Grafton Street and he swore he'd come. It's such a job to get him round to Millie's. I do find your aunt rather a strain and I know he does too. Thank heavens it's stopped raining, so perhaps he'll wait for us outside. You say everything looked just the same at Blessington Street? I really must get round there and see the boys, Kathleen keeps pestering me. I am surprised she does not re-do her drawing-room. She could easily afford it, and it must look so shabby and old-fashioned now."

"It looked exactly as I always remember it."

It was a room that receded into his earliest childhood like a long dirty corridor, always twilit, stuffy, melancholy, vaguely menacing. And yet perhaps it was not quite the same, or rather he himself had changed. He recalled seeing yesterday, as he checked the massy drifts of furniture and the myriad objects still rooted in their old places, an Oriental table with innumerable pieces of glass set into its gilded legs. He remembered this, which had once seemed to him an object of exotic beauty; it now looked as his mother would see it, tawdry, vulgar. Some glory had gone from the room, something which at least it had had which resembled beauty. The presence of the big crucifix, which had formerly seemed both thrilling and alarming, now just seemed a piece of rotten bad form, characteristic of the particular undiscriminating muddle in which his aunt and uncle lived. Well, well, he would take Frances to England, away from all this. Yes, Andrew, she whispered gratefully, yes, yes. Her little hand sought his, and as he drew her to his breast he could feel the violent beating of her heart.

"Ah, there's Christopher waiting outside, bless him, wearing that comical mackintosh hat. Hello, Christopher, we were hoping you would be punctual. Oh, before I forget, Kathleen was at Claresville just after luncheon and said she'd looked for you at Finglas and there was something special she wanted to see you about."

Christopher seemed a little depressed by this news. "What have I done now? Did she say what it was? Was she upset?"

"No, she didn't say. She wasn't upset. You know Kathleen's never exactly bright and gay. I shouldn't think it's important, so don't worry."

"Ah, well. Once more into the breach, dear friends."

Aunt Millicent's town house was what Hilda called "one of the better-class houses" of Dublin. It was a "double-fronted" house in Upper Mount Street, several times wider than the house in Blessington Street, but otherwise not unlike it in structure. In the watery sunlight the brick façades of Upper Mount Street glowed a rusty pink and yellow, only Millie's house, together with one or two others, had been washed over with a powdery red preparation, currently fashionable, and the interstices between the bricks outlined in black. The sagging steps up to the door were immaculately reddened to match. Beneath its magisterial fanlight the door was a radiant newly painted rose pink, its brass knocker, shaped like a fish, polished as softly bright and smooth as Saint Peter's toe; while at each gleaming window a heavy froth of lace curtain was symmetrically looped back. Just beyond, at the end of the street, the elegant green dome of Saint Stephen's, Church of Ireland, rose into the lucid blue sky. Long green coppery streaks trailed down the light grey stone of the tower and fingered the clock which was just now striking four. Its particular high cracked tone struck with a melancholy authority upon the heart of Andrew, recalling to him the church's rational empty interior where he had sometimes worshipped as a child, if participation in those calm, prosaic rites could be called worship.

A maid with long white streamers depending from her cap informed them that her ladyship was out in the garden. As they passed through the dark belly of the house Andrew tried to revive his memories of it. But it was many years since he had been there, and the rooms seemed unfamiliar. He glimpsed great mahogany surfaces gleaming like black mirrors in twilit interiors. There was a vernal smell of furniture polish.

The garden was more fresh in memory. He recognized, though he could not have pictured it beforehand, the wide terrace of slightly reddish paving stones, with its intermittent clumps of iris and rosemary and rue, and its square fish pool, the brown beech hedge beyond, still clothed in its crisp twirled winter leafage, and the little lawn with the propped-up mulberry tree. The scene was wet and glistening, the paving stones reflecting hints of light and form, the mulberry tree dripping. Then suddenly the sun became brighter and a light seemed switched on in the garden. The great hump of the mulberry tree glowed into a golden green. Aunt Millicent came through the gap in the hedge.

Andrew felt a perceptible pleasurable very rapid shock as if a needle had passed right through his body without hurting him. It was many years since he had seen his aunt, and although he retained intact, like old snapshots, some attractive memories of her, these had been gradually overlaid by his mother's continual though vague remarks about Millie's being so "tiresome," or being about to "go to pieces," a fate which was for some reason persistently foreseen by her sister-in-law. These prognostications, together with the reports of hunting, cigar-smoking, pistol shots, and trousers, had made him, without reflection, expect something slightly, by this time, gaunt and sourly tweedy, something a little weatherbeaten smelling of tobacco and even of whiskey, although drink had not in fact figured so far in his mother's denunciations. What confronted him now was a plump youngish woman with a radiantly smiling face, elegantly dressed in a tight-skirted, slightly old-fashioned mode, and positively, oh, very positively, pretty.

"Oh hello, my dears," shouted Millie across the terrace.

"You've come! Oh, goody!" She swept up to Hilda and began kissing her. "Hello, Christopher. Glad to see you, you old stranger. I absolutely adore your hat. And this is the golden-haired soldier boy! My, doesn't he look fine! I can remember him when he wasn't interested in anything but farthing lucky-bags. Can you remember those farthing lucky-bags, Andrew? Many a penny you begged off me for them, to get them at Nolan's shop. But I mustn't remind you of that now, must I? Why, I think he's blushing, the pet!"

Andrew, smiling rather stiffly, felt he had gained a little insight after all into what his mother meant by "tiresomeness."

"It's very nice to see you, Millie," said Hilda. "You seem to be keeping well. We had such a pleasant walk here. Merrion Square is looking lovely, with the lilac and the laburnum all ready to flower. And I'm glad to say the rain seems to have given up at last."

"Oh, yes, and I thought we'd have tea in the garden," said Millie. "Wouldn't that be fun? I haven't done it yet this year."

"Won't it be a bit wet and cold for tea in the garden?" said Hilda, not concealing her displeasure.

"I'll lend you all woolly shawls from Connemara. I've just got some new ones and they're such pretty colours. And as for a little wet, sure I don't mind it, and you won't either when you've been over here a bit longer. One's getting oneself wet all the time in Ireland, isn't that so, Christopher? Sure I don't mind it at all."

This appeared to be true, as Andrew observed that his aunt's high-necked dress of dove-grey silk, which with the enthusiastic gesturing that accompanied her words constantly swirled against the low bushes, was darkened with water and even muddied all round the lower hem. He also noticed as she swayed the rather old-fashioned flounced bustle effect at the back, unless it was indeed perhaps Aunt Millicent's shape. He looked elsewhere.

"Well, I think we shall be cold," said Hilda firmly. She seemed to have decided it was a matter of principle to show the flag to her sister-in-law straight away.

"The sun's shining and it'll be dry directly," Millie went on inconsequently. "Wouldn't you like to walk down the garden? The little brick path is a dry way."

"How's the camellia?" said Christopher.

"Oh, but it's in *flower*, it's a *sight*. You take Hilda down to the greenhouse to see the camellia and young Andrew shall stay here and help me with the tea things."

Christopher led Hilda away. The murmur of her protests could be heard receding beyond the hedge.

"Aren't they a well-matched couple?" said Millie, looking after them. Then she laughed. "Well now, young Andrew, come and sit down and let me look at you."

She drew him to a wooden seat and they sat down. The long twisting branches of rosemary swept the pavement at their feet. The seat was extremely wet, as Andrew instantly realized. The dove-grey silk took the matter in its stride.

Millie sat for a moment staring at him, and he, half annoyed, half amused, returned her stare. She was not perhaps as handsome as she had seemed at first sight. Her complexion was rather coarse and her mouth too large. She had big dark brown eyes which she continually narrowed, perhaps because she was short-sighted. Her reddish-brown hair, to which a fine and scarcely perceptible scattering of grey gave a metallic patina, was much plaited and entwined. Two small ears held their own against it, adorned with bright blue lapis lazuli earrings. After having been a very laughing face it was now a very serious face. It compelled Andrew, and only after he had been looking into her eyes in silence for half a minute did he realize how unusual this proceeding was.

"Yes," she said. "You *are* like him. I could never really see it before."

"Like—"

"Like your father. You are really very like him now."

"I'm glad," said Andrew lamely. The scrutiny now embarrassed him and he averted his eyes.

"I wonder if you remember a picnic at Howth—well, why should you, you were very young. Tell me about yourself. So you were in France, but not for long, you got pneumonia, and you're still on sick leave?"

Andrew was a bit surprised and flattered at this knowledge of his lot. "Yes. I'm afraid I haven't seen much action yet."

"Don't worry," said Millie. "This old war is going to last quite a while. You'll have plenty of time to behave with reckless courage on some battlefield."

"I hope so."

"Well, you're a fool to hope so. I really think one should be a pacifist. I'm sure they could all make peace now if they tried. But what with the wicked old men and the silly young ones—it's about time women had the vote. Are you political?"

Andrew was not sure how serious she was. He answered lightly. "I don't understand much about politics. I'm leaving that for later."

"I think we should all be political nowadays. I say, my bottom says it's wet, what does yours say? Let's walk about a bit, take a turn, as your mother would say."

She jumped up, and as she did so swept her hand along one of the rosemary branches, collecting the small narrow leaves in her palm. A delicious musty fragrance arose which almost made Andrew sneeze.

"I love things with grey leaves, don't you? Well, rosemary hasn't actually got grey leaves, or rather they're only grey underneath, but that was the idea of this garden, and the rue has, and that stuff called trimalchio or whatever it is. There—" As she took his arm she strewed the leaves of the rosemary over his khaki sleeve.

"That's for remembrance. And rue—what is rue for, I forget?"

"For sorrow, I suppose," said Andrew.

"Such a pretty plant. Well, sorrow we shall all have, especially you, as you are so young. I keep thinking I have grown out of sorrow, but it keeps coming back. Don't worry about the tea, Maudie will lay it inside whatever I say, and I declare I think it's going to rain again after all. Come and see my fish."

She released him, and moved to the other side of the little fish pool, regarding him across it. The brown surface of the pool quivered a little at their feet, perhaps with some preliminary drops of rain. The sky behind Millie was now a bright, hazy yellow.

Andrew stared at his aunt across the pool. The blue earrings glowed in the dark, convoluted hair.

She murmured, "Yes, you are confoundedly like your da. What are you thinking at this moment?"

Andrew framed in his mind the sentence, How beautiful your earrings are, Aunt Millicent. He said, "How beautiful you are, Aunt Millicent."

There was a second's silence before Millie's loud laugh. "Why, you naughty boy, are you flirting? And you engaged to the dearest girl in the world! Well, you must bring her to see me. You must come to tea next Thursday at Rathblane, the pair of you. And next Thursday, but not before, you shall call me Millie."

She knelt down on the pavement beside the pool. Andrew knelt too, embarrassed at what he had so unaccountably said, but also, unaccountably, feeling rather pleased with himself. He pretended to be investigating the fish.

As he looked down into the dense brown vegetable depths of the pool something suddenly flashed past him. There was a glint of blue and a splash and a receding sinking glimmer. "Dear me," said Millie. "One of my earrings has gone west."

With an exclamation of distress Andrew peered down into the pool where the earring had completely disappeared from view, and his first instinctive idea was that it was lost forever. He looked up at Millie and found her regarding him coolly, her eyebrows slightly raised. She seemed unmoved by the incident and only interested in what he would do.

"Of course," said Andrew, as if laboriously working it out,

"the pool's not very deep, is it? I'll get it for you." His hand broke the surface of the warm water. He hesitated. Rather awkwardly he removed his watch and put it in his pocket and then began to take off his jacket. Millie stared at him. He folded the jacket and then could not think what to do with it, being unwilling to lay it on the wet pavement, until Millie reached out and took it from him in silence. He rolled up one sleeve of his shirt to the shoulder and loosened his tie and undid the shirt at the neck where it was a little tight. These preparations seemed to take a ludicrously long time. He plunged his arm into the pool up to the elbow, deeper, without touching bottom. A pale oval, the reflection of Millie's face, danced disjointedly on the disturbed surface. Andrew lay down full length upon the pavement. As the water lapped at his shoulder his hand explored the soft sludgy bottom. He touched something hard, and the next moment had fished up the earring. He handed it quickly to his aunt and they both rose.

Andrew felt distressed and discomfited by the incident, chiefly, as he now confusedly felt, because he had paused to take his jacket off; and yet it would have been idiotic to plunge his arm in without doing so. He quickly resumed his jacket. He coughed and began to brush down his breeches, to which a greenish slime from the pavement adhered in streaks. He was beginning to feel annoyed and put in the wrong.

"Andrew," said Aunt Millicent.

He straightened up to look at her. At once with a quick gesture she dropped the earring down inside the front of his shirt. A second later Hilda and Christopher appeared through the gap in the hedge. The terrace rang with Millie's unexplained laughter. It began to pour with rain.

Five

_____

"I thought they'd never go," said Christopher.

"How did you give them the slip?"

"I said I was going into town."

"You don't think Aunt Hilda suspects?"

"Darling Hilda knows nothing."

"Did she say anything special?"

"Only that it was just like you to want to have tea in the garden. I must say I agree!"

"But that was on purpose," said Millie. "I thought if we were all shivering out on the terrace they'd go all the sooner!"

"So you're not as feckless as I thought. A shrewd, calculating person lives inside you."

"Well, not really. I only invented the reason afterwards."

"Whatever did you do to young Andrew, by the way? You must have bewitched him. He said practically nothing all through tea and just fumbled with the neck of his shirt."

Millie laughed. "Oh, I did something to embarrass him. Never mind what. He is so touchingly like his father, one can't help teasing him. Do you fancy him as a son-in-law?"

"He's all right. He's not as intelligent as Frances, but he's got sense and a very sweet nature. And they know each other very well and love each other."

"Love—ah, well—"

"Ah, well, indeed."

This conversation was taking place in a long upper room, originally a billiard room, which Millie used as a combination of personal boudoir and shooting gallery. The combination of these two atmospheres unnerved, and doubtless was intended to unnerve, Millie's friends. The room was thickly carpeted, and at the near end, by the door, looking obscurely ecclesiastical, stood a low white dressing table with a tall mirror surmounted by a large lace canopy not unlike those which are held above the Host in religious processions. A plump pink stool, gathered in to a waistline of silken roses, was placed before the mirror, which was flanked by a pair of gilded candlesticks containing candles, unlit at the moment. All round about was a cluster of extremely comfortable satin-covered armchairs, all facing the mirror, placed as if for some ceremony at which Millie would adorn herself or possibly undress before an admiring audience. This ceremony, as far as Christopher knew, never took place, nor did he suppose, though he had never investigated, that the jars of Waterford glass on the dressing table actually contained cosmetics. They were more likely to contain liqueurs. As far as he knew: for sometimes, for a fleeting moment, he had the suspicion that Millie led some secret life where, with other recondite suitors, she proceeded to lengths of which he never dreamed. But in fact that was impossible; he knew all about Millie: and even if he lacked, certainly no one else enjoyed, the ultimate privileges.

The wall at the far end of the room, faced with wood and pitted with revolver fire, was bare except for the row of targets at which, standing among the satiny chairs, Millie took aim with her small nickel-plated revolver. The side walls, lined with a furry green vegetational wallpaper, were thickly covered with tolerably good oil paintings of members of the Kinnard family. At these, with suitably pugnacious exclamations, Millie often pointed her weapon, but had only once loosed off a bullet in their direction, which happily lodged in a frame. Christopher disliked these sports. He hated the noise and the horrible sensation of the impact. Millie, armed, cut a pretty figure. But he took the menace of it painfully to himself.

Although it was still light outside, Millie had pulled the curtains and lit the gas, and the fierce bright mantles purred along the room under their red tasselled shades. During the time in which Christopher had been engaged in "giving the slip" to Andrew and Hilda, she had changed out of the tight grey dress into a looser shorter dress of purple crêpe de Chine, rather Oriental in appearance. She kept nudging the skirt of it against her leg as she stood, as if unused to the length, while she played absently with the revolver, spinning the barrel fast and then stopping it abruptly with her finger. Christopher, outstretched in one of the armchairs, watched her with exasperation, fascination, adoration, and fear.

"You know, Christopher, when you play Russian roulette it isn't really dangerous because the weight of the bullet always pulls the loaded chamber down to the bottom."

"I have no intention of playing Russian roulette. You are quite breath-taking enough as a pastime. Don't change the subject, my darling."

The process of falling in love with Millie had, for Christopher, taken place over quite a long period. Yet there had never been any moment when he had both understood clearly what he was doing and been still able to control it. At moments of control he had not understood, and at moments of understanding he had been helpless. He sometimes told himself that if he could have prevented this thing from happening he would have done so. He knew, now, what Millie did, but he did not know what Millie thought, and he feared, coming upon them suddenly, certain blank moments of ruthlessness in her. Yet even the process of coveting Millie, at first as it had seemed so vainly, had renewed the world for him, and in her light he had seen every flower, every leaf, every bird designed with a wiry clarity and plumped out with a celestial untainted colour.

When Christopher had first met Millie, at a time when he himself was courting Heather Kinnard, she was already married to Arthur. He had disliked her, chiefly, as it seemed in retrospect, because she had tended to put Heather in the shade. Yet Heather had adored her dominating sister-in-law and defended her heartily against Christopher's criticisms. He had thought Millie loud, vulgar, and thoroughly selfish. He still thought her loud, vulgar, and thoroughly selfish, only now these things were meat and drink to him; or rather, he saw her faults with a difference, touched by romance into gaiety and by charity into innocence. Kathleen, whose conceptual armoury did not include the idea of vulgarity, disliked and indeed feared in Millie a merciless rapacity upon which she blamed Arthur's early death. Kathleen once said of Millie, "She respects no one. She does not see where another person begins." But Heather enjoyed Millie's flamboyance, her noise. This paler, frailer, quieter soul took from her boisterous sister-in-law the reflection of a more abundant life. Perhaps, Christopher had often felt, Arthur's attitude to Millie was of this kind too. He had enjoyed being digested by this larger organism. And it also occurred to Christopher to wonder: had he himself similarly engulfed Heather? Was he able to "see where another person begins"? No one had seemed to blame him for the way in which Heather had faded from life. Yet perhaps something in himself, less noisy, less overtly colourful, but just as ruthlessly and largely egoistic, had thrust aside that gentler, weaker spirit. But, of course, these were strictly irrational speculations. Heather had died from a disease of the liver and Arthur from cancer of the stomach. Science proclaimed their deaths normal, unavoidable.

Perhaps, in the long run, it was some deep sense of identification with his sister-in-law, some feeling of the similarity of their temperaments, of a profound likeness underneath a superficial unlikeness, which had made Christopher so interested. Arthur's demise had preceded Heather's by some eighteen months, and at the time of these deaths Christopher's dislike of Millie had been at a maximum: possibly because he felt himself associated with her in some kind of guilty pact. All the same, she had by now become an object of speculation, irritation, fascination. Perhaps too he had in a way learnt from Heather to regard Millie as one of the world's more significant objects. When her name came up in conversation he would jump and listen nervously, and when she was present he was always unusually argumentative. Then one day she asked him to lend her some money.

That was now about eight years ago. It had been a significant moment, and Christopher had felt it to be such at the time. It had been, for him, the first indication that all was not well with Millie's finances. She lived extremely lavishly, and it had been and still was confidently assumed by the world at large that Millie Kinnard was "pretty well heeled." Christopher was surprised, interested, and in a prophetic way curiously pleased to find that this was not so. He lent her the money at once, without comment, happy to be, and happy to be tacitly expected to be, supremely discreet. She was grateful; he was politely, reticently dignified; and at once their relationship was altered. Christopher's money had come to him from his father, who had been a teacher of mathematics at Trinity, an amateur economist, and an expert gambler on the Stock Exchange—which expertise had augmented an already comfortable family fortune. Christopher himself was neither rapacious nor mean and had not inherited his father's taste for playing with money. Yet money was important to him, its presence was a deep source of security, and it was somehow a stuff through which he was vitally connected with the world. A part of his life-blood ran through it. And when he became financially connected with Millie some warmth passed from him to her with the connection. It was this primitive touching, more even perhaps than the more obvious sense of a power over her, which made him begin to fall in love.

But, of course, these explanations, upon which he himself later meditated, were in a way otiose. Millie was a gorgeous, desirable object. He wondered why all men were not in love with her, and soon began to suspect that they were. She was an overflowing vessel, a plump, gay, generous woman. There was some coldness, some shivering, shrewd thinness in Christopher which needed her desperately, which clung to her as to a source of warmth and life. He only half concealed his need, watching her with a large affectation of detachment, and enraptured by the cool amused gaze which, in the formality of their new relationship, she with equal affectation adopted. He remembered how, in the old quarrelling days, Millie would sometimes shout out, "But I adore Christopher!" Now, as their poker-faced relation gradually broke down into tenderness and laughter, he realized that Millie was not only grateful, she was prepared in effect to adore him. This made Christopher very happy indeed.

Time passed, and Millie's affairs became more involved and difficult. Christopher lent her more money. He gave her advice too, but he was a prudent rather than an original capitalist, and an ineffective helper. Millie took advice in other quarters, without revealing the seriousness of the situation, and merely increased the muddle she was in. She was incapable of economies. Christopher watched these developments with mixed feelings, and gradually an idea which seemed to him both sinister and delightful formulated itself in his mind. Millie's difficulty would be Christopher's opportunity.

That he might ever ask Millie to marry him was a notion which, after he had fallen in love with her, he had early dismissed. He wanted to be happy, to enjoy the deliciousness of her company, not to ask too much; and it seemed clear that she could not possibly want to marry him. She was a spoilt girl, he was not by any means her only admirer, and she ostentatiously enjoyed her freedom. She "adored" him, but she was not in the least in love with him. "Adoration" was something different. Millie skipped about, bounded like a dog, shouted more than usual when Christopher arrived. But she let him depart without repining. She liked the intermittent character of their converse. He would have wished to be with her day and night. He coveted her body with a passion which his shrewd hedonism constantly quieted and checked. He did not care, at his age, to suffer the sleepless nights of unsatisfied desire, and he did not in fact suffer them. But he wanted Millie; and he knew that she did not, in that way, want him.

Discretion about money had somehow cast a veil of secrecy over their whole relationship. It was not generally known that they were fond of each other or that they met so often; and Christopher kept up for the benefit of some of his relations the fiction that he found Millie "trying." He did this partly out of an innate taste for the clandestine, partly because of the money question, and partly because Millie wanted it that way. Christopher was realistic and resigned about Millie's desire for secrecy. A popular woman who enjoys her admirers and is also kind-hearted will naturally want to keep her friendships strictly sealed off from each other. To each man Millie seemed available with an undivided attention and a full heart. Christopher was consoled by being more in her confidence than most. He at least knew about the others; and he was fairly certain that, at present at any rate, these "relationships" which Millie cultivated remained at a level of innocuous flirtation, although hearts other than hers were sometimes cracked in the process.

There was however yet another and graver reason for Christopher's secrecy, and that was the attitude of Frances. Frances disliked Millie, perhaps because, although Christopher had always, and quite automatically, concealed it from her, she sensed her father's interest and was jealous, or perhaps out of a strong temperamental disparity. "I don't like being bounced at," Frances had once said coldly after some demonstration of Millie's. And Millie indeed, who was always made nervous by the presence of Frances, whom she felt as a critic, had made various effusive but vain attempts to win the girl round. Christopher loved Frances dearly, though he had always treated her, even as a child, in the cool, ironical manner which he used to the world at large. In this respect, he and his daughter, early left to each other's company by the vanishing of Heather, perfectly understood one another, and made no display of a strong affection which passed freely between them under a guise of such calmness that not everyone realized that they loved each other at all.

Before Christopher had formulated the idea of asking Millie to marry him he had not too much troubled about the hostility of Frances. It had merely provided another motive for a total discretion. But when the notion of such a marriage had appeared in the background the view which Frances might take of it became an appalling source of anxiety. That Frances disliked Millie was, of course, in itself a serious impediment; and there was also the possibility that a projected match between her father and "that woman" might produce in Frances some unprecedented reaction of violence. Christopher was aware that in some respects which were relevant to this problem he did not know his daughter very well. Their relations had been, in a sense, too perfectly organized. Being so much in each other's company, they had early developed an adult language of understatement, and their feelings, just because they were so harmonious, had been tacit. But Christopher divined in his daughter the presence of an as yet unpractised stubbornness, the presence of ferocious will.

The marriage question, for some time hovering in the background, had now suddenly and automatically been brought into the foreground by the almost complete collapse of Millie's fortunes. This collapse was not yet known to the world. At Upper Mount Street the maids with the white streamers still tripped confidently about the house and under the windows of Rathblane the hunters still strolled and nibbled the green grass. The chauffeur still polished the brass fitments of the Panhard. But all this must shortly vanish like a dream, dissolve like Aladdin's palace, unless . . .

Christopher, faced with the supreme temptation, did not attempt to resist it, did not even formulate the idea of it as a temptation, so confident did he now suddenly feel in his gods. He would save Millie, he would save her by marrying her. The idea that he was in effect proposing to buy Millie was perfectly clear in his mind, but seemed in the context entirely innocuous. The one who is in love has the significant destiny, and Christopher felt that, beyond his hopes, a path had been made, a door had been opened, especially for him. His significance would felicitously espouse Millie's misfortune. There was indeed an inevitability about it, the other side of which was that it was somehow clearly "impossible" for Christopher to save Millie without marrying her.

Although the idea that there was only one solution had been taking shape over a period of months, as Millie's financial affairs went into the final phases of collapse, it was only in the last four weeks or so that Christopher had used explicitly the words which named his intention. This had happened during scenes in which Millie would say desperately, "I'll sell this house and Rathblane and go into lodgings," and Christopher would say, "Don't be foolish. You know you can't face it. You'll marry me and everything will be all right." Then Millie would laugh loudly, say, "It looks as if I'll have to!" and change the subject. It was true that Millie could not face it, that she would in the end do anything rather than face it; and meanwhile she played a little for time.

This period of their relationship had had, for Christopher, a special, rather sad charm. Millie had been, of late, even in the last year, more subdued, less boisterous. It was not that she seemed older or positively melancholy, but her beauty wore a sort of gauzy veil which perhaps only he could see. She was less rowdy, and her gaiety sometimes seemed "switched on," an effort, and she was often thoughtful. Christopher had her cornered and she knew it. She used now her resources of irony and humour to cover the loss of her dignity as a free being. She seemed without resentment. There was something beautiful and sad in this loss of power which made him feel very tenderly towards her. It was like a stage in taming a wild beast when it becomes suddenly gentle and puss-like. It plunges far off, but feels the rope that draws and draws it. Now it trots more soberly nearby. Soon it will come to the hand. It will have to.

This was how Christopher saw it most of the time; but there were moments of uneasiness when he felt that the closer he came to her the more likely it was that Millie might suddenly bolt. He would have been prepared to let her decide very slowly indeed. He rather enjoyed his state of undeclared sovereignty. But financial pressures set the pace, and Millie herself seemed increasingly anxious to settle her fate, although she still avoided any clear commitment; while Christopher, who had intended not to press her, could not now prevent himself from advancing upon her as the situation itself relentlessly advanced. No, he did not really think that she could escape him. Yet with a woman like Millie one never knew. She was used to doing things on the hunting field which seemed equivalent to suicide; and, although she was probably incapable of facing poverty, she was not incapable of pulling the house down, of provoking some total catastrophe on the assumption that the world was going to end immediately.

"Have some of your special cider and sherry mixture," said Millie. "I've got some here in a jug."

"Thanks." Christopher was partial to a mixture of two parts of Tio Pepe to one part of dry cider.

She released the glass into his fingers but kept her hand lightly resting against his, looking down at him. The purple silk brushed his knee.

"You look Chinese today, Millie. It must be the dress."

"Good. I shall need all my inscrutability for dealing with you." She suddenly laughed and moved away. "Do you know, poor dear Hilda, I was watching her at tea. I think she thinks she's got you hooked."

Christopher laughed too. "Not hooked, no. She pictures us as two ancient craft driven by the storms of fortune into the selfsame anchorage!"

"When is Frances getting married?"

Christopher drew a quiet breath. Millie's jumpy, nervy mood

both frightened and exhilarated him. How endlessly she must have thought about Frances. Yet the name was rarely mentioned between them. "Soon."

"How soon?"

"I don't know. That foolish boy still hasn't fixed it. But he will directly. I'll make him."

It was a sad thing to Christopher, and perhaps the only thing about which he really felt guilt, that he was now actually impatient for Frances to be married. Indeed, she must be married before anything else could happen. He feared that will of hers, roaming unoccupied and uncaged.

"Christopher—"

"Yes, dear?"

"Do you think I'm getting old and ugly?"

"You know perfectly well what I think."

"I must be getting old. I need to hear somebody saying that I am gorgeously attractive. Once I didn't need to be told, except by my looking-glass."

"You are gorgeously attractive, Millie."

She paused by the tall mirror and with a large gesture lit the candles on either side of it. Like a new ghost in the flickering light her reflection gazed at Christopher, and the reflection had suddenly the remote distinction of a work of art, and something too of the eternal sadness of art.

"Well, it's not true, but bless you for saying it. This soft light suits me, don't you think? It makes me hazy. One mustn't look too close. I am getting old. I'm nearly ready to retire. Perhaps I'll retire with you and we'll go and live in the hotel at Greystones and become a well-known old couple taking a turn on the front."

"I wish you would! You know how much I wish—"

"Sssh, Christopher."

"Yes?"

"I like you because you are so clever."

"Oh, Millie, do stop tormenting me." He had not meant to strike this note, but suddenly it was unbearable, the enclosed scene and her proximity. The straight silk dress moved upon her body as if she were naked beneath. She was very close and it was an agony not to touch her.

"I'm sorry," she said in a suddenly desolate tone, and moved out of the soft aura of the candles. After a pause she said, "I don't want to sell Rathblane."

"I know you don't."

"I like being Lady Kinnard of Rathblane."

Christopher gripped his glass. Millie was now going to say something which he had long guessed to be in her mind although she had never explicitly uttered it. "Yes?"

"Yes. Christopher—would we have to change things altogether? You know you could have anything that you wanted. I am that sort of girl. Or rather, I could be for you."

"But I am not that sort of man. Besides—"

"Besides?"

"I should require—shall we say moderate faithfulness."

Millie laughed but became tense again the next moment. "You are modest! I would be faithful to you—moderately."

"That is what you will be with marriage, my dear. Without marriage you would be nothing."

Millie sat down on the stool, smoothing the purple silk over her thighs and gathering it tightly with one hand behind her knees. "Yes, you are clever. I could say that I might find someone else more accommodating. But unfortunately you know quite well that I could only tolerate an arrangement of this sort with a very old friend, and a highly intelligent one at that."

They were silent for a moment.

Christopher said with emotion, "Millie, I want you to be Mrs. Bellman. I want Mrs. Bellman to be you."

"It doesn't sound so good," she said with a sigh. "Well, you are my last temptation, the devil come to buy my soul."

"Hardly your last temptation, darling Millie. But sell, please sell!"

"I'll think about it," said Millie, jumping up. "Or perhaps I shall shoot myself instead. Do you think I have the temperament for suicide?"

"No. You love yourself far too dearly. We are not suicidal types, my darling."

"I'm afraid you're right. And now I'm going to turn you out because I've got another visitor coming."

"Who?" said Christopher. He got up, trembling with irritation and jealousy.

"Barney. He's coming for his evening bowl of milk. And he's to help me sort some papers. He's so devoted and useful."

Christopher could not understand how Millie could encourage the futile, crawling homage of someone like Barnabas Drumm. For many years now Barney had had—unknown, Christopher suspected, to Kathleen—a sort of position as a lackey, or serviceable buffoon, in Millie's household. How this curious relationship had started, or why it continued, Christopher did not know. He supposed that Millie was simply incapable of refusing a devotion, however absurd. He was hurt by this lack of dignity in her, and he was a little affronted too on behalf of Kathleen, whom he respected. This little game of Millie's, he felt, would have to stop. It had, of course, never occurred to him to be jealous of Barney.

Millie had gone to the door. "Barney'll take a knock," she said thoughtfully.

"How do you mean?"

"If I say yes."

"If you say yes. Dearest Millie—"

"All right, all right. Come to me on Wednesday. Come before luncheon, about midday. Or no, I'll come to you. Isn't that the day when Hilda and Frances go to town? I'd like to come to Sandycove. It would feel so dangerous! I'll give you your answer then. Now please go, I'm so tired."

They moved out onto the dark landing. There was a stirring down below and Millie looked over. "Why, I think that's Barney coming up. Come, boy, come, boy!" She whistled shrilly as if for a dog. "Good boy, good boy, come, come!"

Six

When Cathal had asked his question, "When is it to be?" Pat Dumay had not known the answer. He knew the answer now. The armed rising was to begin on Easter Sunday at six o'clock in the evening.

Pat had known for some long time that it would happen, that it would come. He had long felt it as inevitable, had taken it as it were into his own body. It was as if he were fixed to a steel chain the other end of which was hidden in that imagined mystery of violence, and he could feel it almost as a physical pain, a physical pleasure, drawing him towards it. But it was one thing to know, however certainly, that it would come; it was quite another to be given a date and a definite diminishing final interim of five days. What had been imagined had entered time, and now the pattern of the hours lay under its authority. The news, which Pat had received this very morning, Tuesday the eighteenth of April, had been itself like a moment of violence, a blow which spread out through his flesh like a red rosette of anguish and delight. He was afraid. But such fear was a glorious decoration. He was afraid, but he knew himself too to be a brave man. He had not enjoyed the spectacle of others suffering in a war which he could not join, and he had not liked it either when they distinguished themselves. There had been moments when his own war had seemed an unreal sham. But there had been for him no alternative to that war.

It seemed to Pat that he had been born to a vision of fighting for Ireland. His parents had had little Irish patriotism, and this lack was for him a part of their utter commonplaceness. His own recognition of himself as far from commonplace came with his early sense of his Irish destiny, his sense of belonging not to himself but to some design of history. He knew himself, even as a boy, as one chosen and already under orders. His first vivid memories were of the South African war, Dublin decked out in Transvaal flags, Boer songs sung in the streets, and the crowd at the *Irish Times* office to cheer a victory over the English. He had seen the Union Jack burnt and plumed troopers charging a crowd. The shock, the experience of subjection, the knowledge of belonging to a subject race, came into him with his first consciousness, together with a cold, fierce will to freedom. And when, at George the Fifth's coronation visit, the town had been decked with hostile streamers declaring, "Thou art not conquered yet, dear land," Pat had felt himself come of age for Ireland. The enormity of the insult laid upon his people, matched with his own unshaken sense of his worth, produced in him such a charge of power and resentment that at times he felt himself almost capable of acting and succeeding alone.

His patriotism was not of the diffuse and talkative kind, and though it was certainly romantic it was with some distilled essence of romanticism, something bitter and dark and pure. He had small use for "Cathleen ni Houlihan," nor was he interested in Patrick Pearse's archaistic visions of a virtuous, manly society whose manners were somehow to be restored. He had never joined the Gaelic League, and though he had attempted to learn Irish he did not think the language important. He was himself a matter-of-fact practising Catholic, but the pattern of his religion, though it remained secure, did not enter into the chief passion of his life. He was not one of those who made their Catholicism into nationalism. He was unmoved by the Holy Ireland affected by his stepfather, nor was he, like his younger brother, an ardent theorist. His Ireland was nameless, a pure Ireland of the mind, to be relentlessly served by a naked sense of justice and a naked self-assertion. There were in his drama only these two characters, Ireland and himself.

When the Irish Volunteers were founded in nineteen-thirteen Pat joined them at once. He was in fact at the time on the point of attaching himself to James Connolly's Irish Citizen Army. He had been much affected by the Labour troubles and much impressed by the great strike earlier that year. The courage and discipline of the unions stirred him deeply. Here again he had seen uniformed men attacking a crowd and had digested a violence of anger which nearly choked him. He had taken young Cathal to hear Jim Larkin speak, and had received certain new complexities into his concept of justice. So there were two kinds of masters to be reckoned with; and he listened, and his young brother listened even more avidly, to the words of those who said that the fight for freedom was a single fight and that the capitalist tyrant and the English tyrant must be driven out in the self-same battle.

However, when it came to it he joined the Volunteers. Without calling himself a Socialist, for he would never have called himself anything, he had no doubt at all that the capitalist system was irrational, tyrannical, and wicked. The sense of being a subject, a serf, which his sensitive awareness of his nationality had brought home to his pride at such an early age made him ready to identify himself with the Dublin workers. But whereas he envisaged the liberation of Ireland as something singularly simple and pure, he could not picture the liberation of the working class without becoming entangled in ambiguous speculations and theories. He was not convinced that the two fights could be fought at once and he was sure that the affair of Ireland came first.

He joined the Volunteers also out of a sense that here was his place. He despised the genteel snobbery of many of the Volunteer supporters and their "employer's Ireland"; but he felt that the hour of bloodshed would sufficiently separate the sheep from the goats. The men who were prepared to shoot and kill would be men of the right kind, and when the day came they and the Citizen Army would form one brotherhood. Meanwhile there was, of course, much less nonsense about the Citizen Army, whose discipline and fanaticism Pat observed with respect; and when he learnt that Connolly had lately interviewed each Citizen Army man individually and asked him if he would be willing to fight if the Army had to act without the Volunteers, and that each man had said yes, Pat felt something very like envy. But for just this reason, that the Volunteers represented something less compact and clear-headed, Pat had decided that his task lay with them. He conceived that the Volunteers needed backbone: he proposed himself as a stiffening agent; and he was influenced too by the idea that, in the Volunteer organization where there were fewer enthusiasts, he would receive a more rapid promotion.

Soon after joining the Volunteers, however, he discovered two things, first that the desired backbone was already present in the guise of an extensive secret group of the Irish Republican Brotherhood, and secondly, that he was not destined to shoot rapidly to the top of the military hierarchy. He was, he was never quite sure why, a little looked askance at. He overheard himself referred to as "Hotspur" and "that mad boy." He felt the unfairness of this, as he knew that in matters of action he was cold, all cold with a chilly clarity which surprised even him. But he hid his disappointment as he hid everything else. After the beginning of the war, when the Volunteers had divided in two and the traitors had shuffled away into the British Army, Pat rose to the rank of captain. He still felt himself misjudged by those above and he did not seek their friendship. Equally he did not encourage the personal loyalty of his men, though when it sometimes seemed to him that they idolized him he was not displeased. He lived privately, going to his work each day at the solicitor's office, but conceiving of himself entirely as a soldier.

There was another reason why Pat had not joined the Citizen Army. He could not have served under James Connolly. He admired and respected Connolly, and there had been a time when, holding Cathal by the hand, he had followed often in the procession while the great man marched dourly, followed by a supporter with an orange box, to some chosen street corner. Connolly would mount his box and the two boys would listen spellbound, though Pat was always the first one to want to go. But Connolly was both too human and too theoretical to command the devotion which Pat wanted to offer; and given the structure and temper of the Citizen Army it would have been impossible to be in it without feeling an intense emotional loyalty to its leader. Pat was a man of savage independence, and yet it often seemed to him that he would have brooked a limitless discipline from a perfect master. He felt himself as a person surrounded on the whole by second-rate men and dangerous to his surroundings. He would gladly have given up his dangerous will to one who should have been worthy to use him as an instrument. For someone truly great and ruthless he would have embraced both slavery and suffering. But there was no such person. It had once seemed to him that he might so have served Roger Casement. But he had only met Casement twice, and Casement was now in Berlin. There were men in Dublin, such as Thomas MacDonagh and Joseph Plunkett, whom he could respect. But the only one who really moved him was Patrick Pearse.

Pearse troubled Pat, attracted, annoyed, and disturbed him. He had first met Pearse in connection with the Wolfe Tone Memorial Committee, and he had heard him speak at the funeral of O'Donovan Rossa. He recognized there the power of a pure spirit, the sheer selfless strength which was in the end the only thing that Pat bowed to. Hundreds of things about Pearse irritated him. The man was given to all kinds of infantile nonsense. He romanticized Ireland's heroic past, which he peopled not only with Red Branch Knights but also with ghosts and fairies and leprechauns in which he himself seemed half to believe. He was a blatant admirer of

Napoleon, an alleged lock of whose hair he fatuously displayed to his friends. He also romanticized war in a way which Pat found alien and undignified, babbling about "the red wine of the battlefields warming the heart of the earth" and other rubbish of this sort. But nevertheless he was something like a great man, and Pat was emotionally troubled by him in a way he could not entirely understand and would often have been glad to be rid of.

Admirable, too, was Pearse's chastity, his abstemiousness and his solitariness. He never smoked or drank or went to parties; and Pat approved of the absence from his life of women and all that they represented. In a way it made a barrier between them that Pat apprehended in Pearse a man in some ways rather like himself. He sensed in him too a sort of generalized tenderness, a sort of sweetness, something which Pat had long ago recognized in his own bosom as an enemy and attempted to destroy. Pearse was not the iron man who could have made of Pat a slavish tool. But Pat was prepared to accept him as his remote leader, and although Pearse was not officially the head of the Volunteers Pat regarded him as his chief. More near at hand he could perhaps not have brooked him. Pat detested his work in the solicitor's office, and it had once been suggested by some friends that he might apply for a post as a teacher at St. Enda's, the school of which Pearse was headmaster. Pat liked boys and he admired what he knew of St. Enda's, but he could not have had, at such close quarters, Pearse in authority over him. Pat was glad too that circumstances had not taken his brother Cathal to St. Enda's. He would not have wished Pearse to be Cathal's teacher.

Pat had little use for women. He connected them with the part of himself which disgusted him. He found them somehow muddled and unclean, representative of the frailty and incompleteness of human life. He despised the stupidity and frivolity which characterized their talk, and he was positively nervous of being touched by one. He did not, in fact, like being touched by anybody. The human touch reminded him of a fact which he preferred to forget, that he was incarnate. The desires, the disturbances, consequent upon being a sexual being he either suffered with a bitter consciousness or else disposed of by his own means, despising himself for this servitude. In a spirit of pure inquiry, or perhaps to kill within himself a troublesome demon of curiosity, he had made his explorations in the world, both lurid and pathetic, of the Dublin prostitutes. He had discovered there exactly what he sought and took the filth of the sport into which he was initiated as a symbol of what he had in his more respectable surroundings already divined. He avoided married people.

His experience with the prostitutes had been in some ways his most momentous experience so far. It was something to which he had had to bring himself with violence. What seemed the greater part of him had felt such extreme nausea at the mere proximity of these grotesque animals: to force himself to seek their company and actually to embrace their atrocious bodies had been both a supreme degradation and a triumph of pure will. These two conceptions remained for Pat very close together. There was a satisfaction and a certainty in forcing himself to go down to the very bottom, to feel as it were the absolute floor of the world and know there was nothing under it.

Of the regions above him he did not very well know how to think. The pure perfection which he somehow knew about and from which he derived his steel-hard absolutes, his sense of justice, his love of Ireland, remained itself veiled and beyond experience. He did not call it God, nor did he connect it with the simplicities of his Catholic practice. He did not, as it were, even trouble to doubt his religion, but took from it quietly only those disciplines which suited his temperament. What served Pat, perhaps exclusively, as spiritual experience was the ripping apart of his will from the rest of his being. When he had been a boy he had pictured himself as a monk in one of the more ferociously austere religious orders, envisaging this as a supreme triumph of the will: the will riding alone, naked, over the trembling mediocre human desires. Pat had long ceased to dream of the cloister and he did not any more visit the dark doorways off the Dublin quays, but he found in a systematic thwarting of the flesh a partial remedy for the self-loathing which came over him so often. On manoeuvres with the Volunteers in the mountains he would set himself almost impossible physical endurance tests. He avoided all regularity in his eating and sleeping, and would, in the midst of his most ordinary working days, harden himself with hunger and fatigue. He would have welcomed a military discipline more ruthless than anything he had yet encountered: he would glady have accepted, and also inflicted, corporal punishment. It would have pleased him to have his flesh beside him, like a beaten subject animal, entirely cowed by his will.

Yet physical suffering was merely the symbol of what he wanted. If he could have believed himself a poet, a creator of any kind, capable of lifting out of the muck and mess of life some self-contained perfect object, this would have seemed to him a goal worthy of his powers. But he knew, bitterly, that this salvation was not given to him. He could put no name to what he wanted: it was certainly not love. There was in his life only one piece or fragment or strand of ordinary human love, one place where he needed and was needed, and he regarded this, and his inability to erase it, with the utmost dismay. His aim was something very much more like freedom. He despised the ordinary imperfect mechanics of the human personality, wherein the command of the pure Mentor was never obeyed until the impure mass of tissue, the gross living Self, was ready to obey it with ease. The Mentor's command would be only half listened to, half heard, and the gross Self might then slowly, lazily, begin to adjust. This could be suffering, but mild, confused, scarcely conscious, dim. There would be no direct relation between the Mentor and the Self until the moment of easy obedience was reached, and the two could be related emotionally, indulgently, in the making intelligible of an act of coercion now almost completed. This method of operation enabled the gross Self to remain fat and healthy, however often it might be forced to change direction. Whereas, so it seemed to Pat, in perfect life the command would be obeyed immediately, and the Mentor would not be a consoling though reproachful friend, but would be more like an executioner, bringing about a real loss of tissue in the Self and causing extreme pain.

This was the freedom Pat desired for himself in the purest inner recesses of his intent. But in his more ordinary being this desire was almost entirely fused with his resolve to free Ireland and his sense of having been born as a liberator. The Ireland which he loved was not personified or described, it was the refined, purified counterpart of his own Irishness, the necessary magnetic pole of his own resentment of the bondage which he saw about him and most of all within him. For this he would fight, and the fight could only be a bloody one. He agreed with those who said that, after all that had passed, Ireland's freedom must be bought with blood. So it was that for Pat the idea of the rising in arms, now suddenly imminent, had come to be the target of his whole existence.

At this moment, on Tuesday, April the eighteenth, Pat was down in the cellar of Millie Kinnard's house in Upper Mount Street. The cellar, which was lit now by two candles, was big, low-ceilinged, and vaulted like a crypt. Thick blankets of cobwebs, stirred by the warm air rising from the two flames, undulated rhythmically overhead like vegetation in a stream, and cobwebby streaks shivered a little upon the dull white walls. There was a cool, rather pleasant, musty, earthy smell, as of a comfortable, well-cared-for tomb. In a row of domed side chapels at the far end the round bottoms of bottles glinted greenly under long draperies of dust. In the centre, ranged neatly in piles and covering almost the whole floor, was a large collection of miscellaneous weapons.

Pat had been very uneasy, and was still uneasy, about trusting Millie with this secret. He did not greatly like Millie, and, although he knew that she was brave, he thought her incurably frivolous. He saw her as merely playing at politics, enjoying the excitement and the secrecy and the spice of danger. She had observed an impeccable discretion about the contents of her cellar and had also been conveniently discreet about her patriotism, so that hardly anyone knew her for a sympathizer. But Pat did not like having this frail link in the chain, and there had been much speculation and misgiving about Millie's loyalty. However, it had been necessary, on an initial occasion two years ago, very rapidly to find a hiding place for a quantity of arms, and Pat had made the quick decision, for which he still felt entirely responsible, to trust her.

The occasion of his originally trusting Millie had also been the occasion of his fist bit of active service with the Volunteers, when Erskine Childers had landed a load of rifles at Howth. That was a summer Sunday of two years before when, in a contingent of eight hundred unarmed and unsuspecting Volunteers, Pat had marched down to Howth harbour. As they came onto the quay and saw the yacht waiting, there was a sudden thrilling suspicion, and then they were told to advance at the double. They unloaded the yacht in ten minutes, taking possession of more than nine hundred German Mausers. As they passed the guns from hand to hand, so happy was each man to hold a real weapon at last that he kept the first gun he touched and passed on the second. Marching back with his rifle on his shoulder, Pat could have wept with emotion, and several of his comrades actually did. Now they were armed men. Nor did they have to wait long before confronting their enemy. A company of the Kings Own Scottish Borderers awaited them at Clontarf. Happily, perhaps, the newly acquired Mausers were not loaded. Cunning prevailed over force, and while the leaders on both sides were parleying, the Volunteers melted away into the gardens at the side of the road. The British soldiers marched back to Dublin and later that day fired upon a hostile crowd. Three people were killed, and Pat's next public appearance with his rifle was when he carried it reversed in the slow march at the funeral.

But these seemed old, childish days now. Then they had been

clumsy recruits. Now they were hard, well-trained troops, real soldiers as good as their enemy and better. They had felt their power. This year on St. Patrick's day they had taken the city over. They had marched straight from mass, two thousand strong, to College Green to be inspected by MacNeill. Traffic came to a standstill, police were swept aside, as they marched, disciplined and armed, to the sound of their pipe bands. Dublin stood and watched them like a breathess, enchanted girl. Pat felt they could have taken Dublin that day.

Not that he had any illusions about either the difficulty or the sheer ugliness of the kind of struggle he was engaged in. He felt a detached envy of the simple, open, public war which he could not join. Although in a curious way he was not really a man of action, he knew himself to be brave, and if he had any identity now he had the identity of a soldier. He would have liked a cleaner, straighter fight, "a steed, a rushing steed, on the Curragh of Kildare, a hundred yards and English guards. . . ." The sort of song that Cathal sang. As it was, his choice and his justification would be lonely and secret, and the killing he would do would look like murder. But that was how it had to be.

He had no illusions about the difficulties. Bernard Shaw had justly likened their struggle to an encounter between a pram and a Pickford's van. Nor was Pat at all reassured by the military strategy of his superior officers. There had been a long controversy about uniforms. Pat had been opposed to a uniformed force. He envisaged nebulous, mobile, irregular columns which could strike and disappear. He had studied the methods of the Boers, who, with a much larger army, had preferred guerrilla tactics. In the face of heavy artillery, mobility seemed an obvious essential. But the military mind in the Volunteers, and even in the I.C.A., seemed old-fashioned in cast. There was much talk of *esprit de corps*, and other even wilder talk of status under International Law. It was imagined that the green puttees, the slouch hats, and the Sam Brownes would bestow on their wearers the status of belligerents, and entitle them to the privileges of the

International Code in battle and as prisoners. Whereas Pat knew perfectly well that if they failed they would be treated as murderers and traitors.

Although the troops were tough and the discipline good, the training was not always very rational. There had been some excellent courses in street fighting, but there were still too many textbook exercises out of old British Army drill manuals. The chief difficulty always, of course, was arms. Here again many illusions were cherished. There were those who spoke of the imminent arrival of fifty thousand German troops with Roger Casement at their head. Pat neither believed in these men nor wanted them on Irish soil. He disliked the Germans as much as he disliked the English, and echoed Casement's own bitter cry: the Germans want cheap Irish blood. German arms, German technicians even, that was another thing. Give the Irish the weapons and they could do the job themselves. But, though there were frequent rumours of German arms ships that were to slip through the blockade, nothing came of it, and Pat dismissed this too as a myth.

On the other hand, he did not hold with Connolly that they should "start first and get the rifles afterwards." It was a matter of scraping together a minimum armament. Every week brought in, from various sources, fresh rifles. But what was chiefly needed was machine guns, machine guns, machine guns. James Connolly had hopefully set his engineers to devise a simplified Lewis gun, which was then to be mass-produced in the basements of Liberty Hall, but the men had been simply unable to do it. There had also been some experiments with bombs, but these instruments turned out to be far more dangerous to their inventors than to the British. Pat cursed them all for incompetent oafs. He felt that if he had been an engineer he would have solved the problems involved by sheer will-power.

In the flickering light of the two candles Pat surveyed his arsenal. It was extremely miscellaneous. Besides the Howth Mausers, there were old big-game guns, German sporting rifles, old Italian weapons, British rifles stolen from soldiers on leave or bought from their drunken owners outside pubs for the price of a drink. There were a good many bayonets, mainly slim Italian ones, but these would not always fit the guns for which they were intended. There were also a number of old Fenian pikes, weapons much favoured by Eamon de Valera, a young man of whom Pat was emulous. Ammunition was plentiful, not all of it very straightforward. This was a subject which caused Pat a good deal of doubt and anxiety. There were a lot of sporting cartridges with heavy slugs and leaden blunt-nosed big-game bullets. These would make terrible wounds, and Pat felt almost persuaded that it would be improper to use them. Yet bayonets and shells could make terrible wounds, too, and no one thought that they were unsporting. He recalled his mother's view that warfare was all right when it was bows and arrows. Then he bitterly concluded that bows and arrows were just about what they had.

But the shortage of weapons and even the fallibility of the men were not the last difficulties. Pat knew of another and yet more demoralizing problem which concerned the leadership. The apparent structure of the Volunteers was not its real structure. The actual power in the movement, together with the plans for the rising and for co-operation with the Irish Citizen Army, lay with a group of militants, mainly men of the Republican Brotherhood, who had kept these plans secret from the more moderate nominal leaders such as Eoin MacNeill and Bulmer Hobson. The soldiers would obey their militants—at least they would in Dublin. But the divided leadership was a possible source of confusion; and Pat had been dismayed to hear of a speech made by Hobson at the weekend in which he had said that the duty of the Volunteers was "to influence the Peace Conference" and that no one should "take the responsibility for shedding blood." This suggested both that Hobson had heard a certain rumour, and that he might be prepared to act vigorously upon his own beliefs. There was no doubt that the situation was tricky. If Pat had had his way he would have ordered Hobson, MacNeill, and several other persons to be taken into immediate custody. It was not safe, at this stage, to let their voices be heard at all.

Pat had now completed his survey and checked his list. He let the strange blue daylight in through the heavy cellar door and then returned to blow out the candles. He locked the door behind him. He hoped that he would not meet Millie on the way out. She was often hanging about to accost him after his visits to the cellar, hiding in doorways or leaning over bannisters. As a precaution Pat had acquired copies of the keys of the Upper Mount Street house and of Rathblane, where various other items were in store. He had not mentioned this fact to Millie. He did not like women playing at soldiers, and Millie must be regarded as dispensable. He mistrusted her curiosity and abhorred her almost sexual excitement about the possibility of bloodshed. He saw her as depraved and frivolous, a mixture of prostitute and adolescent boy.

As Pat reached the dark hallway there was the tap of a shoe and a pale flurry as Millie appeared from the direction of the garden, where she had evidently been waiting. He saw her plump, eager face thrust forward in the half light, her big rather damp eyes glistening and bulging with interest.

"Oh, Pat—any news?"

"News? No. I've just been looking things over, as usual."

Millie swept round him and the stiffish satin of her skirt ran rat-like over his foot. She leaned her back against the hall door, her hands spread out, breathing hard, barring his way. "There *must* be some news."

"I don't know what you mean. There's nothing particular."

" 'Thou wilt not utter what thou dost not know, and thus far will I trust thee, gentle Millie.' Is that it?"

"I must be getting along."

"I have a very *special* reason for wanting to know. Things can't go on like this, can they? Something is going to happen, isn't it? Something is going to happen soon?"

"Nothing whatever is going to happen."

Millie gave a long sigh and her arms dropped to her sides. "Well, it makes an easy war."

Pat ignored this. Lowering his voice he said, "You shouldn't talk so. Now please let me out."

There was a sudden sound from behind the half-open door of one of the front rooms. The room was in semi-darkness as the huge red-velvet curtains had been released from the cords and covered half the window. In the centre a little yellow light entered through the thickly worked lace. It was raining outside.

Millie gave a startled hiss, and then darted to the door of the room, throwing it wide open. Pat followed her. In the soupy twilight he saw a rotund figure stretching and uncurling in a big leather armchair. It was his stepfather, Barnabas Drumm.

Millie was transfigured. She bounded furiously forward and cracked the flat of her hand down upon the table. "What are you doing in here, you beast? Why are you spying on us? What do you mean by it? Get up!"

Barnabas got to his feet, gaping miserably at Millie and over her shoulder at Pat. He was hunched up, shrinking into himself like a disturbed spider. "Sure, I just fell asleep. I wasn't spying, Millie, word of honour. I meant no harm. I don't know why, I just fell asleep."

"I know you creep about and listen. I know your mean ways. Well, take your drunken sleep somewhere else. Go on, get away with you!" Her long skirt swirled as she aimed a kick at him.

Barney edged round the chair and then bolted past them as if fearing another kick. He fled, not out of the house but toward the back quarters as if to take refuge, dog-like, in the kitchen.

The incident disgusted Pat. He knew, but preferred not to reflect on, the fact that Barnabas trailed about after Millie and she contemptuously tolerated him. But what angered him now was that Millie simply did not seem to have realized that the person she was thus humiliating was Pat's stepfather.

Millie herself seemed to become aware of this a second later. She put her hands to her face and said, "I'm sorry—"

"Well, good-bye." Pat quickly opened the front door and let himself out into the rain. He turned up his coat collar. She is trash, he thought as he strode away, She is trash, she is trash.

Seven

At this period of my life I imperceptibly became aware that I was becoming steadily estranged from my sister Hilda. Perhaps such slow partings, who knows, are our inevitable rehearsals for the final severance. Hilda and I had been united, at an obscure but effectively deep level, during childhood by our joint opposition to our parents. But, as time and circumstance shook our characters into position, it became clear that we abhorred the parental way of life for different reasons: Hilda, because it was brittle, noisy, shrewdly inexpensive, and not socially grand; I, because it was utterly unspiritual.

There was also, and I felt this increasingly whenever Hilda visited Ireland, the fact that she did not understand either of the women in my life nor appreciate the subtle threads of my relationship with them. She was simply not "in the picture"! The dumb devotion of Kathleen, the tender possessive raillery of Millie: Hilda could make little of all this. Indeed, self-absorbed as always, she *saw* very little; but what her intuition silently told her was that there were women, and women whom she variously deemed unworthy, who were rivals for the monopoly of her adored brother.

Barnabas Drumm had penned these words that very afternoon as he sat at his "work" in the National Library, and they now ran through and through his head, all pure and glittering like a clear brook. Or perhaps the words were the stones in the brook, speckled and smooth, which through a trembling translucent medium he saw steadfastly arrayed before him. His words, it seemed to him, rang out with a quiet authority; and when he had uttered a convincing passage it remained with him and eased his spirit for the rest of the day. For several years now Barney had been secretly working on his Memoir. The tattered notebooks about the Irish saints had been touched more intermittently and lately not touched at all. Barney had become completely absorbed in the more interesting task of self-analysis.

Barney had commenced this task when, after a Lenten retreat, he had decided that he must make a serious effort to find out "what had gone wrong." He must, in the most relentless way, examine himself. He had for too long assumed that he could lay it all at *her* door, could count himself a man ruined by a single catastrophe, a catastrophe which passed in a matter of weeks. But a man's life is not so easily destroyed; and as he realized this later he wished that he had known it *then*. He could have picked himself up. So if he was now the wreck that he was it could not simply be *her* fault. There must have been ancient reasons why he had made of himself the young man that he had, so lately it seemed to him, been, and other reasons, or perhaps the same ones, why he had gone on, with all the appearance of a ruthless intention, driving himself into a wilderness of the spirit. He was very unhappy and he felt that he deserved not to be. He did not especially hope that finding out what had gone wrong would help to put it right. He started his project in a mood of pure self-castigation. Sometimes he felt very old and told himself that the least he could do before he died was to face, clear-eyed and squarely, the wreck of his life. Later he found that the task he had undertaken was curiously consoling.

He had been a talented boy for whom much was hoped. He gained a top classical scholarship at Cambridge and mastered Hebrew while still at the university. He was a crack shot and a noted rowing man. He had loving parents, an adoring sister, and plenty of friends. He had loving parents, and yet somehow from the earliest times he could remember Barney had resented his parents. He could not think what, in a small child, that resentment could have been. Later on it took form as a thorough impatience with the noisy frolicsome frivolity of the parental world. His fashionable-on-a-shoestring mother laughed, or rather screamed, too much, and his father's ingenious set-piece parties and elaborate much-screamed-over practical jokes seemed to him unbearably vulgar. He was hurt by their whole mode of being, although when he reflected upon their misdemeanours they did not really seem very grave. He decided to go to Ireland.

Barney's mother, Grace Drumm, *née* Richardson, was Anglo-Irish, a connection of the Kinnard family, and Barney and his sister had had their share of Irish holidays, during which Hilda had had her eyes dazzled by the splendours of Rathblane. Other things impressed Barney. Ireland was for him a dark place, slow, dignified, and mystical: everything that was unlike the gay little, bright little flat in South Kensington. He lost his heart; and it was not long before, the focus shifting a little, he perceived that the mystic beauty of Ireland resided in the Catholic Church.

This perception developed into a great spiritual crisis during which it became clear to him that he had an extreme destiny. He must forswear the world and aim at perfect sanctity: anything less would be, for him, a meaningless, perhaps a disastrous, goal. He took himself away alone to the saint-haunted solitude of Clonmacnoise and stood beside the round tower in the holiest place in Ireland. Here he felt himself, in what later seemed to be a mystical experience, confronted, captured, claimed. What claimed him then was something very old and pure, a Christianity still simple and innocent of blood, whose humble and unpretentious saints lived in little low-roofed cells. The sacred river Shannon, flooding yellow-reeded between the small barrow-like hills, turned under his gaze from pewter-grey to blue, and Barney decided that he must become a priest.

To the despair of the family he entered Maynooth and soon donned the soutane. He lived in a perpetual exaltation, giving himself up to austerities and enthusiasms which earned him many a shrewd rebuke from his spiritual advisers. He developed a passionate relationship to the Eucharist. He constantly pictured himself, as it was soon to be, holding the very Body of Christ in his hands and feeding a starving kneeling flock which stretched away to the confines of the earth. At nights he dreamed of the Chalice from which the blood of his Master streamed to take away the sins of the world. He held the cup in his hands, turning with an unspeakable happiness to say, *Ite, missa est.* But he was never ordained. He quite suddenly fell in love with Millie.

Millie, in fact, as it seemed later, simply coerced him into love. She was recently widowed and in a condition of intoxication with her new freedom. She had been but vaguely aware of him, had largely ignored him, at their few meetings since her marriage, and Barney had been equally unobservant of her. But when Millie saw him in his soutane she suddenly, recklessly, coveted him. She never deceived him, at least not verbally. She simply wanted this black-robed priestling as her slave, a pet to fondle and caress. She wanted to arouse a blasphemous passion in this pale, long-skirted half-man. She told him constantly that she was not in love with him. She just needed him to be in love with her. Barney found this absolutely pure-hearted wickedness quite irresistible.

He had had some vague emotional involvements with girls at Cambridge and had counted these as his wild oats. The experience with Millie was entirely different. He was shattered, scattered; and he could not help in fact believing that she loved him. She certainly behaved as if she did. His body, which had seemed a pure vessel, a spiritual temple, scoured, empty, and awaiting the final installation of a ghostly visitor, now hotly and needfully enclosed him, a tugging animal of unquiet flesh. It was as if his veins had been emptied and given new blood. He became horribly incarnate; and when the desperately beautiful, desperately desirable Millie looked meltingly into his eyes and inclined her warm lips slowly upon his he felt that god was become man indeed. Of course Millie restricted her favours to the most superficial caresses, thereby reducing him to a state near to madness. The end came with a party at Maynooth, where Barney was discovered with Millie sitting on his knee. He left the college shortly afterwards.

In what order things happened then was never very clear to Barney in his memory: whether he repented and gave up Millie, or whether Millie dropped him and he repented. He often felt able to give himself the benefit of the doubt, since the shock of his dismissal brought back to him an appalling sense of what he had lost. While falling in love he had not explicitly told himself that this meant the end of his vocation. He suffered continual sharp pangs of guilt about what he was doing, but he still felt that he was acting somehow within the framework of his former intention. When that whole numinous world vanished from him and he found himself outside, with nothing to help him except the daily bread of the Church and the penny-plain machinery of repentance, he felt himself so broken that he could hardly envisage himself any more as a man. Here Millie, even if she had not at once removed herself, could have been no use to him. In fact, when Millie saw Barney outside Maynooth, stripped of his soutane, a miserable, confused young man running round Dublin looking for a job, her interest in him ceased abruptly; and, after a meeting at which she treated the whole matter as a joke and then practically accused him of having invented it all, she ceased seeing him altogether. Perhaps she felt ashamed. If so, the only sign of it was that she kept this interlude a close secret and never spoke of it to anyone. Barney's superiors at Maynooth were discreet, and Barney himself had no motives for being talkative, so the part which Millie had played in his life remained almost entirely unknown. It was thought that "some woman" had been involved in his decision not to be ordained, but beyond this even rumour did not go.

Kathleen, however, knew. By a curious accident, which Barney later felt to have been decisive in his life, Kathleen, admitted unexpectedly to the house in Upper Mount Street, found Millie and Barney in an embrace. Barney was never sure whether, if that had not happened, he would have chosen to confide in Kathleen; very possibly not. In any case the shock, the sudden appearance of Kathleen as a spectator, and her continued existence as one of the few people "in the know" gave her, for him, a privileged position. Through her surprised, censorious eyes he saw himself, a robed ordinand passionately embracing a pretty widow of dubious reputation. He resented her knowledge, but it also brought her near to him. In his dereliction, with both Millie and the priesthood lost to him, he had to turn to someone, and he turned to Kathleen.

But why did he despair so quickly, he often asked himself. Why did he not accept the full force of the blow, regard himself as someone who, for years perhaps, must remain a broken, humbled man? He ought to have left Dublin and joined himself in a menial capacity to some remote religious house. There were places for such as he. For the disaster had not broken his faith. It had not broken it, but it must, he later felt, have temporarily cracked it, or he would not so quickly have attempted to rearrange the whole pattern of his wishes. He ought to have kept his attention fixed upon the priesthood, regarding that great treasure, which had been so nearly within his grasp, as having simply receded far away, perhaps impossibly far away, but still presenting itself as the only good. He ought to have repented relentlessly, ferociously, and been prepared to lie upon the ground. He ought, strip by strip, to have divested himself of his former mind, of everything that had made him frail and false. Instead of which, without hope, turning his back entirely upon all that had happened, he sought an immediate consolation.

Kathleen, herself lately left a widow, was several years his senior, and he turned to her at first as to a mother or an elder sister. He told her everything, everything not only about Millie but about his whole life, his childhood, his parents, everything. He came to her again and again; and Kathleen listened to him with a plain gentleness and wisdom which made her seem to him a supremely good woman, the first good woman that he had ever met. She uttered no reproaches but she made no allowances, and he was grateful for her willingness to judge him. Then there began to be a kind of meaning in his escape from the bad woman to the good woman. With an easeful sweetness which was quite unlike his recent frenzy he started to love her. And it seemed that she loved him too, loved him for his history and for his need of her. She represented suddenly and as it were all complete the possibility of the good life which he had previously sought in a mistaken quarter. He now saw himself as a Catholic husband, a Catholic father, the upholder of a pure, robust, cheerful Catholic home, his house renowned as a refuge for the guilty and the unfortunate. He saw a way here which led straight back to innocence. He proposed to Kathleen and she accepted him.

What went wrong? It seemed to him that he was settling down. He found himself a small job in the civil service and started work upon his history of the early Irish church. He published an article, which was lengthily though adversely criticized in *The Sword of the Spirit*, entitled "Some Druidic Origins of Christian Mysteries." He became interested in the struggle between the Irish and the Roman Church which preceded the Council of Whitby. He began to perceive important affinities between the Irish church and the Eastern church. Ireland and the East, he proposed to demonstrate, had spoken the pure tongue of the Gospels, preserving a mystical freedom and a spirit of love which were increasingly lost to the over-organized and over-theorized Roman machine. He published a tract called *From Athos to Athlone* and began to correspond with some very sophisticated French Jesuits who chaffed him about the dangers of heresy. He made a detailed study of the origins of monasticism in Ireland and formed a strong attachment to Saint Brigid—generous, gentle, miraculous saint—and went on devout pilgrimages upon her tracks. He projected a book entitled *The Significance of Brigid* as the first volume of his *oeuvre*. It seemed like the good life. Yet during all this time he had not consummated his marriage with Kathleen.

Perhaps it was that after all there was really no short way back to innocence. As soon as he had tied himself to Kathleen, Barney began to feel subdued resentment which had to do both with the priesthood and with Millie. At a conscious reflective level he made out the irrevocable and tedious nature of the marriage bond which linked him to a material, cheated him of a spiritual, destiny; while in the deeper thoughts of his flesh he hopelessly missed Millie and knew it would be sacrilege without zeal to accept a second best. He had missed two absolutes and was left with a compromise. Symbol of two losses, he retained his virginity.

Of course Kathleen never reproached him, never indeed mentioned his remarkable failure. But of course, too, after a while she began to withdraw. It seemed to him that she had withdrawn slowly, step by step, her eyes fixed upon him, waiting for a sign or gesture which he simply could not make. If he could only, as in the old days, have sought her forgiveness. But he could not. He needed now to defend himself against her, to make fortifications. He began to feel a little afraid of her. He kept formulating and then of course rejecting the theory that she had married him to spite Millie. He formulated more confidently the theory that what she had loved in him was not the whole muddled human person but simply his fallen state. As he put it much later in his Memoir, "Millie loved me because I was a blasphemer, Kathleen loved me because I was a penitent."

He regretted what he had lost; he wished that he had waited. With a curious pain, which was like remorse in reverse, he judged that he had been far too hard on himself at the time of the original fault with Millie. He had exaggerated his guilt. He had been guilty of nothing but inopportunely falling in love. It now began to seem to him that he had done something far worse in marrying Kathleen. He became moody, gave up his job in the excise department, and tried to concentrate on his work on the Irish church. He spent a great deal of time away from home, ostensibly at the Library, but in fact more and more frequently sitting in bars by himself or with chance acquaintances. Then one day by accident he met Millie in Sackville Street.

She immediately began to laugh. She laughed and laughed while Barney scowled at her sickly. Then she took his arm and said he must come to her house forthwith for a glass of sherry. He came there and immediately fell at her feet. Extreme love is like certain kinds of conditioning in animals. It exists at a level where there is no such thing as time. Barney was simply back where he was. A few kind words, a touch, from Millie re-established and confirmed his servitude. He did not accuse her of the past but told her in a trembling voice that *now, now* she must never send him away again. Moved herself, she promised that she would never send him away, that he could always come to her. Carried away, she even expressed a sort of love for him. Perhaps, being older, she was now more appreciative of an absolute devotion. And when Barney began, slightly sobered, to explain that of course he didn't exactly mean that he was going to leave Kathleen, she began to laugh again, and laughed and shook him until he laughed too. Barney was very happy on that day.

Later times were less happy. He took to frequenting the house at Upper Mount Street. He said nothing to Kathleen about having met Millie and nothing about these visits. He noticed too that Millie, following the instincts of a much-courted woman, quite automatically made a secret of his status with her. When others were present he was merely "a relation"; and indeed most of Millie's grander friends were in any case incapable of focussing their attention upon so drab a figure. Barney, for his part, watched Millie closely, more closely than she realized, coming with relief to the conclusion that she had no lover. He began to feel a little security in his new life. Christopher Bellman, who knew vaguely of his existence as Millie's friend, was a man of the world and no gossip. Barney had been shaken, surprised, and rather especially pained at twice meeting Pat Dumay at the house. But he knew of Pat's morbid reticence. Nothing would reach Kathleen from that quarter.

Kathleen did not know; but Barney's secret life with Millie took nourishment, took blood, from his existence at home, and Kathleen certainly felt this extra deprivation, this increased rate of emaciation of their common world. And Kathleen, as it seemed to Barney, took perhaps unconsciously her own steps to punish him. Since his re-instatement with Millie, Barney had been less than constant in his attendance at mass. He had taken no stand with himself, formulated no policy; he just found that, giving this or that explanation to his wife, he just went to church less often. He shunned confession or else went through it in a kind of dream. During this time Kathleen became noticeably more devout. She began to go to mass daily and, almost ostentatiously, to collect "lame ducks" of all kinds. She spent a lot of time in the poorer parts of Dublin doing strenuous kinds of social work, and became an organizer of a league for helping ex-prisoners. She had never been particularly house-proud, but her attention to the house was now minimal. She was too busy helping people in distress. Her appearance also she neglected, and began to look noticeably shabby, untidy, old. She was often up half the night with her charges and invariably seemed tired. It was as if she had taken over the pastoral function which had once seemed reserved for her husband. She was the priest now.

Barney felt these excesses to be directed against himself. What charm, what beauty, she had had she was now deliberately destroying; and when he saw her trudging along Blessington Street, her shoulders hunched with tiredness and preoccupation, her old unfashionable serge dress bobbing on the pavement, her bulging shopping bag knocking on the railings, he felt both exasperation and pity, but the pity was the more fleeting of the two. This was her way of being merciless to him. His reaction was a further withdrawal, more drink, and more Millie. More of the Mountjoy bar and considerably less of St. Joseph's Church. At the same time he still felt capable of judging himself; things had not yet gone too far. He still had a fairly clear head and could measure where he was. But effectively his repentances took the form of isolated orgies of regret: if only he had not married he could still have conceived of finding a way back into the priesthood. *Then* he could really have tried to be good; *then* it would have made sense for him to ask perfection of himself. Well, did it not make sense now? In an ephemeral moment of humility he went to a retreat house. On his return he started to write his Memoir. And he made jokes about the retreat to Millie.

At the same time, with a self-tormenting casuistry, he kept alive the pain of his other total loss. If only he had not been married he could have been so content to be Millie's fool. Perhaps after all he was not so unlike his father. How much he enjoyed making her laugh! He would be her ass and she should drive him in harness. It was only the nagging thought of Kathleen that spoiled this happiness for him. He started to spend a great deal more time reflecting about himself. The book on the Irish church began to seem to him a piece of mushy devotional nonsense; or rather, the factual parts now seemed dried up and devoid of interest and the speculative parts seemed pure sentimentality. The whole thing collapsed, went soft; and Barney soon abandoned it and concentrated on the Memoir.

His failures to practise his religion, for which his wife reproached him only by her own increased piety, did not indicate any slackening of the bond which united him to his church. On the contrary, it seemed to Barney that this bond grew ever closer and more painful. He had so much thought himself into the priesthood and he could not now undo this. He was ordained in his mind and his heart, and he had no other profession. He was by vocation a failed priest. Yet it was an almost unlivable vocation. Barney would ask himself: could not even now some miracle of regeneration occur? It seemed as if, all along the way, he had exaggerated his faults, he had despaired too soon: suppose he had turned back then, or then; for what happened later was worse, whereas then it would have been possible to hope. Well, he found himself saying, yet again, was it not still possible to hope? His life was like the Sybil's leaves; there was always, for the same price, less to salvage. And he followed, as it were at a distance, the yearly cycle of the Church, the pilgrimage of Christ from birth to death. Even now He was drawing near to Calvary. He was riding upon an ass into Jerusalem to die.

"And a very great multitude spread their garments in the way: others cut down branches from the trees and strewed them in the way. And the multitudes that went before and that followed cried saying, Hosannah to the Son of David: Blessed is he that cometh in the name of the Lord; Hosannah in the highest. And when He was come into Jerusalem, all the city was moved, saying Who is this?" Who indeed? Barney felt that if he could really believe, even for a moment, in redemption by love he would be instantly, automatically redeemed. He dreamed of being punished and then restored to the flock: when even punishment would fade within that love and be transformed, becoming the spectacle itself of the suffering induced in a pure being by the existence of evil. But for all his cries of *Kyrie eleison* the faith eluded him that would have made him whole. His self-abasement provided a not wholly disagreeable emotional occupation; and not only was there no large change, there was not even the smallest, most momentary change in the pattern of life which he deplored. He was inside, indeed he was, the machine.

Tears started into Barney's eyes. He had been drinking that afternoon with some friendly *bona fides* in the Big Tree in Dorset Street. Just lately he had noticed that he was never entirely sober. Tracts of time were blotted out and he was not always sure where the line came between what he had imagined and what was real, what he had intended and what he had done. He recalled with pain the scene of that morning when Millie had abused him in front of his stepson. Unfortunately, that was no dream. He had been cuffed and sent about his business. He felt a physical pain to think that Pat had witnessed this. Barney loved his step-children, though feeling rather in awe of both of them. He knew they could not respect him; but it seemed so very sad that therefore his love for them must be wasted and nullified. He had made one effort to draw closer to Pat by joining up with the Volunteers in the early days, and this had gained him one moment of pure pleasure, when Pat had made the discovery that Barney was a good shot. Barney had been moved too by a vague notion that he was going to strike a blow against social injustice. He had long had fantasies of himself as a slum priest defending the poor against the rich. He now proposed to divert his attention from his own sufferings to the sufferings of humanity. But humanity proved too elusive an object, and the Volunteers, like everything else, turned out not to be the answer.

As Barney mused painfully upon his humiliation of that morning he was walking down the hill from the tram in Kingstown, down past the People's Park, over the mysterious cleft of the railway, towards the sea. Praise be to God it wasn't raining, for it was his day for Frances. Every Tuesday Barney met Frances in the afternoon and they walked down the pier and then had tea at O'Halloran's Bun Shop. Barney looked forward to this time: it was a time of innocence. Barney had a happy relationship with Frances, his only relationship which was not now in some way soured and twisted. Frances was the only person who had always *simply* loved him. He had known her since she was a child and had got to know her well since her move to Sandycove. He was aware that, for Frances too, he had the fascinating role of a sinner. His religion also fascinated her; and for her he could somehow wear all the complicated tragic finery of his story, although of course she knew none of the details. She sensed the wreckage within and felt compassion, although there was also something of the self-conscious stooping of the pure young girl towards the fallen man. Frances knew nothing of his relations with Millie, though she had heard the rumour that "some woman" had got him slung out of Maynooth. She was very curious about his past and often tried to draw him on to talk about it. Barney had amused himself by hinting at a liaison with a notable prostitute. Keeping it up, he gave Frances to understand that he had once been a great frequenter of Dublin's brothels. This idea, which seemed to Barney to have a sort of symbolic truth, gave a certain thrill both to him and to the girl.

Barney had known from long ago, as everybody had, that Frances was destined to marry his nephew Andrew. He used to feel pleased about this, as it represented an inclusion of Frances more closely in the family. But now that the time for the marriage had drawn so very near he had other feelings. He guessed that Andrew intended to take Frances to England. There Barney could not go. He too much needed, not only to see Millie, but also almost superstitiously in the intervals of seeing her to watch her. Now the withdrawal of Frances seemed suddenly to abandon him to the devices of nightmare. Frances had been a source of light. There was also, Barney was surprised to find, an element of pure jealousy in his attitude to this marriage. He was fond of his nephew, but he simply did not want him to have Frances. This was an absurd thought, from which Barney rapidly switched to edifying pictures of dear old Uncle Barnabas, grown curiously ancient and sage-like, dandling little children upon his knee. This sometimes worked. But he was now very unhappy about Frances.

It was a windy day. The wind pursued spherical golden and black cloudlets through a yellowish sky over Kingstown and out towards the soft hazy bands of more slowly shifting sea-cloud which always lay upon the horizon like a distant range of hills. The sea would be rough. Barney could see it ahead of him now, a cold and scaly green with flecks of white. He reached the bottom of the hill and entered the gloomy patch of vegetation known as the Crocks' Garden. This consisted of paths of blackish earth which trailed about between the thick clumps of veronica bushes which clothed the slope down to the sea: a sad place which had seemed a labyrinth of mystery to him when he had been young. Below it the waves roared onto a little muddy beach of green untidy stones and foamed along a broken breakwater which had seemed to the youthful Barney like some piece of Roman antiquity. Beyond, like a strange yellow coastline, stretched the great rocky arm of the pier, on this side of which, hollow and majestic as Egyptian temples to the eyes of the child, rose two stone shelters wherein he had spent many happy hours of his holidays watching the rain falling interminably into the sea.

Barney now took the way past the shelters before climbing up onto the top of the pier, where he was to meet Frances. The shelters, whose speckled stony concrete looked like living rock, had been decorated, as usual, by small posters which the Royal Irish Constabulary had not yet had time to remove. *England's Last Ditch. Pretence of the Realm Act. Fight for Catholic Ireland not for Catholic Belgium.* Barney passed by and climbed up to the top, where he could pass through the thick wall to the harbour side of the pier. He looked back for a moment as a touch of sun illumined the multicoloured stucco fronts of the marine terraces, and behind them the two tall rival spires of Kingstown, Catholic and Protestant, shifting constantly in their relation to each other except when from the Martello tower at Sandycove they could be seen superimposed.

The pier itself, upon which he now set foot, had always seemed to Barney an object ancient and numinous, like some old terraced ziggurat, composed of immense rocks of yellow granite and scarcely raised by human labour: something "built by the hands of giants for god-like kings of old." Its two great arms, ending in lighthouse fortresses, enclosed a vast space of gently rolling indigo water and a miscellany of craft riding at anchor. The inner side of the pier was terraced and decorated at intervals by strange stone edifices, wind towers and obelisks and great cubes with doors, which made it seem all the more like some pagan religious monument. Beyond were the waters of Dublin Bay, now a harsh streaky blue, the outskirts of Dublin to the left, a purplish mass in the uncertain light, the dark low line of Clontorf, and the rising hump of Howth. Barney noticed uneasily that it appeared to be raining on Howth. But then it was always raining on Howth.

And there was the dear girl herself down below, waving and hurrying on towards him.

"Are you all right, Barney?"

"Oh, all right, struggling along. A bit battered, you know, a bit battered. But struggling along."

Frances always asked this question and Barney always gave this sort of answer. That anxious "Are you all right?" of Frances was perhaps the nearest he ever got to a token of the love for which his heart craved.

Frances was wearing a mackintosh cape and motoring hood, and a tartan pleated skirt which swirled about her ankles. She took a firm grip upon the skirt as she walked, gathering several of the pleats carefully between her fingers. They set off along the pier in silence, mounting again to the upper terrace, where a gleam of sunshine made the powerful stones a chilly, sandy gold. They did not always talk then. The wind often made talking impossible.

"What's that, Frances?"

"I just said there's the mail boat."

"Why, so it is."

"How very clear and bright its colours are in the sun, though it's still so far away. Which one is it?"

"The *Hibernia*." From long experience Barney could tell the almost identical boats apart. He hardly knew how he did it. He added, "She's late. There must have been a U-boat alert."

"How awfully frightened they must be."

"You mean the passengers—"

"No, the Germans down in the U-boats. It must be terrible."

It had never occurred to Barney to feel sorry for the Germans down in the U-boats. But of course Frances was right, it must be terrible. His thoughts reverted to himself. With a perverse desire to cause himself pain he said to Frances, "You'll be off on the mail boat one of these days."

"What?"

"I said you'll be off on the mail boat one of these days."

"Why?"

"I mean young Andrew will take you, I mean when you're married."

Frances was silent.

"When will you be married?" said Barney. He had put off asking Frances this question; he did not want to know; it would be horrible to know.

"I'm not sure, Barney, Andrew hasn't actually fixed anything yet, and until—"

"Oh, well, he'll fix it soon. He'll have to before he— He's a lucky boy." Some people have all the luck, Barney thought. Why had he not grown up with a dear lovely girl just holding out her arms and waiting for him?

Frances thrust her arm through Barney's and they forged ahead together against the wind. "Well, even then, you know, I probably wouldn't leave Ireland—"

"Yes, you would. You know Andrew hates Ireland."

She squeezed his arm in comfort or protest and they went on for a while in silence. When they got as far as one of the "temples," a square stone hut with a pediment, surmounted by three iron cups which whirled, chasing each other with desperate speed, they stopped for a moment to give their whipped, glowing faces a rest from the wind, and leaned back against the great wall of the pier. The sun had gone in now and the landward clouds had turned to a bright pewter grey. The spires of Kingstown rose blackened as if dipped into some infusion of darkness, but a mysterious glow lit the terraces of houses, and reflected light gleamed in the windows. Beyond, the mountains were almost black save where the sun fell very far away upon a slope of rusty green. Barney began to try to light his pipe.

"Are you still in the Volunteers, Barney?"

"I suppose so. I haven't actually resigned. But I've rather fallen out of things lately."

Frances was silent for a while, looking towards Kingstown. The spire of the Mariners' Church emerged from its veil of darkness and shone a silvery grey.

She said suddenly, "I can't think why it doesn't all blow up."

"What?"

"Oh, I don't know—I mean society, everything. Why do the poor people put up with us? Why do the men go and fight in that stupid, ghastly war? Why don't they all say, no, no, no?"

"I agree with you, Frances. It's extraordinary what people will put up with. But they just feel helpless. What can they do? What can any of us do?"

"People shouldn't feel helpless. Something ought to be done. I saw today by Stephen's Green—I was in town this morning—oh, it was so sad—a girl, a mother, she must have been my age, with clothes, well they weren't clothes, just jumbled bits of stuff, and four little children, all of them barefoot, and she was begging, and the little kids were sort of dressed up like little monkeys, and trying to dance, and they were crying all the time—"

"I expect they were hungry."

"Well, it's scandalous, wicked, and a society which allows it deserves to be blown to bits."

"But dearest Frances, you must have seen girls like that girl a hundred times. Dublin is full of them."

"Yes, I know, and that's awful. One gets used to it. I've just been thinking more about it lately. It shouldn't be. And I can't think why they don't attack us, jump on us like wild animals, instead of just humbly holding out their hands for a penny."

Barney agreed with her that it shouldn't be. But, after all, what could one do? The begging mother, the starving children, the men in the trenches, the Germans down in the U-boats. It was mad and a tragic world. Now if he had been a priest—

"Barney, do you think there'll be any trouble in Ireland?"

"You mean fighting here?"

"Yes, about Home Rule and so on."

"No, of course not. Home Rule will come automatically after the war."

"So there's nothing to fight about, is there?"

"Nothing at all."

"And anyway Father was saying they have no arms. They *can't* fight."

"No, they can't."

"Barney, what will Home Rule do for that woman begging in the street?"

Barney thought for a moment. "Absolutely nothing."

"It won't really touch that level of people at all?"

"Well, they'll have the pleasure of being exploited by P. Flanagan instead of J. Smith."

"Then the thing's not *worth* fighting for anyway."

"Wait a minute. It's worth having one's national freedom," said Barney. He felt a bit vague about it. "Once Ireland's free of England it'll be easier to set the house in order."

"I don't see why. Some people say there ought to be a rising against the whole thing, against the English and against the Irish employers too. James Connolly says that, doesn't he?"

"Yes, but it's all dreams, Frances. They couldn't do it. And it would be just a very nasty mess if they tried. Those people don't know how to run the country."

"Do the people who let that woman beg and her children starve know how to run the country?"

"Well, I see what you mean. But law and order are important too. The workers should stick to the Trade Unions, that's how they'll better themselves."

"But the government and the employers won't allow the Trade Unions."

"They will, they'll have to. You're getting quite a political woman these days, Frances. We'll see you in uniform next!"

"I ought to be in uniform. But I don't know which one to wear!" She spoke bitterly, striking the palms of her hands against the damp stone behind her. The wind had spread the tartan skirt and flattened it against the wall. She added, "Oh, I don't know what I'm talking about. How I wish I'd had some proper education. I'm so muddled. Perhaps women really can't understand politics. It can't be right to shed blood for anything. I do think this dreadful war against Germany is so wrong. All those terrible things in the trenches, and the shell fire. There must be some way of stopping it. The soldiers should all just throw down their arms."

"Come, come. You wouldn't like to see Andrew being a conchie!"

"If Andrew became a conchie I'd fall down and worship him."

As Barney turned in some surprise to look at her she jerked from him impatiently saying, "Let's go through and look at the rocks."

This was something they always did. On the inside of the pier were the great terraces and the temples. On the outside, where the open sea beat against it, was a mountainside of immense jagged rocks heaped together. Periodic gaps in the upper wall allowed one to pass through to this side. Barney and Frances went through and stood looking down.

The blows and caresses of the sea had made no impression upon the shape of the rocks or even upon their colour. They remained senselessly jagged and yellow, a random pile of unalterable many-surfaced solids. Here and there a huge stone, balanced between two neighbours, would tilt to and fro at the touch of the waves. In other places the rocks seemed more closely fused as if some semi-intelligent hand had wedged them together. But mostly they lay like things tossed down, one idly resting upon another. And between them were great holes and crevasses, ugly slits and irregular gashes, within which the sea would roar or come suddenly surging upward to boil out over the indifferent granite surfaces. Barney had always felt frightened of these rocks, even when as a boy he had leapt familiarly from one to another. He feared the deep crevasses down which a man might slide into some awful sea cavern. More perhaps he feared the huge weight, the appalling hardness, the senselessness of them. They were like the great weighty stupid world which had rolled off the lap of God. They were the most meaningless things that he knew, as meaningless as death.

He looked at Frances. She seemed to feel as he did, looking down with a puckered, alarmed face at the huge waves which were rushing in in quick succession to destroy themselves upon the rocks with a deafening ferocity of foam. It was impossible to speak here. A mist of spray, picked up by the wind, was carried rainily into their faces. Frances shivered and turned back through the opening. Over her shoulder as he came through Barney saw that the mail boat was just entering the harbour.

Back again on the inside of the pier he realized that it was, in fact, raining. The sky above was hazily grey, and thick bunches of ebony cloud were coming up from behind Dublin. The waters of the harbour were black now.

"Come on," said Frances. "Oh, it's so *cold*!" She sounded almost tearful. Lifting her skirt well up, she set off at a smart pace along the pier. For a while, not trying to catch up, he followed her. The *Hibernia* had docked. It had turned its lights on dimly and stood out strangely vivid in the darkened scene. The people were coming off it now, hundreds of people streaming off it and streaming away in all directions into rainy Ireland.

Eight

"Charge it again, boys, charge it again,
  Pardonnez moi je vous en prie,
  As long as you have any ink in your pen,
  With never a penny of money!"
"Don't sing that song, Cathal."
"Why not?"
"I don't like it."
"Why don't you like it?"
"I don't like that sort of song."
"Why don't you like that sort of song?"
"Do you want your ears boxed?"
"You're in a nice friendly mood today, I don't think. All right,
I'll sing another sort of song.
    'Sure 'twas for this Lord Edward died and Wolfe Tone sunk
      serene,
    Because they could not bear to leave the red above the
      green.' "
"If you sing that song you ought to sing it seriously."
"Sure I am singing it seriously. How does one sing a song

seriously or not seriously? One just sings it. Anyway, you know I love Wolfe Tone and I wouldn't—"

"Your head is full of bad poetry. 'Sunk serene' is rotten. And it's not grammar either. Dying isn't 'sinking serene.' Bad poetry is lies."

"Well, it's better than no poetry at all, and no one has told us about Lord Edward and Wolfe Tone in good poetry yet. I wish I'd been called after him. Wolfe Tone Dumay.

> 'As I lay on the sod that lay over Wolfe Tone
> And thought how he perished in prison alone—'

I did that, too."

"Did what?"

"Lay on the sod. Last time we went out to Bodenstown. When you and the others went off to the meeting, I lay down there and thought about him. Not right on top, but nearby."

"You're too young to go lying on people's graves."

"I'm going to die young, so I'm really older. Like cats and dogs, you have to reckon my age differently."

"You're a tiresome little brat now, and you'll live to be a tiresome old fellow with a grey beard spouting bad verse."

It was Tuesday evening, and the ceremony of Pat's bath was in progress. This ritual had started long ago, when the boys shared a cabin in Connemara for part of a summer and Pat had trained his young brother to heat the water in iron pots on the range and then to pour it for him into the big tin bath and to stand by with warm towels while Pat washed off the mud of the bogs and the ferocious coldness of the sea. Although he complained ceaselessly of being "enslaved," Cathal enjoyed this ritual, which had somehow continued in the less primitive surroundings of Blessington Street, a piece of religious drama surviving in a modified form perhaps because it represented for the participants some half-conscious, half-forgotten spiritual need.

So Cathal always attended Pat's bath, his role as acolyte now limited to the handing over of the towels. It was a time, traditionally, of communication between the two brothers, or at least a time when Pat made himself more than usually approachable, so that advice could be covertly asked or misdemeanours defiantly owned to. Sometimes thinking himself rather ridiculous in the role of a steamy oracle, Pat had been inclined to discontinue the custom, but Cathal now claimed his attendance as a right, attaching himself like a small child to "the way things had always been."

Now, while Pat meditated or splashed gently, Cathal sat opposite to him on the large wooden cover of the lavatory, on top of Pat's clothes. The lavatory, in an arched recess, fitted discreetly inside a long chest of reddish highly polished mahogany, one section of which lifted on a hinge. The wall behind was papered with a design of ivy and blue cabbage roses upon which Cathal's head, inclined always in the same place, had made a blurred brown mark. Lazily relaxed, one leg tucked under, the other crooked at the knee, Cathal displayed the long brown trousers of Irish tweed to which he had lately been promoted. Self-consciously he smoothed them and leaned forward from time to time to smell them appreciatively. He seemed, since the trousers, taller, a very slim boy with a narrow intent face, smooth and straight as a piece of ivory, rather close eyes, and longish blackish straight hair. The long-nosed crested head resembled that of a bird, and he had, too, a bird's capacity for alternating between darting speed and stillness. He sat now perfectly still, watching Pat.

At such moments Pat was conscious of resembling his younger brother, though usually they were held to be unlike. Pat's face, which he shaved clean twice a day, was broader and more ruggedly bony, and his eyes were cold blue while Cathal's were brown. Cathal laughed oftener. But his mouth in repose was harder than Pat's. Yet at times when Cathal looked at him Pat saw his brother's face as a mirror, the mask of expression, something poised and fierce, as of a head glimpsed inside a helmet, seeming the image of a grimness which he felt to flow outwards from himself.

Pat turned on the hot tap again. He had noticed lately that he was a little troubled at being seen naked by Cathal. He would not of course have let any other person see him bare. But the brothers had never troubled themselves about this. What had changed? Perhaps it was simply that Cathal was growing up; and Pat perceived this growing up as something very purely, sharply painful, like the touch of a clean knife or a flame. Something here, he scarcely knew what, hurt him and made him wish to withdraw and to hide. Was it this which made him suddenly conscious of his body, which though it was so supple and hard was also white, white as an underground defenceless thing? Or perhaps this whiteness seemed to him now so especially shameful and pathetic since, as he touched his warm limbs in the sticky water, he apprehended himself in an entirely new and urgent way as destructible and mortal. Since the news about Sunday every cell in his body announced itself as precious.

After a pause Cathal said, reverting to a topic which they had in fact been discussing almost continually since the arrival of the afternoon papers, "So you think it's a forgery?"

"Yes, of course."

The papers had carried the text of a most alarming document, which had just "come into somebody's hands," which purported to be a British military plan for a concerted swoop upon the Citizen Army and the Volunteers. All "nationalists" in arms were to be disarmed and all "disaffected" premises seized. The places which were to be occupied, including Liberty Hall, the Volunteer headquarters in Dawson Street and a number of other institutions and private houses, were listed in the document, which had many, perhaps too many, marks of authenticity. Dublin was outraged. And the British authorities had at once declared the thing to be forged.

"Well, *they* say so, but of course they would. What makes you think it's not genuine?"

"The bit about the Archbishop's house at Drumcondra. The English wouldn't be so stupid as to interfere with the Archbishop. He's not an extremist, he's well known to be against violence. He's useful to the English. Besides, if they were to touch him Dublin would go mad with rage."

In fact Pat, who had been startled by the document, had rapidly formed his own theory about its provenance. He attributed it to the Machiavellian pen of the romantic and devious Joseph Plunkett, and when he had taken in its purpose he paid homage to the ingenuity of his comrade. Patriotic indignation spiced with fear—this was just the stimulant which Dublin needed now on the eve of her trial. All the same, it was just possible that the document was genuine, and it was just possible that its publication might lead the authorities to carry out their plan quickly before the threatened persons could take counter-measures.

"But the English *are* stupid," said Cathal. "Well, let them try! Then there'll be ructions. General Friend will get a pretty hot reception if he tries to walk into Liberty Hall."

That was what Pat had for some time feared. If the English had been a little less stupid and a little more callous they would long ago have attempted to disarm their potential foes, and when resisted would have used machine guns. Such a very excusable "incident" might well be overlooked in the midst of a war where casualties on an astronomic scale were happening elsewhere. A scheme like that could have destroyed the whole movement overnight. Pat wondered if it had been mooted. Fortunately one could rely upon the English, who were certainly not intelligent, to be also less than ruthless. Against a ruthless enemy there would have been no chance at all.

"Do you know what happened at Liberty Hall last Sunday?" said Cathal, pursuing his own line of thought.

"I neither know nor care what happened at Liberty Hall last Sunday."

"Connolly said anyone who didn't want to fight was to drop out of the ranks. He said it was better for them to go now than later on when they might be needed. He said there'd be no reproaches. No one dropped out."

"Of course no one dropped out! That theatre business has gone to Connolly's head. He thinks he's the great dramatist of the Irish nation. He's on the stage all the time. It doesn't mean those fellows will actually fight. It's all moonshine anyway."

"Fight? Of course they'll fight. It's the Volunteers that'll be hiding their heads when the day comes. And the Volunteers are beastly to the Citizen Army. They keep trying to prevent them from having halls and—"

"You shouldn't be surprised. Isn't it the Class Struggle? And I thought I told you to keep away from Liberty Hall."

"Well, I was there on Sunday and I heard a jolly good lecture on street fighting."

"Cathal—"

"And I saw those pictures of the civil war in Cuba. One's got to pick up tips. Did you know that you ought to learn to shoot with your left hand? Tom Clarke was telling me—"

"I told you not to be hanging round Tom Clarke's shop either."

"Think of Tom Clarke being fifteen years in prison. He was in prison longer than my whole life. If I'd been fifteen years in prison I'd hate everybody. But he doesn't seem to hate anyone, not even the English."

"Sure he's a great man."

"Then why don't you want me to go and see him?"

"You're too young for this, Cathal. Your turn will come. This isn't for you."

"So there *is* a plan?" Cathal was rigid with attention. His body, scarcely moving, became taut.

Pat cursed his incautious words. Almost anything he said to Cathal now could be dangerous. "Of course there's no plan! I just don't want you to be wasting your time romancing with a lot of old Fenians when you ought to be working for your exams."

"Exams! Connolly says that the failure to take the offensive is the death of all revolutions."

"How can you take the offensive when you're armed with

broken bottles and old shotguns tied together with twine?"

"If I were Connolly I'd bring the I.C.A. out, and that'd force the Volunteers to follow."

"Well, thank God you're not Connolly, so maybe we'll have a bit of peace."

"Anyway, the Germans will be coming soon."

"Oh, will they? I see you know all about it!"

"Yes. I don't much like the Germans but I'm quite prepared to use them."

"Listen who's talking!"

"Yes, and then we'll carry out Robert Emmett's plan. Take Dublin Castle, while the Germans will be landing in Kerry and arming all the south and the west, and they'll advance, and Roger Casement's Irish Brigade will come—"

"All three of them."

"And at the same time the Germans will attack all along the front in France, and they'll bombard the English coast and there'll be Zeppelin raids on London—"

"All to set the Irish free."

"And the U-boats will come streaming up the Irish Sea and cut off the English in Ireland so no more troops can come over and no one will feed the English and they'll have to surrender."

"The British Navy seems to have been pretty successful so far at keeping the U-boats out of the Irish Sea. The mail boat arrives every day, doesn't it?"

"But there are secret U-boat bases all round Ireland now, and wireless transmitters—"

"Besides, even if we did maroon the English troops, which we couldn't, they're still armed to the teeth, aren't they? What about all those field guns?"

"The Irish regiments wouldn't fight against their own people. The Dublin Fusiliers—"

"They'd fight. They'd fight, not 'against their own people,' but against a little gang of terrorists. And when one of them was killed they'd fight with hatred."

"Besides, Connolly says a capitalist power will never use artillery against capitalist property."

"That's the stupidest argument I ever heard. The French used artillery against the Paris workers in eighteen-seventy-one. Your great hero ought to read some history."

"Well, and then the Americans—"

"The Americans! The only sensible thing your hero ever said was that the snakes that Saint Patrick drove out of Ireland swam the Atlantic and became Irish Americans."

"It may interest you to know that the Americans are going to make a special treaty with Germany because of the submarines and declare war on England because of the blockade."

"Why not the other way round? The Americans will never fight the English. It's inconceivable."

"Well, they don't like the British Empire, do they? A blow in Ireland against the British Empire has a hundred times more political significance than an equal blow struck in Asia or Africa. A child may stick a pin in a giant's heart."

"Who said that, as if I didn't know?"

"Well, it wasn't. It was someone called Lenin, he's a Russian, and I bet you've never heard of him."

"Well, I have so."

"The eyes of the world are upon us—"

"That's what the poor Irish always think."

"Whenever it's the turn of a country, however small, to rise against its tyrants it represents the oppressed peoples of the whole world."

"I thought William Martin Murphy and the Dublin employers were the tyrants your friends hated, more than the English."

"Have you heard that Murphy has persuaded all the employers to sack all the able-bodied workers to force them to enlist?"

"If I were your schoolmaster I'd beat a bit of accuracy into you. The employers would do no such thing, it would hit their pockets."

"Well, there's no call for you to sneer—"

"I'm not sneering."

"You are so."

"I am not."

"The Irish worker is the worst-fed and the worst-housed in the British Isles, and that's saying something. And it was a Government Commission said that, not James Connolly. Have you been over to Jinny's place ever and seen how she lives? Do you know that they're living six in a room all over Dublin? Do you know how cold they are in winter? Do you know what they have to eat? Do you know what happens to them when they're ill?"

"I know these things, Cathal, don't shout."

"Well, once we get started we'll shift the whole lot. We'll shift the bloody English and William Martin Murphy all at the same time. And they can put the Home Rule bill where the monkey put the nuts."

"Haven't I told you not to be using that bad language?"

"We'll hail the English workers as our brothers. And all over Europe the workers will rise to stop the war. We'll ride on top of the workers' movement like Toomai on the elephant. 'Kala Nag, Kala Nag, take me with you—' "

"I'm surprised to hear you quoting that Imperialist writer!"

Cathal was silent for a moment. Then as if deliberately putting his exaltation from him he lifted his other knee and began with wrinkled nostrils to sniff the tweed of his trouser leg. He massaged his ankles and then slowly lowered his feet to the ground, leaning far forward so that his straight heavy sheet of hair fell down over his brow. With face hidden he said, "So you think it is —impossible—to fight?"

Pat stared at the bowed head. Then he answered slowly. "Yes, impossible."

Impossible. That was what all his arguments had proved it to be. But on Sunday they were going to do the impossible.

"Pass me the towel, Cathal."

The boy jumped up quickly and then laughed. "Why are you covering yourself up like that, like a girl? Patrick Pearse says the

Red Branch heroes went naked into battle. He says shame of nakedness is a modern English thing—"

"Pearse talks almost as much nonsense as your friend at Liberty Hall. Shove over the bath mat, would you?"

For a while Cathal watched Pat drying himself. Then he said, almost under his breath, "When you go, I am going with you."

Pat said nothing. His fierce love for his younger brother had expressed itself in a tyranny which had deceived many outsiders. He loved Cathal, and only Cathal, with all the intensity of that place of weakness which he called his heart; and he had always known and knew it now with an especial terror, that Cathal was his vulnerable point, his Achilles heel. Though he were to make himself into a man of iron, here he would always be naked and totally without defence. When Sunday came, what could he do about Cathal?

Nine

On Wednesday, at about five o'clock in the morning, Christopher Bellman, who had been unable to sleep, arose from his bed. It was today that Millie was to give him her momentous answer. Since last meeting her he had pursued an inward dialogue of great length and complexity. He could not clearly remember doing anything else, though in fact he must somehow have conversed with Frances, Andrew, and Hilda, and gone about a semblance of his daily work. In fact he had sat for long hours in his study, staring out of the window and listening to the uproar of his thoughts which rattled away in his ears, sounding now like schoolmen and now like fishwives.

He was chiefly troubled by two things. First and most fundamentally he was afraid that Millie might say no. His view of her as "cornered" depended upon an assumption about her rationality which could very well prove false. Of course Millie did not want to sell Rathblane and the house in Upper Mount Street and go into cheap lodgings. But was Millie rational enough to keep this prospect steadily before her face? Might she not prefer to drift vaguely on, trusting that her luck would change? This might result, indeed would certainly soon result, in her ruin, the dissolution of her empire: and at that moment, or on the brink of it, she might well turn to him again. Yet if things went that far, and especially if her situation were to become public, would she in fact turn to him? She might, when really faced with it, positively prefer the catastrophe and feel that it was now too late to buy back the continuity and the splendour of her previous existence. He could negotiate with an unrealistic, comfort-loving, imperial Millie who simply wanted the preservation of her advantages, provided she was just rational enough to know what must be done to ensure this. But Millie was also capable of enjoying disaster. A desperate, exposed Millie would be an entirely different person, and one who might well find the strength within herself to prefer her freedom. He must see to it that this person did not come into existence.

The other thing that troubled him was the plain thought that he was acting wrongly. Of course he had had this thought before, but in a different form. He had been ruthless with a certain dash. It seemed to him that after a lifetime of quiet decency this sudden act of selfishness had some elegance about it. For once, and in a wonderful cause, he was going to go straight for what he wanted. Millie was a rich prize, and he would take her in spite of the demon of morality. He had pictured his wrong-doing entirely in terms of himself, in terms of a really rather brave, and certainly rather stylish, overthrowing of moral barriers which perhaps his timidity rather than his virtue had previously respected. Now he began to think more closely about Millie.

Of course if he pressed her too much against her will to marry him she might well resent it in ways which would later make his own life a misery, so there were clear self-interested motives for caution. But Christopher somehow did not fear this. He knew Millie very well, and knew the sturdy cheerfulness of her temperament. She would make the best of a bad job. But if it was indeed such a bad job why force it upon her at all? Ought he not simply to rescue her financially, which he could fairly easily do, and expect no reward? The trouble was, he would probably get no reward. He had been exact in saying that moderate faithfulness was all he could expect from a Millie married. Not that he anticipated positive love affairs, though that was possible too, but Millie would never be able to resist a conquest or to contain her roving affections, and he could not reasonably, in all the circumstances, ask her, if she became Mrs. Bellman, to do so. From a Millie unmarried, however greatly indebted, he knew he could expect very little. Millie would, in a short while, almost literally *forget* what had happened.

Nevertheless it now appeared before him more precisely, like an alien tablet held up before his face, that his duty was to make the money available and lightly and generously to drop the other idea which would never, except in this graceless context, have occurred to him as in the least feasible or to Millie as in the least interesting. When the argument reached this point the question promptly arose in a new form: was he going to do his duty? He had been prepared to perform the stylish act. Was he equally prepared to perform the ugly act? But here his desire for Millie, the sheer dazzling image of her, like a miraculous icon suddenly laid open before him, struck him dumb with a comforting sense of the inevitable. He simply could not resist her. Then almost at once the whisper of the argument would begin again from the beginning. And now on the morning of Wednesday he was still unresolved, weakly inclined to wait for Millie's words to bring about some new mood in him. With a supreme frailty, of which he was thoroughly conscious, he handed the moral decision over to his future self.

These matters had occupied Christopher for a greater part of the night, in the intervals of storms of nightmare which had departed from memory, leaving only a dark stain behind. Unable now to lie still, he got up into the twilight, rather shakily pushing himself out of bed and lowering his feet, which curled stiffly and reluctantly on contact with the floor. Sleep still buzzed and swarmed about him. Drooping his head, he noticed how extremely thin his legs were. He sat on the edge of the bed and contemplated his bony knees and ankles and the narrow white shaft in between, sparsely scattered with long, spidery black hairs. The flesh seemed like a kind of solidified paste, rigidly tubular yet without significant shape or colour. With this came a disagreeable intuition of his whole body as stiff and old and flaky. Unclothed, he would be found to be a stick-like puppet, something so crude and primitive that its connection with the human form was merely conjectural. He would ask nothing of Millie. But at that moment it was not even the thought of her that appalled him: it was some old fear of death which had not visited him now for many years.

He got up and mixed himself a little chlorodyne in some water. Then, holding the glass, he went over to the window. The garden was very still, hazily present in a bluish twilight which only just allowed the eyes to see. It seemed to him now an alien scene, something reflected in an old dim looking-glass, a strangely altered mirror garden. Never by day did the trees and plants look so monumentally quiet and abstractedly aware, as in a wide-eyed trance. He shivered and then found that he was listening, perhaps for the sound of the dew dripping from the spikey tips of the palm trees. But the blue air was silent, no sound diffused in it even of the sea, an opaque and sterile air. He was about to turn away to the comfort of his room when he became aware of something unusual in the dim space before him. He saw, or thought he saw, a human figure standing in the garden. He stared, trying in vain to make his eyes see clearly. The bewitchment had shifted, the diffused menace of the blue twilight concentrated in this motionless intruder, quieter and more intent than the waiting trees. Christopher drew in his breath slowly; then suddenly his vision shifted again and he recognized the figure. It was his daughter Frances.

Frances began to move slowly across the lawn. She was wearing a long dressing gown of a whitish colour which dragged behind her, leaving a dark trail in the dew. She came as far as the swing. She was now, underneath the chestnut tree, barely visible. Her pale gown moved behind the leaves, and for a moment she seemed to be kneeling on the seat of the swing. Then she emerged and stood looking up at the tree. She touched one of the lower branches and made it sway as if to be sure that something other than herself could move. Her gestures had the dreadful completeness and self-absorption of those who do not think they are observed. Then she swung slowly away and began to drift across the grass, abruptly pausing from time to time to think or listen. She moved heavily, in a way quite unlike her normal gait, as if her entry into the mirror world had weighed her down, powdered her over with some resistant silvery stuff; and indeed her figure seemed now to shimmer slightly, perhaps in the increasing light, like something metallic. Then when she stood still she was very still, fading a little, gathered into the dim morning silence where not even a bird was stirring.

Christopher was extremely troubled. There was something distraught about the quiet figure with its heavy, menaced gait. He would have been unwilling now to see her face. She seemed like a person deliberately frightening herself, trying perhaps to still one fear by another. Yet what was so appalling about the garden? It was the girl's own fear which he had seen in the twilit garden, diffused in the blue grains of the dawn light. With a quick horror of being seen by her he moved back from the window. The figure watching from inside could only seem a terrible demon to the figure wandering without. He sat down shuddering upon his bed. How did he so certainly know that she was afraid? And what was it that she was afraid of?

"Oh what fun, you've had the old swing mended!"
"Yes, Andrew mended it."

The sun was shining brightly and the birds were singing. It had been raining in the earlier part of the morning, but now the sun shone upon the sparkling wet garden which smelt and looked a sort of light, salty green.

"Has the dear boy popped the question?"

"Not yet."

Christopher followed Millie down the garden. He was uneasy at her presence here, uneasy at her insistence on coming to his house, although he knew that Hilda and Frances were safely in Dublin. He would have kept her indoors, but she had, on her arrival, walked straight through the house into the garden.

"Have Andrew and Hilda moved yet?"

"They slept last night at Claresville, just camping out. The furniture from England arrives tomorrow."

"I must go down and inspect. Do you approve of Hilda's new place?"

"I don't like a sloping garden, but the house is pretty enough. Millie—"

"Your gardener hasn't pruned the roses properly. Look at all those spindly branches."

"I know. His mind hasn't been on his job lately. Millie—"

"How early the roses are in bud here. But the buds won't open, will they, for nearly another month."

"More than that. Millie—"

"Isn't it funny the way one *forgets* every year the way things happen in the spring? I never know what order the flowers come in, do you?"

"I envy you all those surprises. Dearest Millie—"

"Is the Castle going to raid all those Sinn Feiners and take their guns away? Did you see that thing in the paper yesterday?"

"No, of course not. That order was obviously a fake. I rang up MacNeill's brother about it and he just laughed. Mr. Birrell has gone off to England for Easter as usual. This country's the same on both sides of the fence. All talk and no action."

"And you think the others won't do anything beyond their usual playing at soldiers?"

"No, they'll sit about waiting for the peace conference. They can't lose by waiting. Now, please—"

"It's so sad. I always thought something wonderful would come out of Ireland. Some great glittering event that would change everything, some great act. But no, it's all toy, it's tiny and provincial after all."

"There could be no great event, Millie, there aren't the historical conditions for a great event. A few people might commit a few murders—"

"Well, perhaps it was just something in my own life I was waiting for, some golden thing which never came."

"Millie, I do wish you'd come inside."

"No, I like it out here. It's so gorgeously wet. It keeps my ankles cool."

"Dearest, there was something you were going to tell me today."

"Oh, the future, the future! I keep on consulting the cards but I draw nothing but the Queen of Spades."

"You ought to be consulting your heart."

"My *what?*"

"Millie, please don't torture me."

"You refer to your suggestion that we should get married?"

"Of course."

"Well, naturally the answer's yes."

Christopher stared at Millie, who was now retreating from him across the grass. She was still wearing her grey outdoor coat with its militaristic trimmings in red velvet. Beneath it her silk skirt was visible, patchily darkened by the rain water, and her neat little boots. Christopher watched her plump, slightly swaying figure moving away and now leaning a little over the roses. For a moment it all seemed a picture, as if a golden light had shone upon a stage and made uncertain random things into a beautiful tableau. The relief he felt made him quite dazed with joy. He wanted to kneel down on the wet grass. Instead he stooped and touched it and drew his wet rainy hand across his brow. He followed her. "Oh, Millie, I'm so glad."

"Yes, I give in, I surrender. I'm coming out with the white flag. You have all the big guns."

"Is it as bad as that?"

"Oh, worse. But no, I'm only jesting! Here, I've picked you a lovely green rosebud. Mind the thorns."

"May there be no thorns in our life together."

"Nothing sharp with which we can hurt each other. Oh if you knew how frightened I am of being hurt by you, Christopher."

"Millie! As if I could ever hurt you. I worship you."

The unexpectedness of her cry pierced him, causing a little sweet pain which became a warm glow of power. As he spoke he knew still that he ought to be saying something very different to her, he ought to be using all the intelligence he could command to make her, at this last minute, feel utterly free of him. He should be offering her his help and her freedom too. But already, loaded deep with joy and absolutism, the new situation had gained its own historical momentum.

"You think Frances won't mind, really?"

"No, no," said Christopher. "When she's married, when she's got her man and her own place, she won't be troubled about this." He recalled the haunted figure that he had seen that morning. But that was a ghost, and this sunny garden and its certainties were the real world.

"I wonder why men always think that about women. Well, I hope you won't falter for Frances. For myself, for what's left of my heart, I've got to think of you as desperate about me." She gave him a quick look and then turned her back again, going toward the swing.

"But I am desperate about you, Millie."

"Could you dry the seat for me?"

He dried the seat of the swing with his handkerchief and she sat upon it, digging the heel of her boot into the lawn.

"You know, Christopher, I did love Arthur. A lot of people thought I didn't but I did."

"I'm sure you did."

"Really, I don't know any way of being fond of people except being in love with them. Arthur was very beautiful when he was young. Well, I suppose in a way he's still young. And I am old."

"You know you're not old, Millie—"

"Yes I am. I'm doing an old person's thing. I'm giving up waiting. Christopher—"

"Yes?"

"I shall want another motor car. We shall want another motor car."

" 'We'—oh, yes—whatever you say, my darling. But we shall have to have a mechanic. I couldn't manage—"

"We won't need a mechanic. We'll use my young men. I shall have a troop of young men, you know, to follow me about. Like young Andrew. He knows all about engines. You won't mind, will you?"

"If you marry me I won't mind anything."

"I wonder. Will you give me an engagement ring?"

"Of course! But we can't make anything, you know, public for a bit—"

"What an ardent, impetuous fellow you are! I suppose I could wear my ring underneath a glove! No, you'd better not buy the ring just yet. You may still change your mind."

"Millie, I'll get you a ring this afternoon—"

"No, no, of course not! Anyway, I want a little breathing space. I want a little time, time for a sort of holiday—"

"You don't mean a last fling do you, my darling?"

"A last fling? Good heavens, no. Whoever could I have a last fling with? No, don't swing me, I can swing myself."

She began to move the swing to and fro. She had opened the front of her coat, revealing a high-necked blouse of innumerable white frills pulled tightly over her bosom. Her legs bent and straightened vigorously with a flash of plump grey-stockinged calf and a hint of petticoat. The rope groaned on the tree and the fragments of bark fluttered down onto the red velvet epaulettes. Millie swung higher. Then something solid and glittering, dislodged from one of her pockets, plopped heavily onto the grass at Christopher's feet. It was a revolver. He picked it up and saw that it was loaded.

Millie let the swing lose speed and in a moment, with a great swirl of skirts, she jumped out of it, her hand seizing Christopher's shoulder. Her other hand gripped the revolver, crushing it against his palm and slipping it from him. As Christopher felt the weight of her body suddenly against him he made as if to embrace her, but she moved quickly from him to the other side of the swing.

Someone appeared at the side of the house and was now going in through the glass doors of the conservatory. It was Barnabas Drumm. He noticed them, hesitated, gave a vague wave, and went inside.

Christopher felt suddenly uneasy. "He must be looking for Hilda. He doesn't know she's moved. He can't have seen or heard anything, can he?"

"No, of course not. He's only just come."

"I don't trust him. He's full of malice, and I believe he spies on you."

"Nonsense, he's just a dear old sheepdog. Let's go in, shall we? I think it's beginning to rain again."

They moved out from under the tree into the first drops of the rain. The weak sun still touched the tips of white flowering cherry trees against a leaden sky. Christopher halted. There was, to make his happiness complete, one thing he must say, one hazard more he must run. And surely now it was safe to run it. He meant to say, You know you needn't marry me. I'll do it all, but if you don't want to you needn't marry me.

The words came out differently. "You know you can always do anything that you want, Millie."

She looked away from him. The small rain was already laying

its drops in her dark hair and upon the shoulders of her coat. "I won't want to do anything."

"You may do. You know you can command me. You can do what you please with me."

"So you think *now*," she murmured. "But there are deep roots of selfishness in both of us. And when we struggle you will always win, always."

Ten

At this period of my life I again became a frequent visitor at the house in Upper Mount Street, where I knew that a gay welcome always awaited me. It was, I knew, improper, doubtless unjust, to prefer the lively affection of the light-hearted "Millie" to the dour and dumb attachment of my wife. But the order of the world is unjust and with a natural spontaneity like moves to like and life flows towards life. My own congenital gaiety, so muted in the gloomy atmosphere of my home "had its fling" at Upper Mount Street, and at times Lady Kinnard and I would make each other laugh until the tears ran. The return to Blessington Street was always something of a penance. The house was usually untidy and often far from clean; and I was, I confess, offended by the, as it seemed to me, deliberate tawdriness and ill-kempt appearance not of my home only, but of my wife's person. That most regrettable, that unexpected but implacable physical distaste which had led me so unforgivably to fail my wife in the central sanctum of our marriage, early and silently divined by her, had led the poor sufferer perversely to accentuate just those features of her personal appearance which had been the initial occasion of my abstinence.

These words, which he had penned early that morning in the National Library, ran automatically through Barney's head, giving him but little pleasure since his thoughts were by now engaged elsewhere as he sat in the Butt Bar in Beresford Place on the afternoon of Wednesday April the nineteenth. Previous to his arrival at the Butt Bar he had been in Little's Public House in Harcourt Street, and before that in Nagle's Bar in Earl Street, and before that at Bergin's in Amiens Street. He had lunched, or it seemed likely that he had lunched, at the Red Bank Restaurant, but that was a long time ago by this time.

Barney was still in a shocked condition. Seeking Hilda that morning at Finglas, he had, coming up the lane at the side of the house, become aware of Millie in the garden. From behind the hedge he had heard the greater part of her conversation with Christopher. Millie flirting with Christopher was one thing, Millie married to Christopher was quite another, and Barney had immediately felt: I cannot endure it. If Millie were married he could not go to her any more. This, which he had never thought, since he had never conceived of her second marriage, was instantly and horribly clear. His presence at Millie's depended on certain assumptions, certain—he had to admit it—perhaps fictions or illusions. He had to feel himself, with her, "as good as anybody." He had to feel her somehow potentially his. And Millie was often so gay with him, might he not really be the most necessary man of them all? He could be Millie's spaniel now, but not the tolerated pet of a married Millie, even if he were in fact tolerated.

He was appalled too, almost frightened, by the sudden image of Millie under duress. With an ear attuned by love, or by his own specialized self-interest, he had heard in her bantering voice the hidden whine of despair. Millie was acting under coercion, and there could be only one reason for this coerced decision: she was marrying money. Barney was not so much shocked by this revelation as horrified by it on Millie's behalf. Millie was so essentially a free animal. What awful desperation must lie behind this choice to wear the collar of slavery? Barney could not envisage her as in love with Christopher. That pain, at least, was spared him. She was not in love; but she would with all the vitality and all the duplicity of her nature play the part of a rapturously happy wife. And she would be utterly lost to him.

At a certain point in these miserable reflections, possibly in Little's Public House, Barney felt an obscure lightening. This sense of relief shortly became explicit as the resolution: it must not be. She would certainly regret her decision: better, then, if she were prevented from carrying it out. Whatever Millie's financial embarrassments—and Barney had for some time had an inkling of their existence—they were better for her than a forced marriage which her free nature would resent and soon detest. Barney, who, after all, knew her better than anyone else did, was certain of this. It was for him, doubtless not unrewarded, to rescue Millie from herself. She must be stopped. But how?

To turn from fruitless grinding pain to the envisaging, however vague, of counter-measures, is an invigorating change. Barney had sat up, ordered another whiskey, and focused his eyes sternly upon the Meeting of the Waters, which was wanly represented in a diamond of stained glass in the window of the bar. And at once there arose, commanding the new perspective of his thoughts, the figure of Frances. Frances was not yet to be told of her father's intentions. Why? Clearly because Christopher wished the girl to be safely married and packed away before he made his move. Again why? Because he was afraid of his daughter's reactions. Barney, who had by now conveyed himself as far as the Butt Bar, beat his forehead and tried to focus his eyes upon the Snowy Breasted Pearl, who was wanly represented in a diamond of stained glass in the window of the bar. The young lady, who would otherwise have been hard to identify, was thus labelled. The letters danced before his eyes, but he had read them on a previous occasion. The matter of Frances was complicated.

Barney had always experienced with Frances a simplicity and gentleness of communication which he had otherwise hoped for in vain from the world of women. Through Frances he had glimpsed that absolute of love, which is the only thing which heals the humiliated spirit. But he was aware too, inside this quiet girl, of a woman both strong and complex. The will of Frances was a powerful machine. If he were to release that machine into

the situation he had just discovered, what would happen? That
Frances was capable of preventing her father's marriage Barney
did not doubt. Though whether she would decide to do so was
another thing. The beginning of the argument was that Millie
ought not to marry Christopher. But granted that, it was still not
absolutely clear that it was wise to involve Frances. Frances
would be desperately upset; and was it right to upset her just
upon the verge of her own marriage? Though, of course, if
Frances did engage in a struggle with her father this might induce
her to put off leaving Ireland or even to put off getting married,
especially if her struggle was successful. She would feel it necessary to stay with her father and comfort him if she had effectively crossed him.

This introduced a new consideration so interesting to Barney
that, scarcely noticing, he put on his hat, heaved himself up, and
walked with dignity out of the Butt Bar onto the quay. The Butt
Bar stood next door to Liberty Hall, the headquarters of the
Transport and General Workers' Union, and now of James Connolly's Citizen Army. As Barney crossed the cobbles in the direction of the Loop Line Railway he noticed that a number of
people were gathered outside Liberty Hall. There was a familiar
figure in the group. He realized that it was Pat, and stopped with
a quick instinct of concealment. Pat was dressed in the vivid
green uniform of the Volunteers, complete with slouch hat and
Sam Brown. He carried a revolver at his belt and a rifle slung at
his back. The other men in the group wore the darker green
uniform of the Citizen Army. Some sort of argument seemed to
be going on. After a moment they all moved inside the building.

The glimpse of Pat sobered Barney and made him realize that
he had in fact drunk quite a lot of whiskey. He was glad that Pat
had not seen him; and he felt a spasm of that special, unique pain
which was caused in him by his stepsons. This pain was com-
pounded of love, shame, and an acute sense of injustice. Barney
saw his stepchildren as superior, almost perfect, beings, and he
loved them with a peculiar, private, incapsulated love. He had

never been able to find any language for this love. There was no touch, no look, no gesture, no tone of voice which could give expression to it at all. At the same time he knew, and knew it daily, that he was a cause of scandal to the two boys. They resented what they saw of his attitude to their mother. Even more perhaps they simply resented their stepfather as an object upon the scene, as a debased version of human existence. The contrast between the purity and perfection of his inward love and the meanness and absurdity of his outward performance, between the gravity of his heart and the oafishness of his manner, seemed to Barney something miserably unjust. At the same time he felt ashamed before the two boys with a genuine piercing shame which seemed itself to belong to what was most profound and uncorrupted in him, and which was sometimes almost pleasurable in its intensity.

Barney walked a little way and then leaned against the warm rounded granite of the quay. The sky above him was that particular sort of cold Irish pale blue, looking like thin wet paper down which highly diluted blue paint is almost imperceptibly running. A steady wind tilted the masts of ships outside the Customs House and kept the rippling Union Jack squarely on display. Dublin, or perhaps it was the Liffey, smelt of yeast. Barney looked down at the river. Great iron rings hung upon the river walls, joined by loops of rope, shaggy with seaweed, resembling huge coarse Georgian decorations, and below the gluey water passed slowly by, foaming a little like stout, its dark, dirty brown smudged with rusty white lights and thin overlaid blues and shimmers of old tarnished gold. A flight of whitewashed steps was chalkily reflected, and now a tower of white gulls descending to investigate some more than usual opacity in the viscous stream. As Barney stared at it and smelt it, and listened to the clatter of the traffic and the quarrelling of the gulls, he thought about the silent unpolluted Shannon at Clonmacnoise and the big open-handed Christ upon His ancient cross, and the empty land there.

He walked on as far as the bridge. Ahead of him the multicoloured quays of the cluttered city meandered away, starkly clear, in the direction of the Four Courts with its green pencilled dome. A construction of clouds, whitish brown like the light upon the Liffey, was rising above Guinness's brewery. Perhaps it was going to rain after all. Barney stroked his moustache, sniffing the whiskey from it. He paused to gaze idly at the array of posters on St. George's quay. A large one affirmed, with a modesty which always puzzled him, that Monkey Brand would not wash clothes. Smaller notices announced that *Vaseline Helped the British to Victory*, and *His Skin Turned Black, Zam-buk the Only Cure*. A recruiting poster showed a white-haired woman admonishing her dubious son, *Go, Lad, It's Your Duty*. A photographer's advertisement claimed a willingness to *Enlarge Any Photo of Your Wife, Sweetheart, Child or Dearest Friend to Full Life Size* for only one and sixpence. Did they really mean it? Barney imagined himself in possession of a Full Life Size picture of Millie. He would have to keep it locked in his room. Probably the only safe place would be under the mattress. This led to other disturbing thoughts.

He began to walk up toward the Pillar. Sackville Street was full of the blue uniforms of wounded soldiers, conspicuous in the weak sunshine. A small detachment of lancers, armed with carbines and lances, trotted past in the direction of Phoenix Park, and after them a brake full of police. Barney detached his mind from the interesting possibilities of a life-size replica of Millie, and began to wonder again about Frances and whether her deep dislike of Millie, which he had observed but never fully understood, would lead, her, should she be apprised of the situation, to oppose her parent's wishes in the matter of his marriage. As it began to seem to him bleakly probable that Frances would prove all that a magnanimous daughter should be, it occurred to him that there was yet another card which he might play. He might tell Frances about what had happened at Maynooth. He paused at the corner of Rutland Square. The clouds were massing now above the green dome of the Rotunda Hospital, and the clock on

Findlater's Church stood at ten minutes to five. Frances had always wanted to know what woman "had been his downfall," and Barney had often wished to tell her, not in order to discredit Millie, but simply in order to draw Frances closer to him. He had sometimes envisaged telling her everything and making her his confessor and his judge. But a sense of loyalty to Millie had always prevented him from unfolding to Frances the full pattern of his woes, though she herself had often prompted him to do so in O'Halloran's Bun Shop. Frances intuited wickedness in Millie. Should he not, in revealing that this woman was to marry Christopher, also reveal how far that intuition had been correct?

Barney let himself in very quietly at the front door of the house in Blessington Street. It was just beginning to rain. He paused in the dark hall to hang his hat upon the stand, and drew out of the drawer a velvet skull cap which he had lately bought at Finnegans, the Gentleman's Outfitter, and which he liked because it kept his bald head warm and gave him a slightly ecclesiastical appearance. He noticed that the hall-stand was thick with dust. He drew a face quickly in the dust, then carefully fitted on his velvet cap and peered at his dim image in the mirror. The cap, in a way which he found satisfactory, made him look much older. He observed how white his eyebrows had become. He was aware of an urgent desire to lie down somewhere and close his eyes. He began to creep quietly up the stairs. He always went up like a mouse so as to avoid any possible interview with his wife.

He passed the stained-glass lavatory window, inhaling the smell and avoiding the stair that creaked. On these occasions he eschewed the ostentation of the lavatory, reserving himself for the discreet quiet of his own chamber-pot. He passed through the glass-bead curtain, grasping it with a practised hand to prevent the jangle, and had his foot upon the next flight of stairs when he heard Kathleen's voice calling from the drawing-room. "Barney, is that you? Could you come in for a minute?"

Barney groaned. He turned back and inserted himself noncommittally through the drawing-room door. It now seemed to be raining hard outside, and the room was dark and cold. No fire had been lit in the grate, which was still full of yesterday's ashes. There was the usual stuffy, musty smell of dust and old thick feathery textiles.

Kathleen was standing at the far end of the room by the window, plucking at the lace curtain. She must have seen him come in. As she turned her head he saw the big outline of her bun, from which some untidy hairs were sprouting. Her face was a worried pale blur out of which those big light-brown eyes glared at him with a luminous intensity. She was wearing her usual old-fashioned brown skirt down to the ground and had drawn a knitted shawl round her for warmth. Not feeling very strong, Barney sat down on an upright chair near the door. The shiny slippery seat, unaccustomed to being sat on, nearly ejected him. He experienced the immediate physical sense of guilt which a confrontation with Kathleen always occasioned. His skin turned black. Zam-buk the only cure.

"Barney, I'm so worried."

"What about, dear?" Had Kathleen found out something?

"About Pat."

"Oh, about Pat. I shouldn't worry about Pat."

"Barney, do you know of anything, anything Pat's going to —do?"

"No, nothing at all. Funny, I saw Pat today by Liberty Hall. He was just going inside."

"Liberty Hall? But that's not his headquarters. His headquarters is in Dawson Street."

"I know. But I expect they were just planning a joint march or something with the I.C.A. boys. We're great pals with them these days."

"Yes, I've noticed that. So you don't know anything about it, Barney? I really think you ought to tell me if you do."

"Honest, Kathleen, I don't know anything. I just don't know what you're worrying about."

"Oh, well—they wouldn't tell you, anyway." She came and sat down by the untidy hearth, and crumbled a piece of half-burnt coal with her boot.

Barney was a bit annoyed by this. He got off the reluctant chair and came over to the mantelpiece. "Of course I'd know if anything was on. I don't understand what you're imagining anyway. What makes you say that about Pat?"

"Oh, I don't know. Nothing definite. He's been two days away from his job without giving any explanation, and Mr. Monaghan called in last night to see him. He asked me if Pat was ill and of course I told him he wasn't. It's so discourteous. And when I said Mr. Monaghan had been, Pat just laughed and said something about not going back at all. He seems to be living in another world."

"Oh, I shouldn't worry," said Barney. He was relieved that what troubled Kathleen was not something about himself. He shuffled his feet to produce an atmosphere of departure.

"And now every time he goes out he carries a gun. And he was wearing that uniform again today. And he seems terribly excited and unnatural, and Cathal's excited too."

"Cathal's always excited."

"He spends so much *time* out. What's he doing all day? And he simply ignores things I say to him, he doesn't even bother to reply. Barney, couldn't you say something to him?"

"Good heavens, what could I say?"

"Well, ask him if they're thinking of—" Kathleen stopped, and Barney suddenly realized that she was in some state of extreme emotion. She did not weep, but her white face puckered blindly and she covered her mouth with her hand.

"Come, come, Kathleen," he said, touched and infected by her agitation. "You know nothing will happen. Nothing ever happens in Ireland."

"Please speak to him, Barney."

"I have no authority over Pat."

"Just to find out. Oh, it's so *wrong*—"

"What is?"

"This hatred, these guns—"

"You don't understand," said Barney. "Women don't understand." Did he understand himself? He was flattered by Kathleen's appeal, but he was also frightened by it. Could her intuition have told her of something which was really the case? But that was impossible.

"You see, it *is* sometimes right to fight—" Barney began. His words sounded blundering and childish in the cold, darkened room. Was he only now trying to think about those possibilities which the sheer physical infection of Kathleen's fear had conjured up? He felt sudden fear himself, coldness.

"I'm so frightened about Pat." Kathleen had turned back to her particular concern. She murmured it as if she knew that there was no help and that she was alone again. Barney saw that she was shivering.

"Don't worry," he said in a loud voice. "I've seen these young people getting excited. It comes to nothing." He felt he would have to get out of the room quickly. He began to move away. "Shall I light the gas? It's gloomy in here."

"And that rifle of yours upstairs—" Kathleen went on, suddenly addressing herself to Barney as she saw that he was going to go. "You oughtn't to have that rifle, it's wrong, it's a wrong thing. You older men should set an example. What can you expect of the young? You should get rid of that rifle. One can't live by violence. The whole world is mad with violence."

"Oh, well, that's just an old thing," said Barney. In fact it was a new Lee Enfield in beautiful condition.

"All the guns ought to be dropped into the sea. It's a man's world, a world of hate. Why do you always lock your door now? You're getting as bad as Pat."

Kathleen had an intuitive gift, a sort of artistic talent, for jumbling together the personal and the impersonal into a sort of inconsequent yet compulsive ensemble. This, Barney often thought, was what made her so good at making people feel guilty. All Kathleen's complaints were threaded together and then somehow attached to her interlocutor. "Well, you see—" Barney, who now locked his door because the Memoir had reached such monumental proportions that it was impossible to hide it, fumbled for an invention.

Fortunately Kathleen went straight on. "Must you wear that ridiculous little hat in the house? It makes you look like a Jew."

"I like looking like a Jew."

"Have you been to confession?"

"No."

"Oughtn't you to go?"

"Maybe."

"Will you go?"

"I don't know."

"It's nearly Easter."

"I know it's nearly Easter. I've been thinking about Easter."

"Won't you go to Father Ryan?"

"I don't like Father Ryan."

"Confession isn't a personal thing."

"I know it isn't."

"Well, go to some other priest. Go to some priest that you don't know somewhere in town."

"Perhaps I will, perhaps I won't," said Barney. There was something timeless about his quarrels with Kathleen. It was as if it was always the same quarrel. She reduced him to the status of a petulant child and then goaded him to naughtiness. Helplessly on each occasion he watched himself move from a condition of humiliated stupidity to a condition of spiteful rage.

"Go to Tenebrae. You always like going to Tenebrae."

"I will if I choose."

"We are all sinners. At this holy time of all times we must remember it."

"I know I'm a sinner."

"We are in Lent, and that speaks of austerity. Religion is a great simplicity, Barney. Is not that what your life needs, simplicity?"

"It's simple enough already if by simple you mean dull!"

"You know I don't mean that. What troubles you is that you are ashamed."

"I'm damned if I'm ashamed!" Of course the central trouble of his life was that he was ashamed, but that meant to him something that Kathleen would never, never understand, so that he was right to reject her words which had a meaning so far away from the truth. He was not ashamed in her way. He writhed before her, half turning towards the door but unable to escape. She was looking up at him. He could not see her face in the gloom, but he somehow felt the naked, careworn piety of her expression. It drove him mad.

"Sometimes I think you're just going to pieces, Barney."

"Well, if I am going to pieces whose fault is that?" If he had not married this woman he could have been a good man. If he had not married he would have known how to perfect himself and how to achieve that simplicity which Kathleen was quite right to say was the essence of religion. It was she who prevented him from being simple.

"What's to stop me going to pieces?" said Barney. "No one looks after me or loves me. And you go round looking like an old hag just to spite me. Why don't you get yourself some proper clothes? You go round looking like an old hag from the tenements. Cathal said the new people down the road thought you were my mother. You're punishing yourself just to punish me. You even use your religion to spite me."

"That's a wicked thing to say," said Kathleen quietly.

"Well, you do. You're eating me up. And I'm not looked after. No one does my room upstairs—"

"You lock your door."

"And the house is a shambles. Look at this room, with the fire not even cleared out. And there's dust everywhere. What does Jinny think she's doing? She's a single girl, she hasn't got a place of her own to look after, you'd think she'd have enough time in the day to dust the place a little. You haven't trained her properly. You should be getting after her with a stick."

"Jinny's away."

"What's the matter with her?"

"She's pregnant."

"Oh—" This sudden intrusion of someone else's troubles into the recital of his own left him for the moment confused.

"Didn't you see her crying the other day on the stairs?"

"No." In fact Barney had noticed Jinny crying on the stairs, but he had been hurrying to see Millie at the time and he had forgotten her tears the moment after. The lie was too base. He put his hand to his cheek and muttered, "Yes, I did see her crying, but I was in a hurry and I forgot."

"You're always in a hurry. You're always forgetting. You're only half here."

"Poor Jinny. What can we do?"

"Very little. But you might go and see her, for instance. The doctor's told her to stop work. And you know what that place she lives in is like."

"Go and see her?" Barney was about to pronounce it impossible. Then he sat down abruptly in the nearest chair. He had been ready in imagination to open his compassionate arms to the whole world. And now he was scarcely able to bring himself to visit a poor servant girl who was in trouble. He said aloud, "What is the matter with me?"

"You know what's the matter with you. You're so sunk in yourself you hardly know that anybody else exists at all. Why don't you this Easter—"

"Well and what about you?" said Barney raising his head. He forgot all about Jinny. "Aren't you sunk in yourself? Do you know that I exist? You don't seem to. All you—"

The door of the drawing-room swung silently open and a figure appeared. It was Cathal, carrying a tray. He circled Barney adroitly and put the tray down on one of the brass-topped tables with a light clatter. "Why, mother, how dark it is in here! It's raining cats and dogs outside. Shall I light the gas?"

A match flared at once in his hand, and Cathal was moving along the wall lighting up the gas mantels. Each mantel flickered a pale orange under its silk, beaded shade, and then as Cathal turned the tap glowed into a globe of brilliant white. The room lightened and the rainy window darkened as the gas hissed quietly.

"I just wet the tea," said Cathal, returning to the tray. "I thought I'd bring some up. Oh, I wish I'd remembered to light the fire, I meant to now poor Jinny's away. There, Mother." He poured out a cup of tea and handed it to Kathleen.

Kathleen looked up at him, smiling. Her face, pearly-golden in the soft glow of the gas, seemed still a little tearful and puckered, as if it had been lightly plucked at, but her features drooped with a calm, loving weariness, the brow bland and the big eyes bright with affection as she lifted an almost ecstatic gaze upon her son. Cathal, with his gauchely deliberate grace, trampled about her for a moment as if he were weaving some invisible protective cocoon. He pressed his dark hair back behind his ears, giving his mother his intense close-eyed stare. His whole figure was sharp with youth and brilliant with consciousness. Then he turned to Barney.

"Here, for you," he said. He never called Barney by any name, but he spoke now in a low coaxing voice as if to an ill person. He handed him the tea. "And look, I've got you your biscuits. Those special biscuits you like. The lemon creams. I got them at Lipton's. I had to queue up."

Barney looked at the tray. He saw the plate with his special biscuits, the lemon creams, which Cathal had queued up to get at Lipton's.

He felt the tears rising to his eyes. He saw Cathal close to him and saw as if it were a separate thing, a passing bird, Cathal's hand moving in a gesture towards the tray, urging him to eat. He took hold of the boy's hand. Some sort of confused words seemed to be coming up with the tears. "You are so good to me. You are innocent and pure in heart. Oh, remain so always. Do not ever let evil into your life. Forgive me." He lifted Cathal's hand to his lips and kissed it.

There was a moment of silence and immobility. Then Cathal stepped back, a little confused and embarrassed. He hesitated, and then put his hand on Barney's shoulder, squeezing it slightly. He turned quickly to his mother. "Well, I'll go and get the sticks to light the fire." He was gone from the room.

Barney stood up. His sudden consciousness of Cathal's goodness, his equally sudden and automatic unconsciousness of himself, made him light and buoyant. He felt he had had a revelation.

"So you're drunk," said Kathleen. "I hadn't realized it. But I might have known."

"I'm not drunk!" Was he? Did he always know now whether he was drunk or not? He turned his back to her and the tears spilled out onto his cheeks. It was unjust. He had, for one good moment, spoken to his stepson with the voice of pure love, and all his wife could think of to say was that he was drunk. All right, he was drunk. The tears seemed uncontrollable. They were drunken tears.

He saw through a haze the crucifix upon the wall. He said, "Where did we lose the way, Kathleen? Can we not find some love for each other?"

His wife was silent.

Barney blundered to the door. He did not want to meet Cathal again. And as he went up the stairs to his room the awful black consciousness of Millie returned to him. He unlocked his door. There was the Lee Enfield rifle leaning in the corner. He sat down at the table and rubbed his tears away. Then he gathered together the scattered pages of his Memoir and began quickly to write.

Eleven

The misty rosary of morn, my fair,
Marks me your footprints in the holy dew.
Daylight is amethystine where you are
And every floweret of the dawn is you!
Such festal favours feed the sanguine day,
Our plighting day that blushes graciously!
You are its glow, its glimmer and its ray
Which falls from far into the deeps of me.
Now as you trip with little tiny steps,
Your petal hands and water-crystal voice,
Your flower-fragrant, oh-so-sighed-for lips
Make my dull essence tremble and rejoice.
Oh thou my dawn, in thee my noonday glints,
In thee my sun sets with a million tints.

It was early on Thursday morning and Andrew had at last decided that it was time formally to propose to Frances. He was glad that he had waited. He knew now that he had not been idly prevaricating. They had been parted, after all, for a matter of over a year, since Frances' visit to England early in the war, and there was a little strangeness to be got over. He had been upset by his return to Ireland, upset by the fuss and flurry of his mother, upset by his relations. Only now had he, with a certain cool relentlessness, calmed himself and begun to favour Frances with his complete attention.

He had penned the sonnet late last night at Claresville, where he had been camping out with his mother for two nights now, doing the innumerable jobs which had to be finished before the furniture arrived. He looked his effort over with satisfaction. He was pleased with "amethystine," which provided just that vivid dash of colour which Andrew, a disciple of Gautier, knew that any poem must have. "Amethystine" emphasized and developed the image of the sparkling dew in which Frances' footsteps, from which of course the epithet "holy" was transferred, were spread out like a rosary or rosy necklace. "Little tiny steps" was not perhaps quite realistic, as Frances rather tended to stride along, but it was symbolically right, expressing the tripping, gliding motion of the beloved compared to the slow breaking of the dawn. The half-rhymes which he had failed to eliminate troubled him a little, but a friend at Cambridge who published poetry in the *Cornhill* magazine had told him that half-rhymes were now an allowable device. Andrew himself had once nearly had a poem in the *Cornhill*. The editor had sent it back with a very friendly note.

The thought that he was shortly going to make himself and Frances so extremely happy made Andrew quite dazed with pride. Suddenly he was omnipotent, the benevolent despot of his little world. He would make everybody happy. He would lay an egg of pure good which would nourish them all. Humility followed pride. He did not deserve this sweet, clever girl. A sort of laughing rapture followed the humility, because, of course, he knew he did deserve her, or rather knew he didn't really feel he didn't! This peculiar private exultation merged into a diffused physical desire. His physical feelings about Frances had always been muddled and fluctuating. He had never really wanted any other girl. Yet he had not always sharply wanted her. Now it was as if his desires were coming into focus and revealing Frances unambiguously as their object. In this self-finding and self-defining Andrew more plainly realized how much he had been afraid of physical love. He had not shared the obvious and obsessive fears which drove his brother officers to places he would shudder to visit. But he had deep, deep fears all the same. And with a calmness of resolution it occurred to him that if he could properly conquer those fears all other fears would be conquered too; or, if not conquered, at least they would receive an intelligible place. The blind black hole in his consciousness which was the awful prospect of returning to France would be lightened, filled with manageable items. Once married, there would be no more nightmare.

Andrew had been extremely upset by his encounter with Pat Dumay. The memory that he had been so undignified and stupid as to taunt his cousin made him hot with shame, and on the following day he had been able to think of nothing else. Immediately afterwards he had wished to apologize but had been prevented, perhaps fortunately, by the presence of Cathal. A straight apology stammered out upon the occasion of the fault would only have made things worse. He had, however, very much wanted to see Pat alone—had, in fact, all through Tuesday pined and fretted simply with this desire. He felt, with an almost physical humiliation, how absurdly much he had counted on achieving with Pat, now that they were both grown up, some quite remarkable friendship. Pat's magic for him had not faded, and entering the Blessington Street drawing room on Monday he had felt the pang of a delicious fear.

On Wednesday morning, in order to escape from his mother and to think some decisive thoughts about Frances, he walked over from Dalkey to Killiney and stood on the beach in a hollow of blue conical mountains. Here there came to him a great enlightenment and a great peace. He would never be friends with Pat. Pat belonged to some other race of men. Even if he were to seek Pat out and somehow beg his pardon, even if he were to seek Pat out and somehow defy him, the response would be the same.

Pat would be cool, ironical, amused, polite, distant, and finally bored. The realization that there are people we shall never conquer comes to us as a part of the process of growing up. With a clarity of mind which he felt did him credit, and which brought with it a new moral vigour, Andrew faced the fact that Pat was a lost cause. Now was the time to think of Frances and of Frances only.

Standing with his bare feet in the freezing sea he told himself that he had become a realist. He would take Frances away to England, at once if possible. And after the war he would insist on his mother's return to England. After all, he was a man and a soldier and must be expected to exert some authority over a female parent. The obvious idea that his mother need not stay over here forever came to him with a revelation of how much, up to now, he had sheerly been afraid of Ireland. It had seemed like a dark pit full of demons. Now it was suddenly clear that he had only to snap his fingers at these chained-up bogeys. Having "given up" Pat Dumay was perhaps the crucial step. Henceforth he would act like a free person. He saw himself suddenly in the future, a strong paterfamilias, ruling his womenfolk and his children with a benevolent firmness. Even the idea of making Frances pregnant before he returned to the front was no longer distasteful. Even the idea that he might never survive to see his son was now something at which he could look.

The sand and pebbles in the shallow foam beat on his feet, which were almost too cold to feel pain. He stepped back and hobbled to a rock and began to dry his benumbed feet on his socks. A moving shaft of sunlight came across the beach and made the sea sparkle in front of him and gave him a shadow on the sand. His thoughts reverted to the matter of his Aunt Millicent. Millie, as he now rather self-consciously thought of her, had never, in fact, been very far from his mind since the incident of the lapis lazuli earring. He had wondered again and again whether she had dropped the earring into the pool on purpose. He kept coming to the delightful conclusion that probably she had, and smiled every time he reached it. The situation in which she had put him, of having to make tea-time conversation while at the same time keeping the earring under control in some reasonably secure part of his underclothing, had embarrassed him exceedingly at the time and amused him exceedingly afterwards. He felt, about it all, a sense of achievement. He had returned the earring in an envelope next day with a short note which, after numerous re-writings, simply read: *And thank you for my tea!* Really, the little drama had excited Andrew quite considerably. He was not sure whether he had been played with as a child or flirted with as an adult, but again successive examinations of the subject brought the more flattering conclusion. His charming aunt had flirted with him. Andrew had never been flirted with in quite this way by an older woman. There came with it, with Millie herself, the faintest whiff of wickedness which he laughed to find so attractive. Women were gay and beautiful and he was young and free. But, of course, he knew this in any case. And Millie was only his aunt.

He was young and free, but now he was going to bind himself to the dearest girl in the world. He was so happy to find himself eager, to find, when it came to it, no grain of regret. He could give his whole heart. He had rehearsed the scene so often in imagination. Only he had not anticipated the sonnet. That arrived, sent by the gods at just the right moment, like an engagement present. He decided that he would, her clothes permitting, tuck the sonnet into the front of Frances' dress. Then he laughed to think that he was copying Millie. There was also the matter of the ring. On the previous day Hilda, displaying for once some sense of the tempo of others, had produced for him a gold ring set with a ruby and two diamonds which she had got in Dublin with Christopher's help and which she said she was sure would fit Frances. She handed it over to him with no further admonitions. The ring, when Andrew brooded over it later, seemed an almost heart-breakingly beautiful and significant object. Suddenly the romance, the sweetness, the innocence of his union with Frances came before him with an intensity which wrought him to tears.

Now on Thursday morning he was waiting in the garden, waiting near the red swing for Frances to come out of the house. She had been busy with some domestic task when he arrived and had told him to await her outside. Andrew, who had earlier envisaged, indeed planned, the scene quite calmly, now felt dizzy with excitement. He had the sonnet in one pocket of his jacket and the ring wrapped up in his handkerchief in the other pocket. He kept fingering them both, and the sonnet was becoming rather crumpled. His heart was hitting his side as if it wanted to fly out of him like a cannon ball, and his breath came in short, desperate sniffs of the quiet, stifling morning air. The day, bright to begin with, had clouded over. He began to fiddle with the swing, and then turned to find Frances quite close to him.

The dear girl was looking so beautiful this morning, her plump round face rosy and smooth, cool and sleek as the surface of an apple. It was one of the days when she revealed her big brow, and her hair was pushed back, still in something of an early-morning tangle, behind her ears. She was wearing a long grey dress of coarse cotton, rather like a nurse's overall, caught in at the waist, and over it rather quaintly one of Christopher's tweed jackets, caught up, no doubt, as she left the house. She had turned up the collar of the jacket round her neck, and her hands were thrust into the pockets. She had never looked sweeter.

Seeing something portentous in Andrew's look, Frances was silent, waiting for him to speak.

Trembling all over, he began. "My dearest Frances, I have something of very great importance to ask you. I wonder if you can at all guess what it is?" His voice trembled and quavered too.

"No," said Frances.

"I wish you to do me the honour of becoming my wife."

There was a silence. Then Frances abruptly turned her back upon him.

Andrew stood quite still, staring at the tousled pile of Frances' dark hair appearing over the top of Christopher's jacket. He felt startled and breathless, as if he had inadvertently struck her. He had not realized that his sudden words would arouse so much emotion in her. But, of course, the gracious imaginary Frances was not thus taken by surprise. He put out a reassuring hand to touch her sleeve. Without turning she moved a step away.

"Frances—"

"Hang on a minute, Andrew."

The silence continued. Andrew stood staring at her back. His hands in his two pockets twisted the sonnet and fumbled the ring. A light wind was blowing now from the sea, stirring the chestnut tree and the tall leaves of the montbretia, stirring the red swing.

Frances began to turn slowly about. Her hands had not left her pockets. But now she raised one and drew it over her face as if erasing whatever expression had been there before. She coughed, as if a cough would set some helpful tone of ordinariness. Then she said, "Thank you very much, Andrew."

Andrew stared at her face. It was the strongest face he had ever seen her wear, and the grimmest. Her long mouth curved downward at the corners with a positive force and her eyes were wrinkled into what seemed two dark narrow rectangles.

"Frances—"

"Oh, my dear—"

"Frances, darling, what is it? Don't be upset."

"Andrew, it's that I can't say yes. At least, I can't just say yes."

Andrew opened his fingers and drew them out of his pockets. He wiped his hands together. "I see." He felt completely confused and frightened. He felt as if he were in the presence of Frances for the first time, as if the real Frances had just broken through a screen upon which a picture of her had been painted. It was difficult to put words together. Speech between them had been a kind of silence. Now suddenly it had become something noisy, crackling, arduous. "What do you mean by 'just,' that you can't just say yes?"

Frances seemed to find it equally difficult to speak. She stared down at the ground. "Well, I can't say yes. But I mean it isn't that things are different. It's just—oh, dear—"

"But, but—you do love me? You haven't stopped loving me?" He had never known a world without Frances' love.

"Of course I love you."

"And I love you, dearest Frances, and I want you to be my wife. I expect you're cross with me because I didn't say anything sooner, but you see—"

"It's not that, and I'm not cross with you. I'm cross with myself."

"I don't understand."

"We've both taken it—so much for granted—too much for granted. And everyone else assuming it too. It hasn't somehow been quite right—"

"I see. You feel I ought to have courted you properly—that we know each other too well. But I *will* court you—"

"No, no nonsense like that. You see, in a way we are like brother and sister."

"I don't feel we are like brother and sister at this moment," said Andrew. He had never found Frances more ferociously attractive. She looked up at him quickly. "And neither do you," he added.

She gazed at him, her fiercely controlled face relaxing a little. "Yes. Odd. Well, not odd. But, Andrew, I'm sorry. I've given you a rotten answer."

"You've given me an incomprehensible answer. But I do understand about—how it's all been taken for granted. As if we weren't private people. I've felt funny about that too. But that can't have spoilt everything. Suppose we were to start again at the beginning as if we'd never met?"

"But we can't—"

"I don't know. For the last five minutes I've been talking to a most exciting stranger."

"I feel like that too. But it's just that our friendship has had a shock. Oh, dearest Andrew, I do love you—"

"In that case—Frances, is there somebody else?"

"No, of course not."

"Well, then, is it just that you'd like to wait a bit? We may have known each other since childhood, but we haven't seen a lot of each other lately. Maybe we need time to get used to each other again."

"There's been so much sort of—quiet pressure—"

"Of course, of course. I know, all these people expecting us to get married next week—it's awful—and I know—for a girl—oh, Frances, I'm sorry I've been so stupid. What you're really saying to me is yes, only let's wait a longer time before getting married. That's it, isn't it?"

"Well, no, it isn't quite. I'm not saying that."

"Then you're saying no?"

"Not exactly, but I have to be fair—I can't tie you—"

"But I am tied—I love you. You mean you *are* saying no?"

"You're forcing me to say no!"

"No, I'm not. I'm just trying to understand," he said miserably.

"I can't tie you," she repeated, "so if you force me to say something I've got to say no."

"I'm not forcing you to say anything. I'm just asking you to marry me. I would have asked you much sooner if I'd thought you'd changed."

"But I haven't changed."

"You must have. I just want to know what your feelings are. Do you want me to wait a while and ask you again?"

"Perhaps I do—but this is so unfair, so unfair. I should only say no again. It's that I don't want to hurt you and I want everything to be happy like it was." She closed her eyes and a great many tears streamed down her cheeks. She took a large white handkerchief smelling of tobacco out of the pocket of Christopher's jacket and blew her nose. It was beginning to rain.

"Well," said Andrew, "I'll ask you again later."

"I should only say no again," she said in a frantic tone.

"I'll ask you all the same."

They stood for a moment silently in the light rain, each looking down at the other's feet. Frances said, "Please don't say anything about this to anyone just yet, not for a few days. I'll have to break it to my father first—and I'll have somehow to find the right moment."

"All right. But I can't hold out very long. My mother will be so upset—and I'm not very good at telling lies."

"Oh, Andrew, forgive me. Oh, dear, I must think, I must think. Won't you come in and have some coffee? It's really going to rain hard."

"No," said Andrew, "I won't come in. I suppose I won't be able to come here any more."

"But of course you must come here—"

"I don't think I'll want to, with everything different."

They looked at each other suddenly terrified. Even the most dreadful words can be treated as a bad dream through which one reels with a kind of intoxication of horror. But the cold touch of action awakens the spirit to a world where what is dreadful has slowly and minutely to be lived.

For a second Andrew felt it all beyond his strength. He reached out clumsily to Frances as if to seize her arm, perhaps embrace her. But she drew back. They faced each other for a moment. Then she whispered, "I am sorry, I am so very sorry," and turned and ran into the house.

Andrew went out of the garden gate, turning up the collar of his greatcoat against the rain. He walked down the road to the sea. The very calm sea was lazily washing the rocks and for miles and miles over its level grey surface the heavy rain was falling.

Twelve

Pat was giddy with impatience. It was still only Thursday morning. Sunday rose up in front of him like a black cliff. The mountain must open to admit him, how he knew not. He could foresee nothing except that he would be fighting. This time next week he would have been fighting. Perhaps he would be dead. His first startled fear was diffused now into an aching desire for action, and his body was weary of the interim. In the two days since he had been told he had grimly lived the reality of it into himself. To the mystery of Sunday he was dedicated and resigned, become in every cell of his being a taut extension of that violent future. When it came he would enter upon it coldly. It was only the waiting which was an agony and a fever. He could hardly sleep at night but lay telling himself vividly and lucidly how much he needed sleep. His flesh twitched and ached with expectation.

There was much to do each day. He had attended a staff conference at Liberty Hall about the dovetailing of plans between the Citizen Army and the Volunteers, and had been impressed, as always, by the efficiency of Connolly's men. He had visited a quarry at Brittas where some gelignite was hidden which was to be rushed into Dublin on Sunday morning. He had checked over all the ammunition allotted to his own company, which was hidden, often in small quantities, in various places throughout the city, and made arrangements for it to be moved at short notice. He had made a point of seeing individually all the men under his command, and, without revealing anything, satisfying himself that they were equipped and ready.

Pat was one of the most junior officers to have been told of the plan. The great majority of the Volunteers, including some officers, knew nothing except that "very important manoeuvres" were to take place on Sunday and that "the absence of any Volunteer would be treated as a serious breach of discipline." Of course the men had been told, from long ago, that they must be prepared for anything on any occasion when they marched out in arms. But they had marched out in arms so often and returned afterwards to their tea. There was a ferment in Dublin all the same, which it was to be hoped was not attracting the attention of the Castle. Visiting Lawlor's gun shop in Fownes Street, Pat had found it almost emptied of stock. Streams of people had been in to buy bandoliers and water bottles and even sheath knives; and it was said that you could not get hold of a bayonet from one end of Dublin to the other. Perhaps the men were simply "stocking up," for the "important manoeuvres." Or perhaps the news was gradually leaking out to the rank and file. If so, this was dangerous. It was still only Thursday.

To most of us at most times past history seems like a brightly lit and faintly clamorous procession, while the present is a dark rumbling corridor off which, in hidden shafts and private rooms, our personal stories are enacted. Elsewhere in that obscure continuum, and out of quite other stuff, history is manufactured. Rarely are we able to be the intelligent spectators of an historical event, more rarely still its actors. At such times the darkness lightens and the space contracts until we apprehend the rhythm of our daily actions as the rhythm of a much larger scheme which has included us within its composition. Pat felt for the first time this nearness of history, this almost physical sense of a connection with it, when he learned that on the previous day at a secret meeting Patrick Pearse had been appointed President of the Irish Republic.

At the same meeting James Connolly had been appointed commandant general of the Dublin district and MacDonagh commandant of the Dublin brigade. Final decisions had also been taken about what points of the city should be occupied. There was argument about where the military headquarters should be. Connolly had favoured the ready-made fortress of the Bank of Ireland. But eventually the choice fell upon the General Post Office in Sackville Street. The fate of Dublin Castle was then debated. Pearse had been for attacking the Castle, but Connolly had opposed this. The "Castle," in fact, consisted of a straggle of buildings which would be hard to defend, and there was also a Red Cross hospital inside it. A full attack on the Castle seemed to present too many problems, and it was resolved instead to isolate it by occupying the City Hall and the offices of the *Evening Mail* opposite the gates.

Pat, who had thought long and soberly about the shortage of arms, had food now for further gloomy reflection as he reviewed the gratuitous folly of his leaders. It was surely essential that Dublin Castle should be attacked and preferably burnt. It was the Bastille of the regime, the symbol of its brutality. The Post Office was an insane choice as headquarters: a building hemmed in by others and quite unsuitable for a prolonged defence. In any case, the whole scheme of establishing fixed strong points inside the city was ill-considered. Faced with an enemy who possessed and would use artillery, some degree of mobility was essential. Mobile troops could also make more use of the good will of the civilian population. A number of flying columns, able to retire rapidly out of the city if necessary, would do the enemy more damage, and baffle and scare him far more than a number of isolated strongholds, however bravely defended. There were two thousand five hundred British troops in the city itself and more at the

Curragh. The joint forces of the I.C.A. and the Volunteers might reach twelve or fifteen hundred at a good turn-out. Mobile forces could seem more numerous than they were. Static forces could be studied and counted. But revolutionary leaders can be just as childish and old-fashioned and romantic as the most reactionary of regular soldiers. There was even a plan to occupy Stephen's Green and dig trenches there, although it was agreed that there were not enough men to take the Shelbourne Hotel; and this particular "strong point" could be dealt with in a matter of minutes by a Lewis gun on top of the Shelbourne.

Pat reflected coolly on the folly of it all, the shortage of arms, the absence of sensible plans, the lack of elementary medical supplies and medical skill. He thought that he could accept death now, for himself and others, a death for Ireland. But driving his imagination on to savour the worst that was possible he pictured himself, unaided and horribly wounded, unable to stop from moaning and crying out, lying in the back of some wrecked blood-spattered room, while his comrades knelt at the window returning the enemy fire. At that time he would be empty of destiny. History would exist no more. Even Ireland would exist no more. There would be just a half-crushed animal screaming to be allowed to live: screaming perhaps to be allowed to die. He wanted now to be beyond prayer, to ask nothing more for himself as if he had already ceased to be. But he could not help clasping to him, as an amulet, the hope that if he were to die he might die quickly.

Yet in spite of all these reasons for a steady pessimism Pat could not, at the same time, at the back of his blackest arguments, help feeling a most tremendous glow of hope. He had heard Pearse say that the armed rising was to be thought of simply as a sacrifice of blood, after which Ireland would be spiritually reborn. Pearse said that Ireland needed martyrs. Pat agreed that Ireland needed martyrs. But he felt, felt within his own body, as if it came up out of the old tortured soil, the great angry strength of Ireland. At one with this power he felt superhumanly strong;

and if there were but a few others like him they would make an irresistible tide. These were feelings rather than thoughts, and did not belong to his rational part. Eamonn Ceannt, who had given him the news of the secret council, had said, "If we can last a month the British will come to terms," and Pat had replied, "We won't last a week!" But he had not judged this with his heart. He could not stop imagining that as soon as the first shot was fired the whole of Ireland would rise.

It was only Thursday, and between now and Sunday much could happen for good or ill. There were the persistent rumours about German arms, constantly revived from some mysterious source, to which Pat gave little credit. There was, more seriously, the possibility that the Castle might strike first. The document giving details of the planned military "swoop" was, he was still sure, a clever provocative forgery by some such genius as Joseph Plunkett. But it was just possible that it was not, and it was always possible that with so many men in Dublin in the secret the news of the rising would leak out and the military would act quickly. If that happened, Pat knew that he would resist, he would fight, even if he were alone. To be, at this last moment, tamely disarmed would break his heart forever.

There was also the problem of MacNeill and Hobson, nominal leaders of the Volunteers, indeed in the eyes of the innocent rank and file the true leaders: MacNeill and Hobson, the "moderates," who viewed the idea of fighting with horror and who were entirely unaware that the organization which they headed had been hollowed out by a secret hierarchy of power which left them at the top, isolated. At some point before Sunday they would be told, or would find out. At some point, somehow, the real leaders had got to sweep the nominal leaders aside. Pat felt uneasily that his masters had not got the answer to this problem: that they were waiting to see and hoping for the best. They would act on the spur of the moment. He also, with a pain that never left his consciousness, knew that there was a personal problem to which he himself had not found the solution and which he too would perhaps have to solve, when it came up, on the spur of the moment.

Pat was about to leave Millie's house in Upper Mount Street. He had detailed men to remove the arms and ammunition from the cellar on Saturday night and take it to a house in Ballybough Road which was being used as an arsenal. Dublin would be full of mysterious horses and carts on that night. But these risks had to be run, and Pat, who had often performed such operations under the noses of the British, did not regard them very seriously. He had just now, with the help of his sergeant, packed the goods up into manageable bundles, and the man had left unobtrusively by the side door. Millie's servants were, happily, creatures of habit. For Millie herself Pat had invented a good enough story about why the arms had to be moved. In any case, she might well be at Rathblane for the weekend.

Pat had been frequently questioned by his superior officers concerning Millie, initially concerning her reliability. He had on one occasion been disgusted to detect an assumption that his relationship with Millie must be of a sentimental kind. He had satisfied others, as he had satisfied himself, concerning her trustworthiness. Millie was a very silly woman; in a word, she was a woman. But she was capable of a strength of discretion which Pat somehow connected with her undoubted physical courage. More lately his superiors had asked him different questions. Millie had been trained as a nurse. She was also a good shot. Should she not simply be enlisted? To this Pat had said curtly no. It was not that he was not prepared to trust Millie all the way or that he thought she would necessarily draw back if asked. She was reckless enough for anything and might well embrace the project simply as an adventure. But he just did not want, at this sacred and holy crisis of his life, to have to bother about Millie at all. When Sunday came Millie and all she stood for would be left behind.

"Pat!"

He stopped in the hallway and cursed. In another minute he would have been clear of the house.

"Pat, come up here. I've got something important to tell you."

He looked up through the dim cage of the stairs and saw her somewhere farther up sitting on a step and peering down. He hesitated and decided he had better hear what she had to say. He came slowly up.

When she saw him coming she jumped up, enticingly, like a dog, and ran ahead of him. He noticed with repulsion that she was wearing trousers.

The door of Millie's "shooting gallery" stood open, and it was grey and murky within. A light rain tapped the skylight and ran steadily down the big window at the near end of the room, where the small satiny chairs, thickly fringed down to the carpet, stood grouped about Millie's white dressing table. The mirror was leaden, reflecting nothing, like a dull slab of metal behind the altar-like table. There was a faint unpleasant smell of flowers. In the dim light the scene had the air of a derelict chapel which had been perverted to some other purpose.

Pat came in reluctantly, and Millie at once whisked round behind him to close the door. She returned to the dressing table and stood there poised, as if at attention, her prominent eyes glistening with appetitie. In the black tight trousers she looked like a principal boy in an operetta, vivacious, vulgar, and about to become extremely noisy.

"Well?" He wondered if she had heard something. If she had, this was going to be awkward.

"Pat, do sit down."

He looked round for a hard chair. There wasn't one. "I'll stand, thank you."

"Have some madeira. I've got some awfully good madeira here and some cake. See, it's all set out."

"No, thank you. You had something to say?"

"It's so dark in here. It always gets so dark when it rains. I wonder if I should light the gas? One might as well draw the curtains really, it's like the night-time."

"I've only got a minute."

"Do you like these white daffodils? They're rather unusual, aren't they? They're from Rathblane. I think it's so uncanny when flowers don't have their proper colours. How late the spring is this year. Well, I suppose one says that every year. Do you mind if I have some madeira?"

Pat watched her silently. Her hand shook as she poured out the madeira, and the decanter struck the rim of the glass with a loud clang.

Millie examined the glass to see if it was cracked. "How clumsy I am. Pat, do sit down."

"I can't, I'm in a hurry."

"Don't be. I do wish you'd come down to Rathblane now and again. You haven't been there since you were a boy, have you. And I've got such a fine grand horse for you to ride, he's called Owen Roe, and you could have him any time."

"If you've got something to say, say it."

"Well, it's nothing special, really. I just wanted to talk to you. We never seem to meet and talk to each other properly, and that seems such a shame."

"I have very little time for social conversation. You must excuse me." Pat began to make the movements of departure. He did not think now that Millie knew anything about Sunday.

There was a sudden noisy flurry in the dark room and Millie moved quickly, plunging forward as if she were going to pick something up from the floor. She half fell, half darted forward, grunting like an animal, and blundered past him, butting him with her shoulder. In a moment she was leaning back against the closed door holding something in her hand. He saw her mouth open, moist and almost round as she drew breath, and saw that what she held in her hand was a revolver pointed at him.

For about two seconds Pat speculated. He had once, at the start, put it to himself that Millie might be or might become anything. She was an irresponsible, a person without a centre. She could be a spy in the pay of the Castle. Now suddenly and vividly he saw her as a traitor. In the third second he realized that of course this was only a piece of play-acting, a piece of Millie's usual tomfoolery. He stepped towards her and took the gun out of her hand. She held it lightly, scarcely resisting his fingers. He laid it down on the dressing table, and as he turned back to her he inhaled the sweet disagreeable odour of the white daffodils.

Millie was still leaning against the door, but her body, which had been taut and fierce, was now quite limp. She seemed like a figure made of soft wax which might bend or sag slowly to the floor, at any moment. Her face was vague and dazed, her eyes half closed. She said very softly, "Just for a second you were afraid of me. Oh, oh, oh—"

"You shouldn't play with those things," said Pat. Of course he had not been afraid of her, but he was angry that she should have seen his mind, and disgusted at the way she had suddenly transformed herself into an animal.

"I was in earnest, you know—for a moment anyway. You were so *rude*. Why can't you be ordinarily polite to me? I've stored all that stuff for you and never questioned you or bothered you. And you know I've told nobody."

"If I've been rude I apologize."

"You can't apologize just by saying 'I apologize,' not in that tone of voice. Of course you've been rude. But it's not that I mind. Sit down."

Pat sat down.

He felt Millie lean heavily on the back of his chair, and then she had sat down close opposite to him, staring. Her face resembled a Roman mask, huge-eyed and open-mouthed, strained and painful and yet at the same time lewd. The rain seemed to have stopped, and there was a little more light and colour in the room. Beyond her head the daffodils were a white blur against the wet, silvery window pane. Near to him Millie's features trembled for a moment, quivered all over like something seen through disturbed water. "You don't like me very much, do you, Pat?"

"I wouldn't say that."

"And yet in a way too you do like me, I feel it."

"I don't know you at all—"

"That's just it. But you will get to know me, you will. I wish we could meet sometimes and talk, just talk of anything at all that's in our minds. It would be good, wouldn't it? I feel we have so much to give each other. I wish you'd come sometimes, here or to Rathblane. Just to talk. I so much want to know you better. I need to."

"I doubt if we'd have much to say to each other."

"Please, Pat, please, please, please. I beg you to come and see me."

"Really—I have no time for visiting—I shall have to go directly."

"I beg you."

"I've got to go." He got up hastily and kicked the soft chair aside, shuffling backwards.

"Pat, I'm so useless, my life is so useless, so empty. You could help me. You could tell me what to do to be of use. I would obey you."

"There's nothing I can do—"

"I might really have shot you just now. Shot you first and myself after. Do you know how often I think of killing myself? Every day, every hour."

Pat had got to the door. Fumbling behind him he found the handle, opened the door an inch, and closed it again. He had been almost prepared to find it locked.

"I can't help you."

"How can you be so cruel? You can help me with your little finger, with any look, any word. Don't you understand what I'm telling you? I love you."

Pat's immediate feeling was simply of an embarrassed shock.

Then there was something darker, like intense anger. He said at once, "That's a foul lie."

There was a pause in which he heard Millie's indrawn breath, a gasp like a gasp of triumph. She rose and circled behind her chair, keeping her distance from him. He curled with loathing but his hand upon the door handle seemed paralysed. The directness of his response to her seemed to have flung out a taut, tingling connection between them and they were, as never before, present to each other.

Millie breathed slowly and deeply. Her face, clear in the brightening light from the window, wore an intense expression of happy cunning. She said softly, coaxingly, argumentatively, "Well, it may be that it is not love. Yet it is fierce enough, deep enough to be love. Will you not test it? I want you."

"Don't talk like that."

"And you want me. All right, I know I disgust you. Strike me then."

"Stop—"

"I know you better than you think. I know the twistings and turnings of your heart. I know you because at the bottom you and I are as like as two pins. You want to humiliate yourself. You want your will to drive you like a screaming animal into some dark place where you will be crushed utterly. You want to test yourself to the point where you can will the death of all that you are and stand aside coolly and watch it die. Come to me then. I will be your slave and your executioner. No other woman can please you. Only I, because I am hard and clever like a man. Only I can understand you and lift to you the face of the beauty that you really desire. Come to me, Pat."

"Stop—"

"Come soon. Come before the month ends. Think that I shall be at Rathblane, in my bed, waiting for you. Come."

Pat fumbled desperately with the door. He seemed to be turning the handle the wrong way. Then before he could get it open she had tumbled herself at his feet in a sort of animal onslaught.

Her arms entwined him fiercely, pinching and pawing, while she babbled out incoherent supplications. Pat jerked the opening door violently against her and kicked himself free. As he rushed down the stairs and out of the house he felt his trousers damp at the knee from Millie's tears or kisses. He ran away as fast as he could along the shining wet pavements in the direction of Merrion Square.

Thirteen

Andrew was riding to Rathblane on a bicycle borrowed from his mother's new gardener. It was Thursday afternoon and he was going to have tea with Millie. On Monday she had asked him and Frances to come to tea. Now he was going there by himself.

Andrew felt that he had received a violent blow which had in reality killed him, although he was still moving blindly about. He felt as he had felt when his father died. Grief had destroyed his ordinary self, and now there was nothing but the grief and a body racked with physical pain which somehow accompanied it. Frances had been there so long, so long, an ultimate and invincible source of comfort. He had taken her to be eternal, and this deep sense of the permanence of love had been the essence of all his joys, even those apparently unconnected with her. To lead a life without her he would have to remake himself entirely. But there was no vital being left. She had been the hidden sun of his world. He had thought that world was beautiful just for him, an offering to his youth and his hope, whereas it was only she who had lent it brightness. Her affection and her intelligence had gilded every-thing. Now all that beauty was withdrawn into her veiled, forbid-den figure and the world was ashen. He turned to and fro in despair, seeking a familiar support which should enable him to live through such misery, but the support was Frances.

Getting up from a sleepless bed he had tried resolutely to become more rational and to confront his situation. He realized how dreadfully he had undervalued Frances, how stupidly he had taken her for granted. He ought to have behaved like one of Malory's Knights and treated her as a great and difficult trial of his worth. Yet they had known each other so well, with a simplicity which now seemed to him a source of infection. Surely things *had* been all right, their long love had not been illusion? What had gone wrong? Was it perhaps that Frances had thought him too casual, and was thrusting him away so that he might return again more ardently? But such a policy was inconceivable in her. She was incapable of ruse. There were no mysteries here out of which dramas could be made. She was his oldest friend, and if she wanted him she would take him as he was, without gallantry. The truth was that she was exercising her last inalienable and terrible natural right, the free disposition of the heart. She simply did not want him.

Absolute devotion of one human being to another is comparatively rare, yet such is the dazzling light of egoism in which each of us lives that when devotion fails us in some quarter where we have looked to find it we feel amazement, shocked surprise, that so great a value should not be an object of love. And amid his shame and his misery Andrew felt also quite distinctly this surprise, which he did not then recognize as the germ of a healing selfishness which would in time make his pain diminish. How *could* Frances abandon him? It seemed inconceivable that she should have deliberately ended their long, happy companionship and made it impossible for him to come to her any more. Would it not, tomorrow, be as it was? But he knew in a kind of madness at night, and more soberly in the light of day, that he had not been teased, provoked, played with, or simply asked to wait. He had been rejected.

He was already nearing Rathblane, which he had not visited

for a number of years, and was surprised to notice that he had found his way there quite unconsciously. Looking at the road now he found it uncomfortably memorable, loaded with some pungent but undeclared consciousness out of his childhood. Some vanished self had made that landscape live. And it accosted him now like an old friend who fails to realize that one has changed utterly.

Rathblane was about fifteen miles south of Dublin, situated in a fold of the Dublin mountains not far from the river Dodder. Without reflection Andrew had taken the road through Stillorgan and turned inland at Cabinateely. It was a windy day. Little round clouds like smoke rings hung high over the sea, but inland the sky was crowded with bulbous folds of grey and golden stuff which formed a huge and alarmingly three-dimensional world, gathering, rearing, and toppling with slow speed only just above the tops of the mountains. The peak of Kippure, now coming into view, was a dark slatey blue against a diminishing strip of fading yellow sky, as if the peak had already absorbed the dark ray of the coming night. But the little won fields of the nearer mountainsides, pressing upward almost vertically against the thick, rusty surge of the heather, were an almost silvery light green, and the gorse hillocks, round which the black-faced sheep stood in circles, glowed a rich yellow in the afternoon sun with a light which seemed to come from within their dense humps of golden flowers.

Andrew had dismounted now and was walking on the rough road up the ridge which separated him from Rathblane. The crumbling domain wall on his right, overgrown with brambles and valerian, seemed like a natural excrescence. A little rain had welcomed him into the wilder country, but now it was dry again. Nearby the left side of the road they had been cutting turf, and the thick dark undersoil of the bog, the consistency of sticky fudge, glistened in the momentary sun. Weary with pushing his bike over the stones, Andrew wondered why he had bothered to come at all. There was little point in it now, and he could easily have sent an excuse. Well, it was something to do. And it was a pretext for escaping from Claresville, where the arrival of the furniture had sent his mother into a state of unbearable excitement, setting up all sorts of painfully domestic trains of thought. Hilda had even uttered the word "nursery." His imposed silence was a torture to him, and to be taken to be happy when he was in fact the most wretched man in the world. He mounted the bicycle again and jolted down the hill, through the entrance gates between the battered stone griffins, into a sudden windless hush.

Rathblane was a Georgian house of moderate size, grey and rather tall, with an irregular front, bowed and buttress-like at one end, and smooth and balustraded at the other. Some further extension of the house had been intended but never built. It stood in a large square of trees which separated it entirely from the open country. An eighteenth-century print showed the house in a vista, but nineteenth-century Kinnards had zealously planted innumerable varieties of trees, many of them rare ones, so that boughs of gingko and catalpa and liquidambar, grown into a dense matrix, now concealed the house in a web of closely woven quietness so intense, after the windy expanse of the mountain road, as to make the unsuspecting visitor gasp. Seen only at the last moment within its thick green architecture, Rathblane had that formidable sinister stillness of the Irish country house, a stillness which is perhaps something to do with the Irish air, or is more simply due to the continued absence of the owners or to the premonition that, on coming close to the handsome façade, one will suddenly see the open sky through the upper windows.

Andrew turned the last corner of the drive and saw the big grey buttresses still deep in trees. The bumpy drive led on beside a stone wall towards the stables, but the front door of the house had to be approached across a small unmown lawn where a semicircular stone staircase with white painted railings descended directly into the rough rye grass. Andrew propped his bicycle against the wall and walked across to the steps. He pushed open the heavy door and came into the hall which always smelt of stale

"I don't like horses."

"You *what?*" This information for some reason amused Millie very much. It seemed to cheer her up. "The little pet! And you a cavalry officer! I hope you've kept it a secret. But of course I don't believe you. Now I want nothing so much as to see you on board. You shall come down here often, and we'll have a gallop together. I've got such a fine grand horse for you to ride, he's called Owen Roe, and you could have him any time."

"I'm afraid I shall be leaving for Longford almost at once, Aunt Millicent."

"Aunt Millicent, indeed! It was today, wasn't it, that you were to start calling me Millie. What a pity dear Frances isn't here, you could have begun the new regime together. Eh, Andrew? Now you must say 'Yes, Millie.' "

"Yes, Millie."

"That's better. Well, well, Longford is it? I suppose King and Country are after you. What's your regiment, I always forget."

"King Edward's Horse."

"And a fine lot of fellows they are too. How the uniform suits you, especially those boots. I'm sure you'll distinguish yourself. Have some of Maudie's lemon cake. Dear God, I think it's going to rain again, what a country. Listen, can you hear the nuthatches singing? Quee, quee, quee. They always sing like that just before it rains, or maybe it's just that the air is clearer then and one hears them. They're building in the old wall, I'll show you the nest. You'll stay for dinner and the night of course?"

"No, sorry, I've got to get back, Aunt Millicent."

"Well, I won't keep you from your Frances. But I shall have to punish you every time you call me Aunt Millicent! You're getting a bit big to slap. How old are you now, dear boy?"

"Twenty-one."

"You lucky child. I wish I were. You look quite the young man, I must say, and I adore your moustache. I shall come and sit beside you."

Millie drove the tea trolley away with her feet and bounced heavily onto the sofa beside Andrew.

Andrew edged himself away from her. He fumbled in his pocket for his handkerchief to wipe the lemon cake off his fingers. As he drew out the handkerchief something else came out too and fell onto the rug at his feet. It was the ruby and diamond ring.

Millie saw the ring and promptly picked it up. At once she slipped it onto her finger and held it up to admire it, flashing it to and fro. "What an awfully pretty ring! And it just fits me. But of course, it must be Frances' engagement ring. How romantic! Am I the first person to see it? You shouldn't carry it loose like that in your pocket, silly boy, you'll lose it. Haven't you got a little box for it?"

Andrew said, "I've got a box—" Then he stopped. His voice was not under his control and he felt that if he continued to talk he would croak and then burst into tears. He sat in paralysed silence staring at the carpet.

After a pause he felt Millie touching his shoulder. "Something's happened, something's gone wrong?"

He nodded.

"Very wrong?"

He nodded.

"Oh, God. She's refused you."

"Yes." He put his hand to his eyes, which were suddenly wet with tears. He realized that Millie had left him, getting up abruptly and going to the window.

"Why?" she said. "Why?"

"Why not?" said Andrew, mopping up the tears with his handkerchief. "Just because we've always been sort of promised to each other it doesn't mean—in fact, perhaps that's the reason. In a way we've been too close. She says we've been like brother and sister."

"Brother and sister!" Millie laughed shortly. "You don't think there's any special reason, anything to do with her father perhaps?"

"No. Christopher's always been in favour."

"She'll come round surely?"

"No, I'm certain she won't. That's why I'm going away as soon as I can."

"Your mother must be knocked by this."

"She doesn't know yet. Frances asked me to tell nobody for a few days until she's had time to break it to Christopher."

"Ah— Don't worry, I'll be discreet. I *can* be. But I'm being so thoughtless questioning you like this. Why, the child's in tears! Come now, let's have some sherry, shall we? You need a drink. And I rather think I do too!"

In fact Millie's brisk questions had done Andrew good. The tears had come and gone. He felt a little better. He sipped the sherry and felt warmer and more alive.

Millie came and sat beside him and took hold of his hand. "You're infernally like my dear brother, your father. Did you love poor Henry?"

"Yes, of course."

"I'm glad. Not all children love their parents these days. I loved him dearly. Well, well, so it's not to be Frances after all. But don't grieve. You're young and quite confoundedly good-looking. Just keep your head and you can have your pick of the fine girls of England and Ireland. I'll help you choose one."

Andrew shook his head. He looked wearily at the sulky flames of the turf fire. "No. There won't be anything else for me. Anyway, I'm going to die young." The thought was curiously cheering.

"That's always a solution, isn't it? Nonsense! I'm already looking forward to teaching your children to ride."

"I don't think I could marry anybody but Frances. Maybe I'm not the marrying type."

"Sweet boy, just look in the mirror! I wonder if you're really afraid of it, though. Have you ever had a girl?"

"No, of course not."

"Now I've shocked you. But really never? Don't you want to terribly? Have some more sherry."

Andrew settled back in the sofa, drawing his knees up. He found that he was still holding Millie's hand, and released it. Millie wriggled into a more comfortable position with her knee touching his. He was very embarrassed by the turn the conversation had taken, yet the sudden crudeness of it was a distraction, almost a consolation. "I suppose I am frightened. I'm afraid it would be, well, a failure. Anyway, the question doesn't arise any more."

"It *will* arise, my child. You are a soldier. Damn it, Andrew, you are a man. You are inconceivably young. The next two or three years will be more full of events and changes than you can possibly imagine. Here, give me your hand again. How did it get away?"

"Oh, Millie, I don't know. Sometimes I feel frightened of everything. I'm so frightened of going back to France."

"Any rational person would be frightened of that." She pressed his hand, kneading it comfortably between her palms.

"It's good to talk to you."

"You're a lonely chap, really, aren't you? I wish you were staying here, there's a lot I could do for you! I must cheer you up, though. Don't you feel, even now, a little tiny bit pleased to be free, pleased to think that after all the big wide unpredictable world lies in front of you?"

"No, I just feel utterly wretched."

"Well, it's a bit early. But that feeling will come. God, if I were your age and free, knowing what I know now! *Si la juenesse savait, si la vieiellesse pouvait!*"

"But you aren't in the least *vieille*, Millie, and I'm sure you can *pouvait* anything you like."

"You're very sweet. Let me kiss you."

The silky mauve knees edged a little over the khaki knees and Millie put her arm round Andrew's neck. She drew his head down towards her and kissed him on the cheek. Then, shifting her arm to his shoulder and sliding more closely up against him, she kissed him on the lips.

Andrew accepted her kiss with a kind of surprise. He had been conscious of her as a diffuse, warm, comforting animal presence. Now he became precisely aware of her body, aware of its posture and its closeness, of just where it touched his own and how it might be taken hold of. With a hurried gesture, half impulsive, half grateful, he slid his arm round her back and pressed his face awkwardly against hers. Then he drew away in confusion.

They stared at each other. Millie said softly, "I didn't expect this." She lifted his hand and laid it against her cheek. "There you are—the big wide unpredictable world at its tricks already."

"I'm sorry," said Andrew.

"What for? You've done me so much good. I'm a disappointed person like you. And a person in a terrible fix. Never mind. But your coming today, and *this*—it's part of something just happy and innocent. You aren't frightened of me, are you?"

"No."

"Then come kiss me, sweet and twenty, and kiss me properly this time."

Andrew took a deep breath and then as Millie's body moved to him promptingly he took her firmly in his arms and, thrusting her head back against the cushions of the sofa, kissed her. It was difficult to let go. Half horrified and half exhilarated, he pulled himself away and stood up. "I'm terribly sorry, Aunt Millicent."

"There you go again. I shall really slap you in a minute. Do sit down. There at the far end, I won't touch you. That's right. Dear Andrew, you've altered the world for me. I was utterly miserable when you came. You remember what I said about the scyllas being so blue? Well, they weren't blue, they were grey. They're blue now. You've made them blue."

Andrew sat down. He felt both alarmed and ashamed, but he could not help also apprehending, in the very glow of his shame, his sheer male power over this handsome older woman.

"And you know, you know, Andrew, we can't leave it at that. It would be a crime."

"What do you mean?"

"You said you were frightened of it. You said it might somehow be a failure. Well, let me teach you. With me it won't be a failure."

For a moment Andrew did not understand her. Then he stared at her, silent, appalled.

"I've shocked you again. But let me persuade you. There's nothing wrong in it, no sin, you know. With you and me it would be just innocent and lovely. And it would take away all your fears."

Andrew looked at her and his eyes were really frightened like those of a scared child. "No, no, it's not—no—"

"Don't be a coward, Andrew. It's a beautiful, wonderful, God-sent chance. Nobody would know. And after that you would be really free. And you would make me so happy."

"I couldn't—"

"I want you, Andrew. And you want me. That's something one can't be mistaken about."

"No, really—Millie, I think I'd better be going."

"What a cowardy custard you are. But I know I've rather sprung it on you. Well, I've rather sprung it on myself! And you're shocked to the core, too. Just think about it. But oh, think quickly, my dear and beautiful boy, think quickly!"

They had both risen and Andrew was struggling into his greatcoat.

"Dear Andrew, you're not angry with me?"

"No—forgive me—" He took her hand and kissed it and laid it against his eyes, bowing before her.

"Well, I'll let you go now. Why, I'm still wearing Frances' ring. I'll give it back to you now. But when you come, when you *really* come, you shall give it to me as a present. No, no, sure I'm only joking. Are you going back on that bicycle? Wouldn't you like to ride back on Owen Roe? You could leave him at the stables in Harcourt Street."

"No, thanks."

She had led him to the front door and out into the damp, darkening evening. A little light rain was just beginning to fall. The woolly black-faced sheep had come close to the steps, a crowd of quiet presences. The sky was a thin papery yellow and the peak of Kippure, just lifting above the trees, was jet black.

"I love it when the animals come right up to the house. You will come back, won't you, I mean come back anyway, just to talk. Why I'm almost crying, how absurd. There now, dear boy, you move me so—and I envy you. And it's not your freedom or your youth I'm after envying at this moment, it's your innocence."

Fourteen

Were there four candles or eight candles? Barney wondered as he knelt in extreme discomfort on the stone floor. He ought to know from the number of the psalm. The fifteen candles, burning upon the triangular candlestick, were extinguished one by one at the close of each psalm. But Barney had long ago lost his place. All he knew was that he had been there some time and that the floor was not only hard but also rather wet from the rain water which had trickled off the mackintoshes and umbrellas of the people who surrounded him. He had been there some time and before that he had been in a bar. He could not remember coming from the bar to the chapel. He had decided after all to come to Tenebrae, or evidently he had decided, since here he was.

The chapel, which belonged to a small Dominican community, was a narrow concrete cave, situated off an obscure courtyard in Upper Gardiner Street. Barney knew none of the community, had found the place by accident, and liked it because of the austerity of its furnishings and because it was anonymous and unfrequented. Even now on the Thursday night the chairs provided for the congregation were only half filled. The chapel was entirely dark now except for the sanctuary light and the flickering candles which dimly and intermittently illuminated the two bowed lines of hooded black and white figures stretching away to the altar whereon rose the blurred shape of the shrouded crucifix. In the body of the chapel people knelt here and there in untidy heaps, hunched and sagging in the attitudes of those who have been kneeling for a long time, their mackintoshes piled up beside them. There was a smell of wet clothing and of wet stone.

Tenebrae factae sunt, dum crucifixissent Jesum Judaei: et circa horam nonam exclamavit Jesus voce magna: Deus meus, ut quid me dereliquisti? Barney shifted his knees a little on the floor and then sat back on his heels. In order to be more acutely uncomfortable he had refused himself a hassock, and now his knees felt like two cold alien metal plates rather roughly attached to his legs. His thighs ached, his shoulders ached, and there was a little creeping chilly pain in the small of his back. He resisted the temptation to sit side ways on the floor. He screwed up his eyes to look at the candles again and decided there were four of them.

The intoning of the brothers continued monotonously, expressionlessly, wearily. The penitents were huddled upon the floor, a few of them peering at the words in their books, but most of them humped in attitudes of stupefied abandonment induced by spiritual misery or physical discomfort. What does it all mean? thought Barney. Why had he come here? Wasn't it the same to him now whether he was here or in the Mountjoy bar? His emotions were the same, the familiar round of his intentions and compulsions the same. He could have enacted all this elsewhere. Even here it was only play-acting, only, despite the dull voices of the brothers, despite the pain in his knees, indeed because of these things, a kind of cosiness. He was no stranger to remorse. Bitterly every day he regretted what he had done, bitterly he regretted what he was doing in the moment when he lifted his hand to do it. And the power to change himself by an iota was simply not included in the complex that he was. That power, if it existed, resided in some other world, and since it was not native to him it could not help him. Then he must cast himself on God's mercy. But could there be such a thing, was it not, must it not be, a contradiction? Could a perfect being be merciful to what was imperfect? If he were to go *there* would he not simply be burnt up automatically? *Ego autem sum vermis et non homo.*

Barney wondered if he ought to go to confession. Well, of course he ought. Yet now the great austere impersonal machinery of the church which had once so much drawn him seemed a hollow clattering mumbo-jumbo. Perhaps he had never become entirely used to the sacrament of confession. He could go at random to some unfamiliar priest, interrupting him in his perusal of the *Irish Times*, and kneel down and whisper some vague uncriticized account of what he had been doing and receive a flimsy penance and a preoccupied absolution. But he ought to be interrogated, he ought to be beaten. Punishment had no meaning where there was no personal relation between the punisher and the punished. And only punishment, it seemed to him, could now reintegrate him into the order of love. He would have to be punished by God Himself, nothing less would serve. *Quoniam ego in flagella paratus sum.*

How can guilt be taken away, how can it not drag the guilty one down and down? Did redemption exist, *could* it exist, was it not a strictly senseless idea? Could another save me by his suffering? If someone who is good suffers because I am evil and I see and contemplate that suffering might that not alter me and purify me almost automatically? But such contemplation is impossible precisely because I am evil. Human beings cannot look at affliction with uncorrupted eyes. If the suffering of a good person on my behalf could redeem me Kathleen would be an instrument of my salvation instead of being, as she is, an instrument of my damnation. *O vos omnes qui transitis per viam, attendite et videte.* But though he might look and look he could not really attend and see. The spectacle of Christ crucified changed nothing in his heart.

Why should not the sight of any innocent suffering have

power to save? He remembered live fowls he had seen in the market, their legs tied together, thrown into dusty corners. Every hour, every second, the young rabbit squealed in the jaws of the fox, the owl flew silently through the night with the vole hanging limp from its beak. He knew of these things, this terrible knowledge was in him as it was in all human beings. But because of his own darkness it was all turned to darkness too and not to light. The appalling tenderness and guilt he had felt before the helpless creatures in the market made him in the end turn away with a curse. That the innocent suffer: this should startle the spirit into a self-denying purity forever. But instead there is only the callous indifference of a guilt felt to be ineradicable. He was on the side of the bad thief. *Me minavit et adduxit in tenebras et non in lucem.*

Was not even the bad thief saved perhaps in the end? Yet what could save him? It is as oneself that one must be saved, and not as another, if salvation has meaning at all. Barney could see plainly, as if a surgical light had been shone within him, that the machinery of his virtuous intent was simply not attached to the living animal that he really was. Nothing that moved here touched the great powerful thing underneath which went its way regardless. It was the strength of that thing, its fat strength, which made him despair. He had thought of himself as a man haunted at least by goodness, but these hauntings were merely the bog fires of his own psyche. His "good resolutions" were not even play-acting, they were babbling. He did not know what the word "good" meant. It was a parrot cry in his mouth. His whole substance was fit only for burning. *Non est sanitas in carne mea a facie irae tuae, non est pax in ossibus meis a facie peccatorum meorum.*

Barney had not yet made up his mind to tell Frances about Christopher's intentions. He wanted to desperately, if only in order to be able to act somehow in a situation which tortured him. He told himself that it was his duty to bring the truth out into the open so that everybody should be able to understand what they were doing. But ought people always to understand what they were doing, and would that anyway be the result in this case? How was he, sunk in the muddle of his own life, to distinguish between virtuous truth-telling and wicked trouble-making? Frances would be extremely upset. But what would she do? She might postpone her own marriage and prevent her father's, both things which Barney wanted. Then what would Millie's vengeance be? Could he hope to survive as Millie's favourite? It was too risky. Yet how tempting it was to tell Frances and see what happened. Had he really anything to lose? These debates, which usually began on a high moral level, ended inconclusively with the yapping and scratching tug-of-war of different forms of self-interest.

Of course there was one way in which Barney could be fairly sure that in telling Frances his motives would be good, and that was if he really resolved to give up Millie. It was odd how often he came back to this idea, odd considering how sunk he was in his devotion to her, sunk and drowned like a fly in treacle. It was meaningless to think of giving her up. Yet, quite abstractly, he would think of it again; and he would think of it because he knew perfectly well that what utterly poisoned his life was the beastliness of his relation to Kathleen. Kathleen was his wife, she was *there*, with the authority of an obligation which was rooted so deep in the nature of things that it continually compelled the attention if not the respect of the corrupted will. Kathleen could not be ignored, got round, shuffled away to suffer quietly in a dusty corner like the poor birds in the market. She could not suffer quietly, however silent she was, because she was a human being to whom he was irrevocably bound and he had to see her suffer, he had to see himself making her suffer.

There was no limit to his offence against her, or the limit came only with the limit of himself. Everything he was was offence. It was the sense of this which made him despair and curse. She seemed to turn every part of him into the stuff of his own damnation. His Memoir, into which he had put so much of his creative power and which had proved such a consolation, was in the end simply a weapon against Kathleen. There had to be somewhere which was safe from her, some place where he was justified and she was judged. In real life she was all judge, even when she said nothing. In the Memoir everything was reversed and the unfairness of life was done away with and that dreadful power was quenched. There were times when the Memoir seemed to Barney the only clean and clear thing in the world. Yet there were always other times when he knew that it was a sin, perhaps his greatest sin, the final corruption of what might have remained unstained, his intellect, his talents. What he wrote in the Memoir was not quite true, and that "not quite" was the stuff of a most wicked lie. *Vinea mea electa, ego te plantavi. Quomodo conversa es in amaritudinem ut me crucifigeres et Barabbam dimitteres?*

Barney opened his eyes. He was sitting sideways on the floor and leaning against the next chair, which he had pulled towards him. His head and arm were resting on the chair. He must have fallen asleep.

The chapel was dark and silent and empty. The office had ended and everyone had gone away, leaving him there sleeping. The plain walls of the chapel seemed like a dark tunnel at the far end of which the sanctuary light flickered dimly, seeming to give out no illumination but to be a light completely surrounded by darkness up to the very confine of itself.

Barney looked at the light. The last thing he remembered before sleeping was that piercing reproach, *Vinea mea electa . . .* It seemed to him that it was the most annihilating reproach in the whole world. Yet why was it so? Because it was also, in a way which one could not possibly mistake, the voice of love. Could reproach and love become so nearly identical? Yes, for this is the nature of the magnet by which what is good draws what is partly evil, by which perhaps mysteriously it may even draw what is wholly evil. The light cast from a perfect centre cannot but define what is imperfect in a revelation which is both rebuke and summons.

Barney returned to his knees. He was extremely stiff and cold, and his head ached. It must be very late now, perhaps it was already the morning of Good Friday. He stared at the sanctuary light and felt the certain, almost bodily, presence of perfect Goodness. And with this he felt, as he had not felt it before, an absolute certainty of his own existence. He existed and God, opposite to him, existed too. And if he was not, by that juxtaposition, simply dissolved into nothing it could only be because God was love.

At the same moment it also became perfectly clear to Barney that everything which he had dreamt of vaguely as good in some way which simply did not concern him was not only possible but even easy. He could give up Millie, he could tear up his Memoir, he could confess everything to Kathleen and start a new life with her and learn to love her properly. He could make everything simple and innocent once again, and in that instant he knew too that if he lifted so much as a finger to attempt that simplicity and that innocence he would receive, from the other region which had seemed so far away outside him, the inrush of an entirely new strength. He had thought himself so lost, so astronomically far removed that there was no nearer or further any more and no sense in the idea of a way. But all the time he had been held so close that he could not escape even if he would. *Quoniam sagittae tuae infixae sunt mihi et confirmasti super me manum tuam.*

Fifteen

"Oh, I feel so happy!"

Hilda threw her gloves down on a packing case in the hall and began with delicate exact movements to pluck the hatpin out of her large velvet hat. She had just returned from attending the earlier part of the three-hour Good Friday service at the Mariners' Church.

"I'm as hungry as a hunter. I expect you are too, Andrew. I'll bring out the cold luncheon directly. You really should have come to church, it was wonderful. Such inspiring addresses. I suppose one ought to be feeling sad on Good Friday, but I always feel so exalted, even more than on Easter day."

Andrew looked down at her gloomily through the bannisters. He was engaged in tacking down the carpet on the upper landing. "Yes, Mother. I'm just coming down. Where do you want the gilt mirror put? I've found the hooks for it."

"Oh, opposite the door, I think, it will enlarge the hall, and we'll put the tropical birds in front of it. It's going to be such a pretty house, isn't it, Andrew? It really makes me terribly happy. Christopher is coming round to see it after luncheon. I saw Frances at church, but she said she couldn't come as she had a

Comforts for the Troops meeting. But of course she'll have told you."

Hilda bustled away into the kitchen, humming loudly. A moment later he heard her voice raised in rather self-conscious shrillness above the purr of the taps. *"When I survey the Wondrous Cross . . ."*

Claresville was indeed a charming little house, but everything about it filled Andrew with misery. It was situated in the steep labyrinthine part of Dalkey below the Loreto convent and above Bullock Harbour, convenient (as the prospectus said) to St. Patrick's (Church of Ireland) and commanding from its upper window a handsome view of Dublin Bay. It was a solid nineteenth-century villa with Gothic windows and a high-peaked lattice porch, "quaint" features also commended in the prospectus. The smooth stucco was painted a dark, dusty pink, except for the raised bands of white which outlined the windows. There was an extensive garden on several levels with two fine eucalyptus trees, an old ragged monkey puzzle, and a rockery made out of large sea shells which delighted Hilda. To the drawbacks of the house, obvious to Andrew, Hilda was blind. It was a long way up the hill to the shops and the tram. The road was dark and lonely at night. The steepness of the slope made the house feel precarious as well as making the garden difficult to work. Andrew was even prepared to accept Kathleen's view, scornfully quoted by Hilda, that Claresville was damp. Exploring earlier to find Hilda's nearest shops, he had entered a bar and for the first time since his arrival in Ireland had had his uniform sneered at. He decided that he hated Dalkey.

The inside of the house was at present in extreme confusion. The removal men had arrived on the morning of the previous day, and after hastily pushing everything in through the front door had gone away, to some religious service they said, promising to come back shortly to complete the installation of the heavy furniture. Hilda had incautiously tipped them and Christopher had laughed and prophesied that they would be seen no more. Meanwhile Hilda's grand piano, dismantled and perched on its side, a very large bookcase, and a substantial tallboy were left standing in the hall. Andrew thought that he and Christopher could probably manage the bookcase and the tallboy, but the piano would need three or four men. Hilda's suggestion that Pat Dumay should be asked to come and help was received by Andrew with a silence so profound that even his mother quickly changed the subject.

Andrew was tormented by the fact that Hilda did not yet know. Her little gaieties, her joy in the house, her coy references to Frances, her even more coy references to "when we're a bigger family," continually beset him with detailed images of the happiness he had lost. He measured, too, the shock which Hilda herself was going to receive. He had not thought of it at once, but of course for her everything, Ireland, everything would be utterly ruined by this new situation. He knew that his mother was assuming that when he had to go away Frances would remain, a married, perhaps even a pregnant Frances, to be fussed over by Hilda, and that this represented a very real consolation. And then there was Christopher. Hilda was deeply attached to Christopher and relied upon him completely. "Christopher will know," or "Christopher will arrange it," was her answer to any practical difficulty. What would happen to her relationship to the Bellmans when she knew that her darling boy had been rejected? Would she want to stay on in the pretty house with the monkey puzzle and the sea-shell rockery? And if she did not stay on, where should she go?

The dreadful blank pain of deprivation and the frightened, miserable tenderness for Hilda did not however compose quite the whole of Andrew's mind. There was also the thought of Millie. What this thought exactly was was not entirely clear to him; it was persistent, significant, but veiled. At intervals, like a small spark in his memory, the events at Rathblane kept recurring to him, always with a little impetus of interest. And he recalled, too, as if this were something unimportant now but which he must not on any account forget, what Millie had said about freedom and about the big unpredictable world. He had certainly not expected what had happened at Rathblane, and the mere fact that, after Frances' rejection of him, anything at all could still *happen* was in itself a kind of salve. He recalled reading once in some French writer that the interpolation of anything, even if it is only a broken arm, between oneself and the experience of unhappy love is a consolation. Andrew had been extremely shocked by Millie's unthinkable proposal. But it was an event, it must be admitted, as momentous as a broken arm and certainly more agreeable.

Now he could hear from the sounds below that Christopher had arrived. Hilda was saying, "You've caught us just at the start of luncheon. Everything gets late on Good Friday, doesn't it, because of the service. Will you have a bite? Oh, you've eaten already. Well, you'll excuse us, won't you? It looks as if we'll have to eat off sheets of the *Irish Times*, so it's not very elegant anyway! Andrew! Christopher's come!"

Andrew went down reluctantly. Christopher and Hilda were standing in the bright bay window of what was to be the drawing-room. Against the deep, feathery leafage of the garden the sunny room floated in space, dotted with objects, not yet anchored down by the heavy significance of furniture. The keen sunlight revealed the ghosts of old pictures upon its rose-sprigged walls. Christopher and Hilda turned about with faces radiant with happiness. It was clear that Christopher did not yet know. Andrew had never seen him looking so happy.

Andrew's boots resounded in the unmuffled space. "Hello."

"Hello, Andrew. Are you going to conscript me to deal with that piano?"

"I'd rather not think about the piano." Their voices echoed like distant halloos.

"Those men will come back," said Hilda. "They said they would."

"Precisely. But this is Ireland." Christopher laughed with the ready, pointless laughter of the happy man. "Hilda shouldn't have tipped them," he said to Andrew. "They went straight off to the bar. And Hilda was imagining them on their knees!"

"Well, I thought they were very nice men," said Hilda complacently, pleased to be teased by Christopher.

Andrew thought miserably how pleasant to him this little family scene would have been if only all were well. He would have been glad to see his mother so happy and so befriended.

"Don't let me keep you from your grub," said Christopher. "The godless must not prevent the godly from eating!"

"Andrew, would you mind lifting those boxes off the chairs? Be careful with them. The Royal Worcester dinner service is in that one, at least I *hope* it is. And the flower vases should be in that one. Oh, how I am longing to bring some flowers in from the garden and make it really look like home!"

Andrew moved the boxes, and Hilda seated herself at a green baize card table, putting down the sheets of newspaper under the plates of cold tongue and salad. "Come, Andrew. It's our first meal in Claresville. Isn't that exciting?"

Andrew scraped his knife and fork on his plate in a pretence of eating. He wanted to weep. He loved his mother so much.

Christopher, humming and almost skipping about the room, kept up a disjointed chatter. "You should lay down a pavement, really. It's not expensive. That grass is so damp and mossy. And I do think you should cut a vista through those bamboos. You might even get a glimpse of the sea from here. Oh—"

Andrew looked up sharply. In the haze of sunlight he saw Christopher suddenly stiff, looking with surprise and alarm towards the door. In that instant Andrew was sure that Frances had come herself, grim and unsmiling, to accuse him publicly of having failed her. He leapt to his feet. But the figure in the doorway was Kathleen.

Kathleen, her long coat pulled shapelessly about her like a cloak, stared into the room with a face haggard with fear and distress. The features were strained and pulled downward in a grotesque, terrified leer.

Hilda, looking up short-sightedly, noticed nothing amiss. She was annoyed at Christopher's visit's being spoilt by the arrival of Kathleen. "Why, what a nice surprise!"

"What is it, Kathleen?" said Christopher.

"I just thought I'd call," said Kathleen in a voice which was surprisingly calm, only just slightly too monotonous to be natural.

"Would you like to join us? It's just a cold meal, I'm afraid."

"No, thank you."

"I expect you'd like to look round the house and garden. You haven't really seen it except on that wet afternoon."

"I'll take Kathleen round," said Christopher. "I'll show her the garden while you're finishing luncheon." He marched Kathleen out again into the hall and out through the back door.

Andrew went to the window. He watched Christopher and Kathleen walking slowly down the little pebbled path in the direction of the rockery. Something awful had happened to Aunt Kathleen, but he didn't care. He hated them all.

"What is it, Kathleen?"

Christopher was in that condition of sensitive availability to the troubles of others which is produced by certain kinds of happiness. His world had been made perfect, and by that perfection he was himself increased, filled suddenly to the brim with a new abundance of free affections. He felt, positively, a better man. He longed to help others and almost felt that he could do so miraculously just by touching them.

He had not seen Millie since Wednesday, when she had given him her world-changing yes. She had told him, though not at all solemnly, that she was going into an Easter "retreat" at Rathblane and that she wished to be left alone. She had spoken again, with a laugh, of the "holiday" which she needed before what she called, even more laughingly, "the fatal event." Prayer and fasting and meditation were her programme just now. Spiritually refreshed, she would return to Christopher to celebrate the new era with rivers of champagne.

Christopher understood her wish and even welcomed it. With a slightly grim affection he appreciated her need to steel herself in solitude to carry out a plan which was not entirely to her liking. She would succeed in reorganizing her mind and even her heart to meet this new necessity. Millie was an amazingly efficient organism. Christopher had been, in fact, a little uneasy in case she should press him, once it was all decided, into some immediate action. He was anxious lest she should hold against him his continued silence on account of Frances. He feared the charge of being insufficiently in love to carry all before him, even the opposition of Frances. Well, perhaps he was insufficiently in love. But in any case it would all be much easier and more agreeable if Frances could first be married off and, amid the preoccupations of a newly married girl, be unable to bend her formidable will against her parent. "Abandoned" by his daughter, Christopher's act must look more understandable, more forgivable. A married Frances would be in a less strong position to object, might indeed, Christopher suspected, not be on the scene at all: though he had not mentioned this to Hilda, he anticipated that young Andrew would promptly remove his bride to England. So, since everything pointed to silence and discretion, it was as well that the interval should be imposed by Millie herself and not by him. Thus deprived, he could by gentle complaints forestall her possible protestations about his own pusillanimity. In a more straightforward way, having achieved his end at last he was content to be alone for a little while simply to gloat. Lotus-like he floated, sufficient to himself, upon his own felicity.

"What's happened, Kathleen? You look quite distracted." He propelled her down the humpy path, between two straggling roses bushy with briars, past the chipped muddy shells of the rockery, to a wooden seat. The damp air smelt of eucalyptus.

"Nothing's happened yet. I'm sorry, Christopher. I looked for you at Finglas and when I couldn't find you I got upset."

Kathleen and Christopher had known each other for a very long time without becoming close friends. Each accepted the other as a familiar feature of the landscape, and this acceptance had become, with the years, a sort of affection. Though she was quite unlike himself, and though he found her outlook in many ways depressing, Christopher respected Kathleen as a decent independent character. In his view, most people were slaves; but Kathleen was no slave, and this was noticeable. His contempt for Barney partly took the form of sympathy for Kathleen; and he liked her, too, because she appreciated Frances. Kathleen sometimes afflicted him, as she afflicted so many, with feelings of guilt; but since he was more rational than other persons thus stricken he understood the ailment and forgave her for it.

"Well now, tell me all about it." He was rather touched that she should have sought him out.

"I'm sorry to trouble you with this, but you're the only man who's near and I've got to talk to somebody. I said something to Barney, though I wasn't sure *then,* but Barney can't do anything, and anyway he's part of it himself."

"What on earth are you talking about, Kathleen?"

"They're going to fight."

"Who are?"

"The Sinn Feiners, the Volunteers."

"My dear, they're always going to fight, only they never do."

"But there really is a definite plan. I don't know when it'll be, but soon. They're going to take over Dublin."

"Oh, nonsense, Kathleen. What in heaven's name makes you think this?"

"I broke into Pat's room. He was so secretive and so excited about something, I had to try to find out. So I broke in and there were some plans. I couldn't really understand them, but they were plans for a military occupation of Dublin. And there was a map of Dublin showing what buildings were to be occupied."

"But, my dear Kathleen, they've been doing this for years. Don't you know that James Connolly 'captures' Dublin Castle practically every weekend? They thoroughly enjoy it! I'm sure every young man in the movement has got a plan for the military occupation of Dublin in his pocket."

Kathleen stared at the black, rain-sifted earth of the rockery. Her face had lost the haggard look of terror and was stern and thoughtful. Christopher saw her old, lost handsomeness. "No," she said. "It's serious this time. I'm quite sure. I'm sure because of the way Pat is."

"Pat's young and excitable. He might be that way for lots of reasons. Perhaps he's in love."

"He's not in love. He isn't interested in girls."

Christopher was about to suggest that he might conceivably be interested in boys, but decided that this speculation, which was not new to him, was not suitable for Kathleen's ears. "Have you said anything to Pat yourself?"

"No. He's almost entirely stopped talking to me about anything. Up to now I've simply prayed."

"Shall I have a word with him?"

"Oh, if only you would! This was really what I came to ask you. I felt I must do something. You might be able to use logic with him."

"Logic! How like a woman to think that logic is a kind of stuff you just apply to a situation! Anyway I don't know what the logic of this one is."

"But you might be able to persuade him that it's mad."

"I doubt if anyone could persuade that young fellow of anything. Besides, it's not clear that it is mad."

"What do you mean?"

"It's arguable that the only way for Ireland to become really independent is to fight. England will delay Home Rule and pare it away until there's practically nothing left. An imperialist power won't really budge without a show of force. And a show of force is one thing one can't be too rational about, it comes when it has to. Anyway, Ireland's honour demands a fight. Only I mustn't say things like that to you."

"It's wicked and insane what you say. Why should Ireland be really independent? How can she be really independent? Ireland's honour means nothing but the vanity of a few murderous men."

"Well, you argue like a woman. If you like I'll certainly see Pat and try to find out something. But I do assure you there's nothing in it. I know the MacNeills, and I'd have heard if anything was in the air. These plans you saw are just for the usual routine manoeuvres."

Kathleen stood up. She looked down at Christopher with eyes big and dazed with thought. "I wonder if I ought to tell the Castle."

"*What?*"

"If the Castle knew now they could circumvent them, they could take their arms away."

"Kathleen, are you mad? That would certainly be the way to start a fight! Anyway, the Castle wouldn't believe you any more than I do. And it would be such, well, treachery. Do you want to break Pat's heart?"

"I don't want to lose both my sons."

"Cathal's only in the Fianna! No one's going to give him a gun!"

"He'd follow Pat anywhere, and it would be impossible to stop him."

"No, no, Kathleen, do stop worrying. All this is in your imagination. Now I must take you back to the house or Hilda will be cross. Anyway it's starting to rain. Have I convinced you you're wrong to worry?"

"Well, perhaps—"

"Good. But I will talk to Pat. And I'll use logic with him, oh, I'll use logic!"

Sixteen

It was Saturday afternoon. Barney had enveloped his Lee Enfield rifle in a long roll of brown paper and was binding it around with twine. He had at last come to a decision.

When it had seemed to him, at his moment of illumination in the Dominican chapel, that if he were simply to lift a finger he would gain a great access of spiritual strength, he had not foreseen how difficult the lifting of his finger would prove to be. He had returned home in the early hours of Good Friday moving in a spiritual rapture which seemed as intense and as pure as his numinous experience at Clonmacnoise. He was resolved on three things, to stop seeing Millie, to confess everything to Kathleen, and to destroy the Memoir. He had lain down and slept, in anticipation, the sleep of the just.

Later on on Friday, and this morning, it had all appeared less simple. The thought of not seeing Millie any more was not just painful it was absurd. It now seemed morbidly gratuitous, like punishing himself for nothing. He might go and see Millie less often, but the difference between less often and never was the difference between sanity and madness. To drop Millie would be a pointless act of self-mutilation. His little visits to her did no harm. It was all in his mind. Yes, that was it, it was all in his mind. He did no real harm to Kathleen by cheering himself up with Millie; on the contrary, he was a more kindly person at home just because he had this consolation. The idea of making a general confession to Kathleen now also seemed somehow an unnecessary penance. He would upset Kathleen, he would upset himself; and anyway, Kathleen probably understood the essence of the matter already. To set it out crudely in words was just to make extra trouble. It would not make things simple and inno- cent, it would make them nasty, emotional, and complicated. He had much better keep quiet and try hard, within the structure of his life as it now again seemed to him that it had to be, to be a better husband to Kathleen. Didn't that make sense? Yet he felt, with all this, disappointed. He knew in some refined pinpoint of his heart that what he had glimpsed in the chapel was true and was far more important than the reasoning which could make such nonsense of it. The trouble was that his quick vision of the truth was not commensurable with any plan of action which suited his capabilities. The acts it enjoined now seemed, not neces- sary, but isolated, arbitrary, and senseless. He had no energy for them. Sure it's all in my mind, he came back to saying.

The conclusion he had reached about his Memoir, that it was a sin against his wife, had seemed, even late on Friday night, both more clearly right and more practically manageable. He knew, as soon as he started to reflect seriously on the matter at all, that the Memoir provided a continual source of bitterness against Kath- leen. He was not really soberly and before God trying to write down what was the truth of their relationship, he was deploying an elaborate private argument against her. He was using his intelli- gence simply to take her captive in the imagination and belittle her, and correspondingly to enlarge himself. He was the wise, detached, shrewd observer, ironical and invulnerable. This must stop. If he was going to lead, even in a rather modified way, a new life, he must destroy the Memoir and blot out from his mind the picture of Kathleen which it contained.

He took out the manuscript and opened it at random.

I observed with sorrow the progressive estrangement of my wife from her two sons. On one or two occasions I even felt bound to upbraid the boys separately for an "off-hand" treatment of their mother which amounted almost to rudeness. They heard my admonitions with respect but seemed unable to promise any amelioration. It was clear that their mother afflicted them, as she afflicted so many people, with an uneasiness similar in structure to a sense of guilt. That this was not "true" guilt it took me indeed some years to perceive. A prolonged study of my wife's character led me in the end to conclude that the phenomenon was caused, not by any moral superiority on her part, but by something much more simple, her curious lack of vitality. She was, in the end, one of those who "have not" and from whom therefore, in the harsh words of the Gospel, "shall be taken away even that which they have." There was a negative quality in her, an un-life, in the presence of which ordinary healthy persons, such as myself and my stepsons, quite perceptibly shuddered.

The trouble was, it was so dashedly well written; and it was the only thing he had ever really created. It seemed a pity just to tear it up, in fact it seemed rather a crime. The Memoir existed now in its own right as a sort of personality, and the violent physical act of destroying it would seem like a murder and surely quite a needless one. He would stop writing it, of course. Well, it was almost finished, anyway. Perhaps he would just quickly finish it and put it away. And in case anyone ever found it he would write at the bottom in large letters ALL THIS IS NOT QUITE TRUE. Or perhaps one day he might change all the names and turn it into a novel.

He reached this conclusion on Saturday morning, and after reaching it, feeling distinctly more cheerful, he went out to the Reading Room in Lord Edward Street and looked at the newspapers and thought about Frances. If he had decided, which he had not, to give up Millie it would have simplified the decision whether to tell Frances about Christopher since, as he would have lost Millie anyway, he would not have to fear her displeasure, nor would he have to worry about the purity of his motives. But, given that he was still aiming at the preservation of Millie not only from herself but for himself, if Millie knew that Barney had told Frances that Christopher . . . He decided that he would read the newspapers first and think about all this afterwards.

There were two articles in the newspapers which interested him. The first one, which was in the *Irish Volunteer*, gave an account of how to ambush your enemy at a crossroads. Suppose you have forty men, armed with five rifles, twenty shotguns, fifteen pikes, and as many revolvers or automatics. Find a reasonably high wall and build up a footing behind it and put sandbags on top with loopholes between. Know your left-hand shuts and where to place them. For yourself, if you use a revolver or pistol with lance or bayonet, practise shooting with your left hand. Keep open your lines of communication and retreat. Throw up a barricade on the road in front, always on the right side of a bend so as not to be visible to an enemy till he comes right up to it. Do not put men behind it. Place the shotgun men and the pike men behind hedges at the side. When the column comes down the road hold your fire until it is well into range; while it is thrown into confusion by fire let your pike men charge through it and back; then another volley.

It sounded easy. Barney liked reading things like that in the *Volunteer* and feeling that they were meant for men like himself. "Know your left-hand shots and where to place them." He would know. "Practise shooting with your left hand." Left-hand shooting was child's play to him. Being an expert marksman had always made him feel himself to be an honorary soldier. Yet he had never, in fact, joined the Territorials, nor had he been distinguished either for zeal or performance in the Volunteers, although he was respected as a crack shot by the younger men. Perhaps after all he had not got a soldier's temperament. He read the instructions for the ambush over again. Could he really imagine himself there? Hold your fire. . . . Let your pike men charge . . . then another volley. He had seen men training with pikes, though he had never handled one himself. What would it be like to thrust one of those things into a human body? Then another volley. He pictured the men lying in the road, some lying still, some twisting and crying out. Could he be there? He closed the *Volunteer* with a shudder. The Irish spent so much of their time imagining what they would do to the English once they got hold of them. Perhaps these fancies really were, as Kathleen thought them, a poison of the imagination, a corruption of the heart.

He next opened the *Irish Times* and started reading an article, reprinted from the *New York Times*, by Bernard Shaw called "Irish Nonsense about Ireland." Shaw was at his usual game of deriding Irish nationalism. "I invite America to contemplate the spectacle of a few manifesto-writing stalwarts from the decimated population of a tiny green island at the back of Godspeed, claiming its national right to confront the world with its own army, its own fleet, its own tariff, and its own language which not five percent of its population could speak or read or write even if they wanted to. . . . If Ireland were cut loose from the British fleet and army tomorrow she would have to make a present of herself the day after to the United States, or France, or Germany, or any big Power that would condescend to accept her: England for preference."

Of course Shaw was right. Could Ireland stand alone? No, of course she couldn't. No little nation could stand alone in these days. And it was true, as Shaw said later in the article, that Ireland's first natural ally was England. Barney had heard the exalted talk of his stepsons, had heard Pat speak of a transfigured Ireland that would shine in the eyes of the nations, had heard Cathal tell how a magnanimous Ireland would raise a defeated England from the dust. But these were dreams. Ireland would always be the half-potty second-rate provincial dump which it had always been, with its stupid clergy and its stupid poor. It was not worth shedding men's blood, sticking them through with pikes or knocking them off with shotguns at country crossroads, to try to change what could never really be changed.

And yet was Shaw entirely right? All over Europe men had fought savagely for their freedom in scenes just as petty and hopeless as the Irish scene. Was it a bad thing that they had done this, and not chaffered rationally with their local tyrants for a slightly better bargain? Like almost all the Anglo-Irish, Barney had a strong peppering of Irish patriotism in his blood. He felt what it was like to belong to the persecuted and the broken, though he himself had never suffered hunger or blows. The history of Ireland was such a tale of misery and wretchedness, enough to make the angels howl and stamp their golden feet. England had destroyed Ireland slowly and casually, without malice, without mercy, practically without thought, like someone who treads upon an insect, forgets it, then sees it quivering and treads upon it again. Was there under heaven no tribunal where such a wrong could be set right and where the voices of the starved dead could mount into a mighty tempest at last? Were the young men wrong to imagine that an Ireland set free by its own righteous anger would be an unimaginably different place?

What could he do? As his thoughts returned to himself, taking him unawares, he felt a familiar pain which was his timeless assumption that he was a priest and then the quick jolt of the truth. He might, for all the horrors of the crossroads, endorse the fighting of others. He could not fight himself. His battles were battles of the spirit, his only task his own regeneration. And then as he remembered again the pure yet untranslatable summons of the little light which shone so withdrawn and self-contained in the thickness of the dark, he suddenly realized what the thing was which he could do for Kathleen. He could sacrifice his rifle.

The one clear idea which had remained with Barney from his spiritual half hour in the Dominican chapel was that he ought to act. He ought to do *something*. He ought to lift his finger. He ought, as he put it to himself, to give God a chance. He should shake himself into performing some movement which might be just violent enough to let loose the avalanche of goodness which he had, in that dazed but indubitable encounter, apprehended as reserved in especial for his own address. But there seemed, after all, to be no action which he could perform. He had decided that at least he could go and visit poor Jinny at the "little hell" and bring her a present. But Kathleen had told him that Jinny had gone back to her parents in County Meath. So even that little decent act was taken from him. There was nothing left except lighting a candle in a church and resolving to be more polite to his wife. Was that all that had come of such an overwhelming sense of the presence of the Almighty?

The idea of sacrificing his Lee Enfield suddenly seemed the perfect solution. It was something that would cause him pain. It was something that would please Kathleen and win her approval. She had said that she wanted that rifle out of the house. It was a gesture that would symbolize a return to a purer and simpler life. Guns and uniforms were all very well for young ones like Pat and Cathal, who were not dedicated men, but he had much better stay away and purge his imagination utterly of these pictures of violence. He must become a man of peace, asking little, harming no one. And he felt in an almost superstitious way that if he could undertake this positive penance this might indeed be the lifting of the finger, the joining of action to good intent from which a whole sequence of improvement might follow.

But how was he to get rid of the rifle? It seemed improper and insufficiently dramatic to sell it or give it away; he could not destroy it bodily and could scarcely leave it on a tram. Again the answer came to him as if from a divine source: he must take it to Kingstown Pier and cast it down a hole in the rocks! Feeling himself once more a man guided and inspired, he ate a hearty meal of sausages at the Red Bank Restaurant and then returned to Blessington Street and tied up the Lee Enfield into a brown paper parcel.

It was an extremely cold day, and there was nobody about on the front at Kingstown. Holding his parcel cradled in front of him like a child, Barney began to walk along the pier. The sharpened wind blew into his face and brought tears. He felt, with his strange burden, like a man dressed for a part, one garbed for a Passion-tide procession who by back streets makes his way toward the Cathedral. Yesterday Christ had been crucified. To-day He lay in the tomb. Tomorrow He would rise victorious over death. Barney felt, as never before, that he was a part of that mystery. His instinct had been right. An action, even a mad, arbitrary action, was needed to break the spell of his despair and set free the promised grace. Penance, sacrifice—these were symbolic movements whose effects were incommensurable in the world of the spirit. His single act would bring the full circle of his reconciliation. God, who had asked for Isaac, had also sent the ram.

He had gone about a third of the way along the pier on the upper terrace. There was nobody about. He approached one of the gaps in the wall through which one could pass to the other side. The wind screamed in the aperture. In a drenching of spray Barney went through and shuffled sideways with his back to the wall facing the open sea. The sea was extremely rough. It roared into the mountainous random rocks in a break-neck surge which creamed almost as far as Barney's feet and was withdrawn with an equal ferocity, sucked back through holes and crevasses to howl in chambers far below, vanishing in boiling foam under the high, dissolving front of the next wave. In a mist of spray Barney gazed, wondering which was more horrible, the huge savage sea or the piled rocks with their shapeless crannies. He found suddenly that he had to sit down against the wall.

A veil of rain farther out concealed Howth and even Sandy-cove from view. There was nothing ahead of him except that line of great, glistening, light yellow rocks stretching away on either side, on which a sort of diffused sunshine fell, and the rolling backs of the waves, dark grey, almost black, coming steadily towards him out of the wall of rain. Barney sat with the salt trickling upon his face and stared, stared at a manifestation of something far older and more primitive than the god who today lay sleeping in the quiet tomb and tomorrow would rise out of a casket of daffodils and lilies.

He could not think why he was so affected by the sea. After all, he had seen rough seas before. Or perhaps it was something to do with the rocks. He had always hated and feared those rocks, and now, perhaps, catching him in this rarefied, this spiritual condition, they were suddenly able to get at him. He closed his eyes to blot them out for a moment and to collect his strength. The din of the sea inside his head, the clatter of Chaos and Old Night, dulled into a ghastly replica of silence, and he almost feared to fall into a drugged, perilous slumber. He opened his eyes quickly and began to look about for a suitable hole or crevice down which to drop the Lee Enfield. There were plenty of huge triangles of blackness between the rocks into which the broken waves drained and echoed away. Once thrust in there and released from the hand, the rifle would slip away into some other world. It would not just disappear; it would cease to be. Barney sat still for a while. Then he began to wipe the spray slowly off his face with a handkerchief. He had realized that he could not do it.

He had known that the surrender of the rifle would be painful for him, but he had not foreseen that it would be like a mutilation. At that moment the Lee Enfield seemed like an extension of himself. He could not sever it, he could not thrust it into one of those appalling caves and let it go. He felt that he might perish himself at the moment of release. The prospect was like a descent into madness. He pitied the rifle, he loved it. He could not surrender a part of himself to that evil, howling power. He got up hastily and went through the gap and began to run back along the pier, clasping the rifle against his chest.

He went on running with occasional gasping pauses until he got as far as the Crock's Garden. The misty rain had receded momentarily, and the sea was a blackish blue scattered with points of light. There was a luminous pallor at the horizon. Overhead, the sky was suddenly clear, and a weak yellow sun shone onto the Crock's Garden. Barney had again that sense of dream, of belonging to another dimension from the people about him, of taking part in a ritual. Only before he had felt himself the glad master of his steps. Now, in some mysterious enactment into which he had not been initiated, he was being conveyed along.

There were a few people sitting gloomily in their mackintoshes upon the wet seats of the garden looking at the sea. Barney took one of the labyrinthine paths which wound uphill between the thick, round veronica bushes. He felt now that he must get rid of the rifle as quickly as possible. If he kept the thing in his hands much longer, some doom would fall upon him. He looked quickly about. There was no one to be seen. He thrust the long brown paper parcel far in under one of the bushes and out of sight. Then he walked quickly on till he came to a seat at the top of the hill and sat down.

He was panting with exertion and excitement. He stared at the Martello tower at Sandycove, caught in a grey, luminous shaft of sunny rainy light. After a few minutes he thought he would go again and look at where the rifle was. Perhaps, after all, he should now simply pick it up and go back to Dublin on the tram. He had performed the movements of an act of penance. It was all symbolic, anyhow. It's all in my mind, he said to himself. Could he remember under which bush he had put the gun? He started off down the hill, panting again. But several elderly ladies were now coming up the winding path. He returned to the seat at the top. It was raining now in Sandycove, and the Martello tower was almost obscured. He waited three minutes and then began to descend the hill again.

He turned the corner of the path and saw a group of people beside a bush. Some children had already found the rifle and pulled it out onto the path. The paper was being unwrapped. Someone was saying confusedly to someone else that hadn't a policeman better be called. Barney pushed quickly past and went down the hill. He expected at any moment to be called back and accused of something. Then it suddenly began to rain extremely hard. Everyone started to run. Barney ran.

He ran towards the nearest of the big Egyptian temples, the

concrete shelter upon the near end of the pier. The rain was spilling down, beating violently upon the heads of the running people. It stretched away in front of him like a series of bright metal curtains. Just as he reached the shelter he heard somebody call his name. An umbrella jerked against his shoulder. Underneath the umbrella he saw the pale face of Kathleen.

Barney slithered into the damp gloom of the shelter. There were a lot of people already there and others arriving in haste. Kathleen followed him in, closing her umbrella. They made their way into a corner.

The sudden appearance of his wife did not surprise Barney very much. In his present weird state of mind it seemed to him natural that Kathleen should materialize, since she had been in a sense the spiritual agent of whatever it was that had just been happening to him. She was a performer in the same ritual and perhaps its directing genius. However, he asked her, "How did you know I was here?" It seemed natural, too, that she should have been out looking for him.

"I asked you when you were leaving the house where you were going and you said Kingstown Pier."

"Oh. I'd forgotten."

"I came to look for Christopher, really, but there was no one at Finglas, so I came down here in case you might be here with Frances and she might know where Christopher was."

"It's not my day for Frances." So Kathleen had not been looking for him after all. "Would you like to sit down? It's terribly wet."

Kathleen spread out a newspaper on the rough concrete seat at the back of the shelter, and they sat down. Behind them out of holes in the wall a little water trickled over the pebbly surface. The dreary damp smell of wet concrete mingled with a human smell of wet tweed. A large number of persons were standing up just in front of them, hemming them in, and steaming slightly in the sudden closeness. Their voices echoed in the hollow space.

Barney suddenly felt that he and Kathleen were very private here at the back of the crowd, sitting together in the dark. He felt a desire to touch her, to pat her knee, but felt too shy to do so. A moment later he decided that he must make his confession. The sacrifice of the rifle had worked. "Kathleen—"

"Barney, I'm so worried—"

"Listen, Kathleen, I must tell you something. I've got to tell you now and it'll make everything all right again between us. I know it'll upset you but it's right to tell the truth isn't it and won't you forgive me for it? It's about Millie, well it's about me really, but there are two things and one of them is about Millie, that I've been going to see Millie still. You didn't know that did you? Well, for ages now I've been going to see her at her house, just to talk like, but it was very wrong and I'm very sorry and I won't go there any more at all. And the other thing is about Saint Brigid, I mean about the early church that I'm supposed to be writing. I haven't been writing it at all but I've been writing another thing a sort of autobiography thing about you and me in a way I shouldn't but I'll stop doing that too and—"

"Saint Brigid?" said Kathleen. Perhaps she could not hear very well in the crowded, echoing shelter.

"I say I'm not writing about Saint Brigid but about you and me in a sort of Memoir like I shouldn't have been. But did you hear what I said about Millie?"

"Don't talk so loudly. I can hear you quite well. You mustn't talk like that here."

"But did you hear?"

"Yes. I knew you went to see Millie."

"Oh. Well and wasn't it wrong of me to?"

"I still don't understand what it has to do with Saint Brigid."

"That's *another* thing, I'm doing two wrong things but they're not connected, forget about Saint Brigid, it's just that all the time I've been at the National Library I've been writing that thing about you and me, and—"

"Sure why shouldn't you?"

Barney had often imagined himself making this confession to Kathleen, but it had been in a scene quite unlike this one. He had pictured himself shaken by emotion, the words rent from his breast. He had pictured Kathleen's stricken face, perhaps her tears, her bitter reproaches, and then the great reconciliation. But this was as random and senseless as the sea roaring through the rocks.

"Barney, I'm so worried—"

The people in front of them suddenly surged forward. There were exclamations—"It's stopped!" The sun was shining outside. Everyone started to troop out of the shelter.

Barney and Kathleen got up automatically. Kathleen began to pull pieces of damp newspaper off her coat, and Barney pawed at the seat of his trousers, which felt very uncomfortable indeed. Automatically they walked out towards the sun.

The sunshine was warm and fragrant after the chill atmosphere of the shelter. The wind had dropped, and the sea below them was a thick glassy green. The people dispersed along the promenade, whose drenched surface steamed in the sun. Kathleen started to speak again, but before Barney could hear what she was saying they both saw, with a sudden dismayed premonition, someone running towards them. There was a sort of explosion and Cathal arrived, cannoning into Barney and saving himself by grasping him violently round the waist. The boy was in a state of incoherent excitement.

"Pat wants you," he said to Barney, and had to say it twice because the words got all mixed up.

"Whatever is it, Cathal?" said Kathleen, her hands at her mouth with fright.

"I knew you were coming down here and I told Pat I could find you at once and he says you're to report to him directly, so come now."

"Cathal, *what is it?*"

Cathal turned to his mother. He was almost tearful with emotion. "We're going to fight them now. We're going to take over Dublin tomorrow."

He darted away, receding along the wet promenade, dodging the people who were standing about, enjoying the sunshine. Kathleen ran after him awkwardly, her half-closed umbrella underneath her arm. Barney ran after Kathleen.

Seventeen

"Pat, Pat, let me in!"

Pat groaned. He had hoped to avoid seeing his mother. He had intended, indeed, to be out of the house entirely that day, but it had been necessary to come back to destroy some documents and to remove a copy of his will, which he wished to leave with a solicitor. He had also wanted to interview Barney about a particular matter. And now he was caught.

When he had noticed on the previous day that the door of his room had been forced he had immediately thought of the police, but Cathal had then appeared and told him what had happened. Kathleen after searching his room had gone away in great agitation, saying she was going to see Christopher, and had returned rather more calm later in the afternoon. She had said nothing to either of her sons.

Pat, who had jammed a tilted chair against the door handle so that the door could not be opened from the outside, said, "All right, Mother, I'll come down in a moment." Her steps receded.

Pat stamped on the smouldering ash in the grate and thrust the copy of the will into the pocket of his green jacket. The other copy was in the unlocked drawer of his desk. All his papers were neat and in order, the room bared and tidied, already unfamiliar. He looked about him. He would not come back that night. Perhaps he would not come back at all.

The authority of tomorrow had made him by now utterly hard and quiet. He had received his final orders, and now knew as much as he would know until the firing of the first shot. To his profound joy, he had been appointed to be at the centre of the conflict at headquarters, with Pearse and MacDonagh in the General Post Office. He closed the door and went down to his mother.

"Pat, what is this about tomorrow?"

He looked at his mother coldly down the length of the long, narrow drawing room. It seemed to be raining again outside and he could not see her face very well. "Do sit down, Mother, and take your coat off. You seem to have got soaked."

"Pat, what are you going to do? They've planned an armed rising for tomorrow, I *know* it, so don't pretend. What are you going to do?"

Pat decided there was no point in a denial. "How did you find out?"

"Cathal told me."

"Damn Cathal." Pat had, of course, not told his brother anything of the plan. Cathal must have found it out from someone at Liberty Hall. The Citizen Army men had always encouraged Cathal, treating him as if he were grown up.

"So it is true. And you are going to be in it."

"I'm going to be where every decent Irishman will be on that day."

"I would do anything to stop you," said Kathleen in a low gruff voice, uttering every word with an effort.

"Fortunately, there is nothing you can do."

"I could reveal everything to the Castle."

"That would not stop us from fighting. It would merely increase our chances of defeat. It's too late. There is nothing whatever that you can do, Mother."

Kathleen slowly took off her wet coat and let it fall to the floor. "And if I beg and implore you not to—"

"My dear Mother, your disapproval is not likely to weigh with me very much at this stage."

"Not my disapproval, my misery—"

"Or your misery either. I thought of all these things long ago. Be sensible now. Would you really be pleased to have a son who kept out of danger for the sake of his mother's tears? I'm sorry to cause you pain, but I know where my duty lies."

"It *can't* be your duty," she said. "It *can't* be. What's wrong can't be your duty."

"It's not wrong to fight to free your country."

"But you won't be *doing* that. You'll just be killing people pointlessly. You'll have innocent blood on your hands. And you may be killed yourself, or maimed for life. That's what it will be. And what for? Think about later on, think when people will look back and see that nothing has been changed. You cannot change Ireland by firing a few shots. Don't you see? Nothing can be *done* in this way at all. All that great action is in your mind only. You'll commit crimes and you'll destroy yourself utterly and break my heart, and for nothing. Can't you see it all from that place in the future and see that it's for nothing?"

"I don't inhabit that place in the future, Mother, and neither do you. This is the moment when Ireland has got to fight, and she's come to it over a long road."

"She! She! Who is Ireland indeed? Are you and your friends Ireland? You use these grand jumped-up words but they mean nothing at all. They're empty words. You're caught all of you in the tangle of your dreams, and it just needs a few sane men to halt you. Have you not the courage to stop this thing?"

"It's too late to argue."

"And what about Cathal?"

Pat was silent.

"Have you thought about your young brother in this? Have you the right to destroy him, too?"

"We'll keep Cathal out of it."

"And how will you do that? You know he'll go wherever you go. Are we to tie him up or what?"

"No one will let him do anything. He's too young."

"Who'll trouble about his age? Those fellows of James Connolly's he's always about with will take him with them if you don't."

"I'll manage about Cathal."

"Pat, child, please don't go. You must have some influence with these men. Put it off at any rate, think a little longer. You know you haven't got a chance against the English, sure you all know you haven't a chance. MacNeill must know that. He's not a madman."

"It's not the point whether we have a chance."

"You're going out there to be killed for nothing, to die for nothing."

"It won't be for nothing. If I die I shall die for Ireland."

"There is no such thing as dying for Ireland," she said.

There was a heavy sound of running feet upon the stairs and along the landing, and as they both turned quickly towards the door it burst open and Christopher Bellman rushed into the room.

"Kathleen, would you mind leaving me alone with Pat for a few minutes?"

Kathleen said, "They are going to fight tomorrow." She went to the door.

"Tomorrow is it?" Christopher stared at Pat. He waited for Kathleen to be gone and then strode forward and gripped Pat's arms above the elbow. He shook Pat with a violence which was half affection and half anger and then suddenly, closing his eyes and baring his teeth, he dropped his hands and turned away. "Tomorrow? Oh, God, you fools, you fools, you fools. You haven't heard what's happened down in Kerry?"

"What?"

"Your precious German arms. A whole shipload of them. Now they're at the bottom of Queenstown harbour. Oh, you idiots, you dolts— But tomorrow—Pat, you're mad."

"What's this about German arms?"

"You didn't know? A ship crammed with arms for you from Germany—God knows how they did it. I heard it all from Mac-Neill—got through the blockade—they were disguised as Norwegian fishermen or something—got as far as Tralee harbour—and there they sat for nearly two days waiting for some of your people to pay some attention to them! God, how can you have been so *stupid?* The Germans do this absolutely marvellous thing for you and you have to muff it. Why, why, why, didn't somebody get those arms ashore? But no one seems even to have noticed the wretched Germans! God, what were your people thinking of? And then they felt they had to move and they sailed a bit along the coast and ran smack into a British sloop, which took them into Queenstown harbour. Even then the Germans were beautiful, beautiful—the captain got everyone off and blew his ship up under the nose of the Royal Navy! My God, the Germans know how to do things. But they might have known the Irish would mess up their end of it. All that stuff sitting in Tralee bay and no one there to land it! God, what a nation of dunces!"

Pat turned away. He was silent for a moment. "Well, that's gone."

"Yes, it's gone all right! And they've got Casement."

"Casement? But Casement isn't in Ireland."

"He is now. He's in the R.I.C. barracks at Tralee. The Germans landed him from a submarine and he walked straight into the arms of the police."

"Oh, God," said Pat. "Casement." He sat down heavily in a chair. "They'll hang him." He covered his face with his hands.

Christopher was in a state of intense excitement which he hardly himself understood. He had comforted Kathleen, but after she had gone he had suddenly felt quite certain that she was right. MacNeill evidently knew nothing of it, but it now seemed to him obvious that if violence was planned MacNeill *would* know nothing of it. Something was going to happen. The certainty came upon him not as a thought-out conclusion but more like a physical visitation, making him leap to his feet and gasp and tremble; and like a man for whom an ambiguous picture has abruptly shifted he saw only the new shape and could not now recapture the old.

Christopher had always played the cynic in political discussions. But in fact, though this would not have led him to lift a finger himself, he felt a strong romantic sympathy with the whole tradition of rebellion in Ireland and with the Sinn Feiners as the present representatives of that tradition. He loved the history of Ireland as if it were a personal possession; and although he freely mocked the person of the "tragic woman," there was more than a touch of heated gallantry in his reaction to the whole miserable story. He enjoyed here an indignation which he kept entirely private. Like many scholars who ostentatiously eschew the field of action, he had a strongly developed sense of the heroic, while with the sensibility of an artist he apprehended an epic splendour always latent in the tragedy of Ireland.

Now he felt in the most terrible confusion. His misery, his fury at learning the news about the German arms made him realize how utterly he identified himself with the rebels. He was desolated too by the plight of Casement, a man whom he greatly admired. His heart was already in revolt. Yet he knew, too, that whatever happened now could only be another miserable failure. He had lightly agreed to Kathleen's request to "use logic" with Pat; but now that he saw the boy in front of him, illuminated in Christopher's sensitive vision by the bright light of history, he could not think what to say, nor what to do with the sudden tumult of energy with which the new situation had filled him.

"Yes, they'll hang Casement," he said to Pat. "They'll hang you all. If you want to end your young life on an English gallows you're certainly going the right way about it."

Pat lifted his head and smiled slightly. "Don't worry. They won't hang us, they'll shoot us. After all, we are soldiers."

"They won't treat you as soldiers. They'll treat you as murderers. They'll treat you as rats."

"They'll soon find out we're soldiers. Where did you hear this about Casement? I suppose it's true?"

"I heard it at MacNeill's. I'm very sorry about Casement. But oh, that you should have muffed those arms—"

"I don't understand about the arms ship," said Pat, "but our men in Tralee will rescue Casement."

"You won't have time. You'll all be disarmed by tonight."

"Then we'll all be fighting by tonight. You'll keep your mouth shut about what my mother said just now?"

"Yes, I will, God forgive me, but I think you're insane."

"I don't think they will jump on us before tomorrow. We may be stupid but they're stupider. What is it, Mother?"

Kathleen had opened the door. She went up to her son and struck him fiercely upon the arm. "Someone has just seen Cathal going away down the road with a rifle—"

Pat put her aside and left the room at a run.

Eighteen

Pat had put off solving the problem, had put it off because he could see no solution. In a way he simply could not think about Cathal at all, could not treat him as an object of rational reflection, could not put to himself questions of the form would this or that be "advantageous" to Cathal. His brother had always been as close and as connected to him as his own hand. He had always associated Cathal with his view of his own life as if they looked out through the same eyes; and his long tyranny over him had been a form of self-discipline, an experience of living in two bodies. There would be, at moments, the sudden apprehension of the boy's separateness, making him gasp with surprise as at a felicitous audacity. Then as they returned again into each other Pat would feel, in an easing and enlargement of time, his own childhood not only preserved and continued, but perfected.

Would he not have risked Cathal if they were to climb a mountain together or swim a flooded river together? He had indeed so risked him. But this was simply a way of risking himself, and in those open solitudes their joint strength and their youth had seemed invincible. Pat had always so closely associated Cathal in his mind with all his decisions, they had seemed to exist together in perfect unity at a level only a little below that at which they constantly bickered. Pat had indeed been aware of this unity simply as a sense of including his brother. So it was that even in this thing he had seemed to bring Cathal along with him, to bring him absolutely to the threshold over which he was now so determined not to take him.

Pat had, of course, asked himself if it were not really best, after all, to keep Cathal with him, to have him, in whatever ensued, positively beside him and under his eye. Then at least he could be sure the boy would do nothing insane: which, if left uncontrolled, he would be certain to do. But Pat knew at once how unrealistic this idea was. He could not help seeing the coming events in a heroic light; but he also knew, though not with his heart, that when these events arrived they would be incoherent and terrible. He would simply not be able to keep an eye on Cathal or to protect him. And to be less than single-minded would be a gross failure of duty.

Pat was well aware that he himself, at Cathal's age, would have reacted in exactly the same way, and he asked himself whether, in trying to keep him out of the conflict, he were not somehow tampering with the boy's honour. But he could not sufficiently make sense of this idea or see Cathal as having, in this respect, separate rights. If the boy had been a little older, even two years older, even perhaps one year older, the sacrifice would have had to be consented to, it would have had to be accepted as part of the ordinary world. Where he was together with his brother was still the sacred land of childhood.

It was not exactly that he wanted Cathal to survive him, that he wanted to keep that most precious piece of himself out of danger; nor did he care at all about his mother's need for sons. He had a deeper, more physical, sensation of being, where Cathal was, entirely exposed and naked, and his instinct was to hide and cherish this unprotected part. He wanted to stand entirely in front of Cathal, to shield him completely, to press him back behind him into a place of safety. He was ready to expose himself to the English bullets, he had thought about them often enough, and it was as if he were already physically hardened, a veteran of the imagination. But the idea that any harm might come to his brother made him writhe and shrink. It made an utter coward of him.

When Pat emerged into Blessington Street there was no sign of Cathal anywhere, and Pat began to run down the hill into a light misty rain which was materializing softly out of the warm air. It occurred to him that Cathal might have gone to confession at St. Joseph's church in Berkeley Road. It was a time when confessions were heard there. And that day all over Dublin, as intimations of the morrow spread wider through all ranks of the movement, men in green uniforms were to be seen queuing up outside the confessionals. Pat himself had been to confess that morning; and it was possible that Cathal, apeing here his brother, or whichever of Connolly's men was his latest mentor, had had the same idea.

Pat shouldered his way through the door into the stale, incense-laden darkness of the church and peered about him. The east window glimmered faintly, bleakly, above the Lenten simplicity of the high altar, and between vegetable pillars the many lights of adoration flickered, blue before the Queen of Heaven, red for Saint Joseph, and yellow for the Little Flower. A few old women, black murmuring bundles, crouched or trotted here and there, but the body of the church was full of men, and there was a deep buzz of men's voices, only just quiet enough for reverence. Looking about him Pat saw everywhere the uniforms of the I.C.A. and the Volunteers. The interior of the church seemed like a busy encampment. The chairs, which had been moved out of their neat rows, stood higgledy-piggledy, piled with knapsacks, with rifles leaning up against them; and the men waited in long, patient lines beside the confessionals, or knelt among the chairs or out in the open aisles. The gathering seemed impromptu, unorganized, yet strangely solemn. The men bowed their heads low, or when they lifted them threw them back in a free way and their faces were clear and relaxed and seemed to shine in the darkness. The men smiled at each other as they passed, took hands in silence, or spoke briefly, holding each other's shoulders. There was a sense of happiness in the church, a sense of all sins forgiven.

Pat pushed his way forward, brushing against people that he knew. As he passed the confessionals he scanned the army boots of various types whose soles were displayed while their owners murmured quietly to the priest. But in fact the queues were so long that Cathal would not have had time to get to the front. He passed through into the side chapel where innumerable candles, dazzling not illuminating, mingled with the dark without dispelling it, and God's Blessed Mother, muffled from head to foot in purple cloth, leaned over him as he scanned the kneeling figures. Eyes which did not see him were lifted in the darkness and rosaries clicked, bumped on wooden chairs or trailed upon the floor as hands fell to sides in unconscious gestures of self-surrender. Cathal was not there.

Pat pushed his way back again through the murmuring, shifting crowd, reached the door, and jostled out again, shading his eyes, into the very pale clear light of the late afternoon. The rain had just stopped and there was a diffused sunny atmosphere, thick and low, over Dublin, which made the pavements shine cruelly and outlined every brick in the façades of the houses. Pat started to run down the hill toward Rutland Square. Now he must go to Liberty Hall.

Thick and huge, gross with imperial confidence, the Pillar rose above Sackville Street, and from its summit Nelson gazed thoughtfully over the head of the Liberator to the Liffey and the masts of the ships and the open sea. The street was full of people, the usual Saturday crowds, ambling the pavements with deliberate slowness and trailing in slow mobs to and from the trams. Under the low ceiling of sunny light the voices of women and children were mainly heard, producing a continuous animated clacking. As Pat forced himself along, the surge of cheerful faces resisted him, clear, detailed little human surfaces, glowing in the brightening air, thrust close up against him and jerked past. Frantic now with need and fear, Pat struggled on through the herd of happy people. He hated them all. Tomorrow this cackling would be put to silence and he would be separated from the like of these by a line of English soldiers. As he came to the middle of the street he looked quickly across at the Post Office.

Near to the Liffey the crowds were less dense, and Pat turned to the left along the quay. The sun was coming out properly now, patterning the pavements with reflections and shadows, and there was a sky of the faintest, feeblest blue above the glistening wet dome of the Customs House. As Pat approached Beresford Place he saw the gaping doorway of the Butt Bar and heard the sound within of drunken men singing the Soldier's Song. Groups of men in Citizen Army uniform were standing about in the roadway. On the façade of Liberty Hall the dripping banner still proclaimed *We serve neither King nor Kaiser but Ireland*.

Then Pat saw Cathal, standing on the pavement opposite, underneath the shadow of the Loop Line railway, talking to one of Connolly's men. He was holding the rifle awkwardly, like an acolyte holding a very large candle, and conversed with the man with a solemn air, nodding his head in an exaggerated way. As Pat drew near, the Citizen Army man turned away, leaving Cathal, and made for the main entrance of Liberty Hall. Cathal stood still for a moment looking down at the rifle, hesitating whether to rest the butt of it upon the wet pavement. Pat recognized the gun as his own crack Italian rifle, which Cathal had evidently purloined from his room. Pat crossed the road at a run and almost cannoned into his brother. He took the rifle lightly out of his hand and struck Cathal hard across the side of the face. Then he took Cathal's wrist in a firm grip and began to pull him back in the direction of the quay. Cathal resisted him and began to sob.

As Pat forced him along, ignoring the sobs, a large group of uniformed men were seen approaching Liberty Hall at the double. They thrust Pat and Cathal back against the wall as they passed, and Pat saw the figure of James Connolly in the midst of them. As the bright light fell upon Connolly Pat felt a sudden shock of apprehension. Connolly's face expressed an appalled, shocked grief.

Following the group of men with Connolly came three Volunteer officers, all known to Pat and senior to himself. As he pressed forward now, still automatically dragging Cathal with him by the wrist, one of these, a man called Owen Magillivray, saw Pat and at once beckoned to him. Magillivray's face expressed the same misery and shock. Pat and Cathal followed the Volunteer officers in through the door of Liberty Hall and on into a dark office where a number of men were talking in low, agitated voices. Magillivray, shouldering the others aside, half pushed Pat into a corner of the room. He said nothing to him, but thrust a folded piece of paper into his hand. Pat fumbled it open and read. *Owing to the very critical position, all orders given to Irish Volunteers for tomorrow, Easter Sunday, are hereby rescinded and no parades, marches or other movements of Irish Volunteers will take place. Each individual Volunteer will obey the order strictly in every particular.* The signatures were those of MacNeill, MacDonagh, and de Valera. The rising had been cancelled.

Nineteen

Pat Dumay propped his bicycle against the wall and looked up at the darkened house. The moon, shining through a brown haze, was a large, vague blur of light, seeming to move rapidly through the disturbed night sky. In this faint illumination Rathblane looked thicker, squatter, more like a fortress than a country house. Its shadow, an indeterminate hump or blot of darkness hanging from the walls, contained half of the expanse of rough grass, while on the other half, just fading into visibility, the sheep, grouped near the steps, were motionless, fuzzy, seemingly spherical. The windows of the house, very lightly smirched by the moon, bore upon their blackness little streaks and drips of light, as if some liquid silver had been thrown upon them and almost all washed away. Although it was not yet midnight the house and the countryside were deep, not exactly in sleep, but in trance. There was a profound silence in which the wall, the trees, the great black and grey block of the house seemed submerged, more completely full and present than by daylight, as if the night and the stillness had filled them to the brim and weighted them with a quieter, denser element. The plantation beyond, faintly animate, seemed to breathe without moving, not exactly visible, but perceived in some further solidifying of murky air. Pat fingered the key in his pocket like a man fingering a weapon.

What had happened in the last two days in Dublin Pat had by now largely discovered. On Thursday a rumour had reached Bulmer Hobson that an armed rising was planned for Easter Sunday. He went at once to MacNeill, who was still of course the nominal head of the Volunteers, and in the early hours of Good Friday morning he and MacNeill visited Pearse, who admitted to them that the rumour was true. MacNeill said, "I will do everything I can to stop it, except ringing up Dublin Castle." There was a violent and inconclusive dispute, after which MacNeill went home. A little later Pearse went with MacDermott and MacDonagh to MacNeill's house to argue with him again. MacNeill refused to see Pearse and MacDonagh, but allowed MacDermott to come in. MacDermott told MacNeill that the rising was now unavoidable and that the real command of the Volunteers was no longer in MacNeill's hands. He also told him of the German arms which were about to be landed in Kerry, and pointed out that after the arrival of the arms the British were certain to attempt to disarm the Volunteers, and this would mean a fight anyway. So it was better to strike first. MacNeill gave in and agreed to sanction the rising.

On Saturday morning came the news of the catastrophe to the German arms ship. MacNeill began to waver. He was visited by the O'Rahilly and other officers who were opposed to the rising. At last he went to St. Enda's to see Pearse, and there was bitter argument. After that MacNeill went home and wrote out countermanding orders which were dispatched with couriers to the Volunteer organization throughout the country. He prepared a statement, cancelling all "manoeuvres," which was to be published in the *Sunday Independent* next day, and cycled personally to the office to deliver it. Finally he ordered MacDonagh, as commandant of the Dublin Brigade, to inform all his men officially of the cancellation. MacDonagh, who judged that by now the plan was irrevocably spoilt, agreed, and sent out a Brigade Order over his own signature and that of his adjutant de Valera. It was the end of the enterprise.

"If we don't fight now, all we have left to hope and pray for is that an earthquake will come and swallow Ireland up, and our shame." These words of James Connolly expressed what Pat felt, what they all felt, in those amazed and disappointed hours. Pat went back to Blessington Street. He sent Cathal on ahead to tell his mother. He could not have endured her happy, relieved face. He climbed to his room and shut the door and fell face downwards on his bed.

It seemed that life was over. He had only, ever, had but one purpose, and now that had been quite suddenly twisted away from him. It was snatched, gone, quickly, meanly, quietly, and without remedy. Pat knew that what was lost here could not be retrieved. If they did not act at once, they could not act at all. The impetus would be spent, the movement discredited, the moment missed. There was to have been martyred blood, but now everything would collapse into absurdity and those who had called them shirkers and dreamers would have been proved right. The English would disarm them. Pat, who had felt that he would surrender his weapons with his life, now felt that it no longer mattered whether he kept his gun or not. Everything had been betrayed.

He cursed the leaders, he cursed Pearse. He grieved unutterably for Casement. MacNeill ought to have been arrested days ago. Why could the Irish get nothing right? Such dunces deserved their slavery. But it was no use cursing and grieving. There was the rest of the day to be got through, there was the rest of his life to be got through, without a plan or purpose. He sat up and stared about him. He felt as if he had been pushed through a very small aperture into a completely other world. He felt giddy and unable to focus his eyes upon the little room, which had become an entirely different place. He had nodded for a moment and awakened in prison. The rush of time in his ears had ceased, and there was empty space and idleness and silence.

Leaning his head forward in his hands, Pat felt that he could hardly bear to go on being conscious. He wanted death.

How and when the idea of Millie came into his mind he was not sure. Somewhere in the flashing centre of his unfocused gaze her image had come to be, like a deity seen by a saint in an ellipse of light. The wretchedness of his body demanded violence, the whip, the brand. Thought, even consciousness, must be choked in feeling, drowned in pain. He recalled how Millie had offered herself, and the disgust he had felt for her, and yet also, as it seemed to him now, how in a totally horrible way she had attracted him. She was a slut, not exactly a woman, but a kind of degraded boy. He pictured her as dirty, sallow, dishevelled, stinking. She had said that she would be waiting for him in her bed, and he pictured her bed. Could he force himself to that?

He sat very quiet now. If this was despair, it was a deeper pit than any he had ever dreamed of. And then it seemed to him almost like a duty to go there, to perform this, as it appeared, quite final act of will. There would be an action and an ending after all, not this well-lighted idleness but a swift rush into the dark. This would be the last triumph of his will over his fastidious mind, and over the foul animal of his body, for although he now desired Millie he knew that it was only by pure volition that he could so degrade himself. He went downstairs and found his bicycle.

Now that he had reached Rathblane, desire and cool intent had fused into a single thrust. He wanted Millie as an enemy, a victim, a quarry. What she had asked for she would get. He moved forward through the wet grass towards the steps, bringing out the key. It was fortunate that he had provided himself with a key to Rathblane. He did not want to be seen by the servants, not because of any discretion—he was far beyond discretion—but because he did not wish the momentum of his action to be checked. He edged the big key into the lock and the door gave quietly in front of him.

Pat was fairly familiar with the interior of Rathblane but he did not know which was Millie's bedroom. He did not want any apparitions of screaming house maids. He guessed that it would be safe to try the big bow-windowed room above the drawing-room. He began very cautiously to mount the stairs, which creaked at every step. It was extremely dark, and the darkness seemed to be getting inside his eyes and mouth. For a moment he felt stifled, as if the black air were foul with soot. He paused on the landing, trying hard to see, and made out the window with difficulty. The moon must be obscured now, and there was a soft, hissing sound of rain. Something white glimmered nearby, and, reaching out his hand, Pat touched the cold smooth globe of an oil lamp. He struck a match and lit the lamp, still breathing hard, and turned it up slowly. Furniture, flowers, pictures, and the half-curtained window, with its rainy whisper, came into shadowy being about him.

He had no qualms about waking Millie suddenly. She was not the kind of woman who would scream. In fact, he was so dazed with his own purposes that he hardly conceived that he would surprise her. He moved across the landing, carrying the lamp, and very quietly opened a door. He leaned through, holding the light above him, and saw a small, empty room, perhaps a dressing room, with the low embers of a fire in the grate. There was a smell of turf and a slight smell of whiskey. Some clothes lay untidily upon a sofa beside the fire. At the far side of the room there was another door.

Pat closed the first door carefully behind him and crossed the room. He was gasping for breath as his hand touched the handle of the second door. As the door moved and the dark aperture widened before him he lifted the lamp high and tried to murmur Millie's name. At once, in the sudden wavering light, he discovered a bed. And a second later he saw that there were two people in it. Millie was not alone.

Pat closed the door abruptly and stepped back. He put the lamp down on a table. He covered his eyes and shook his head to and fro. He felt shocked, ashamed, and stupid, and intensely hurt, though whether this was pain for damage he had received or damage he had done he was not sure. Stupidity had come upon him like a physical condition, like an ass's head. He could have taken hold of Millie without a thought for her mind or her heart. But now he was suddenly related to her differently, shocked into some more childish puritanism. He thought, I have been made an utter fool of. He had not conceived of a rival, that a rival could exist. When Millie had said that she would be waiting for him he had believed her quite simply, quite naïvely. He had imagined her like a helpless quarry, like a victim tied to a post. Now in an instant he had been robbed of his active role, reduced to a gaping spectator, a shameful watcher. He had expected, he had wanted, violence and pain, not muddle.

He wondered if he should not just go away straight out of the house, and he pictured himself going, but his body stood there stiff and paralysed. Then, as he still stood, almost at attention, and uncovered his eyes, the door of the bedroom opened and Millie came out, wearing a white frilled dressing gown.

The appearance of Millie, the movement of the door, made Pat suddenly aware of his rival as an individual. Who was in there with her? But he could not feel angry. He felt humiliated and utterly, primitively, shocked. That another should do *that* was simply something horrible.

Millie, not looking at him, moved to the lamp and turned it up. The white scalloped frills of the silky gown dragged slowly upon the carpet. She leaned over the fire, thrust a long spill into the embers, and lit another lamp. Then she faced him.

Millie looked unfamiliar. Her hair, which he had never seen undone, fell in thin dark sheets about the shoulders of her gown and down onto her breast, making her look like a young girl, vulnerable, caught. Her plump face wore an expression of rueful, quizzical sadness. With the conscious dignity of a youthful princess facing her executioner, she seemed perfectly calm.

"What a pity, what a very great pity. If I had known you

might come I would have been more than ready. I despaired of you too soon." She spoke in a detached way, as if to herself, as if knowing the words could not have much significance for him.

Pat stared at her and then looked down at the floor. One bare foot, half emerged beneath the frilly hem, seemed to clutch the carpet like a clenching hand. He had no way of dealing with her now; he felt like a child. He was almost ready to say that he was sorry.

"How did you get in, Pat?"

"I had a key of the place," he said in a hoarse low voice.

"Ah, well. I know this can never be mended or forgiven or even explained. But I think I regret it more than anything that has ever happened to me. I did not conceive that you might come. If you had given me the least hint, I would have been eternally patient. I most bitterly regret not having been alone when you came, and I shall regret it forever." Millie spoke softly, but very slowly and clearly.

"Sure I—" Pat started. He could not face her. He could not feel angry. He felt the hurt, confused, ashamed resentment of a child who, without understanding, has spoilt some grown-up plan. He half turned as if to go.

"I don't want to act stupidly now," said Millie, speaking more quickly. "I know we can't talk now. But your having come, it's so important. If there was any satisfaction I could give you I would undergo anything. I suppose it's hopeless, but I can't help saying—"

"Who's that in there?" said Pat. Even this question, which should have been brutal, was broken, hang-dog. He stared at the closed bedroom door.

Millie hesitated. Then she said. "Well, I'll give you this, and remember that I gave it to you." She walked over to the door and opened it wide. "Come out, Andrew."

Andrew Chase-White, clad in shirt and breeches, emerged from the bedroom and leaned against the jamb of the door. He was very pale and shuddering slightly. He too appeared entirely different. He stared Pat full in the face with a look of dazed, bleak misery.

Millie said, "I'm sorry, Andrew. I'm sorry, Pat. There's nothing more I can say." Then she added, "All the same, it's quite an achievement, isn't it," and gave a short laugh.

The two young men gazed at each other. Then Pat turned abruptly and left the room. He half fell down the stairs in the dark and found the front door and the moist night air. The rain had stopped and the moon shone clearly through a jagged gap in the clouds. The figure of a man materialized close in front of him upon the steps. Pat thrust the man violently aside and heard him fall with an exclamation into the long grass. Without looking back, Pat reached his bicycle where it stood against the wall. He now saw, revealed by the brighter moon, two other bicycles near it. He swung his left hand hard against the wall, and swung it again and then a third time, until the moonlight showed a dark stain upon the stone.

Twenty

Christopher Bellman had suddenly decided that he absolutely must see Millie. After her wonderful "yes" to him, he had felt happy and at peace and quite content not to see her for a while. He had felt her to be delightfully stored up and safe, a prize reserved and labelled, a perfume sealed, and he had returned to his work and felt more serene, he thought, than ever in his life. This serenity had been disturbed by two things. First, he had been extremely excited and upset by the news of the projected rebellion, which had been followed so soon by the news of its cancellation. This sudden glimpse of another Ireland, so close and yet so hidden, filled him with a distress which seemed like guilt. For a second he had felt the warm, quick movement of Irish history risen out of books alive, alive-o. He was stirred, magnetized, then disappointed, relieved. The second thing was that Frances, later that afternoon, had told him that she was not going to marry Andrew. Then it became essential to see Millie.

He set off on his bicycle and would have arrived at Rathblane earlier in the evening, only just as he was beginning to get into the mountains he had a puncture. He left the bicycle and walked on, imagining that the distance was shorter than it was. Then it became dark and he missed his way. When, very tired and drenched with rain, he at last reached Millie's front door he was extremely startled at being jumped upon by a man suddenly issuing from the doorway. As he picked himself up it seemed that the man, who had now faded into the moonlight, was Pat Dumay. He went in through the open door.

The hall was very dark and as soon as he came in it seemed to him that someone who was standing in the darkness moved away, with a soundless displacement of air, into one of the rooms. Almost at once a moving light was seen up above and Millie appeared, wearing a white gown. She began to glide quickly down the stairs, carrying the lamp, her gown flowing out behind her, her loose hair lifted. When she was halfway down, the lamplight showed her Christopher and she stopped abruptly.

"Millie, what on earth's happening? Somebody rushed out at me. I thought it was—"

"Hello, Christopher," said Millie. "Good evening." She put the lamp down on the stairs and sat down beside it. Then she began to laugh helplessly. She rocked quietly to and fro, moaning with laughter.

"I'm sorry I've come so late," said Christopher. "I'd have got here much earlier, only I got a puncture and had to walk the last bit. But, Millie, what—"

Millie stopped laughing. "Please, Christopher, would you go into the drawing-room and wait there? I'll put on some clothes and join you in a few minutes." She went back up the stairs, taking the lamp with her and leaving Christopher in darkness.

Christopher fumbled his way to the drawing-room door and fell through it, knocking his head on the big Chinese screen whose position just inside the door he had forgotten. There was no fire, and the room smelt of damp textile and turf ash. He stood still until he could discern the squares of the windows and shuffled towards them. There was a sound of scuffling overhead, and he thought he heard voices.

Christopher was feeling very confused. During his long walk along the dark mountain road he had been all the time anxious simply to arrive. He disliked walking. The mountains were frightening at night; there were sounds, presences. He had hurried on, looking forward to finding Millie up, a blazing fire, a welcoming glass of whiskey. But the uphill walk had taken such a long time. And now here he was, hustled away, left in the dark and the cold, not looked after in the least. And who was that person who had rushed out of the door and knocked him down? He realized that his arm was hurting from the fall and his head was aching from the encounter with the Chinese screen. Was it Pat Dumay? What was he doing bursting out of the house as if the devil was after him? And who was the mysterious moving figure in the hallway? And what was all that curious scuffling going on in the room above? Christopher felt very puzzled and very ill-used. He pawed several tables, looking for matches, but only succeeded in overturning something which fell onto the floor with a crash. It sounded as if it was broken. He began to feel his way back to the door.

Before he could reach it, Millie came in with the lamp. She was wearing her plainest grey walking dress, with a red woollen shawl over her head. She put the lamp down, carefully pulled the curtains, and then lit another lamp.

"Please sit down, Christopher."

"I'm so sorry, I've broken that vase. I was looking for the matches."

"It doesn't matter. It's only Ming or something. For God's sake, Christopher, sit down."

"My dear Millie, I'm only too anxious to sit down once you've given me time to take off this extremely damp mackintosh. And I think you might give me some whiskey. I've had a very long walk."

"Oh, yes, of course, whiskey, there's some in the cupboard. Wait a moment. Here you are."

"Millie, is something funny going on here? Was that Pat Dumay? And is there somebody else in the house? I thought I saw someone in the hall as I came in."

"No, there's no one here but me. The maids all sleep in the annexe."

"What was Pat doing here and why did he push me like that? I nearly broke my arm. I'm sorry I came so late, but as I told you I had a puncture and—"

"I should think he pushed you like that because you were in his way when he wanted to go out of the door. I'm sorry about your arm and I'm sorry about your bicycle and I'm sorry—"

"But what did he *want?*"

"What did he want? He wanted me." Millie laughed. She kicked a piece of the broken vase across the floor and turned to stare at Christopher.

He now took in her elated, excited face, flushed with an onset of laughter or tears. Her hair was plaited in a single plait, which she had drawn forward over her shoulder and was convulsively clutching and tugging together with the folds of the red shawl.

"What on earth do you mean?"

"He came here to seduce me."

"Millie! Surely you hadn't given him any reason to think—"

"No, of course I hadn't given him any reason to think. I sent him away with a flea in his ear."

"But he can hardly just have taken it into his head—"

"Why shouldn't he just have taken it into his head? Or do you think I'm not attractive enough?"

"Of course I think you're attractive enough—"

"Then there's nothing more to explain, is there?"

"Millie, I'm very surprised indeed."

"Well, I can't help that. Nothing happened. I just sent him off. That's why he was in such a hurry. You do believe me, don't you?"

"Of course I believe you. But, as I say—"

"Why did *you* take it into your head to come, Christopher?"

"I had to see you. So many things have been happening. I'm sorry to arrive so late, but as I told you—"

"Yes, yes, your bike. Tell me some of the things that have been happening."

'Well—Frances has decided not to marry Andrew."

"Ah—" Millie let go of the red shawl, which fell in a heap behind her. She moved forward and began quickly picking up the fragments of the Chinese vase. "It's so cold in here, we could do with a fire, couldn't we." She put the fragments of the vase on the table. She advanced on the fireplace and bent to put a match to the paper and sticks. "Hand over a couple of those little logs, would you?"

"Millie, did you hear what I said?"

"Of course I did, but what am I supposed to say about it? I'm sorry."

"It won't make any difference to us, of course. That's what I wanted to come and tell you. I'll manage about Frances."

"Have you told Frances about us?"

"No."

"That's just as well, perhaps."

"Why?"

"Christopher, I think I can't marry you after all."

"Millie, what on earth are you talking about?"

"I just can't. I'd be no use to you."

"Is this because of Frances?"

"No, it's nothing to do with Frances. I just can't do it, it would be wrong. Please forgive me. I should never have let the idea exist at all."

"Millie, I can't let you say this—" He got awkwardly and stiffly to his feet stretching out his arms towards her. Millie continued to stare down at the crackling sticks, whose light flickered on her face, showing a serene exhausted smile.

"Millie, my darling—" Christopher took her hand, lifting it from her side. It was heavy and limp. Her hand was familiar to him, and as he touched her his fingers became aware of something unusual. He looked down and saw that she was wearing a ring adorned with diamonds and rubies. He recognized the ring.

When Millie saw Christopher's expression and saw what he was looking at she withdrew her hand with an exclamation and moved away from him.

"Millie, why are you wearing Andrew's ring?"

She pulled it quickly off and laid it on the table. "Because Andrew has been wearing my ring."

"I don't understand."

"Well, why should you, with such an awful lot going on? I've just seduced your would-be son-in-law. I didn't mean to tell you. I just forgot about the ring. I never seem to be able to do wrong with impunity. What an unlucky girl I am!"

"Millie, do you actually mean that you—"

"Yes. I was in bed with Andrew when Pat turned up. I'd invited Pat to be my lover, only I didn't think he would oblige, so I made do with Andrew instead. It was all most unfortunate, and I'm a very disappointed woman."

"Millie, are you seriously saying that you and Andrew—"

"Yes! I've said it as clearly as I can. Do you want me to say it again?"

"How can you talk in that tone?"

"Well, a woman caught in my situation has got to adopt some tone, and it's not easy to combine devastating frankness with calm dignity. What tone do you suggest?"

"I just can't believe you."

"Have a good try. The fact is I'm in love with Pat, I'm desperately in love with Pat and I have been for ages, only of course it's hopeless, and it would have been hopeless even if Andrew hadn't been here tonight. And our thing would have been hopeless even if you hadn't found out about Andrew. I really think you'd better go, Christopher. Oh, hang it, you can't, you haven't got a bike."

"In love with Pat. I see."

"Yes, the real thing. I'd let him walk on me. If only I'd just wanted the best and stayed true to it, it would have come to me. It *did* come to me, and I muffed it."

"But you said it would have been hopeless anyway. And you have a rather quaint idea of the best. One night in bed with Pat Dumay. You know he'd have hated you in the morning."

"Yes, you understand Pat. But you don't quite understand me. I'm an odder fish than you imagine, Christopher. Perhaps one night would have been enough, perhaps it would have been everything, and perhaps such hatred would be purer than the purest love. But it's all lost now. I've been unfaithful to my own code. You muddled me, the money business muddled me. And now he despises me and I expect you do too. I think I'll have some whiskey."

"So you took Andrew. And that was why Frances refused him. I see it all now. It was because of you. I knew you were pretty irresponsible but I didn't think you were utterly wicked."

"Oh, God, you don't think *that?*" Millie jarred the whiskey bottle back onto the table. "I'm not that bad. I didn't do anything with Andrew, it didn't enter my head, until after he'd told me Frances had turned him down. Honest, Christopher. You can't really believe I'm capable of—"

"I'm afraid, Millie, that I think you capable of anything."

They stared at each other in silence. Then Millie took the bottle again and unsteadily poured some whiskey into her glass. She murmured, "It's funny. At this moment I think I'm almost in love with you. I told you I was a bit odd."

"There was obviously some guilty secret between you last Monday when you had the boy to tea with Hilda. I thought he was behaving very strangely. But I didn't dream—"

"Oh, that. That was just a silly joke I played on him, it's not even worth explaining."

"Frances could have had no other reason for refusing Andrew. It was all fixed up."

"It wasn't all fixed up. And she could have had any reason for refusing him. He's not very clever. He's not even all that good-looking."

"You say this just after you've dragged him into bed with you."

"All right, I'm vulgar as well as wicked. But it's true."

"Where is he now, by the way?"

"Halfway back to Dublin, I hope. He was supposed to slip out just after I came down again. What a pity, you might have borrowed his bike." Millie started to laugh again, but stopped abruptly. "You *can't* believe it, Christopher, you just can't believe that I would have seduced Andrew while he was engaged to Frances. I couldn't possibly have done anything so cruel, I'm not cruel, I'm just silly. And anyway I wanted Andrew to marry Frances just as you did because of us."

"But you said just now you were in love with Pat and you knew our thing was no good anyway."

"Yes—I do seem in rather a muddle, don't I? But I swear I didn't—"

"You might have done this deliberately to break up Frances' engagement so as to have an excuse for dropping me. I regard you as an utterly mad and destructive person, and I always have."

"Then you shouldn't have envisaged marrying me."

"I entirely agree I shouldn't."

They stood now facing each other across the table. What on earth is happening, Christopher asked himself, why are we shouting like this, am I dreaming? His weariness, his wet clothes, the strong dose of whiskey, made him feel dazed and light-headed. The figure of Millie stood out before him with a ghastly sharpness, an object detached from a flat background. He swayed, then went and sat down heavily.

"Anyway it's not going to happen now," said Millie in a dull voice. She began to push the ring about the surface of the table with her finger. "I know it all serves me right. If you behave rottenly you can't complain when other people don't realize just *how* rottenly you're prepared to behave. But, Christopher, you must believe what I said. Andrew came and told me that Frances had turned him down, and then, just to cheer him up you know, I suggested—"

"How long had it been going on?"

"It had been going on for about two hours when Pat arrived, and—"

"I don't mean that! How long before today?"

"Not at all before today."

"Why did you say our thing would have been no good even if I hadn't found out?"

"Because of Pat. Well, no, not because of Pat. Pat wasn't really anything to do with that. I thought of these things in separate parts of my mind. It was no good anyway, it was a bad kind of idea. We don't love each other enough, Christopher."

"I suppose it's true," he said slowly. "We don't."

It was raining again. The wind blew the light rain against the windows in intermittent sighing gusts that were like a soft ripple of waves.

"Well, there it is. God, I feel wretched. Damn, we've let the fire go out."

Christopher got up and found his mackintosh. "I must go now."

"You can't go in all this rain. And I haven't got a bike to lend you."

"Don't worry, I'll walk."

"Don't be idiotic, Christopher, you know perfectly well you've got to stay here. There's a room ready. You'd die of exposure walking all the way down the mountain."

Christopher threw down his coat. He was ready to weep. "All right, all right."

"And here, you'd better take the ring to give back to Andrew. I don't suppose I'll ever see *him* again. Everybody hates me now."

"I don't want the ring— Oh, all right, I'll take it."

"Well, no, maybe you'd better not. It would hurt him so terribly to know you knew—"

"I don't care how hurt he is."

"You must forgive Andrew. He was very miserable, and he's so young."

"Oh, hang Andrew."

"You know, you should have given me a ring, Christopher, it might have protected me. Ah, well. I'll show you to your room. The bed's not aired, but I'll get you a hot-water bottle."

"Don't bother, I just want to be left alone now."

They went out, Millie carrying the lamp, and mounted the stairs slowly together like an old couple.

"This is your room. Are you sure you wouldn't—"

"No, thanks."

"I'll light your candle for you. There. Oh, I forgot, would you like anything to eat?"

"No, thank you, Millie."

"Christopher, you do believe me, don't you, that I didn't—"

"Yes, yes, yes, I believe you."

"Christopher, I'm awfully sorry about everything."

"It doesn't matter."

"Well, it does, but anyway. May I kiss you?"

"Oh, go away, Millie."

"Good night, my dear, sleep well."

"Good night."

Twenty-one

The movement of renewal with which I had hoped to associate my wife failed largely because of a complete lack of response on her part. I appreciated later that it was of course foolish of me to expect from her any understanding of the symbolic nature of my action and its sheer difficulty, or even any conceptual grasp of what I had to tell her. A being devoid of theory, living almost entirely at the level of intuition, she condemned me for what I was, but when I positively desired, even needed, her judgment upon what I had done, she withheld it, and seemed incapable of censuring, even of perceiving, anything as definite as an act. Absolution requires a definition of sin. My wife was unable to give me absolution.

Barney inhaled the fragrance of this paragraph and returned refreshed to consider the pad of paper on which, earlier that day, he had several times begun to compose a letter. It was Sunday afternoon.

Dear Frances,
    I feel it is my duty to pass on to you a piece of information which has lately come into my possession. I know for a positive fact that your fiancé has been having a love affair with Lady Kinnard. I am sorry to be a bringer of bad news, but I feel it is my duty . . .

He thrust the sheet aside and picked up a second version.

My dear Frances,
  It is sad to be a bringer of bad news to one one loves—and I think you do, you must, know the sincerity of my attachment to you. But there are moments when it is one's tragic duty to shatter a peace of mind which rests upon a misconception.

He studied this for some time, altered "sincerity of my attachment" to "warmth of my affection," and then put the paper down again.

Was it really his tragic duty to shatter a peace of mind which rested upon a misconception? Barney was in a state of excited distress with which his experience that morning at the Easter mass had mingled to produce a turmoil of emotions, now dark, now singularly light and glittering. The crowded church, the high exultation of the choir, the unveiled images, the heaped-up flowers: these impressions, as of emergence into a place of dazzling brightness, contrasted strangely and yet significantly with the sinister, dangerous, thief-like adventures of the night.

Barney had yielded to the temptation to go to Rathblane knowing quite well that he was doing something idiotic and improper. He was increasingly aware of all his activities as a mode of warfare against his wife, and the very fact that it was not altogether for Millie that he wanted to go made the action seem at first even more a wrong one. If Kathleen had only co-operated with him and entered into the drama of his change of heart she could, he felt, really have changed him. He would have given up seeing Millie. But in order to be able to do what he so pure-heartedly intended he needed a motive which only Kathleen could give him. Her inability to see the mechanics, as it were, of his good intentions he read as a condemnation of him far deeper than any he had ever before experienced. He felt suddenly that Kathleen regarded him as hopeless. All right, he would behave accordingly.

This was what he thought at first. But as he cycled towards Rathblane in the evening and breathed the mountain air and saw

the quick fugitive sun on distant green fields and watched a rainbow grow slowly from the lower slopes of Kippure he experienced a youthful sensation of pleasure at being a man going
towards a woman he loved. He no longer felt that this was part
of his fight with Kathleen or had anything to do with Kathleen at
all. In thus obeying his heart he was doing something essentially
innocent. He needed to see Millie, and there was a redeeming
simplicity in satisfying the need. Perhaps his whole moral scheme
had become too complicated? If he could only get out of the old
familiar web of guilt and justification and back to the things he
just wanted to do and the doing of them, then he might become
innocent and harmless as he had once been. As the sun went
down behind Kippure and the fields glowed a luminous dusty
gold before becoming dark, it began to seem to Barney that his
wants and his needs were very simple and without corruption.

He had obeyed the impulse to go where Millie was without
having any special plan about what he would do when he arrived.
He hoped, of course, to find Millie alone, to come to her as at
their happiest times and be received by that especial laughter
which she reserved for him, to be called to her joyously like an
animal. The thought that this could still happen made him smile
happily as he pushed his bicycle up the steeper parts of the road.
If, however, he was unlucky and Millie had company he would
have to decide whether to let her know that he had come or
whether to remain concealed. At various times in the past Barney
had observed Millie without revealing his presence. These expe-
riences, invariably painful, yet gave him a guilty thrill and a
pleasure even more obscure and profound. It was something that
took him straight back to certain pleasures of childhood. And
more reflectively he could treat this pleasure-pain as a gift which
he gave to Millie, as a form of homage.

The thought that someone else might be there brought back
again to his mind the melancholy prospect of her marriage to
Christopher. Since what now seemed to him his mystical experience on Thursday Barney had set aside the whole problem of

Christopher and had ceased to feel the temptation to tell Frances her father's intentions. Now the problem and the temptation had reappeared, and constituted, in fact, an extra motive for going at once to see Millie. Unable in certain moods to believe in his misfortune, Barney felt that perhaps, after all, it was unlikely that Millie would really marry Christopher. Nothing was fixed, the future was still uncertain. And, although he did not really think that he could positively ask Millie what she intended to do, he needed to see her as a sort of reassurance. He felt that when he actually saw her he would be quite sure that everything between him and her was going to be all right, and, indeed, better than ever.

On arriving at Rathblane in the darkness Barney had noticed a bicycle which he knew not to be Christopher's leaning against the wall. On penetrating into the house by methods well known to him he had heard voices. With the thrilled curiosity which caused him such painful pleasure he had crept closer. He had then learnt first the identity, and then the errand, of Millie's visitor. This discovery caused him at first simply an intense moral shock. Millie and Andrew were both quite suddenly revealed to him as wicked, and wicked with a blackness which faded his own moral frailty to the palest grey. After the first shock he felt amazed, indignant jealousy, sheer fright at being the possessor of so potent a secret, and finally a childish misery that his Millie, who had played such harmless, pretty games with him, should elect to play *this* game with another. These reflections were interrupted by the arrival of Pat. Barney, who had been standing in the dark on the landing, heard someone enter below and hid himself quickly in one of the rooms opposite. Later he heard Pat's voice in the dressing-room.

Barney, who had been feeling scared before, was now terrified. He was in a state of total confusion concerning the nature and consequences of his discovery, and he had just made a colossal moral judgment which he was still entirely unable to assimilate. With Pat's arrival Barney became suddenly sensitive to another aspect of the matter, his own guilt as an eavesdropper, a guilt vastly potentiated by the magnitude of what he had overheard. If they were to find him there listening to them in the dark there could be no forgiveness then. Pat, moreover, was the last person in the world before whom Barney could have endured to feel that particular shame.

He did not speculate about Pat's visit or attempt to overhear any more. He tiptoed down the stairs and stood at the back of the hall, wondering if it was safe to leave the house. As he was still hesitating Pat came running down the stairs and out of the front door. A moment later the door reopened and Pat, as it seemed to Barney, came back into the house again. Barney waited no longer, but slid away into the kitchen quarters and out into the paved yard, where he waited a while until the moon was again obscured and then went to rejoin his bicycle.

The next morning the pattern of his feelings had shifted. His indignation against Andrew was more extreme, while his indignation against Millie was tempered by a kind of pity which made him feel for the first time superior to her. He felt also a kind of triumphant relief at having found out so much and escaped with impunity. His jealousy had diminished, merging into a tender sense of responsibility for Millie, and a sober recognition that he now held a very powerful weapon against her. His previous temptation, to reveal Christopher's intentions to Frances, now seemed a feeble, pointless affair. It was, it remained, unclear what could be the result of this revelation. But now Barney had at his disposal an infallible method of achieving both his objects, the separation of Millie from Christopher and the separation of Frances from Andrew. Would he employ this method?

Perhaps it was better not to meddle. Since *that* had happened and would presumably be happening again, it was unlikely that the two marriages that he feared would come off anyway. The apple cart was sure to be upset without his intervention. If by any chance, however, Frances or Millie did marry, not only would Barney never be able to forgive himself for not having spoken sooner, he knew that he would be irresistibly impelled to make the revelation later on when it was too late to do anything but damage. So was it not, considering all the facts including his own weakness, his plain duty to write to Frances?

Barney went to the Easter mass like a sleep-walker. He had decided on the previous day to go, and now went automatically. Then quite suddenly, as if someone had come into the room and lightly touched him as he sat absent-mindedly, he was reminded of where he was and what occasion was being honoured. He recalled his good resolutions of three days ago, when he had decided to simplify his life and make peace with Kathleen. Had that been mere meaningless emotion or had it been truly the pressure of another world upon his darkness? He remembered how he had felt sunk in himself beyond the possibility of change. Then, when this freedom had suddenly been breathed upon him, he had jerked up, he had certainly moved; but he had moved still in the old way, projecting his stale self in a new direction; and as soon as there was any check to his fantasy he had despaired at once. He had wanted a formal punishment. But perhaps his penance was simply informality. The terrible thought occurred to him that possibly he ought simply to act rightly and expect no one even to notice it.

The mass impressed him with the notion of an event, a change. Attending to it, he began to feel an obscure distress, a pang as at the loss of something. He never really liked the ending of Lent. He was never quite ready to finish with mourning when the great peal of joy rang out. Suddenly now it occurred to him why.

> *Dic nobis, Maria,*
> *Quid vidisti in via?*
> *Sepulcrum Christi viventis*
> *Et gloriam vidi resurgentis.*

Mary Magdalen might indeed have glimpsed Him in the garden somewhere, but for the rest of us there remained only the empty tomb. "He is not here." The Christ who travels towards Jerusalem and suffers there can be made into a familiar. The risen Christ is something suddenly unknown. This metamorphosis had always in the past represented for Barney simply a disappointment, like the ending of a play. He had never thought of it as a starting point. He thought of it so now for the first time; and, with this shift of view, it became clear to him, with a sudden authoritative clarity, that it was the risen Christ and not the suffering Christ who must be his saviour: the absent Christ hidden in God and not that all too recognizable victim. He was too horribly, too intimately connected with his own degraded image of the Christ of Good Friday. Easter must purge that imagery now. The scourged, tormented flesh appealed to something in him that was too grossly human, since he had not the gift of compassion. These sufferings ended for him in self-pity and further on and shamefully in pleasure. This could not alter him a jot though he contemplated it forever. What was required of him was something which lay quite outside the deeply worked pattern of suffering, the plain possibility of change without drama and even without punishment. Perhaps after all that was the message of Easter. Absence, not pain, would be the rite of his salvation.

As Barney walked home from mass he also recalled to his mind events of yesterday which his visit to Rathblane had made him totally forget. For a short time, a period perhaps of two hours, he had believed that the Volunteers were about to start an armed rising. Even though he had so incomprehensibly, and it now seemed to him stupidly, surrendered his rifle, a sacrifice not to God but to his own vanity, he was nevertheless an Irish Volunteer. He was a careless, lax, muddle-headed one, but still he was a Volunteer, and he had pledged himself to fight for Ireland should the moment ever come. Then by a connection of thought which led him back through what seemed to him the best moments of his life, he recalled Clonmacnoise, and the little roofless chapel and the abandoned stones and the great empty sweep of the

Shannon. *Numen inerat.* And the presence there had been not only God but Ireland. Tears sprang into his eyes.

Barney had joined the Volunteers partly but not entirely to please Pat. He had joined, too, because he loved Ireland and pitied that history of suffering and because he knew that it might in the end be necessary to fight for rights which had been too long withheld. Barney had a strong sense of history but very little sense of politics, and he acted here by intuition. He had expected everything from Ireland, from her darkness and her beauty, he had run to her as to a mother and a place of shriving. And, although his life had been a disappointment and a muddle, it did not occur to him to blame Ireland for this. He had abandoned his book on the saints. It was he who was the traitor. That dark perfection remained near him and untouched, and he loved it. He owed Ireland that service. He had thought so when he joined the Volunteers and he had ineluctably thought so again during the dreadful two hours of yesterday. He had been intensely relieved to learn that he had not got to fight after all.

Barney now sat in his room and looked at the letters to Frances which he had begun earlier in the morning before he went to mass. He could still not think quite clearly about the problem, but it seemed to him that the letters were unworthy. Perhaps Frances ought to know, and perhaps Christopher ought to know, what had happened, but this did not yield the result that he ought to tell them. Any meddling of his here would be evil. He could not, just automatically could not, act with a pure interest, and he ought not to cause fear, misery, and hatred without one. Andrew, Millie, Frances, and Christopher must take their chance and work out the design of their fate without interference from him. It must be as if he had never known, never seen, that which he knew and saw, or as if he must forever admit that he could not understand it. Inaction, agnosticism, were for him the lessons of the empty tomb. And then it had come to him that with Kathleen, too, it must be the same. He must not expect to understand Kathleen or to be understood by her. He must not expect her to help him to make a tidy drama out of his infidelities or to make him suffer in exactly the way he wanted. He must just do the right thing simply, even surreptitiously, and let what would follow follow mechanically.

Barney, having come through this maze of speculation, now felt himself brought up with a jerk like a horse that has browsed its way to the end of its tether. So he had come to the same conclusion again but by a different route. Now that the working out was different could the act be done? Could he really surrender Millie? He leaned his head forward on the table, closing his eyes, resting, and then realized that he was praying.

"Barney, I'm so sorry, I've wakened you up. There was no answer when I knocked, so I just came in to leave a note."

Frances was there.

Barney sat up abruptly.

"Oh, Frances, come in. I must have been asleep for a moment. I'm so glad to see you. I've been so wanting to see you."

He got up, fussing round about her, murmuring, touching her, and her presence in the room made him intensely happy. He felt as if somehow while he slept a problem had been solved, a burden lifted.

"Here, let me help you off with your wet things. Your umbrella will be all right there in the corner, let it drip, it won't hurt. Would you like some tea? But oh, my dear, what is it?"

Barney, now that Frances had taken off her hood, saw her face and that she must have been crying. She sat down beside the table, flattening the damp streaky hair back against her head.

"I've just come to say good-bye."

"Good-bye? But are you going away?"

"Yes, I'm going to England. I'm going to be a V.A.D. I'm going to the war." She did not look at him but stared across the little heaped-up table at the lines of faded cottage gardens upon the powdery dry wallpaper. Her mouth drooped.

"But why ever—"

"Why not? One ought to do one's bit. I may be totally uneducated, but at least I can cut bread and butter."

"But what about, what about—Andrew?" Barney felt as if his guilty knowledge must all come tumbling out of his mouth attached to the name.

"Oh, that. That's all over. I'm not going to marry Andrew, you know. We've decided not to get married after all."

Barney circled the room, rebounding from the walls in his excitement. He longed to question Frances, but could not think how to do it. "Not marry Andrew. All over. Well, fancy. Oh, dear. I'm so sorry. What a surprise, though. I do hope you're not sad about it. I do wish you weren't going away."

"I'm sorry to go, Barney, and I'm specially sorry to leave you. I'll miss you. But it'll do me good to get out of Ireland. With the war and so on, Ireland is a bit of a hole. And I have been in such a stupid mood lately. I won't stay more than a minute now. I see you're working. Is it Saint Brigid?"

Frances picked up a sheet of paper from the table.

"Wait, not that!" Too late Barney jumped. She was already reading the letter.

There was a moment's silence as she read it, put it down, then rested her head in her hand with an almost inaudible "Oh."

After another moment she said in a tired, spiritless voice, "How did you know this, Barney?"

Interpreting her tone he said quickly, "So you know?"

"Yes."

"How did you find out?"

"First tell me how you did?"

"I was there last night, at Rathblane. I went to see Millie and found—"

"Pat and Andrew. Yes. You didn't see my father. He was there too. There was quite a gathering. Just like comic opera."

"Christopher—so he knows—"

"Yes, and he told me this morning."

"And then you broke things off with Andrew."

"No, no. I'd refused Andrew days ago, I mean we'd decided not to marry. That was nothing to do with Millie. Millie's not a monster. She didn't grab Andrew until after I'd dropped him. And he still thinks no one knows about his little adventure."

Barney held his head. It was complicated. But was it not now all right, utterly all right? Christopher knew, and Millie was innocent. Well, not quite, but almost. So everything would be all right. He would not have to lose Millie after all. But what was he saying?

Frances' voice interrupted him. "I'm reading the other letter now. I like the bit about your tragic duty. You must have enjoyed writing that. Which one were you going to send?"

Barney suddenly became aware of a different Frances, a Frances with a new vocabulary, a Frances who could talk in a cynical way, who could assess and sentence him. He felt hurt, then appallingly guilty. His instinct had been right. One could not so intrude one's abominable knowledge. He deserved to be hated for what he knew.

"Frances, darling, I was not going to send either of those letters, honest. It would have been utterly wrong and I'd decided not to. I was just going to tear them up."

"Oh." She did not believe him.

Barney jerked himself about, jostling the table and spilling the greater part of the Memoir onto the floor. He trampled the pages underfoot. He felt frantic. He was not going to get the credit for anything with anybody. And now she would never forgive him simply for knowing. "Frances, I *swear* I was not going to send those letters. I know I ought never to have written them—"

"Don't shout, Barney. It doesn't matter, I knew anyway, it doesn't matter. I really must go now. I've got so much to do."

"When are you going?"

"Tuesday or Wednesday."

"So you'll be on the mail boat after all. Frances, you do believe me?"

"Yes, yes, of course."

There was a sudden loud bang on the door and they both jumped. The door swung wide open to reveal the large form of Pat Dumay.

"I must be off," said Frances. She whipped her things together and was gone, fading thinly away under Pat's right arm.

Barney stared at where she had been, and then formed the face of Pat, huge, excited, grinning. "What is it, Pat?"

"Sit down. I want to ask you two questions."

Barney sat by the table and Pat closed the door carefully and sat beside him, placing his large hand on Barney's shoulder.

Barney sat open-mouthed, staring up at his stepson. He felt he was being apprehended for some fault. But the pressure of the hand was affectionate. Pat seemed to be in a state of anxious rapture. His left hand, which was bandaged, kneaded Barney's shoulder with a rhythmic clutch and caress, while he pressed his other hand flat upon the table as if he were about to vault. He leant over his stepfather.

"Listen now. You know the plan that you heard of yesterday? Well, we are going to carry it out tomorrow."

"You mean you're going to fight after all, the Volunteers, just like—"

"Yes. It's for tomorrow. I want to ask you first, do you want to join us, or would you rather be left out? No one will think the worse of you."

"I'll come with you, of course," said Barney.

There was silence between them for a moment. Then Pat released him and stood up. "You mean you're willing to fight?"

"Yes."

Pat stared at him doubtfully. Then he gave a grunt which might have been a sigh or a laugh. "Good for you."

"When is it to be tomorrow?"

"Twelve noon at the first stroke of the Angelus. I'll give you full instructions."

"What was the other thing you wanted to ask me?"

"It doesn't arise now. It was something about Cathal. But it would only have come up if you'd said no to the first question. I'm afraid I thought that you would. I apologize."

"Don't mention it," said Barney. "By the way, you'll have to issue me with another rifle."

When Pat was gone Barney stood beside his cluttered table and started at the powdery cottage gardens deep in the old wallpaper. He was extremely frightened. He had too, in a way that was not entirely disagreeable, a sense of being finally cornered. Whatever the state of his soul might be, his old existence was over, a life beyond his own had taken charge of him.

Would he have sent those letters to Frances in the end? Would he really have managed to give up Millie? He would get no credit. He was justly judged. Or rather it did not much matter now how he was judged. That was not so very important, after all.

He reached out for the two letters and took them and tore them into long strips. Then he picked up the crumpled sheets of the Memoir from the floor and began systematically to tear each sheet into small pieces.

Twenty-two

Pat Dumay began to mount the dark stairs to the attic. A lamp placed on the floor at the top cast thick shadows down beneath each stair and illuminated the figure of a man in Volunteer uniform who had just come to attention. Pat swayed with fatigue. He had been unceasingly active since the news had reached him on Sunday afternoon that the rebellion was to take place after all. Now it was already after midnight, it was already Easter Monday morning.

On Sunday morning MacNeill's countermanding order had appeared in the *Sunday Independent*. At the same time, Pearse, Connolly, MacDonagh, and all the chief militants came together for a meeting at Liberty Hall. At this meeting it was decided that in spite of MacNeill they must act. The rising was fixed again for twelve noon on Monday. Couriers were sent out to all parts of Ireland with the new order.

They all knew, and Pat knew perfectly well, that MacNeill's action had damaged the project perhaps irrevocably. The men, who had been keyed up, had relaxed. Some of them had gone away. A few had even destroyed their uniforms in disgust. There was an atmosphere of *détente* and disappointment and irresponsibility. Monday was the day of the Fairyhouse races, the Irish Grand National. Even if the messengers could, in time, reach every part of the organization, would the order be obeyed? Faint-hearts would find an excuse in the obvious confusion of the leadership. The first plan had administered a fright. Those who had learnt with relief of its cancellation would be in no mood to start again. They would say that they knew not whom to believe and they would go off to the races.

On Sunday Pearse and Connolly could have been sure of their numbers. On Monday it was anybody's guess how many men would turn up. This meant that a lot of quite new arrangements had to be made in a hurry, and crucial projects had to be abandoned, such as the cutting of all telephone contact with England, since there would now not be enough men to occupy the Dublin telephone exchange. An elaborate plan, the product of weeks and months of work, had to be scrapped in favour of a congeries of last-minute improvisations.

However, it was necessary to fight. The English might be slow-witted, but they were capable of reflection upon the events in Kerry; and, since so many people in Dublin now knew what had been intended, an informer would soon find his way to the Castle. It was surprising that he had not already done so. Then the English would have to act, they would have to disarm the whole movement; and the Irish would have the choice of firing a few disorganized shots or submitting tamely. These were compelling reasons for fighting. But they were haunted by another reason which nobody mentioned. History now required of them that they should shed their blood. They had planned and schemed and hoped for so long, and set going a train of events which now seemed to have a momentum of its own. On the morning of Sunday, April the twenty-third, at Liberty Hall, they could, in some quite ordinary sense of could, have decided otherwise. But everyone present felt their decision to be inevitable.

Pat reached the top of the stairs and the uniformed man saluted.

"How is my prisoner?"

"All safe, Sir."

"You may go now."

The guard unlocked the door and stepped aside, and Pat entered the room. The prisoner was Cathal.

Pat had decided to spend the night of Sunday to Monday at Blessington Street. This had been made possible by the timely departure of his mother to the country. Because of anxiety about Pat, she had been putting off a visit to an ailing elderly cousin. Now her mind had been entirely set at rest. Pat thought that what had impressed his mother most was reading MacNeill's notice in the *Sunday Independent*. After a Sunday paper had said that all was well, Kathleen was entirely reassured. Her joy took form immediately as an extreme concern for her ailing cousin, and she left Dublin by train after mass on Sunday.

Late on Sunday afternoon Pat had made the decision to detain Cathal. He knew that this was only a temporary solution, but he did not want a repetition of Saturday's drama. He had, of course, not told Cathal that the rebellion was going to take place after all, but Cathal might at any moment find this out and decide to hide himself from his brother. Hurrying back from the other end of Dublin, Pat was extremely relieved to find the boy in the house, and decoyed him upstairs and locked him in an attic, setting one of his own men there to guard him. He informed Cathal briefly about the renewed plan and told him that he would let him know later what his own part in it might be. Pat said this out of prudence so that Cathal might not be driven into a frenzy and attempt to climb out of the window. Pat was, in fact, determined that Cathal should have no part at all in the coming events.

But how on earth was he to bring this about? Pat was now more certain than ever that if his brother were exposed to danger he himself would become totally ineffective. He realized, realized it only perhaps now on Sunday with absolute clarity, that Cathal was as important to him as Ireland: was conceivably more important. When he knew this he was appalled. If this were so, then anything might happen, anything might be decided. Only then slowly he moved again in automatic performance of his tasks, for he knew that there was something else which would always weigh down the balance on the side of Ireland, and that was his own honour. He could not conceivably in any last or smallest particular fail the cause to which he was engaged. But he could not put it to himself that he must be ready to sacrifice Cathal. If anything happened to Cathal he would become incapable, blind, a mad man. He had got to save Cathal, not only because of Cathal but because of Ireland. But how?

When he had seen this problem, as, of course, he had seen it, from further back, it had seemed to Pat that he would manage either by arranging for his brother to be out of Ireland at the crucial moment or else by somehow incarcerating him. Pat had had too short a warning to adopt the former plan; he now saw at the last moment the difficulties of the latter. It was not realistic to imagine that Cathal could simply be imprisoned until the rising either was successful or was crushed. This might take weeks, months. All that could possibly be achieved would be to keep him prisoner until the fighting had started and hope that it would then be physically impossible for him to reach any of the places where the rebels were. If he could prevent Cathal from marching with Connolly's men he would have done all that he could. But even this was difficult, since—and Pat did not fully understand this until Sunday night—it was not just a matter of ropes or handcuffs or a locked door. Cathal would have to be guarded.

Cathal would have to be guarded or else he would do himself some serious damage. The problem of imprisoning him was like the problem of restraining, without an adequate cage, a strong and desperate animal. Obviously a locked door was not enough; and it is not so very simple to tie someone up in such a way that he cannot escape and also cannot hurt himself seriously in trying to. If Pat was to march away on Monday morning without the most crippling anxiety he must find somebody to stay with Cathal; but who? It was, after all, unfortunate that his mother had

gone away and could not now be reached. He could not honoura-
bly spare one of his own soldiers for this odd, entirely personal
task. He had thought first of his stepfather. But when Barney had
so simply and so unexpectedly elected to fight, Pat, taken aback,
had felt unable to deny him what was, after all, every Irishman's
right. To keep his stepfather well out of his own way he had
arranged for him to join the contingent at Boland's Mill, and
Barney had already gone to spend the night with a comrade in
the vicinity. Pat telephoned Christopher several times but got no
reply. He even thought of Millie, but she was presumably still at
Rathblane, which was not on the telephone. He continued with
his duties, acting as courier between Dawson Street and Liberty
Hall, without solving the problem. Would it be all right just to tie
Cathal up and lock the door? He visited the storeroom at Dawson Street and came away with a pair of handcuffs. The problem
obsessed and paralysed him; and now, late at night and almost
unconscious with tiredness, he had still not resolved it.

There was a small lamp burning inside the room. Cathal was
huddled on the bed in a rather unnatural position, and did not stir
when Pat came in. He seemed to have been sitting thus for a long
time, staring at the door.

Pat was now in full uniform. He had left his rifle and knapsack
downstairs but was wearing his bandolier and revolver. The
handcuffs were in his pocket. He closed the door and sat down
on the floor, leaning against it.

The attic had once been a maid's bedroom in the days when
there were maids at the house in Blessington Street, and it still
contained an iron bedstead and mattress, a washstand and an
upright chair and a coloured picture representing the Sacred
Heart. The little lamp, which was on the floor, showed the under-
side of innumerable cobwebs upon the yellow stained walls.
Close, pattering rain enclosed the room, the roof, the window,
made of rain. Pat looked at the picture and thought, But the heart
is not there in the middle of the body, it is on the left. Then he

recalled someone saying that in fact it was really in the middle though it was popularly said to be on the left. What would it be like to be shot in the heart? He realized that on sitting down he had almost fallen asleep and that Cathal had said something.

"What did you say, Cathal?"

"I said what are you going to do with me?"

What, what, what? Pat saw from the outline of Cathal's shadow on the wall that the boy was trembling. He could not see his face clearly through the rain and the sleep.

"That mattress must be damp," said Pat. "You shouldn't be sitting on it." He simply must not fall asleep. He got up, half staggering, opened the door, transferred the key to the inside, locked the door, and put the key in his pocket. He sagged down again to the floor.

"What are you going to do?"

"I don't know," said Pat. "You're a problem. Let's start at the beginning." He felt that there was some sort of logic here, some sort of consequential procedure which if he could go through step by step he might keep awake and reach a conclusion with independent authority. "Logic," he said aloud.

"What?"

"I said logic. Listen. Let's start at the beginning. I don't want you to take part in this business—you're too young."

"You can skip that bit," said Cathal. He began to uncurl his legs, which were obviously very stiff. He grimaced and rubbed his ankles and then knelt up on the mattress. "You're right about the damp."

"You're too young," said Pat, "and you must simply obey me and promise me that you'll stay at home tomorrow and not put yourself in danger. This is a job for professionals. You're not trained and you would only be a hindrance. Someone would have to look after you and you would do harm and not good to the cause. I know this is very hard, but you must be old enough and brave enough to understand it."

"I'm old enough and brave enough to fight," said Cathal. "You may still treat me as a child, but other people don't. And I can use a rifle, one of the I.C.A. fellows taught me. And—"

"I'm not arguing. I'm telling you what you are going to do."

"You're not my da. You used to beat me when you were stronger, but I'm just as strong now, and if I decide to go out of that door you can't stop me."

"You know perfectly well I can stop you with one hand. Cathal, be sensible—"

"I'm not going to obey you and I am going to fight tomorrow. Imagine you were me. Would you stay at home because your elder brother told you you were a little boy?"

Pat was silent. His head swayed. He must keep on talking. What was the next step? Logic. "In that case," said Pat, "you'll have to stay a prisoner." He touched the handcuffs in his pocket.

"Just you try and cage me."

It was evident to Pat that Cathal had thought just as hard on this subject as he had. "I can easily cage you. I'll lock the door."

"I'll kick the door to bits or get out of the window."

"I'll tie you up. I've got some handcuffs too."

"I'll scream the place down and drum on the wall with my feet. There are people in these rooms on either side. The whole street would come and rescue me."

"I'd have to gag you."

"I'd swallow my gag and choke or else get a scream out somehow."

Pat knew that he could not gag Cathal. It is very difficult to gag a desperate person with safety. Pat's head swayed again. He was beginning to feel almost tearful with self-pity. He must sleep tonight and soon. He must make himself ready for tomorrow. Oh, God, tomorrow. There must be some way out of this agony. Logic.

"Pat," said Cathal. His face was indistinct among the cobwebs and the clatter of the rain. "Understand that it is no use trying to tie me up. I'd be like a wild animal in a trap that would bite its own leg off to get away. I'd get out or kill myself doing it. Imagine yourself—"

"I'll leave someone with you."

"There's no one you can spare. Everyone who knows will be out tomorrow and you can't trust anyone else. Besides, I'd get away whoever you left with me. It's too late now to keep me out of it. Let me come with you, Pat, I want to be with you, see that you've got to let me be with you."

Cathal's voice now was strained and childish, and Pat realized that Cathal, too, was in the last stages of exhaustion. Something had got to be decided, and he must not go to sleep. If he went to sleep now he would wake to find Cathal gone.

Pat moved, trying to keep himself conscious, and his arm brushed the holster of his revolver. He opened his eyes wide. It was perfectly simple, after all. He had only to shoot his brother in the leg.

Pat saw the room very clearly, as if it had only now been lighted up, the cobwebs slightly swaying in the air from the lamp, the blotched, sloping walls where the rain tapped, Christ displaying His Sacred Heart. Cathal was crouched on the bed underneath his shadow, moving himself about slightly, stiff and chilled upon the damp mattress. Pat saw his face sharply defined, pinched together about his long nose with tiredness and anxiety. There was a pathetic, exhausted defiance about the pouting mouth. Cathal's dark hair kept falling forward as if it were wearily trying to draw his head down.

Does he know what I am thinking? thought Pat as he stared. He fingered the revolver. Then somehow out of the dream he was almost in, out of the Sacred Heart, came the thought that he would kill Cathal. That would be simpler still. That would make him entirely safe. If Cathal were dead he would be beyond harm, and tomorrow Pat would be free to die himself. Was that not, after all, the best thing? He loved Cathal too much to allow him to be hurt by anyone else. Only Pat should hurt him, and that would be no hurt but simply to lay him to sleep. He loved Cathal too much.

Pat grunted and tried to get up and lurched to his knees. He had been thinking something that was insane or else he had been in a dream. He groaned and said, "Cathal, I've got to sleep, I've got to rest. Have some mercy on me."

"Promise that you'll let me go tomorrow."

"I can't, I can't."

"Promise, and then we can both sleep."

"I shall be lying here on my face in a minute," said Pat. He was not sure whether he had said the words aloud. Cathal would soon get the key out of his pocket. The room was indistinct again as if it were full of fumes.

"Promise."

"I promise," said Pat. "All right, I promise."

It was a lie. But what else could he do? He groaned, leaning against the door, trying to get up. He had to sleep. He would solve the problem tomorrow.

"You do really promise, you do?"

"Yes, yes. Where's the key? Here. Come down from here. You must go to your own room. We've both got to sleep now. Come."

The stairway opened and the lamp was still burning at the top of it. It was dark below like a pit. Pat held onto the bannisters. "Can you carry that lamp, Cathal?"

He pushed open the door of Cathal's room, and the light showed it. The lamp jolted down onto the table. Cathal, his head drooping, took off his shoes and his trousers and got into bed. He started to say something, but it turned into a drowsy mumble and in a moment he was fast asleep.

Pat looked about the familiar little room: the bookcase with Cathal's books staggering upon the shelves, the pictures of birds pinned to the wall, Cathal's model yacht. It seemed his own childhood that was present here. He had had indeed, with Cathal, a second boyhood, a second innocence. For the first time he grasped what was going to happen tomorrow as a nightmare, as something terrible. He had so often seen his brother lie down to sleep like that on holidays when they were as tired as they were tonight; and they slept and in the early morning went swimming in the cold sea. Would it never be like that again? Tomorrow he would be killing men. Could the nightmare not pass away and leave them innocent and free in the morning? He leaned over his brother, thrusting back the dark lock of hair from his face and touching that place upon his temple where the muzzle of a revolver might be pressed. Had Cathal got to die? Had he got to die? They were so young. He suddenly recalled and understood his mother's words: there is no such thing as dying for Ireland.

Twenty-three

Soon after nine o'clock on Easter Monday morning Second Lieutenant Andrew Chase-White was walking briskly up Blessington Street. He had decided that he must have some sort of explanation with his cousin Pat.

Andrew had decided to go to Rathblane not really because his interest in Millie had increased: that interest steadily diminished, reaching zero when he was actually in bed with her. His best, he thought afterwards his purest, moment with Millie had been when he first kissed her. This event, like a rocket suddenly bursting and slowly descending, had cast a shower of fading light over his subsequent movements. He felt drugged, romantic; but it was despair that made him act. The loss of Frances, as the news of it came to the different, the outlying, regions of his consciousness made his whole being into something restless and diseased. He could not see how, moment to moment, to exist any more. He put off informing his mother of the catastrophe and suffered her questions with churlish writhing. He resolved to return at once to England, but recalled that he had to report to Longford at the end of the week. This obligation, which might have seemed a consoling necessity of fate, tormented him too, and he thought: I shall be sent out *there*, I shall be killed, and nothing will have had any meaning. I shall have done nothing, I shall not even have understood. Frances was the whole meaning of my life, and now my life has no meaning and is empty.

The sense was one of emptiness and of strewn pieces and of the sudden disappearance of any picture of himself. A week ago he had occupied himself, packed himself tight with satisfied being, and glimpsed all about him the reflection of a handsome young British officer, the darling of the world, a fine young man with a bride. Now he could scarcely believe that his physical appearance was not utterly altered. He could indeed feel the expression of his face puckering and sagging as if his head were shrinking. He was empty and ragged within: and he felt at moments that his whole body must collapse in obedience to a vacuum.

He went to Millie simply in order to have some action, something, to fill up the void. He felt that Millie might make him into a person again. His altered being must acquire a history. He must have something to remember that was un-Frances. What sort of new person Millie might make of him, and whether she might not, like Circe, change him into a brute, it did not occur to him to wonder. He was in the state of misery which dispenses with all question of right and wrong. He wanted an experience, a transformation. The little glow, not yet faded, from the moment of the kiss, cast a rosy light upon Millie's image, like a cult statue seen by the light of a fire. She was all that was electrical, and magical, and naked. And Andrew did not want to die without having been to bed with a beautiful woman.

Even so he would have funked it if Millie had not, directly on his arrival, made him very drunk with whiskey. He hardly remembered how he had got into her bedroom. But he remembered the rest. Millie reclining unclothed in the lamplight, her hair undone, her legs relaxed and slightly parted, her hands folded on her shiny plump stomach, Millie propped up by pillows, revealed, offered, seemed to him an utter stranger and filled him

with fright. He did not know where to look at her. Her face, at
once dazed, complacent, and vulnerable, seemed to him unrecog-
nizable and obscene. He undressed miserably, hiding himself, and
felt as he took off his trousers that he was become spindly and
shrimp-like, a little white thing that might at any moment fall
through a crack in the floor.

Of course it had been no good. He had been almost in tears.
He shivered all over as if he were cold, and did indeed feel very
cold. Pimply gooseflesh rose leprously along his thighs. He did
not know how to touch Millie. His hands would not obey him,
but like recalcitrant animals curled up or sought refuge beneath
his arms or behind his back. He sagged and lumbered in the bed
like a paralytic; and Millie's brisk attempts to arouse his interest
filled him with a disgust of himself which approached nausea. At
the same time he felt intensely sorry for Millie and ashamed for
her, wanting to veil, to conceal her too eager face, working away
so close to his. The rest of her body he dared not look at, and to
conceal his shrinking he became like stone. He longed to leave
her, longed for the decency of clothes, but still he slumped there
in the bed, sinking into an insensibility which was almost like
sleep.

The arrival of Pat awoke him to a pain of quite a different
order. He was like someone lying half conscious on the mud who
suddenly receives a bayonet in the ribs. With clumsy haste he got
himself dressed, listening to the voices of Pat and Millie in the
next room. He had no doubt that Pat had recognized him; and
when he pictured what it was that Pat had seen from the doorway he wondered whether he had not better just shoot himself
and be done with it. When Millie called him out he could hardly
force himself through the door and leaned there helplessly, trying
to control a pitiful shuddering in his face. He did not then reflect
why Pat had come. He only knew that he had been seen thus,
and seen by the person who, it was suddenly clear to him, mattered most in the world.

On Sunday Andrew took his bicycle and set off early for the

country. He wanted to avoid his mother, who was asking whether he and Frances would not come with her to the Easter service at the Mariners' Church. He intended to cycle to Howth, which had nothing to recommend it except that it was the opposite way from Rathblane. In fact, he got as far as Clontarf and took refuge from the rain in a bar, where he sat for several hours. It did then occur to him to wonder why Pat had arrived so late at Millie's house and had come straight up to her bedroom. He had been far too agitated to overhear any of their conversation. But he could not really attend to this problem, nor indeed did he care about it. Millie herself had been blotted out of his mind. All that remained was his shame and Pat as the witness of it. With this there returned to him, flooding and burning his heart, all his childhood love for his cousin. Sitting in the dingy bar in Clontarf, he buried his face in his hands.

Andrew thought, at first hopelessly and as of something impossible, of going to see Pat and demanding from him some kind of help, some healing touch. Only Pat could heal this wound of which Andrew now felt himself likely to die. If he could only remove that picture of himself from Pat's consciousness forever; or, if that was impossible, at least in some way modify or overlay it. But how could he do this? There was no possible explanation of what Pat had seen which would make it less disgusting and less base than it was. Yet if he could only talk to Pat about it, perhaps tell him about Frances, or accuse himself in Pat's presence, this might a little lessen the pain. The idea was impossible; Pat would be cold and scornful or would refuse to talk at all. He would simply not participate in Andrew's scene. The idea was absurd; and yet it was also impossible to report at Longford, to return to France, with this horror unresolved and some alleviation, however small, unattempted. By Sunday night Andrew was beginning to be certain that he would make the attempt. On Monday morning, after a sleepless night, he knew that he could not endure any more hours without seeing Pat.

A light rain was drifting down as Andrew approached the

Dumays', house and flashes of bright sunlight were making the wet pavements dazzling. The door of the house was unlocked as usual. Andrew did not knock but pushed the door cautiously open. He did not want to meet Cathal or Aunt Kathleen and hoped that he might be able to slink straight upstairs to Pat's room. Sick with anticipation, he stood for a moment in the hall to listen. He heard voices in the kitchen.

Andrew moved quietly towards the kitchen door, deciding that if Pat was in there he would just go on up to Pat's room and wait. He did not want to meet him in company. He listened.

"And you won't worry any more about letting me fight? I'll be all right, surely."

"Yes, yes."

"And you'll let me have a gun? Sure I can use a rifle."

"I don't know."

"Will we be firing on them directly when it all starts at twelve?"

"I'll do what I'm told and so will you."

"Why can't we go straight to Dublin Castle and throw them out of there?"

"We haven't enough men."

"What I like to think of is the surprise there'll be this day! And they all saying we'd never fight!"

"Do shut up, will you, Cathal?"

"And when the shooting starts it'll be a revolution, just like James Connolly said. Sure Ireland will go mad."

"Did you lock the front door like I told you?"

"Yes, I did. Well, I'll just see. God, we'll fry the English! They'll—" Cathal opened the door and came face to face with Andrew.

Andrew had been listening with curiosity. He was struck by Cathal's excited tone, but he had not taken in the meaning of what was said. He now saw over Cathal's shoulder Pat Dumay in full Volunteer uniform and armed. At the same instant he grasped himself as a British officer in uniform and armed. But he still did not understand.

Cathal jumped back with an exclamation and then turned to Pat. "He was listening at the door!"

Pat said, or rather drawled, "Come inside, Andrew, come inside."

Andrew obeyed him automatically. His own private emotions and expectations in coming to the house were still clouding about his head, and this entirely new crisis left him bewildered.

Pat said, "Did you hear what we were speaking of just now?"

"Yes, but—"

"I'm afraid you must consider yourself my prisoner. Put your hands up, please."

Andrew realized that Pat was pointing a revolver at him. He tried to think how he should react, but all he felt was blinding surprise and shock. He did not raise his hands, but moved them a little from his sides in a gesture of helpless inquiry.

"Disarm him, Cathal."

Cathal quickly took Andrew's revolver from the holster and pushed it across the kitchen table. When he saw his revolver lying on the table Andrew began to understand the conversation he had overheard.

"Can I have that gun?" said Cathal, wide-eyed.

"Shut up. Go and lock that door as you ought to have done before. Move over here, will you, and sit down on that chair."

Andrew moved and sat down. Cathal returned to the room and stood against the door. Andrew knew that he ought to take some initiative now, to try to get out quickly, while his cousins were both as surprised at his arrival as he had been surprised at his reception. He could see doubt, even bewilderment, in Pat's eyes. He ought to act now before Pat had formed any policy or reached any decision. He glanced about, noting the scullery door, the door into the side passage. He began to get up.

"Sit down, I said."

Andrew sat down. The habit of obedience to Pat, formed in remotest childhood, was too strong in him. He knew then that it was no good and the moment of possibility had passed. He was indeed a prisoner. He stared at Pat with gradual appalled comprehension.

"You're a fine nuisance turning up now."

"I wanted to see you," said Andrew. "I wanted to tell you—" But this was meaningless talk. Now he was only a factor in a situation, a British officer in a damnably awkward fix. He noticed a rifle leaning against the gas stove, a pair of handcuffs hung upon the back of a chair. He stared at his revolver, which was lying on the check lino tabletop where so often as a child he had sat eating bread and honey. He saw the little shut-in room and the figure of the armed man. Andrew realized that he was in action for the first time.

He said, "Oh God, whatever are we going to do?" But this was not the right way of speaking either.

"I'm thinking," said Pat. "It's unfortunate that you heard that conversation. I ought to be court-martialled for having left that door open. You appreciate that I can't just let you go?"

Andrew was silent. He looked down at his highly polished boots and his khaki breeches and his empty holster.

"I don't want to have to shoot you," Pat's voice went on coolly, "and it won't be very nice for you if I tie you up and gag you. Suppose we save ourselves trouble and damage and you give me your word as an officer and a gentleman that you will remain quietly in this house until midday and communicate with nobody."

Andrew looked up. "I know perfectly well what my duty is as an officer and a gentleman, and you know it too."

Pat suddenly smiled at him. "Well, well, and how else could you answer? Cathal, go and fetch that rope from my room, and any handkerchiefs and scarves you can lay your hands on."

Cathal paused, fascinated. "Would you really think of shooting him, Pat?"

"Go on! And don't be after touching that." Pat tossed Andrew's revolver onto the gas stove with a clang.

When Andrew said he knew what his duty was, he at last understood perfectly and grasped what was about to occur not just as the occasion of a conflict between him and his cousin, but as a general catastrophe. When he left this place he would be going into the firing line not to shoot at Germans but to shoot at Pat and his comrades. He gave a groan of pain. "Why did this have to happen?"

Pat understood him. "It's necessary."

"It's insane. You can't hold out against the British Army. You're forcing us to fight you when we don't want to, and we're the same people, we're brothers, we *can't* fight—" Andrew felt the outrage of it. He wanted to explain that he did not want to fight the Irish, they had done him no harm, there must be some mistake. It could not be that he would have to kill his first man here in Dublin, here where his mother had just moved into a pretty house, where Frances—

"Cousins, not brothers. Thank you, Cathal. Now, Andrew, I'm sorry, but I'm to be out of this place in twenty minutes and I want to leave you behind in a neat bundle. You'll be rescued this afternoon when my mother comes home. Could you just stand up and turn round and put your hands behind your back."

Andrew stood up, facing Pat. Then as he turned about to face the window he said, as he had used to say as a child when about to be beaten, "Oh, *no*, oh, *no*—" He felt the cold touch of the handcuffs on his wrists.

The square frame of the window opposite Andrew was suddenly darkened by a figure which rose up from below. The sun was shining now outside, and the figure appeared bulky and startling against the dirty sunny brick wall. All three inside the room jumped and exclaimed, and Andrew found himself stumbling against Pat. The handcuffs clattered to the floor. Then Andrew recognized through the window, close to his own face, the round, eager face of Millie. She tapped urgently on the glass, mouthing something.

"Cathal, go and let her in. You sit down again. Oh, Mother of God!"

As Pat grimaced, Andrew knew again that he ought to act. He did not think that Pat would shoot him if he made a dash for it. Pat was physically the stronger, but should he not at least try to force his way out, lock his cousin in a wrestling hold with all the force he had? But his body was timid, submissive, defeated. He sat down where he had been told to sit.

The next moment Millie was in the room. She was wearing trousers and a thick overcoat.

"Well, what a to-do," said Millie, "and Andrew's here too. What is Andrew doing? We three are always meeting." She picked up the handcuffs and put them on the table.

"What do you want here, Millie?"

"I know all about it and I've come to offer you my services and I'm certainly coming with you and you're not going to stop me."

Millie's hair was curly and shaggy, bundled against the upturned coat collar. Her whole figure looked stiffly youthful and impromptu, like a schoolgirl acting a man in a play. But she stared at Pat, not provocatively and not defiantly. She was cool and bitter with determination.

Pat was gazing at Millie with a strange look. He put his fingers to his parted lips like one calculating. He said very slowly, "You can't come with me, but there's something very important indeed which you can do for me. Will you do it?"

Millie looked at him, still with her face hard. "Pat, I want this thing. It's more than you."

"Will you hear what it is I want?"

"All right."

"Cathal, will you go outside a moment, please."

"Why?" said Cathal.

"Go outside because I tell you. I want to talk to her alone."

Cathal left the room.

Pat suddenly drew Millie right up against him, jerking her half off her feet. Andrew remembered afterwards how Pat's arm sank deep into the folds of her overcoat, how Millie gasped as her feet slithered upon the kitchen floor, and how Pat, all the time he was talking to her, kept staring over her shoulder at Andrew. He spoke in a quick whisper of which Andrew could catch only a word here and there.

"No, Pat dear, I can't. This thing is made for me. Don't ask me to stay out of it. I can't help you. Just let me come along."

Pat released, or rather dropped her, and she staggered. "I can't stop you from getting yourself murdered, but you're not coming along with any of us."

Millie stared at him, biting her lip. She looked at Andrew. "I still don't understand about *him*."

"He knows. He wouldn't give us his parole so he's going to be tied up and left here."

"Hmmm. I see. Wait a minute, wait a minute. If I solve your little problem for you will you let me come with you today?"

Pat hesitated. "I don't see how you—"

"But if I can, will you promise?"

"Well, yes—"

"Listen, then."

Millie put her two hands on Pat's shoulders and jolted him back against the frame of the window. She stood on tiptoe, hauling herself up towards his face as she hissed out an inaudible stream of words. Again Andrew saw Pat's eyes fixed upon him, now widening a little as Millie's whisper continued. What a nightmare, thought Andrew. And he thought, how jerky and unreal. Surely nothing connected him to this cardboard catastrophe. Should he not just get up and walk away through the door and leave these grimacing puppets? He moved, or twitched himself, like someone under a spell, trying to find if he is still sentient. But Millie and Pat had stepped apart, and Pat now blocked his way.

"All right," said Pat.

"Shall I take him in there?" Millie pointed to the scullery door. "There's no way out, is there?"

"No way out."

"Come in here for a moment, would you, Andrew?"

Andrew followed Millie into the dark scullery, and she shut the door. A little square window gave onto the dirty wall on which the sun was obliquely shining. There was a small table, a sink full of unwashed dishes, and a smell of decaying wood and tea leaves. Andrew thought, I have been taken to the end of the world, and at the end there is nothing but idiocy. I am in hell, and hell is gibberish. He was standing close against Millie and saw her face below him looking up, not with the obscene vulnerability of the last time, but with a cruel intentness, like a stalking cat's face. This is insanity, he thought, this is dishonour, to be standing in this little room up against this woman.

Millie pushed him as she had pushed Pat, her two hands hooked upon his shoulders, her chin poking into his chest, her hair, which now seemed to issue from her mouth, spread onto his khaki sleeve. She began to speak in a low voice. As he looked over her shoulder Andrew saw the sun fading in the window square. He looked at the pile of dishes. He listened to Millie and began to take in what she was saying.

"I don't believe you," said Andrew.

"I have the evidence."

Andrew thrust her violently away from him. He saw her evil cat face, the eyes screwed with purpose, the lips wet, bobbing near him in the scullery, which had suddenly become dark.

"I don't believe you."

"She would."

"And I couldn't trust you."

"You've got to."

"Don't touch me."

"If you will do what I want I will have everything destroyed. Otherwise—"

"Oh, shut up. Let me think."

"Well, think quickly, Andrew. Believe me, dear boy, it is true. Look, I will write you a letter to take to Upper Mount Street. I swear to you I won't cheat. And will you then do what I ask? Otherwise I shall be completely ruthless."

"What is it that you want me to do?"

"Simply to promise to stay inside this house until twelve and keep your mouth shut."

Andrew sat down and laid his head on the table. The surface of the table was damp, soft, and rotten. He said, gazing along the grain of the wood, "A promise given under duress is not a promise."

"You are not under duress. You are perfectly free to refuse and take the consequences. You are perfectly free to promise and to break your promise. But if I find out later that you have, I'll tell everything, evidence or no evidence."

Andrew lifted his head. "All right. I'll do as you ask. Write that letter and give it to me at once. And if you cheat here I'll kill you."

"Ah—" Millie breathed with satisfaction and flung open the scullery door. Pat and Cathal were talking on the other side of the kitchen. Millie went through and Andrew followed her. He sat down in a corner and laid his head awkwardly against the wall, turning his face away from them.

"He will," said Millie.

The three of them came and stood round Andrew. He did not look up at them, but fixed his eyes upon the gas stove. He saw his revolver there. It had fallen down inside the iron framework of the gas burners and hung there suspended. Andrew felt as if he had had a stroke. His eyes seemed to be askew, his limbs recalcitrant and twisted. He listened dully for his sentence.

Pat said, "Andrew, do you give me your promise, your most honourable promise, that you will stay inside this house and say nothing of what you know until twelve o'clock today?"

"Yes."

"You have a watch, haven't you? Well, you'll hear the Angelus. You do faithfully promise?"

"Yes."

Pat seemed to hesitate. Andrew looked up at their three faces. Cathal was looking puzzled and frightened. Millie's face was plumped with triumph, her cat eyes slanting. Pat was perspiring. The sweat trickled down past his eyes to his cheeks, and his lower lip palpitated. What is it, thought Andrew, what is happening, what are they going to do to me? At that moment it seemed to him that they were intending to kill him.

Cathal said, "You're not surely—"

"Could you stand up?" said Pat.

Andrew stood up.

"Turn round."

He turned round and saw again the brick wall, sunny now, its crust of dirt shadowed by the slanting sun.

"I'm sorry to use the handcuffs," said Pat's voice. "I have to make sure. Cathal, could you just help me hold his wrist. *There.*"

There was a click. Andrew felt the steel on one wrist. Then there was a wild outcry, an animal howl, and Andrew's wrist was jerked and seared. He staggered, exclaimed, and then for a moment everyone stood still. He was handcuffed to Cathal.

"Ingenious, eh?" said Millie.

The moment of stillness passed. Cathal began to shout out something in a loud voice and ran towards the door, dragging Andrew with him. Pat caught Cathal in his arms and smothered his shouting mouth against his chest. He called out something to Millie.

"Don't worry," said Millie. "I'll gag him. Just hold him tight. I learnt all about that in the South African war. We used to gag troublesome patients. You'd be surprised what goes on in military hospitals. The trouble with gagging is the shape of the human head. Those scarves are no use. I need four yards of surgical bandage. In that drawer? What luck. Get him down on his knees, would you."

Pat forced Cathal down, and Andrew was pulled down too, slipping half under the table. The dragging handcuff bit into his wrist and his arm moved jerkily, following the convulsive movements of his fellow-prisoner, shifting so as to ease the pain. He did not look at the struggle which was going on beside him.

"Open his mouth. That's right. Keep your tongue down, boy. Ouch, he bites! There, that's comfy and safe. Don't worry, I know what I'm doing, he won't choke. Now wind the bandage so, plenty of room to breathe, over the bridge of the nose is the important bit. It's all a matter of mechanics. Just as well I was here, isn't it? You couldn't have managed this alone. Now he won't be able to shout for help. Safety pins are best. That's done it."

Millie and Pat stood up.

Now Millie had placed a sheet of paper against the window and was writing on it. Andrew shifted along the floor as Pat pushed Cathal to the wall and began to bind his free hand. Pat groaned softly and rhythmically as he tied Cathal's hand to the foot of the stove. Over Pat's shoulder Andrew could now see Cathal's thrown-back head. His head, entirely swathed in bandage which thickly covered his mouth, wound over his nose and round his brow, leaving only eyes and nostrils free, looked like an old picture of Lazarus, or some faceless monster glimpsed in a dream. As Andrew watched, tears filled Cathal's eyes and streamed down onto the bandage and darkened it. Andrew turned away, saw Pat's feet in army boots, peered up at Pat's face which was red and quivering. Pat looked down, his mouth opening, the lips drawing back in a snarl of pain; then he turned and leaned his head against the door.

"There's your letter." Andrew held it automatically. "I'm sorry, Andrew. I'm a desperate woman. Hadn't we better go, Pat? You will keep your promise, won't you?"

Pat was on his knees beside Cathal. "I should have been useless if you had come with me. I had to do this."

"I must say I don't understand why," said Millie. "You are

destroying the child. If the world ends, let it end, is how I feel."

Pat sat back on his heels. He turned to Andrew, and his face was the face of a weeping man although his eyes were tearless. "Andrew, I just want you to know that I don't know what it was that Millie told you."

Andrew nodded slightly.

Pat had turned back to Cathal. He knelt awkwardly and his cheek grazed the bandaging as he bowed his head for a moment onto his brother's shoulder. Then he rose and picked up his rifle and Andrew's revolver.

"Cheer up." Millie squeezed Andrew's arm. She opened the door and moved out. Andrew saw the boots and the green leg-bands follow her. The front door banged. There was a long silence. Cathal was crying with a soft hissing sound behind the bandage.

Andrew said, "Do you mind if I lie flat for a while?" He lifted his pinioned hand, edging the wrist round inside the handcuff, and managed to adjust himself supine upon the floor. The sun, rising higher, began to shine into the kitchen. The muffled weeping continued.

Twenty-four

It was twenty-five minutes to twelve, Easter Monday morning, on the clock at Findlater's Church, as Christopher and Frances Bellman hurried through Rutland Square and on up the hill towards Blessington Street. The sun shone from a sky of pallid, exhausted blue upon the green domes of Dublin, the majestic dome of the Customs House, the lace-cap dome of the Four Courts, the elegant little dome of the Rotunda Hospital. The two figures moved urgently onward against the slow crowd of holiday-makers who were sauntering down to enjoy the sudden sunshine in the centre of the city.

Christopher had spent the previous day, Sunday, in a condition of frenzy. He had woken early at Rathblane to a state of consciousness which he could scarcely endure. It was not just the sense of having lost Millie, it was the sense of having lost her in such a horrible, muddled, undignified way. He recalled with misery and disgust the pathetic, defensive, frivolous tone which Millie had adopted. This hurt him more than jealousy. He could have borne a firm, even a mysterious no from Millie. He could even more easily have borne a tragic severance with tears. But this confused matter of having "found her out" made his own position not only painful but unmanageably absurd. Neither he nor Millie knew how to behave. Christopher hated muddle, hated the plunging to and fro in confusion of half-guilty half-frantic human beings caught up together like carriage horses in an accident.

He decided to leave the house early before anyone was up, and, in fact, set off on foot shortly before seven o'clock. He walked for nearly an hour, and began to feel extremely tired, and it began to rain. Then there was the sound of a galloping horse behind him, and he was overtaken by Millie. A ridiculous conversation followed, during which Millie tried to persuade him to mount behind her and return to Rathblane. Christopher turned and walked on, stumbling in the mud out of sheer anger and misery, and Millie followed, leading her horse and expostulating. Finally, as it was now raining very hard indeed, he consented to wait under a tree while she rode to the factor's cottage and got the factor to come down bringing a bicycle. After an exceedingly long time the factor arrived riding his own bicycle and pushing his daughter's. Millie once more galloped up and there was another confused conversation in the factor's hearing, with Millie saying she wanted to talk to Christopher and Christopher saying he must be going. Finally, as he began to wobble down the stony track on the factor's daughter's bicycle, he could hear, behind him, Millie addressing friendly remarks to her horse.

Christopher arrived back at Finglas wet, exhausted, shivering, to find an extremely upset and anxious Frances waiting for him. He had forgotten to tell her that he would be away for the night; he had not even reflected on whether he would be away for the night. His daughter's distress and reproaches, and the fact that there was no warm meal waiting for him and that the fires had not been lit, sent Christopher into a paroxysm of self-pity in the course of which he told Frances everything: Millie, Pat, Andrew, the engagement ring, everything. He regretted this immediately after. If he had been calmer and less self-absorbed he would have spared her a revelation which was unnecessary and could not but be intensely painful. But a little later still, when he had had his hot meal, and in the lucid brutality of a renewed concern with self, he decided it had been right to tell her after all: for her sake, because she would now have fewer regrets about Andrew, and for his sake, because the bitterness of Frances would now support him in the loss of Millie. He did not really conceive that Frances might have changed her mind again about Andrew.

Yet her reaction to his news was extreme, and she gave herself up to weeping and declared, which he did not take too seriously, that she was forthwith going to England to become a nurse. Christopher thought that it was probably the bit about the ring which hurt most. Frances had not even known about the existence of the ring. How touching to know that Andrew had had it ready for her. How humiliating to know that he had almost directly after her refusal given it, and in such circumstances, to another. It is enough to refuse a man without experiencing also the muddy splash of his too precipitate departure. As Christopher imagined the chagrin of his daughter he had dark thoughts about Andrew, and then, returning to his own hurt, even darker ones about Millie. He was still utterly unsure whether or not to believe Millie's assurance that she had not tampered with Andrew until after his refusal by Frances. He began to wonder again whether Frances had not somehow found out something. He went early to bed, to lie sleepless with these speculations, hearing the soft sound of weeping in the next room.

On Monday morning Christopher became aware that his daughter was in some quite new frame of mind. She was no longer tearful, but seemed excited, frightened, yet resolute. When he asked her what was now the matter, she explained at last that she had seen the gardener that morning and she felt sure that something was going on. Further questioned, she explained that she had found the gardener in Citizen Army uniform searching frantically in the potting shed for something which, when found, looked like a box of ammunition. He had mumbled something about "manoeuvres" and departed at a run, but, Frances said, something about the *way* he ran, and his excitement, and his confusion at being discovered, suggested that something extreme might be going to happen after all. And, having got this idea into her head, it was evident that Frances could do nothing now but worry about it.

Christopher argued, and ended by being infected by her anxiety. He was a little irritated by this evidence of a continued concern about young Andrew, who might, if Frances' guess was correct, find himself in the firing line sooner than he bargained for. But this piece of drama was at least something new to think about; and the idea that, after all the talk and the anti-climax, something violent *was* perhaps going to occur upset and moved Christopher in a great many ways when, even momentarily, he gave it credence. He let himself become worried, too, and readily agreed when Frances herself suggested that they should go over to Blessington Street and see if anything could be found out from Barney. It was at least something to do, and something which was not connected with Millie.

Blessington Street was deserted, as usual, except for a few scratching dogs and Keogh's laundry van, whose horse had mounted the pavement to eat as much as he could of an elder tree which was growing out of one of the areas. Once out of the crowd, the particular desolate peace of Dublin established itself round about them: the wide, pale sky, low down even when it was cloudless, the open, dusty, cliff-like streets, the endless dark façades, spongy with dirt, absorbing light and sound. A half-clad child emerged slowly from a gaping doorway. Keogh's van moved on a few yards. Surely nothing could happen in this quiet city.

Frances had quickened her pace as they got into Blessington Street, her boots briskly kicking back the skirts of her coat, and Christopher was panting and falling behind when they reached the door of the Dumays' house. Christopher started to say something to her about not alarming Kathleen, but she had already rung the bell. The bell jangled harshly inside the dark hallway, and they waited until it had stammered itself into silence. Frances rang again. Then she tried the door, which was usually left unfastened. It was locked. Christopher, who did not want to meet Pat and who had been having misgivings about the whole project as they came up the hill, was beginning to suggest that they should go and have some coffee and that Frances might come back again later, when Frances, who had been peering through the letter box, gave a startled exclamation.

"What is it, Frances?"

"I don't know. Something very odd. It looks as if someone's lying on the floor in the kitchen. I can see their foot. You look."

Christopher stooped and looked through the aperture. He saw and smelt the dark hall and saw beyond it the half-open door of the kitchen and a sunny segment of the kitchen floor. Something was lying just inside the doorway which looked like a foot, or at least a boot. The rest of the person, if person it was, was hidden. Christopher felt a thrill of fright. A foot, a leg, extended there upon the kitchen floor while the bell pealed in vain seemed to him at first uncanny. What could it mean? An equally vague but more rational fear followed.

"Let me look again." Frances straightened up with a frightened face. "Do you think there can have been—an accident?"

"It might be just someone's boot lying there."

"No, I'm sure it's someone's foot. I can see part of the leg."

Something about his daughter's agitation made Christopher push her aside. As he looked more carefully it seemed to him that the immobile object in the kitchen doorway resembled the booted foot of a British cavalry officer.

Christopher shouted through the letter box. "Hello, there! Barney, Kathleen, Pat! Hello, hello!" He pulled the bell again so violently that it gave one yelp and jolted to silence. The stillness of the house absorbed the din.

Frances was now stooping at the slot. She exclaimed, "It's gone."

"What?"

"The foot. It's gone."

Christopher looked again. The boot-like object had disappeared. Had they imagined it? They stared at each other.

"I must get inside," said Christopher. "There's a lane at the back. You'd better wait here."

He ran to the corner of Mountjoy Street and round into the lane, a narrow track of cinders and black earth, smelling of cats and dust-bins, which ran along behind the yards of the houses. The houses looked entirely different at the back, made ugly and formless by every kind of jutting annexe and out-building. The yards, behind earthy, weedy walls, were full of sheds and wash-houses and high lines of tossing linen. As Christopher hesitated, wondering which house belonged to the Dumays, Frances appearing from behind his shoulder said "This is the one," and began to push the door of the yard. It was locked.

"Look, *you stay here*," said Christopher. "I'll see what's happened, if anything's happened."

The wall was not high. He dragged an empty dust-bin up against it and mounted. The top of the wall crumbled under his knee and he jumped down on the other side. But before he could advance to the house he saw the shadow of Frances, who was trying to pull herself up onto the wall. She got one leg over the top and then almost fell into his arms, bringing down a shower of broken brick and earth.

"*Please* stay here, Frances, and don't come till I tell you."

But her eyes, large and vague with fear, looked past him, and he had to push forward to intercept her. Together they approached the kitchen window.

The sun was shining directly into the kitchen. At the moment of looking in Christopher felt extremely afraid. He had no notion what he expected, except that now, somehow through Frances, he expected something dreadful. The combination of the disappearing foot and the silence of the house had produced an effect both of catastrophe and of eeriness. What he now saw, though it was less catastrophic than his fears, was perhaps ever more eerie.

Two people were sitting on the kitchen floor opposite to the window with their backs against the wall. They looked unreal, too big, like outsize dolls. Their faces looked so strange that it took Christopher several seconds to recognize them as Andrew and Cathal, and to be certain that they were both alive. What was unusual was their expression, or rather something which had communicated itself to their entire posture. Andrew, in uniform as usual, had taken off half his jacket and loosened his tie. He sat slack and limp, his feet spread out rather wide apart in front of him. He was caressing his moustache in a curiously absent manner. Cathal, who had a great deal of white stuff which looked like bandage hanging loose around his neck, sat with hunched shoulders half turned away from Andrew, his legs drawn right up and his cheek against the wall. Both heads moved slightly as the two figures appeared in the window, and with a shock of horror Christopher saw on both faces a look of utter lassitude and indifference. It was impossible not to think of drugs, insanity. Sitting there vacantly on the floor, the one crouched, the other with outspread feet, they looked like two derelict beings in a madhouse.

Frances was pulling at the kitchen door, and now at the window. "Help me push this up, I think it's unlatched." Christopher pawed at the window frame, and it moved a little. Frances got her fingers underneath it, and in a moment had thrust her arm through and unbolted the door. They went into the kitchen.

Cathal had leaned his head back against the wall and was wiping his face with a piece of the bandage. He appeared to have been crying. His eyes moved a little, observing the newcomers, but he did not change his posture. Andrew peered up with a frightened hostile look but seemed unable to focus his gaze upon them. The blank expression returned. It was as if some appalling meditation had been momentarily interrupted.

"What's the matter with you, what's happened?" cried Christopher. "Are you ill?" He stooped over Andrew.

"Look," said Frances behind him.

He followed her pointing finger and saw that Andrew and Cathal were handcuffed together.

Christopher jumped back as promptly as if he had touched a metal limb. The comatose propped-up figures, and now the handcuffs, produced an effect of the mechanical, the less than human. Frances, who was looking down with a grimace of fascination, had backed away to the window.

"Andrew, Andrew," said Christopher, "how did this happen? Who did it? Are you hurt? Have you been here long?"

After a moment's silence Andrew answered, speaking rather slowly and laboriously. "I've been here several hours. Well, two or three perhaps. No, I'm not hurt." Lifting the wrist that was bound to Cathal's, he looked at his watch, frowning a little. It was nearly five minutes to twelve. His eyes widened again into the vacant stare and he looked away into the corner of the kitchen. He seemed oblivious of Frances.

"Why are you sitting here on the floor?"

"Well, you see, until about five minutes ago Cathal was tied onto the gas stove."

"*What?* But who tied him? And who put these handcuffs on you?"

"Pat did."

"Pat?" Frances swept round the table to Cathal's side and shook the boy by the shoulder. "Cathal, are you all right? Tell us what happened? What's all that bandaging for?"

Cathal shrunk slightly away from her touch, but did not otherwise move or speak.

"Are you both bewitched?"

"It was a gag," said Andrew, with the same slow, stolid enunciation.

"A gag? Cathal gagged? But why? Who did it?"

"Pat. Or rather Millie."

"*Millie*," said Christopher. "Was she here?"

"Yes. She went with them."

"With *who?*" cried Frances. "Oh, do talk properly!"

"With Pat. With the Sinn Feiners."

"But where to?"

"To fight."

"Oh, God, I was right." Frances clapped her hands over her mouth.

"Millie gone with the Sinn Feiners, to fight?" said Christopher stupidly. "But there isn't any fighting."

"There will be soon," said Andrew. "They're going to start at twelve." He drew his legs up in front of him, twitching his shoulder. He said, "I'm deucedly stiff."

"But it's almost twelve now!" Frances started convulsively towards the door, then returned to stare down at Andrew. "But you—why are you here like this? What happened, what *happened?*"

"I shall never be able to explain that to anybody," said Andrew, speaking in the same slow way and staring past Christopher at a point on the wall.

"At twelve. It can't be. It's impossible." Christopher stood there stupefied, his arms hanging down as if he, too, had become a doll. Millie gone to join the rebels, gone away with Pat with a gun in her hand. "But why did you just stay here? Why didn't you go and do something, tell somebody, if you knew about it?"

"It was your *duty*, what were you thinking of?" Frances was looking down at Andrew now almost with fury.

"I can't explain," said Andrew. "I found out about it quite accidentally. Then I gave Pat my word of honour that I'd tell no one and that I'd stay here in this house until twelve. And he handcuffed Cathal to me because he wanted Cathal kept out of the fight. And he gagged him, or rather Millie did, so that he shouldn't shout for help. And I took the gag off and undid his hand just before you arrived because he was crying so much I thought he might stifle and the time was almost up anyway." He offered the account in a dull voice as if, after all, it were something obvious. He shifted awkwardly, tugging Cathal's arm with a petulant movement.

"But why, why, why?" cried Frances, "Why did you give in? Why did you promise? How could he have frightened you so? Why didn't you run out and try to stop it all? Why did you just sit here for hours doing nothing? Have you forgotten you're an Army officer?"

Andrew simply shook his head. He looked up at Frances for a moment, and then screwed up his eyes as if he had been dazzled.

Frances stamped her foot. Her hands clawed at the muddied skirts of her coat. She advanced on Andrew as if she would have kicked him. "Your word of honour! Gave Pat your word of honour! You ought to have shot him as a traitor! You've betrayed your King and country. You've dishonoured your uniform. How could you do it? I can't understand!"

"I don't think Pat understood either," said Andrew slowly.

"You did it because you were afraid of Pat. You've always been afraid of Pat. Oh, I shall never forgive you—"

As her voice dissolved into an incoherence of tears the clear sound of a bell was heard. It was the Angelus ringing at St. Joseph's church in Berkeley Road.

They all paused for a moment. Then with a jerk Cathal threw himself forward and began to rise. Andrew tried to crouch but was pulled sharply onto his knees. The handcuffed pair swayed awkwardly together and at last managed to get up onto their feet. Frances began to sob again. The Angelus went on slowly ringing. There was a distant noise which sounded like rifle fire.

Twenty-five

Andrew and Cathal raced down Blessington Street in the bright sunshine. The sky, cloudless and pale golden with light, dazzled their eyes. Swinging between them and concealing the handcuffs was a mackintosh which Andrew had had the presence of mind to pick up as Cathal dragged him through the hall and out of the house. Their feet clapped and slithered upon the still rainy pavements, and the wet sunny houses gave back an echo, as they rushed along, now jerking apart, now drawn violently together by their bound wrists.

The sun was hot. The two figures were running now in step. But by the time they got as far as Findlater's church Andrew forced Cathal to slow down. Cathal's breath came in wailing gasps, like quick little screams, and his face, as Andrew glimpsed it, strained and moulded by fear, looked no less grotesque than his Lazarus head of an hour ago. They continued at a quick, jolting walk. People eyed them uneasily as they passed; and here and there from side streets men with grimmer faces emerged and began to hurry down towards the centre of the city. One or two people now passed them at a run. An increasing murmur of anxious talk hung like a light canopy above their heads. Dublin, a little startled, a little puzzled, seemed already to be aware that this was no ordinary day in her history.

As they came past the Rotunda towards the upper end of Sackville Street there was a sound of rifle fire ahead of them and then, as in reply, a burst of firing in another part of the city. The murmur of talk fell almost to silence and the moving people, not yet numerous, seemed to draw together with an uneasy, eager purposiveness, already aware of themselves as a crowd compelled onward by the mystery of an historical event. Someone laughed nervously. The rifle fire was heard again.

The police had already formed a cordon across the end of Sackville Street, and people were standing four and five deep behind them. Andrew and Cathal pushed their way forward until they could see, over the policemen's shoulders, the wide expanse of the street, empty. That sudden utter emptiness, more perhaps than anything else, showed to the wondering gaze of the on-lookers the extraordinary nature of what had happened. The Post Office had a strange look. The glass in all the windows had been broken and the spaces barricaded with piles of furniture. The building already had a huddled, beleaguered appearance, the air weirdly of a fortress. A large placard hung upon the façade read: *Headquarters of the Provisional Government of the Irish Republic.* While up above, in place of the Union Jack, a green flag blew out taut a ⌐ clear, with the words *Irish Republic* written upon it in white letters. There was something miniature, amateurish, improbable about this scene, as if the line between dream and reality had been crossed in a blundering manner and almost unaware.

As they watched, the crowd almost silent now, a figure emerged onto the Post Office portico and began to speak, reading aloud to the empty street from a piece of paper which fluttered in his hand. While the sound of the voice, too far off to be understood, rang out thinly in the clear sunny air, a man near to Andrew who had some field glasses said, "That's Patrick Pearse." Andrew could not hear Pearse's words, but he read them later many times and on many days as they nightly appeared upon posters all over the city. "Irishmen and Irishwomen. In the name of God and of the dead generations from which she receives her old traditions of nationhood, Ireland, through us, summons her children to her flag and strikes for her freedom. . . ."

The figure had vanished now from the Post Office portico and the deserted street seemed quiet, almost sleepy, in the sun. The crowd began to talk again in low voices. There was a baffled painful excitement which was like guilt.

"Why didn't the English take a pot shot at him while he was out there?"

"Sure that lot have no guns."

"He's after declaring the Irish Republic, whatever the hell that is."

"Isn't it the like of the bloody Sinn Feiners to do this on the day of the races, and it fine for once."

"The murderin' idjuts, they've killed a horse."

Andrew, peering between the shifting heads of the police, saw that they had indeed killed a horse. The horse lay in the middle of the street opposite the main door of the Post Office, a huge, brown, glossy mound. Looking at the dead horse Andrew felt a piercing fright, an anguish which he scarcely understood. Then looking sideways he saw on the nearby pavement, some mounted and some dismounted, a group of Lancers in colourful uniforms and very evident disarray. Bound for Phoenix Park, the Lancers, who carried no firearms, had passed unsuspectingly down Sackville Street at a minute or two after twelve and had received the first volley from the rebels. Four men had been hit and had already been pulled away into the shops opposite. The horse remained. Andrew looked at the Lancers and looked at the horrified, frightened face of the young officer, a boy of his own age. Andrew's heart expanded and contracted with a violence which almost broke it, as if the blood were trying to burst from his body with shame and despair. He touched himself, touched his cap and jacket to be sure that he was indeed wearing them, touched his shoulder with the single pip. He, too, was a British officer.

He was then at once aware that people in the crowd were looking at him. The crowd was detached, confused, if anything hostile to the Sinn Feiners. But they stared at Andrew and at his uniform without friendliness. By the violence which had already occurred a breach had been opened, and through that breach inevitably would flow the bitterness of centuries.

Andrew began to struggle back. People were pushing now alarmingly from behind. He edged through, pulling Cathal after him. He tried to manoeuvre his pinioned hand so as to get a grip on the boy's wrist, but managed only to catch hold of his limp fingers. Cathal followed him unresistingly now, his head hanging forward. They picked their way back out of the densest part of the crowd.

Why had he done it? He was a dead man now, he had died there in that little room sitting there beside Cathal with his back against the wall measuring the slow hours and minutes of his dissolution. Frances and Millie—the figures of the women paled to nothing; he scarcely now recalled who it was that had been with him when the Angelus began to ring. What was colossal, irrevocable, and insupportable was the destruction of his honour. He had been murdered in that little room just as surely as if they had shed his blood. Why had he given in and let them destroy him?

Even as he replied, Andrew knew that this was not the answer and that he was without defence against the appalling nature of his act. When Millie had whispered to him, driving him with her knee up against the scullery wall, that she had had a certain relationship with her brother, his father, and that there were letters to prove it, he had for a second not believed her. Then when she had gone on murmuring into his ear that unless he surrendered she would have those letters sent to his mother, his mind was overwhelmed with a pity for Hilda which had seemed to bring belief with it and to leave him with no other course but to protect her. Such knowledge could blacken his mother's life back through time to its very roots. He could not risk, by any gambling with Millie, the possibility of so hideous a disclosure. He decided to give in at once.

Now he could doubt it all. The first shock, felt for his mother, brought belief. The second shock, felt for himself, brought disbelief. How could anything so horrible have really happened, anything so, as he now apprehended it, insulting to him? Perhaps there were letters, but they might mean nothing or be construed as harmless. Perhaps Millie would not, or could not, in fact have carried out her threat. Or perhaps, with a grotesque ingenuity, she had invented the whole story to terrify him with. That afternoon, he supposed, he would go to Upper Mount Street and find out. After that he would report to Longford.

But the thought of Longford and of his shame brought him to what lay deeper. He ought, whatever else he had done, to have faced Pat. He ought to have ignored Pat's revolver and to have fought Pat with his bare hands. His cousin would not have killed him. Or if he had, that would have been better, far better, than this other death. He had been near to Pat, nearer perhaps than ever in his life, when Pat had smiled and said, "How else could you answer?" At that moment there had been a bond between them of dignity and respect. But Andrew had merely spoken of his duty. He ought to have done it. He ought to have fought then and there in the Dumays' kitchen with all the fury of his manhood. This was the encounter for which his whole life had been a training. He loved and he had always loved Pat Dumay. To have fought with Pat then up to any extremity of destruction and disaster would have been the last perfect expression of that love. But precisely because he had always idolized Pat the spring of power was broken inside him. He could not command the splendour of will which would have taken his cousin into a wrestler's embrace. He had dishonoured his uniform, and this dishonour could not be forgiven, or blotted out by any degree of heroism ever. And he had done it, in the end, because of Pat and for Pat; and in doing it he had done the one thing·which would make Pat despise him eternally.

Andrew found that he was still holding Cathal's hand. He looked at the boy. Cathal's face was oblivious, flushed and running with tears. Andrew felt near to tears himself. He said, "Come on, Cathal, we must find someone to get these things off us. Do you know where we could go?" He pulled the boy along with him, pulling him away from the ominous dreadful emptiness of Sackville Street.

As they walked together, people were hurrying past them from all sides in ever-increasing numbers, their talk filling the sunny air, louder now, more confident, already less amazed.

"Is it mad they all are?"

"They're bringing field guns up into Trinity."

"They've got the Irish Lights boat up the river to shell them out of that."

"Please God they've got a priest in there with them."

"God and His Blessed Mother help them now, the poor bloody fools."

"Ah sure isn't this a grand day for Ireland."

Epilogue

Blessington Street
April 1938

Dearest Frances,

I know I should have written to you ages ago but I've been rushed off my feet what with the work for the settlement and getting the house ready for the new lodgers, it's a lot of small things really but there hasn't been a moment. Jinny's a great blessing of course, and her son has been painting the kitchen and scullery, a useful decent boy and not like the run of those kids at all. I hope the new lodgers will be all right. I got so fond of the other lot, we were quite like a big family here at Blessington Street! But I expect I shall soon get just as fond of the new ones. Did I tell you one had been a major in the British Army, a very nice kind of a man, who's taking the two rooms at the top.

I loved to have the news of your family, how quickly they are growing up, it makes me feel so old to think you've got nearly grown children now, Frances. Well, God help us we can none of us escape from anno domini and I'm lucky to have my health and strength, not like poor Millie. She's a lot better now of course, but she was never the same since her operation. I think I told you I got her out of that damp place in Eccles Street and now she has a dear little room in Dargle Road, that's off the Drumcondra Road. There's a lot of other old crocks in the house and they all call her "my lady," and that's still good for a wet of whiskey! I took her out to lunch the other day at Jammet's and a waiter recognized her and said she hadn't changed a bit and that pleased her so much, poor thing, though God knows it isn't true. And she started telling the waiter all about Easter Week at Boland's Mill, and I suppose she was very heroic all that time in the back room tying bandages, but she talks so loud now she's a bit deaf and all the restaurant was listening and passing remarks and I was quite embarrassed. Then after that she was on at me about Barney and how good he was to her and how she misses him yet and in the end we were both of us quite wretched. It's hard to believe it's all of ten years since poor Barney passed away, God rest his soul.

And when are you coming over here? I could make room for the lot of you at Blessington Street, there's that big sofa still in the drawing-room and one of the kids could have the camp bed. It'd be so good to talk about the old days. I've found an album full of old snaps I'd love to show you, including such a nice one of your poor father in that old mackintosh hat of his, you remember the old mackintosh hat. And there's one of Hilda at Claresville, such a pretty house and so sad that she never really lived in it. Now that you've all the children away at school couldn't you be spared to give us a visit, even if you couldn't persuade all the family to come? They say there'll be a heat wave this summer and I know it would please Millie so much if you came, she's always asking after you. And we could go and visit all the old places, Kingstown's just the same, though I still can't get used to calling it Dun Laoghaire, and Sandycove and the baths and all. I was down there the other week and went down past Finglas and looked into the garden. The old red swing's still there. You remember the old swing and how poor Andrew mended it for you and took such trouble with it. Only they've painted the house pink now which I don't like and they've renamed it Hillcrest, which is a silly name as it isn't on the crest of the hill at all. I don't know who the people are who are there now since the Porters left. I think they're English people.

Well, I must stop this scrawl and do the laundry. Give my love to the family. And do come over this summer all of you to the Emerald Isle and "we'll talk of old times till they put out the light" like it says in the song!

Yours with fondest love,
Kathleen

P.S. I've sent you some spiced beef. Don't undo the cloth, just boil it for two hours.

"Who's that great fat letter from?" said Frances' tall son.

"From Aunt Kathleen."

"Is she complaining as usual?" said Frances' English husband.

"Not specially."

"I suppose she wants us to go over?"

"She always wants us to go over."

"Well, you can go. You're not getting me over there a-gain."

"Oh, I don't really want to go," said Frances.

She saw her husband folding the newspaper in the careful way in which he always folded it at the end of breakfast to make it into a flat, square package which would fit into his briefcase. She saw folding inwards the headline *Franco Threatens Barcelona*. She looked at the face of her tall son and quickly withdrew her eyes. Since her son's best friend had gone to join the International Brigade Frances had lived with fear daily.

"What's the latest in your Irish family?" asked Frances' son.

Her children always spoke of her "Irish family." It did not occur to them to regard themselves as half Irish. They did not even regard their mother as Irish. They had visited Ireland four times and expressed no wish to go again.

"Oh, they're very quiet as usual. Aunt Millie's a bit better."

"Quiet! Quiet as the grave, I'd say," said Frances' husband.

"Well, after all, Kathleen—"

"Oh, I don't mean Kathleen, I mean the whole island. Do you remember how depressed we got last time? I never saw anything deader."

"Well, perhaps they enjoy it—"

"I hope so, they certainly asked for it. They wanted to be by themselves alone, and they're by themselves alone."

"I liked that place on the west coast," said Frances' son.

"No, you didn't. You complained all the time because it was too cold to bathe. And it rained every day. I must say, Ireland's an object lesson."

"Well, I don't mind things being quiet," said Frances. "There's too much noise and rush over here. And I like rain."

"A provincial dump living on German capital. A dairy-farming country that can't even invent its own cheese. And if there's another war they won't fight, any more than they did last time. And that'll really finish them."

"They did fight last time," said Frances. "The Irish regiments were famous."

"Yes, and where are those regiments now? Oh, a collection of madcaps enlisted. But most of the Irish were looking after number one. And all that nineteen-sixteen nonsense that your family was mixed up in."

"I don't think it was nonsense," said Frances' son.

"It was unadulterated nonsense," said Frances' husband. "Can you tell me what good it did?"

"I don't know—" said Frances.

"It made no sense at all. Home Rule was coming anyway. Only a lot of disgruntled fanatics wanted to draw attention to themselves. It was pure bloody-minded romanticism, the sort of thing that makes people into Fascists nowadays."

"They weren't like Fascists," said Frances' tall son, "because they were on the right side."

"When you're grown up," said Frances' husband, "which let me once again remind you that you're not, you'll realize that politics is not a matter of sides, it's a matter of methods. That's why there isn't a pin to choose between those two lots in Spain. If you ask me, it's one gang of barbarians against another gang of barbarians."

Frances quickly intercepted her son's reply. She was used to this task of oiling the waters, a task that consisted in turning all serious discussion between her husband and children into vague generalities or harmless personal chat. "Father might have agreed with you. He was always against any kind of extremism. He said the Irish talked nothing but history, but had no historical sense at all."

"Your father sounds a most sensible man," said Frances' husband. "I'm sure we would have seen eye to eye on many subjects. I wish I had known him."

For some reason Frances had never told her husband of the circumstances of Christopher Bellman's death. Christopher died on April the twenty-seventh, nineteen-sixteen. What exactly happened was never very clear. As the days of that interminable week succeeded one another, and the rebels, surrounded, bombarded, shelled, still somehow miraculously held out, Christopher became more and more frenzied. On the Thursday morning he set off on his bicycle for Dublin. That evening someone brought the bicycle back to Finglas, together with the news of Christopher's death. It appeared that he had attempted to make his way into the Post Office through Moore Street. He was killed by a sniper's bullet, no one knew from which side.

"Well, I think those nineteen-sixteen men would have gone to fight in Spain," said Frances' tall son.

"Yes. But on which side!"

"You know perfectly well on which side I mean."

"Storms in teacups," said Frances' husband. "Who's heard of nineteen-sixteen now? *You* wouldn't have heard of it if you hadn't heard your mother going on about it. It'll be the same in twenty years with these Spanish war events you make such a fuss over. Guernica, Irun, Toledo, Teruel. No one will remember."

"Your father may be right," said Frances. "People will only remember Guernica, and that will be because of Picasso."

"I don't agree," said Frances' son. He had become almost alarmingly good at keeping his temper lately. "These names are part of European history. Like Agincourt."

"There is no such thing as European history," said Frances' husband. "Each country tells a selective story creditable to itself. No Frenchman has heard of Agincourt."

"No Englishman has heard of Fontenoy, if it comes to that," said Frances.

"How have you heard of Fontenoy?" said Frances' husband. "It's new to me that you know any history."

"Some Irish soldiers were there, fighting for the French. The Wild Geese, you know. There was a long poem about it. How did it go?

> King Louis drew his rein.
> 'Not so, my liege,' Saxe interposed,
> 'The Irish troops remain'—"

"Playing traitors as usual! No, no, I'm only teasing. You mustn't take me so seriously, my dear. Now I must go for my train."

Frances' husband slid the neat square of newspaper into his briefcase, and after it the white handkerchief, fresh every morning, which he used to clean his glasses. The case clicked shut.

He paused at the door. "What was the fancy name you used to call Ireland by?"

"Cathleen ni Houlihan."

"Well, in my view Cathleen ni Houlihan is a great bore. In this century, small nations have got to pack up, and the sooner they realize it the better. You've got to belong to a big show nowadays, and you may as well do it with sense and with a good grace. I'm sure your excellent father would have agreed with me. There." He kissed Frances. He was a kindly man, though much given to sarcasm.

The front door banged.

Frances and her tall son sat down again at the breakfast table with the slightly guilty air of a relieved complicity which was part of their morning ritual.

"Well, I think nineteen-sixteen was wonderful," said Frances' tall son.

"So do I, really. Though I don't quite see what good it did."

"It was a reminder that people can't be enslaved forever. Tyrannies end because sooner or later people begin automatically to hit back. That's the only thing which really impresses the tyrant and makes him give way. Freedom belongs to human nature, and it can't vanish from the earth. Even though we forget the details of the fight, the fight goes on, and men have to be ready to go down among the details that are forgotten. And whenever it's the turn of a country, however small, to rise against its tyrants, it represents the oppressed peoples of the whole world."

Frances felt the chill touch again. "What a speech! You sound just like Cathal Dumay when you say that. He used to say that sort of thing. You're even beginning to look a bit like him."

"What happened to all those people you knew in those days?" said Frances' tall son. "Do tell me again. I remember you used to tell us all about them, when we were children. But you haven't talked about them for years now, and I've got them all mixed up together in my mind. What happened to Uncle Barney, for instance? He was a real comic. I always remember the touching way he told us he'd have been a vegetarian if it wasn't for his passion for sausages! Something awfully funny happened to him in that nineteen-sixteen business, but I can't recall what it was."

Frances gave a long sigh. "It wasn't very funny, really. Barney was going to fight with the rebels, but before they reached the place they were going to, he accidentally shot himself in the foot, and he had to be left behind."

Frances' son laughed. "That sounds just like Uncle Barney as I knew him! I expect he did it unconsciously on purpose. You know hardly anything we do is really accidental. I was reading about it in a book the other day. Nearly everything we do is our unconscious mind, only we don't know."

"You might be right that it was somehow on purpose. I couldn't imagine Barney really harming anyone but himself. He was the gentlest of men."

"What happened to Cathal Dumay, the chap you said I was like?"

"He was killed in nineteen-twenty-one, in the Irish civil war."

"The Irish civil war? I'd forgotten there was an Irish civil war. What was it about?"

"Some of the Irish thought that we, they, shouldn't accept the Treaty, that it didn't give Ireland enough freedom, and they were prepared to fight about it. And the English helped the more moderate Irish, who accepted the Treaty, to put down the extremists."

"I bet Cathal was with the extremists."

"Yes, he was with the I.R.A. He was very brave, he led a flying column. He was only nineteen when he died."

"Was he killed in a battle?"

"No. A Black and Tan officer came up and shot him one night in his bed."

Frances' son looked thoughtful. "A civil war—that must be a dreadful thing to have in your own country. Were you in Ireland then?"

"No, I was married. I was over here. You existed. It was a terrible business. Your father says the Irish have managed to hush it up completely, and in a way that's true. It was too painful to think about."

"Well, no one will be able to hush up the Spanish civil war. We're not going to forget *that*. What about Cathal's brother, what's his name, Pat Dumay?"

"Oh, he was one of the nineteen-sixteen rebels, he was with Pearse and Connolly in the Post Office. He was killed in the fighting, on the Thursday of Easter week, the day before they surrendered. He was killed by a shell."

"And then there was that other fellow, the English chap—"

"You mean Andrew Chase-White? He wasn't English, he was Irish."

"I always think of him as English. What happened to him?"

"He was killed at Passchendaele in nineteen-seventeen. He got an M.C."

"I remember now. And his mother died of grief."

"I don't know whether Aunt Hilda died of grief. She developed cancer very soon after the news of Andrew's death."

"Heroic lot, weren't they."

"They were inconceivably brave men," said Frances, suddenly gripping the table.

"And all those leaders, Patrick Pearse and company?"

"They shot most of them. Pearse, Connolly, MacDonagh, Mac-Dermott, MacBride, Joseph Plunkett— And they hanged Roger Casement."

"It's rather a miracle de Valera survived. Up Dev! You remember how you used to say that to us when we were children?"

Frances smiled, relaxing her hold. "Up Dev!"

She did not really think all that much about the old days; and yet now for a moment it seemed to her that these thoughts were always with her, and that she had lived out, in those months, in those weeks, the true and entire history of her heart, and that the rest was a survival. Of course this was unfair to her children and to the man with whom she had journeyed so far into this workaday middle of her life. They, those others, had a beauty which could not be eclipsed or rivalled. They had been made young and perfect forever, safe from the corruption of time and from those ambiguous second thoughts which dim the brightest face of youth. In the undivided strength of their first loves they had died, and their mothers had wept for them, and had it been for nothing? Because of their perfection she could not bring herself to say so. They had died for glorious things, for justice, for freedom, for Ireland.

"Yes, I do muddle them up, though," said Frances' tall son. "I remember you said you were in love with one of them. Which one was that?"

"Me?" said Frances. "Oh, I was in love with Pat Dumay."

She got up and went to the window to hide some sudden tears. She looked out at the neat garden and at the houses opposite. Tears flowed more freely now; and she heard drumming in her ears, heard, as she had heard it all through that dreadful week in nineteen-sixteen, battering and breaking her heart, the thunder of the English guns.

The
INVISIBLE
LIFE of
ADDIE
LARUE

The
INVISIBLE
LIFE *of*
ADDIE
LARUE

V. E. SCHWAB

TOR

A TOM DOHERTY ASSOCIATES BOOK
New York

This is a work of fiction. All of the characters, organizations, and events portrayed in this novel are either products of the author's imagination or are used fictitiously.

THE INVISIBLE LIFE OF ADDIE LARUE

Copyright © 2020 by Victoria Schwab

All rights reserved.

Edited by Miriam Weinberg

Interior illustrations by Jennifer Hanover

A Tor Book
Published by Tom Doherty Associates
120 Broadway
New York, NY 10271

www.tor-forge.com

Tor® is a registered trademark of Macmillan Publishing Group, LLC.

The Library of Congress Cataloging-in-Publication Data is available upon request.

ISBN 978-0-7653-8756-1 (hardcover)
ISBN 978-1-250-79399-7 (signed edition)
ISBN 978-1-250-78453-7 (international, sold outside the U.S., subject to rights availability)
ISBN 978-0-7653-8758-5 (ebook)

Our books may be purchased in bulk for promotional, educational, or business use. Please contact your local bookseller or the Macmillan Corporate and Premium Sales Department at 1-800-221-7945, extension 5442, or by email at MacmillanSpecialMarkets@macmillan.com.

First U.S. Edition: October 2020
First International Edition: October 2020

Printed in the United States of America

10 9 8 7 6 5 4 3 2 1

To Patricia—
For never once forgetting.

The old gods may be great, but they are neither kind nor merciful. They are fickle, unsteady as moonlight on water, or shadows in a storm. If you insist on calling them, take heed: be careful what you ask for, be willing to pay the price. And no matter how desperate or dire, *never* pray to the gods that answer after dark.

Estele Magritte
1642–1719

The
INVISIBLE
LIFE of
ADDIE
LARUE

A girl is running for her life.

The summer air burns at her back, but there are no torches, no angry mobs, only the distant lanterns of the wedding party, the reddish glow of the sun as it breaks against the horizon, cracks and spills across the hills, and the girl runs, skirts tangling in the grass as she surges toward the woods, trying to beat the dying light.

Voices carry on the wind, calling her name.

Adeline? Adeline? Adeline!

Her shadow stretches out ahead—too long, its edges already blurring—and small white flowers tumble from her hair, littering the ground like stars. A constellation left in her wake, almost like the one across her cheeks.

Seven freckles. One for every love she'd have, that's what Estele had said, when the girl was still young.

One for every life she'd lead.

One for every god watching over her.

Now, they mock her, those seven marks. Promises. Lies. She's had no loves, she's lived no lives, she's met no gods, and now she is out of time.

But the girl doesn't slow, doesn't look back; she doesn't want to see the life that stands there, waiting. Static as a drawing. Solid as a tomb.

Instead, she runs.

PART ONE

THE GODS THAT ANSWER
AFTER DARK

Title of Piece: *Revenir*

Artist: Arlo Miret

Date: 1721–22 AD

Medium: ash wood, marble

Location: On loan from the Museé d'Orsay

Description: A sculptural series of five wooden birds in various postures and stages of pre-flight, mounted on a narrow marble plinth.

Background: A diligent autobiographer, Miret kept journals that provide insight into the artist's mind and process. Regarding the inspiration for *Revenir,* Miret attributed the idea to a figurine found on the streets of Paris in the winter of 1715. The wooden bird, found with a broken wing, is reputedly re-created as the fifth in the sequence (albeit intact), about to take flight.

Estimated Value: $175,000

The girl wakes up in someone else's bed.

She lies there, perfectly still, tries to hold time like a breath in her chest; as if she can keep the clock from ticking forward, keep the boy beside her from waking, keep the memory of their night alive through sheer force of will.

She knows, of course, that she can't. Knows that he'll forget. They always do.

It isn't his fault—it is never their faults.

The boy is still asleep, and she watches the slow rise and fall of his shoulders, the place where his dark hair curls against the nape of his neck, the scar along his ribs. Details long memorized.

His name is Toby.

Last night, she told him hers was Jess. She lied, but only because she can't say her real name—one of the vicious little details tucked like nettles in the grass. Hidden barbs designed to sting. What is a person, if not the marks they leave behind? She has learned to step between the thorny weeds, but there are some cuts that cannot be avoided—a memory, a photograph, a name.

In the last month, she has been Claire, Zoe, Michelle—but two nights ago, when she was Elle, and they were closing down a late-night café after one of his gigs, Toby said that he was in love with a girl named Jess—he simply hadn't met her yet.

So now, she is Jess.

Toby begins to stir, and she feels the old familiar ache in her chest as he stretches, rolls toward her—but doesn't wake, not yet. His face is now inches from her, his lips parted in sleep, black curls shadowing his eyes, dark lashes against fair cheeks.

Once, the darkness teased the girl as they strolled along the Seine, told her that she had a "type," insinuating that most of the men she chose—and even a few of the women—looked an awful lot like *him*.

The same dark hair, the same sharp eyes, the same etched features.

But that wasn't fair.

After all, the darkness only looked the way he did because of *her*. She'd given him that shape, chosen what to make of him, what to see.

Don't you remember, she told him then, *when you were nothing but shadow and smoke?*

Darling, he'd said in his soft, rich way, *I was the night itself.*

Now it is morning, in another city, another century, the bright sunlight cutting through the curtains, and Toby shifts again, rising up through the surface of sleep. And the girl who is—was—Jess holds her breath again as she tries to imagine a version of this day where he wakes, and sees her, and *remembers.*

Where he smiles, and strokes her cheek, and says, "Good morning."

But it won't happen like that, and she doesn't want to see the familiar vacant expression, doesn't want to watch as the boy tries to fill in the gaps where memories of her *should* be, witness as he pulls together his composure into practiced nonchalance. The girl has seen that performance often enough, knows the motions by heart, so instead she slides from the bed and pads barefoot out into the living room.

She catches her reflection in the hall mirror and notices what everyone notices: the seven freckles, scattered like a band of stars across her nose and cheeks.

Her own private constellation.

She leans forward and fogs the glass with her breath. Draws her fingertip through the cloud as she tries to write her name. *A—d—*

But she only gets as far as that before the letters dissolve. It's not the medium—no matter how she tries to say her name, no matter how she tries to tell her story. And she *has* tried, in pencil, in ink, in paint, in blood.

Adeline.

Addie.

LaRue.

It is no use.

The letters crumble, or fade. The sounds die in her throat.

Her fingers fall away from the glass and she turns, surveying the living room.

Toby is a musician, and the signs of his art are everywhere.

In the instruments that lean against the walls. In the scribbled lines and notes scattered on tables—bars of half-remembered melodies mixed in with grocery lists and weekly to-do's. But here and there, another hand—the flowers he's started keeping on the kitchen sill, though he can't remember when the habit started. The book on Rilke he doesn't remember buying. The things that last, even when memories don't.

Toby is a slow riser, so Addie makes herself tea—he doesn't drink it, but it's already there, in his cupboard, a tin of loose Ceylon, and a box of silk pouches. A relic of a late-night trip to the grocery store, a boy and a girl wandering the aisles, hand in hand, because they couldn't sleep. Because she hadn't been willing to let the night end. Wasn't ready to let go.

She lifts the mug, inhales the scent as memories waft up to meet it.

A park in London. A patio in Prague. A team room in Edinburgh.

The past drawn like a silk sheet over the present.

It's a cold morning in New York, the windows fogged with frost, so she pulls a blanket from the back of the couch and wraps it around her shoulders. A guitar case takes up one end of the sofa, and Toby's cat takes up the other, so she perches on the piano bench instead.

The cat, *also* named Toby ("So I can talk to myself without it being weird . . ." he explained) looks at her as she blows on her tea.

She wonders if the cat remembers.

Her hands are warmer now, and she sets the mug on top of the piano and slides the cover up off the keys, stretches her fingers, and starts to play as softly as possible. In the bedroom, she can hear Toby-the-human stirring, and every inch of her, from skeleton to skin, tightens in dread.

This is the hardest part.

Addie could have left—*should* have left—slipped out when he was still asleep, when their morning was still an extension of their night, a moment trapped in amber. But it is too late now, so she closes her eyes and continues to play, keeps her head down as she hears his footsteps underneath the notes, keeps her fingers moving when she feels him in the doorway. He'll stand there, taking in the scene, trying to piece together the timeline of last night, how it could have gone astray, when he could have met a girl and then taken her home, if he could have had too much drink, why he doesn't remember any of it.

But she knows that Toby won't interrupt her as long as she's playing, so she savors the music for several more seconds before forcing herself to trail off, look up, pretend she doesn't notice the confusion on his face.

"Morning," she says, her voice cheerful, and her accent, once country French, now so faint that she hardly hears it.

"Uh, good morning," he says, running a hand through his loose black curls, and to his credit, Toby looks the way he always does—a little dazed, and surprised to see a pretty girl sitting in his living room wearing nothing but a pair of underwear and his favorite band T-shirt beneath the blanket.

"Jess," she says, supplying the name he can't find, because it isn't there. "It's okay," she says, "if you don't remember."

Toby blushes, and nudges Toby-the-cat out of the way as he sinks onto the couch cushions. "I'm sorry . . . this isn't like me. I'm not that kind of guy."

She smiles. "I'm not that kind of girl."

He smiles, too, then, and it's a line of light breaking the shadows of his face. He nods at the piano, and she wants him to say something like, "I didn't know you could play," but instead Toby says, "You're really good," and she is—it's amazing what you can learn when you have the time.

"Thanks," she says, running her fingertips across the keys.

Toby is restless now, escaping to the kitchen. "Coffee?" he asks, shuffling through the cupboards.

"I found tea."

She starts to play a different song. Nothing intricate, just a strain of notes. The beginnings of something. She finds the melody, takes it up, lets its slip between her fingers as Toby ducks back into the room, a steaming cup in his hands.

"What was that?" he asks, eyes brightening in that way unique to artists— writers, painters, musicians, anyone prone to moments of inspiration. "It sounded familiar . . ."

A shrug. "You played it for me last night."

It isn't a lie, not exactly. He did play it for her. After she showed him.

"I did?" he says, brow furrowing. He's already setting the coffee aside, reaching for a pencil and a notepad off the nearest table. "God—I must have been drunk."

He shakes his head as he says it; Toby's never been one of those songwriters who prefer to work under the influence.

"Do you remember more?" he asks, turning through the pad. She starts playing again, leading him through the notes. He doesn't know it, but he's been working on this song for weeks. Well, *they* have.

Together.

She smiles a little as she plays on. This is the grass between the nettles. A safe place to step. She can't leave her own mark, but if she's careful, she can give the mark to someone else. Nothing concrete, of course, but inspiration rarely is.

Toby's got the guitar up now, balanced on one knee, and he follows her lead, murmuring to himself. That this is good, this is different, this is *something*. She stops playing, gets to her feet.

"I should go."

The melody falls apart on the strings as Toby looks up. "What? But I don't even know you."

"Exactly," she says, heading for the bedroom to collect her clothes.

"But I *want* to know you," Toby says, setting down the guitar and trailing her through the apartment, and this is the moment when none of it feels fair, the only time she feels the wave of frustration threatening to break. Because she has spent *weeks* getting to know him. And he has spent hours forgetting her. "Slow down."

She hates this part. She shouldn't have lingered. Should have been out of sight as well as out of mind, but there's always that nagging hope that this time, it will be different, that this time, they will remember.

I remember, says the darkness in her ear.

She shakes her head, forcing the voice away.

"Where's the rush?" asks Toby. "At least let me make you breakfast."

But she's too tired to play the game again so soon, and so she lies instead, says there's something she has to do, and doesn't let herself stop moving, because if she does, she knows she won't have the strength to start again, and the cycle will spin on, the affair beginning in the morning instead of at night. But it won't be any easier when it ends, and if she has to start over, she'd rather be a meet-cute at a bar than the unremembered aftermath of a one-night stand.

It won't matter, in a moment, anyways.

"Jess, wait," Toby says, catching her hand. He fumbles for the right words, and then gives up, starts again. "I have a gig tonight, at the Alloway. You should come. It's over on . . ."

She knows where it is, of course. That is where they met for the first time, and the fifth, and the ninth. And when she agrees to come, his smile is dazzling. It always is.

"Promise?" he asks.

"Promise."

"I'll see you there," he says, the words full of hope as she turns and steps through the door. She looks back, and says, "Don't forget me in the meantime."

An old habit. A superstition. A plea.

Toby shakes his head. "How could I?"

She smiles, as if it's just a joke.

But Addie knows, as she forces herself down the stairs, that it's already happening—knows that by the time he closes the door, she'll be gone.

II

March is such a fickle month.

It is the seam between winter and spring—though *seam* suggests an even hem, and March is more like a rough line of stitches sewn by an unsteady hand, swinging wildly between January gusts and June greens. You don't know what you'll find, until you step outside.

Estele used to call these the restless days, when the warmer-blooded gods began to stir, and the cold ones began to settle. When dreamers were most prone to bad ideas, and wanderers were likely to get lost.

Addie has always been predisposed to both.

It makes sense then, that she was born on the 10th of March, right along the ragged seam, though it has been so long since Addie felt like celebrating.

For twenty-three years, she dreaded the marker of time, what it meant: that she was growing up, growing old. And then, for centuries, a birthday was a rather useless thing, far less important than the night she signed away her soul.

That date a death, and a rebirth, rolled into one.

Still, it is her birthday, and a birthday deserves a gift.

She pauses in front of a boutique, her reflection ghosted in the glass.

In the broad window, a mannequin poses mid-stride, its head tilted ever so slightly to one side, as if listening to some private song. Its long torso is wrapped in a broad-striped sweater, a pair of oil-slick leggings vanishing into knee-high boots. One hand up, fingers hooked in the collar of the jacket that hangs over one shoulder. As Addie studies the mannequin, she finds herself mimicking the pose, shifting her stance, tilting her head. And maybe it's the day, or the promise of spring in the air, or maybe she's simply in the mood for something new.

Inside, the boutique smells of unlit candles and unworn clothes, and Addie runs her fingers over cotton and silk before finding the striped knit sweater, which turns out to be cashmere. She throws it over one arm, along with the featured leggings. She knows her sizes.

They haven't changed.

"Hi there!" The cheerful clerk is a girl in her early twenties, like Addie herself, though one is real and aging and the other is an image trapped in amber. "Can I get a room started for you?"

"Oh, that's okay," she says, plucking a pair of boots from a display. "I've got everything I need." She follows the girl to the three curtained stalls at the rear of the shop.

"Just give me a shout if I can help," says the girl, turning away before the curtain swings shut, and Addie is alone with a pillowed bench, and a full-length mirror, and herself.

She kicks off her boots, and shrugs out of her jacket, tossing it onto the seat. Change rattles in the pocket as it lands, and something tumbles out. It hits the floor with a dull clack and rolls across the narrow changing room, stopping only when it meets the baseboard.

It is a ring.

A small circle carved of ash-gray wood. A familiar band, once loved, now loathsome.

Addie stares at the thing a moment. Her fingers twitch, traitorous, but she doesn't reach for the ring, doesn't pick it up, just turns her back on the small wooden circle and continues undressing. She pulls on the sweater, shimmies into the leggings, zips up the boots. The mannequin was thinner, taller, but Addie likes the way the outfit hangs on her, the warmth of the cashmere, the weight of the leggings, the soft embrace of the lining in the boots.

She plucks the price tags off one by one, ignoring the zeroes.

Joyeux anniversaire, she thinks, meeting her reflection. Inclining her head, as if she too hears some private song. The picture of a modern Manhattan woman, even if the face in the mirror is the same one she's had for centuries.

Addie leaves her old clothes strewn like a shadow across the dressing room floor. The ring, a scorned child in the corner. The only thing she reclaims is the discarded jacket.

It's soft, made of black leather and worn practically to silk, the kind of thing people pay a fortune for these days and call it vintage. It is the only thing Addie refused to leave behind and feed to the flames in New Orleans, though the smell of him clung to it like smoke, his stain forever on everything. She does not care. She loves the jacket.

It was new then, but it is broken in now, shows its wear in all the ways she can't. It reminds her of Dorian Gray, time reflected in cowhide instead of human skin.

Addie steps out of the little curtained booth.

Across the boutique, the clerk startles, flustered at the sight of her. "Everything fit?" she asks, too polite to admit she doesn't remember letting someone into the back. God bless customer service.

Addie shakes her head ruefully. "Some days you're stuck with what you've got," she says, heading for the door.

By the time the clerk finds the clothes, a ghost of a girl on the changing room floor, she won't remember whose they are, and Addie will be gone, from sight and mind and memory.

She tosses the jacket over her shoulder, one finger hooked in the collar, and steps out into the sun.

Adeline sits on a bench beside her father.

Her father, who is, to her, a mystery, a solemn giant most at home inside his workshop.

Beneath their feet, a pile of woodwares make shapes like small bodies under a blanket, and the cart wheels rattle as Maxime, the sturdy mare, draws them down the lane, away from home.

Away—*away*—a word that makes her small heart race.

Adeline is seven, the same as the number of freckles on her face. She is bright and small and quick as a sparrow, and has begged for months to go with him to market. Begged until her mother swore she would go mad, until her father finally said yes. He is a woodworker, her father, and three times a year, he makes the trip along the Sarthe, up to the city of Le Mans.

And today, she is with him.

Today, for the first time, Adeline is leaving Villon.

She looks back at her mother, arms crossed beside the old yew tree at the end of the lane, and then they round the bend, and her mother is gone. The village rolls past, here the houses and there the fields, here the church and there the trees, here Monsieur Berger turning soil and there Madame Therault hanging clothes, her daughter Isabelle sitting in the grass nearby, twining flowers into crowns, her tongue between her teeth in concentration.

When Adeline told the girl about her trip, Isabelle had only shrugged, and said, "I like it here."

As if you couldn't like one place and want to see another.

Now she looks up at Adeline, and waves as the cart goes by. They reach the edge of the village, the farthest she has ever gone before, and the cart hits a divot in the road, and shakes as if it too has crossed a threshold. Adeline holds her breath, expecting to feel some rope draw tight inside her, binding her to the town.

But there is no tether, no lurch. The cart keeps moving, and Adeline feels a little wild and a little scared as she turns back to look at the shrinking picture of Villon, which was, until now, the sum of her world, and is now only a part, made smaller with the mare's every step, until the town seems like one of her father's figurines, small enough to nest within one calloused palm.

It is a day's ride to Le Mans, the trek made easy with her mother's basket and her father's company—one's bread and cheese to fill her belly, and the other's easy laugh, and broad shoulders making shade for Adeline beneath the summer sun.

At home he is a quiet man, committed to his work, but on the road he begins to open, to unfold, to speak.

And when he speaks, it is to tell her stories.

Those stories he gathered, the way one gathers wood.

"Il était une fois," he will say, before sliding into stories of palaces and kings, of gold and glamour, of masquerade balls and cities full of splendor. Once upon a time. This is how the story starts.

She will not remember the stories themselves, but she will recall the way he tells them; the words feel smooth as river stones, and she wonders if he tells these stories when he is alone, if he carries on, talking to Maxime in this easy, gentle way. Wonders if he tells stories to the wood as he is working it. Or if they are just for her.

Adeline wishes she could write them down.

Later, her father will teach her letters. Her mother will have a fit when she finds out, and accuse him of giving her another way to idle, waste the hours of the day, but Adeline will steal away into his workshop nonetheless, and he will let her sit and practice writing her own name in the fine dust that always seems to coat the workshop floor.

But today, she can only listen.

The countryside rolls past around them, a jostling portrait of a world she already knows. The fields are fields, just like her own, the trees arranged in roughly the same order, and when they do come upon a village, it is a watery reflection of Villon, and Adeline begins to wonder if the world outside is as boring as her own.

And then, the walls of Le Mans come into sight.

Stone ridges rising in the distance, a many-patterned spine along the hills. It is a hundred times the size of Villon—or at least, it is that grand in memory—and Adeline holds her breath as they pass through the gates and into the protected city.

Beyond, a maze of crowded streets. Her father guides the cart between houses squeezed tight as stones, until the narrow road opens onto a square.

There is a square back in Villon, of course, but it is little bigger than their yard. This is a giant's space, the ground lost beneath so many feet, and carts, and stalls. And as her father guides Maxime to a stop, Adeline stands on the bench and marvels at the marketplace, the heady smell of bread and sugar on the air, and people, people, everywhere she looks. She has never seen so many of them, let alone ones she does not know. They are a sea of strangers, unfamiliar faces in unfamiliar clothes, with unfamiliar voices, calling unfamiliar words. It feels as if the doors of her world have been thrown wide, so many rooms added to a house she thought she knew.

Her father leans against the cart, and talks to anyone who passes by, and all the while his hands move over a block of wood, a small knife nested in one palm. He shaves at the surface with all the steady ease of someone peeling an apple, ribbons falling between his fingers. Adeline has always loved to watch him work, to see the figures take shape, as if they were there all along, but hidden, like pits in the center of a peach.

Her father's work is beautiful, the wood smooth where his hands are rough, delicate where he is large.

And mixed among the bowls and cups, tucked between the tools of his trade, are toys for sale, and wooden figures as small as rolls of bread—a horse, a boy, a house, a bird.

Adeline grew up surrounded by such trinkets, but her favorite is neither animal nor man.

It is a ring.

She wears it on a leather cord around her neck, a delicate band, the wood ash gray, and smooth as polished stone. He carved it when she was born, made for the girl she'd one day be, and Adeline wears it like a talisman, an amulet, a key. Her hand goes to it now and then, thumb running over the surface the way her mother's runs over a rosary.

She clings to it now, an anchor in the storm, as she perches on the back of the cart, and watches *everything*. From this angle she is almost tall enough to see the buildings beyond. She stretches up onto her toes, wondering how far they go, until a nearby horse jostles their cart as it goes past, and she nearly falls. Her father's hand closes around her arm, pulling her back into the safety of his reach.

By the end of the day, the wooden wares are gone, and Adeline's father gives her a copper sol and says she may buy anything she likes. She goes from stall to stall, eying the pastries and the cakes, the hats and the dresses and the dolls, but in the end, she settles on a journal, parchment bound with waxy thread. It is the blankness of the paper that excites her, the idea that she might fill the space with anything she likes.

She could not afford the pencils to go with it, but her father uses a second coin to buy a bundle of small black sticks, and explains that these are charcoal, shows her how to press the darkened chalk to the paper, smudge the line to turn hard edges into shadow. With a few quick strokes, he draws a bird in the corner of the page, and she spends the next hour copying the lines, far more interesting than the letters he's written beneath.

Her father packs up the cart as the day gives way to dusk.

They will stay the night in a local inn, and for the first time in her life, Adeline will sleep in a foreign bed, and wake to foreign sounds and smells, and there will be a moment, as brief as a yawn, when she won't know where she is, and her heart will quicken—first with fear, and then with something else. Something she does not have the words for yet.

And by the time they return home to Villon, she will already be a different version of herself. A room with the windows all thrown wide, eager to let in the fresh air, the sunlight, the spring.

It is a Catholic place, Villon. Certainly the part that shows.

There is a church in the center of town, a solemn stone thing where everyone goes to save their souls. Adeline's mother and father kneel there twice a week, cross themselves and say their blessings and speak of God.

Adeline is twelve now, so she does, too. But she prays the way her father turns loaves of bread upright, the way her mother licks her thumb to collect stray flakes of salt.

As a matter of habit, more automatic than faith.

The church in town isn't new, and neither is God, but Adeline has come to think of Him that way, thanks to Estele, who says the greatest danger in change is letting the new replace the old.

Estele, who belongs to everyone, and no one, and herself.

Estele, who grew like a tree at the heart of the village by the river, and has certainly never been young, who sprang up from the ground itself with gnarled hands and woody skin and roots deep enough to tap into her own hidden well.

Estele, who believes that the new God is a filigreed thing. She thinks that He belongs to cities and kings, and that He sits over Paris on a golden pillow, and has no time for peasants, no place among the wood and stone and river water.

Adeline's father thinks Estele is mad.

Her mother says that the woman is bound for Hell, and once, when Adeline repeated as much, Estele laughed her dry-leaf laugh and said there was no such place, only the cool dark soil and the promise of sleep.

"And what of Heaven?" asked Adeline.

"Heaven is a nice spot in the shade, a broad tree over my bones."

At twelve, Adeline wonders which god she should pray to now, to make her father change his mind. He has loaded up his cart with wares bound for Le Mans, has harnessed Maxime, but for the first time in six years, she is not going with him.

He has promised to bring her a fresh pad of parchment, new tools with which to sketch. But they both know she would rather go and have no gifts, would rather see the world outside than have another pad to draw on. She is running out of subjects, has memorized the tired lines of the village, and all the familiar faces in it.

But this year, her mother has decided that it isn't right for her to go to market, it isn't fitting, even though Adeline *knows* she can still fit on that wooden bench beside her father.

Her mother wishes she was more like Isabelle Therault, sweet and kind and utterly incurious, content to keep her eyes down upon her knitting instead of looking up at clouds, instead of wondering what's around the bend, over the hills.

But Adeline does not know how to be like Isabelle.

She does not *want* to be like Isabelle.

She wants only to go to Le Mans, and once there, to watch the people and see the art all around, and taste the food, and discover things she hasn't heard of yet.

"Please," she says, as her father climbs up into the cart. She should have stowed away among the woodworks, hidden safe beneath the tarp. But now it is too late, and when Adeline reaches for the wheel, her mother catches her by the wrist and pulls her back.

"*Enough,*" she says.

Her father looks at them, and then away. The cart sets out, and when Adeline tries to tear free and run after the cart, her mother's hand flashes out again, this time finding her cheek.

Tears spring to her eyes, a vivid blush before the rising bruise, and her mother's voice when it lands is a second blow.

"You are not a child anymore."

And Adeline understands—and still does not understand at all—feels as if she's being punished for simply growing up. She is so angry then that she wants to run away. Wants to fling her mother's needlework into the hearth and break every half-made sculpture in her father's shop.

Instead, she watches the cart round the bend, and vanish between trees, with one hand clenched around her father's ring. Adeline waits for her mother to let her go, and send her on to do her chores.

And then she goes to find Estele.

Estele, who still worships the old gods.

Adeline must have been five or six the first time she saw the woman drop her stone cup into the river. It was a pretty thing, with a pattern pressed like lace into its sides, and the old woman just let it fall, admiring the splash. Her eyes were closed, and her lips were moving, and when Adeline ambushed the old woman—she was already old, has always been old—on the path home, Estele said she was praying to the gods.

"What for?"

"Marie's child isn't coming as it should," she said. "I asked the river gods to make things flow smooth. They are good at that."

"But why did you give them your cup?"

"Because, Addie, the gods are greedy."

Addie. A pet name, one her mother scorned as boyish. A name her father favored, but only when they were alone. A name that rang like a bell in her bones. A name that suited her far more than *Adeline.*

Now, she finds Estele in her garden, folded in among the wild vines of squash, the thorny spine of a blackberry bush, bent low as a warping branch.

"Addie." The old woman says her name without looking up.

It is autumn, and the ground is littered with the stones of fruit that didn't ripen as it should. Addie nudges them with the toe of her shoe. "How do you talk to them?" she asks. "The old gods. Do you call them by name?"

Estele straightens, joints cracking like dry sticks. If she's surprised by the question, it doesn't show. "They have no names."

"Is there a spell?"

Estele gives her a pointed look. "Spells are for witches, and witches are too often burned."

"Then how do you pray?"

"With gifts, and praise, and even then, the old gods are fickle. They are not bound to answer."

"What do you do then?"

"You carry on."

She chews on the inside of her cheek. "How many gods are there, Estele?"

"As many gods as you have questions," answers the old woman, but there is no scorn in her voice, and Addie knows to wait her out, to hold her breath until she sees the telltale sign of Estele's softening. It is like waiting at a neighbor's door after you've knocked, when you know they are home. She can hear the steps, the low rasp of the lock, and knows that it will give.

Estele sighs open.

"The old gods are everywhere," she says. "They swim in the river, and grow in the field, and sing in the woods. They are in the sunlight on the wheat, and under the saplings in spring, and in the vines that grow up the side of that stone church. They gather at the edges of the day, at dawn, and at dusk."

Adeline's eyes narrow. "Will you teach me? How to call on them?"

The old woman sighs, knowing that Adeline LaRue is not only clever, but also stubborn. She begins wading through the garden to the house, and the girl follows, afraid that if Estele reaches her front door before she answers, she might close it on this conversation. But Estele looks back, eyes keen in her wrinkled face.

"There are rules."

Adeline hates rules, but she knows that sometimes they are necessary.

"Like what?"

"You must humble yourself before them. You must offer them a gift. Something precious to you. And you must be careful what you ask for."

Adeline considers. "Is that all?"

Estele's face darkens. "The old gods may be great, but they are neither kind nor merciful. They are fickle, unsteady as moonlight on water, or shadows in a storm. If you insist on calling them, take heed: be careful what you ask for, be willing to pay the price." She leans over Adeline, casting her in shadow. "And no matter how desperate or dire, *never* pray to the gods that answer after dark."

Two days later, when Adeline's father returns, he comes bearing a fresh pad of parchment, and a bundle of black lead pencils, bound with string, and the first thing she does is pick the best one, and sink it down into the ground behind their garden, and pray that next time her father leaves, she will be with him.

But if the gods hear, they do not answer.

She never goes to market again.

Blink, and the years fall away like leaves.

Adeline is sixteen now, and everyone speaks of her as if she is a summer bloom, something to be plucked, and propped within a vase, intended only to flower and then to rot. Like Isabelle, who dreams of family instead of freedom, and seems content to briefly blossom and then wither.

No, Adeline has decided she would rather be a tree, like Estele. If she must grow roots, she would rather be left to flourish wild instead of pruned, would rather stand alone, allowed to grow beneath the open sky. Better that than firewood, cut down just to burn in someone else's hearth.

She hefts the laundry on her hip and crests the rise, making her way down the weedy slope to the river. When she reaches the banks, she turns the basket out, dumping the soiled clothes into the grass, and there, tucked like a secret between the skirts and aprons and undergarments, is the sketchbook. Not the first—she has gathered them year after year, careful to fill every inch of space, to make the most of each blank page.

But every one is like a taper burning on a moonless night, always running out too fast.

It does not help that she keeps giving bits away.

She kicks off her shoes and slumps back against the slope, her skirts pooling beneath her. She runs her fingers through the weedy grass and finds the fraying edge of the paper, one of her favorite drawings, folded into a square and driven down into the bank last week, just after dawn. A token, buried like a seed, or a promise. An offering.

Adeline still prays to the new God, when she must, but when her parents are not looking she prays to the old ones, too. She can do both: keep one tucked in her cheek like a cherry pit while she whispers to the other.

So far, none of them have answered.

And yet, Adeline is sure that they are listening.

When George Caron began to look at her a certain way last spring, she prayed for him to turn his gaze, and he began to notice Isabelle instead. Isabelle has since become his wife, and is now ripe with her first child, and worn with all the torments that come with it.

When Arnaud Tulle made his intentions clear last fall, Adeline prayed that he would find another girl. He did not, but that winter he took ill and died, and Adeline felt terrible for her relief, even as she fed more trinkets to the stream.

She has prayed, and someone must have heard, for she is still free. Free from courtship, free from marriage, free from everything except Villon. Left alone to grow.

And dream.

Adeline sits back on the slope, the sketchpad balanced on her knees. She pulls the drawstring pouch from her pocket, bits of charcoal and a few worn-down precious pencils rattling like coins on market day.

She used to bind a bit of cloth around the stems to keep her fingers clean, until her father fashioned narrow bands of wood around the blackened sticks, and showed her how to hold the little knife, how to shave away the edges, and trim the casing into points. And now the images are sharper, the edges contoured, the details fine. The pictures bloom like stains across the paper, landscapes of Villon, and everyone in it, too—the lines of her mother's hair and her father's eyes and Estele's hands, and then there, tucked into the seams and edges of each page—

Adeline's secret.

Her stranger.

Every bit of unused space she fills with him, a face drawn so often that the gestures now feel effortless, the lines unfurling on their own. She can conjure him from memory, even though they have never met.

He is, after all, only a figment of her mind. A companion crafted first from boredom, and then from longing.

A dream, to keep her company.

She doesn't remember when it started, only that one day she cast her gaze about the village and found every prospect wanting.

Arnaud's eyes were pleasant, but he had no chin.

Jacques was tall, but dull as dirt.

George was strong, but his hands were rough, his moods rougher still.

And so she stole the pieces she found pleasant, and assembled someone new.

A stranger.

It began as a game—but the more Adeline draws him, the stronger the lines, the more confident the press of her charcoal.

Black curls. Pale eyes. Strong jaw. Sloping shoulders and a cupid's bow mouth. A man she'd never meet, a life she'd never know, a world she could only dream of.

When she is restless, she returns to the drawings, tracing over the now familiar lines. And when she cannot sleep, she thinks of him. Not the angle of his cheek, or the shade of green she has conjured for his eyes, but his voice, his touch. She lies awake and imagines him beside her, his long fingers tracing absent patterns on her skin. As he does, he tells her stories.

Not the kind her father used to tell, of knights and kingdoms, princesses and thieves. Not fairy tales and warnings of venturing outside the lines, but stories that feel like truths, renditions of the road, cities that sparkle, of the world beyond Villon. And even though the words she puts in his mouth are surely full of errors and lies, her stranger's conjured voice makes them sound so wonderful, so real.

If only you could see it, he says.

I would give anything, she answers.

One day, he promises. *One day, I'll show you. You'll see it all.*

The words ache, even as she thinks them, the game giving way to want, a thing too genuine, too dangerous. And so, even in her imagination, she guides the conversation back to safer roads.

Tell me about tigers, Adeline says, having heard of the massive cats from Estele, who heard of them from the mason, who was part of a caravan that included a woman who claimed to have seen one.

Her stranger smiles, and gestures with his tapered fingers, and tells her of their silken fur, their teeth, their furious roars.

On the slope, the laundry forgotten beside her, Adeline turns her wooden ring absently with one hand as she draws with the other, sketching out his eyes, his mouth, the line of his bare shoulders. She breathes life into him with every line. And with every stroke, coaxes out another story.

Tell me about dancing in Paris.

Tell me about sailing across the sea.

Tell me everything.

There was no danger in it, no reproach, not when she was young. All girls are prone to dreaming. She will grow out of it, her parents say—but instead, Adeline feels herself growing *in,* holding tighter to the stubborn hope of something more.

The world should be getting larger. Instead, she feels it shrinking, tightening like chains around her limbs as the flat lines of her own body begin to curve out against it, and suddenly the charcoal beneath her nails is unbecoming, as is the idea that she would choose her own company over Arnaud's or George's, or any man who might have her.

She is at odds with everything, she does not fit, an insult to her sex, a stubborn child in a woman's form, her head bowed and arms wrapped tight around her drawing pad as if it were a door.

And when she does look up, her gaze always goes to the edge of town.
"A dreamer," scorns her mother.
"A dreamer," mourns her father.
"A dreamer," warns Estele.
Still, it does not seem such a bad word.
Until Adeline wakes up.

There is a rhythm to moving through the world alone.

You discover what you can and cannot live without, the simple necessities and small joys that define a life. Not food, not shelter, not the basic things a *body* needs—those are, for her, a luxury—but the things that keep you sane. That bring you joy. That make life bearable.

Addie thinks of her father and his carvings, the way he peeled away the bark, whittled down the wood beneath to find the shapes that lived inside. Michelangelo called it the angel in the marble—though she'd not known that as a child. Her father had called it the secret in the wood. He knew how to reduce a thing, sliver by sliver, piece by piece, until he found its essence; knew, too, when he'd gone too far. One stroke too many, and the wood went from delicate to brittle in his hands.

Addie has had three hundred years to practice her father's art, to whittle herself down to a few essential truths, to learn the things she cannot do without.

And this is what she's settled on: she can go without food (she will not wither). She can go without heat (the cold will not kill her). But a life without art, without wonder, without beautiful things—she would go mad. She has gone mad.

What she *needs* are stories.

Stories are a way to preserve one's self. To be remembered. And to forget.

Stories come in so many forms: in charcoal, and in song, in paintings, poems, films. And *books*.

Books, she has found, are a way to live a thousand lives—or to find strength in a very long one.

Two blocks up Flatbush, she sees the familiar green folding table on the sidewalk, covered in paperbacks, and Fred hunched in his rickety chair behind it, red nose buried in *M is for Malice*. The old man explained to her once, back when he was on *K is for Killer*, how he was determined to get through Grafton's entire alphabet series before he dies. She hopes he makes it. He has a nagging cough, and sitting out here in the cold doesn't help, but here he is, whenever Addie comes by.

Fred doesn't smile, or make small talk. What Addie knows of him she has pried out word by word over the last two years, the progress slow and halting. She knows he is a widower who lives upstairs, knows the books belonged to his wife, Candace, knows that when she died, he packed up all her books and brought them down to sell, and it's like letting her go in pieces. Selling off his grief. Addie knows that he sits down here because he's afraid of dying in his apartment, of not being found—not being missed.

"I keel over out here," he says, "at least someone will notice."

He is a gruff old man, but Addie likes him. Sees the sadness in his anger, the guardedness of grief.

Addie suspects he doesn't really want the books to sell.

He doesn't price them, hasn't read more than a few, and sometimes his mood is so coarse, his tone so cold, he actually scares the customers away. Still, they come, and still, they buy, but every time the selection seems to thin a new box appears, the contents are unpacked to fill the gaps, and in the last few weeks, Addie has once more begun to spot new releases among the old, fresh covers and unbroken spines in with the battered paperbacks. She wonders if he is buying them, or if other people have begun donating to his strange collection.

Addie slows, now, her fingers dancing over the spines.

The selection is always a medley of discordant notes. Thrillers, biographies, romance, battered mass markets, mostly, interrupted by a few glossy hardcovers. She has stopped to study them a hundred times, but today she simply tips the book on the end into her hand, the gesture light and swift as a magician's. A piece of legerdemain. Practice long given way to perfect. Addie tucks the book under her arm and keeps walking.

The old man never looks up.

The market sits like a cluster of old wives at the edge of the park.

Long thin from winter, the number of white-capped stalls is finally beginning to swell again, drops of color dotting the square where new produce springs up between the root vegetables, meat and bread, and other staples resistant to the cold.

Addie weaves between the people, heading to the little white tent nestled by the front gates of Prospect. Rise and Shine is a coffee and pastry stall run by a pair of sisters that remind Addie of Estele, if the old woman had been two instead of one, divided along the lines of temper. If she had been kinder, softer, or perhaps if she had simply lived another life, another time.

The sisters are here year-round, come snow or sun, a small constant in an ever-changing city.

"Hey, sugar," says Mel, all broad shoulders, and wild curls, and the kind of sweetness that makes strangers feel like family. Addie loves that, the easy warmth, wants to nestle into it like a well-worn sweater.

"What can we get for you?" asks Maggie, older, leaner, laugh lines around her eyes belying the idea she rarely smiles.

Addie orders a large coffee and two muffins, one blueberry and the other chocolate chip, and then hands over a crumpled ten that she'd found on Toby's coffee table. She could steal something from the market, of course, but she likes this little stand, and the two women who run it.

"Got a dime?" asks Maggie.

Addie digs the change from her pocket, coming up with a few quarters, a nickel—and there it is again, warm among the cold metal coins. Her fingers graze the wooden ring and she clenches her teeth at the feel of it. Like a nagging thought, impossible to shed. Sifting through the coins, Addie is careful not to touch the wooden band again as she searches her change, resists the urge to fling the ring into the weeds, knows it will not make a difference if she does. It will always find its way back.

The darkness whispers in her ear, arms wrapped like a scarf around her throat.

I am always with you.

Addie plucks out a dime and pockets the rest.

Maggie hands back four dollars.

"Where you from, doll?" asks Mel, noticing the faintest edge of an accent in the corners of Addie's voice, reduced these days to the vanishing end of an *s,* the slight softening of a *t.* It has been so long, and yet, she cannot seem to let it go.

"Here and there," she says, "but I was born in France."

"Oh la la," says Mel in her flat Brooklyn drawl.

"Here you go, sunshine," says Maggie, passing her a bag of pastries and a tall cup. Addie curls her fingers around the paper, relishing the heat on her cold palms. The coffee is strong, and dark, and when she takes a sip, she feels the warmth all the way down, and she is back in Paris again, in Istanbul, in Naples.

A mouthful of memory.

She starts toward the park gates.

"Au revoir!" calls Mel, landing hard on every letter, and Addie smiles into the steam.

The air is crisp inside the park. The sun is out, fighting for warmth, but the shade still belongs to winter, so Addie follows the light, sinking onto a grassy slope beneath the cloudless sky.

She sits the blueberry muffin on top of the paper bag, and sips her coffee, examining the book she borrowed from Fred's table. She hadn't bothered to look at what she was taking, but now her heart sinks a little at the sight of the paperback, the cover soft with wear, the title in German.

Kinder und Hausmärchen it reads, by Brüder Grimm.

Grimm's Fairy Tales.

Her German is rusty, kept in the back of her mind, in a corner she hasn't used much since the war. Now she dusts it off, knows that beneath the layer of grime she will find the space intact, undisturbed. The boon of memory. She turns through the fragile old pages, eyes tripping over the words.

Once upon a time, she loved this kind of story.

When she was still a child, and the world was small, and she dreamed of open doors.

But Addie knows too well now, knows that these stories are full of foolish humans doing foolish things, warning tales of gods and monsters and greedy mortals who want too much, and then fail to understand what they've lost. Until the price is paid, and it's too late to claim it back.

A voice rises like smoke inside her chest.

Never pray to the gods who answer after dark.

Addie tosses the book aside and slumps back into the grass, closing her eyes as she tries to savor the sun.

VIII

Adeline had wanted to be a tree.

To grow wild and deep, belong to no one but the ground beneath her feet, and the sky above, just like Estele. It would be an unconventional life, and perhaps a little lonely, but at least it would be hers. She would belong to no one but herself.

But here is the danger of a place like Villon.

Blink—and a year is gone.

Blink—and five more follow.

It is like a gap between stones, this village, just wide enough for things to get lost. The kind of place where time slips and blurs, where a month, a year, a life can go missing. Where everyone is born and buried in the same ten-meter plot.

Adeline was going to be a tree.

But then came Roger, and his wife, Pauline. Grown up together, and then married, and then gone, in the time it took for her to lace up a pair of boots.

A hard pregnancy, a ruinous birth, two deaths instead of one new life.

Three small children left behind, where there should have been four. The earth still fresh over a grave, and Roger looking for another wife, a mother for his children, a second life at the cost of Adeline's one and only.

Of course, she said no.

Adeline is three and twenty, already too old to wed.

Three and twenty, a third of a life already buried.

Three and twenty—and then gifted like a prize sow to a man she does not love, or want, or even know.

She said no, and learned how much the word was worth. Learned that, like Estele, she had promised herself to the village, and the village had a need.

Her mother said it was duty.

Her father said it was mercy, though Adeline doesn't know for whom.

Estele said nothing, because she knew it wasn't fair. Knew this was the risk of being a woman, of giving yourself to a place, instead of a person.

Adeline was going to be a tree, and instead, people have come brandishing an ax.

They have given her away.

She lies awake the night before the wedding, and thinks of freedom. Of fleeing. Of stealing away on her father's horse, even as she knows the thought is madness.

She feels mad enough to do it.

Instead, she prays.

She has been praying, of course, since the day of her betrothal, given half her possessions to the river and buried the other half in the field or at the slope of dirt and brush where the village meets the woods, and now she is almost out of time, and out of tokens.

She lies there in the dark, twists the old wooden ring on its leather cord, and considers going out and praying again now, in the dead of night, but Adeline remembers Estele's fearsome warning about the ones who might answer. So instead, she clenches her hands together and prays to her mother's God instead. Prays for help, for a miracle, for a way out. And then in the darkest part of night, she prays for Roger's death—anything for her escape.

She feels guilty at once, sucks it back into her chest like an expelled breath, and waits.

Day breaks like an egg yolk, spilling yellow light across the field.

Adeline slips out of the house before dawn, having never slept at all. Now she winds her way through the wild grass beyond the vegetable garden, skirts wicking up the dew. She lets herself sink with the weight of them, her favorite drawing pencil clutched in one hand. Adeline does not want to give it up, but she is running out of time and out of tokens.

She presses the pencil point down into the damp soil of the field.

"Help me," she whispers to the grass, its edges limned with light. "I know you are there. I know you are listening. Please. Please."

But the grass is only grass, and the wind is only wind, and neither answers, even when she presses her forehead to the ground and sobs.

There is nothing *wrong* with Roger.

But there is nothing *right*, either. His skin is waxy, his blond hair thinning, his voice like a wisp of wind. When his hand lays itself upon her arm, the grip is weak, and when he inclines his head toward hers, his breath is stale.

And Adeline? She is a vegetable left too long in the garden, its skin gone stiff, its insides woody, gone to ground by choice, only to be dug up and made into a meal.

"I do not want to marry him," she says, fingers tangled in the weedy earth.

"Adeline!" calls her mother, as if she is one of the livestock, gone astray.

She drags herself up, empty with anger and grief, and when she goes inside her mother sees only the dirt caking her hands, and orders her daughter to the basin. Adeline scrubs the soil from beneath her nails, bristles biting her fingers as her mother scolds.

"What will your husband think?"

Husband.

A word like a millstone, all weight and no warmth.

Her mother tuts. "You will not be so restless once you have children to tend."

Adeline thinks again of Isabelle, two small boys clinging to her skirts, a third in a basket by the hearth. They used to dream together, but she has aged ten years in two, it seems. She is always tired, and there are hollows in her face where once her cheeks were red from laughter.

"It will be good for you," says her mother, "to be somebody's wife."

The day passes like a sentence.

The sun falls like a scythe.

Adeline can almost hear the whistle of the blade as her mother braids her hair into a crown, weaves flowers in the place of jewels. Her dress is simple and light, but it might as well be made of mail for how it weighs on her.

She wants to scream.

Instead, she reaches up and grips the wooden ring around her neck, as if for balance.

"You must take that off before the ceremony," instructs her mother, and Adeline nods, even as her fingers tighten around it.

Her father comes in from the barn, dusted with wood shavings and smelling of sap. He coughs, a faint rattle, like loose seeds, inside his chest. It has been there for a year, that cough, but he will not let them talk of it.

"You are almost ready?" he asks.

What a foolish question.

Her mother talks about the wedding dinner as if it has already come and gone. Adeline looks out the window at the sinking sun, and doesn't listen to the words, but she can hear the light in her mother's voice, the vindication in it. Even in her father's eyes, there is a measure of relief. Their daughter tried to carve her own road, but now things are being set right, a wayward life dragged back on course, propelled down its proper path.

The house is too warm, the air heavy and still, and Adeline cannot breathe.

Finally the church bell tolls, the same low tone it calls at funerals, and she forces herself to her feet.

Her father touches her arm.

His face is sorry, but his grip is firm.

"You will come to love your husband," he says, but the words are clearly more wish than promise.

"You will be a good wife," says her mother, and hers are more command than wish.

And then Estele appears in the doorway, dressed as if she is in mourning. And why shouldn't she be? This woman who taught her of wild dreams and willful gods, who filled Adeline's head with thoughts of freedom, blew on the embers of hope and let her believe a life could be her own.

The light has gone watery and thin behind Estele's gray head. There is still time, Adeline tells herself, but it is fleeting, faster now with every breath.

Time—how often has she heard it described as sand within a glass, steady, constant. But that is a lie, because she can feel it quicken, crashing toward her.

Panic beats a drum inside her chest, and outside, the path is a single dark line, stretched straight and narrow toward the village square. On the other side, the church stands waiting, pale and stiff as a tombstone, and she knows that if she walks in, she will not come out.

Her future will rush by the same as her past, only worse, because there will be no freedom, only a marriage bed and a deathbed and perhaps a child-bed between, and when she dies it will be as though she never lived.

There will be no Paris.

No green-eyed lover.

No trips on boats to faraway lands.

No foreign skies.

No life beyond this village.

No life at all, unless—

Adeline pulls free of her father's grip, drags to a stop on the path.

Her mother turns to look at her, as if she might run, which is exactly what she wants to do, but knows she can't.

"I made a gift for my husband," says Adeline, mind spinning. "I've left it in the house."

Her mother softens, approving.

Her father stiffens, suspicious.

Estele's eyes narrow, knowing.

"I'll just fetch it," she continues, already turning back.

"I'll go with you," says her father, and her heart lurches and her fingers twitch, but it is Estele who reaches out to stop him.

"Jean," she says in that sly way, "Adeline cannot be your daughter *and* his wife. She is a woman grown, not a child to be minded."

He finds his daughter's eyes, and says, "Be quick."

Adeline has already taken flight.

Back up the path, and past the door, into the house, and through, to the other side, to the open window, and the field, and the distant line of trees. The woods standing sentinel at the eastern edge of the village, opposite the sun. The woods, already cloaked in shadow, though she knows there is still light, still time.

"Adeline?" calls her father, but she doesn't look back.

Instead, she climbs through the window, wood snagging on the wedding dress as she stumbles out, and runs.

"Adeline? Adeline!"

The voices call out after her, but they stretch thinner with every step, and soon she is across the field, and into the woods, breaking the line of trees as she sinks to her knees in the dense summer dirt.

She clutches the wooden ring, feels the loss of it even before she tugs the leather cord over her head. Adeline does not want to sacrifice it, but she has used up all her tokens, given every gift she could spare back to the earth, and none of the gods have answered. Now this is all she has left, and the light is thin, and the village is calling, and she is desperate to escape.

"Please," she whispers, her voice breaking over the word as she plunges the band down into the mossy earth. "I will do anything."

The trees murmur overhead, and then go still, as if they too are waiting, and Adeline prays, to every god in the Villon woods, to anyone and anything who will listen. This cannot be her life. This cannot be all there is.

"Answer me," she pleads as the damp seeps into her wedding dress.

She squeezes her eyes shut, and strains to hear, but the only sound is her own voice on the wind and her name, echoing in her ears like a heartbeat.

"Adeline . . ."

"Adeline . . ."

"Adeline . . ."

She bows her head against the soil and grips the dark earth and screams, "Answer me!"

The silence is mocking.

She has lived here all her life and never heard the woods this quiet. Cold settles over her, and she doesn't know if it's coming from the forest or from her own bones, giving up the last of their fight. Her eyes are still shut tight, and perhaps that is why she doesn't notice that the sun has slipped behind the village at her back, that dusk has given way to dark.

Adeline keeps praying, and doesn't notice at all.

IX

The sound, when it comes, is a low rumble, deep and distant as thunder.

Laughter, Adeline thinks, opening her eyes and noticing, finally, how the light has faded.

She looks up, but sees nothing. "Hello?"

The laughter draws itself into a voice, somewhere behind her.

"You need not kneel," it says. "Let us see you on your feet."

She scrambles up, and turns, but she is met only by darkness, surrounded by it, a moonless night after the summer sun has fled. And Adeline knows, then, that she has made a mistake. That this is one of the gods she was warned against.

"Adeline? Adeline?" call the voices from the town, as faint and faraway as the wind.

She squints into the shadows between the trees, but there is no shape, no god to be found—only that voice, close as a breath against her cheek.

"Adeline, Adeline," it says, mocking, ". . . they are calling for you."

She turns again, finding nothing but deep shadow. "Show yourself," she orders, her own voice sharp and brittle as a stick.

Something brushes her shoulder, grazes her wrist, drapes itself around her like a lover. Adeline swallows. "What are you?"

The shadow's touch withdraws. "What am I?" it asks, an edge of humor in that velvet tone. "That depends on what you believe."

The voice splits, doubles, rattling through tree limbs and snaking over moss, folding over on itself until it is everywhere.

"So tell me—tell me—tell me," it echoes. "Am I the devil—the devil—or the dark—dark—dark? Am I a monster—monster—or a god—god—god—or . . ."

The shadows in the woods begin to pull together, drawn like storm clouds. But when they settle, the edges are no longer wisps of smoke, but hard lines, the shape of a man, made firm by the light of the village lanterns at his back.

"Or am I this?"

The voice spills from a perfect pair of lips, a shadow revealing emerald eyes that dance below black brows, black hair that curls across his forehead, framing a face Adeline knows too well. One that she has conjured up a thousand times, in pencil and charcoal and dream.

It is the stranger.

Her stranger.

She knows it is a trick, a shadow parading as a man, but the sight of him still robs her breath. The darkness looks down at his shape, seeing himself as if for the first time, and seems to approve. "Ah, so the girl believes in something after all." Those green eyes lift. "Well now," he says, "you have called, and I have come."

Never pray to the gods that answer after dark.

Adeline knows—she *knows*—but this is the only one who answered. The only one who would help.

"Are you prepared to pay?"

Pay.

The price.

The ring.

Adeline drops to her knees, scours the ground until she finds the leather cord, and frees her father's ring from the soil.

She holds it out to the god, its pale wood now stained with dirt, and he draws closer. He may look like flesh and blood, but he still moves like shadow. A single step, and he is there, filling her vision, folding one hand around the ring, and resting the other on Adeline's cheek. His thumb brushes the freckle beneath her eye, the edge of her stars.

"My dear," says the darkness, taking the ring, "I do not deal in trinkets."

The wooden band crumbles in his hand, and falls away, nothing more than smoke. A strangled sound escapes her lips—it hurt enough to lose the ring, hurts more to see it wiped from the world like a smudge on skin. But if the ring is not enough, then what?

"Please," she says, "I will give anything."

The shadow's other hand still rests against her cheek. "You assume I want *anything*," he says, lifting her chin. "But I take only one coin." He leans closer still, green eyes impossibly bright, his voice soft as silk. "The deals I make, I make for souls."

Adeline's heart lurches in her chest.

In her mind, she sees her mother on her knees in church, speaking of God and Heaven, hears her father talking, telling stories of wishes and riddles. She thinks of Estele, who believes in nothing but a tree over her bones. Who would say that a soul is nothing more than a seed returned to soil—though she's the one who warned against the dark.

"Adeline," says the darkness, her name sliding like moss between his teeth. "I am here. Now tell me why."

She has waited so long to be met—to be answered, to be asked—that at first the words all fail her.

"I do not want to marry."

She feels so small when she says it. Her whole life feels small, and she sees that judgment reflected in the god's gaze, as if to say, *Is that all?*

And no, it is more than that. Of course it is more.

"I do not want to belong to someone else," she says with sudden vehemence. The words are a door flung wide, and now the rest pour out of her. "I do not want to belong to anyone but myself. I want to be free. Free to live, and to find my own way, to love, or to be alone, but at least it is my choice, and I am so tired of not having choices, so scared of the years rushing past beneath my feet. I do not want to die as I've lived, which is no life at all. I—"

The shadow cuts her off, impatient. "What use is it, to tell me what you do *not* want?" His hand slides through her hair, comes to rest against the back of her neck, drawing her close. "Tell me instead what you want most."

She looks up. "I want a chance to live. I want to be free." She thinks of the years slipping by.

Blink, and half your life is gone.

"I want more time."

He considers her, those green eyes changing shade, now spring grass, now summer leaf. "How long?"

Her mind spins. Fifty years. One hundred. Every number feels too small.

"Ah," says the darkness, reading her silence. "You do not know." Again, the green eyes shift, darken. "You ask for time without limit. You want freedom without rule. You want to be untethered. You want to live exactly as you please."

"Yes," says Adeline, breathless with want, but the shadow's expression sours. His hand drops from her skin, and then he is no longer there, but leaning against a tree several strides away.

"I decline," he says.

Adeline draws back as if struck. "What?" She has come this far, has given everything she has—she made her choice. She cannot go back to that world, that life, that present and past without a future. "You cannot decline."

One dark brow lifts, but there is no amusement in that face.

"I am not some genie, bound to your whim." He pushes off the tree. "Nor am I some petty forest spirit, content with granting favors for mortal trinkets. I am stronger than your god and older than your devil. I am the darkness between stars, and the roots beneath the earth. I am promise, and potential, and when it comes to playing games, I divine the rules, I set the pieces, and I choose when to play. And tonight, I say no."

Adeline? Adeline? Adeline?

Beyond the edge of the woods, the village lights are closer now. There are torches in the field. They are coming for her.

The shadow looks over his shoulder. "Go home, Adeline. Back to your small life."

"Why?" she pleads, grabbing his arm. "Why do you refuse me?"

He brushes his hand along her cheek, the gesture soft and warm as hearth-smoke. "I am not in the business of charity. You ask for too much. How many years until you're sated? How many, until I get my due? No, I make deals with endings, and yours has none."

She will come back to this moment a thousand times.

In frustration, and regret, in sorrow, and self-pity, and unbridled rage.

She will come to face the fact that she cursed herself before he ever did.

But here, and now, all she can see is the flickering torchlight of Villon, and the green eyes of the stranger she once dreamed of loving, and the chance to escape slipping away with his touch.

"You want an ending," she says. "Then take my life when I am done with it. You can have my soul when I don't want it anymore."

The shadow tips his head, suddenly intrigued.

A smile—just like the smile in her drawings, askance, and full of secrets—crosses his mouth. And then he pulls her to him. A lover's embrace. He is smoke and skin, air and bone, and when his mouth presses against hers, the first thing she tastes is the turning of the seasons, the moment when dusk gives way to night. And then his kiss deepens. His teeth skim her bottom lip, and there is pain in the pleasure, followed by the copper taste of blood on her tongue.

"Done," whispers the god against her lips.

And then the world goes black, and she is falling.

Adeline shivers.

She looks down, and sees that she is sitting on a bed of wet leaves.

A second ago, she was falling—for only a second, barely the length it takes to draw a breath—but time, it seems, has skipped ahead. The stranger is gone, and so are the last dregs of light. The summer sky, where it shows through the canopied trees, is smoothed to a velvet black, marked only by a low-hanging moon.

Adeline rises, studying her hands, looking past the dirt for some sign of transformation.

But she feels . . . unchanged. A little dizzy, perhaps, as if she's stood too quickly, or drunk too much wine on an empty stomach, but after a moment even that unsteadiness has passed, and she's left feeling as if the world has tipped, but not fallen, leaned, and then rebalanced, settled back into the same old groove.

She licks her lips, expecting to taste blood, but the mark left by the stranger's teeth is gone, swept away with every other trace of him.

How does one know if a spell has worked? She asked for time, for life— will she have to wait a year, or three, or five, to see if age leaves any mark? Or take up a knife and cut into her skin, to see if and how it heals? But no, she had asked for life, not a life *unscathed,* and if Adeline is being honest, she is afraid to test it, afraid to find her skin still too yielding, afraid to learn that the shadow's promise was a dream, or worse, a lie.

But she knows one thing—whether or not the deal was real, she will not heed the ringing church bells, will not marry Roger. She will defy her family. She will leave Villon, if she must. She knows she will do whatever it takes now, because she was willing in the dark, and one way or another, from this moment forward, her life *will* be her own.

The thought is thrilling. Terrifying, but thrilling, as she leaves the forest.

She is halfway across the field before she realizes how quiet the village is. How dark.

The festive lanterns have been put out, the bells have stopped ringing, there are no voices calling her name.

Adeline makes her way home, the dull dread growing a little sharper with every step. By the time she gets there, her mind is buzzing with worry. The front door hangs open, spilling light onto the path, and she can hear her mother humming in the kitchen, her father chopping wood around the side of the house. A normal night, made wrong by the fact it was not meant to be a normal night.

"Maman!" she says, stepping inside.

A plate shatters to the floor, and her mother yelps, not in pain, but surprise, her face contorted.

"What are you doing here?" she demands, and here is the anger Addie expected. Here is the dismay.

"I'm sorry," she starts. "I know you must be mad, but I couldn't—"

"Who are you?"

The words are a hiss, and she realizes then, that fearsome look on her mother's face is not the anger of a mother scorned, but that of a woman scared.

"Maman—"

Her mother cringes away from the very word. "Get out of my house."

But Adeline crosses the room, grabs her by the shoulders. "Don't be absurd. It's me, A—"

She is about to say *Adeline*.

Indeed, she tries. Three syllables should not be such a mountain to climb, but she is breathless by the end of the first, unable to manage the second. The air turns to stone inside her throat, and she is left stifled, silent. She tries again, this time attempting *Addie*, then at last their family name, *LaRue*, but it is no use. The words meet an impasse between her mind and tongue. And yet, the second she draws breath to say *another* word, any other word, it is there, lungs filled and throat loose.

"Let go," pleads her mother.

"What's this?" demands a voice, low and deep. The voice that soothed Adeline on sick nights, that told her stories as she sat on the floor of his shop.

Her father stands in the doorway, his arms full of wood.

"Papa," she says, and he draws back, as if the word were sharp.

"The woman is mad," sobs her mother. "Or cursed."

"I am your daughter," she says again.

Her father grimaces. "We have no child."

Those words, a duller knife. A deeper cut.

"No," says Adeline, shaking her head at the absurdity. She is three and twenty, has lived every day and every night beneath this roof. "You know me."

How can they not? The resemblance between them has always been so keen, her father's eyes, her mother's chin, one's brow and the other's lips, each piece clearly copied from its source.

They see it, too, they *must*.

But to them, it is only proof of devilry.

Her mother crosses herself, and her father's hands close around her, and she wants to sink into the strength of his embrace, but there is not warmth in it as he drags her to the door.

"No," she begs.

Her mother is crying now, one hand to her mouth and the other clutching the wooden cross around her neck, as she calls her own daughter a demon, a monster, a demented thing, and her father says nothing, only grips her arm tighter as he pulls her from the house.

"Be gone," he says, the words half-pleading.

Sadness sweeps across his face, but not the kind that comes with knowing. No, it is the sadness reserved for lost things, a storm-torn tree, a horse made lame, a carving split one stroke before it's done.

"Please," she begs. "Papa—"

His face hardens as he forces her out into the dark and slams the door. The bolt scrapes home. Adeline stumbles back, shaking with shock and horror. And then she turns and runs.

"Estele."

The name begins as a prayer, soft and private, and grows to a shout as Adeline nears the woman's cottage.

"Estele!"

A lamp is lit within, and by the time she reaches the edge of the light, the old woman stands in the open doorway, waiting for her caller.

"Are you a stranger or a spirit?" Estele asks warily.

"I am neither," says Adeline, though she knows how she must look. Her dress tattered, her hair wild, streaming words like witchcraft on the step. "I am flesh and blood and human, and I have known you all my life. You make charms in the shape of children to keep them well in winter. You think peaches are the sweetest fruit, and that church walls are too thick for prayers to get through, and you want to be buried not beneath a stone, but in a patch of shade under a large tree."

Something flashes across the old woman's face, and Adeline holds her breath, hoping it is recognition. But it is too brief.

"You are a clever spirit," says Estele, "but you will not cross this hearth."

"I am not a spirit!" shouts Adeline, storming into the light of the old woman's door. "You taught me about the old gods, and all the ways to summon them, but I made a mistake. They wouldn't answer, and the sun was going down so fast." She wraps her arms tight around her ribs, unable to stop shaking. "I prayed too late, and something answered, and now everything is wrong."

"Foolish girl," chides Estele, sounding like herself. Sounding as if she knows her.

"What do I do? How do I fix it?"

But the old woman only shakes her head. "The darkness plays its own game," she says. "It makes its own rules," she says. "And you have lost."

And with that, Estele draws back into her house.

"Wait!" calls Adeline as the old woman shuts the door.

The bolt drives home.

Adeline hurls herself against the wood, sobbing until her legs give way, and she sinks to her knees on the cold stone step, one fist still pounding against the wood.

And then, suddenly, the bolt draws back.

The door swings open, and Estele stands over her.

"What is this?" she asks, surveying the girl folded on her steps.

The old woman looks at her as if they've never met. The moments before erased by an instant and a closed door.

Her wrinkled gaze flicks over the stained wedding dress, the wild hair, the dirt under her nails, but there's no knowing in her face, only a guarded curiosity.

"Are you a spirit? Or a stranger?"

Adeline squeezes her eyes shut. What is happening? Her name is still a rock lodged deep, and when she was a spirit, she was banished, so she swallows hard and answers, "A stranger." Tears begin to slide down Adeline's face. "Please," she manages. "I have nowhere to go."

The old woman looks at her for a long moment, and then nods.

"Wait here," she says, slipping back into the house, and Adeline will never know what Estele was going to do then, because the door swings shut, and stays shut, and she is left kneeling on the ground, trembling more from shock than cold.

She doesn't know how long she sits there, but her legs are stiff when she forces them to bear her weight. She rises, and walks past the old woman's house to the line of trees beyond, past their sentinels' edge into the crowded dark.

"Show yourself!" she calls out.

But there is only the ruffle of feathers, the crackle of leaves, the ripple of a forest disturbed in sleep. She conjures his face, those green eyes, those black curls, tries to will the darkness into shape again, but moments pass, and she is still alone.

I do not want to belong to anyone.

Adeline walks deeper into the forest. This is a wilder stretch of wood, the floor a nest of bramble and brush. It claws at her bare legs, but she doesn't stop, not until the trees have closed around her, their branches blotting out the moon overhead.

"I call on you!" she screams.

I am not some genie, bound to your whim.

A low limb, half buried by the forest floor, rises just enough to catch her feet, and she goes down hard, knees hitting ragged earth and hands tearing through weedy soil.

Please, I will give anything.

The tears come, then, sudden and heaving. Fool. Fool. Fool. She pounds her fists against the ground.

This is a vile trick, she thinks, a horrid dream, but it will pass.

That is the nature of dreams. They do not last.

"Wake up," she whispers into the dark.

Wake up.

Adeline curls into the forest floor, closes her eyes, and sees her mother's tearstained cheeks, her father's hollow sadness, Estele's weary gaze. She sees the darkness, smiling. Hears his voice as he whispers that single, binding word.

Done.

A Frisbee lands in the grass nearby.

Addie hears the rumble of running feet, and opens her eyes in time to see a giant black nose rushing at her face before the dog covers her in wet kisses. She laughs and sits up, runs her fingers through thick fur, catching the dog by his collar before he can get ahold of the paper bag with the second muffin.

"Hello, you," she says as, across the park, someone calls out an apology.

She flings the Frisbee back in their direction, and the dog is off again. Addie shivers, suddenly wide awake, and cold.

That's the trouble with March—the warmth never lasts. There's that narrow stretch when it parades as spring, just enough for you to thaw if you're sitting in the sun, but then it's gone. The sun has moved on. The shadows have swept in. Addie shivers again, and pushes up from the grass, brushing off her leggings.

She should have stolen warmer pants.

Shoving the paper bag in her pocket, Addie tucks Fred's book under her arm and abandons the park, heading east down Union and up toward the waterfront.

Halfway there, she stops at the sound of a violin, the notes picked out like ripened fruit.

On the sidewalk, a woman perches on a stool, the instrument tucked beneath her chin. The melody is sweet and slow, drawing Addie back to Marseilles, to Budapest, to Dublin.

A handful of people gather to listen, and when the song ends, the sidewalk fills with soft applause, and passing bodies. Addie digs the last change out of her pocket, and drops it into the open case, and carries on, lighter, and fuller.

When she reaches the theater in Cobble Hill, she checks the posted timetable and then pushes open the door, quickening her pace as she crosses the crowded lobby.

"Hey," Addie says, flagging down a teen boy with a broom. "I think I left my purse in theater three."

Lying is easy, so long as you choose the right words.

He waves her on without looking up, and she ducks beneath the velvet ticket-taker's rope and into the darkened hall, the urgency falling away with every step. Muted thunder rolls beneath the doors of an action film. Music seeps into the hall from a romantic comedy. The highs and lows of voices, and scores. She ambles down the corridor, studying the COMING SOON posters and the ticker tapes announcing the showings above each door. She's seen them all a dozen times, but she doesn't care.

The credits must be rolling on number five, because the doors swing open, and a stream of people spill out into the corridor. Addie ducks past them, into the emptying room, and finds an overturned bucket of popcorn in the second row, golden pebbles littering the sticky floor. She scoops it up and marches back to the lobby, and the concession stand, waits in line behind a trio of preteen girls before reaching the counter, and the boy behind it.

She runs a hand through her hair, mussing it slightly, and blows out her breath.

"I'm sorry," she says, "some little boy kicked over my popcorn." She shakes her head, and so does he, a mimic, echoing her exasperation. "Is there any way you could charge me the refill cost instead of . . ." She is already reaching in her pocket, as if to pull out a wallet, but the boy takes the bucket.

"Don't worry about it," he says, glancing around. "I've got you."

Addie beams. "You're a star," she says, meeting his eyes, and the boy blushes fiercely, and stammers that it's really no problem, no problem at all, even as he scans the lobby for a superior. He dumps out the rest of the spilled popcorn and fills it fresh, passing it like a secret back across the counter.

"Enjoy your show."

Of all the inventions Addie has seen ushered into the world—steam-powered trains, electric lights, photography, and phones, and airplanes, and computers— movies might just be her favorite one.

Books are wonderful, portable, lasting, but sitting there, in the darkened theater, the wide screen filling her vision, the world falls away, and for a few short hours she is someone else, plunged into romance and intrigue and comedy and adventure. All of it complete with 4K picture and stereo sound.

A quiet heaviness fills her chest when the credits roll. For a while she was weightless, but now she returns to herself, sinking until her feet are back on the ground.

By the time Addie gets out of the theater it is almost six, and the sun is going down.

She winds her way back through the tree-lined streets, past the park, the market now shuttered and the stalls already gone, and toward the rusted green table at the other edge. Fred is still sitting there in his chair, reading *M*.

The pattern of spines on the table has shifted a little, an empty space here where a book has sold, a new rise there where another has been added. The light is getting low, and soon he'll have to go in, pack up the boxes and carry them one by one back into the house, and up the two floors to his one-bedroom. Addie has offered many times to help, but Fred insists on doing it himself. Another echo of Estele. Stubborn as stale bread.

Addie crouches down beside the table, and rises with the borrowed book in hand, as if it had simply fallen off the end. She sets it back, careful not to upset the stack, and Fred must be at a good spot in the story, because he grunts without ever looking up at her, or the book, or the paper bag she sets on top, the one with the chocolate-chip muffin inside.

It's the only kind he likes.

Candace always gave him hell for his sweet tooth, he told Addie one morning, said it would kill him, but life's a bitch with a crooked sense of humor—'cause she's gone, and he's still eating shit (his words, not hers).

The temperature is falling, and Addie tucks her hands in her pockets and wishes Fred a good night before continuing down the block, her back to the low sun and her shadow long ahead.

It's dark by the time Addie gets to the Alloway—one of those places that seems to relish its status as a dive bar, a reputation tarnished by the fact it's become a favorite among headliners who want that Brooklyn feel. A handful of people mill around on the curb, smoking, chatting, waiting for friends, and Addie lingers among them a moment. She bums a cigarette, just to have something to do, resisting the easy draw of the door for as long as she can, that tipping sense of the familiar, *déjà vu.*

She knows this road.

Knows where it leads.

Inside, the Alloway is shaped like a bottle of whisky, the narrow stem of the entry, the dark wooden bar widening to a room of tables and chairs. She takes a seat at the counter. The man on her left buys her a drink, and she lets him.

"Let me guess," says the man. "A rosé?"

And she thinks of ordering whisky just to see the surprise on his face, but that was never her drink; she's always gone for sweet.

"Champagne."

He orders, and they make small talk until he gets a call, and steps away, promising to be right back. She knows he won't, is grateful for it as she sips her drink and waits for Toby to go onstage.

He takes a seat, one knee up to steady his guitar, and flashes that bashful smile, almost apologetic. He hasn't learned yet how to take up space, but she's sure he will. He looks out at the small crowd before he starts to play, and Addie closes her eyes and lets herself vanish into the music. He plays a few covers. One of his own folk tunes. And then, this.

The first chords float through the Alloway, and Addie is back in his place. She is sitting at the piano, coaxing out notes, and he is there, beside her, fingers folded over hers.

It is coming together now, words wrapped over melody. It is becoming his. It is like a tree, taking root. He will remember, on his own; not her, of course—not her, but this. Their song.

It ends, the music replaced by applause, and Toby sidles up to the bar, orders a Jack and Coke because they'll give it to him for free, and somewhere between the first sip and the third he sees her, and smiles, and for an instant Addie thinks—hopes, even now—that he remembers something, because he looks at her as if he knows her, but the truth is simply that he wants to; attraction can look an awful lot like recognition in the wrong light.

"Sorry," Toby says, head ducking the way it does whenever he's embarrassed. The way it did that morning when he found her in his living room.

Someone brushes Addie's shoulder as they reach past her for the bar door. She blinks, and the dream falls away.

She has not gone in. She is still standing on the street, the cigarette burned away to nothing between her fingers.

A man holds open the door. "You coming in?"

Addie shakes her head, and forces herself to step back, away from the door, and the bar, and the boy about to take the stage. "Not tonight," she says.

The rise isn't worth the fall.

Night settles over Addie as she crosses the Brooklyn Bridge.

The promise of spring has retreated like a tide, replaced again by a damp winter chill, and she pulls her jacket close, breath fogging as she starts the long stretch up the length of Manhattan.

It would be easy enough to take the subway, but Addie has never liked being underground, where the air is close and stale, the tunnels too much like tombs. Being trapped, buried alive, these are the things that scare you when you cannot die. Besides, she doesn't mind walking, knows the strength of her own limbs, relishes the kind of tired she used to dread.

Still, it's late, and her cheeks are numb, her legs weary, by the time she reaches the Baxter on Fifty-sixth.

A man in a trim gray coat holds the door, and her skin tingles at the sudden flush of central heat as she steps into the Baxter's marble lobby. She is already dreaming of a hot shower and a soft bed, already moving toward the open elevator, when the man behind the desk rises from his seat.

"Good evening," he says. "Can I help you?"

"I'm here to see James," she says, without slowing. "Twenty-third floor."

The man frowns. "He isn't in."

"Even better," she says, stepping into the elevator.

"Ma'am," he calls, starting after her, "you can't just—" but the doors are already closing. He knows he will not make it, is already turning back toward the desk, reaching for the phone to call security, and that is the last thing she sees before the doors slide shut between them. Perhaps he will get the phone to his ear, even begin to dial before the thought slips from his mind, and then he will look down at the receiver in his hand and wonder what he was thinking, apologize profusely to the voice on the line before sinking back into his seat.

The apartment belongs to James St. Clair.

They had met at a coffee shop downtown a couple months ago. The seats were all taken when he came over, wisps of blond escaping the hem of a winter hat, glasses fogging from the cold. That day Addie was Rebecca, and before he'd even introduced himself, James had asked if he could share her table, saw that she was reading Colette's *Chéri*, and managed a few lines of broken, blushing French. He sat, and soon easy smiles gave way to easy conversation. Funny, how some people take an age to warm, and others simply walk into every room as if it's home.

James was like that, instantly likable.

When he asked, she said that she was a poet (an easy lie, as no one ever asked for proof), and he told her he was between jobs, and she nursed her coffee for as long as she could, but eventually her cup was empty, and so was his, and new customers were circling, buzzard-like, in search of chairs, but when he began to rise, she'd felt that old familiar sadness. And then James asked if she liked ice cream, and even though it was January, the ground outside slicked with ice and paving salt, Addie said she did, and this time when they stood, they stood together.

Now she types the six-digit code into the keypad on his door and steps inside.

The lights come on, revealing pale wood floors, and clean marble counters, lush curtains and furniture that still looks unused. A high-backed chair. A cream sofa. A table neatly stacked with books.

She unzips her boots, steps out of them beside the door, and pads barefoot through the apartment, tossing her jacket over the arm of a chair. In the kitchen, she pours herself a glass of merlot, finds a block of Gruyère in a fridge drawer and a box of gourmet crackers in the cupboard, carries her makeshift picnic into the living room, the city unfolding beyond the floor-to-ceiling windows.

Addie sifts through his records, puts on a pressing of Billie Holiday, and retreats to the cream sofa, knees tucked up beneath her as she eats.

She would love a place like this. A place of her own. A bed molded to her body. A wardrobe full of clothes. A home, decorated with markers of the life she's lived, the material evidence of memory. But she cannot seem to hold on to anything for long.

It is not as though she hasn't tried.

Over the years, she's collected books, hoarded art, hidden fine dresses away in chests and locked them there. But no matter what she does, things always go missing. They vanish, one by one, or all at once, stolen by some strange circumstance, or simply time. Only in New Orleans did she have a home, and even that was not hers, but theirs, and it is gone.

The only thing she cannot seem to rid herself of is the ring.

There was a time when she couldn't bear to part with it again. A time when she mourned its loss. A time when her heart soared to hold it, so many decades later.

Now, she cannot stand the sight of it. It is an unwelcome weight in her pocket, an unwanted reminder of another loss. And every time her fingers skim the wood, she feels the darkness kissing her knuckle as he slides the band back on.

See? Now we are even.

Addie shudders, upsetting her glass, and drops of red wine splash over the rim, landing like blood on the cream sofa. She does not curse, does not spring to her feet to fetch club soda and a towel. She simply watches as the stain soaks in, and through, and disappears. As if it was never there.

As if *she* was never there.

Addie rises, and goes to run herself a bath, soaks away the city grime with scented oil, scrubs herself clean with hundred-dollar soap.

When everything slips through your fingers, you learn to savor the feel of nice things against your palm.

She settles back into the tub, and sighs, breathing in a mist of lavender and mint.

They went for ice cream that day, she and James, ate it inside the shop, heads bowed together as they stole toppings from each other's cups. His hat sat discarded on the table, his blond curls on full display, and he was striking, yes, but it still took her a while to notice the looks.

Addie was used to passing glances—her features are sharp, but feminine, her eyes bright above the constellation of freckles on her cheeks, a kind of timeless beauty, she's been told—but this was different. Heads were turning. Gazes lingered. And when she wondered why, he looked at her with such cheerful surprise, and confessed that he was, in fact, an actor—in a show that was currently quite popular. He blushed when he said it, looked away, then back to study her face, as if braced for some fundamental change. But Addie has never seen his work, and even if she had, she is not one to blush at fame. She has lived too long, and known too many artists. And even still, or perhaps more to the point, Addie prefers the ones who aren't yet finished, the ones still looking for their shape.

And so James and Addie carried on.

She teased him about his loafers, his sweater, his wire-frame glasses.

He told her he was born in the wrong decade.

She told him she was born in the wrong century.

He laughed, and she didn't, but there *was* something old-fashioned in his manner. Only twenty-six, but when he talked, he had the easy cadence, the slow precision, of a man who knew the weight of his own voice, belonged to the class of young men who dressed like their fathers, the charade of those too eager to grow old.

Hollywood had seen it, too. He kept getting cast in period pieces.

"I've got a face for sepia," he joked.

Addie smiled. "Better than a face for radio."

It was a lovely face, but there was something wrong, the too-steady smile of a man with a secret. They made it through the ice cream before he came undone. That easy joy of his flickered, and went out, and he dropped the plastic spoon down into the cup and closed his eyes, and said, "I'm sorry."

"What for?" she asked, and he flung himself back in his seat, and ran his fingers through his hair. To the strangers on the street it might have looked like such a careless gesture, a feline stretch, but she could see the anguish in his face as he said it.

"You are so beautiful, and kind, and fun."

"But?" she pressed, sensing the turn.

"I'm gay."

The word, like a hitch in his throat, as he explained that there was so much pressure, that he hated the gaze of the media and all its demands. That people were beginning to whisper, to wonder, and he wasn't ready for them to know.

Addie realized, then, that they were on a stage. Propped before the plate-glass windows of the ice-cream shop, for everyone to see, and James was still apologizing, saying that he shouldn't have flirted, shouldn't have used her in this way, but she wasn't really listening. His blue eyes went somewhat glassy as he spoke, and she wondered if this was what he called on when the script ordered tears. If this was the place he went. Addie has secrets, too, of course, though she cannot help but keep them.

Still, she knows what it's like, to have a truth erased.

"I understand," he was saying, "if you want to go."

But Addie didn't stand up, didn't reach for her coat. She simply leaned in, and stole a blueberry from the edge of his bowl.

"I don't know about you," she said lightly, "but *I'm* having a lovely day."

James let out a shaky breath, blinking away tears, and smiled.

"So am I," he said, and things were better after that.

It is so much easier to share a secret than to keep one, and when they stepped outside again, hand in hand, they were conspirators, made giddy by their private knowledge. She was not worried about being noticed, being seen, knew that if there were photos, they would never turn out.

(There *were* photos, but her face was always conveniently in motion or obscured, and she remained a mystery girl in the tabloids for the next week, until the headlines inevitably moved on to juicier fare.)

They had come back here, to his apartment at the Baxter, for a drink. His tables were covered in a flurry of books and papers, all relating to the Second World War. He was preparing for a role, he told her, reading every firsthand account he could find. He showed them to her, these printed reproductions, and Addie said that she'd been fascinated by the war, that she knew a few stories, told them as if they were someone else's, a stranger's experience instead of her own. James listened, folded into the corner of the cream sofa, his eyes pressed shut and a glass of whisky balanced on his chest as she spoke.

They fell asleep side by side in the king-sized bed, in the shadow of each other's warmth, and the next morning, Addie woke before dawn and slipped away, sparing them both the discomfort of a good-bye.

She has the sense that they would have been friends. If he'd remembered. She tries not to think about that—she swears sometimes her memory runs forward as well as back, unspooling to show the roads she'll never get to travel. But that way lies madness, and she has learned not to follow.

Now she is back here, but he is not.

Addie wraps herself in one of James's plush terry robes, and throws open the French doors, stepping out onto the bedroom balcony. The wind is up, the cold stinging the soles of her bare feet. The city sprawls around her like a low night sky, full of artificial stars, and she shoves her hands into the pockets of the robe, and feels it, resting on the bottom of the empty fold.

A small circle of smooth wood.

She sighs, closes her hand around the ring, and draws it out, leans her elbows on the balcony, and forces herself to look at the band in her open palm, to study it, as if she has not already memorized every warp and whorl. She traces the curve with her free hand, resists the urge to slip the band onto her finger. She has thought of it, of course, in darker moments, tired moments, but she will not be the one to break.

She tips her hand, and lets the ring fall over the edge of the balcony, down, down, into the dark.

Back inside, Addie pours herself another glass of wine and climbs into the magnificent bed, folds herself beneath the down duvet and between the Egyptian sheets, and wishes she'd gone into the Alloway, wishes that she'd sat at the bar and waited for Toby, with his messy curls and shy smile. Toby, who smells of honey, and plays bodies like instruments, and takes up so much space in bed.

XIII

+ + + + +

A hand shakes Adeline awake.

For a moment, she is out of place, out of time. Sleep clings to her edges, and with it, the dream—it must have been a dream—of prayers made to silent gods, of deals made in the dark, of being forgotten.

Her imagination has always been a vivid thing.

"Wake up," says a voice, one she has known all her life.

The hand again, firm on her shoulder, and she blinks away the last of sleep to find the wooden planks of a barn ceiling, straw pricking her skin, and Isabelle kneeling beside her, blond hair braided into a crown, brows drawn tight with worry. Her face has waned a little with every child, each birth stealing a little more of her life.

"Get up, you fool."

That is what Isabelle *should* say, the chiding softened by the kindness in her voice. But her lips are pursed with worry, her forehead furrowed with concern. She has always frowned like that, fully, with her whole face, but when Adeline reaches out to press one thumb into the space between the other girl's brows (to smooth away the worry, the way she has a thousand times before) Isabelle draws back, away from the touch of a stranger.

Not a dream, then.

"Mathieu," Isabelle calls over her shoulder, and Adeline sees her oldest son standing in the barn's open doorway, clutching a pail. "Go and get a blanket."

The boy vanishes into the sun.

"Who are you?" asks Isabelle, and Adeline starts to answer, forgetting that the name won't come. It lodges in her throat.

"What happened to you?" presses Isabelle. "Are you lost?"

Adeline nods.

"Where did you come from?"

"Here."

Isabelle's frown deepens. "Villon? But that's not possible. We would have met. I've lived here all my life."

"So have I," she murmurs, and Isabelle must see the truth as a delusion, because she shakes her head as if clearing away a thought.

"That boy," she mutters, "where has he gone?"

She turns her gaze fully back to Adeline. "Can you stand?"

Arm in arm, they walk into the yard. Adeline is filthy, but Isabelle doesn't let go, and her throat tightens at the simple kindness, the warmth of the other girl's touch. Isabelle treats her like a wild thing, her voice soft, her motions slow as she leads Adeline to the house.

"Are you hurt?"

Yes, she thinks. But she knows Isabelle is speaking of scrapes and cuts and simple wounds, and of those, she is less certain. She looks down at herself. In the darkness, the worst was hidden. In the light of morning, it's on display. Adeline's dress, spoiled. Her slippers, ruined. Her skin, painted with the forest floor. She felt the scratch and tear of brambles in the woods last night, but she can find no angry welts, no cuts, no signs of blood.

"No," she says softly, as they step inside the house.

There is no sign of Mathieu, or Henri, their second child—just the baby, Sara, sleeping in a basket by the hearth. Isabelle sits Adeline in a chair across from the infant, and sets a pot of water over the fire.

"You're being so kind," Adeline whispers.

"'I was a stranger and you welcomed me,'" says Isabelle.

It is a Bible verse.

She brings a basin to the table, along with a cloth. Kneeling at Adeline's feet, she coaxes the dirty slippers off, sets them by the hearth, then takes Adeline's hands and begins to clean the forest floor from her fingers, the soil from beneath her nails.

As she works, Isabelle peppers her with questions, and Adeline tries to answer, she really does, but her name is still a shape she cannot say, and when she speaks of her life in the village, of the shadow in the woods, of the deal she made, the words make it across her lips, but stop before they reach the other girl's ears. Isabelle's face goes blank, her gaze flat, and when Adeline finally trails off, she gives her head a quick shake, as if throwing off a daydream.

"Sorry," says her oldest friend, with an apologetic smile. "What were you saying?"

She will learn in time that she can lie, and the words will flow like wine, easily poured, easily swallowed. But the truth will always stop at the end of her tongue. Her story silenced for all but herself.

A mug is pressed into Adeline's hands as the infant begins to fuss.

"It is an hour's ride to the nearest village," Isabelle says, lifting the swaddled child. "Did you walk all this way? You must have . . ." She is speaking to Adeline, of course, but her voice is soft, sweet, her attention on Sara, breathing into the soft down of the baby's hair, and Adeline must admit, her friend was seemingly made to be a mother—too content to even notice the attention.

"What will we do with you?" she coos.

Footsteps sound on the path outside, heavy and booted, and Isabelle straightens a little, patting the infant's back. "That will be my husband, George."

Adeline knows George well, had kissed him once when they were six, back when kisses were traded like pieces in a game. But now her heart flutters with panic, and she is already on her feet, the cup clattering to the table.

It is not George she fears.

It is the doorway, and what happens when Isabelle is on the other side.

She catches Isabelle's arm, her grip sudden and tight, and for the first time, fear flits across the other woman's face. But then she steadies, and pats Adeline's hand.

"Don't worry," she says. "I'll talk to him. It will all be well." And before Adeline can refuse, the infant is pressed into her arms, and Isabelle is out of reach.

"Wait. Please."

Fear beats inside her chest, but Isabelle is gone. The door stays open, voices rising and falling in the yard beyond, the words themselves reduced to windsong. The infant murmurs in her arms and she sways a little, trying to soothe the child, and herself. The baby quiets, and she's just returning her to the basket when she hears a short gasp.

"Get away from her."

It is Isabelle, her voice high and tight with panic. "Who let you in?"

All the Christian kindness, erased in an instant by a mother's fear.

"*You* did," says Adeline, and she has to fight the urge to laugh. There is no humor in the moment, only madness.

Isabelle stares in horror. "You're lying," she says, surging forward, halted only by her husband's hand upon her shoulder. He has seen Adeline, too, marked her as a different kind of wild thing, a wolf inside their house.

"I meant no harm," she says.

"Then *go*," orders George.

And what else can she do? She abandons the baby, leaves behind the mug of broth, the basin on the table, and her oldest friend. She hurries out into the yard and glances back, sees Isabelle press her daughter to her chest before George blocks the doorway, ax in hand as if she is a tree to fell, a shadow set upon their house.

And then he too is gone, and the door is shut and bolted.

Adeline stands on the path, uncertain what to do, where to go. There are grooves in her mind, worn smooth and deep. Her legs have carried her to and from this place too many times. Her body knows the way. Go down this road, and take a left, and there is her own house, which is not her home anymore, even though her feet are already moving toward it.

Her feet—Adeline shakes her head. She left her slippers by Isabelle's hearth to dry.

A pair of George's boots lean against the wall beside the door, and she takes them and begins to walk. Not to the house she grew up in, but back to the river where her prayers began.

The day is already warm, the air edged with heat as she drops the boots onto the bank and steps out into the shallow stream.

Her breath catches with the cold as the river laps up around her calves, kisses the backs of her knees. She looks down, seeking out her warped reflection and half expects not to find it there, to see only the sky behind her head. But she is still there, distorted by the stream.

Hair once braided, now wild, sharp eyes wide. Seven freckles like flecks of paint across her skin. A face drawn in fear, and anger.

"Why didn't you answer?" she hisses to the sunlight on the stream.

But the river only laughs, in its soft, slippery way, the burble of water over stone.

She wrestles with the laces of her wedding dress, peels the soiled thing away, plunges it down into the water. The current drags at the fabric, and her fingers long to let go, to let the river claim this last vestige of her life, but she has too little now to give up more.

Adeline plunges herself in, too, freeing the last flowers from her hair, rinsing the woods from her skin. She comes up feeling cold, and brittle, and new.

The sun is high, the day hot, and she lays the dress out in the grass to dry, sinks onto the slope beside it in her shift. They sit, side by side in silence, one a ghost of the other. And she realizes, looking down, that this is all she has.

A dress. A slip. A pair of stolen shoes.

Restless, she takes up a stick and begins to draw absent patterns in the silt along the bank. But every stroke she makes dissolves, the change too quick to be the river's doing. She draws a line, watches it begin to wash away before she even finishes the mark. Tries to write her name, but her hand stills, pinned under the same rock that held her tongue. She carves a deeper line, gouges out the sand, but it makes no difference, soon that groove is gone, too, and an angry sob escapes her throat as she casts the stick away.

Tears prick her eyes as she hears the shuffle of small feet, blinks to find a round-faced boy standing over her. Isabelle's four-year-old son. Addie used to swing him in her arms, spin until they both were dizzy and laughing.

"Hello," says the boy.

"Hello," she says, her voice a little shaky.

"Henri!" calls the boy's mother, and in a moment Isabelle is there, on the rise, a basket of washing on her hip. She sees Adeline sitting in the grass, holds out a hand not for her friend, but for her son. "Come here," she orders, those blue eyes lingering on Adeline.

"Who are you?" asks Isabelle, and she feels as if she's at the edge of a steep hill, the ground plunging away beneath her feet. Her balance, tipping forward, as the dreaded descent begins again.

"Are you lost?"

Déjà vu. Déjà su. Déjà vécu.

Already seen. Already known. Already lived.

They have been here before, walked this road, or something like it, and so Adeline now knows where to put her feet, knows what to say, which words will draw out kindness, knows that if she asks in the right way, Isabelle will take her home, and wrap a blanket around her shoulders, and offer her a cup of broth, and it will work until it doesn't.

"No," she says. "I'm just passing through."

It is the wrong thing to say, and Isabelle's expression hardens.

"It is not fitting for a woman to travel alone. And certainly not in such a state."

"I know," she says. "I had more, but I was robbed."

Isabelle blanches. "By who?"

"A stranger in the woods," she says, and it is not a lie.

"Are you hurt?"

Yes, she thinks. *Grievously.* But she forces herself to shake her head and answer, "I will live."

She has no choice.

The other woman sets the washing down.

"Wait here," says Isabelle, the kind and generous Isabelle again. "I will come right back."

She swings her young son up in her arms, and turns back toward her house, and the moment she is out of sight, Adeline gathers her dress, still damp at the hem, and pulls it on.

Isabelle will, of course, forget again.

She'll get halfway to her house before she slows and wonders why she started back without her clothes. She'll blame her tired mind, addled from three children, the infant's distemper, and return to the river. And this time, there will be no woman sitting on the banks, no dress spread in the sun, only a stick, abandoned in the grass, a canvas of silt laid smooth.

* * *

Adeline has drawn her family house a hundred times.

Memorized the angle of the roof, the texture of the door, the shadow of her father's workshop, and the limbs of the old yew tree that sits like a sentinel at the edge of the yard.

That is where she's standing now, tucked behind the trunk, watching Maxime graze beside the barn, watching her mother hang linens out to dry, watching her father whittle down a block of wood.

And as Adeline watches, she realizes she cannot stay.

Or rather, she could—could find a way to skip from house to house, like stones skating across the river—but she will not. Because when she thinks of it, she feels neither like the river nor the stone, but like a hand, as it tires of throwing.

There is Estele, closing her door.

There is Isabelle, one moment kind, and the next filled with horror.

Later, much later, Addie will make a game of these cycles, will see how long she can step from perch to perch before she falls. But right now, the pain is too fresh, too sharp, and she cannot fathom going through those motions, cannot weather the weary look on her father's face, the rebuke in Estele's eyes. Adeline LaRue cannot be a stranger here, to these people she has always known.

It hurts too much, watching them forget her.

Her mother slips back inside the house, and Adeline abandons the shelter of the tree and starts across the yard; not for the front door, but for her father's shop.

There is a single shuttered window, an unlit lamp, the only light a stripe of sun spilling through the open door, but that is enough to see by. She knows the contours of this place by heart. The air smells like sap, earthy and sweet, the floor is covered in shavings and dust, and every surface holds the bounty of her father's work. A wooden horse, modeled from Maxime, of course— but here no bigger than a cat. A set of bowls, decorated only by the rings of the trunk from which they were cut. A collection of palm-sized birds, their wings spread, or folded, or stretched mid-flight.

Adeline learned to sketch the world in charcoal and pressed lead, but her father has always created with a knife; whittled the shapes out of nothing, giving them breadth, and depth, and life.

She reaches out now, and runs her finger down the horse's nose, the way she has a hundred times before.

What is she doing here?

Adeline does not know.

Saying good-bye, perhaps, to her father—her favorite person in this world.

This is how she would remember him. Not by the sad unknowing in his eyes, or the grim set of his jaw as he led her to church, but by the things he loved. By the way he showed her how to hold a stick of charcoal, coaxing shapes and shades with the weight of her hand. The songs and stories, the sights from the five summers she went with him to market, when Adeline was old enough to travel, but not old enough to cause a stir. By the careful gift of a wooden ring, made for his first and only daughter when she was born—the one she then offered to the dark.

Even now, her hand drifts to her throat to thumb the leather cord, and something deep inside her cringes when she remembers it is gone forever.

Scraps of parchment scatter the table, covered in drawings and dimensions, the markings of past and future work. A pencil sits on the edge of the desk, and Adeline finds herself reaching for it, even as a dread echo sounds inside her chest.

She brings it to the page, and begins to write.

Cher Papa—

But as the pencil scratches across the paper, the letters fade in its wake. By the time Adeline has finished those two, unsteady words, they are gone, and when she slams her hand down on the table, she upsets a tiny pot of varnish, spilling the precious oil onto her father's notes, the wood beneath. She scrambles to collect the papers, staining her hands and knocking over one of the little wooden birds.

But there is no need for panic.

The varnish is already soaking through, sinking in and down like a rock in a river, until it's gone. It is such a strange thing, to make sense of this moment, to count what has and hasn't been lost.

The varnish is gone, but not back into the pot, which lies empty on its side, the contents lost. The parchment lies unmarked, untouched, as is the table beneath. Only her hands are stained, the oil tracing the whorls of her fingers, the lines of her palms. She is still staring at them when she steps back, and hears the terrible snap of wood splitting beneath her heel.

It is the little wooden bird, one of its wings splintered on the packed-earth floor. Adeline winces in sympathy—it was her favorite of the flock, frozen in a moment of upward motion, the first rise of flight.

She crouches to gather it up, but by the time she straightens, the splinters on the ground are gone, and in her hand, the little wooden bird is whole again. She nearly drops it in surprise, doesn't know why *this* is the thing that seems impossible. She has been made a stranger, has seen herself slide from the minds of those she's known and loved like the sun behind a cloud, has watched every mark she tries to make as it's undone, erased.

But the bird is different.

Perhaps because she can hold it in her hands. Perhaps because, for an instant, it seems a blessing, this undoing of an accident, a righting of a wrong, and not simply an extension of her own erasure. The inability to leave a mark. But Adeline doesn't think of it that way, not yet, has not spent months turning the curse over in her hands, memorizing its shape, studying the smooth surfaces in search of cracks.

In this moment, she simply clutches the small, unbroken bird, grateful that it's safe.

She is about to return the figure to its flock when something stops her— perhaps the oddness of the moment, perhaps the fact that she is already missing this life, even if it will never miss her—but she tucks the bird into the pocket of her skirts, and forces herself out of the shed, and away from her home.

Down the road, and past the twisted yew tree, and around the bend, until she has reached the edge of town. Only then does she let herself look back, let her gaze drift one last time to the line of trees across the field, the dense shadow stretched beneath the sun, before she turns her back on the forest, and the village of Villon, and the life that is no longer hers, and begins to walk.

Villon vanishes like a cart around a bend, the rooftops swallowed up by the trees and the hills of the surrounding country. By the time Adeline musters the courage to look back, it is gone.

She sighs, and turns, and walks, wincing at the strange shape of George's boots.

They are too large by half. Adeline found socks on a washing line, shoved them into the toes of the shoes to make them fit, but by the fourth hour of walking she can feel the places where her skin has rubbed raw, the blood pooling in the leather soles. She is afraid to look, and so she doesn't, focuses only on the path ahead.

She has decided to walk toward the walled city of Le Mans. It is the farthest she has ever gone, and even still, she has never made the trip alone.

She knows the world is so much larger than the towns along the Sarthe, but right now she cannot think beyond the road in front of her. Every step she takes is a step away from Villon, away from a life that is no longer hers.

You wanted to be free, says a voice in her head, but it is not hers; no, it is deeper, smoother, lined with satin and woodsmoke.

She skirts the villages, the farms alone in their fields. There are whole stretches when the world seems to empty around her. As if an artist drew the barest lines of the landscape, then turned, distracted, from the task.

Once, Adeline hears a cart trundling down the road, and ducks into the shade of a nearby grove and waits for it to pass. She does not want to stray too far from the road, or the river, but over her shoulder, through a copse of trees, she sees the yellow blush of summer fruit, and her stomach aches with longing.

An orchard.

The shade is lovely, the air cool, and she picks a ripened peach from a low branch and sinks her teeth greedily into the fruit, her empty stomach cramping around the sugared bite. Despite the pain, she eats a pear as well, and a handful of mirabelles, scoops palm and after palm of water from a well at the orchard's edge, before forcing herself forward, out of the shelter and back into the summer heat.

The shadows are stretching long when she finally sinks onto the riverbank and pulls off the boots to assess the damage to her feet.

But there is none.

The socks are unbloody. Her heels, uncut. No sign of the miles walked, the wear and tear of so many hours on the packed-earth road, though she felt the pain of every step. Nor are her shoulders burned from the sun, though all day she felt its heat. Her stomach twists, aching for something more than stolen fruit, but as the light ebbs, and the hills darken, there are no lanterns, no homes in sight.

Exhausted, she would curl up right there on the river's edge and give in to sleep, but insects float above the water, nipping at her skin, and so she retreats into an open field, and sinks down amid the tall grass the way she did so many times when she was young, and wanted to be somewhere else. The grass would swallow the house, the workshop, the rooftops of Villon, everything except the open sky overhead, a sky that could belong to anywhere.

Now, as she stares up at the mottled dusk, she longs for home. Not for Roger, or the future she did not want, but the woody grip of Estele's hand on hers as the old woman showed her how to wind raspberry bushes, and the soft hum of her father's voice as he worked in his shed, the scent of sap and wood dust in the air. The pieces of her life she never meant to lose.

She slips her hand into the pocket of her skirt, fingers searching for the little carved bird. She has not let herself reach for it before, half-sure it would be gone, its theft undone like every other act—but it is still there, the wood smooth and warm.

Adeline draws it out, holds it up against the sky, and wonders.

She could not break the figurine.

But she could *take* it.

Amid the growing list of negatives—she cannot write, cannot say her name, cannot leave a mark—this is the first thing she has been *able* to do. She can *steal*. It will be a long time before she knows the contours of her curse, longer still before she understands the shadow's sense of humor, before he looks at her over a glass of wine and observes that a successful theft is an anonymous act. The absence of a mark.

In this moment, she is simply grateful for the talisman.

My name is Adeline LaRue, she tells herself, clutching the little wooden bird. *I was born in Villon in the year 1691, to Jean and Marthe, in a stone house just beyond the old yew tree . . .*

She tells the story of her life to the little carving, as if afraid she'll forget herself as easily as others do, unaware that her mind is now a flawless cage, her memory a perfect trap. She will never forget, though she'll wish she could.

As the night creeps through, purple giving way to black, Adeline looks up into the dark, and begins to suspect that the dark is staring back, that god, or demon, with its cruel gaze, its mocking smile, features contorted in a way she never drew.

As she stares, head craned, the stars seem to pick out the lines of a face, the cheekbones and brow, the illusion drawing together until she half expects the blanket of night to ripple and twist as the shadows did in the woods, the space between stars splitting to reveal those emerald eyes.

She bites her tongue to keep from calling to him, lest something else decide to answer.

She is not in Villon, after all. She does not know which gods might linger here.

Later, her strength will falter.

Later, there will be nights when her need will smother caution, and she will scream and curse and dare him to come out and face her.

Later—but tonight she is tired, and hungry, and loath to waste what little energy she has on gods that will not answer.

So she curls onto her side, squeezes her eyes shut, and waits for sleep, and as she does, she thinks of torches in the field beyond the woods, of voices calling her name.

Adeline, Adeline, Adeline.

The words pound against her, drumming on her skin like rain.

She wakes sometime later with a start, the world inky black and the downpour already soaking through her dress, the rainstorm sudden and heavy.

She hurries, skirts dragging, across the field to the nearest line of trees. Back home she loved the patter of rain against the walls of the house, used to lie awake and listen to the world washed clean. But here she has no bed, no shelter. She does her best to wring the water from the dress, but it is already cooling on her skin, and she huddles among the roots, shivering beneath the broken canopy.

My name is Adeline LaRue, she tells herself. *My father taught me how to be a dreamer, and my mother taught me how to be a wife, and Estele taught me how to speak to gods.*

Her thoughts drag on Estele, who used to stand out in the rain, palms open as if to catch the storm. Estele, who never cared as much for the company of others as for her own.

Who probably would have been content to be alone in the world.

She tries to imagine what the old woman would say, if she could see her now, but every time she tries to summon those keen eyes, that knowing mouth, she sees only the way Estele looked at her in those last moments, the way her face furrowed, and then cleared, a lifetime of knowing brushed away like a tear.

No, she should not think of Estele.

Adeline wraps her arms around her knees, and tries to sleep, and when she wakes again, sunlight is pouring through the trees. A finch stands on the mossy ground nearby, pecking at the hem of her dress. She brushes it away, checking her pocket for the little wooden bird as she stands, sways, dizzy with hunger, realizes she has not had more than fruit in a day and a half.

My name is Adeline LaRue, she tells herself as she makes her way back to the road. It is becoming a mantra, something to pass the time, measure her steps, and she repeats it, over and over.

She rounds a bend, and stops, blinking fiercely, as if the sun is in her eyes. It's not, and yet the world ahead has been plunged into a sudden, vivid yellow, the green fields devoured by a blanket the color of egg yolk.

She looks back over her shoulder, but the way behind her is still green and brown, the ordinary shades of summer. The field ahead is mustard seed, though she doesn't know it then. Then, it is simply beautiful, in an overpowering way. Addie stares, and for a moment she forgets her hunger, her aching feet, her sudden loss, and marvels at the shocking brightness, the all-consuming color.

She wades through the field, flower buds brushing her palms, unafraid to crush the plants underfoot—they have already straightened in her wake, steps erased. By the time she reaches the far edge of the field, and the path, and the steady green, it looks dull, her eyes searching for another source of wonder.

Shortly after, a larger town comes into sight, and she is about to weave around it when she catches a scent on the air that makes her stomach ache.

Butter, yeast, the sweet and hearty smell of bread.

She looks like a dress that fell from the line, wrinkled and dirty, her hair a tangled nest, but she is too hungry to care. She follows the scent between the houses, and up a narrow lane toward the village square. Voices rise with the smell of baking, and when she rounds the corner she sees a handful of women sitting around a communal oven. They perch on the stone bench around it, laughing and chatting like birds on a branch as the loaves rise within the oven's open mouth. The sight of them is jarring, ordinary in an aching way, and Adeline lingers in the shaded lane a moment, listening to the trill and chirp of their voices, before the hunger forces her forward.

She doesn't have to search her pockets to know she has no coins. Perhaps she could barter for the bread, but all she has is the bird, and when she finds it in the folds of her skirt, her fingers refuse to loosen on the wood. She could beg, but her mother's face comes to mind, eyes tight with scorn.

That leaves only theft—which is wrong, of course, but she is too hungry to weigh the sin of it. There is only the matter of how. The oven is hardly unmanned, and despite how fast she seems to fade from memory, she is still flesh and blood, not phantom. She cannot simply walk up and take the bread without causing a stir. Sure, they might forget her soon enough, but what danger would she be in before they did? If she got to the bread, and then away, how far would she have to run? How fast?

And then she hears it. A soft, animal sound, almost lost beneath the chatter.

She circles the stone hut and finds her chance, across the lane.

A mule stands in the shade, lazily chewing its bit beside a sack of apples, a stack of kindling.

All it takes is a single, sharp smack, and the mule lurches, more in shock, she hopes, than pain. It jostles forward, upsetting the apples and the wood as it sets off. And just like that, the square is startled, thrown into a brief but noisy state as the beast trots away, dragging a bag of grain, and the women leap to their feet, the trills and warbles of their laughs dissolving into taut shouts of dismay.

Adeline slips across the oven like a cloud, swiping the nearest loaf from the stone mouth. Pain sears across her fingers as she grabs it, and she nearly drops the bread, but she is too hungry, and pain, she is learning, doesn't last. The loaf is hers, and by the time the mule is settled, and the grain set right, and the apples gathered, and the women returned to their place by the oven, she is already gone.

She leans in the shade of a stable on the edge of town, teeth tearing into the under-baked bread. The dough collapses in her mouth, heavy, sweet, and hard to swallow, but she doesn't care. It is filling enough, wearing the edges off her hunger. Her mind begins to clear. Her chest loosens, and for the first time since she left Villon, she feels something like human, if not whole. She pushes off the stable wall and begins to walk again, following the line of the sun, and the path of the river, toward Le Mans.

My name is Adeline . . . she starts again, then stops.

She never loved the name, and now she cannot even say it. Whatever she calls herself, it will be only in her head. *Adeline* is the woman she left in Villon, on the eve of a wedding she did not want. But *Addie*—Addie was a gift from Estele, shorter, sharper, the switch-quick name for the girl who rode to markets, and strained to see over roofs, for the one who drew and dreamed of bigger stories, grander worlds, of lives filled with adventure.

And so, as she walks on, she starts the story over in her head.

My name is Addie LaRue . . .

It is too quiet without James.

Addie never thought of him as loud—charming, cheerful, but hardly raucous—but now she realizes how much he filled this space when they were in it.

That night, he put on a record and sang along as he made grilled cheese on the six-burner stove, which they ate standing up because the place was new, and he hadn't bought kitchen chairs. There are still no kitchen chairs, but now there is no James, either—he's off on location somewhere—and the apartment stretches out around her, too silent and too large for one person, the high floor and the double-paned glass combining to block out the sounds of the city, reducing Manhattan to a picture, still and gray, beyond the windows.

Addie plays record after record, but the sound only echoes. She tries to watch TV, but the drone of news is more static than anything, as is the tinny choir of voices on the radio, too far away to feel real.

The sky outside is a static gray, a thin mist of rain blurring the buildings. It is the kind of day designed for wood fires, and mugs of tea, and well-loved books.

But while James has a fireplace, it's only gas, and when she checks the cupboard for her favorite blend, she finds the box nestled at the back, but it is empty, and all the books he keeps are histories, not fiction, and Addie knows she cannot pass the day here, with only herself for company.

She gets dressed again, in her own clothes, and smooths the covers back onto the bed, even though the cleaners will surely return before James does. With a last glance at the dreary day, she steals a scarf from a closet shelf, a soft plaid cashmere with the tags still on, and sets out, the lock chiming behind her.

She does not know, at first, where she is going.

Some days she still feels like a lion caged, pacing its enclosure. Her feet have a mind of their own, and soon they are carrying her uptown.

My name is Addie LaRue, she thinks to herself as she walks.

Three hundred years, and some part of her is still afraid of forgetting. There have been times, of course, when she wished her memory more fickle, when she would have given anything to welcome madness, and disappear. It is the kinder road, to lose yourself.

Like Peter, in J. M. Barrie's *Peter Pan*.

There, at the end, when Peter sits on the rock, the memory of Wendy Darling sliding from his mind, and it is sad, of course, to forget.

But it is a *lonely* thing, to be forgotten.

To remember when no one else does.

I remember, whispers the darkness, almost kindly, as if he's not the one who cursed her.

Perhaps it is the bad weather, or perhaps it is this maudlin mood that leads Addie up along the eastern edge of Central Park, to Eighty-second and into the granite halls of the Met.

Addie has always had a fondness for museums.

Spaces where history gathers out of place, where art is ordered, and artifacts sit on pedestals, or hang on walls above little white didactics. Addie feels like a museum sometimes, one only she can visit.

She crosses the great hall, with its stone arches and colonnades, weaves her way through Greco-Roman and past Oceania, exhibits she has lingered in a hundred times, continues until she reaches the European sculpture court, with its grand marble figures.

One room over, she finds it, where it always is.

It sits in a glass case along one wall, framed on either side by pieces made of iron, or silver. It is not large, as far as sculptures go, the length of her arm, from elbow to fingertips. A wooden plinth with five marble birds perched atop it, each about to fly away. It is the fifth that holds her gaze: the lift of its beak, the angle of its wings, the soft down of its feathers captured once in wood, and now in stone.

Revenir, it's called. *To come back.*

Addie remembers the first time she found the work, the small miracle of it, sitting there on its clean white block. The artist, Arlo Miret, a man she never knew, never met, and yet here he is, with a piece of her story, her past. Found, and made into something memorable, something worthwhile, something beautiful.

She wishes she could touch the little bird, run her finger along its wing, the way she always did, even though she knows it's not the one she lost, knows this one wasn't carved by her father's strong hands, but by a stranger. Still, it is there, it is real, it is, in some way, hers.

A secret kept. A record made. The first mark she left upon the world, long before she knew the truth, that ideas are so much wilder than memories, that they long and look for ways of taking root.

Le Mans lies likes a sleeping giant in the fields along the Sarthe.

It has been more than ten years since Addie was allowed to make the trek to the walled city, perched beside her father in the family cart.

Now her heart quickens as she steps through the city gates. There is no horse this time, no father, no cart, but in the late-afternoon light, the city is just as busy, just as bustling, as she remembered. Addie doesn't bother trying to blend in—if, now and then, someone glances her way, notices the young woman in the stained white dress, they keep their opinions to themselves. It is easier to be alone among so many people.

Only—she doesn't know where to go. She pauses a moment to think, only to hear hooves clattering, too sudden and too close, and narrowly escapes being trampled by a cart.

"Out of the way!" shouts the driver, as she lunges back, only to collide with a woman carrying a basket of pears. It tips, spilling three or four onto the cobbled path.

"Watch where you're going," snarls the woman, but when Addie bends to help her fetch the fallen fruit, the woman screeches and stomps at her fingers.

Addie backs away and thrusts her hands into her pockets, clings to the little wooden bird as she continues through the winding streets toward the center of the city. There are so many roads, but they all look the same.

She thought this place would feel more familiar, but it only feels strange. A figment from a long-ago dream. When Addie was last here, the city seemed a wonder, a grand and vital place: the bustling markets, bathed in sun; the voices ringing off of stone; her father's broad shoulders, blocking out the city's darker sides.

But now, alone, a menace has crept in, like fog, erasing the buoyant charm, leaving only the sharp edges jutting through the mist. One version of the city replaced by another.

Palimpsest.

She doesn't know the word just yet, but fifty years from now, in a Paris salon, she will hear it for the first time, the idea of the past blotted out, written over by the present, and think of this moment in Le Mans.

A place she knows, and yet doesn't.

How foolish to think it would stay the same, when everything else has changed. When *she* has changed, grown from a girl into a woman, and then into this—a phantom, a ghost.

She swallows hard, and stands up straight, determined not to fray or fall apart.

But Addie cannot find the inn where she and her father stayed, and even if she could, what did she plan to do there? She has no way to pay, and even if she had the coin, who would rent to a woman on her own? Le Mans is a city, but it is not so big that such a thing would pass beneath a landlord's notice.

Addie's grip tightens on the carving in her skirts as she continues through the streets. There is a market just past the town hall, but it is closing up, tables empty, the carts pulling away, the ground littered only with the dregs of lettuce and a few moldy potatoes, and before she can think of scrounging for them, they are gone, swept away by smaller, quicker hands.

There is a tavern inn at the edge of the square.

She watches a man dismount his horse, a dappled mare, and pass the reins to a stable hand, already turning toward the noise and hustle of the open doors. She watches the stable hand lead the mare across the way to a broad wooden barn, and vanish into the relative dark. But it's not the barn that's caught her eye, or the horse—it's the pack still thrown across its back. Two heavy satchels, bulging like sacks of grain.

Addie crosses the square and slips into the stable behind the man and the mare, her steps as light and quick as possible. Sunlight streams weakly through the beams in the stable roof, casting the place in soft relief, a few highlights amid the layered shadow, the kind of place she would have loved to draw.

A dozen horses shuffle in their stalls, and across the barn, the stable hand hums to the mare as he strips away its tack, tosses the saddle over the wooden divide, and brushes down the beast, his own hair a nest of knots and snarls.

Addie ducks low, creeping toward the stalls at the back of the barn, the sacks and satchels strewn on the wooden barriers between the horses. Her hands dart hungrily across the trappings, searching beneath buckles and under flaps. There are no purses, but she finds a heavy riding coat, a skin of wine, a boning knife the length of her hand. The coat she drapes around her shoulders, the blade goes into one deep pocket and the wine in the other as she creeps on, quiet as a ghost.

She doesn't see the empty bucket until her shoe cracks against it with a sharp clatter. It falls with a muffled thud onto the hay, and Addie holds her breath and hopes the sound is lost among the shuffling hooves. But the stable hand stops humming. She sinks lower, folds herself into the shadows of the nearest stall. Five seconds pass, then ten, and then at last the humming starts again, and Addie straightens and makes her way to the final stall, where a stout draft horse lounges, munching grain, beside a belted bag. Her fingers drift toward the buckle.

"What are you doing?"

The voice, too close, behind her. The stable hand, no longer humming, no longer brushing the dappled mare, but standing in the alley between berths, a crop in his hand.

"Sorry, sir," she says, a shade breathless. "I came looking for my father's horse. He wanted something from his satchel."

He stares at her, unblinking, his features half-swallowed by the dark sprawl of his hair. "Which horse would that be?"

She wishes she'd studied the horses as well as their packs, but she cannot hesitate, it would reveal the lie, so she turns quickly toward the workhorse. "This one."

It is a good lie, as far as lies go, the kind that could have easily been true, if she'd only picked another horse. A grim smile twitches beneath the man's beard.

"Ah," he says, flicking the crop against his palm, "but you see, that one's *mine*."

Addie has the strange and sickening urge to laugh.

"Can I pick again?" she whispers, inching toward the stable door.

Somewhere nearby, a mare whinnies. Another stamps its hoof. The crop stops snapping against the man's palm, and Addie lurches sideways, between the stalls, the stable hand on her heels.

He's fast, a speed clearly born from catching beasts, but she is lighter, and has far more to lose. His hand grazes the collar of her stolen coat, but he cannot catch her; his heavy steps falter and slow, and Addie thinks she's free, right before she hears the crisp, bright sound of a bell ringing on the stable wall, followed by the sound of boots coming from outside.

She is nearly to the mouth of the barn when the second man appears, cutting like a wide shadow across the doorway.

"Has a beast got free?" he shouts before he sees her, wrapped in the stolen coat, her too-large boots catching on the hay. She scrambles backward, right into the arms of the stable hand. His fingers close around her shoulders, heavy as shackles, and when she tries to twist free, his grip digs deep enough to bruise.

"Caught her thieving," he says, the coarse bristles on his cheek scraping hers.

"Let me go," she pleads as he pulls her tight.

"This isn't a market stall," sneers the second, drawing a knife from his belt. "Do you know what we do with thieves?"

"It was a mistake. Please. Let me go."

The knife wags like a finger. "Not until you've paid."

"I don't have any money."

"That's all right," says the second man, drawing closer. "Thieves pay in flesh."

She tries to tear free, but the grip on her arms is iron as the knife comes to rest against the laces of her dress, plucking them like strings. And when she twists again, she is no longer trying to get free, simply trying to reach the boning knife inside the pocket of her stolen coat. Twice her fingers brush the wooden hilt before she manages to catch it.

She drives the blade down and back into the first man's thigh, feels it sink into the meat of his leg. He cries out before he thrusts her away like a hornet, flinging her forward, right onto the other man's blade.

Pain screams through her shoulder as the knife bites in, skates along her collarbone, leaving a trail of searing heat. Her mind goes blank with it, but her legs are already moving, carrying her through the stable doors and out into the square. She throws herself behind a barrel, out of sight, as the men come stumbling, swearing, out of the barn behind her, their faces twisted with rage and something worse, something primal, hungry.

And then, between one step and the next, they begin to slow.

Between one step and the next, the urgency falters, and fades, the purpose slipping, like a thought, out of reach. The men look around, and then at each other. The one she stabbed stands straighter now, no sign of the tear in his trousers, no blood soaking through the fabric. The mark she left on him, erased.

They jostle, and rib, and head back into the barn, and Addie slumps forward, her head coming to rest against the wooden barrel. Her chest throbs, pain tracing a vivid line along her collar, and when she presses her hand to the wound, her fingers come away red.

She cannot stay there, curled behind the barrel, forces herself up, and sways, feeling faint, but soon the wave of sickness passes, and she is still on her feet. She walks, one hand pressed to her shoulder, and the other closed tight around the knife beneath her stolen coat. She doesn't know when she decides to leave Le Mans, but soon enough she is crossing the courtyard, away from the stable and through the winding streets, past bawdy inns and tavern houses, past crowded steps and raucous laughter, giving the city up with every step.

The ache in her shoulder fades from a searing heat to a dull throb, and then, to nothing. She runs her fingers over the gash, but it is gone. As is the blood on her dress, swallowed up like the words she scrawled across her father's parchment, the lines she drew in the silt on the riverbank. The only traces of it are on her skin, a crust of drying blood along her collarbone, a smear of browning red across her palm. And Addie marvels a moment, despite herself, at the strange magic of it, the proof that in one way, the shadow kept his word. Twisted it, yes, warped her wishes into something wrong and rotten. But granted her this, at least.

To live.

A small, mad sound escapes her throat, and there is relief in it, perhaps, but also horror. For the truth of her hunger, which she is only just discovering. For the ache in her feet, though they do not cut or bruise. For the pain of the wound in her shoulder, before it healed. The darkness has granted her freedom from death, perhaps, but not from this. Not from suffering.

It will be years before she learns the true meaning of that word, but in this moment, as she walks into the thickening dusk, she is still relieved to be alive.

A relief that flickers when she reaches the edge of the city.

This is as far as Adeline has ever gone.

Le Mans looms at her back, and ahead the high stone walls give way to scattered towns, each one like a copse of tress, and then, to open field, and then, to what, she does not know.

When Addie was young, she would surge up the slopes that rose and fell around Villon, fling herself to the very edge of the hill, the place where the ground fell away, and stop, heart racing as her body leaned forward, longing for the fall.

The slightest push, and weight would do the rest.

There is no steep hill beneath her now, no slope, and yet, she feels her balance tilt.

And then, Estele's voice rises to meet her in the dark.

How do you walk to the end of the world? she once asked. And when Addie didn't know, the old woman smiled that wrinkled grin, and answered.

One step at a time.

Addie is not going to the end of the world, but she must go *somewhere,* and in that moment, she decides.

She is going to Paris.

It is, beside Le Mans, the only city she knows by name, a place that played so many times across her stranger's lips, and featured into every tale her father told, a place of gods and kings, gold and majesty, and promise.

This is how it starts, he would have said, if he could see her now.

Addie takes the first step, and feels the ground give way, feels herself tip forward, but this time, she does not fall.

XVII

✦ ✦ ✦ ✦
✦ ✦ ✦

It is a better day.

The sun is out, the air is not so cold, and there is so much to love about a city like New York.

The food, the art, the constant offerings of culture—though Addie's favorite thing is its scale. Towns and villages are easily conquered. A week in Villon was enough to walk every path, to learn every face. But with cities like Paris, London, Chicago, New York, she doesn't have to pace herself, doesn't have to take small bites to make the newness last. A city she can consume as hungrily as she likes, devour it every day and never run out of things to eat.

It is the kind of place that takes years to visit, and still there always seems to be another alley, another set of steps, another door.

Perhaps that's why she hasn't noticed it before.

Set off from the curb, and down a short flight of steps, there is a shop half-hidden by the line of the street. The awning was clearly once purple, but has long faded toward gray, though the shop's name is still legible, picked out in white lettering.

The Last Word.

A used bookstore, judging by the name, and the windows brimming with stacked spines. Addie's pulse thrills a little. She was certain she'd found them all. But that is the brilliant thing about New York. Addie has wandered a fair portion of the five boroughs, and still the city has its secrets, some tucked in corners—basement bars, speakeasies, members-only clubs—and others sitting in plain sight. Like Easter eggs in a movie, the ones you don't notice until the second or third viewing. And not like Easter eggs at all, because no matter how many times she walks these blocks, no matter how many hours, or days, or years she spends learning the contours of New York, as soon as she turns her back it seems to shift again, reassemble. Buildings go up and come down, businesses open and close, people arrive and depart and the deck shuffles itself again and again and again.

Of course, she goes in.

A faint bell announces her arrival, the sound quickly smothered by the crush of books in various conditions. Some bookstores are organized, more gallery than shop. Some are sterile, reserved for only the new and untouched.

But not this one.

This shop is a labyrinth of stacks and shelves, texts stacked two, even three deep, leather beside paper beside board. Her favorite kind of store, one that's easy to get lost in.

There is a checkout counter by the door, but it is empty, and she wanders, unmolested, through the aisles, picking her way along the well-loved shelves. The bookshop seems fairly empty, save for an older white man studying a row of thrillers, a gorgeous Black girl sitting cross-legged in a leather chair at the end of a row, silver shining on her fingers and in her ears, a giant art book open in her lap.

Addie wanders past a placard marked POETRY, and the darkness whispers against her skin. Teeth skimming like a blade along a bare shoulder.

Come live with me and be my love.

Addie's refrain, worn smooth with repetition.

You do not know what love is.

She doesn't stop, but turns the corner, fingers trailing now along THEOLOGY. She has read the Bible, the Upanishads, the Quran, after a spiritual bender of sorts a century ago. She passes Shakespeare, too, a religion all his own.

She pauses at MEMOIR, studying the titles on the spines, so many *I*'s and *Me*'s and *My*'s, possessive words for possessive lives. What a luxury, to tell one's story. To be read, remembered.

Something knocks against Addie's elbow, and she looks down to see a pair of amber eyes peering over her sleeve, surrounded by a mass of orange fur. The cat looks as old as the book in her hand. It opens its mouth, and lets out something between a yawn and a meow, a hollow, whistling sound.

"Hello." She scratches the cat between the ears, eliciting a low rumble of pleasure.

"Wow," says a male voice behind her. "Book doesn't usually bother with people."

Addie turns, about to comment on the cat's name, but loses her train of thought when she sees him, because for a moment, only a moment, before the face comes into focus, she is certain it is—

But it is not him.

Of course it is not.

The boy's hair, though black, falls in loose curls around his face, and his eyes, behind their thick-frame glasses, are closer to gray than green. There is something fragile to them, more like glass than stone, and when he speaks, his voice is gentle, warm, undeniably human. "Help you find anything?"

Addie shakes her head. "No," she says, clearing her throat. "Just browsing."

"Well then," he says with a smile. "Carry on."

She watches him go, black curls vanishing into the maze of titles, before dragging her gaze back to the cat.

But the cat is gone, too.

Addie returns the memoir to the shelf and continues browsing, attention wandering over ART and WORLD HISTORY, all the while waiting for the boy to reappear, to start the cycle over, wondering what she'll say when he does. She should have asked for help, let him lead her through the shelves—but he doesn't come back.

The shop bell chimes again, announcing a new customer as Addie reaches the Classics. *Beowulf. Antigone. The Odyssey.* There are a dozen versions of this last, and she's just drawing one out when there's a sudden burst of laughter, high and light, and she glances through a gap in the shelves and sees a blond girl leaning on the counter. The boy stands on the other side, cleaning his glasses on the edge of his shirt.

He bows his head, dark lashes skimming his cheeks.

He isn't even looking at the girl, who's rising on her toes to get closer to him. She reaches out and runs one hand along his sleeve the way Addie just did along the shelves, and he smiles, then, a quiet, bashful grin that erases the last of his resemblance to the dark.

Addie tucks the book under her arm and heads for the door, and out, taking advantage of his distraction.

"Hey!" calls a voice—his voice—but she continues up the steps onto the street. In a moment, he will forget. In a moment, his mind will trail off, and he'll—

A hand lands on her shoulder.

"You have to pay for that."

She turns, and there's the boy from the shop, a little breathless, and very annoyed. Her eyes flick past him to the steps, the open door. It must have been ajar. He must have been right behind her. But still. He followed her out.

"Well?" he demands, hand dropping from her shoulder and coming to rest, palm open, in the space between them. She could run, of course, but it's not worth it. She checks the cost on the back of the book. It isn't much, but it's more than she has on her.

"Sorry," she says, handing it back.

He frowns, then, a furrow too deep for his face. The kind of line carved by years of repetition, even though he can't be more than thirty. He looks down at the book, and a dark brow lifts behind his glasses.

"A shop full of antique books, and you steal a battered paperback of *The Odyssey*? You know this won't fetch anything, right?"

Addie holds his gaze. "Who says I wanted to resell it?"

"It's also in Greek."

That, she hadn't noticed. Not that it matters. She learned the classics in Latin first, but in the decades since, she's picked up Greek.

"Silly me," she says dryly, "I should have stolen it in English."

He almost—*almost*—smiles, then, but it's a bemused, misshapen thing. Instead, he shakes his head. "Just take it," he says, holding out the book. "I think the shop can spare it."

She has to fight the sudden urge to push it back.

The gesture feels too much like charity.

"Henry!" calls the pretty Black girl from the doorway. "Should I call the cops?"

"No," he calls back, still looking at Addie. "It's fine." He narrows his eyes, as if studying her. "Honest mistake."

She stares at this boy—at *Henry*. Then she reaches out and takes back the book, cradling it against her as the bookseller vanishes back into the shop.

PART TWO

THE DARKEST PART
OF THE NIGHT

Title: *One Forgotten Night*

Artist: Samantha Benning

Date: 2014

Medium: Acrylic on canvas over wood

Location: On loan from the Lisette Price Gallery, NYC

Description: A largely monochromatic piece, paint layered into a topography of black, charcoals, and grays. Seven small white dots stand out against the backdrop.

Background: Known largely on its own, this painting also serves as the frontispiece for an ongoing series titled *I Look Up to You,* in which Benning imagines family, friends, and lovers as different iterations of the sky.

Estimated Value: $11,500

Henry Strauss heads back into the shop.

Bea's taken up residence again in the battered leather chair, the glossy art book open in her lap. "Where did you go?"

He looks back through the open door and frowns. "Nowhere."

She shrugs, turning through the pages, a guide to neoclassical art that she has no intention of buying.

Not a library. Henry sighs, returning to the till.

"Sorry," he says to the girl by the counter. "Where were we?"

She bites her lip. Her name is Emily, he thinks. "*I* was about to ask if you wanted to grab a drink."

He laughs, a little nervously—a habit he's beginning to think he'll never shake. She's pretty, she really is, but there's the troublesome shine in her eyes, a familiar milky light, and he's relieved he doesn't have to lie about having plans tonight.

"Another time," she says with a smile.

"Another time," he echoes as the girl takes her book and goes. The door has barely closed when Bea clears her throat.

"What?" he asks without turning.

"You could have gotten her number."

"We have plans," he says, tapping the tickets on the counter.

He hears the soft stretch of leather as she rises from the chair. "You know," she says, swinging an arm around his shoulder, "the great thing about plans is that you can make them for other days, too."

He turns, hands rising to her waist, and now they're locked like kids in the throes of a school dance, limbs making wide circles like nets, or chains.

"Beatrice Helen," he scolds.

"Henry Samuel."

They stand there, in the middle of the store, two twenty-somethings in a preteen embrace. And maybe once upon a time Bea would have leaned a little harder, made some speech about finding someone (new), about deserving to be happy (again). But they have a deal: she doesn't mention Tabitha, and Henry doesn't mention the Professor. Everyone has their fallen foes, their battle scars.

"Excuse me," says an older man, sounding genuinely sorry to interrupt.

He holds up a book, and Henry smiles and breaks the chain, ducking back behind the counter to ring him up. Bea swipes her ticket from the table and says she'll meet him at the show, and Henry nods her off and the old man goes on his way, and the rest of the afternoon is a quiet blur of pleasant strangers.

He turns the sign over at five to six, and goes through the motions of closing up the shop. The Last Word isn't his, but it might as well be. It's been weeks since he saw the actual owner, Meredith, who's spending her golden years traveling the world on her late husband's life insurance. A fall woman indulging in a second spring.

Henry scoops a handful of kibble into the small red dish behind the counter for Book, the shop's ancient cat, and a moment later, a ratty orange head pokes up over the chapbooks in POETRY. The cat likes to climb behind a stack and sleep for days, his presence marked only by the emptying dish and the occasional gasp of a customer when they come across a pair of unblinking yellow eyes at the back of the shelves.

Book is the only one who's been at the bookstore longer than Henry.

He's worked there for the last five years, having started back when he was still a grad student in theology. At first it was just a part-time gig, a way to supplement the university stipend, but then school went away, and the store stayed. Henry knows he should probably get another job, because the pay is shit and he has twenty-one years of expensive formal education, and then of course there's his brother David's voice, which sounds exactly like their father's voice, calmly asking where this job *leads,* if this is really how he plans to spend his life. But Henry doesn't know what else to do, and he can't bring himself to leave; it's the only thing he hasn't failed out of yet.

And the truth is, Henry loves the store. Loves the smell of books, and the steady weight of them on shelves, the presence of old titles and the arrival of new ones and the fact that in a city like New York, there will always be readers.

Bea insists that everyone who works in a bookstore wants to be a writer, but Henry's never fancied himself a novelist. Sure, he's tried putting pen to paper, but it never really works. He can't find the words, the story, the voice. Can't figure out what he could possibly add to so many shelves.

Henry would rather be a storykeeper than a storyteller.

He turns off the lights and grabs the ticket and his coat, and heads over to Robbie's show.

Henry didn't have time to change.

The show starts at seven, and The Last Word closed at six, and anyways he isn't sure what the dress code is for an off-off-Broadway show about faeries in the Bowery, so he's still in dark jeans and a tattered sweater. It's what Bea likes to call Librarian Chic, even though he doesn't work in a library, a fact she cannot seem to grasp. Bea, on the other hand, looks painfully fashionable, as she always does, with a white blazer rolled up to her elbows, thin silver bands wrapped around her fingers and shining in her ears, thick dreads coiled in a crown atop her head. Henry wonders, as they wait in the queue, if some people have natural style, or if they simply have the discipline to curate themselves every day.

They shuffle forward, presenting their tickets at the door.

The play is one of those strange medleys of theater and modern dance that only exist in a place like New York. According to Robbie, it's loosely based on *A Midsummer Night's Dream,* if someone had filed Shakespeare's cadence smooth, and cranked up the saturation.

Bea knocks him in the ribs.

"Did you see the way she looked at you?"

He blinks. "What? Who?"

Bea rolls her eyes. "You are entirely hopeless."

The lobby bustles around them, and they're wading through the crowd when another person catches Henry's arm. A girl, wrapped in a tattered bohemian dress, green paint flourishes like abstract vines on her temples and cheeks, marking her as one of the actors of the show. He's seen the remnants on Robbie's skin a dozen times in the last few weeks.

She holds up a paintbrush and a bowl of gold. "You're not adorned," she says with sober sincerity, and before he can think to stop her, she paints gold dust on his cheeks, the brush's touch feather-light. This close, he can see that faint shimmer in the girl's eyes.

Henry tips his chin.

"How do I look?" he asks, affecting a model's pout, and even though he's joking, the girl flashes him an earnest smile and says, "Perfect."

A shiver rolls through him at the word, and he is somewhere else, a hand holding his in the dark, a thumb brushing his cheek. But he shakes it off.

Bea lets the girl paint a shining stripe down her nose, a dot of gold on her chin, manages to get in a solid thirty seconds of flirting before bells chime through the lobby, and the artistic sprite vanishes back into the crowd as they continue toward the theater doors.

Henry threads his arm through Bea's. "You don't think I'm perfect, do you?"

She snorts. "God, no."

And he smiles, despite himself, as another actor, a dark-skinned man with rose-gold on his cheeks, hands them each a branch, the leaves too green to be real. His gaze lingers on Henry, kind, and sad, and shining.

They show their tickets to an usher—an old woman, white-haired and barely five feet tall—and she holds on to Henry's arm for balance as she shows them to their row, pats his elbow when she leaves them, murmuring, "Such a good boy" as she toddles up the aisle.

Henry looks at the number on his ticket, and they sidestep over to their seats, a group of three near the middle of the row. Henry sits, Bea on one side, the empty seat on the other. The seat reserved for Tabitha, because of course they'd bought their tickets months ago, when they were still together, when everything was a plural instead of a singular.

A dull ache fills Henry's chest, and he wishes he'd paid the ten dollars for a drink.

The lights go down, and the curtain goes up on a kingdom of neon and spray-painted steel, and there is Robbie in the middle of it all, lounging on a throne in a pose that is pure goblin king.

His hair curls up in a high wave, streaks of purple and gold carving the lines of his face into something stunning and strange. And when he smiles, it is easy to remember how Henry fell in love, back when they were nineteen, a tangle of lust, and loneliness, and far-off dreams. And when Robbie speaks, his voice is crystal, reflecting across the theater.

"This," he says, "is a story of gods."

The stage fills with players, the music begins, and for a while, it is easy.

For a while, the world falls away, and everything quiets around them, and Henry disappears.

Toward the end of the play there is a scene that will press itself into the dark of Henry's mind, exposed like light on film.

Robbie, the Bowery king, rises from his throne as rain falls in a single sheet across the stage, and even though, moments earlier, it was crowded with people, now, somehow, there is only Robbie. He reaches out, hand skimming the curtain of rain, and it parts around his fingers, his wrist, his arm as he moves forward inch by inch until his whole body is beneath the wave.

He tips his head back, the rain rinsing gold and glitter from his skin, flattening the perfect wave of curls against his skull, erasing all traces of magic, turning him from a languid, arrogant prince into a boy; mortal, vulnerable, alone.

The lights go out, and for a long moment, the only sound in the theater is the rain, fading from a solid wall to the steady rhythm of a downpour, and after, to the soft patter of drops on the stage.

And then, at last, nothing.

The lights come up, and the cast takes the stage, and everyone applauds. Bea cheers, and looks at Henry, the joy bleeding from her face.

"What's wrong?" she asks. "You look like you're about to faint."

He swallows, shakes his head.

His hand is throbbing, and when he looks down, he's dug his nails into the scar along his palm, drawing a fresh line of blood.

"Henry?"

"I'm fine," he says, wiping his hand on the velvet seat. "It was just. It was good."

He stands, and follows Bea out.

The crowd thins until it's mostly friends and family waiting for the actors to reappear. But Henry feels the eyes, attention drifting like a current. Everywhere he looks, he finds a friendly face, a warm smile, and sometimes, more.

Finally Robbie comes bounding into the lobby, and throws his arms around both of them.

"My adoring fans!" he says, in a thespian's ringing alto.

Henry snorts, and Bea holds out a chocolate rose, a long inside joke since Robbie once bemoaned that you had to choose between chocolates and flowers, and Bea pointed out that that was Valentine's Day, and that for performances, flowers were typical, and Robbie said he wasn't typical, and besides, what if he was hungry?

"You were great," says Henry, and it's true. Robbie *is* great—he's always been great. That trifecta of dance, music, and theater required to get work in New York. He's still a few streets off Broadway, but Henry has no doubt he'll get there.

He runs his hand through Robbie's hair.

Dry, it is the color of burnt sugar, a tawny shade somewhere between brown and red, depending on the light. But right now it's still wet from the final scene, and for a second, Robbie leans into the touch, resting the weight of his head in Henry's hand. His chest tightens, and he has to remind his heart it is not real, not anymore.

Henry pats his friend's back, and Robbie straightens, as if revived, renewed. He holds his rose aloft like a baton and announces, "To the party!"

Henry used to think that after-parties were only for last shows, a way for the cast to say good-bye, but he's since learned that, for theater kids, every performance is an excuse to celebrate. To come down from the high, or in the case of Robbie's crowd, to keep it going.

It's almost midnight, and they're packed into a third-floor walk-up in SoHo, the lights low and someone's playlist pumping through a pair of wireless speakers. The cast moves through the center like a vein, their faces still painted but their costumes shed, caught between their onstage characters and their offstage selves.

Henry drinks a lukewarm beer and rubs his thumb along the scar on his palm, in what's quickly becoming a habit.

For a while, he had Bea to keep him company.

Bea, who much prefers dinner parties to theater ones, place settings and dialogues to plastic cups and lines shouted over stereos. A groaning compatriot, huddled with Henry in the corner, studying the tapestry of actors as if they were in one of her art history books. But then another Bowery sprite whisked her away, and Henry shouted *traitor* in their wake, even though he was glad to see Bea happy again.

Meanwhile, Robbie is dancing in the middle of the room, always the center of the party.

He gestures for Henry to join him, but Henry shakes his head, ignoring the pull, the easy draw of gravity, the open arms waiting at the end of the fall. At his worst, they were a perfect match, the differences between them purely gravitational. Robbie, who always managed to stay alight, while Henry came crashing down.

"Hey, handsome."

Henry turns, looking up from his beer, and sees one of the leads from the show, a stunning girl with rust-red lips and a white lily crown, the gold glitter on her cheeks stenciled to look like graffiti. She is looking at him with such open want he should *feel* wanted, should feel something besides sad, lonely, lost.

"Drink with me."

Her blue eyes shine as she holds out a little tray, a pair of shots with something small and white dissolving on the bottom. Henry thinks of all the stories about accepting food and drink from the fae, even as he reaches for the glass. He drinks, and at first all he tastes is sweetness, the faint burn of tequila, but then the world begins to fuzz a little at the edges.

He wants to feel lighter, to feel brighter, but the room darkens, and he can feel a storm creeping in.

He was twelve when the first one rolled through. He didn't see it coming.

One day the skies were blue and the next the clouds were low and dense, and the next, the wind was up and it was pouring rain.

It would be years before Henry learned to think of those dark times as storms, to believe that they would pass, if he could simply hold on long enough.

His parents meant well, of course, but they always told him things like *Cheer up,* or *It will get better,* or worse, *It's not that bad,* which is easy to say when you've never had a day of rain. Henry's oldest brother, David, is a doctor, but he still doesn't understand. His sister, Muriel, says she does, that all artists suffer through their storms, before offering him a pill from the mint container she keeps in her purse. Her little pink umbrellas, she calls them, playing on his metaphor; as if it's just a clever turn of phrase and not the only way Henry can try to make them understand what it's like inside his head.

It is just a storm, he thinks again, even as he pulls away from the scene, makes some excuse about going to find air. The party is too warm, and he wants to be outside, wants to go onto the roof and look up and see there is no bad weather, only stars, but of course, there are no stars, not in SoHo.

He makes it halfway down the hall before he stops, remembering the show, the sight of Robbie in the rain, and shivers, deciding to go down instead of up, deciding to go home.

And he's almost to the door when she catches his hand. The girl with ivy curling over her skin. The one who painted him gold.

"It's you," she says.

"It's you," he says.

She reaches out and wipes a fleck of gold from Henry's cheek, and the contact is like static shock, a spark of energy where skin meets skin.

"Don't go," she says, and he's still trying to think of what to say next when she pulls him close, and he kisses her, quick, searching, breaks off when he hears her gasp.

"Sorry," he says, the word automatic, like *please,* like *thank you,* like *I'm fine.*

But she reaches up and grabs a handful of his curls.

"What for?" she asks, drawing his mouth back to hers.

"Are you sure?" he murmurs, even though he knows what she will say, because he's already seen the light in her eyes, the pale clouds sweeping through her vision. "Is this what you want?"

He wants the truth—but there is no truth for him, not anymore, and the girl just smiles, and draws him back against the nearest door.

"This," she says, "is *exactly* what I want."

And then they are in one of the bedrooms, the door clicking shut and blotting out the noises of the party beyond the wall, and her mouth is on his, and he cannot see her eyes now in the dark, so it's easy to believe that this is real.

And for a while, Henry disappears.

Addie makes her way uptown, reading *The Odyssey* by streetlight. It's been a while since she read anything in Greek, but the poetic cadence of the epic poem draws her back into the stride of the old language, and by the time the Baxter comes into sight, she is half-lost in the image of the ship at sea, looking forward to a glass of wine and a hot bath.

And destined for neither.

Her timing is either very good, or very bad, depending on how you look at it, because Addie rounds the corner onto Fifty-sixth just as a black sedan pulls up in front of the Baxter and James St. Clair steps out onto the curb. He's back from his filming, tan and seemingly happy, wearing a pair of sunglasses despite the fact it's after dark. Addie slows, and stops, hovers across the street as the doorman helps him unload and carry his bags inside.

"Shit," she mutters under her breath as her night dissolves. No bubble baths, no bottles of merlot.

She sighs and retreats to the intersection, trying to decide what to do next.

To her left, Central Park unravels like a dark green cloth in the center of the city.

To her right, Manhattan rises in jagged lines, block after block of crowded buildings from Midtown down to the Financial District.

She goes right, making her way down toward the East Village.

Her stomach begins to growl, and on Second, she catches sight of dinner. A young man on a bicycle dismounts on the curb, unpacks an order from the zippered case behind the seat, and jogs the plastic bag up to the building. Addie drifts up to the bike and reaches in. It's Chinese, she guesses, going by the size and shape of the containers, the paper edges folded and bound with thin metal handles. She plucks out a carton, and a pair of disposable chopsticks, and slips away before the man at the door has even paid.

There was a time she felt guilty about stealing.

But the guilt, like so many things, has worn away, and even though the hunger can't kill her, it still hurts as though it will.

Addie makes her way toward Avenue C, scooping lo mein into her mouth as her legs carry her through the Village to a brick building with a green door. She dumps the empty carton in a trash can on the corner and reaches the building entrance just as a man is coming out. She smiles at him, and he smiles back and holds the door.

Inside, she climbs four flights of narrow steps to a steel door at the top, reaches up, and feels along the dusty frame for the small silver key, discovered last fall, when she and a lover stumbled home, the two a tangle of limbs on the stairs. Sam's lips pressed beneath her jaw, paint-streaked fingers sliding beneath the waistband of her jeans.

It was, for Sam, a rare impulsive moment.

It was, for Addie, the second month of an affair.

A passionate affair, to be sure, but only because time is a luxury she can't afford. Sure, she dreams of sleepy mornings over coffee, legs draped across a lap, inside jokes and easy laughter, but those comforts come with the knowing. There can be no slow build, no quiet lust, intimacy fostered over days, weeks, months. Not for them. So she longs for the mornings, but she settles for the nights, and if it cannot be love, well, then, at least it is not lonely.

Her fingers close around the key, the metal scraping softly as she drags it from its hiding spot. It takes three tries in the rusted old lock, just like it did that first night, but then the door swings open, and she steps out onto the building's roof. A breeze kicks up, and she shoves her hands in the pocket of her leather jacket as she crosses the roof.

It's empty, save for a trio of lawn chairs, each of them imperfect in its own way—seats warped, stuck in different poses of recline, one arm hanging at a broken angle. A stained cooler sits nearby, and a string of fairy lights hangs between laundry posts, transforming the roof into a shabby, weather-worn oasis.

It's quiet up here—not *silent*, that is a thing she's yet to find in a city, a thing she is beginning to think lost amid the weeds of the old world—but as quiet as it gets in this part of Manhattan. And yet, it is not the same kind of quiet that stifled her at James's place, not the empty, internal quiet of places too big for one. It is a living quiet, full of distant shouts and car horns and stereo bass reduced to an ambient static.

A low brick wall surrounds the roof, and Addie lets herself lean forward against it, resting her elbows and looking out until the building falls away, and all she can see is the lights of Manhattan, tracing patterns against the vast and starless sky.

Addie misses stars.

She met a boy, back in '65, and when she told him that, he drove her an hour outside of L.A., just to see them. The way his face glowed with pride when he pulled over in the dark and pointed up. Addie had craned her head and looked at the meager offering, the spare string of lights across the sky, and felt something in her sag. A heavy sadness, like loss. And for the first time in a century, she longed for Villon. For *home*. For a place where the stars were so bright they formed a river, a stream of silver and purple light against the dark.

She looks up now, over the rooftops, and wonders if, after all this time, the darkness is still watching. Even though it has been so long. Even though he told her once that he doesn't keep track of every life, pointed out that the world was big and full of souls, and he had far more to occupy himself than thoughts of her.

The rooftop door crashes open behind her, and a handful of people stumble out.

Two guys. Two girls.

And Sam.

Wrapped in a white sweater and pale gray jeans, her body like a brush-stroke, long and lean and bright against the backdrop of the darkened roof. Her hair is longer now, wild blond curls escaping a messy bun. Streaks of red paint dab her forearms where the sleeves are pushed up, and Addie wonders, almost absently, what she's working on. She is a painter. Abstracts, mostly. Her place, already small, made smaller by the stacks of canvas propped against the walls. Her name, crisp and easy, only Samantha on her finished work, or when traced across a spine in the middle of the night.

The other four move in a huddle of noise across the roof, one of the guys in the middle of a story, but Sam lags behind a step, head tipped back to savor the crisp night air, and Addie wishes she had something else to stare at. An anchor to keep her from falling into the easy gravity of the other girl's orbit.

She does, of course.

The Odyssey.

Addie is about to bury her gaze in the book, when Sam's blue eyes dip down from the sky and find her own. The painter smiles, and for an instant, it is August again, and they are laughing over beers on a bar patio, Addie lifting the hair off her neck to calm the flush of summer heat. Sam leaning in to blow on her skin. It is September, and they are in her unmade bed, their fingers tangled in the sheets and with each other as Addie's mouth traces the dark warmth between Sam's legs.

Addie's heart slams in her chest as the girl peels away from her group and casually wanders over. "Sorry for crashing your peace."

"Oh, I don't mind," says Addie, forcing her gaze out, as if studying the city, even though Sam always made her feel like a sunflower, unconsciously angling toward the other girl's light.

"These days, everyone's looking down," muses Sam. "It's nice to see some-one looking up."

Time slides. It's the same thing Sam said the first time they met. And the sixth. And the tenth. But it's not just a line. Sam has an artist's eye, present, searching, the kind that studies their subject and sees something more than shapes.

Addie turns away, waits for the sound of retreating steps, but instead, she hears the snap of a lighter, and then Sam is beside her, a white-blond curl dancing at the edge of her sight. She gives in, glances over.

"Could I steal one of those?" she asks, nodding at the cigarette.

Sam smiles. "You could. But you don't need to." She draws another from the box and hands it over, along with a neon blue lighter. Addie takes them, tucks the cigarette between her lips and drags her thumb along the starter. Luckily the breeze is up, and she has an excuse, watching the flame as it goes out.

Goes out. Goes out. Goes out.

"Here."

Sam steps closer, her shoulder brushing Addie's as she steps in to block the wind. She smells like the chocolate-chip cookies that her neighbor bakes whenever he's stressed, like the lavender soap she uses to scrub paint from her fingers, the coconut conditioner she leaves in her curls at night.

Addie has never loved the taste of tobacco, but the smoke warms her chest, and it gives her something to do with her hands, a thing to focus on besides Sam. They are so close, breaths fogging the same bit of air, and then Sam reaches out and touches one of the freckles on Addie's right cheek, the way she did the first time they met, a gesture so simple and still so intimate.

"You have stars," she says, and Addie's chest tightens, twists again.

Déjà vu. Déjà su. Déjà vecu.

She has to fight the urge to close the gap, to run her palm along the long slope of Sam's neck, to let it rest against the nape, where Addie knows it fits so well. They stand in silence, blowing out clouds of pale smoke, the other four laughing and shouting at their backs, until one of the guys—Eric? Aaron?—calls Sam over, and just like that, she is slipping away, back across the roof. Addie fights the urge to tighten her grip, instead of letting go—again.

But she does.

Leans against the low brick wall and listens to them talk, about life, about getting old, about bucket lists and bad decisions, and then one of the girls says, "Shit, we're gonna be late." And just like that, beers get finished, cigarettes put out, and the group of them drifts back toward the rooftop door, all five retreating like a tide.

Sam is the last to go.

She slows, glances over her shoulder, flashing a last smile at Addie before she ducks inside, and Addie knows she could catch her if she runs, could beat the closing door.

She doesn't move.

The metal bangs shut.

Addie sags against the brick wall.

Being forgotten, she thinks, is a bit like going mad. You begin to wonder what is real, if *you* are real. After all, how can a thing be real if it cannot be remembered? It's like that Zen koan, the one about the tree falling in the woods.

If no one heard it, did it happen?

If a person cannot leave a mark, do they *exist?*

Addie stubs the cigarette out on the brick ledge, and turns her back on the skyline, makes her way to the broken chairs and the cooler wedged between them. She finds a single beer floating amid the half-frozen melt and twists off the cap, sinking onto the least-damaged lawn chair.

It is not so cold tonight, and she is too tired to go looking for another bed.

The glow of the fairy lights is just enough to see by, and Addie stretches out in the lawn chair, and opens *The Odyssey,* and reads of strange lands, and monsters, and men who can't ever go home, until the cold lulls her to sleep.

Heat hangs like a low roof over Paris.

The August air is heavy, made heavier still by the sprawl of stone build-ings, the reek of rotting food and human refuse, the sheer number of bodies living shoulder to shoulder.

In a hundred and fifty years, Haussman will set his mark upon the city, raise a uniform facade and paint the buildings in the same pale palette, cre-ating a testament to art, and evenness, and beauty.

That is the kind of Paris Addie dreamed of, and one she will certainly live to see.

But right now, the poor pile themselves in ragged heaps while silk-finished nobles stroll through gardens. The streets are crowded with horse-drawn carts, the squares thick with people, and here and there spires thrust up through the woolen fabric of the city. Wealth parades down avenues, and rises with the peaks of each palace and estate, while hovels cluster in narrow roads, the stones stained dark with grime and smoke.

Addie is too overwhelmed to notice any of it.

She skirts the edge of a square, watching as men dismantle market stalls, and kick out at the ragged children who duck and weave between them, searching for scraps. As she walks, her hand slips into the hem pocket of her skirts, past the little wooden bird to the four copper sols she found in the lining of the stolen coat. Four sols, to make a life.

It is getting late, and threatening to rain, and she must find a place to sleep. It should be easy enough—there is, it seems, a lodging house on every street—but she is hardly across the threshold of the first when she is turned away.

"This is no brothel," chides the owner, glaring down his nose.

"And I'm no whore," she answers, but he only sneers, and flicks his fingers as if casting off some unwanted residue.

The second house is full, the third too costly, the fourth harbors only men. By the time she steps through the doors of the fifth the sun has set, and her spirits with it, and she is already braced for the rebuke, some excuse as to why she is unfit to stay beneath the roof.

But she isn't turned away.

An older woman meets her in the entry, thin, and stiff, with a long nose and the small, sharp eyes of a hawk. She takes one look at Addie and leads her down the hall. The rooms are small, and dingy, but they have walls and doors, a window and a bed.

"A week's pay," demands the woman, "in advance."

Addie's heart sinks. A week seems an impossible stretch when memories only seem to last a moment, an hour, a day.

"Well?" snaps the woman.

Addie's hand closes around the copper coins. She is careful to draw out only three, and the woman snatches them as fast as a crow stealing crusts of bread. They vanish into the pouch at her waist.

"Can you give me a bill?" asks Addie. "Some proof, to show I've paid?"

The woman scowls, clearly insulted. "I run an honest house."

"I'm sure you do," fumbles Addie, "but you have so many rooms to keep. It would be easy to forget which ones have—"

"Thirty-four years I've run this lodge," she cuts in, "and never yet forgotten a face."

It is a cruel joke, thinks Addie, as the woman turns and shuffles away, leaving her to her rented room.

A week she paid for, but she knows that she will be lucky to have a day. Knows that in the morning she will be evicted, the matron three crowns richer, while she herself will be out on the street.

A little bronze key rests in the lock, and Addie turns it, relishes the solid sound, like a stone dropped into a stream. She has nothing to unpack, no change of clothes; she casts off the traveling coat, draws the little wooden bird from her skirts and sets it on the windowsill. A talisman against the dark.

She looks out, expecting to see Paris's grand rooftops and dazzling buildings, the tall spires, or at least the Seine. But she has walked too far from the river, and the little window looks out only onto a narrow alleyway, and the stone wall of another house that could be anywhere.

Addie's father told her so many stories of Paris. Made it sound like a place of glamour and gold, rich with magic and dreams waiting to be uncovered. Now she wonders if he ever saw it, or if the city was nothing but a name, an easy backdrop for princes and knights, adventurers and queens.

They have bled together in her mind, those stories, become less a picture than a palette, a tone. Perhaps the city was less splendid. Perhaps there were shadows mixed in with the light.

It is a gray and humid night, the sounds of merchants and horse-carts muted by the soft rain beginning to fall, and Addie curls up on the narrow bed and tries to sleep.

She thought at least she'd have the night, but the rain hasn't even stopped, the darkness barely settled when the woman bangs upon her door, and a key is thrust into the lock, and the tiny room is plunged into noise. Rough hands haul Addie from the bed. A man grips her arm as the woman sneers and says, "Who let you in?"

Addie fights to wipe away the dregs of sleep.

"You did," she says, wishing the woman had only swallowed her pride and given a receipt, but all Addie has is the key, and before she can show it, the woman's bony hand cuts hard across her cheek.

"Don't lie, girl," she says, sucking her teeth. "This isn't a charity house."

"I paid," says Addie, cupping her face, but it is no use. The three sols in the pouch at the woman's waist will not serve as proof. "We spoke, you and I. Thirty-four years you said you've run this house—"

For an instant, uncertainty flashes across the woman's face. But it is too brief, too fleeting. Addie will one day learn to ask for secrets, details only a friend or intimate would know, but even then it will not always gain their favor. She will be called a trickster, a witch, a spirit, and a madwoman. Will be cast out for a dozen different reasons, when in truth, there is only one.

They don't remember.

"Out," orders the woman, and Addie barely has time to grab her coat before she's forced from the room. Halfway down the hall, she remembers the wooden bird still resting on the windowsill, and tries to twist free, to go back for it, but the man's grip is firm.

She's cast out onto the street, shaking from the sudden violence of it all, the only consolation that before the door swings shut, the little wooden bird is tossed out, too. It lands on the stones beside her, one wing cracking with the force.

Though this time, the bird doesn't mend itself.

It lies there, beside her, a sliver of wood chipped off like a fallen feather as the woman vanishes back inside the house. And Addie stifles the horrible urge to laugh, not at the humor but the madness of it, the absurd, inevitable ending to her night.

It is very late, or very early, the city quieted and the sky a cloudy, rain-slicked gray, but she knows the dark is watching as she scoops up the carving, buries it in her pocket with the last copper coin. Gets to her feet, drawing the coat tight around her shoulders, the hem of her skirts already damp.

Exhausted, Addie makes her way down the narrow street and takes shelter beneath the wooden lip of an awning, sinking down into the stone crook between buildings to wait for dawn.

She slips into a feverish almost-sleep, and feels her mother's hand against her brow, the faint rise and fall of her voice as she hums, smoothing a blanket over Addie's shoulders. And she knows she must be ill; that is the only time she saw her mother gentle. Addie lingers there, holding fast to the memory even as it fades, the harsh clop of hooves and strain of wooden carts encroaching on her mother's whispering song, burying it note by note until she jerks forward out of the haze.

Her skirts are stiff with grime, stained and wrinkled from the brief but restless sleep.

The rain has stopped, but the city looks just as dirty as it did on her arrival.

Back home, a good storm would wash the world clean, leave it smelling crisp and new.

But it seems nothing can rinse the grime from the streets of Paris.

If anything, that storm has only made things worse, the world wet and dull, puddles brown with mud and filth.

And then, amid the muck, she smells something sweet.

She follows the scent until she finds a market in full swing, the vendors shouting prices from tables and stalls, chickens still squawking as they're hauled off the backs of carts.

Addie is famished, cannot even remember the last time she ate. Her dress doesn't fit, but it never did—she'd stolen it from a washing line two days outside of Paris, tired of the one she'd worn the day of her wedding. Still, it hangs no looser now, despite the days without food or drink. She supposes she does not *need* to eat, will not perish from hunger—but tell that to her cramping stomach, her shaking legs.

She scans the busy square, thumbs the last coin in her pocket, loath to spend it. Perhaps she does not need to. With so many people in the market, it should be easy to steal what she needs. Or so she thinks, but the merchants of Paris are as cunning as its thieves, and they keep twice as tight a grip on every ware. Addie learns this the hard way; it will be weeks before she learns to palm an apple, longer still to master it without the faintest tell.

Today, she makes a clumsy effort, tries to swipe a seeded roll from a bread-baker's cart, and is rewarded with a meaty hand vised around her wrist.

"Thief!"

She catches a glimpse of men-at-arms weaving through the crowd, and is flooded with the fear of landing in a cell, or stock. She is still flesh and bone, has not learned yet to pick locks, or charm men out of charges, to free herself from shackles as easily as her face slips from their minds.

So she pleads hastily, handing over her last coin.

He plucks it from her, waves the men away as the sol vanishes into his purse. Far too much for a roll, but he gives her nothing back. Payment, he says, for trying to steal.

"Lucky I don't take your fingers," he growls, pushing her away.

And that is how Addie comes to be in Paris, with a crust of bread and a broken bird, and nothing else.

She hurries from the market, slowing only when she reaches the bank of the Seine. And then, breathless, she tears into the roll, tries to make it last, but in moments it is gone, like a drop of water down an empty well, her hunger barely touched.

She thinks of Estele.

The year before, the old woman developed a ringing in her ears.

It was always there, she said, day and night, and when Addie asked her how she could bear the constant noise, she shrugged.

"With time," she said, "you can get used to anything."

But Addie does not think she will ever get used to this.

She stares out at the boats on the river, the cathedral rising through the curtain of mist. The glimpses of beauty that shine like gems against the dingy setting of the blocks, too far away and flat to be real.

She stands there until she realizes she is waiting. Waiting for someone to help. To come and fix the mess she's in. But no one is coming. No one remembers, and if she resigns herself to waiting, she will wait forever.

So she walks.

And as she walks, she studies Paris. Makes a note of this house, and that road, of bridges, and carriage horses, and the gates of a garden. Glimpses roses beyond the wall, beauty in the cracks.

It will take years for her to learn the workings of this city. To memorize the clockwork of arrondissements, step by step, chart the course of every vendor, shop, and street. To study the nuances of the neighborhoods and find the strongholds and the cracks, learn to survive, and thrive, in the spaces between other people's lives, make a place for herself among them.

Eventually, Addie will master Paris.

She will become a flawless thief, uncatchable and quick.

She will slip through fine houses like a filigreed ghost, move through salons, and steal up onto rooftops at night and drink pilfered wine beneath the open sky.

She will smile and laugh at every stolen victory.

Eventually—but not today.

Today, she is simply trying to distract herself from her gnawing hunger and her stifling fear. Today she is alone in a strange city, with no money, and no past, and no future.

Someone dumps a bucket from a second-floor window, without warning, and thick brown water splashes onto the cobbles at her feet. Addie jumps back, trying to avoid the worst of the splash, only to collide with a pair of women in fine dress, who look at her as if she were a stain.

Addie retreats, sinking onto a nearby step, but moments later a woman comes out and shakes a broom, accuses her of trying to steal away her customers.

"Go to the docks if you plan to sell your wares," she scolds.

And at first, Addie doesn't know what the woman means. Her pockets are empty. She's nothing to sell. But when she says as much, the woman gives her such a look, and says, "You've got a body, don't you?"

Her face flushes as she understands.

"I'm not a whore," she says, and the woman flashes a cold smirk.

"Aren't we proud?" she says, as Addie rises, turns to go. "Well," the woman calls after in a crow-like caw, "that pride won't fill your belly."

Addie pulls the coat tight about her shoulders and forces her legs forward down the road, feeling as if they're about to fold, when she sees the open doors of a church. Not the grand, imposing towers of Notre-Dame, but a small, stone thing, squeezed between buildings on a narrow street.

She has never been religious, not like her parents. She has always felt caught between the old gods and the new—but meeting the devil in the woods has got her thinking. For every shadow, there must be light. Perhaps the darkness has an equal, and Addie could balance her wish. Estele would sneer, but one god gave her nothing but a curse, so the woman cannot fault her for seeking shelter with the other.

The heavy door scrapes open, and she shuffles in, blinking in the sudden dark until her eyes adjust, and she sees the panels of stained glass.

Addie inhales, struck by the quiet beauty of the space, the vaulted ceiling, the red and blue and green light painting patterns on the walls. It is a kind of art, she thinks, starting forward, when a man steps into her path.

He opens his arms, but there is no welcome in the gesture.

The priest is there to bar her way. He shakes his head at her arrival.

"I'm sorry," he says, coaxing her like a stray bird back up the aisle. "There is no room here. We're full."

And then she is back out on the steps of the church, the heavy grind of the bolt sliding home, and somewhere in Addie's mind, Estele begins to cackle.

"You see," she says, in her rasping way, "only new gods have *locks*."

Addie never decides to go to the docks.

Her feet choose for her, carry her along the Seine as the sun sinks over the river, lead her down the steps, stolen boots thudding on the wooden planks.

It's darker there, in the shadow of the ships, a landscape of crates and barrels, ropes and rocking boats. Eyes follow her. Men glance over from their work, and women look on, lounging like cats in the shade. They have a sickly look about them, their color too high, their mouths painted a violent gash of red. Their dresses tattered and dirty, and still finer than Addie's own.

She has not decided what she means to do, even when she slips the coat from her shoulders. Even when a man comes up to her, one hand already roving, as if testing fruit.

"How much?" he asks in a gruff voice.

And she has no idea what a body is worth, or if she is willing to sell it. When she does not answer, his hands grow rough, his grip grows firm.

"Ten sols," she says, and the man lets out a bark of laughter.

"What are you, a princess?"

"No," she answers, "a virgin."

There were nights, back home, when Addie dreamed of pleasure, when she conjured the stranger beside her in the dark, felt his lips against her breasts, imagined her hand was his as it slipped between her legs.

"My love," the stranger said, pressing her down into the bed, black curls tumbling into gem-green eyes.

"My love," she breathed as he entered her, her body parting around his solid strength. He pushed deeper, and she gasped, biting her hand to keep from sighing too loud. Her mother would say that a woman's pleasure was a mortal sin, but in those moments, Addie didn't care. In those moments, there was only the longing and the want and the stranger, whispering against her skin as the tension deepened, the heat building like a storm in the bowl of her hips, and then in her mind, Adeline would pull his body down on hers, drawing him deeper and deeper until the storm broke, and thunder rolled through her.

But this is nothing like that.

There is no poetry to this unknown man's grunts, no melody or harmony, save the steady noise of thrusting as he pushes himself against her. No rolling pleasure, only pressure, and pain, the tightness of one thing being forced inside another, and Addie looks up at the night sky so she won't have to look at his body moving, and she feels the darkness looking back.

Then they are in the woods again, and his mouth is on hers, blood bubbling up on her lips as he whispers.

"Done."

The man finishes with a final thrust, and slumps against her, leaden, and this cannot be it, this cannot be the life Addie traded everything for, this cannot be the future that erased her past. Panic grips her chest but *this* stranger doesn't seem to care, or even notice. He simply straightens up, and tosses a handful of coins onto the cobbles at her feet. He trundles off and Addie sinks to her knees to collect her reward, and then empties her stomach into the Seine.

When asked about her first memories of Paris, those terrible few months, she will say it was a season of grief blurred into a fog. She will say she can't remember.

But, of course, Addie remembers.

She remembers the stench of rotten food, and waste, the brackish waters of the Seine, the figures on the docks. Remembers moments of kindness erased by a doorway or a dawn, remembers mourning her home with its fresh bread and warm hearth, her family's quiet melody, and Estele's strong beat. The life she had, the one she gave up for the one she thought she wanted, stolen and replaced by this.

And yet, she remembers, too, how she marveled at the city, the way the light swept through in the mornings and evenings, the grandeur carved out between the unhewn blocks; how, despite all the grime, and grief, and disappointment, Paris was full of surprises. Beauty glimpsed through cracks.

Addie remembers the brief respite of that first fall, the brilliant turning of leaves over footpaths, going from green to gold like a jeweler's showcase, before the short, sharp plunge into winter.

Remembers the cold that gnawed at her fingers and toes before swallowing them whole. Cold, and hunger. They had lean months in Villon, of course, when the cold snap stole the last of a harvest, or a late freeze ruined new growth—but this is a new kind of hunger. It rakes at her from the inside, drags its nails along her ribs. It wears her down, and while Addie knows it cannot kill her, the knowing does nothing to dull the urgent ache, the fear. She has not lost an ounce of flesh, but her stomach twists, gnawing on itself, and just as her feet refuse to callus, so her nerves refuse to learn. There is no numbing, none of the ease that comes with a habit. This pain is always fresh, brittle and bright, the feeling as sharp as her memory.

And she remembers the worst, too.

Remembers the sudden freeze, the brutal chill that stole upon the city, and the wave of sickness that blew in behind it like a late-fall breeze, scattering mounds of dead and dying leaves. The sound and sight of the carts rattling past, carrying grim cargo. Addie, turning her face away, trying not to look at the bony shapes piled carelessly in the back. She pulls a stolen coat close around her as she stumbles down the road, and dreams of summer heat, while the cold climbs down into her bones.

She does not think she will ever be warm again. Twice more she has gone to the docks, but the cold has forced the callers in, to the warm shelters of brothels, and around her, the cold snap has turned Paris cruel. The rich board themselves up inside their homes, cling to their hearth fires, while out in the streets, the poor are whittled down by winter. There is nowhere to hide from it—or rather, the only spots have all been claimed.

That first year, Addie is too tired to fight for space.

Too tired to search for shelter.

Another gust whips through, and Addie folds herself against it, eyes blurring. She shuffles sideways, onto a narrow street, just to escape the violent wind, and the sudden quiet, the breezeless peace, of the alley is like down, soft and warm. Her knees fold. She slumps into a corner against a set of steps, and watches her fingers turn blue, thinks she can see frost spreading over her skin, and marvels quietly, sleepily, at her own transformation. Her breath fogs the air in front of her, each exhale briefly blotting out the world beyond until the gray city fades to white, to white, to white. Strange, how it seems to linger now, a little more with every breath, as if she's fogging up a pane of glass. She wonders how many breaths until the world is hidden. Erased, like her.

Perhaps it is her vision blurring.

She does not care.

She is tired.

She is so tired.

Addie cannot stay awake, and why should she try?

Sleep is such a mercy.

Perhaps she will wake again in spring, like the princess in one of her father's stories, and find herself lying in the grassy bank along the Sarthe, Estele nudging her with a worn shoe and teasing her for dreaming again.

This is death.

At least, for an instant, Addie thinks it must be death.

The world is dark, the cold unable to hold back the reek of rot, and she cannot move. But then, she remembers, she cannot die. There is her stubborn pulse, fighting to beat, and her stubborn lungs, fighting to fill, and Addie realizes her limbs aren't lifeless at all, but weighted down on every side. Heavy sacks above, below, and panic flutters through her, but her mind is still sluggish with sleep. She twists, and the sacks shift a little on top of her. The dark splits, and a sliver of gray light shines through.

Addie writhes and wriggles until she frees one arm and then the other, drawing them in against her body. She begins to push up through the sacks, and only then does she feel bones beneath the cloth, only then does her hand meet waxy skin, only then do her fingers tangle in the strands of someone else's hair, and now she is awake, so awake, scrambling, tearing, desperate to get free.

She claws her way up, and out, hands splayed across the bony mound of a dead man's back. Nearby, milky eyes stare up at her. A jaw hangs open, and Addie stumbles out of the cart and collapses to the ground, retching, sobbing, alive.

A horrible sound tears free from her chest, a harsh cough, something snagged halfway between a sob and a laugh.

Then, a scream, and it takes a moment for her to realize it is not coming from her own cracked lips. A ragged woman stands across the road, hands to her mouth in horror, and Addie cannot even blame her.

What a shock it must be, to see a corpse drag itself free from the cart.

The woman crosses herself, and Addie calls out in a hoarse and broken voice, "I am not dead." But the woman only shuffles away and Addie turns her fury on the cart. "I am not dead!" she says again, kicking at the wooden wheel.

"Hey!" shouts a man, holding the legs of a frail and twisted corpse.

"Stay back," shouts a second, gripping its shoulders.

Of course, they do not remember throwing her in. Addie backs away as they swing the newest body up into the cart. It lands with a sickening thud atop the others, and her stomach churns to think she was among them, even briefly.

A whip cracks, the horses shuffle forward, the wheels turn on the cobbled stones, and it is not until the cart has gone, not until Addie thrusts her trembling hands into the pockets of her stolen coat, that she realizes they are empty.

The little wooden bird is gone.

The last of her past life, carried away with the dead.

For months, she will keep reaching for the bird, hand drifting to her pocket the way it might to a stubborn curl, a motion born of so much habit. She cannot seem to remind her fingers it is gone, cannot seem to remind her heart, which stutters a little every time she finds the pocket empty. But, there, blooming amid the sorrow, is a terrible relief. Every moment since she left Villon, she has feared the loss of this last token.

Now that it is gone, there is a guilty gladness tucked among the grief.

This last, brittle thread to her old life has broken, and Addie has been set well, and truly, and forcibly free.

IV

Dreamer is too soft a word.

It conjures thoughts of silken sleep, of lazy days in fields of tall grass, of charcoal smudges on soft parchment.

Addie still holds on to dreams, but she is learning to be sharper. Less the artist's hand, and more the knife, honing the pencil's edge.

"Pour me a drink," she says, holding out the bottle of wine, and the man pries out the cork and fills two glasses from the low shelf of the rented room. He hands her one, and she doesn't touch it as he throws his back in a single swallow, downs a second before abandoning the glass and reaching for her dress.

"Where's the rush?" she says, guiding him back. "You've paid for the room. We have all night."

She is careful not to push him away, careful to keep the pressure of her resistance coy. Some men, she's found, take pleasure in disregarding the wishes of a woman. Instead, Addie lifts her own glass to his hungry mouth, tips the rust-red contents between his lips, tries to pass the gesture off as seduction instead of force.

He drinks deep, then knocks the glass away. Clumsy hands paw at her front, fighting with the laces and the stays.

"I cannot wait to . . ." he slurs, but the drug in the wine is already taking hold, and soon he trails off, his tongue going heavy in his mouth.

He sags back onto the bed, still grasping at her dress, and a moment later his eyes roll back and he slumps sideways, lost to sleep before his head strikes the thin pillow.

Addie leans over and pushes until he rolls off the bed, hitting the floor like a sack of grain. The man lets out a muted groan, but does not wake.

She finishes his work, loosening the laces of her dress until she can breathe again. Paris fashion—twice as tight as country clothes, and half as practical.

She stretches out on the bed, grateful to have it to herself, at least for the night. She does not want to think about tomorrow, when she is forced to start again.

That is the madness of it. Every day is amber, and she is the fly trapped inside. No way to think in days or weeks when she lives in moments. Time begins to lose its meaning—and yet, she has not lost track of time. She cannot seem to misplace it (no matter how she tries) and so Addie knows what month it is, what day, what night, and so she knows it has been a year.

A year since she ran from her own wedding.

A year since she fled into the woods.

A year since she sold her soul for this. For freedom. For time.

A year, and she has spent it learning the boundaries of this new life.

Walking the edges of her curse like a lion in its cage. (She has *seen* lions now. They came to Paris in the spring as part of an exhibit. They were nothing like the beasts of her imagination. So much grander, and so much less, their majesty diminished by the dimensions of their cells. Addie went a dozen times to see them, studied their mournful gazes, looking past the visitors to the gap in the tent, the single sliver of freedom.)

A year she's spent bound within the prism of this deal, forced to suffer but not die, starve but not waste, want but not wither. Every moment pressed into her own memory, while she herself slips from the minds of others with the slightest push, erased by a closing door, an instant out of sight, a moment of sleep. Unable to leave a mark on anyone, or anything.

Even the man slumped on the floor.

She draws the stoppered bottle of laudanum from her skirts, and holds it to the meager light. Three tries, and two bottles of the precious medicine wasted before she realized she could not drug the drinks herself, could not be the hand that did the harm. But mix it in the bottle of wine, reset the cork, and let them pour their own glass, and the action is no longer hers.

See?

She is learning.

It is a lonely education.

She tips the bottle, the last of the milky substance shifting inside the glass, and wonders if it might buy her a night of dreamless sleep, a deep and drugged peace.

"How disappointing."

At the sound of the voice, Addie nearly drops the laudanum. She twists around in the small room, scouring the dark, but cannot find its source.

"I confess, my dear, I expected more."

The voice seems to come from every shadow—then, from one. It gathers in the darkest corner of the room, like smoke. And then he steps forward into the circle cast by the candle flame. Black curls tumble across his brow. Shadows land in the hollows of his face, and green eyes glitter with their own internal light.

And for a traitorous instant, her heart lurches at the familiar sight of her stranger, before she remembers it is only *him*.

The darkness from the woods.

A year she's lived this curse, and in that time, she's called for him. She's pleaded with the night, sunk coins she could not spare into the banks of the Seine, begged for him to answer just so she could ask why, why, why.

Now, she throws the bottle of laudanum straight at his head.

The shadow does not move to catch it, does not need to. It passes straight through, shatters against the wall behind him. He gives her a pitying smile.

"Hello, Adeline."

Adeline. A name she thought she'd never hear again. A name that aches like a bruise, even as her heart skips to hear it.

"You," she snarls.

The barest incline of his head. The curl of his smile. "Have you missed me?"

She hurtles toward him like the stoppered bottle, throws herself against his front, half expecting to fall through and shatter as it did. But her hands meet flesh and bone, or at least, the illusion of it. She pounds against his chest, and it is like striking a tree, just as hard and just as pointless.

He looks down at her, amused. "I see you have."

She tears herself away, wants to scream, to rage, to sob. "You left me there. You took everything from me, and you left. Do you know how many nights I begged—"

"I heard you," he says, and there is an awful pleasure in the way he says it.

Addie sneers with rage. "But you never came."

The darkness spreads his arms, as if to say, *I am here now.* And she wants to strike him, useless as it is, wants to banish him, cast him from this room like a curse, but she must ask. She must know. "Why? Why did you do this to me?"

His dark brows knit with false worry, mock concern. "I granted your wish."

"I asked only for more time, for a life of freedom—"

"I have given you both." His fingers trail along the bedpost. "This past year has taken no toll—" A stifled sound escapes her throat, but he continues. "You are whole, are you not? And uninjured. You do not age. You do not wither. And as for freedom, is there any keener liberation than what I've gifted you? A life with no one to answer to."

"You know this isn't what I wanted."

"You did not know *what* you wanted," he says sharply, stepping toward her. "And if you did, then you should have been more careful."

"You deceived—"

"You *erred*," says the darkness, closing the last space between them. "Don't you remember, Adeline?" His voices drops to a whisper. "You were so brash, so brazen, tripping over your words as if they were roots. Rambling on about all the things you did *not* want."

He is so close to her now, one hand drifting up her arm, and she wills herself not to give him the satisfaction of retreat, not to let him play the wolf, and force her into the part of sheep. But it is hard. For all that he is painted as her stranger, he is not a man. Not even human. It is only a mask, and it does not fit. She can see the thing beneath, as it was in the woods, shapeless and boundless, monstrous, and menacing. The darkness shimmers behind that green-eyed gaze.

"You asked for an eternity and I said no. You begged, and pleaded, and then, do you remember what you said?" When he speaks again, his voice is still his voice, but she can hear her own, echoing through it.

"You can have my life when I am done with it. You can have my soul when I don't want it anymore."

She draws back, from the words, from him, or tries to, but this time he does not let her. The hand on her arm tightens; the other rests like a lover's touch behind her neck.

"Was it not in my best interest, then, to make your life unpleasant? To press you toward your inevitable surrender?"

"You did not have to," she whispers, hating the waver in her voice.

"My dear Adeline," he says, hand sliding up her neck into her hair. "I am in the business of souls, not mercy." His fingers tighten, forcing her head back, her gaze up to meet his own, and there is no sweetness in his face, only a kind of feral beauty.

"Come," he says, "give me what I want, and the deal will be done, this misery ended."

A soul, for a single year of grief and madness.

A soul, for copper coins on a Paris dock.

A soul, for nothing more than this.

And yet, it would be a lie to say she does not waver. To say that no part of her wants to give up, give in, if only for a moment. Perhaps it is that part that asks.

"What would become of me?"

Those shoulders—the ones she drew so many times, the ones *she* conjured into being—give only a dismissive shrug.

"You will be nothing, my dear," he says simply. "But it is a kinder nothing than this. Surrender, and I will set you free."

If some part of her wavered, if some small part wanted to give in, it did not last beyond a moment. There is a defiance in being a dreamer.

"I decline," she growls.

The shadow scowls, those green eyes darkening like cloth soaked wet.

His hands fall away.

"You will give in," he says. "Soon enough."

He does not step back, does not turn to go. He is simply gone. Swallowed by the dark.

Henry Strauss has never been a morning person.

He *wants* to be one, has dreamed of rising with the sun, sipping his first cup of coffee while the city is still waking, the whole day ahead and full of promise.

He's *tried* to be a morning person, and on the rare occasion he's managed to get up before dawn, it was a thrill: to watch the day begin, to feel, at least for a little while, like he was ahead instead of behind. But then a night would go long, and a day would start late, and now he feels like there's no time at all. Like he is always late for something.

Today, it is breakfast with his younger sister, Muriel.

Henry hurries down the block, his head still ringing faintly from the night before, and he would have canceled, should have canceled. But he's canceled three times in the last month alone, and he doesn't want to be a shitty brother; she just wants to be a good sister and that's nice. That's new.

He's never been to this place before. It's not one of his local haunts—though the truth is, Henry's running out of coffee shops in his vicinity. Vanessa ruined the first. Milo the second. The espresso at the third tasted like charcoal. So he let Muriel pick one, and she chose a "quaint little hole in the wall" called Sunflower that apparently doesn't have a sign or an address or any way to find it except by some hipster radar that Henry obviously lacks.

At last he spots a single sunflower stenciled on a wall across the street. He jogs to make the light, bumping into a guy on the corner, mumbles apologies (even as the other man says it's fine, it's fine, it's totally fine). When Henry finally finds the entrance, the hostess is halfway through telling him there's no space, but then she looks up from the podium, and smiles, and says she'll make it work.

Henry looks around for Muriel, but she's always considered time a flexible concept, so even though he's late, she's definitely later. And he's secretly glad, for once, because it gives him a moment to breathe, to smooth his hair and wrest himself free of the scarf that's trying to strangle him, even order a coffee. He tries to make himself look presentable, even if it doesn't matter what he does; it won't change what she sees. But it still matters. It has to.

Five minutes later, Muriel sweeps in. She is, as usual, a tornado of dark curls and unshakable confidence.

Muriel Strauss, who at twenty-four only ever talks about the world in terms of *conceptual authenticity* and *creative truth,* who's been a darling of the New York art scene since her first semester at Tisch, where she quickly realized she was better at critiquing art than creating it.

Henry loves his sister, he does. But Muriel's always been like strong perfume.

Better in small doses. And at a distance.

"Henry!" she shouts, shedding her coat and dropping into the seat with a dramatic flourish.

"You look great," she says, which isn't true, but he simply says, "You too, Mur."

She beams, and orders a flat white, and Henry braces for an awkward silence, because the truth is, he has no idea how to talk to her. But if Muriel's good at anything, it's holding up a conversation. So he drinks his black coffee and settles in while she rolls through the latest pop-up gallery drama, then her schedule for Passover, raves about an experiential art festival on the High Line, even though it isn't open yet. It isn't until after she finishes a rant on a piece of street art that was definitely not a pile of trash, but in fact a commentary on capitalist waste, to the echo of Henry's mhm's, and nods, that Muriel brings up their older brother.

"He's been asking about you."

This is a thing Muriel has never said. Not about David; never to Henry.

So he cannot help himself. "Why?"

His sister rolls her eyes. "I imagine it's because he *cares.*"

Henry nearly chokes on his drink.

David Strauss cares about a lot of things. He cares about his status as the youngest head surgeon at Sinai. He cares, presumably, about his patients. He cares about making time for Midrash, even if it means he has to do it in the middle of a Wednesday night. He cares about his parents, and how proud they are of what he's done. David Strauss does *not* care about his younger brother, except for the myriad ways in which he's ruining the family reputation.

Henry looks down at his watch, even though it doesn't tell the time, or any time, for that matter.

"Sorry, sis," he says, scraping back his chair. "I've got to open the store."

She cuts herself off—something she never used to do—and rises from the chair to wrap her arms around his waist, squeezing him tight. It feels like an apology, like affection, like *love*. Muriel is a good five inches shorter than Henry, enough that he could rest his chin on her head, if they were that kind of close, which they're not.

"Don't be a stranger," she says, and Henry promises he won't.

Addie wakes to someone touching her cheek.

The gesture is so gentle, at first she thinks she must be dreaming, but then she opens her eyes, and sees the fairy lights on the roof, sees Sam crouched beside the lawn chair, a worried crease across her forehead. Her hair has been set free, a mane of wild blond curls around her face.

"Hey, Sleeping Beauty," she says, tucking a cigarette back into its box, unlit.

Addie shivers and sits up, pulling the jacket tight around her. It's a cold, cloudy morning, the sky a stretch of sunless white. She didn't mean to sleep this long, this late. Not that she has anywhere to be, but it certainly seemed like a better idea last night, when she could feel her fingers.

The Odyssey has fallen off her lap. It lies facedown on the ground, the cover slick with morning dew. She reaches to pick it up, does her best to dust the jacket off, smooth the pages where they got bent, or smudged.

"It's freezing out here," says Sam, pulling Addie to her feet. "Come on."

Sam always talks like that, statements in place of questions, imperatives that sound like invitations. She pulls Addie toward the rooftop door, and Addie is too cold to protest, simply trails Sam down the stairs to her apartment, pretending she doesn't know the way.

The door swings open onto madness.

The hall, the bedroom, the kitchen are all stuffed full of art and artifact. Only the living room—at the back of the apartment—is spacious and bare. No sofa or tables there, nothing but two large windows, an easel, and a stool.

"This is where I do my living," she said, when she first brought Addie home.

And Addie answered, "I can tell."

She's crammed everything she owns into three-quarters of the space, just to preserve the peace and quiet of the fourth. Her friend offered her a studio space at an insane deal, but it felt cold, she said, and she needs warmth to paint.

"Sorry," says Sam, stepping around a canvas, over a box. "It's a bit cluttered right now."

Addie has never seen it any other way. She would love to see what Sam is working on, what put the white paint under her nails and led to the smudge of pink just below her jaw. But instead Addie forces herself to follow the girl around and over and through the mess into the kitchen. Sam snaps on the coffeemaker, and Addie's eyes slide over the space, marking the changes. A new purple vase. A stack of half-read books, a postcard from Italy. The collection of mugs, some sprouting clean brushes, and always growing.

"You paint," she says, nodding at the stack of canvases leaning against the stove.

"I do," says Sam, a smile breaking over her face. "Abstracts, mostly. Nonsense art, my friend Jake calls it. But it's not really nonsense, it's just—other people paint what they see. I paint what I feel. Maybe it's confusing, swapping one sense for another, but there's beauty in the transmutation."

Sam pours two cups of coffee, one mug green, as shallow and wide as a bowl, the other tall and blue. "Cats or dogs?" she asks, instead of "green or blue," even though there are no dogs or cats on either of them, and Addie says, "cats," and Sam hands her the tall blue cup without any explanation.

Their fingers brush, and they are standing closer than she realized, close enough for Addie to see the streaks of silver in the blue of Sam's eyes, close enough for Sam to count the freckles on her face.

"You have stars," she says.

Déjà vu, thinks Addie, again. She wills herself to pull away, to leave, to spare herself the insanity of repetition and reflection. Instead, Addie wraps her hands around the cup and takes a long sip. The first note is strong and bitter, but the second is rich and sweet.

She sighs with pleasure, and Sam flashes her a brilliant grin. "Good, right?" she says. "The secret is—"

Cacao nibs, thinks Addie.

"Cacao nibs," says Sam, taking a long sip from her cup, which Addie is convinced now is really a bowl. She drapes herself over the counter, head bowed over the coffee as if it were an offering.

"You look like a wilted flower," teases Addie.

Sam winks and lifts her cup. "Water me, and watch me bloom."

Addie has never seen Sam like this, in the morning. Of course, she's woken up beside her, but those days were tinged with apologies, unease. The aftermath of the absence of memory. It is never fun to linger in those moments. Now, though. This is new. A memory made for the first time.

Sam shakes her head. "Sorry. I never asked your name."

This is one of the things she loves about Sam, one of the first things she ever noticed. Sam lives and loves with such an open heart, shares the kind of warmth most reserve only for the closest people in their lives. Reasons come second to needs. She took her in, she warmed her up, before she thought to ask her name.

"Madeline," says Addie, because it is the closest she can get.

"Mmm," says Sam, "my favorite kind of cookie. I'm Sam."

"Hello, Sam," she says, as if tasting the name for the first time.

"So," says the other girl, as if the question only just occurred to her. "What were you doing up there on the roof?"

"Oh," says Addie with a small, self-deprecating laugh. "I didn't mean to fall asleep up there. I don't even remember sitting down on the lawn chair. I must have been more tired than I thought. I just moved in, 2F, and I don't think I'm used to all the noise. I couldn't sleep, finally gave up and went up there to get some fresh air and watch the sun rise over the city."

The lie rolls out so easily, the way paved with practice.

"We're neighbors!" says Sam. "You know," she adds, setting her empty cup aside, "I'd love to paint you sometime."

And Addie fights the urge to say, *You already have.*

"I mean, it wouldn't *look* like you," Sam rambles on, heading into the hall. Addie follows, watches her stop and run her fingers over a stack of canvases, turning through them as if they were records in a vinyl shop.

"I've got this whole series I'm working on," she says, "of people as skies."

A dull pang echoes through Addie's chest, and it's six months ago, and they are lying in bed, Sam's fingers tracing the freckles on her cheeks, her touch as light and steady as a brush.

"You know," she'd said, "they say people are like snowflakes, each one unique, but I think they're more like skies. Some are cloudy, some are stormy, some are clear, but no two are ever quite the same."

"And what kind of sky am I?" Addie had asked then, and Sam had stared at her, unblinking, and then brightened, and it was the kind of brightening she had seen with a hundred artists, a hundred times, the glow of inspiration, as if someone switched on a light beneath their skin. And Sam, suddenly animated, wound to life, sprang from the bed, taking Addie with her into the living room.

An hour of sitting on the hardwood floor, wrapped in only a blanket, listening to the murmur and scrape of Sam mixing paint, the hiss of the brush on the canvas, and then it was done, and when Addie came around to look at it, what she saw was the night sky. Not the night sky as anyone else would have painted it. Bold streaks of charcoal, and black, and thin slashes of middle gray, the paint so thick it rose up from the canvas. And flecked across the surface, a handful of silver dots. They looked almost accidental, like spatter from a brush, but there were exactly seven of them, small and distant and wide apart as stars.

Sam's voice draws her back to the kitchen.

"I wish I could show you my favorite piece," she's saying now. "It was the first in the series. *One Forgotten Night.* I sold it to this collector on the Lower East Side. It was my first *major* sale, paid my rent for three months, got me into a gallery. Still, it's hard, letting go of the art. I know I have to—that whole starving artist thing is overrated—but I miss it every day."

Her voice dips softer.

"The crazy thing is, every one of the pieces in that series is modeled after someone. Friends, people here in the building, strangers I found on the street. I remember all of them. But I can't for the life of me remember who she was."

Addie swallows. "You think it was a girl?"

"Yeah. I do. It just had this *energy.*"

"Maybe you dreamed her."

"Maybe," says Sam. "I've never been good at remembering dreams. But you know . . ." She trails off, staring at Addie the way she did that night in bed, beginning to glow. "You remind me of that piece." She puts a hand over her face. "God, that sounds like the worst pickup line in the world. I'm sorry. I'm going to take a shower."

"I should get going," says Addie. "Thanks for the coffee."

Sam bites her lip. "Do you have to?"

No, she doesn't. Addie knows she could follow Sam right into the shower, wrap herself in a towel, and sit on the living room floor and see what kind of painting Sam would make of her today. She could. She could. She could fall into this moment forever, but she knows there is no future in it. Only an infinite number of presents, and she has lived as many of those with Sam as she can bear.

"Sorry," she says, chest aching, but Sam only shrugs.

"We'll see each other again," she says with so much faith. "After all, we're neighbors now."

Addie manages a pale shadow of a smile. "That's right."

Sam walks her to the door, and with every step, Addie resists the urge to look back.

"Don't be a stranger," says Sam.

"I won't," promises Addie, as the door swings shut. She sighs, leaning back against it, listens to Sam's footsteps retreating down the cluttered hall, before she forces herself up, and forward, and away.

Outside, the white marble sky has cracked, letting through thin bands of blue.

The cold has burned off, and Addie finds a café with sidewalk seating, busy enough that the waiter only has time to make a pass of the outside tables every ten minutes or so. She counts the beats like a prisoner marking the pace of guards, orders a coffee—it isn't as good as Sam's, all bitter, no sweet, but it's warm enough to keep the chill at bay. She puts up the collar of her leather coat, and opens *The Odyssey* again, and tries to read.

Here, Odysseus thinks he is heading home, to finally be reunited with Penelope after the horrors of war, but she has read the story enough times to know how far the journey is from done.

She skims, translating from Greek to modern English.

I fear the sharp frost and the soaking dew together
will do me in—I'm bone-weary, about to breathe my last,
and a cold wind blows from a river on toward morning.

The waiter ducks back outside, and she glances up from the book, watches him frown a little at the sight of the drink already ordered and delivered, the gap in his memory where a customer should be. But she looks like she belongs, and that's half the battle, really, and a moment later he turns his attention to the couple in the doorway, waiting for a seat.

She returns to her book, but it's no use. She's not in the mood for old men lost at sea, for parables of lonely lives. She wants to be stolen away, wants to forget. A fantasy, or perhaps a romance.

The coffee is cold now, anyway, and Addie stands up, book in hand, and sets off for The Last Word to find something new.

VII

She stands in the shade of a silk merchant.

Across the way, the tailor's shop bustles, the pace of business brisk even as the day wears on. Sweat drips down her neck as she unties and reties the bonnet, salvaged from a gust of wind, hoping the cloth cap will be enough to pass her off as a lady's maid, to grant her the kind of invisibility reserved for help. If he thinks her a maid, Bertin will not look too close. If he thinks her a maid, he might not notice Addie's dress, which is simple but fine, slipped from a tailor's model a week before, in a similar shop across the Seine. It was a pretty thing at first, until she snagged the skirts on an errant nail, and someone cast a bucket of soot too near her feet, and red wine somehow got onto one of the sleeves.

She wishes her clothes were as resistant to change as she appears to be. Especially because she has only the one dress—there's no point collecting a wardrobe, or anything else, when you've nowhere to put it. (She will try, in later years, to gather trinkets, hide them away like a magpie with its nest, but something will always conspire to steal them back. Like the wooden bird, lost among the bodies in the cart. She cannot seem to hold on to much of anything for long.)

At last, the final customer steps out—a valet, one beribboned box beneath each arm—and before anyone else can beat her to the door, Addie darts across the street and steps inside the tailor's shop.

It is a narrow space: a table piled high with rolls of fabric; a pair of dress forms modeling the latest fashions. The kind of gowns that take at least four hands to get on, and just as many to take off—all bolstered hips and ruffled sleeves and bosoms cinched too tight to breathe. These days the fine society of Paris is wrapped like parcels, clearly not meant to be opened.

A small bell on the door announces her arrival, and the tailor, Monsieur Bertin, looks up at her through brows as thick as brambles, and makes a sour face.

"I am closing," he says curtly.

Addie ducks her head, the picture of discretion. "I am here on behalf of Madame Lautrec."

It is a name plucked from the breeze, overheard on a handful of her walks, but it is the right answer. The tailor straightens, suddenly keen. "For the Lautrecs, anything." He takes up a small pad, a charcoal pencil, and Addie's own fingers twitch, a moment of grief, a longing to draw as she so often did.

"It is strange, though," he is saying, shaking the stiffness from his hands, "that she would send a lady's maid in place of her valet."

"He's ill," Addie answers swiftly. She is learning to lie, to bend with the current of the conversation, follow its course. "So she sent her lady's maid instead. Madame wishes to throw a dance, and is in need of a new dress."

"But of course," he says. "You have her measurements?"

"I do."

He stares, waiting for her to produce a slip of paper.

"No," she explains. "I *have* her measurements—they are the same as mine. That's why she sent me."

She thinks it is a rather clever lie, but the tailor only frowns, and turns toward a curtain at the back of the shop. "I will get my tape."

She catches a brief glimpse of the room beyond, a dozen dress forms, a mountain of silks, before the curtain falls again. But as Bertin slips away, so does she, vanishing between the dress forms and the rolls of muslin and cotton propped against the wall. It is not her first visit to the shop, and she has learned well its crevices and crooks, all the corners large enough to hide in. Addie folds into one such space, and by the time Bertin returns to the front of the shop, the tape in one hand, he has forgotten all about Madame Lautrec and her peculiar maid.

It is stuffy among the rolls of cloth, and she's grateful when she hears the rattle of the bell, the shuffling sound of Bertin closing up his shop. He will go upstairs, to the room he keeps above, will have some soup, and soak his aching hands, and go to bed before it is full night. She waits, letting the quiet settle around her, waits until she can hear the groan of his steps overhead.

And then she is free to wander, and peruse.

A weak gray light seeps through the front window as she crosses the shop, pulls aside the heavy curtain, and steps through.

The fading light slides in through a single window, just enough to see by. Along the back wall there are cloaks, half-finished, and she makes a mental note to return when summer gives way to fall, and the cold sweeps through. But her focus falls on the center of the room, where a dozen dress forms stand like dancers taking up their marks, their narrow waists wrapped in shades of green and gray, a navy gown piped white, another pale blue with yellow trim.

Addie smiles, and casts the bonnet off onto a table, shaking loose her hair. She runs her hand over skeins of patterned silk and richly dyed cotton, savoring the textures of linen and twill. Touches the boning of the corsets, the bustles at the hips, imagining herself in each. She passes the muslin and wool, simple and sturdy, lingers instead on worsted pleats and layered satin, finer than anything she saw back home.

Home—it is a hard word to let go of, even now, when there is nothing left to bind her to it.

She plucks at the stays of a bodice, the blue of summer, and stops, breath held, when she catches movement out of the corner of her eye. But it is only a mirror, leaning against the wall. She turns, studies herself in the silvered surface, as if she were a portrait of someone else, though the truth is, she looks entirely herself.

These last two years have felt like ten, and yet, they do not show. She should have long been whittled down to skin and bone, hardened, hewn, but her face is just as full as it was the summer she left home. Her skin, unlined by time and trial, untouched in any way, save for the familiar freckles on the smooth palette of her cheeks. Only her eyes mark the change—an edge of shadow threaded through the brown and gold.

Addie blinks, forces her gaze away from herself, and the dresses.

Across the room, a trio of dark shapes—men's forms, in trousers and waistcoats and jackets. In the low light, their headless forms seem alive, leaning into one another as they study her. She considers the cut of their clothes, the absence of bone stays or bustled skirts, and thinks, not for the first time, and certainly not for the last, how much simpler it would be to be a man, how easily they move through the world, and at such little cost.

And then, she is reaching for the nearest form, sliding off its coat. Unfastening the buttons down its front. There is a strange intimacy to the undressing, and she enjoys it all the more for the fact that the man beneath her fingers is not real, and therefore cannot grope, or paw, or push.

She frees herself from the laces of her own dress, and finds her way into the trousers, fastening them below her knee. She pulls on the tunic and buttons the waistcoat, shrugs the striped coat over her shoulders, fastens the lace cravat at her throat.

She feels safe in the armor of their fashion, but when she turns to the mirror, her spirits sink. Her chest is too full, her waist too narrow, her hips flaring to fill the trousers in the wrong place. The jacket helps, a little, but nothing can disguise her face. The bow of her lips, the line of her cheek, the smoothness of her brow, all too soft and round to pass for anything but female.

She takes up a pair of shears, tries to trim the loose coil of her hair to her shoulders, but seconds later, it is back, the locks on the floor swept away by some invisible hand. No mark made, even on herself. She finds a pin and fastens the light brown waves back in the style she has seen men wear, plucks a tricorne hat from one of the forms and rests it above her brow.

At a distance, perhaps; at a passing glance, perhaps; at night, perhaps, when the darkness is thick enough to smudge the details; but even by lamplight, the illusion does not hold.

The men in Paris are soft, even pretty, but they are still men.

She sighs, and casts off the disguise, and passes the next hour trying on dress after dress, already longing for the freedom of those trousers, the stayless comfort of that tunic. But the dresses are fine, and lush. Her favorite among them is a lovely green and white—but it isn't finished yet. The collar and hem lie open, waiting for lace. She'll have to check back in a week or two, hope that she catches the dress before it's gone, wrapped in paper and sent on to the home of some baroness.

In the end, Addie chooses a dark sapphire dress, its edges trimmed in gray. It reminds her of a storm at night, the clouds blotting out the sky. The silk kisses her skin, the fabric crisp and new and utterly unblemished. It is too fine for her needs, a dress for banquets, for balls, but she does not care. And if it draws strange looks, what of it? They will forget before they have the chance to gossip.

Addie leaves her own dress draped around the naked form, does not bother with the bonnet, lifted from a line of clothes that morning. She slips back through the curtain and across the shop, skirts rustling around her, finds the spare key Bertin keeps in the table's top drawer, and unlocks the door, careful to still the bell with her fingers. She pulls the door shut behind her, crouching to slip the iron key back through the gap beneath the door, then rises and turns, only to collide with a man standing on the street.

It is no wonder she didn't see him; dressed in black, from his shoes to his collar, he blends right into the dark. She is already murmuring apologies, already backing away when her gaze lifts, and she sees the line of his jaw, the raven curls, the eyes, so green despite the lack of light.

He smiles down at her.

"Adeline."

That name, it strikes like flint on his tongue, sparks an answering light behind her ribs. His gaze drifts over her new dress. "You're looking well."

"I look the same."

"The prize of immortality. As you wanted."

This time she does not rise to take the bait. Does not scream or swear or point out all the ways he's damned her, but he must see the struggle on her face, because he laughs, soft and airy as a breeze.

"Come," says the shadow, offering his arm. "I will walk you."

He does not say that he will walk her *home*. And if it were midday, she would scorn the offer just to spite him. (Of course, if it were midday, the darkness would not be there.) But it is late, and only one kind of woman walks alone at night.

Addie has learned that women—at least, women of a certain class—never venture forth alone, even during the day. They are kept inside like potted plants, tucked behind the curtains of their homes. And when they do go out, they go in groups, safe within the cages of each other's company, and always in the light of day.

To walk alone in the morning is a scandal, but to walk alone at night, that is something else. Addie knows. She has felt their looks, their judgment, from every side. The women scorn her from their windows, the men try to buy her on the streets, and the devout, they try to save her soul, as if she hasn't already sold it. She has said yes to the church, on more than one occasion, but only for the shelter, and never the salvation.

"Well?" asks the shadow, holding out his arm.

Perhaps she is lonelier than she would say.

Perhaps an enemy's company is still better than none.

Addie does not take his arm, but she does start walking, and she does not need to look to know that he has fallen in step beside her. His shoes echo softly on the cobblestones, and a faint breeze presses like a palm against her back.

They walk in silence, until she cannot bear it. Until her resolve slips, and she looks over, and sees him, head tipped slightly back, dark lashes brushing fair cheeks as he breathes in the night, fetid though it is. A faint smile on those lips, as if he's perfectly at ease. His very image mocks her, even as his edges blur, dark into dark, smoke on shadow, a reminder of what he is, and what he isn't.

Her silence cracks, the words spill out.

"You can take any shape you please, isn't that right?"

His head tips down. "It is."

"Then change," she says. "I cannot bear to look at you."

A rueful smile. "I rather like this form. I think you do as well."

"I did once," she says. "But you have ruined it for me."

It is an opening, she sees too late, a crack in her own armor.

Now he will never change.

Addie stops on a narrow, winding street, before a house, if it can be called that. A slumping wooden structure, like a pile of kindling, deserted, abandoned, but not empty.

When he is gone, she will climb through the gap in the boards, trying not to ruin the hem of her new skirts, will cross the uneven floor and go up a set of broken stairs to the attic, and hope that no one else has found it first.

She will climb out of her storm-cloud dress, and fold it carefully within a piece of tissue paper, and then she will lie down on a pallet of burlap and board, and stare up through the split planks of the ceiling two feet over her head, and hope it does not rain, while the lost souls creep through the body of the house below.

Tomorrow, the little room will be taken, and in a month, the building will burn down, but there is no sense worrying about the future now.

The darkness shifts like a curtain at her back.

"How long will you carry on?" he muses. "What is the point of dragging yourself through another day, when there is no reprieve?"

Questions she has asked herself in the dead of night, moments of weakness when winter sank its teeth into her skin, or hunger clawed against her bones, when a space was taken, a day's work undone, a night's peace lost, and she could not bear the thought of rising to do it all again. And yet, hearing the words parroted back like this, in his voice instead of hers, they lose a measure of their venom.

"Don't you see?" he says, green eyes sharp as broken glass. "There is no end besides the one I offer. All you have to do is yiel—"

"I saw an elephant," says Addie, and the words are like cold water on coals. The darkness stills beside her, and she continues, gaze fixed on the ramshackle house, and the broken roof, and the open sky above. "Two, in fact. They were in the palace grounds, as part of some display. I didn't know animals could be so large. And there was a fiddler in the square the other day," she presses on, her voice steady, "and his music made me cry. It was the prettiest song I'd ever heard. I had Champagne, drank it straight from the bottle, and watched the sun set over the Seine while the bells rang out from Notre-Dame, and none of it would have happened back in Villon." She turns to look at him. "It has only been two years," she says. "Think of all the time I have, and all the things I'll see."

Addie grins at the shadow then, a small, feral smile, all teeth, feasting on the way the humor falls from his face.

It is a small victory, and yet so sweet, to see him falter, even for an instant.

And then, suddenly, he is too close, the air between them snuffed like a candle. He smells of summer nights, of earth, and moss, and tall grass waving beneath stars. And of something darker. Of blood on rocks, and wolves loose in the woods.

He leans in until his cheek brushes against hers, and when he speaks again, the words are little more than whispers over skin.

"You think it will get easier," he says. "It will not. You are as good as gone, and every year you live will feel a lifetime, and in every lifetime, you will be forgotten. Your pain is meaningless. Your life is meaningless. The years will be like weights around your ankles. They will crush you, bit by bit, and when you cannot stand it, you will *beg* me to put you from your misery."

Addie pulls back to face the darkness, but he is already gone.

She stands alone on the narrow road. Inhales a low, unsteady breath, forces it out again, and then straightens, and smooths her skirts, and makes her way into the broken house that, tonight at least, is home.

The bookshop is busier today.

A kid plays hide-and-seek with his imaginary friend while his father turns through a military history. A college student crouches, scanning the different editions of Blake, and the boy she met yesterday stands behind the counter.

She studies him, the habit like thumbing through a book.

His black hair tumbles forward into his eyes, unruly, untamable. He pushes it back, but in seconds it has fallen forward again, making him look younger than he is.

He has the kind of face, she thinks, that can't keep secrets well.

There is a short queue, so Addie hangs back between POETRY and MEMOIR. She raps her nails along a shelf, and a few moments later an orange head pokes itself out from the dark above the spines. She pets Book absently, and waits for the queue to thin from three, to two, to one.

The boy—*Henry*—notices her, lingering nearby, and something crosses his face, too fast for even her to read, before his attention flicks back to the woman at the counter.

"Yes, Ms. Kline," he's saying. "No, that's fine. And if it's not what he wants, just bring it back."

The woman toddles off, clutching her store bag, and Addie steps up. "Hi there," she says brightly.

"Hello," Henry says, an edge of caution in his voice. "Can I help you?"

"I hope so," she says, all practiced charm. She sets *The Odyssey* on the counter between them. "My friend bought me this book, but I already have it. I was hoping I could exchange it for something else."

He studies her. A dark brow lifts behind his glasses. "Are you serious?"

"I know," she says with a laugh, "hard to believe I already own this one in Greek but—"

He rocks back on his heels. "You *are* serious."

Addie falters, thrown off by the edge in his voice. "I just thought it was worth asking . . ."

"This isn't a library," he chides. "You can't just trade one book for another."

Addie straightens. "Obviously," she says, a little indignant. "But like I said, *I* didn't buy it. My friend did, and I just heard you tell Ms. Kline that—"

His face hardens, the flat regard of a door slammed shut. "Word of advice. Next time you try to return a book, don't return it to the same person you stole it from the first time."

A rock drops inside her chest. "What?"

He shakes his head. "You were just in here yesterday."

"I wasn't—"

"I remember you."

Three words, large enough to tip the world.

I remember you.

Addie lurches as if struck, about to fall. She tries to right herself. "No you don't," she says firmly.

His green eyes narrow. "Yes. I do. You came in here yesterday, green sweater, black jeans. You stole this used copy of *The Odyssey*, which I gave *back* to you, because who steals a used copy of *The Odyssey* in Greek anyways, and then you have the nerve to come back in here and try to trade it out for something else? When you didn't even buy the first one . . ."

Addie closes her eyes, vision swimming.

She doesn't understand.

She can't—

"Now look," he says, "I think you better go."

She opens her eyes, and sees him pointing to the door. Her feet won't move. They refuse to carry her away from those three words.

I remember you.

Three hundred years.

Three hundred years, and no one has said those words, no one has ever, *ever* remembered. She wants to grab him by the sleeve, wants to pull him forward, wants to know why, how, what is so special about a boy in a bookstore—but the man with the military history is waiting to pay, the kid clinging to his leg, and the boy with the glasses is glaring at her, and this is all wrong. She grips the counter, feels like she might faint. His eyes soften, just a fraction.

"Please," he says under his breath. "Just go."

She tries.

She can't.

Addie gets as far as the open door, the four short steps from the shop to the street, before something in her gives.

She slumps onto the lip at the top of the stairs, puts her head in her hands, feels like she might cry, or laugh, but instead, she stares back through the beveled glass insert of the shop door. She watches the boy every time he comes into the frame. She cannot tear her eyes away.

I remember you. I remember you. I remember you. I remember you. I remember you. I remember you. I remember you. I remember you. I remember you. I remember you. I remember you. I remember you. I remember you. I remember you. I remember you. I remember—

"What are you doing?"

She blinks, and sees him standing in the open doorway, arms crossed. The sun has shifted lower in the sky, the light going thin.

"Waiting for you," she says, cringing as soon as she says it. "I wanted to apologize," she continues. "For the whole book thing."

"It's fine," he says curtly.

"No, it's not," she says, rising to her feet. "Let me buy you a coffee."

"You don't have to do that."

"I insist. As an apology."

"I'm working."

"*Please.*"

And it must be something in the way she says it, the sheer mix of hope and need, the obvious fact it means more than a book, more than a sorry, that makes the boy look her in the eyes, makes her realize that he hadn't really, not until now. There's something strange, searching in his gaze, but whatever he sees when he looks at her, it changes his mind.

"One coffee," he says. "And you're still banned from the shop."

Addie feels the air rush back into her lungs. "Deal."

Addie lingers on the bookstore steps for an hour until it closes.

Henry locks up, and turns to see her sitting there, and Addie braces again for the blankness in his gaze, the confirmation that their earlier encounter was only some strange glitch, a slipped stitch in the centuries of her curse.

But when he looks at her, he knows her. She is certain he knows her.

His brows go up beneath his tangled curls, as if he's surprised that she's still there. But his annoyance has given way to something else—something that confuses her even more. It's less hostile than suspicion, more guarded than relief, and it is still wonderful, because of the knowing in it. Not a first meeting, but a second—or rather, a third—and for once she is not the only one who knows.

"Well?" he says, holding out his hand, not for her to take, but for her to lead the way, and she does. They walk a few blocks in awkward silence, Addie stealing glances that tell her nothing but the line of his nose, the angle of his jaw.

He has a starved look, wolfish and lean, and even though he's not unnaturally tall, he hunches his shoulders as if to make himself shorter, smaller, less obtrusive. Perhaps, in the right clothes, perhaps, with the right air, perhaps, perhaps; but the longer she looks at him, the weaker the resemblance to that other stranger.

And yet.

There is something about him that keeps catching her attention, snagging it the way a nail snags a sweater.

Twice he catches her looking at him, and frowns.

Once she catches him stealing his own glance, and smiles.

At the coffee shop, she tells him to grab a table while she buys the drinks, and he hesitates, as if torn between the urge to pay and the fear of being poisoned, before retreating to a corner booth. She orders him a latte.

"Three eighty," says the girl behind the counter.

Addie cringes at the cost. She pulls a few bills from her pocket, the last of what she took from James St. Clair. She doesn't have the cash for two drinks, and she can't just walk out with them, because there's a boy waiting. And he remembers.

Addie glances toward the table, where he sits, arms folded, staring out the window.

"Eve!" calls the barista.

"Eve!"

Addie startles, realizing that means her.

"So," says the boy when she sits down. "Eve?"

No, she thinks. "Yeah," she says. "And you're . . ."

Henry, she thinks just before he says it.

"Henry." It fits him, like a coat. Henry: soft, poetic. Henry: quiet, strong. The black curls, the pale eyes behind their heavy frames. She has known a dozen Henrys, in London, Paris, Boston, and L.A., but he is not like any of them.

His gaze drops to the table, his cup, her empty hands. "You didn't get anything."

She waves it away. "I'm not really thirsty," she lies.

"It feels weird."

"Why?" She shrugs. "I said I'd buy you a coffee. Besides," she hesitates, "I lost my wallet. I didn't have enough for two."

Henry frowns. "Is that why you stole the book?"

"I didn't *steal* it. I wanted to trade. And I said sorry."

"Did you?"

"With the coffee."

"Speaking of," he says, standing. "How do you take it?"

"What?"

"The coffee. I can't sit here and drink alone, it makes me feel like an asshole."

She smiles. "Hot chocolate. Dark."

Those brows quirk up again. He walks away to order, says something that makes the barista laugh and lean forward, like a flower to the sun. He returns with a second cup and a croissant, and sets them both in front of her before taking his seat, and now they are uneven again. Balance tipped, restored, and tipped again, and it is the kind of game she's played a hundred times, a sparring match made of small gestures, the stranger smiling across the table.

But this is not her stranger, and he is not smiling.

"So," says Henry, "what *was* all that today, with the book?"

"Honestly?" Addie wraps her hands around the coffee cup. "I didn't think you'd remember."

The question rattles like loose change in her chest, like pebbles in a porcelain bowl; it shakes inside her, threatening to spill out.

How did you remember? How? How?

"The Last Word doesn't get *that* many customers," Henry says. "And even fewer try to leave without paying. I guess you made an impression."

An impression.

An impression is like a mark.

Addie runs her fingers through the foam on her hot chocolate, watches the milk smooth again in her wake. Henry doesn't notice, but he noticed her, he remembered.

What is happening?

"So," he says, but the sentence goes nowhere.

"So," she echoes, because she cannot say what she wants. "Tell me about yourself."

Who are you? Why are you? What is happening?

Henry bites his lip and says, "Not much to tell."

"Did you always want to work in a bookshop?"

Henry's face turns wistful. "I'm not sure it's the job that people dream of, but I like it." He's lifting the latte to his mouth when someone shuffles past, knocking against his chair. Henry rights the cup in time, but the man begins to apologize. And doesn't stop.

"Hey, I'm so sorry." His face twists with guilt.

"It's fine."

"Did I make you spill?" asks the man with genuine concern.

"Nope," says Henry. "You're good."

If he registers the man's intensity, he gives no sign. His focus stays firmly on Addie, as if he can will the man away.

"That was weird," she says, when he's finally gone.

Henry only shrugs. "Accidents happen."

That isn't what she meant. But the thoughts are passing trains, and she can't afford to be derailed.

"So," she says, "the bookshop. Is it yours?"

Henry shakes his head. "No. I mean, it might as well be, I'm the only employee, but it belongs to a woman named Meredith, who spends most of her time on cruises. I just work there. What about you? What do you do when you're not stealing books?"

Addie weighs the question, the many possible answers, all of them lies, and settles for something closer to the truth.

"I'm a talent scout," she says. "Music, mostly, but also art."

Henry's face hardens. "You should meet my sister."

"Oh?" asks Addie, wishing she'd lied. "Is she an artist?"

"I think she'd say she *fosters* art, that it's a type of artist, maybe. She likes to"—he makes a flourish—"nurture the raw potential, shape the narrative of the creative future."

Addie thinks she *would* like to meet his sister, but she doesn't say it.

"Do you have siblings?" he asks.

She shakes her head, tearing a corner off the croissant because he hasn't touched it, and her stomach's growling.

"Lucky," he says.

"Lonely," she counters.

"Well, you're welcome to mine. There's David, who's a doctor, a scholar, and a pretentious asshole, and Muriel who's, well—Muriel."

He looks at her, and there it is again, that strange intensity, and maybe it's just that so few people make eye contact in the city, but she can't shake the feeling he's looking for something in her face.

"What is it?" she asks, and he starts to say one thing, but changes course.

"Your freckles look like stars."

Addie smiles. "I've heard. My own little constellation. It's the first thing everyone sees."

Henry shifts in his seat. "What do you see," he says, "when you look at *me*?"

His voice is light enough, but there is something in the question, a weight, like a stone buried in a snowball. He's been waiting to ask. The answer matters.

"I see a boy with dark hair and kind eyes and an open face."

He frowns a little. "Is that all?"

"Of course not," she says. "But I don't know you yet."

"Yet," he echoes, and there's something like a smile in his voice.

She purses her lips, considers him again.

For a moment, they are the only silent spot in the bustling café.

Live long enough, and you learn how to read a person. To ease them open like a book, some passages underlined and others hidden between the lines.

Addie scans his face, the slight furrow where his brows go in and up, the set of his lips, the way he rubs one palm as if working out an ache, even as he leans forward, and in, his attention wholly on her.

"I see someone who cares," she says slowly. "Perhaps too much. Who feels too much. I see someone lost, and hungry. The kind of person who feels like they're wasting away in a world full of food, because they can't decide what they want."

Henry stares at her, all the humor gone out of his face, and she knows she's gotten too close to the truth.

Addie laughs nervously, and the sound rushes back in around them.

"Sorry," she says, shaking her head. "Too deep. I probably should have just said you were good-looking."

Henry's mouth quirks, but the smile doesn't reach his eyes. "At least you think I'm good-looking."

"What about me?" she asks, trying to break the sudden tension.

But for the first time, Henry won't look her in the eyes. "I've never been good at reading people." He nudges the cup away, and stands, and Addie thinks she's ruined it. He's leaving.

But then he looks down at her and says, "I'm hungry. Are you hungry?"

And the air rushes back into her lungs.

"Always," she says.

And this time, when he holds out his hand, she knows he's inviting her to take it.

Addie has discovered *chocolate*.

Harder to come by than salt, or Champagne, or silver, and yet the marchioness keeps an entire tin of the dark, sweet flakes beside her bed. Addie wonders, as she holds a melting sliver on her tongue, if the woman counts the pieces every night, or if she only notices when her fingers skim the empty bottom of the tin. She is not home to ask. If she were, Addie wouldn't be sprawled atop her down duvet.

But Addie and the lady of the house have never met.

Hopefully, they never will.

The marquis and his wife keep quite a social calendar, after all, and over the last few years their city house has become one of her favorite haunts.

Haunt—it is the right word, for someone living like a ghost.

Twice a week they have friends to dinner in their city house, and every fortnight they host a grander party there, and once a month, which happens to be tonight, they take a carriage across Paris to play cards with other noble families, and do not return until the early morning.

By now, the servants have retreated to their own quarters, no doubt to drink and savor their small measure of freedom. They will take shifts, so that at any given time, a single sentinel stands watch at the base of the stairs, while the rest enjoy their peace. Perhaps they play cards, too. Or perhaps they simply relish the quiet of an empty house.

Addie rests another bit of chocolate on her tongue and sinks back onto the marchioness's bed, into the cloud of airy down. There are more cushions here than in all of Villon, she is certain, and each is twice as full of feathers. Apparently nobles are made of glass, designed to break if laid upon too rough a surface. Addie spreads her arms, like a child making angels in the snow, and sighs with pleasure.

She spent an hour or so combing over and through the marchioness's many dresses, but she doesn't have enough hands to climb into any of them, so she has wrapped herself in a blue silk dressing gown finer than anything she's ever owned. Her own dress, a rust-colored thing with a cream lace trim, lies abandoned on the chaise, and when she looks at it she remembers the wedding gown, cast-off in the grass along the Sarthe, the pale white linen shed like a skin beside her.

The memory clings like spider silk.

Addie pulls the dressing gown close, inhales the scent of roses on the hem, closes her eyes, and imagines this is her bed, her life, and for a few minutes, it is pleasant enough. But the room is too warm, too still, and she's afraid if she lingers in the bed, it might swallow her. Or worse, she might fall asleep, and find herself shaken awake by the lady of the house, and what a pain that would be, since the bedroom is on the second floor.

It takes a full minute to climb out of the bed, hands and knees sinking into the down as she scrambles toward the edge, tumbles gracelessly onto the rug. She steadies herself against a wooden post, delicate branches carved into the oak, thinks of trees as she surveys the room, deciding how to occupy herself. A glass door leads out onto the balcony, a wooden one leads into the hall. A chest of drawers. A chaise. A dressing table, topped by a polished mirror.

Addie sinks onto a cushioned stool before the vanity, her fingers dancing over the bottles of perfume and pots of cream, the soft plume of a powder puff, a bowl of silver hairpins.

Of these last, she takes a handful, and begins to twist up locks of hair, fastening the coils back and up around her face as if she has the faintest idea what she is doing. The current style is reminiscent of a sparrow's nest, a bundle of curls. At least she is not yet expected to wear a wig, one of those monstrous, powdered things like towers of meringue that will come into fashion fifty years from now.

Her nest of curls is set, but needs a final touch. Addie lifts a pearl comb in the shape of a feather and slides the teeth into the locks just behind her ear.

Strange, the way small differences add up.

Perched there on the pillowed seat, surrounded by luxury, in her borrowed blue silk robe with her hair pinned up in curls, Addie could almost forget herself, could almost be someone else. A young mistress, the lady of the house, able to move freely with the safeguard of her reputation.

Only the freckles on her cheeks stand out, a reminder of who Addie was, is, will always be.

But freckles are easily covered.

She takes up the powder puff, the bloom halfway to her cheek when a faint breeze stirs the air, carrying the scent not of Paris, but open fields, and a low voice says, "I would rather see clouds blot out the stars."

Addie's gaze cuts to the mirror, and the reflection of the room behind her. The balcony doors are still shut fast, but the chamber is no longer empty. The shadow leans against the wall with all the ease of someone who has been there for a while. She is not surprised to see him—he has come, year after year—but she is unsettled. She will always be unsettled.

"Hello, Adeline," says the darkness, and though he is across the room, the words brush like leaves against her skin.

She turns in her seat, free hand rising to the open collar of her robe. "Go away."

He clicks his tongue. "A year apart, and that is all you have to say?"

"No."

"What, then?"

"I mean *no*," she says again. "That is my answer, to your question. The only reason you're here. You've come to ask if I will yield, and the answer is no."

His smile ripples, shifts. Gone is the gentleman; again, the wolf.

"My Adeline, you've grown some teeth."

"I am not yours," she says.

A flash of warning white, and then the wolf retreats, pretends to be a man again as he steps into the light. And yet, the shadows cling to him, smudging edges into the dark. "I grant you immortality. And you spend your evenings eating bonbons in other people's beds. I imagined more for you than this."

"And yet, you condemned me to less. Come to gloat?"

He runs a hand along the wooden post, tracing the branches. "Such venom on our anniversary. And here I came only to offer you dinner."

"I see no food. And I do not want your company."

He moves like smoke, one moment across the room and the next beside her. "I would not be so quick to scorn," he says, one long finger grazing the pearl comb in her hair. "It is the only company you'll ever have."

Before she can pull away, the air is empty; he is across the room again, hand resting on the tassel beside the door.

"Stop," she says, lunging to her feet, but it's too late. He pulls, and a moment later the bell rings, splitting the silence of the house.

"Damn you," she hisses as footsteps sound on the stairs.

Addie is already turning to take up her dress, to snag what little she can before she flees—but the darkness catches her arm. He forces her to stay there at his side like some misbehaving child as a lady's maid opens the door.

She should startle at the sight of them, two strangers in her master's home, but there is no shock in the woman's face. No surprise, anger, or fear. There is nothing at all. Only a kind of vacancy, a calm unique to the dreaming and the dazed. The maid stands, head bowed and hands laced, waiting for instruction, and Addie realizes with dawning horror and relief that the woman is bewitched.

"We will dine in the salon tonight," says the darkness, as if the house were his. There is a new timbre to his voice, a film, like gossamer drawn over stone. It ripples in the air, wraps itself around the maid, and Addie can feel it sliding along her own skin, even as it fails to hold.

"Yes, sir," says the maid with a small bow.

She turns to lead them down the stairs, and the darkness looks to Addie and smiles.

"Come," he says, eyes gone emerald with arrogant glee. "I heard the marquis's chef is one of the best in Paris."

He offers her his arm, but she does not take it.

"You don't really expect me to dine with *you*."

He lifts his chin. "You would waste such a meal, simply because I'm at the table? I think your stomach is louder than your pride. But suit yourself, my dear. Stay here in your borrowed room, and glut yourself on stolen sweets. I'll eat without you."

With that, he strides away, and she is torn between the urge to slam the door behind him and the knowledge that her night is ruined, whether she eats with him or not, that even if she stays here in this room, her mind will follow him down the stairs to dinner.

And so she goes.

Seven years from now, Addie will see a puppet show being put on in a Paris square. A curtained cart, with a man behind, hands raised to hold aloft the little wooden figures, their limbs dancing up and down with twine.

And she will think of this night.

This dinner.

The servants of the house move around them as if on strings, smooth and silent, every gesture done with that same, sleepy ease. Chairs pulled back, linens smoothed, bottles of Champagne uncorked and poured into waiting crystal flutes.

But the food comes out too quickly, the first course arriving as the glasses are filled. Whatever hold the darkness has on the servants of this house, it began before his entrance in her stolen room. It began before he rang the bell, and called the maid, and summoned her to dinner.

He should seem so out of place in the filigreed room. He is, after all, a wild thing, a god of forest nights, a demon bounded by the dark, and yet he sits with the poise and grace of a nobleman enjoying his dinner.

Addie fingers the silver cutlery, the gilt trim of the plates.

"Am I supposed to be impressed?"

The darkness looks at her across the table. "Are you not?" he asks as the servants bow, and draw back against the walls.

The truth is, she is scared. Unsettled by the display. She knows his power—at least, she thought she did—but it's one thing to make a deal, and another to be the witness of such control. What could he make them do? How far could he make them go? Is it as easy for him as pulling strings?

The first course is placed before her, a cream soup the pale orange of dawn. It smells wonderful, and the Champagne sparkles in its glass, but she does not let herself reach for either.

The darkness reads the caution in her face.

"Come, Adeline," he says, "I am no fae thing, here to trap you with food and drink."

"And yet, everything seems to have a price."

He exhales, eyes flashing a paler shade of green.

"Suit yourself," he says, taking up his glass and drinking deeply.

After a long moment, Addie gives in, and lifts the crystal to her lips, taking her first sip of Champagne. It is unlike anything she's ever tasted; a thousand fragile bubbles race across her tongue, sweet and sharp, and she would melt with pleasure, if it were any other table, any other man, any other night.

Instead of savoring each sip, she immediately empties her glass, and by the time she sets it on the table, her head is fizzing slightly, and the servant is already at her elbow, pouring her a second drink.

The darkness sips his own, and watches, saying nothing as she eats. The silence in the room grows heavy, but she does not break it.

Instead she focuses first on the soup, and then on fish, and then on a round of pastry-crusted beef. It is more than she has eaten in months, in *years*, and she feels full in a way that goes beyond her stomach. And as she slows, she studies the man, who is not a man, across the table, the way the shadows bend in the room at his back.

This is the longest they have ever spent together.

Before, there were only those mere moments in the woods, the minutes in a shoddy room, half an hour along the Seine. But now, for the first time, he does not loom behind her like a shadow, does not linger like a phantom at the edges of her sight. Now, he sits across from her, on full display, and though she knows the static details of his face, having drawn them a hundred times, still she cannot help but study him in motion.

And he lets her.

There is no shyness in his manner.

He seems, if anything, to relish her attention.

As his knife slices across the plate, as he lifts a bite of meat to his lips, his black brows lift, his mouth tugs at the corner. Less a man than a collection of features, drawn by a careful hand.

In time, that will change. He will inflate, expand to fill the gaps between the lines of her drawing, wrest the image from her grip until she cannot fathom that it was ever hers.

But for now, the only aspect that is his—entirely his—are those eyes.

She imagined them a hundred times, and yes, they were always green, but in her dreams they were a single shade: the steady green of summer leaves. *His* are different.

Startling, inconstant, the slightest change in humor, in temper, reflected there, and only there.

It will take Addie years to learn the language of those eyes. To know that amusement renders them the shade of summer ivy, while annoyance lightens them to sour apple, and pleasure, pleasure darkens them to the almost-black of the woods at night, only the edges still discernible as green.

Tonight, they are the slippery color of weeds caught in the current of a stream.

By the end of dinner, they will be another shade entirely.

There is something languid in his posture. He sits there, one elbow on the tablecloth, his attention drifting, head tipped ever so slightly as if listening to a far-off sound, while his elegant fingers trace the line of his chin as if amused by his own form, and before she knows it, she has broken the silence again.

"What is your name?"

His eyes slide from a corner of the room back to her. "Why must I have one?"

"All things have names," she says. "Names have purpose. Names have power." She tips her glass his way. "You know that, or else you wouldn't have stolen mine."

A smile tugs at the corner of his mouth, wolfish, amused. "If it is true," he says, "that names have power, then why would I hand you mine?"

"Because I must call you something, to your face and in my head. And right now I have only curses."

The darkness does not seem to care. "Call me whatever you like, it makes no difference. What did you call the stranger in your journals? The man after whom you fashioned me?"

"You fashioned yourself to mock me, and I would rather you take *any* other form."

"You see violence in every gesture," he muses, running a thumb over his glass. "I fashioned myself to suit you. To put you at ease."

Anger rises in her chest. "You have ruined the one thing I still had."

"How sad, that you had only dreams."

She resists the urge to fling the crystal at him, knowing it will do no good. Instead, she looks to the servant by the wall, holds out the glass for him to fill it. But the servant doesn't move—none of them do. They are bound to his will, not hers. And so she rises, and takes the bottle up herself.

"What was his name, your stranger?"

She returns to her seat, refills her glass, focuses on the thousand shining bubbles that rise through the center. "He had no name," she says.

But it is a lie, of course, and the darkness looks at her as if he knows it.

The truth is, she'd tried on a dozen names over the years—Michel, and Jean, Nicolas, Henri, Vincent—and none of them had fit. And then, one night, there it was, tripping off her tongue, when she was curled in bed, wrapped in the image of him beside her, long fingers trailing through her hair. The name had passed her lips, simple as breath, natural as air.

Luc.

In her mind it stood for Lucien, but now, sitting across from this shadow, this *charade*, the irony is like a too-hot drink, an ember burning in her chest.

Luc.

As in Lucifer.

The words echo through her, carried like a breeze.

Am I the devil, or the darkness?

And she does not know, will never know, but the name is already ruined. Let him have it.

"Luc," she murmurs.

The shadow smiles, a dazzling, cruel imitation of joy, and lifts his drink as if to toast.

"Then Luc it is."

Addie drains her glass again, clinging to the lightheadedness it brings. The effects won't last, of course, she can feel her senses fighting back with every empty glass, but she presses on, determined to best them, at least for a while.

"I hate you," she says.

"Oh, Adeline," he says, setting down his glass. "Without me, where would you be?" As he speaks, he turns the crystal stem between his fingers, and in its faceted reflection, she sees another life—her own, and not her own—a version where Adeline didn't run to the woods as the sun went down and the wedding party gathered, didn't summon the darkness to set her free.

In the glass, she sees herself—her old self, the one she might have been, Roger's children at her side and a new baby on her hip and her familiar face gone sallow with fatigue. Addie sees herself beside him in the bed, the space cold between their bodies, sees herself bent over the hearth the way her mother always was, the same frown lines, too, fingers aching too much to stitch the tears in clothes, far too much to hold her old drawing pencils; sees herself wither on the vine of life, and walk the short steps so familiar to every person in Villon, the narrow road from cradle to grave—the little church waiting, still and gray as a tombstone.

Addie sees it, and she is grateful he doesn't ask if she would go back, trade this for that, because for all the grief and the madness, the loss, the hunger, and the pain, she still recoils from the image in the glass.

The meal is done, and the servants of the house stand in the shadows, waiting for their master's next instruction. And though their heads are bowed, and their faces are blank, she cannot help but think of them as hostages.

"I wish you would send them away."

"You are out of wishes," he says. But Addie meets his eyes, and holds them—it is easier, now that he has a name, to think of him as a man, and men can be challenged—and after a moment, the darkness sighs, and turns to the nearest servant, and tells them to open a bottle for themselves, and go.

And now they are alone, and the room seems smaller than it was before.

"There," says Luc.

"When the marquis and his wife come home and find their servants drunk, they will suffer for it."

"And who will be blamed, I wonder, for the missing chocolates in the lady's room? Or the blue silk robe? Do you think no one suffers when you steal?"

Addie bristles, heat rising to her cheeks.

"You gave me no *choice*."

"I gave you what you asked for, Adeline. Time, without constraint. Life without restriction."

"You cursed me to be forgotten."

"You asked for freedom. There is no greater freedom than that. You can move through the world unhindered. Untethered. Unbound."

"Stop pretending you did me a kindness instead of a cruelty."

"I did you a *deal*."

His hand comes down hard on the table as he says it, annoyance flashing yellow in his eyes, brief as lightning. "You came to me. You pleaded. You begged. You chose the words. I chose the terms. There is no going back. But if you have already tired of going forward, you need only say the words."

And there it is again, the hatred, so much easier to hold on to.

"It was a mistake to curse me." Her tongue is coming loose, and she doesn't know if it's the Champagne, or simply the duration of his presence, the acclimation that comes with time, like a body adjusting to a too-hot bath. "If you had only given me what I asked for, I would have burned out in time, would have had my fill of living, and we would, both of us, have won. But now, no matter how tired I am, I will *never* give you this soul."

He smiles. "You are a stubborn thing. But even rocks wear away to nothing."

Addie sits forward. "You think yourself a cat, playing with its catch. But I am *not* a mouse, and I will not be a meal."

"I do hope not." He spreads his hands. "It's been so long since I had a challenge."

A game. To him, *everything* is a game.

"You underestimate me."

"Do I?" One black brow lifts as he sips his drink. "I suppose we'll see."

"Yes," says Addie, taking up her own. "We will."

He has given her a gift tonight, though she doubts he knows it. Time has no face, no form, nothing to fight against. But in his mocking smile, his toying words, the darkness has given her the one thing she truly needs: an enemy.

It is here the battle lines are drawn.

The first shot may have been fired back in Villon, when he stole her life along with her soul, but this, this, is the beginning of the war.

She follows Henry to a bar that's too crowded, too loud.

All the bars in Brooklyn are like that, too little space for too many bodies, and the Merchant is apparently no exception, even on a Thursday. Addie and Henry are crammed into a narrow patio out back, bundled together under an awning, but she still has to lean in to hear his voice over the noise.

"Where are you from?" she starts.

"Upstate. Newburgh. You?"

"Villon-sur-Sarthe," she says. The words ache a little in her throat.

"France? You don't have an accent."

"I moved around."

They are sharing an order of fries and a pair of happy-hour beers because, he explains, a bookstore job doesn't pay that well. Addie wishes she could go back in and fetch them some proper drinks, but she's already told him the lie about the wallet, and she doesn't want to pull any more tricks, not after *The Odyssey*.

Plus, she's afraid.

Afraid to let him walk away.

Afraid to let him out of sight.

Whatever this is, a blip, a mistake, a beautiful dream, or a piece of impossible luck, she's afraid to let it go. Let him go.

One wrong step, and she'll wake up. One wrong step, and the thread will snap, the curse will shudder back into place, and it will be over, and Henry will be gone, and she will be alone again.

She forces herself back into the present. Enjoy it while it lasts. It cannot last. But right here, right now—

"Penny for your thoughts," he calls over the crowd.

She smiles. "I can't wait for summer." It's not a lie. It has been a long, damp spring, and she is tired of being cold. Summer means hot days, and nights where the light lingers. Summer means another year alive. Another year without—

"If you could have one thing," cuts in Henry, "what would it be?"

He studies her, squinting at her as if she's a book, not a person; something to be read. She stares back at him like he's a ghost. A miracle. An impossible thing.

This, she thinks, but she lifts her empty glass and says, "Another beer."

XII

Addie can account for every second of her life, but that night, with Henry, the moments seem to bleed together. Time slides by as they bounce from bar to bar, happy hour giving way to dinner and then to late-night drinks, and every time they hit the point where the evening splits, and one road leads their separate ways and the other carries on ahead, they choose the second road.

They stay together, each waiting for the other to say "It's getting late" or "I should be going," or "See you around." There is some unspoken pact, an unwillingness to sever whatever this is, and she knows why she's afraid to break the thread, but she wonders about Henry. Wonders at the loneliness she sees behind his eyes. Wonders at the way the waiters and the bartenders and the other patrons look at him, the warmth he doesn't seem to notice.

And then it is almost midnight, and they are eating cheap pizza, walking side by side through the first warm night of spring, as the clouds stretch overhead, low and lit by the moon.

She looks up, and so does Henry, and for a moment, only a moment, he looks overwhelmingly, unbearably sad.

"I miss the stars," he says.

"So do I," she says, and his gaze drops back to her, and he smiles.

"Who are you?"

His eyes have gone glassy, and the way he says *who* almost sounds like *how*, less a question of how she's doing and more a question of how she's here, and she wants to ask him the same thing, but she has a good reason, and he's just a little drunk.

And simply, perfectly, normal.

But he *can't* be normal.

Because normal people don't remember her.

They've reached the subway. Henry stops.

"This is me."

His hand slips free of hers, and there it is, that old familiar fear, of endings, of something giving way to nothing, of moments unwritten and memories erased. She doesn't want the night to end.

Doesn't want the spell to break. Doesn't—

"I want to see you again," says Henry.

The hope fills her chest until it hurts. She's heard those words a hundred times, but for the first time, they feel real. Possible. "I want you to see me again, too."

Henry smiles, the kind of smile that takes over an entire face.

He pulls out his cell, and Addie's heart sinks. She tells him that her phone is broken, when the truth is, she's never needed one before. Even if she had someone to call, she could not call them. Her fingers would slip uselessly over the screen. She has no e-mail, either, no way to send a message of any kind, thanks to the whole thou-shalt-not-write part of her curse.

"I didn't know you could exist these days without one."

"Old-fashioned," she says.

He offers to come by her place the next day. Where does she live? And it feels as if the universe is mocking her now.

"I'm staying at a friend's while they're out of town," she says. "Why don't I meet you at the store?"

Henry nods. "The store, then," he says, backing away.

"Saturday?"

"Saturday."

"Don't go disappearing."

Addie laughs, a small, brittle thing. And then he's walking away, he's got a foot down the first step, and the panic grips her.

"Wait," she says, calling him back. "I need to tell you something."

"Oh god," Henry groans. "You're with someone."

The ring burns in her pocket. "No."

"You're in the CIA and you leave for a top-secret mission tomorrow."

Addie laughs. "No."

"You're—"

"My real name isn't Eve."

He pulls back, confused. ". . . okay."

She doesn't know if she can say it, if the curse will let her, but she has to try. "I didn't tell you my real name because, well—it's complicated. But I like you, and I want you to know—to hear it from me."

Henry straightens, sobering. "Well then, what is it?"

"It's A—" The sound lodges, for just a second, the stiffness of a muscle long since fallen to disuse. A rusty cog. And then—it scrapes free.

"Addie." She swallows, hard. "My name's Addie."

It hangs in the air between them.

And then Henry smiles. "Well, okay," he says. "Goodnight, Addie."

As simple as that.

Two syllables falling from a tongue.

And it's the best sound she's ever heard. She wants to throw her arms around him, wants to hear it again, and again, the impossible word filling her like air, making her feel solid.

Real.

"Goodnight, Henry," Addie says, willing him to turn and go, because she doesn't think she can bring herself to turn away from him.

She stands there, rooted to the spot at the top of the subway steps until he's out of sight, holds her breath and waits to feel the thread snap, the world shudder back into shape, waits for the fear and the loss and the knowledge that it was just a fluke, a cosmic error, a mistake, that it is over now, that it will never happen again.

But she doesn't feel any of those things.

All she feels is joy, and hope.

Her boot heels tap out a rhythm on the street, and even after all these years, she half expects a second pair of shoes to fall in step beside her own. To hear the rolling fog of his voice, soft, and sweet, and mocking. But there is no shadow at her side, not tonight.

The evening is quiet, and she is alone, but for once it is not the same as being lonely.

Goodnight, Addie, Henry said, and Addie cannot help but wonder if he has somehow broken the spell.

She smiles, and whispers to herself. "Goodnight, Ad—"

But the curse closes around her throat, the name lodging there, as it always has.

And yet.

And yet.

Goodnight, Addie.

Three hundred years she's tested the confines of her deal, found the places where it gives, the subtle bend and flex around the bars, but never a way out.

And yet.

Somehow, impossibly, Henry has found a way *in.*

Somehow, he remembers her.

How? How? The question thuds with the drum of her heart, but in this moment, Addie does not care.

In this moment, she is holding to the sound of her name, her real name, on someone else's tongue, and it is enough, it is enough, it is enough.

The stage is set, the places ready.

Addie smooths the linen on the table, arranges the porcelain plates, the cups—not crystal, but still glass—and draws the dinner from its hamper. It is no five-course meal, served by glamoured hands, but it is fresh and hearty fare. A loaf of bread, still warm. A wedge of cheese. A pork terrine. A bottle of red wine. She is proud of her collection, prouder still of the fact *she* had no magic, save the curse, by which to gather it, could not simply cut her gaze, say a word, and will it so.

It is not only the table.

It is the room. No stolen chamber. No beggar's hovel. A place, for now at least, to call her own. It took two months to find, a fortnight to fix up, but it was worth it. From the outside it is nothing: cracked glass and warping wood. And it's true, the lower floors have fallen into disrepair, home now only to rodents and the occasional stray cats—and, in winter, crowded with bodies seeking any form of shelter—but it is the height of summer now, and the city's poor have taken to the streets, and Addie has claimed the top floor for herself. Boarded up the stairs and carved a way in and out through an upper window, like a child in a wooden fort. It is an unconventional entrance, but it is worth it for the room beyond, where she has made herself a home.

A bed, piled high with blankets. A chest, filled with stolen clothes. The windowsill brims with trinkets, glass and porcelain and bone, gathered and assembled like a line of makeshift birds.

In the middle of the narrow room, a pair of chairs set before a table covered in pale linen. And in its center, a bundle of flowers, picked in the night from a royal garden and smuggled out in the folds of her skirt. And Addie knows none of it will last, it never does—a breeze will somehow steal away the totems on her mantel; there will be a fire, or a flood; the floor will give way or the secret home will be found and claimed by someone else.

But she has guarded the pieces this past month, gathered and arranged them one by one to make a semblance of a life, and if she's being honest, it is not only for herself.

It is for the darkness.

It is for *Luc*.

Or rather, it is to spite him, to prove that she is living, she is free. That Addie will give him no hold, no way to mock her with his charity.

The first round was his, but the second will be hers.

And so she has made her home, and readied it for company, fastened up her hair and dressed herself in russet silk, the color of fall leaves, even cinched herself into a corset despite her loathing of bone stays.

She has had a year to plan, to design the posture she will strike, and as she straightens up the room she turns barbs over in her mind, sharpening the weapons of their discourse. She imagines his thrusts, and her parries, the way his eyes will lighten or darken as the conversation turns.

You have grown teeth, he said, and Addie will show him how sharp they have become.

The sun has gone down now, and all that's left to do is wait. An hour passes, and her stomach growls with want as the bread goes cold in its cloth, but she doesn't allow herself to eat. Instead, she leans out the window and watches the city, the shifting lights of lanterns being lit.

And he doesn't come.

She pours herself a glass of wine, and paces, as the stolen candles drip, and wax pools on the table linen, and the night grows heavy, the hours first late, and then early.

And still he doesn't come.

The candles gutter and snuff themselves out, and Addie sits in the dark as the knowledge settles over her.

The night has passed, the first threads of daylight creeping into the sky, and it is tomorrow now, and their anniversary is over, and five years have become six without his presence, without his face, without his asking if she's had enough, and the world slips, because it is unfair, it is cheating, it is wrong.

He was supposed to come, that was the nature of their dance. She did not *want* him there, has never wanted it, but she *expected* it, he has *made* her expect it. Has given her a single threshold on which to balance, a narrow precipice of hope, because he is a hated thing, but a hated thing is still *something*. The only thing she has.

And that is the point, of course.

That is the reason for the empty glass, the barren plate, the unused chair.

She gazes out the window, and remembers the look in his eyes when they toasted, the curve of his lips when they declared war, and realizes what a fool she is, how easily baited.

And suddenly, the whole tableau seems gruesome and pathetic, and Addie can't bear to look at it, can't breathe in her red silk. She tears at the laces of the corset, pulls the pins from her hair, frees herself from the confines of the dress, sweeps the settings from the table, and dashes the now empty bottle against the wall.

Glass bites into her hand, and the pain is sharp, and real, the sudden scald of a burn without the lasting scar, and she does not care. In moments, her cuts have already closed. The glasses and bottle lie whole. Once she thought it was a blessing, this inability to break, but now, the impotence is maddening.

She ruins everything, only to watch it shudder, mocking, back together, return like a set to the beginning of the show.

And Addie screams.

Anger flares inside her, hot and bright, anger at Luc, and at herself, but it is giving way to fear, and grief, and terror, because she must face another year alone, a year without hearing her name, without seeing herself reflected in anyone's eyes, without a night's respite from this curse, a year, or five, or ten, and she realizes then how much she's leaned on it, the promise of his presence, because without it, she is falling.

She sinks to the floor among the ruins of her night.

It will be years before she sees the sea, the waves crashing against the jagged white cliffs, and then she will remember Luc's goading words.

Even rocks wear away to nothing.

Addie falls asleep just after dawn, but it is fitful, and brief, and full of nightmares, and when she wakes to see the sun high over Paris, she cannot bring herself to rise. She sleeps all the day and half the night, and when she wakes the shattered thing in her has set again, like a badly broken bone, some softness hardened.

"Enough," she tells herself, rising to her feet.

"Enough," she repeats, feasting on the bread, now stale, the cheese, wilted from the heat.

Enough.

There will be other dark nights, of course, other wretched dawns, and her resolve will always weaken a little as the days grow long, and the anniversary draws near, and treacherous hope slips in like a draft. But the sorrow has faded, replaced by stubborn rage, and she resolves to kindle it, to shield and nurture the flame until it takes far more than a single breath to blow it out.

XIV

Henry Strauss walks home alone through the dark.

Addie, he thinks, turning the name over in his mouth.

Addie, who looked at him and saw a boy with dark hair, kind eyes, an open face.

Nothing more. And nothing else.

A cold gust blows, and he pulls his coat close, and looks up at the starless sky.

And smiles.

PART THREE

THREE HUNDRED YEARS—
AND THREE WORDS

Title: *Untitled Salon Sketch*
Artist: Bernard Rodel
Date: c. 1751–3
Medium: Ink pen on parchment
Location: On loan from *The Paris Salon* exhibition at The British Library
Description: A rendering of Madame Geoffrin's famous salon, brimming with figures in various stages of conversation and repose. Several recognizable personages—Rousseau, Voltaire, Diderot—can be discerned among the group, but the most interesting inclusion is the three women circling the room. One is clearly Madame Geoffrin. Another is believed to be Suzanne Necker. But the third, an elegant woman with a freckled face, remains a mystery.
Background: In addition to his contributions to Diderot's *Encyclopedia,* Rodel was an avid draftsman, and appears to have made use of his rendering skill during many of his installments in Madame Geoffrin's salon. The freckled woman appears in several of his sketches, but is never named.
Estimated Value: Unknown

I

✦ ✦ ✦ ✦ ✦
✦ ✦ ✦

Freedom is a pair of trousers and a buttoned coat.

A man's tunic and a tricorne hat.

If only she had known.

The darkness *claimed* he'd given her freedom, but really, there is no such thing for a woman, not in a world where they are bound up inside their clothes, and sealed inside their homes, a world where only *men* are given leave to roam.

Addie saunters up the street, a stolen basket hooked over the elbow of her coat. Nearby, an old woman stands in a doorway, beating out a rug, and laborers lounge on café steps, and none of them so much as blink, because they do not see a woman, walking alone. They see a young man, barely more than a youth, dawdling in the dying light; they do not think how strange, how scandalous it is to see her strolling. They do not think anything at all.

To think, Addie might have saved her soul, and simply asked for these clothes.

It has been four years now without a visit from the dark.

Four years, and at the dawn of every one, she swears she will not waste the time she has in waiting. But it is a promise she cannot fully keep. For all her effort, Addie is like a clock wound tighter as the day draws near, a coiled spring that cannot loosen until dawn. And even then, it is a grim unwinding, less relief than resignation, the knowledge that it will start again.

Four years.

Four winters, four summers, four visitless nights.

The other ones, at least, are hers, to spend as she likes, but no matter how she tries to pass the time, this one belongs to Luc, even when he is not here.

And yet, she will not declare it forfeit, will not sacrifice the hours as if they are already lost, already his.

Addie passes a group of men and tips her hat in greeting, uses the gesture to pull the tricorne lower on her own brow. Day has not quite given way to night, and in the long summer light she is careful to keep her distance, knowing the illusion will falter under scrutiny. She could have waited an hour longer and been safe within the veil of night, but the truth is, she could not bear the stillness, the creeping seconds of the clock.

Not tonight.

Tonight, she has decided to celebrate her freedom.

To climb the steps of Sacré Coeur, sit at the top of the pale stone stairs, the city at her feet, and have a picnic.

The basket swings from her elbow, brimming with food. Her fingers have gotten light and quick with practice, and she has spent the last several days assembling her feast—a loaf of bread, a side of cured meat, a wedge of cheese, and even a palm-sized jar of honey.

Honey—an indulgence Addie hasn't had since Villon, where Isabelle's father kept a row of hives and skimmed the amber syrup out for markets, leaving them to suck on rinds of honeycomb until their fingers were stained with sweetness. Now she holds her bounty to the waning light, lets the setting sun turn the contents gold.

The man comes out of nowhere.

A shoulder knocks into her arm, and the precious jar slips from her hand and shatters on the cobbled street, and for an instant Addie thinks she is being attacked, or robbed, but the stranger is already stammering out his apologies.

"You fool," she hisses, attention flicking from the golden syrup, now glittering with glass, to the man who caused her loss. He is young, and fair, and lovely, with high cheeks and hair the color of her ruined honey.

And he is not alone.

His companions hang back, whooping and cheering at his mistake—they have the happy air of those who began their evening revels back at midday—but the errant youth blushes fiercely, clearly embarrassed.

"My apologies, truly," he begins, but then a transformation sweeps across his face. First surprise, and then amusement, and she realizes, too late, how close they are, how clearly the light has fallen on her face. Realizes, too late, that he has seen through her illusion, that his hand is still there, on her sleeve, and for a moment she is afraid he will expose her.

But when his companions call for him to hurry on, he tells them to go ahead, and now they are alone on the cobbled street, and Addie is ready to pull free, to run, but there is no shadow in the young man's face, no menace, only a strange delight.

"Let go," she says, lowering her voice a measure when she speaks, which only seems to please him more, even as he frees her arm with all the speed of someone grazing fire.

"Sorry," he says again, "I forgot myself." And then, a mischievous grin. "It seems you have, too."

"Not at all," she says, fingers drifting toward the short blade she's kept inside her basket. "I have misplaced myself on purpose."

The smile widens then, and he drops his gaze, and sees the ruined honey on the ground, and shakes his head.

"I must make that up to you," he says. And she is about to tell him not to bother, about to say that it is fine, when he cranes his head down the road, and says, "Aha," and loops his arm through hers, as if they are already friends.

"Come," he says, leading her toward the café on the corner. She has never been inside one, never been brave enough to chance it, not alone, not with such a tenuous hold on her disguise. But he draws her on as if it's nothing, and at the last moment he swings an arm around her shoulders, the weight so sudden and so intimate she is about to pull away before she catches the edge of a smile, and realizes that he has made a game of it, conscripted himself into the service of her secret.

Inside, the café is a place of energy and life, overlapping voices and the scent of something rich and smoky.

"Careful now," he says, eyes dancing with mischief. "Stay close, and keep your head down, or we will be found out."

She follows him to the counter, where he orders two shallow cups, the contents thin and black as ink. "Sit over there," he says, "against the wall, where the light is not too strong."

They fold themselves into a corner seat, and he sets the cups between them with a flourish, turning the handles just so, as he tells her it is coffee. She has heard of the stuff, of course, the current toast of Paris, but when she lifts the china to her lips and takes a sip, she is rather disappointed.

It is dark, and strong, and bitter, like the chocolate flakes she first tasted years ago, only without the edge of sweetness. But the boy stares at her, as eager as a pup, and so she swallows, and smiles, cradles the cup, and looks out from beneath the brim of her hat, studying the tables of men, some with their heads bowed close, while others laugh, and play at cards, or pass sheaves of paper back and forth. She watches these men and wonders anew at how open the world is to them, how easy the thresholds.

Her attention flicks back to her companion, who's watching her with the same unbridled fascination.

"What were you thinking?" he asks. "Just now?"

There is no introduction, no formal exchange. He simply dives into the conversation, as if they have known each other for years instead of minutes.

"I was thinking," she says, "that it must be so easy to be a man."

"Is that why you put on this disguise?"

"That," she says, "and a hatred of corsets."

He laughs, the sound so open and easy Addie finds a smile rising to her lips.

"Do you have a name?" he asks, and she doesn't know if he's asking for her own, or that of her disguise, but she decides on "Thomas," watches him turn the word over like a bite of fruit.

"Thomas," he muses. "A pleasure to meet you. My name is Remy Laurent."

"Remy," she echoes, tasting the softness, the upturned vowel. It suits him, more than *Adeline* ever suited her. It is young and sweet, and it will haunt her, as all names do, bobbing like apples in the stream. No matter how many men she meets, *Remy* will always conjure *him*, this bright and cheerful boy—the kind she could have loved, perhaps, if given the chance.

She takes another sip, careful not to hold the cup too gingerly, to lean the weight on her elbow, and sit in the unselfconscious way men have when they do not expect anyone to study them.

"Amazing," he marvels. "You have studied my sex well."

"Have I?"

"You are a splendid mimic."

Addie could tell him that she's had the time to practice, that it has become a kind of game over the years, a way to amuse herself. That she has added a dozen different characters by now, knows the exact differences between a duchess and a marchioness, a docksman and a merchant.

But instead, she only says, "We all need ways to pass the time."

He laughs again at that, lifts his cup, but then, between one sip and the next, Remy's attention wanders across the room, and he lands on something that startles him. He chokes on his coffee, color rushing into his cheeks.

"What is it?" she asks. "Are you well?"

Remy coughs, nearly dropping the cup as he gestures to the doorway, where a man has just walked in.

"Do you know him?" she asks, and Remy sputters, "Don't *you*? That man there is Monsieur Voltaire."

She shakes her head a little. The name means nothing.

Remy draws a parcel from his coat. A booklet, thin, with something printed on the cover. She frowns at the cursive title, has only managed half the letters when Remy flips the booklet open to show a wall of words, printed in elegant black ink. It has been too long since her father tried to teach her, and those were simple letters; loose, handwritten script.

Remy sees her studying the page. "Can you read it?"

"I know the letters," she admits, "but I haven't the learning to make much sense of them. And by the time I manage a line, I fear I've lost its meaning."

Remy shakes his head. "It is a crime," he says, "that women are not taught the same as men. Why, a world without reading, I cannot fathom it. A whole long life without poems, or plays, or philosophers. Shakespeare, Socrates, to say nothing of Descartes!"

"Is that all?" she teases.

"And Voltaire," he goes on. "Of course, Voltaire. And essays, and *novels*."

She does not know the word.

"A single long story," he explains, "something of pure invention. Filled with romance, or comedy, or adventure."

She thinks of the fairy tales her father told her, growing up, the stories Estele spun of old gods. But this *novel* that Remy speaks of sounds like it encompasses so much more. She runs her fingers over the page of the proffered booklet, but her attention is on Remy, and his, for the moment, is on Voltaire. "Are you going to introduce yourself?"

Remy's gaze snaps back, horrified. "No, no, not tonight. It is better this way; think of the story." He sits back in his seat, glowing with joy. "See? This is what I love about Paris."

"You are not from here, then."

"Is anyone?" He has come back to her now. "No, I'm from Rennes. A printer's family. But I am the youngest son, and my father made the grave mistake of sending me away to school, and the more I read, the more I thought, and the more I thought, the more I knew I had to be in Paris."

"Your family didn't mind?"

"Of course they did. But I had to come. This is where the thinkers are. This is where the dreamers live. This is the heart of the world, and the head, and it is changing." His eyes dance with light. "Life is so brief, and every night in Rennes I'd go to bed, and lie awake, and think, there is another day behind me, and who knows how few ahead."

It is the same fear that forced her into the woods that night, the same need that drove her to her fate.

"So here I am," he says brightly. "I would not be anywhere else. Isn't it marvelous?"

Addie thinks of the stained glass and the locked doors, the gardens, and the gates around them.

"It can be," she says.

"Ah, you think me an idealist."

Addie lifts the coffee to her lips. "I think it comes more easily to men."

"It does," he admits, before nodding at her attire. "And yet," he says with an impish grin, "you strike me as someone not easily restrained. *Aut viam invenium aut faciam,* and so on."

She does not know Latin yet, and he does not offer a translation, but a decade from now, she will look up the words, and learn their meaning.

To find a way, or make your own.

And she will smile, then, a ghost of the smile he has managed to win from her tonight.

He blushes. "I must be boring you."

"Not at all," she says. "Tell me, does it pay, to be a thinker?"

Laughter bubbles out of him. "No, not very well. But I am still my father's son." He holds out his hands, palms up, and she notices the echo of ink along the lines of his palms, staining the whorls of his fingers, the way charcoal used to stain her own. "It is good work," he says.

But under his words, a softer sound, the rumble of his stomach.

Addie had almost forgotten the shattered jar, the ruined honey. But the rest of the feast sits waiting at her feet.

"Have you ever climbed the steps of Sacré Coeur?"

After so many years, Addie thought she'd come to terms with time.

She thought she'd made her peace with it—or that they'd found a way to coexist—not friends by any means, but at least no longer enemies.

And yet, the time between Thursday night and Saturday afternoon is merciless, every second doled out with the care of an old woman counting pennies to pay for bread. Not once does it seem to quicken, not once does she lose track of it. She can't seem to spend it, or waste it, or even misplace it. The minutes inflate around her, an ocean of undrinkable time between now and then, between here and the store, between her and Henry.

She's spent the last two nights at a place in Prospect Park, a cozy two-bedroom with a bay window belonging to Gerard, a children's book writer she met one winter. A king-size bed, a pile of blankets, the soft hypnotic tick of the radiator, and still she could not sleep. Could not do anything but count and wait, and wish that she had said *tomorrow*, had only to bear one day instead of two.

Three hundred years she's managed to suffer time, but now, now there is a present and a future, now there is something waiting ahead, now she cannot wait to see the look on Henry's face, to hear her name on his lips.

Addie showers until the water goes cold, dries and styles her hair three different ways, sits on the kitchen island tossing kernels of cereal up into the air, trying to catch them on her tongue, as the clock on the wall inches forward from 10:13 a.m. to 10:14 a.m. Addie groans. She isn't supposed to meet Henry until 5:00 p.m. and time is slowing a little more with every minute, and she thinks she might lose her mind.

It has been so long since she felt this kind of boredom, the stir-crazy inability to focus, and it takes her all morning to realize she isn't bored at all.

She's *nervous*.

Nervous, like *tomorrow*, a word for things that have not happened yet. A word for futures, when for so long all she's had are presents.

Addie isn't used to being nervous.

There's no reason to be when you are always alone, when any awkward moment can be erased by a closed door, an instant apart, and every meeting is a fresh start. A clean slate.

The clock reaches 11:00 A.M., and she decides she cannot stay inside.

She sweeps up the few fallen pieces of leftover cereal, sets the apartment back the way she found it, and heads out into the late Brooklyn morning. Flits between boutiques, desperate for distraction, assembling a new outfit because for once the one she has won't do. It is, after all, the same one she wore before.

Before—another word that's lost its shape.

Addie picks out pale jeans and a pair of black silk flats, a top with a plunging neckline, shrugs the leather jacket over the top, even though it doesn't match. It's still the one piece she cannot bear to leave.

Unlike the ring, it won't come back.

Addie lets an enthusiastic girl in a makeup store sit her down on a stool and spend an hour applying various highlighters, liners, shades. When it's over, the face in the mirror is pretty, but wrong, the warm brown of her eyes cooled by the smoky shadow around them, her skin too smooth, the seven freckles hidden by a matte foundation.

Luc's voice rises up like fog against the reflection.

I would rather see clouds blot out the stars.

Addie sends the girl off in search of coral lipstick, and the moment she's alone, Addie wipes the clouds away.

Somehow, she manages to shave off hours until it is 4:00 P.M., but she is outside the bookstore now, buzzing with hope and fear. So she forces herself to circle the block, to count the paving stones, to memorize each and every shop front until it's 4:45 P.M. and she cannot bear it anymore.

Four short steps. One open door.

And a single, leaden fear.

What if?

What if they spent too long apart?

What if the cracks have filled back in, the curse sealed around her once again?

What if it was just a fluke? A cruel joke?

What if what if what if—

Addie holds her breath, opens the door, and steps in.

But Henry isn't there—instead there is someone else behind the counter.

It is the girl. The one from the other day, who sat folded in the leather chair, the one who called his name when Henry ran out to catch Addie on the curb. Now she leans against the till, paging through a large book full of glossy photos.

The girl is a work of art, strikingly pretty, dark skin draped in silver threads, a sweater slouching off one shoulder. She looks up at the sound of the bell.

"Can I help you?"

Addie falters, knocked off-balance by a vertigo of want and fear. "I hope so," she says. "I'm looking for Henry."

The girl stares at her, studying her—

Then a familiar voice comes from the back.

"Bea, do you think this looks . . ." Henry rounds the corner, smoothing his shirt, and trails off when he sees Addie. For an instant, a fraction of a fraction of a moment, she thinks it is over. That he has forgotten, and she is alone again, the thin spell made days before snipped like a stray thread.

But then Henry smiles, and says, "You're early."

And Addie is dizzy with air, with hope, with light.

"Sorry," she says, a little breathless.

"Don't be. I see you've met Beatrice. Bea, this is Addie."

She loves the way Henry says her name.

Luc used to wield it like a weapon, a knife grazing her skin, but on Henry's tongue, it's a bell, something light, and bright, and lovely. It rings out between them.

Addie. Addie. *Addie.*

"*Déjà vu,*" says Bea, shaking her head. "You ever meet someone for the first time, but you're *sure* you've seen them before?"

Addie almost laughs. "Yes."

"I've already fed Book," says Henry, talking to Bea as he shrugs on his coat. "Do *not* sprinkle any more catnip in the horror section." She holds up her hands, bracelets jingling. Henry turns to Addie with a sheepish grin. "You ready to go?"

They're halfway to the door when Bea snaps her fingers. "Baroque," she says. "Or maybe Neoclassical."

Addie stares back, confused. "The art periods?"

The other girl nods. "I have this theory that every face belongs to one. A time. A school."

"Bea is a post-grad," interjects Henry. "Art history, in case you couldn't tell."

"Henry here is obviously pure Romanticism. Our friend Robbie is Postmodern—the avant-garde, of course, not the minimalism. But you . . ." She taps a finger to her lips. "There's something timeless about you."

"Stop flirting with my date," says Henry.

Date. The word thrills through her. A date is something made, something planned; not a chance of opportunity, but time set aside at one point for another, a moment in the future.

"Have fun!" calls Bea cheerfully. "Don't stay out too late."

Henry rolls his eyes. "Bye, Bea," he says, holding the door.

"You owe me," she adds.

"I'm granting you free access to the books."

"Almost like a library!"

"Not a library!" he shouts back, and Addie smiles as she follows him up onto the street. It is obviously an inside joke, some shared, familiar thing, and she aches with longing, wonders what it would feel like to know someone that well, for the knowing to go both ways. Wonders if they could have a joke like that, she and Henry. If they can know each other long enough.

It is a cold evening, and they walk side by side, not intertwined but elbows brushing, each leaning a little into the other's warmth. Addie marvels at it, this boy beside her, his nose burrowed down into the scarf around his throat. Marvels at the slight difference in his manner, the smallest shift in ease. Days ago, she was a stranger to him, and now, she is not, and he is learning her at the same rate she is learning him, and it is still the beginning, it is still so new, but they have moved one step along the road between unknown and familiar. A step she has never been allowed to take with anyone but Luc.

And yet.

Here she is, with this boy.

Who are you? she thinks as Henry's glasses fog with steam. He catches her looking, and winks.

"Where are we going?" she asks when they reach the subway, and Henry looks at her and smiles, a shy, lopsided grin.

"It's a surprise," he answers as they descend the steps.

They take the G train to Greenpoint, backtrack half a block to a nondescript storefront, a WASH AND FOLD sign in the window. Henry holds the door, and Addie steps through. She looks around at the washing machines, the white-noise hum of the rinse cycle, the shudder of the spin.

"It's a laundromat," she says.

But Henry's eyes go bright with mischief. "It's a speakeasy."

A memory lurches through her at the word, and she is in Chicago, nearly a century ago, jazz circling like smoke in the underground bar, the air heavy with the scent of gin and cigars, the rattle of glasses, the open secret of it all. They sit beneath a stained-glass window of an angel lifting his cup, and Champagne breaks across her tongue, and the darkness smiles against her skin, and draws her onto a floor to dance, and it is the beginning and the end of everything.

Addie shudders, drawing herself back. Henry is holding open the door at the back of the laundromat, and she braces herself for a darkened room, a forced retreat into the past, but she's met instead by the neon lights and electronic chime of an arcade game. Pinball, to be precise. The machines line the walls, crammed side by side to make room for the tables and stools, the wooden bar.

Addie stares around, bemused. It is not a speakeasy at all, not in the strictest sense. It is simply one thing hidden behind another. A palimpsest in reverse.

"Well?" he asks with a sheepish grin. "What do you think?"

Addie feels herself smiling back, dizzy with relief. "I love it."

"All right," he says, producing a bag of quarters from one pocket. "Ready to lose?"

It's early, but the place is far from empty.

Henry leads her to the corner, where he claims a pair of vintage machines, and balances a tower of quarters on each. She holds her breath as she inserts the first coin, braces for the inevitable clink of it rolling back into the dish at the bottom. But it goes in, and the game springs to life, emitting a cheerful cacophony of color and sound.

Addie exhales, a mixture of delight and relief.

Perhaps she is anonymous, the act as faceless as a theft. Perhaps, but in the moment, she doesn't care.

She pulls back the lever, and plays.

III

"How are you so good at pinball?" Henry demands as she racks up points.

Addie isn't sure. The truth is, she's never played before, and it's taken her a few times to get the hang of the game, but now she's found her stride.

"I'm a fast learner," she says, just before the ball slips between her paddles.

"HIGH SCORE!" announces the game in a mechanical drone.

"Well done," calls Henry over the noise. "Better own your victory."

The screen flashes, waiting for her to enter her name. Addie hesitates.

"Like this," he says, showing her how to toggle the red box between the letters. He steps aside, but when she tries, the cursor doesn't move. The light just flashes over the letter *A*, mocking.

"It doesn't matter," she says, backing away, but Henry steps in.

"New machines, vintage problems." He bumps it with his hip, and the square goes solid around the *A*. "There we go."

He's about to step aside, but Addie catches his arm. "Enter my name while I grab the next round."

It's easier now that the place is full. She swipes a couple of beers from the edge of the counter, weaves back through the crowd before the bartender even turns around. And when she returns, drinks in hand, the first things she sees are the letters, flashing in bright red on the screen.

ADI.

"I didn't know how to spell your name," he says.

And it's wrong, but it doesn't even matter; nothing matters but those three letters, glowing back at her, almost like a stamp, a signature.

"Swap," says Henry, hands resting on her hips as he guides her over to his machine. "Let's see if I can beat that score."

She holds her breath and hopes that no one ever will.

They play until they run out of quarters and beer, until the place is too crowded for comfort, until they truly can't hear each other over the ring and clash of the games and the shouts of the other people, and then they spill out of the dark arcade. They go back through the too-bright laundromat, and then out onto the street, still bubbling with energy.

It's dark out now, the sky overhead a low canopy of dense gray clouds, promising rain, and Henry shoves his hands in his pockets, looks up and down the street. "What now?"

"You want me to choose?"

"This is an equal opportunity date," he says, rocking from heel to toe. "I provided the first chapter. It's your turn."

Addie hums to herself, looking around, summoning a mental picture of the neighborhood.

"Good thing I found my wallet," she says, patting her pocket. She didn't, of course, but she did liberate a few twenties from the illustrator's kitchen drawer before she left that morning. Judging by the recent profile of him in *The Times*, and the reported size of his latest book deal, Gerald won't miss it.

"This way." Addie takes off down the sidewalk.

"How far are we going?" he asks fifteen minutes later, when they're still walking.

"I thought you were a New Yorker," she teases.

But his strides are long enough to match her speed, and five minutes later they round the corner, and there it is. The Nitehawk lights up the darkening street, white bulbs tracing patterns on the brick façade, the word CINEMA picked out in red neon light across its front.

Addie has been to every movie theater in Brooklyn, the massive multiplexes with their stadium seats and the indie gems with worn-out sofas, has witnessed every mixture of new releases and nostalgia.

And the Nitehawk is one of her favorites.

She scans the board, buys two tickets to a showing of *North by Northwest*, since Henry says he's never seen it, then takes his hand and leads them down the hall into the dark.

There are little tables between each seat with plastic menus and slips of paper to write your order on. She's never been able to order anything, of course—the pencil marks dissolve, the waiter forgets about her as soon as he is out of sight—so she leans in to watch Henry fill out their card, thrilled by the simple potential of the act.

The previews ramble on as the seats fill up around them, and Henry takes her hand, their fingers lacing together like links in a chain. She glances over at him, painted in the low theater light. Black curls. High cheekbones. The cupid's bow of his mouth. The flicker of resemblance.

It is hardly the first time she's seen Luc echoed in a human face.

"You're staring," whispers Henry under the sound of the previews.

Addie blinks. "Sorry." She shakes her head. "You look like someone I used to know."

"Someone you liked, I hope."

"Not really." He shoots her a look of mock affront, and Addie almost laughs. "It was more complicated than that."

"Love, then?"

She shakes her head. "No . . ." But her delivery is slower, less emphatic. "But he was very nice to look at."

Henry laughs as the lights dim, and the movie starts.

A different waiter appears, crouching low as he delivers their food, and she plucks fries from the plate one by one, sinking into the comfort of the film. She glances over to see if Henry's enjoying himself, but he's not even looking at the screen. His face, all energy and light an hour before, is a rictus of tension. One knee bounces restlessly.

She leans in, whispers. "You don't like it?"

Henry flashes a hollow smile. "It's fine," he says, shifting in his seat. "Just a little slow."

It's Hitchcock, she wants to say, but instead she whispers, "It's worth it, I promise."

Henry twists toward her, brow folding. "You've already seen it?"

Of course Addie has seen it.

First, in 1959, at a theater in Los Angeles, and then in the '70s, a double feature with his last film, *Family Plot,* and then again, a few years back, right in Greenwich Village, during a retrospective. Hitchcock has a way of being resurrected, fed back into the cinema system at regular intervals.

"Yeah," she whispers back. "But I don't mind."

Henry says nothing, but he clearly does mind. His knee goes back to bouncing, and a few minutes later he's up and out of the seat, walking out into the lobby.

"Henry," she calls, confused. "What is it? What's wrong?"

She catches up with him as he throws open the theater door and steps out onto the curb. "Sorry," he mumbles. "Needed some air."

But that's obviously not it. He's pacing.

"Talk to me."

His steps slow. "I just wish you'd told me."

"Told you what?"

"That you'd already seen it."

"But *you* hadn't," she says. "And I didn't mind seeing it again. I like seeing things again."

"I don't," he snaps, and then deflates. "I'm sorry." He shakes his head. "I'm sorry. This isn't your problem." He runs his hands through his hair. "I just—" He shakes his head, and turns to look at her, green eyes glassy in the dark. "Do you ever feel like you're running out of time?"

Addie blinks and it is three hundred years ago and she is back on her knees on the forest floor, hands driving down into the mossy earth as the church bells ring behind her.

"I don't mean in that normal, *time flies* way," Henry's saying. "I mean feeling like its surging by so fast, and you try to reach out and grab it, you try to hold on, but it just keeps rushing away. And every second, there's a little less time, and a little less air, and sometimes when I'm sitting still, I start to think about it, and when I think about it, I can't breathe. I have to get up. I have to move."

He has his arms wrapped around himself, fingers digging into his ribs.

It's been a long time since Addie felt that kind of urgency, but she remembers it well, remembers the fear, so heavy she thought it might crush her.

Blink and half your life is gone.

I do not want to die as I've lived.

Born and buried in the same ten-meter plot.

Addie reaches out and grabs his arm. "Come on," she says, pulling him down the street. "Let's go."

"Where?" he asks, and her hand drops to his, and holds on tight.

"To find you something new."

Remy Laurent is laughter bottled into skin. It spills out of him at every turn.

As they walk together through Montmartre, he tips the brow of Addie's hat, plucks at her collar, slings his arm around her shoulders, and inclines his head, as if to whisper some salacious secret. Remy delights in being part of her charade, and she delights in having someone to share it with.

"Thomas, you fool," he jeers loudly when they pass a huddle of men.

"Thomas, you scoundrel," he calls out as they pass a pair of women—girls really, though wrapped in rouge and tattered lace—at the mouth of an alley. They, too, take up the call.

"Thomas," they echo, teasing and sweet, "come be our scoundrel, Thomas. Thomas, come have some fun."

They climb the vaulting steps of the Sacré Coeur, are nearly to the top when Remy stops and spreads his coat on the steps, gesturing for her to sit.

They divide the food between them, and as they eat, she studies her strange companion.

Remy is Luc's opposite, in every way. His hair is a crown of burnished gold, his eyes a summer blue, but more than that, it's in his manner: his easy smile, his open laugh, the vibrant energy of youth. If one is the thrilling darkness, the other is midday radiance, and if the boy is not quite as handsome, well, that is only because he is human.

He is *real*.

Remy sees her staring, and laughs. "Are you making a study of me, for your art? I must say, you have mastered the posture and the manners of a Paris youth."

She looks down, realizes she is sitting with one knee drawn up, her arm hooked lazily around her leg.

"But," adds Remy, "I fear you are far too pretty, even in the dark."

He has moved closer, his hand finding hers.

"What is your real name?" he asks, and how she wishes she could tell him. She tries, she tries—thinking maybe just this once, the sounds will make it over her tongue. But her voice catches after the *A,* so instead she changes course, and says, "Anna."

"Anna," Remy echoes, tucking a stray lock behind her ear. "It suits you."

She will use a hundred names over the years, and countless times, she will hear those words, until she begins to wonder at the importance of a name at all. The very idea will begin to lose its meaning, the way a word does when said too many times, breaking down into useless sounds and syllables. She will use the tired phrase as proof that a name does not really matter—even as she longs to say and hear her own.

"Tell me, Anna," says Remy, now. "Who *are* you?"

And so she tells him. Or at least, she tries—spills out the whole strange and winding journey, and then, when it does not even reach his ears, she starts again, and tells him another version of the truth, one that skirts the edges of her story, smoothing the rough corners into something more human.

Anna's story is a pale shadow of Adeline's.

A girl running away from a woman's life. She leaves behind everything she has ever known, and escapes to the city, disowned, alone, but free.

"Unbelievable," he says. "You simply left?"

"I had to," she says, and it is not a lie. "Admit it, you think me mad."

"Indeed," says Remy with a playful grin. "The maddest. And the most incredible. What courage!"

"It did not feel like courage," Addie says, plucking at the rind of bread. "It felt as if I had no choice. As if . . ." The words lodge in her throat, but she isn't sure if it's the curse, or simply the memory. "It felt as if I'd die there."

Remy nods thoughtfully. "Small places make for small lives. And some people are fine with that. They like knowing where to put their feet. But if you only walk in other people's steps, you cannot make your own way. You cannot leave a mark."

Addie's throat tightens.

"Do you think a life has any value if one doesn't leave some mark upon the world?"

Remy's expression sobers, and he must read the sadness in her voice, because he says, "I think there are many ways to matter." He plucks the book from his pocket. "These are the words of a man—Voltaire. But they are also the hands that set the type. The ink that made it readable, the tree that made the paper. All of them matter, though credit goes only to the name on the cover."

He has misread her, of course, assumed the question stemmed from a different, more common fear. Still, his words hold weight—though it will be years before Addie discovers just how much.

They fall to silence, then, the quiet weighted with their thoughts. The summer heat has broken, given way to a breezy comfort with the thickest part of night. The hour settles on them like a sheet.

"It is late," he says. "Let me walk you home."

She shakes her head. "You do not have to."

"But I do," he protests. "You may disguise yourself as a man, but I know the truth, and so honor will not let me leave you. The darkness is no place to be alone."

He does not know how right he is. Her chest aches at the idea of losing the thread of this night, and the ease beginning to take shape between them, an ease born of hours instead of days or months, but it is something, fragile and lovely.

"Very well," she says, and his smile, when it answers, is pure joy.

"Lead the way."

She has nowhere to take him, but she sets off, in the vague direction of a place she stayed several months before. Her chest tightens a little with every step, because every step brings her closer to the end of this, of them. And when they turn onto the street where she has placed her made-up home, and stopped before her imagined door, Remy leans in and kisses her once, on the cheek. Even in the dark she can see him blushing.

"I would see you again," he says, "in daylight, or in darkness. As a woman, or a man. Please, let me see you again."

And her heart breaks, because of course, there is no tomorrow, only to-night, and Addie is not ready for the thread to snap, the night to end, and so she answers, "Let me walk you home," and when he opens his mouth to protest, she presses on, "The darkness is no place to be alone."

He meets her gaze, and perhaps he knows her meaning, or perhaps he is as loath as she to leave this night behind, because he quickly offers his arm and says, "How chivalrous," and they set off together again, laughing as they realize they are retracing their steps, returning the way they came. And if the walk to her imagined home was leisurely, the walk to his is urgent, threaded with anticipation.

When they reach his lodging house, they do not pretend to say good-bye. He leads her up the stairs, fingers tangled now, steps tripping and breathless, and when they reach his rented room, they do not linger on the threshold.

There is a faint catch in her chest at the idea of what comes next.

Sex has only ever been a burden, a necessity of circumstance, some re-quired currency, and she has, up until now, been willing to pay the price. Even now, she is prepared for him to push her down, to shove her skirts out of the way. Prepared for the longing to break, forced away by the unsubtle act.

But he doesn't thrust himself upon her. There is an urgency, yes, but Remy holds it taut as rope between them. He reaches out a single, steady hand, and lifts the hat from her head, sets it gently on the bureau. His fingers slide up the nape of her neck, and through her hair as his mouth finds hers, the kisses shy, and searching.

For the first time, she feels no reluctance, no dread, only a kind of nervous thrill, and the tension in the air is laced with breathless hunger.

Her fingers fumble for the laces of his trousers, but his own hands move slower, undoing the laces of her tunic, sliding the cloth over her head, unwrapping the muslin bound around her breasts.

"So much easier than corsets," he murmurs, kissing the skin of her collar, and for the first time since those nights in her childhood bed back in Villon, Addie feels the heat rising in her cheeks, across her skin, between her legs.

He guides her back onto the pallet, kisses trailing down her throat, the curve of her breasts, before he frees himself, and climbs onto the bed, and onto her. She parts around him, breath hitching at the first thrust, and Remy pulls back, just enough to catch her eye, to make sure she's okay, and when she nods, he drops his head to kiss her, and only then does he press on, press in, press deep.

Her back arches as that pressure gives way to pleasure, a deep and rolling heat. Their bodies press and move together, and she wishes she could erase those other men, those other nights, their stale breath and awkward bulk, the dull thrusts that ended in a sudden, abrupt spasm, before they pulled out, pulled away. To them, wet was wet, and warm was warm, and she was nothing but a vessel for their pleasure.

She cannot erase the memory of those other nights—so she decides to become a palimpsest, to let Remy write over the other lines.

This is how it should have been.

The name Remy whispers in her hair is not hers, but it doesn't matter. In this moment, she can be Anna. She can be anyone.

Remy's breath quickens as his tempo rises, as he presses deeper, and Addie feels herself quicken, too, her body tightening around him, driven toward the edge by the rocking of his hips and the blond curls tumbling into her face. She coils tighter and tighter, and then she comes undone, and a few moments later, so does he.

Remy collapses down beside her. But he doesn't roll away. He reaches out, and sweeps a lock of hair from her cheek, and kisses her temple, and laughs, little more than a smile given sound, but it warms her all the way through.

He falls back against the pillow, and sleep comes over them, his leaden in the aftermath of pleasure, and hers light, dozing, but dreamless.

Addie no longer dreams.

She hasn't, in truth, since that night in the woods. Or if she has, it is the one thing she never remembers. Perhaps there is no space inside her head, full as it is of memories. Perhaps it is yet another facet of her curse, to live only as she does. Or perhaps it is in some strange sense a mercy, for how many would be nightmares.

But she stays, happy and warm beside him, and for a few hours she almost forgets.

Remy has rolled away from her in sleep, exposing the lean breadth of his back, and she rests her hand between his shoulder blades, and feels him breathing, traces her fingers down the slope of his spine, studying his edges the way he'd studied hers in the midst of passion. Her touch is feather-light, but after a moment, he stirs, and shifts, and rolls to face her.

For a brief moment, his face is wide and open and warm; the face that leaned toward hers in the street and smiled through shared secrets in the café and laughed as he walked her first to her home and then to his.

But in the time it takes for him to fully wake, that face slides away, and all the knowing with it. A shadow sweeps across those warm blue eyes, that welcome mouth. He jerks a little, rises on one elbow, flustered by the sight of this stranger in his bed.

Because, of course, she is a stranger now.

For the first time since they met the night before, he frowns, stammers a greeting, the words too formal, stiff with embarrassment, and Addie's heart breaks a little. He is trying to be kind, but she cannot bear it, so she gets up and dresses as fast as she can, a gross reversal of the time he took to strip the clothes away. She does not bother with the laces or the buckles. Does not turn toward him again, not until she feels the warmth of his hand on her shoulder, the touch almost gentle, and thinks, desperately, wildly, that maybe—maybe—there is a way to salvage this. She turns, hoping to meet his eyes, only to find him looking down, away, as he presses three coins into her hand.

And everything goes cold.

Payment.

It will be many years before she can read Greek, many more before she hears the myth of Sisyphus, but when she does, she will nod in understanding, palms aching from the weight of pushing stones uphill, heart heavy from the weight of watching them roll down again.

In this moment, there is no myth for company.

Only this beautiful boy with his back to her.

Only Remy, who makes no move to follow when she hurries to the door.

Something catches her eye, a bundle of paper askew on the floor. The booklet from the café. The latest of Voltaire. Addie doesn't know what drives her to take it—perhaps she simply wants a token of their night, something more than the dreaded copper in her palm—but one moment the book is on the ground, cast-off among the clothes, and the next it is pressed to her front with the rest of her things.

Her hands have gotten light, after all, and even if the theft was clumsy, Remy would not have noticed, sitting there on the bed, his attention fixed anywhere but her.

Addie leads Henry down the street and around the corner to a nondescript steel door plastered with old posters. A man loiters next to it, chain-smoking and scrolling through pictures on his phone.

"Jupiter," she says, unprompted, and the man straightens, and pushes open the door, exposing a narrow platform, and a set of stairs that drops down out of sight.

"Welcome to the Fourth Rail."

Henry shoots her a wary look, but Addie grabs his hand and pulls him through. He twists, looking back as the door swings shut. "There is no fourth rail," he says, and Addie flashes him a grin.

"Exactly."

This is what she loves about a city like New York. It is so full of hidden chambers, infinite doors leading into infinite rooms, and if you have the time, you can find so many of them. Some she's found by accident, others in the course of this or that adventure. She keeps them tucked away, like slips of paper between the pages of her book.

One stairwell leads to another, the second wider, made of stone. The ceiling arches overhead, plaster giving way to rock, and then tile, the tunnel lit only by a series of electric lanterns, but they're spaced far enough apart that they do little to actually break the dark. A breadcrumb trail, just enough to see by, which is why Addie has the pleasure of seeing Henry's expression when he realizes where they are.

The New York City Subway has nearly five hundred active stations, but the number of abandoned tunnels remains a matter of contention. Some of them are open to the public, both monuments to the past and nods to the unfinished future. Some are little more than closed tracks tucked between functioning lines.

And then some are secrets.

"Addie . . ." murmurs Henry, but she holds up a finger, tilts her head. Listening.

The music starts as an echo, a distant thrum, as much a feeling as a sound. It rises with every downward step, seems to fill the air around them, first a hum, and then a pulse, and then, at last, a beat.

Ahead the tunnel is bricked up, marked only by the white slash of an arrow to the left. Around the corner, the music grows. One more dead end, one more turn and—

Sound crashes over them.

The whole tunnel vibrates with the force of the bass, the reverb of chords against stone. Spotlights pulse blue-white, a strobe reducing the hidden club to still frames; a writhing crowd, bodies bouncing to the beat; a pair of musicians wielding matching electric guitars on a concrete stage; a row of bartenders caught mid-pour.

The tunnel walls are tiled gray and white, wide bands that wrap in arches overhead, bend down again like ribs, as if they are in the belly of some great, forgotten beast, the rhythm pulsing through its heart.

The Fourth Rail is primal, heady. The kind of place Luc would love.

But this? This is *hers*. Addie found the tunnel on her own. She showed it to the musician-turned-manager looking for a venue. Later that night, she even suggested the name, their heads bent over a cocktail napkin. His pen marks. Her idea. She's sure he woke up the next day with a hangover and the first stirrings of the Fourth Rail. Six months later, she saw the guy standing outside the steel doors. Saw the logo they'd designed, a more polished version, tucked beneath the peeling posters, and felt the now-familiar thrill of whispering something into the world and watching it become real.

Addie pulls Henry toward the makeshift bar.

It's simple, the tunnel wall divided into three behind a wide slab of pale stone that serves as a pouring surface. The options are vodka, bourbon, or tequila, and a bartender stands, waiting, before each.

Addie orders for them. Two vodkas.

The transaction happens in silence—there is no point trying to shout over the wall of sound. A series of fingers held up, a ten laid on the bar. The bartender—a slender black guy with silver dusting his eyes—pours two shots, and spreads his hands like a dealer laying down cards.

Henry lifts his glass and Addie raises hers too and their mouths move together (she thinks he's saying *cheers* while she answers *salut*), but the sounds are swallowed up, the clink of their shots nothing but a small vibration through her fingers.

The vodka hits her stomach like a match, heat blossoming behind her ribs.

They set the empty glasses back on the bar, and Addie's already pulling Henry toward the crush of bodies by the stage when the guy behind the bar reaches out and catches Henry's wrist.

The bartender smiles, produces a third shot glass, and pours again. He presses his hands to his chest in the universal gesture for *it's on me*.

They drink, and there is the heat again, spreading from her chest to her limbs, and there is Henry's hand in hers, moving into the crowd. Addie looks back, sees the bartender staring after them, and there is a strange feeling, rising like the last dregs of a dream, and she wants to say something, but the music is a wall, and the vodka smooths the edges of her thoughts until it slips away, and then they are folding into the crowd.

Up above it may be early spring, but down here it is late summer, humid and heavy. The music is liquid, the air thick as syrup as they plunge into the tangled limbs. The tunnel is bricked up behind the stage, making a world of reverb, a place where sound bends back, redoubles, every note carried, thinning, without trailing off entirely. The guitarists play a complicated riff in perfect unison, adding to the echo chamber effect, churning the waters of the crowd.

And then the girl steps into the spotlight.

A teenage sprite—*a fae thing*, Luc would say—in a black baby doll dress and combat boots. Her white-blond hair is piled on her head, done up in twin buns, the ends spiking like a crown. The only color is the slash of her red lips, and the rainbow drawn like a mask across her eyes. The guitarists quicken, fingers flying over strings. The air shakes, the beat thumps through skin and muscle and bone.

And the girl begins to sing.

Her voice is a wail, a banshee's call if a banshee screamed in tune. The syllables bleed together, the consonants blur, and Addie finds herself leaning in, eager to hear the words. But they draw back, slip under the beat, fold into the feral energy of the Fourth Rail.

The guitars play their hypnotic chorus.

The girl singer seems almost like a puppet, pulled along by the strings.

And Addie thinks that Luc would love her, wonders for an instant if he's been down here since she'd found it. She breathes in as if she'd be able to smell the darkness, like smoke, on the air. But Addie wills herself to stop, empties her head of him, makes space instead for the boy beside her, bouncing in time with the beat.

Henry, with his head tipped back, his glasses fogged gray, and sweat sliding down his cheeks like tears. For an instant he looks impossibly, immeasurably sad, and she remembers the pain in his voice when he spoke of losing time.

But then he looks at her and smiles, and it's gone, a trick of the lights, and she wonders who and how and where he came from, knows it is all too good to be true, but in this moment, she is simply glad he's there.

She closes her eyes, lets herself fall into the rhythm of the beat, and she is in Berlin, Mexico City, Madrid, and she is right here, right now, with him.

They dance until their limbs ache.

Until sweat paints their skin, and the air becomes too thick to breathe.

Until there's a lull in the beat, and another silent conversation passed between them like a spark.

Until he draws her back toward the bar and the tunnel, back the way they came, but the flow of traffic is a one-way street, the stairs and the steel door only lead in.

Until she cocks her head the other way, to a dark arch set in the tunnel wall near the stage, leads him up the narrow stairs, the music fading a little more with every upward step, ears buzzing with the white noise left in its wake.

Until they spill out into the cool March night, filling their lungs with fresh air.

And the first clear sound Addie hears is his laughter.

Henry turns toward her, eyes bright, cheeks flushed, intoxicated in a way that has less to do with the vodka than with the power of the Fourth Rail.

He is still laughing when the storm starts.

A crack of thunder, and seconds later, the rain comes down. Not a drizzle—not even the sparse warning drops that soon give way to a steady rain—but the sudden sheet fall of a downpour. The kind of rain that hits you like a wall, soaks you through in seconds.

Addie gasps at the sudden shock of cold.

They are ten feet from the nearest awning, but neither of them runs for cover.

She smiles up into the rain, lets the water kiss her skin.

Henry looks at her, and Addie looks back, and then he spreads his arms as if to welcome the storm, his chest heaving. Water clings to his black lashes, slides down his face, rinsing the club from his clothes, and Addie realizes suddenly that, despite the moments of resemblance, Luc never once looked like this.

Young.

Human.

Alive.

She pulls Henry toward her, relishes the press of his body, warm against the cold. She runs her hand through his hair and for the first time it stays back, exposing the sharp lines of his face, the hungry hollows of his jaw, his eyes, a brighter shade of green than she has seen them yet.

"Addie," he breathes, and the sound sends sparks across her skin, and when he kisses her, he tastes like salt, and summer. But it feels too much like a punctuation mark, and she isn't ready for the night to end, so she kisses him back, deeper, turns the period into a question, into an answer.

And then they are running, not for shelter, but the train.

They stumble into his apartment, wet clothes clinging to their skin.

They are a tangle of limbs in the hallway, unable to get close enough. She pulls the glasses from his face, tosses them onto a nearby chair, shrugs out of her coat, the leather sticking to her skin. And then they are kissing again. Desperate, hungry, wild, as her fingers run over his ribs, hook in the front of his jeans.

"Are you sure?" he asks, and in answer she pulls his mouth to hers, guides his hands to the buttons of her shirt as hers find his belt. He presses her back against the wall, and says her name, and it is lightning through her limbs, it is fire through her core, it is longing between her legs.

And then they are on the bed, and for an instant, only an instant, she is somewhere else, some*when* else, the darkness folding itself around her. A name whispered against bare skin.

But to him she was Adeline, only Adeline. *His* Adeline. *My Adeline.*

Here, now, she is finally Addie.

"Say it again," she pleads.

"Say what?" he murmurs.

"My name."

Henry smiles.

"Addie," he whispers against her throat.

"Addie." The kisses trail over her collar.

"Addie." Her stomach.

"Addie." Her hips.

His mouth finds the heat between her legs, and her fingers tangle in those black curls, her back arching up with pleasure. Time shudders, slides out of focus. He retraces his steps, kisses her again, and then she is on top of him, pressing him down into the bed.

They do not fit together perfectly. He was not made for her the way Luc was—but this is better, because he is real, and kind, and human, and he *remembers.*

When it is over, she collapses, breathless, into the sheets beside him, sweat and rain chilling on her skin. Henry folds around her, pulls her back into the circle of his warmth, and she can feel his heart slowing through his ribs, a metronome easing back into its measure.

The room goes quiet, marked only by the steady rain beyond the windows, the drowsy aftermath of passion, and soon she can feel him drifting down toward sleep.

Addie looks up at the ceiling.

"Don't forget," she says softly, the words half prayer, half plea.

Henry's arms tighten, a body surfacing from sleep. "Forget what?" he murmurs, already sinking again.

And Addie waits for his breath to steady before she whispers the word to the dark.

"Me."

VI

✦ ✦ ✦ ✦ ✦

Addie surges out into the night, swiping tears from her cheeks.

She pulls her jacket close despite the warmth of summer, and makes her way alone across the sleeping city. She is not heading toward the hovel she's called home this season. She is simply moving forward, because she cannot bear the idea of standing still.

So Addie walks.

And at some point, she realizes she is no longer alone. There is a change in the air, a subtle breeze, carrying the leafy scent of country woods, and then he is there, falling in step beside her, stride for stride. An elegant shadow, dressed in the height of Paris fashion, collar and cuff trimmed in silk.

Only his black curls billow around his face, feral and free.

"Adeline, Adeline," he says, his voice laced with pleasure, and she is back in the bed, Remy's voice saying *Anna, Anna* into her hair.

It has been four years without a visit.

Four years of holding her breath, and though she will never admit it, the sight of him is like coming up for air. A terrible, chest-opening relief. As much as she hates this shadow, this god, this monster in his stolen flesh, he is still the only one who remembers her at all.

It does not make her hate him any less.

If anything, she hates him more.

"Where have you been?" she snaps.

Smug pleasure shines like starlight in his eyes. "Why? Have you missed me?" Addie doesn't trust herself to speak. "Come now," Luc presses, "you did not think I would make it easy."

"It's been four years," she says, wincing at the anger in her voice, too close to need.

"Four years is nothing. A breath. A blink."

"And yet, you come tonight."

"I know your heart, my dear. I feel when it falters."

Remy's fingers folding hers over the coins, the sudden weight of sadness, and the darkness, drawn to pain like a wolf to blood.

Luc looks down at her trousers, pinned below the knee, the man's tunic, open at the throat. "I must say," he says, "I preferred you in red."

Her heart catches at the mention of that night four years before, the first time he did not come. He savors the sight of her surprise.

"You saw," she says.

"I am the night itself. I see everything." He steps closer, carrying the scent of summer storms, the kiss of forest leaves. "But that was a lovely dress you wore on my behalf."

Shame slides like a flush beneath her skin, followed by the heat of anger, at the knowledge that he was watching. Had watched her hope gutter with the candles on the sill, watched as she shattered, alone in the dark.

She loathes him, wears that loathing like a coat, wraps it tight around her as she smiles.

"You thought I would wither without your attention. But I have not."

The darkness hums. "It has only been four years," he muses. "Perhaps next time I will wait longer. Or perhaps . . ." His hand grazes her chin, tipping her face to meet his. "I will abandon these visits, and leave you to wander the earth until it ends."

It is a chilling thought, though she does not let him see it.

"If you did that," she says evenly, "you would never have my soul."

He shrugs. "I have a thousand others waiting to be reaped, and you are only one." He is closer now, too close, his thumb tracing up her jaw, fingers sliding along the back of her neck. "It would be so easy to forget you. Everyone else already has." She tries to pull away, but his hand is stone, holding her fast. "I will be kind. It will be quick. Say yes now," he urges, "before I change my mind."

For a terrible moment, she doesn't trust herself to answer. The weight of the coins in her palm is still too fresh, the pain of the night torn away, and victory dances like light in Luc's eyes. It is enough to force her to her senses.

"No," she says, the word a snarl.

And there it is, like a gift, a flash of anger on that perfect face.

His hand falls away, the weight of him vanishing like smoke, and Addie is left alone once more in the dark.

There is a point when the night breaks.

When the darkness finally begins to weaken, and lose its hold over the sky. It's slow, so slow she doesn't notice until the light is already creeping in, until the moon and stars have vanished, and the weight of Luc's attention lifts from her shoulders.

Addie climbs the steps of the Sacré Coeur, sits at the top, with the church at her back and Paris sprawling at her feet, and watches the 29th of July become the 30th, watches the sun rise over the city.

She has almost forgotten the book she took from Remy's floor.

She has clutched it so tight, her fingers ache. Now, in the watery morning light, she puzzles over the title, silently sounding out the words. *La Place Royale*. It is a novel, that new word, though she doesn't yet know it. Addie peels back the cover, and tries to read the first page, manages only a line before the words crumble into letters, and the letters blur, and she has to resist the urge to cast the cursed book away, to fling it down the steps.

Instead, she closes her eyes, and takes a deep breath, and thinks of Remy, not his words, but the soft pleasure in his voice when he spoke of reading, the delight in his eyes, the joy, the hope.

It will be a grueling journey, full of starts and stops and myriad frustrations.

To decipher this first novel will take her almost a year—a year spent laboring over every line, trying to make sense of a sentence, then a page, then a chapter. And still, it will be a decade more before the act comes naturally, before the task itself dissolves, and she finds the hidden pleasure of the story.

It will take time, but time is the one thing Addie has plenty of.

So she opens her eyes, and starts again.

Addie wakes to the smell of toast browning, the sizzle of butter hitting a hot skillet. The bed is empty beside her, the door almost closed, but she can hear Henry moving in the kitchen beneath the soft burble of talk radio. The room is cool, and the bed is warm, and she holds her breath and tries to hold the moment with it, the way she has a thousand times, clutching the past to the present, and warding off the future, the fall.

But today is different.

Because someone remembers.

She throws off the blankets, scavenges the bedroom floor, looking for her clothes, but there's no sign of the rain-soaked jeans or shirt, just the familiar leather jacket draped over a chair. Addie finds a robe beneath and wraps it around her, buries her nose in the collar. It is worn and soft, smells like clean cotton and fabric softener and the faint hint of coconut shampoo, a smell she will come to know as his.

She pads barefoot into the kitchen as Henry pours coffee from a French press.

He looks up, and smiles. "Good morning."

Two small words that move the world.

Not *I'm sorry*. Not *I don't remember*. Not *I must have been drunk.*

Just *good morning.*

"I put your clothes in the dryer," he says. "They should be done soon. Grab yourself a mug."

Most people have a shelf of cups. Henry has a wall. They hang from hooks on a mounted rack, five across and seven down. Some of them are patterned and some of them are plain and no two are the same.

"I'm not sure you have enough mugs."

Henry casts her a sidelong look. He has a way of almost smiling. It's like light behind a curtain, the edge of the sun behind clouds, more a promise than an actual thing, but the warmth shines through.

"It was a thing, in my family," he says. "No matter who came over for coffee, they could choose the one that spoke to them that day."

His own cup sits on the counter, charcoal gray, the inside coated in something that looks like liquid silver. A storm cloud and its lining. Addie studies the wall, trying to make her choice. She reaches for a large porcelain cup with small blue leaves, weighs it in her palm before she notices another. She's about to put it back when Henry stops her.

"I'm afraid all selections are final," he says, scraping butter over toast. "You'll have to try again tomorrow."

Tomorrow. The word swells a little in her chest.

Henry pours, and Addie leans her elbows on the counter, wraps her hands around the steaming cup, inhales the bittersweet scent. For a second, only a second, she is in Paris, hat pulled down in the corner of the café as Remy pushed the cup toward her and said, *Drink*. That is how memories are for her, past rising into present, a palimpsest held up to the light.

"Oh, hey," says Henry, calling her back. "I found this on the floor. Is it yours?"

She looks up and sees the wooden ring.

"Don't touch that." Addie snatches it out of his hand, too fast. The inside of the ring brushes the tip of her finger, rolls around the nail like a coin about to settle, all the ease of a compass finding north.

"Shit." Addie shudders and drops the band. It clatters to the floor, rolling several feet before fetching up against the edge of a rug. She grips her fingers as if burned, heart pounding.

She didn't put it on.

And even if she did—her gaze cuts to the window, but it is morning, sunlight streaming through the curtains. The darkness cannot find her here.

"What happened?" asks Henry, clearly confused.

"Nothing," she says, shaking out her hand. "Just a splinter. Stupid thing." She kneels slowly to retrieve it, careful to touch only the outside of the band.

"Sorry," she says, straightening. She sets the ring on the counter between them, splaying her hands on either side. In the artificial light, the pale wood looks almost gray. Addie glares down at the band.

"Have you ever had something you love, and hate, but can't bear to get rid of? Something you almost wish you'd lose, because then it wouldn't be there, and it wouldn't be your fault . . ." She tries to make the words light, almost casual.

"Yeah," he says quietly. "I do." He opens a kitchen drawer and pulls out something small, and gold. A Star of David. A pendant, missing its chain.

"You're Jewish?"

"I was." Two words, and all he means to say. His attention drifts back to her ring. "It looks old."

"It is." Exactly as old as she is.

They both should have worn to nothing long ago.

She presses her hand down over the ring, feels the smooth wooden rim dig into her palm. "It belonged to my father," she says, and it isn't a lie, though it's only the beginning of the truth. She closes her hand around the ring, and pockets it. The ring is weightless, but she can feel it. She can always feel it.

"Anyway," she says, with a too-bright smile. "What's for breakfast?"

How many times has Addie dreamed of this?

Of hot coffee and buttered toast, of sunlight streaming through the windows, of new days that aren't fresh starts, none of the awkward silence of strangers, of a boy or a girl, elbows on the counter across from her, the simple comfort of a night remembered.

"You must really love breakfast," says Henry, and she realizes she is beaming down at her food.

"It's my favorite meal," she answers, spearing a bite of eggs.

But as she eats, the hope begins to thin.

Addie is not a fool. Whatever this is, she knows it will not last. She has lived too long to think it chance, been cursed too long to think it fate.

She has begun to wonder if it is a trap.

Some new way to torment her. To break the stalemate, force her hand back into play. But even after all these years, Luc's voice wraps around her, soft and low and gloating.

I am all you have. All you will ever have. The only one who will remember.

It was the one card he always held, the weapon of his own attention, and she does not think he'd give it away. But if it is not a trap, then what? An accident? A stroke of luck? Perhaps she has gone mad. It would not be the first time. Perhaps she has frozen up on Sam's roof, and is trapped in a dream.

Perhaps none of it is real.

And yet, there is his hand on hers, there is the soft scent of him on the robe, there is the sound of her name, drawing her back.

"Where did you go?" he asks, and she spears another bite of food and holds it up between them.

"If you could only eat one thing for the rest of your life," she says, "what would it be?"

"Chocolate," Henry answers without missing a beat. "The kind so dark it's almost bitter. You?"

Addie ponders. A life is a very long time. "Cheese," she answers soberly, and Henry nods, and silence settles over them, less awkward than shy. Nervous laughter in between stolen glances, two strangers who are no longer strangers but know so little of each other.

"If you could live somewhere with only one season," asks Henry, "what would it be?"

"Spring," she says, "when everything is new."

"Fall," he says, "when everything is fading."

They have both chosen seams, those ragged lines where things are neither here nor there, but balanced on the brink. And Addie wonders, half to herself, "Would you rather feel nothing or everything?"

A shadow crosses Henry's face, and he falters, looks down at his unfinished food and then to the clock on the wall.

"Shit. I've got to get to the store." He straightens, dropping his plate in the sink. The last question goes unanswered.

"I should go home," says Addie, rising too. "Get changed. Do some work."

There is no home, of course, no clothes, no job. But she is playing the part of a normal girl, a girl who gets to have a normal life, sleep with a boy and wake up to *good morning*s instead of *who are you*s.

Henry finishes his coffee in a single gulp. "How do you go about finding talent?" he asks, and Addie remembers she told him that she was a scout.

"You keep your eyes open," she says, rounding the counter.

But he catches her hand.

"I want to see you again."

"I want you to see me again," she echoes.

"Still no phone?"

She shakes her head, and he raps his fingers for a moment, thinking. "There's a food truck rally in Prospect Park. Meet you there at six?"

Addie smiles. "It's a date." She pulls the robe close. "Mind if I take a shower before I go?"

Henry kisses her. "Of course. Just let yourself out."

She smiles. "I will."

Henry leaves, the front door swinging shut behind him, but for once, the sound doesn't make her stomach drop. It's just a door. Not a period. An ellipsis. A to-be-continued.

She takes a long, hot shower, wraps her hair in a towel, and wanders through the apartment, noticing all the things she didn't see last night.

Henry's apartment is just this side of messy, cluttered in the way so many New York places are, too little space to live and breathe. It's also littered with the remains of abandoned hobbies. A cabinet of oil paints, the brushes gone stale and stiff in a stained cup. Notebooks and journals, most of them empty. A few blocks of wood and a whittling knife—somewhere, in the faded space before her flawless memory, she hears her father humming, and moves on, moves away, slowing only when she reaches the cameras.

A row of them stare down at her from a shelf, their lenses large and wide and black.

Vintage, she thinks, though the word has never held much weight.

She was there when cameras were hulking tripod beasts, the photographer hidden beneath a heavy drape. She was there for the invention of black-and-white film, and then color, there when still frames became videos, when analog became digital, and whole stories could be stored in the palm of a hand.

She runs her fingers across the camera bodies, like carapace shells, feels dust beneath her touch. But there are photographs everywhere.

On the walls, propped on side tables, and sitting in the corner, waiting to be hung. There is one of Beatrice in an art gallery, a silhouette against the brightly lit space. One of Beatrice and Henry, tangled together, her gaze up, and his head down, each caught in the beginning of a laugh. One of a boy that Addie guesses must be Robbie. Bea was right; he looks like he walked out of a party in Andy Warhol's loft. The crowd behind him is a blur of bodies, but Robbie is in focus, mid-laugh, purple glitter tracing his cheekbones, plumes of green along his nose, gold at his temples.

Another photo, in the hall. Here, the three of them sit on a sofa, Bea in the middle, Robbie's legs stretched across her lap, and Henry on the other side, chin resting lazily on his hand.

And across the hall, its opposite. A posed family portrait, stiff against the candids. Again Henry sits on the edge of the sofa, but more upright, and this time placed beside two people who are clearly his brother and sister. The girl, a whirlwind of curls, eyes dancing behind a pair of cat-eye frames, the model of the mother resting a hand on her shoulder. The boy, older, sterner, an echo of the father behind the sofa. And the younger son, lean, wary, smiling the kind of smile that doesn't reach his eyes.

Henry stares back at Addie, from the photos he's in, and the ones he clearly took. She can feel him, the artist in the frame. She could stay there, studying these pictures, trying to find the truth of him in them, the secret, the answer to the question going around and around in her head.

But all she sees is someone sad, lost, searching.

She turns her attention to the books.

Henry's own collection is eclectic, spilling across surfaces in every room. A shelf in the living room, a narrower one in the hall, a stack beside his bed, another on the coffee table. Comics stacked over a pile of textbooks with titles like *Reviewing the Covenant* and *Jewish Theology for the Postmodern Age*. There are novels, biographies, paperbacks and hardcovers mixed together, some old and fraying, others brand new. Bookmarks jut up from the pages, marking a dozen unfinished reads.

Her fingers drift down the spines, hover on a squat gold book. *A History of the World in 100 Objects.* She wonders if you can distill a person's life, let alone human civilization, to a list of things, wonders if that's a valid way to measure worth at all, not by the lives touched, but the things left behind. She tries to build her own list. A History of Addie LaRue.

Her father's bird, lost among the bodies in Paris.

The Place Royale, stolen from Remy's room.

The wooden ring.

But those things have their mark on *her.* What of Addie's legacy? Her face, ghosted in a hundred works of art. Her melodies at the heart of a hundred songs. Ideas taking root, growing wild, the seeds unseen.

Addie continues through the apartment, idle curiosity giving way to a more purposeful search. She is looking for clues, searching for something, anything, to explain Henry Strauss.

A laptop sits on the coffee table. It boots without a password prompt, but when Addie brushes her thumb across the trackpad, the cursor doesn't move. She taps the keys absently, but nothing happens.

The technology changes.

The curse stays the same.

Except it doesn't.

It hasn't—not entirely.

So she goes from room to room, searching for clues to the question she cannot seem to answer.

Who are you, Henry Strauss?

In the medicine cabinet, a handful of prescriptions line the shelf, their names clogged with consonants. Beside them, a vial of pink pills marked with only a Post-it—a tiny, hand-drawn umbrella.

In the bedroom, another bookshelf, a stack of notebooks in various shapes and sizes.

She turns through, but all of them are blank.

On the windowsill, another, older photo—of Henry and Robbie. In this one, they are tangled, Robbie's face pressed against Henry's, his forehead resting on Henry's temple. There's something intimate about the pose, the way Robbie's eyes are almost closed, the way Henry's hand cradles the back of his head, as if holding him up, or holding him close. The serene curve on Robbie's mouth. Happy. Home.

By the bed, an old-fashioned watch sits on the side table. It has no minute hand, and the hour points just past six, even though the clock on the wall reads 9:32. She holds it to her ear, but the battery must be dead.

And then, in the top drawer, a handkerchief, dotted with blood. When she picks it up, a ring tumbles out. A small diamond set in a platinum band. Addie stares down at the engagement ring, and wonders who it was for, wonders who Henry was before he met her, what happened to put him in her path.

"Who *are* you?" she whispers to the empty room.

She wraps the ring in the stained kerchief and returns it to its spot, sliding the drawer shut.

VIII

"I take it back," she says. "If I could only eat one thing for the rest of my life, it would be these fries."

Henry laughs and steals a few from the cone in her hand as they wait in line for gyros. The food trucks form a colorful stripe along Flatbush, crowds of people queuing for lobster rolls and grilled cheese, banh mi and kebabs. There's even a line for ice-cream sandwiches, even though the warmth has dropped out of the March air, promising a crisp, cold night. Addie's glad she picked up a hat and scarf, traded her ballet flats for calf-high boots, even as she leans into the warmth of Henry's arms, until there's a break in the falafel queue, and he ducks away to get in line.

Addie watches him step up to the counter window and order, watches the middle-aged woman working the truck as she leans forward, elbows on the sill, watches them talk, Henry nodding solemnly. The line is growing behind him, but the woman doesn't seem to notice. She's not smiling exactly; if anything, she looks on the verge of tears as she reaches out and takes his hand, squeezes it.

"Next!"

Addie blinks, gets to the front of her own line, spends the last of her stolen cash on a lamb gyro and a blueberry soda, finds herself wishing for the first time in a while that she had a credit card, or more to her name than the clothes on her back and the change in her pocket. Wishes that things didn't seem to slip through her fingers like sand, that she could have a thing without stealing it first.

"You're looking at that sandwich like it broke your heart."

Addie looks up at Henry, cracks a smile. "It looks so good," she says. "I'm just thinking of how sad I'll be when it's gone."

He sighs in mock lament. "The worst part of every meal is when it ends."

They take their spoils and stake out a slope of grass just inside the park, a pool of quickly thinning light. Henry adds the falafel and an order of dumplings to her gyro and fries, and they share, trading bites like cards in a game of gin.

Henry reaches for the falafel, and Addie remembers the woman in the window.

"What was that?" she asks. "Back there at the truck, the woman working, she looked like she was about to cry. Do you know her?"

Henry shakes his head. "She said I reminded her of her son."

Addie stares at him. It isn't a lie, she doesn't think, but it's not entirely the truth, either. There's something he isn't saying, but she doesn't know how to ask. She spears a dumpling and pops it in her mouth.

Food is one of the best things about being alive.

Not just food. *Good* food. There is a chasm between sustenance and satisfaction, and while she spent the better part of three hundred years eating to stave off the pangs of hunger, she has spent the last fifty delighting in the discovery of flavor. So much of life becomes routine, but food is like music, like art, replete with the promise of something new.

She wipes the grease from her fingers and lies back in the grass beside Henry, feeling wonderfully full. She knows it will not last. That fullness is like everything else in her life. It always wears away too soon. But here, and now, she feels . . . perfect.

She closes her eyes, and smiles, and thinks she could stay here all night, despite the growing cold, let the dusk give way to dark, burrow against Henry and hope for stars.

A bright chime sounds in his coat pocket.

Henry answers. "Hey, Bea," he starts, and then abruptly sits up. Addie can only hear half the call, but she can guess at the rest.

"No, of course I didn't forget. I know, I'm late, I'm sorry. I'm on my way. Yeah, I remember."

Henry hangs up, puts his head in his hands.

"Bea's having a dinner party. And I was meant to bring dessert."

He looks back at the food trucks, as if one of them might hold the answer, looks at the sky, which has gone from dusk to dim, runs his hands through his hair, lets out a soft and muttered stream of cursing. But there's no time to wallow now, not when he is late.

"Come on," says Addie, pulling him to his feet. "I know a place."

The best French bakery in Brooklyn has no sign.

Marked by only a butter yellow awning, a narrow glass window between two broad brick storefronts, it belongs to a man named Michel. Every morning before dawn, he arrives, and begins the slow assembly of his art. Apple tarts, the fruit sliced thin as paper, and operas, the tops dusted with cocoa, and petit fours coated in marzipan and small, piped roses.

The shop is closed now, but she can see the shadow of its owner as he moves through the kitchen at its back, and Addie raps her knuckles on the glass door, and waits.

"Are you sure about this?" asks Henry as the shape shuffles forward, cracks the door.

"We are closed," he says, in a heavy accent, and Addie slips from English into French as she explains she is a friend of Delphine's, and the man softens at the mention of his daughter's name, softens more at the sound of his native tongue, and she understands. She can speak German, Italian, Spanish, Swiss, but French is different, French is bread baking in her mother's oven, French is her father's hands carving wood, French is Estele murmuring to her garden.

French is coming home.

"For Delphine," he answers, opening the door, "anything."

Inside the small shop, New York falls away, and it is pure Paris, the taste of sugar and butter still on the air. The cases are mostly empty now, only a handful of the beautiful creations lingering on the shelves, bright and sparse as wildflowers in a barren field.

She does know Delphine, though the young woman does not, of course, know her. She knows Michel as well, visits this shop the way someone else might visit a photograph, linger on a memory.

Henry hovers a few steps behind as Addie and Michel make small talk, each contented by the brief respite of the other's language, and the patissier places each of the remaining pastries in a pink box, and hands them to her. And when she offers to pay, wondering if she can afford the cost, Michel shakes his head, and thanks her for the taste of home, and she wishes him good night, and back on the curb, Henry stares at her as if she's performed a magic act, some strange and wondrous feat.

He pulls her into the circle of his arms.

"You are amazing," he says, and she blushes, having never had an audience.

"Here," she says, pressing the pastry box into his hands. "Enjoy the party."

Henry's smile falls. His forehead rucks up like a carpet. "Why don't you come with me?"

And she doesn't know how to say *I can't* when there is no explaining why, when she was ready to spend all night with him. So she says, "I shouldn't," and he says, "Please," and she knows it is such a terrible idea, that she cannot hold the secret of her curse aloft over so many heads, knows she cannot keep him to herself, that this is all a game of borrowed time.

But this is how you walk to the end of the world.

This is how you live forever.

Here is one day, and here is the next, and the next, and you take what you can, savor every stolen second, cling to every moment, until it's gone.

So she says yes.

They walk, arm in arm, as the evening goes from cool to cold.

"Is there anything I should know?" she says. "About your friends?"

Henry frowns, thinking. "Well, Robbie's a performer. He's really good, but he can be a little . . . difficult?" He exhales a hard breath. "We were together, back in college. He was the first guy I ever fell for."

"But it didn't work out?"

Henry laughs, but the breath is shallow. "No. He dumped me. But look, it was ages ago. We're friends now, nothing more." He shakes his head, as if clearing it. "Then there's Bea, you met her. She's great. She's getting her PhD, and she lives with a guy named Josh."

"Are they dating?"

Henry snorts. "No. Bea's gay. And so is he . . . I think. I don't actually know, it's been the topic of speculation. But Bea will probably invite Mel, or Elise, whichever she's dating now—it's kind of a pendulum swing. Oh, and don't ask about the Professor." Addie looks at him, wondering, and he explains. "Bea had a thing, a few years ago, with a Columbia professor. Bea was in love, but she was married, and it all fell apart."

Addie repeats the names to herself, and Henry smiles.

"It's not a test," he says. "You can't fail."

Addie wishes he were right.

Henry winds a little tighter at her side. He hesitates, exhales. "There's something else you should know," he says at last, "about me."

Her heart stutters in her chest as she braces for a confession, a reluctant truth, some explanation for this, for them. But Henry only looks up at the starless night and says, "There was a girl."

A girl. It does not answer anything.

"Her name was Tabitha," he says, and she can feel the pain in every syllable. She thinks of the ring in his drawer, the bloody kerchief knotted around it.

"What happened?"

"I proposed, and she said no."

It is true, she thinks, some version of it. But Addie is beginning to realize how good Henry is at skirting lies while leaving truths half-told.

"We all have battle scars," she says. "People in our past."

"You too?" he asks, and for a moment, she is in New Orleans, the room in disarray, those green eyes black with rage as the building begins to burn.

"Yeah," she says softly. And then, gently probing, "And we all have secrets, too."

He looks at her, and she can see it swimming in his eyes, the thing he will not say, but he is not Luc, and the green gives nothing away.

Tell me, she thinks. Whatever it is.

But he doesn't.

They reach Bea's building in silence, and she buzzes them in, and as they climb the stairs she turns her thoughts to the party, and thinks, perhaps, it will be okay.

Perhaps, they will remember her, at the end of this evening.

Perhaps, if he is with her—

Perhaps—

But then the door opens, and Bea stands there, oven mitts on hips, voices spilling through the apartment behind her as she says, "Henry Strauss, you are *so late,* that better be dessert." And Henry holds out the pastry box as if it were a shield, but as Bea plucks the box from his hands, she looks past him. "And who's this?"

"This is Addie," he says. "You met in the shop."

Bea rolls her eyes. "Henry, you really don't have enough friends to be getting us mixed up. Besides," she says, flashing Addie a crooked smile, "I wouldn't forget a face like yours. There's something . . . timeless about it."

Henry's frown deepens. "You *have* met, and that's exactly what you said." He looks to Addie. "You remember this, don't you?"

She hesitates, caught between the impossible truth and the easier lie, begins to shake her head. "I'm sorry, I—"

But Addie's saved by the arrival of a girl in a yellow sundress, a bold defiance of the chill beyond the windows, and Henry whispers in her ear that this is Elise. The girl kisses Bea and plucks the box from her hands, and says she cannot find the wine opener, and Josh appears to take their coats, and usher them through.

The apartment is a converted loft, one of those open floor plans where the hall runs into the living room and the living room runs into the kitchen, and it is all mercifully free of walls and doors.

The buzzer rings again, and moments later a boy arrives like a comet crashing through the atmosphere, a bottle of wine in one hand and a scarf in the other. And even though Addie has only seen him in photos on Henry's wall, she knows instantly that this is Robbie.

He sweeps through the front hallway, kissing Bea on the cheek, waves at Josh and hugs Elise, and turns toward Henry, only to notice *her.*

"Who are you?" he says.

"Don't be rude," answers Henry. "This is Addie."

"Henry's date," adds Bea, and Addie wishes she hadn't, because the words are like cold water over Robbie's mood. Henry must see it too, because he takes her hand and says, "Addie's a talent scout."

"Oh?" asks Robbie, rekindling a little. "What kind?"

"Art. Music. All sorts."

He frowns. "Don't scouts usually specialize in something?"

Bea elbows him. "Be nice," she says, reaching for the wine.

"Didn't know I was supposed to bring a date," he says, following her into the kitchen.

She pats his shoulder. "You can borrow Josh."

The dining table sits between the sofa and the kitchen counter, and Bea sets an extra place as Henry opens the first two bottles of wine, and Robbie pours, and Josh carries a salad to the table and Elise checks the lasagna in the oven and Addie stays out of the way.

She is used to having all of the attention, or none of it. To being the brief but sunlit center of a stranger's world, or a shadow at its edges. This is different. This is new.

"Hope you're all hungry," says Bea, setting lasagna and garlic bread in the center of the table.

Henry grimaces a little at the sight of the pasta, and Addie almost laughs, remembering their food truck feast. She is always hungry, the last meal nothing but a memory now, and she gratefully accepts a plate.

IX

✦ ✦ ✦ ✦
✦ ✦ ✦

A woman alone is a scandalous sight.

And yet, Addie has come to revel in the whispers. She sits in the Tuileries, skirts spread around her on the bench, and thumbs the pages of her book, and knows that she is being watched. Or rather, being stared at. But what is the point of worrying? A woman sitting alone in the sun is not a *crime*, and it's not as though the rumors will spread beyond the park. Passersby will, perhaps, be startled, and make note of the strangeness, but they will all forget before they have the chance to gossip.

She turns the page, lets her eyes travel across the printed words. These days, Addie steals books as eagerly as food, a vital piece of daily nourishment. And while she prefers novels to philosophers—adventures and escapes—this particular one is a prop, a key, designed to gain her entry to a specific door.

She has timed her presence in the park, seated herself at the garden's edge along the route she knows Madame Geoffrin tends to favor. And when the woman comes ambling down the path, she knows just what to do.

She turns the page, pretending to be engrossed.

Out of the corner of her eye, Addie can see the woman coming, her hand-maid a step behind, her arms full of flowers, and she rises to her feet, eyes still cast upon her book, turns, and makes two strides before the inevitable collision, careful not to knock the woman down, but simply startle her, while the book falls onto the path between them.

"Foolish thing," snaps Madame Geoffrin.

"I'm so sorry," says Addie at the same time. "Are you hurt?"

"No," says the woman, dropping her gaze from her attacker to the book. "And what has you so distracted?"

The handmaid scoops up the fallen book and passes it to her mistress.

Geoffrin considers the title.

Pensées Philosophiques.

"Diderot," she observes. "And who taught you to read such lofty things as this?"

"My father taught me."

"Himself? You fortunate girl."

"It was a start," answers Addie, "but a woman must take responsibility for her own education, for no man truly will."

"How true," says Geoffrin.

They are playing out a script, though the other woman does not know it. Most people have only one chance to make a first impression, but luckily, Addie has by now had several.

The older woman frowns. "But out in the park with no maidservant? No chaperone? Don't you worry that people will talk?"

A defiant smile flashes across Addie's lips. "I suppose I prefer my freedom to my reputation."

Madame Geoffrin laughs, a short sound, more surprise than amusement. "My dear, there are ways to buck the system, and ways to play it. What is your name?"

"Marie Christine," answers Addie, "La Trémoille," she adds, savoring the way the woman's eyes widen in response. She has spent a month learning the names of noble families, and their proximity to Paris, pruning the ones that might invite too many questions, finding a tree with broad enough limbs that a cousin might go unnoticed. And thankfully, while the salonnière prides herself on knowing everyone, she cannot know all of them equally.

"La Trémoille. *Mais non!*" says Madame Geoffrin, but there is no disbelief in the words, only surprise. "I shall have to chastise Charles for keeping you a secret."

"You must," says Addie with a sheepish grin, knowing it will never come to that. "Well, madame," she continues, holding her hand out for the book. "I should go. I would not want to hurt *your* reputation, too."

"Nonsense," says Geoffrin, eyes glittering with pleasure. "I am quite immune to scandal." She hands Addie back her book, but the gesture is not one of parting. "You must come to my salon. Your Diderot will be there."

Addie hesitates, the barest fraction of a second. She made a mistake, the last time they crossed paths, when she settled on an air of false humility. But she has since learned that the salonnière prefers women who stand their ground, and so this time she smiles in delight. "I would like that very much."

"Superb," says Madame Geoffrin. "Come around in an hour."

And here, her weaving must become precise. One slipped stitch, and it will fall apart.

Addie looks down at herself. "Oh," she says, letting disappointment sweep across her face. "I fear I don't have time to go home and change, but surely this won't be appropriate."

She holds her breath, waiting for the other woman to answer, and when she does, it is to extend her arm. "Don't bother," she says. "I'm sure my ladies will find something that suits you."

They walk together through the park, the maidservant trailing behind.

"Why have we never crossed paths before? We know everyone of note."

"I'm not of note," demurs Addie. "And then I'm only visiting for the summer."

"Your accent is pure Paris."

"Time and practice," she answers, and it is, of course, true.

"And yet, you are unmarried?"

Another turn, another test. Times before Addie has been widowed, has been wed, but today, she decides, she is unmarriable.

"No," she says, "I confess, I do not want a master, and I've yet to find an equal."

That earns a smile from her hostess.

The questioning continues all the way past the park and up to rue Saint-Honoré, when the woman finally peels away to ready for her salon.

Addie watches the salonnière go with some regret.

From here, she is on her own.

The maidservant leads her upstairs, and lays a dress from the nearest wardrobe out on the bed. It is a brocaded silk, a patterned shift, a layer of lace around the collar. Nothing she would choose herself, but it is very fine. Addie has seen a piece of meat trussed up with herbs and readied for the oven, and it reminds her of the current French fashion.

Addie sits before a mirror and adjusts her hair, listening to the doors open and close downstairs, the house stirring with the motions of arriving guests. She must wait for the salon to be in bloom, the rooms crowded enough that she will blend in among them.

Addie adjusts her hair a final time, and smooths her skirts, and when the sound below becomes a steady enough thing, the voices tangling with the clink of glassware, she goes down the stairs to the main room.

The first time Addie ended up in the salon, it was by luck, not staging. She was amazed to find a place where a woman was allowed to speak, or at least to listen, where she could move alone without judgment or condescension. She enjoyed the food, the drink, the conversation, and the company. Could pretend to be among friends instead of strangers.

Until she rounded a corner and saw Remy Laurent.

There he was, perched on a footstool between Voltaire and Rousseau, waving his hands as he spoke, fingers still stained gray with ink.

Seeing him was like missing a step, like fabric snagging on a nail.

A moment thrown off-balance.

Her lover had grown stiff with age, the difference between twenty-three and fifty-one marked in the lines of his face. A brow furrowed from hours reading, a pair of spectacles now balanced on his nose. But then some topic would spark the light in his eyes, and she would see the boy he'd been, the passionate youth who came to Paris to find this, great minds with great ideas.

There is no sign of him today.

Addie lifts a glass of wine from a low table, and moves from room to room like a shadow cast against the wall, unnoticed, but at ease. She listens, and makes pleasant conversation, and feels herself among the folds of history. She meets a naturalist with a fondness for marine life, and when she confesses she has never been to the sea, he spends the next half hour regaling her with tales of crustacean life, and it is a very pleasant way to pass the afternoon, and indeed the night—this night, more than most, in need of such distraction.

It has been six years—but she doesn't want to think of it, of him.

As the sun goes down, and wine is swapped for port, she is having a lovely time, enjoying the company of the scientists, the men of letters.

She should have known then, that he would ruin it.

Luc steps into the room like a gust of cool wind, dressed in shades of gray and black, from his boots to his cravat. Those green eyes, the only drop of color on him.

Six years, and relief is the wrong word for what Addie feels at the sight of him, and yet, it is the closest one. The sensation of a weight set down, a breath expelled, a body sighing in relief. There is no pleasure in it, beyond the simple, physical release—the relief of trading the unknown for the certain.

She was waiting, and now she is not.

No, now she is braced for trouble, for grief.

"Monsieur Lebois," says Madame Geoffrin, greeting her guest, and Addie wonders, for a moment, if their crossing paths is only a coincidence, if her shadow favors the salon, the minds fostering within—but the men who flock here worship progress instead of gods. And already, Luc's attention has fixed squarely on *her*, his face suffused with a coy and menacing light.

"Madame," he says in a voice loud enough to carry, "I fear you have opened your doors too wide."

Addie's stomach drops, and Madame Geoffrin draws back a little, as the conversation in the room seems to peter, still. "What do you mean?"

She tries to back away, but the salon is crowded, the path muddled by legs and chairs.

"That woman, there." Heads begin to turn in Addie's direction. "Do you know her?" Madame Geoffrin does not, of course, not anymore, but she's too well-bred to acknowledge such a misstep.

"My salon is open to many, monsieur."

"This time you have been too generous," says Luc. "That woman is a swindler and a thief. A truly wretched creature. Look," he gestures, "she even wears one of your own gowns. Better check the pockets, and make sure that she hasn't stolen more than the cloth from your back."

And just like that, he has turned her game into his own.

Addie starts toward the door, but there are men around her, on their feet.

"Stop her," announces Geoffrin, and she has no choice but to abandon it all, to rush for the door, to push past them, out of the salon and into the night.

No one comes after her, of course.

Except for Luc.

The darkness follows on her heels, chuckling softly.

She rounds on him. "I thought you had better things to do than plague me."

"And yet I find the task so entertaining."

She shakes her head. "This is nothing. You have marred one moment, ruined one night, but because of my *gift*, I have a million more; infinite chances to reinvent myself. I could walk back in right now, and your slights would be as forgotten as my face."

Mischief glints in those green eyes. "I think you'll find my word won't fade as fast as yours." He shrugs. "They will not remember you, of course. But ideas are so much wilder than memories, so much faster to take root."

It will be fifty years before she realizes that he is right.

Ideas *are* wilder than memories.

And she can plant them, too.

There is a magic to this evening.

A defiant pleasure in a simple act.

Addie spends the first hour holding her breath, bracing for catastrophe, but somewhere between the salad and the main course, between the first glass and the second, she exhales. Sitting there, between Henry and Elise, between warmth and laughter, she can almost believe that it is real, that she belongs, a normal girl beside a normal boy at a normal dinner party. She and Bea talk about art, and she and Josh talk about Paris, and she and Elise talk about wine, and Henry's hand finds her knee beneath the table, and it is all so wonderfully simple and warm. She wants to hold the night like a chocolate on her tongue, savor every second before it melts.

Only Robbie seems unhappy, even though Josh has been trying to flirt with him all night. He shifts in his seat, a performer in search of a spotlight. He drinks too much, too fast, unable to sit still for more than a few minutes. It is the same restless energy Addie saw in Henry, but tonight, *he* seems perfectly at ease.

Once, Elise goes to the bathroom, and Addie thinks that's it, the domino that tips the rest. And sure enough, when she returns to the table, Addie can see the confusion on the girl's face, but it is the kind of embarrassment you cover instead of show, and she says nothing, only shakes her head as if to clear a thought, and smiles, and Addie imagines her wondering if she's had too much to drink, imagines her pulling Beatrice aside before dessert and whispering that she cannot remember her name.

Robbie and their hostess, meanwhile, are deep in conversation.

"Bea," he whines. "Can't we just—"

"My party, my rules. When it was *your* birthday, we went to a sex club in Bushwick."

Robbie rolls his eyes. "It was an exhibitionist-themed music venue."

"It was a sex club," Henry and Bea say at the same time.

"Wait." Addie leans forward in her seat. "Is it your birthday?"

"No," says Bea emphatically.

"Beatrice hates birthdays," explains Henry. "She won't tell us when hers is.

The closest we've gotten is that it's in April. Or March. Or May. So any dinner party in the spring could conceivably be the one nearest to her birthday."

Bea sips her wine and shrugs. "I don't see the point. It's just a day. Why put all this pressure on it?"

"So you can get presents, obviously," says Robbie.

"I understand," says Addie. "The nicest days are always the ones we don't plan."

Robbie glowers. "What did you say your name was? Andy?"

And she goes to correct him, only to feel the letters lodge in her throat. The curse coils tight, strangling the word.

"It's *Addie*," says Henry. "And you're being an ass."

A nervous current runs across the table, and Elise, clearly looking to smooth the energy, cuts into a petit four and says, "This dessert is amazing, Henry."

And he says, "It was all Addie's doing."

And that is enough to tip Robbie like a glass, and send him spilling over. He shoves up from the table with a rush of breath.

"I need a smoke."

"Not in here," says Bea. "Take it to the roof."

And Addie knows that is the end of this beautiful night, the door slamming shut, because she cannot stop them, and once she's out of sight—

Josh rises. "I could use one, too."

"You just want to get out of doing dishes," says Bea, but the two of them are already heading for the door, out of sight and out of mind, and this, she thinks, is midnight, this is how the magic ends, this is how you turn back into a pumpkin.

"I should go," she says.

Bea tries to convince her to stay, says to not let Robbie get to her, and Addie says that it's not his fault, that it's been a long day, says thank you for the lovely meal, thank you for the company; and really, she was lucky to get this far, lucky to have this time, this night, this tiny glimpse of normal.

"Addie, wait," says Henry, but she kisses him, quick, and slips away, out of the apartment, and down the steps and into the dark.

She sighs, and slows, her lungs aching in the sudden cold. And despite the doors and walls between them, she can feel the weight of what she left behind, and she wishes she could have stayed, wishes that when Henry had said *Wait*, she had said, *Come with me*, but she knows it is not fair to make him choose. He is full of roots, while she has only branches.

And then she hears the steps behind her, and slows, shivers, even now, after all this time, expecting Luc.

Luc, who always knew when she brittle.

But it is not the darkness, only a boy with fogging glasses and an open coat.

"You left so fast," says Henry.

"You caught up," says Addie.

And perhaps she should feel guilty, but she is only grateful.

She has gotten good at losing things.

But Henry is still here.

"Friends are messy sometimes, aren't they?"

"Yeah," she says, even though she has no idea.

"I'm sorry," he says, nodding back at the building. "I don't know what got into him."

But Addie does.

Live long enough, and people open up like books. Robbie is a romance novel. A tale of broken hearts. He is so clearly lovesick.

"You said you were just friends."

"We are," he insists. "I love him like family, I always will. But I don't—I never . . ."

She thinks of the photo, Robbie's head bowed against Henry's cheek, thinks of the look on his face when Bea said she was his date, and wonders how he doesn't see it.

"He's still in love with you."

Henry deflates. "I know," he says. "But I can't love him back."

Can't. Not *won't.* Not *shouldn't.*

Addie looks at Henry, meets him eye to eye.

"Is there anything else you want to tell me?"

She doesn't know what she expects him to say, what truth could possibly explain his enduring presence, but for a second, when he looks back at her, there is a brief and blinding sadness.

But then he pulls her close and groans, and says, in a soft and vanquished voice, "I am so full."

And Addie laughs despite herself.

It is too cold to stand, and so they walk together through the dark, and she doesn't even notice they have reached his place until she sees the blue door. She is so tired, and he is so warm; she does not want to go, and he does not ask her to.

Addie has woken up a hundred ways.

To frost forming on her skin, and a sun so hot it should have burned. To empty places, and ones that should have been. To wars raging overhead, and the ocean rocking against the hull. To sirens, and city noise, and silence, and once, a snake coiled by her head.

But Henry Strauss wakes her with kisses.

He plants them one by one, like flower bulbs, lets them blossom on her skin. Addie smiles, and rolls against him, pulls his arms around her like a cloak.

The darkness whispers in her head, *Without me, you will always be alone.*

But instead, she listens to the sound of Henry's heart, to the soft murmur of his voice in her hair as he asks if she is hungry.

It is late, and he should be at work, but he tells her The Last Word is closed on Mondays. He can't possibly know that she remembers the little wooden sign, the hours next to every day. The shop is only closed on Thursdays.

She doesn't correct him.

They pull on clothes, and amble down to the corner shop, where Henry buys egg and cheese rolls from the counter and Addie wanders to the case in search of juice.

And that is when she hears the bell.

That is when she sees a tawny head, and a familiar face, as Robbie stumbles in. That is when her heart drops, the way it does when you miss a step, the sudden lurch of a body off-balance.

Addie has gotten good at losing—

But she isn't ready.

And she wants to stop time, to hide, to disappear.

But for once, she can't. Robbie sees Henry, and Henry sees her, and they are in a triangle of one-way streets. A comedy of memory and absence and terrible luck as Henry wraps an arm around her waist, and Robbie looks at Addie with ice in his eyes and says, "Who's this?"

"That's not funny," says Henry. "Are you still drunk?"

Robbie draws back, indignant. "I'm—what? No. I've never seen this girl. You never said you met someone."

It is a car crash in slow motion, and Addie knew it was bound to happen, the inevitable collision of people and place, time and circumstance.

Henry is an impossible thing, her strange and beautiful oasis. But he is also human, and humans have friends, have families, have a thousand strands tying them to other people. Unlike her, he has never been untethered, never existed in a void.

So it was inevitable.

But she still isn't ready.

"Fuck's sake, Rob, you *just* met her."

"Pretty sure I'd remember." Robbie's eyes darken. "But then again, these days, it's kind of hard to keep them straight."

The space between them collapses as Henry steps in. Addie gets there first, catches his hand as it lifts, pulls him back. "Henry, stop."

It was such a lovely jar she had kept them in. But the glass is cracking now. The water leaking through.

Robbie looks at Henry, stunned, betrayed. And she understands. It is not fair. It is never fair.

"Come on," she says, squeezing his hand.

Henry's attention finally drags toward her. "Please," she says. "Come with me."

They spill out into the street, the morning's peace forgotten, left behind with the OJ and the sandwiches.

Henry is shaking with anger. "I'm sorry," he says. "Robbie can be an ass but that was—"

Addie closes her eyes, sinks back against the wall. "It's not his fault." She could salvage this, hold the breaking jar, keep her fingers over the cracks. But how long? How long can she keep Henry to herself? How long can she keep him from noticing the curse?

"I don't think he remembered me."

Henry squints, clearly confused. "How could he *not*?"

Addie hesitates.

It is easy to be honest when there are no wrong words, because the words don't stick. When whatever you say belongs to only you.

But Henry is different, he hears her, he *remembers*, and suddenly every word is full of weight, honesty such a heavy thing.

She only has one chance.

She can lie to him, like she would anyone else, but if she starts, she'll never be able to stop, and even more than that—she doesn't *want* to lie to him. She's waited too long to be heard, seen.

So Addie throws herself into the truth.

"You know how some people have face blindness? They look at friends, family, people they've known their whole lives, and they don't recognize them?"

Henry frowns. "In theory, sure . . ."

"Well, I have the opposite."

"You remember everyone?"

"No," says Addie. "I mean yes, I do, but that's not what I'm talking about. It's that—people forget me. Even if we've met a hundred times. They forget."

"That doesn't make any sense."

It doesn't. Of course it doesn't.

"I know," she says, "but it's the truth. If we went back in that store right now, Robbie wouldn't remember. You could introduce me, but the moment I walked away, the moment I was out of sight, he'd forget again."

Henry shakes his head. "How? Why?"

The smallest questions. The biggest answer.

Because I was a fool.

Because I was afraid.

Because I wasn't careful.

"Because," she says, slumping back against the concrete wall. "I'm cursed."

Henry stares at her, brow furrowed behind his glasses. "I don't understand."

Addie takes a deep breath, trying to steady her nerves. And then, because she has decided to tell the truth, that's what she does.

"My name is Addie LaRue. I was born in Villon in the year 1691, my parents were Jean and Marthe, and we lived in a stone house just beyond an old yew tree . . ."

The cart rattles to a stop beside the river.

"I can take you further," says the driver, gripping the reins. "We're still a mile out."

"That's all right," she says. "I know the way."

An unknown cart and driver might draw attention, and Addie would rather return the way she left, the way she learned every inch of this place: on foot.

She pays the man and steps down, the edge of her gray cloak skimming the dirt. She hasn't bothered with luggage, has learned to travel light; or rather, to let go of things as easily as she comes into them. It is simpler that way. Things are too hard to hold on to.

"You're from here, then?" he asks, and Addie squints into the sun.

"I am," she says. "But I've been gone a long time."

The driver looks her up and down. "Not *too* long."

"You'd be surprised," she says, and then he cracks the whip, and the cart trundles off, and she is alone again in a land she knows, down to her bones. A place she has not been in fifty years.

Strange—twice as long away as she was here, and still it feels like home.

She doesn't know when she made the decision to come back, or even how, only that it had been building in her like a storm, from the time spring began to feel like summer, the heaviness rolling in like the promise of rain, until she could see the dark clouds on the horizon, hear the thunder in her head, urging her to go.

Perhaps it is a ritual of sorts, this return. A way to cleanse herself, to set Villon firmly in the past. Perhaps she is trying to let go. Or perhaps she is trying to hold on.

She will not stay, that much she knows.

Sunlight glints on the surface of the Sarthe, and for an instant, she thinks of praying, sinking her hands into the shallow stream, but she has nothing to offer the river gods now, and nothing to say to them. They did not answer when it mattered.

Around the bend, and beyond a copse of trees, Villon rises amid the shallow hills, gray stone houses nestled in the basin of the valley. It has grown, a little, widened like a man in middle age, inching outward, but it is still Villon. There is the church, and the town square, and there, beyond the center of the town, the dark green line of the woods.

She does not go through town, instead bends around it to the south.

Toward home.

The old yew tree still stands sentinel at the end of the lane. Fifty years have added a few knotted angles to its limbs, a measure of width around its base, but otherwise, it is the same. And for an instant, when all she can see is the edge of the house, time stutters, and slips, and she is twenty-three again, walking home from the town, or the river, or Isabelle's, washing on her hip, or the drawing pad under her arm, and any moment she will see her mother in the open doorway, flour powdering her wrists, will hear the steady chop of her father's ax, the soft hush of their mare, Maxime, swishing her tail and munching grass.

But then she nears the house, and the illusion crumbles back into memory. The horse is gone, of course, and in the yard, her father's workshop now leans tiredly to one side, while across the weedy grass, her parents' cottage sits, dark and still.

What did she expect?

Fifty years. Addie *knew* they would no longer be there, but the sight of this place, decaying, abandoned, still unnerves her. Her feet move of their own accord, carrying her down the dirt lane, through the yard to the sloping ruins of her father's shop.

She eases the door open—the wood is rotted, crumbling—and steps into the shed.

Sunlight streams through the broken boards, striping the dark, and the air smells of decay instead of fresh-scraped wood, earthy and sweet; every surface is covered in mold, and damp, and dust. Tools her father sharpened every day now lie abandoned, rusted brown and red. The shelves are mostly empty; the wooden birds are gone, but a large bowl sits, half-finished, beneath a curtain of cobwebs and grime.

She runs her hand through the dust, watches it gather again in her wake.

How long has he been gone?

She forces herself back out into the yard, and stops.

The house has come to life, or at least, begun to stir. A thin ribbon of smoke rises from the chimney. A window sits open, thin curtains rippling softly in the draft.

Someone is still here.

She should go, she knows she should, this place isn't hers, not anymore, but she is already crossing the yard, already reaching out to knock. Her fingers slow, remembering that night, the last one of another life.

She hovers there, on the step, willing her hand to choose—but she has already announced herself. The curtain flutters, a shadow crossing the window, and Addie can only retreat two steps, three, before the door opens a crack. Just enough to reveal a sliver of wrinkled cheek, a scowling blue eye.

"Who's there?"

The woman's voice is brittle, thin, but it still lands like a stone in Addie's chest, knocks the air away, and she is sure that even if she were mortal, her mind softened by time, she would still remember this—the sound of her mother's voice.

The door groans open, and there she is, withered like a plant in winter, gnarled fingers clutching a threadbare shawl. She is old, anciently so, but alive.

"Do I know you?" asks her mother, but there is no hint of recognition in her voice, only the doubt of the old and the unsure.

Addie shakes her head.

Afterward, she will wonder if she should have answered yes, if her mother's mind, emptied of memory, could have made room for that one truth. If she might have invited her daughter in, to sit beside the hearth, and share a simple meal, so that when Addie left, she would have something to hold on to besides the version of her mother shutting her out.

But she doesn't.

She tries to tell herself that this woman stopped being her mother when she stopped being her daughter, but of course, it doesn't work that way. And yet, it must. She has already grieved, and though the shock of the woman's face is sharp, the pain is shallow.

"What do you want?" demands Marthe LaRue.

And that is another question she can't answer, because she doesn't know. She looks past the old woman, into the dim hall that used to be her home, and only then does a strange hope rise inside her chest. If her mother is alive, then maybe, maybe—but she knows. Knows by the cobwebs in the workshop door, the dust on the half-finished bowl. Knows by the weary look in her mother's face, and the dark, disheveled state of the cottage behind her.

"I'm sorry," she says, backing away.

And the woman does not ask what for, only stares, unblinking as she goes.

The door groans shut, and Addie knows, as she walks away, that she will never see her mother again.

It is easy enough to say the words.

After all, the story has never been the hard part.

It is a secret she has tried to share so many times, with Isabelle, and Remy, with friends and strangers and anyone who might listen, and every time, she has watched their expressions flatten, their faces go blank, watched the words hang in the air before her like smoke before being blown away.

But Henry looks at her, and listens.

He listens as she tells him of the wedding, and the prayers that went unanswered, the offerings made at dawn, and dusk. Of the darkness in the woods, parading as a man, of her wish, and his refusal, and her mistake.

You can have my soul when I don't want it anymore.

Listens as she tells him of living forever, and being forgotten, and giving up. When she finishes, she holds her breath, expecting Henry to blink away the fog, to ask what she was about to say. Instead, his eyes narrow with such peculiar focus, and she realizes, heart racing, that he has heard every word.

"You made a deal?" he says. There is a detachment in his voice, an unnerving calm.

And of course, it sounds like madness.

Of course, he does not believe her.

This is how she loses him. Not to memory, but to disbelief.

And then, out of nowhere, Henry *laughs.*

He sags against a bike rack, head in his hand, and laughs, and she thinks he's gone mad, thinks she's broken something in him, thinks, even, that he is mocking her.

But it is not the kind of laughter that follows a joke.

It is too manic, too breathless.

"You made a deal," he says again.

She swallows. "Look, I know how it sounds but—"

"I believe you."

She blinks, suddenly confused. "What?"

"I believe you," he says again.

Three small words, as rare as *I remember you,* and it should be enough—but it's not. Nothing makes sense, not Henry, not this; it hasn't since the start and she's been too afraid to ask, to know, as if knowing would bring the whole dream crashing down, but she can see the cracks in his shoulders, can feel them in her chest.

Who are you? she wants to ask. *Why are you different? How do you remember when no one else can? Why do you believe I made a deal?*

In the end, she says only one thing.

"Why?"

And Henry's hands fall away from his face and he looks up at her, his green eyes fever bright, and says—

"Because I made one, too."

PART FOUR

THE MAN WHO STAYED DRY
IN THE RAIN

Title: *Open to Love*
Artist(s): Muriel Strauss (design) and Lance Harringer (manufacture)
Date: 2011
Medium: Aluminum, steel, and glass sculpture
Location: On loan from the Tisch School of the Arts
Description: Originally displayed as an interactive installation, in which the aluminum heart, perforated by small holes, hung suspended over a bucket. On a table beside the metal heart, jars of varying shapes and sizes contained different-colored liquids, some water, some alcohol, some paint, and participants were encouraged to select one of the glass jars, and empty the contents into the heart. The liquid instantly began to leak out, with a speed dependent on the viscosity of the substance poured.
Background: This sculpture formed the central piece of Strauss's senior portfolio, a collection of work on the theme of family. At the time, Strauss did not specify which member of her family was paired with which piece, but insisted that *Open to Love* was designed as "an homage to the exhaustions of serial monogamy and a testament to the dangers of unbalanced affection."
Estimated Value: Unknown; work was given to Tisch by artist for permanent installation

A boy is born with a broken heart.

The doctors go in, and piece it back together, make it whole, and the baby is sent home, lucky to be alive. They say he is better now, that he can live a normal life, and yet, as he grows up, he is convinced something is still wrong inside.

The blood pumps, the valves open and close, and on the scans and screens, everything functions as it should. But something isn't right.

They've left his heart too open.

Forgotten to close back up the armor of his chest.

And now he feels . . . too much.

Other people would call him sensitive, but it is more than that. The dial is broken, the volume turned all the way up. Moments of joy register as brief, but ecstatic. Moments of pain stretch long and unbearably loud.

When his first dog dies, Henry cries for a week. When his parents argue, and he cannot bear the violence in their words, he runs away from home. It takes more than a day to bring him back. When David throws away his childhood bear, when his first girlfriend, Abigail, stands him up at the dance, when they have to dissect a pig in class, when he loses the card his grandfather gave him before he passed, when he finds Liz cheating on him during their senior trip, when Robbie dumps him before junior year, every time, no matter how small, or how big, it feels like his heart is breaking again inside his chest.

Henry is fourteen the first time he steals a swig of his father's liquor, just to turn the volume down. He is sixteen when he swipes two pills from his mother's cabinet, just to dull the ache. He is twenty when he gets so high that he thinks he can see the cracks along his skin, the places where he's falling apart.

His heart has a draft.

It lets in light.

It lets in storms.

It lets in everything.

Time moves so fucking fast.

Blink, and you're halfway through school, paralyzed by the idea that whatever you choose to do, it means choosing *not* to do a hundred other things, so you change your major half a dozen times before finally ending up in theology, and for a while it seems like the right path, but that's really just a reflex to the pride on your parents' faces, because they assume they've got a budding rabbi, but the truth is, you have no desire to practice, you see the holy texts as stories, sweeping epics, and the more you study, the less you believe in any of it.

Blink, and you're twenty-four, and you travel through Europe, thinking—hoping—that the change will spark something in you, that a glimpse of the greater, grander world will bring your own into focus. And for a little while, it does. But there's no job, no future, only an interlude, and when it's over, your bank account is dry, and you're not any closer to anything.

Blink, and you're twenty-six, and you're called into the dean's office because he can tell that your heart's not in it anymore, and he advises you to find another path, and he assures you that you'll find your calling, but that's the whole problem, you've never felt called to any *one* thing. There is no violent push in one direction, but a softer nudge a hundred different ways, and now all of them feel out of reach.

Blink and you're twenty-eight, and everyone else is now a mile down the road, and you're still trying to find it, and the irony is hardly lost on you that in wanting to live, to learn, to find yourself, you've gotten lost.

Blink, and you meet a girl.

The first time Henry saw Tabitha Masters, she was dancing.

There must have been ten of them onstage. Henry was there to see Robbie perform, but *her* limbs had a pull, her form a kind of gravity. His gaze kept falling back toward her. She was the kind of pretty that steals your breath, and the kind you can't really capture in a photo, because the magic is in the movement. The way she moved, it was a story told with nothing but a melody and a bend of her spine, an outstretched hand, a slow descent to the darkened floor.

The first time they met was at an after-party.

Onstage, her features were a mask, a canvas for other people's art. But there, in the crowded room, all Henry could see was her smile. It took up her entire face, from her pointed chin to the line of her hair, an all-consuming kind of joy he couldn't look away from. She was laughing at something—he never found out what—and it was like someone went and turned on all the lights in the room.

And there and then, his heart began to ache.

It took Henry thirty minutes and three drinks to work up the nerve to say hello, but from that moment onward, it was easy. The rhythm and flow of frequencies in sync. And by the end of the night, he was falling in love.

He'd fallen before.

Sophia in high school.

Robbie in college.

Sarah, Ethan, Jenna—but it was always hard, messy. Full of starts and stops, wrong turns and dead ends. But with Tabitha, it was easy.

Two years.

That's how long they were together.

Two years of dinner, and breakfast, and ice cream in the park, of dance rehearsals and rose bouquets, of sleeping over at each other's place, of weekend brunch and bingeing TV shows, and trips upstate to meet his parents.

Two years of drinking less for her, and staying clean for her, dressing up for her, and buying things he couldn't afford, because he wanted to make her smile, wanted to make her happy.

Two years, and not a single fight, and now he thinks that maybe that wasn't such a good thing after all.

Two years—and somewhere between a question and an answer, it fell apart.

Down on one knee with a ring in the middle of the park, and Henry is such a fucking idiot, because she said no.

She said no, and that wasn't even the worst word.

"You're great," she said. "You really are. But you're not . . ."

And she doesn't finish, and she doesn't have to, because he knows what comes next.

You're not right.

You're not enough.

"I thought you wanted to get married."

"I do. One day."

The words, crystal clear, despite never being said.

But not to you.

And then she walked away, and now Henry is here at the bar and he's drunk, but not nearly drunk enough.

He knows, because the world is still there, because the entire night still feels too real, because everything still hurts. He's slumped forward, chin resting on his folded arms, staring through the collection of empty bottles on the table. He looks back from half a dozen warped reflections.

The Merchant is packed with bodies, a wall of white noise, so Robbie has to shout over the din.

"Fuck her."

And for some reason, coming from his ex-boyfriend, it doesn't make Henry feel much better. "I'm fine," he says, in that automatic way people always answer when you ask them how they are, even though his heart is hanging open on its hinges.

"It's for the best," adds Bea, and if anyone else had said it, she would have banished them to the corner of the bar for being trite. Ten-minute time-out for platitudes. But it's all anyone has for him tonight.

Henry finishes the glass in front of him and reaches for another.

"Slow down, kiddo," says Bea, rubbing his neck.

"I'm fine," he says again.

And they both know him well enough to know it is a lie. They know about his broken heart. They've both coaxed him through his storms. They are the best people in his life, the ones who hold him together, or at least, who keep him from falling apart. But right now, there are too many cracks. Right now, there is a chasm between their words and his ears, their hands and his skin.

They are right there, but they feel so far away.

He looks up, studying their expressions, all pity, no surprise, and a realization settles over him like a chill.

"You knew she'd say no."

The silence lasts a beat too long. Bea and Robbie share a glance, as if trying to decide who will take the lead, and then Robbie reaches across for his hand. "Henry—"

He wrenches back. "You *knew*."

He is on his feet now, nearly stumbling into the table behind him.

Bea's face crumples. "Come on. Sit back down."

"No. No. No."

"Hey," says Robbie, steadying him. "I'll walk you home."

But Henry hates the way Robbie is looking at him, so he shakes his head, even though it makes the room blur.

"No," he says. "I just want to be alone."

The biggest lie he's ever told.

But Robbie's hand falls away, and Bea shakes her head at him, and they both let Henry go.

Henry is not drunk enough.

He goes into a liquor store and buys a bottle of vodka from a guy who looks at him like he's already had enough, but also like he clearly needs it. Twists the cap off with his teeth as it begins to rain.

His phone buzzes in his pocket.

Bea, probably. Or Robbie. Nobody else would call.

He lets it ring, holds his breath until it stops. He tells himself that if they call again, he'll answer. If they call again, he'll tell them he is not okay. But the phone doesn't ring a second time.

He doesn't blame them for that, not now, not after. He knows he's not an easy friend, knows he should have seen it coming, should have—

The bottle slips through his fingers, shatters on the sidewalk, and he should leave it there, but he doesn't. He reaches to pick it up, but he loses his balance. His hand comes down on broken glass as he pushes himself back up.

It hurts, of course it hurts, but the pain is dampened a little by the vodka, by the well of grief, by his ruined heart, by everything else.

Henry fumbles for the kerchief in his pocket, the white silk stitched with a silver *T*. He hadn't wanted a box—that classic, impersonal casing that always gave away the question—but now, as he tugs the kerchief out, the ring tumbles free, goes bouncing down the damp sidewalk.

The words echo in his head.

You're great, Henry. You really are. But you're not—

He presses the kerchief to his injured hand. In seconds, the silk is stained red. Ruined.

You're not enough.

Hands are like heads; they always bleed too much.

His brother, David, was the one who told him that. David, the doctor, who's known what he wanted to be since he was ten years old.

Easy to stay on the path when the road is straight and the steps are numbered.

Henry watches the kerchief turn red, stares down at the diamond in the street and thinks of leaving it, but he can't afford to, so he forces himself to bend over and pick it up.

Take a drink every time you hear you're not enough.

Not the right fit.

Not the right look.

Not the right focus.

Not the right drive.

Not the right time.

Not the right job.

Not the right path.

Not the right future.

Not the right present.
Not the right you.
Not you.
(Not me?)
There's just something missing.
(Missing . . .)
From us.
What could I have done?
Nothing. It's just . . .
(Who you are.)
I didn't think we were serious.
(You're just too . . .
. . . sweet.
. . . soft.
. . . sensitive.)
I just don't see us ending up together.
I met someone.
I'm sorry.
It's not you.
Swallow it down.
We're not on the same page.
We're not in the same place.
It's not you.
We can't help who we fall in love with.
(And who we don't.)
You're such a good friend.
You're going to make the right girl happy.
You deserve better.
Let's stay friends.
I don't want to lose you.
It's not you.
I'm sorry.

II

And now he knows he's had too much to drink.

He was trying to reach the place where he wouldn't feel, but he thinks he might have passed it, wandered somewhere worse. His head spins, the sensation long past pleasant. He finds a couple pills in his back pocket, slipped there by his sister Muriel on her last visit. Little pink umbrellas, she told him. He swallows them dry as the drizzle turns to a downpour.

Water drips into his hair, streaking his glasses and soaking through his shirt.

He does not care.

Maybe the rain will rinse him clean.

Maybe it will wash him away.

Henry reaches his building, but can't bring himself to climb the six steps to the door, the twenty-four more to his apartment, that belongs to a past where he had a future, so he sinks onto the stoop, leans back, and looks up at the place where the rooftop meets the sky, and wonders how many steps it takes to reach the edge. Forces himself to stop, press his palms against his eyes, and tell himself it is just a storm.

Batten down the hatches, and wait it out.

It is just a storm.

It is just a storm.

It's just . . .

He is not sure when the man sits down beside him on the step.

One second, Henry is alone, and the next, he is not.

He hears the snap of a lighter, a small flame dancing at the edge of his sight. Then a voice. For just a second, it seems to come from everywhere, and then from right beside him.

"Bad night." A question without the question mark.

Henry looks over and sees a man, dressed in a slick charcoal suit beneath an open black trench, and for a horrible second, he thinks it's his brother, David. Here to remind Henry of all the ways he's a disappointment.

They have the same black hair, the same sharp jaw, but David doesn't smoke, wouldn't be caught dead in this part of Brooklyn, isn't half as handsome. The longer Henry stares at the stranger, the more resemblance fades—replaced by the awareness that the man isn't getting wet.

Even though the rain is still falling hard, still soaking through Henry's wool jacket, his cotton shirt, pressing cold hands against his skin. The stranger in the elegant suit makes no effort to shield the small flame of his lighter, or the cigarette itself. He takes a long drag and leans his elbows back against the soaking steps, and tips his chin up, as if welcoming the rain.

It never touches him.

It falls all around him, but he stays dry.

Henry thinks, then, that the man is a ghost. Or a wizard. Or, most likely, a hallucination.

"What do you want?" asks the stranger, still studying the sky, and Henry cringes, on instinct, but there's no anger in the man's voice. If anything, it's curious, questing. His head drifts back down, and he looks at Henry with the greenest eyes he's ever seen. So bright they glitter in the dark.

"Right now, in this moment," says the stranger. "What do you want?"

"To be happy," answers Henry.

"Ah," says the stranger, smoke sliding between his lips, "no one can give you that."

Not you.

Henry has no idea who this man is, or if he's even real, and he knows, even through the fog of drink and drug, that he should get up, and go inside. But he can't will his legs to move, the world is too heavy, and the words keep coming now, spilling out of him.

"I don't know what they want from me," he says. "I don't know who they want me to be. They tell you to be yourself, but they don't mean it, and I'm just tired . . ." His voice breaks. "I'm tired of falling short. Tired of being . . . it's not that I'm alone. I don't mind alone. But this—" His fingers knot in his shirtfront. "It hurts."

A hand rises beneath his chin.

"Look at me, Henry," says the stranger, who never asked his name.

Henry looks up, meets those luminous eyes. Sees something curl in them, like smoke. The stranger is beautiful, in a wolfish way. Hungry and sharp. That emerald gaze slides over him.

"You're perfect," the man murmurs, stroking a thumb along Henry's cheek.

His voice is silk, and Henry leans into it, into the touch, nearly loses his balance when the man's hand falls away.

"Pain can be beautiful," he says, exhaling a cloud of smoke. "It can transform. It can create."

"But I don't want to be in pain," says Henry hoarsely. "I want—"

"You want to be loved."

A small, empty sound, half cough, half sob. "Yes."

"Then be loved."

"You make it sound simple."

"It is," says the stranger. "If you're willing to pay."

Henry chokes out a laugh. "I'm not looking for that kind of love."

The dark flicker of a smile plays across the stranger's face. "And I'm not talking about money."

"What else is there?"

The stranger reaches out and rests his hand against Henry's sternum.

"The one thing every human has to give."

For an instant, Henry thinks the stranger wants his heart, as broken as it is—and then he understands. He works at a bookstore, has read enough epics, devoured the allegories and myths. Hell, Henry spent the first two-thirds of his life studying scripture, and he grew up on a steady diet of Blake, Milton, and Faust. But it has been a long time since any of them felt like more than stories.

"Who are you?" he asks.

"I am the one who sees kindling and coaxes it to flame. The nurturer of all human potential."

He stares at the stranger, still dry despite the storm, a devil's beauty in a familiar face, and those eyes, suddenly more serpentine, and Henry knows this for what it is: a waking dream. He's had them once or twice before, a consequence of aggressive self-medication.

"I don't believe in devils," he says, rising to his feet. "And I don't believe in souls."

The stranger cranes his head. "Then you have nothing to lose."

The bone-deep sadness, kept at bay the last few minutes by the stranger's easy company, now rushes back. Pressure against cracking glass. He sways a little, but the stranger steadies him.

Henry doesn't remember seeing the other man stand, but now they're eye to eye. And when the devil speaks again, there's a new depth to his voice, a steady warmth, like a blanket drawn around his shoulders. Henry feels himself lean into it.

"You want to be loved," says the stranger, "by all of them. You want to be *enough* for all of them. And I can give that to you, for the price of something you won't even miss." The stranger holds out his hand. "Well, Henry? What do you say?"

And he doesn't think any of this is real.

So it doesn't matter.

Or perhaps the man in the rain is right.

He just has nothing left to lose.

In the end, it's easy.

As easy as stepping off the edge.

And falling.

Henry takes his hand, and the stranger squeezes, hard enough to reopen the cuts along his palm. But at last, he doesn't feel it. He doesn't feel anything, as the darkness smiles, and says a single word.

"Deal."

There are a hundred kinds of silence.

There's the thick silence of places long sealed shut, and the muffled silence of ears stoppered up. The empty silence of the dead, and the heavy silence of the dying.

There is the hollow silence of a man who has stopped praying, and the airy silence of an empty synagogue, and the held-breath silence of someone hiding from themselves.

There is the awkward silence that fills the space between people who don't know what to say. And the taut silence that falls over those who do, but don't know where or how to start.

Henry doesn't know what kind of silence this is, but it is killing him.

He began to talk outside the corner shop, and kept talking as they walked, because it was easier for him to speak when he had somewhere to look besides her face. The words spilled out of him as they reached the blue door of his building, as they climbed the stairs, as they moved through the apartment, and now the truth fills the air between them, heavy as smoke, and Addie isn't saying anything.

She sits on the sofa, her chin in her hand.

Outside the window, the day just carries on as if nothing's changed, but it feels like everything has, because Addie LaRue is immortal, and Henry Strauss is damned.

"Addie," he says, when he cannot stand it anymore. "Please say something."

And she looks up at him, eyes shining, not with some spell, but tears, and he does not know at first if she is heartbroken or happy.

"I couldn't understand," she says. "No one has ever remembered. I thought it was an accident. I thought it was a trap. But you're not an accident, Henry. You're not a trap. You remember me because you made a deal." She shakes her head. "Three hundred years spent trying to break this curse, and Luc did the one thing I never expected." She wipes the tears away, and breaks into a smile.

"He made a *mistake*."

There is such triumph in her eyes. But Henry doesn't understand.

"So our deals cancel out? Is that why we're immune to them?"

Addie shakes her head. "I'm not immune, Henry."

He cringes back, as if struck. "But my deal doesn't work on you."

Addie softens, takes his hand. "Of course it does. Your deal and mine, they nest like Russian dolls together in a shell. I look at you, and I see *exactly* what I want. It's just that what *I* want has nothing to do with looks, or charm, or success. It would sound awful, in another life, but what I want most—what I *need*—has nothing to do with *you* at all. What I want, what I've always truly wanted, is for someone to remember me. That's why you can say my name. That's why you can go away, and come back, and still know who I am. And that's why I can look at *you*, and see you as you are. And it is enough. It will always be enough."

Enough. The word unravels between them, opening at his throat. It lets in so much air.

Enough.

He sinks onto the couch beside her. Her hand slides through his, their fingers knotting.

"You said you were born in 1691," he muses. "That makes you . . ."

"Three hundred and twenty-three," she says.

Henry whistles. "I've never been with an older woman." Addie laughs. "You do look very, very good for your age."

"Why thank you."

"Tell me about it," he says.

"About what?"

"I don't know. Everything. Three hundred years is such a long time. You were there for wars and revolutions. You saw trains and cars and planes and televisions. You witnessed *history* as it was happening."

Addie frowns. "I guess so," she says, "but I don't know; history is something you look back on, not something you really feel at the time. In the moment, you're just . . . living. I didn't want to live forever. I just wanted to *live*."

She curls into him, and they lie, heads together on the couch, intertwined like lovers in a fable, and a new silence settles over them, light as a summer sheet.

And then she says, "How long?"

His head rolls toward her. "What?"

"When you made your deal," she says, voice careful and light, a foot testing icy ground. "How long did you make it for?"

Henry hesitates, and looks up at the ceiling instead of her.

"A lifetime," he says, and it is not a lie, but a shadow crosses Addie's face.

"And he agreed?"

Henry nods, and pulls her back against him, exhausted by everything he's said, and everything he hasn't.

"A lifetime," she whispers.

The words hang between them in the dark.

Addie is so many things, thinks Henry. But she is not forgettable.

How could anyone forget this girl, when she takes up so much space? She fills the room with stories, with laughter, with warmth and light.

He has put her to work, or rather, she has put herself to work, restocking and reshelving while he helps customers.

She has called herself a ghost, and she may be one to other people, but Henry cannot look anywhere but at her.

She moves among the books as if they're friends. And perhaps, in a way, they are. They are, he supposes, a part of her story, another thing she's touched. Here, she says, is a writer she once met, and here is an idea she had, here a book that she read when it first came out. Now and then, Henry glimpses sadness, glimpses longing, but they are only flashes, and then she redoubles, brightens, launching into another story.

"Did you know Hemingway?" he asks.

"We met, once or twice," she says, with a smile, "but Colette was cleverer."

Book trails Addie like a shadow. He has never seen the cat so invested in another human, and when he asks, she draws a handful of treats from her pocket with a sheepish grin.

Their eyes meet now across the store, and he knows she said she's not immune, that their deals simply work together, but the fact remains that there is no shimmer in those brown eyes. Her gaze is clear. A lighthouse through the fog.

She smiles, and Henry's world goes brighter. She turns away, and it is dark again.

A woman approaches the checkout desk, and Henry drags himself back.

"Find everything you need?" Her eyes are already milky with shine.

"Oh yes," the woman says with a warm smile, and he wonders what she sees instead of *Henry*. Is he a son, or a lover, a brother, a friend?

Addie leans her elbows on the counter.

She taps the book he's been turning through between customers. A collection of modern candids in New York.

"I noticed the cameras at your place," she says. "And the photographs. They're yours, aren't they?"

Henry nods, resists the urge to say *It's just a hobby*, or rather, *It was a hobby, once.*

"You're very good," she says, which is nice, especially coming from her. And he's fine, he knows; maybe even a little better than fine, sometimes.

He took headshots for Robbie back in college, but that was because Robbie couldn't afford a real photographer. Muriel called his photos *cute*. Subversive in their conventional way.

But Henry wasn't trying to subvert anything. He just wanted to capture *something*.

He looks down at the book.

"There's this family photo," he says, "not the one in the hall, this other one, from back when I was six or seven. That day was awful. Muriel put gum in David's book and I had a cold, and my parents were fighting right up until the flash went off. And in the photo, we all look so . . . happy. I remember seeing that picture and realizing that photographs weren't real. There's no context, just the illusion that you're showing a snapshot of a life, but life isn't snapshots, it's fluid. So photos are like fictions. I loved that about them. Everyone thinks photography is truth, but it's just a very convincing lie."

"Why did you stop?"

Because time doesn't work like photos.

Click, and it stays still.

Blink, and it leaps forward.

He always thought of taking photos as a hobby, an art class credit, and by the time he figured out that it was something you could *do*, it was too late. Or at least, it felt that way.

He was too many miles behind.

So he gave up. Put the cameras on the shelf with the rest of the abandoned hobbies. But something about Addie makes him want to pick one up again.

He doesn't have a camera with him, of course, only his cell phone, but these days, that is good enough. He lifts it up, framing Addie at rest, the bookshelves rising at her back.

"It won't work," she says, right as Henry takes the picture. Or tries. He taps the screen, but there's no click, no capture. He tries again, and this time the phone takes the photo, but it is a blur.

"I told you," she says softly.

"I don't get it," he says. "It was so long ago. How could he have predicted film, or phones?"

Addie manages a sad smile. "It's not the technology he tampered with. It's me."

Henry pictures the stranger, smiling in the dark.

He sets the phone down.

Henry wakes to the blare of morning traffic.

He winces at the sound of car horns, the sunlight streaming through the window. He reaches for the memories of last night, and for a second, comes up with nothing, a flat black slate, a cottony silence. But when he squeezes his eyes shut, the darkness cracks, gives way to a wave of pain and sadness, a medley of broken bottles and heavy rain, and a stranger in a black suit, a conversation that must have been a dream.

Henry knows that Tabitha said no—that part was real, the memory too stinging to be anything but true. That is, after all, why he started drinking. The drinking is what led him home through the rain, to rest on the stoop before going inside, and that is where the stranger—but no, that part didn't happen.

The stranger and their conversation, that was the stuff of stories, a clear subconscious commentary, his demons played out in mental desperation.

A headache thuds dully in Henry's skull, and he scrubs at his eyes with the back of one hand. A metal weight knocks against his cheek. He squints up and sees a dark leather band around his wrist. An elegant analog watch, with gold numerals set against an onyx ground. On its face, a single golden hand rests the barest fraction off of midnight.

Henry has never worn a watch.

The sight of it, heavy and unfamiliar on his wrist, reminds Henry of a shackle. He sits up, clawing at the clasp, consumed by the sudden fear that it is bound to him, that it won't come off—but at the slightest pressure, the clasp comes free, and the watch tumbles onto the twisted duvet.

It lands facedown, and there, on the reverse, Henry sees two words etched in hairline script.

Live well.

He scrambles out of the bed, away from the watch, stares at the timepiece as if expecting it to attack. But it just lies there, silent. His heart knocks inside his chest, so loud he can hear it, and he is back in the dark, rain dripping through his hair as the stranger smiles and holds out his hand.

Deal.

But that didn't happen.

Henry looks at his palm and sees the shallow cuts, crusted over with blood. Notices the drops of brownish red dotting the sheets. The broken bottle. That was real, then, too. But the devil's hand in his, that was a fever dream. Pain can do that, creep from waking hours into sleep. Once, when he was nine or ten, Henry had strep throat, the pain so bad that every time he drifted off to sleep, he dreamed of swallowing hot coals, of being trapped in burning buildings, the smoke clawing down his throat. The mind, trying to make sense of suffering.

But the watch—

Henry can hear a low, rhythmic knocking as he holds it to his ear. It doesn't make any other sound (one night, soon, he will take the thing apart, and find the body empty of cogs, empty of anything to explain the creeping forward motion).

And yet, it is solid, heavy even, in his hand. It feels real.

The knocking gets louder, and then he realizes it's not coming from the watch at all. It's just the solid thud of knuckles on wood, someone at his door. Henry holds his breath, waits to see if it will stop, but it doesn't. He backs away from the watch, the bed, grabs a clean shirt from the back of a chair.

"I'm coming," he mutters, dragging it over his head. The collar snags on his glasses, and he catches his shoulder on the doorframe, swearing softly, hoping all the way from the bedroom to the front door that the person be-yond will give up, go away. They don't, so Henry opens the door, expecting to see Bea or Robbie or maybe Helen down the hall, looking again for her cat.

But it's his sister, Muriel.

Muriel, who has been to Henry's place exactly twice in the last five years. And once it was because she had too much herbal tea at a lunch meeting and couldn't make it back to Chelsea.

"What are you doing here?" he asks, but she is already brushing past him, unwinding a scarf that's more decorative than functional.

"Does family need a reason?"

The question is clearly rhetorical.

She turns, her eyes sweeping over him, the way he imagines they sweep over exhibits, and he waits for her usual assessment, some variation of *you look like shit.*

Instead his sister says, "You're looking good," which is strange, because Muriel has never been one to lie (she "doesn't like to encourage fallacy in a world rife with empty speech") and a passing glance in the hall mirror is enough to confirm that Henry does, in fact, look almost as rough as he feels.

"Beatrice texted me last night when you didn't answer your phone," she continues. "She told me about Tabitha, and the whole no-go. I'm sorry, Hen."

Muriel hugs him, and Henry doesn't know where to put his hands. They end up hovering in the air around her shoulders until she lets go.

"What happened? Was she cheating?" And Henry wishes the answer were yes, because the truth is worse, the truth is that he simply wasn't interesting enough. "It doesn't matter," continues Muriel. "Fuck her, you deserve better."

He almost laughs, because he can't count how many times Muriel pointed out that Tabitha was out of his league.

She glances around at the apartment.

"Did you redecorate? It's really cozy in here."

Henry surveys the living room, dotted with candles and art and other remnants of Tabitha. The clutter is his. The style was hers. "No."

His sister is still standing. Muriel never sits, never settles, never even perches.

"Well, I can see you're fine," she says, "but next time, answer your phone. Oh," she adds, taking her scarf back, already halfway to the door. "Happy New Year."

It takes him a moment to remember.

Rosh Hashanah.

Muriel sees the confusion on his face and grins. "You would have made such a bad rabbi."

He doesn't disagree. Henry would normally go home—they both would—but David couldn't get away from his hospital shift this year, so their parents had made other plans.

"Are you going to temple?" he asks now.

"No," says Muriel. "But there's a show uptown tonight, a kinky burlesque hybrid, and I'm pretty sure there's going to be some fire play. I'll light a candle on someone."

"Mom and Dad would be so proud," he says dryly, but in truth, he suspects they would. Muriel Strauss can do no wrong.

She shrugs. "We all celebrate in our own way." She twists the scarf back into place with a flourish. "I'll see you for Yom Kippur."

Muriel reaches for the door, then turns back toward him, and stretches up to ruffle Henry's hair. "My little storm cloud," she says. "Don't let it get too dark in there."

And then she's gone, and Henry sags back against the door, dazed, tired, and thoroughly confused.

Henry has heard that grief has stages.

He wonders if the same is true for love.

If it's normal to feel lost, and angry, and sad, hollow and somehow, horribly, relieved. Maybe it's the thud of the hangover muddling all the things he *should* be feeling, churning them into what he *does*.

He stops at Roast, the bustling coffee shop a block shy of the store. It has good muffins, halfway decent drinks, and terrible service, which is pretty much par for the course in this part of Brooklyn, and sees Vanessa working at the till.

New York is full of beautiful people, actors and models moonlighting as bartenders and baristas, making drinks to cover rent until their first big break. He's always assumed Vanessa is one of those, a waifish blonde with a small infinity symbol tattooed inside one wrist. He also *assumes* her name is Vanessa—that's the name on the tag pinned to her apron—but she's never actually told him. Has never said *anything* to him, for that matter, besides, "What can I get you?"

Henry will stand at the counter, and she will ask his order and his name (even though he has been coming here six days a week for the last three years, and she's been there for two of them), and from the time she punches in his flat white to the time she writes his name on the cup and calls out for the next order, she will never look at him. Her gaze will flit from his shirt to the computer to his chin, and Henry will feel like he isn't even there.

That's how it always goes.

Only, today, it doesn't.

Today, when she takes his order, she looks up.

It's such a small change, the difference of two inches, maybe three, but now he can see her eyes, which are a startling blue, and the barista looks at him, not his chin. She holds his gaze, and smiles.

"Hi there," she says, "what can I get you?"

He orders a flat white, and says his name, and that is where it ends.

Then it doesn't.

"Fun day planned?" she asks, making small talk as she writes his name on the cup.

Vanessa has never made small talk with him before.

"Just work," he says, and her attention flicks back to his face. This time he catches a faint shimmer—a *wrongness*—in her eyes. It's a trick of the light, it must be, but for a second, it looks like frost, or fog.

"What do you do?" she asks, sounding genuinely interested, and he tells her about The Last Word, and her eyes light up a little. She has always been a reader, and she cannot think of anywhere better than a bookstore. When he pays for the order, their fingers brush, and she cuts him another glance. "See you tomorrow, Henry."

The barista says his name like she stole it, mischief tugging at her smile.

And he can't tell if she's flirting until he gets his drink, and sees the little black arrow she's drawn, pointing to the bottom, and when he tips it up to see, his heart gives a little thud like an engine turning over.

She's written her name and number on the bottom of the cup.

At The Last Word, Henry unlocks the grate, and the door, while finishing his coffee. He turns the sign and goes through the motions of feeding Book and opening the store and shelving new stock until the bell chimes, announcing his first customer.

Henry winds through the stacks to find an older woman, toddling between the aisles, from HISTORICAL to MYSTERY to ROMANCE and back again. He gives her a few minutes, but when she makes the loop a third time, he steps in.

"Can I help you?"

"I don't know, I don't know," she murmurs, half to herself, but then she turns to look at him, and something changes in her face. "I mean, yes, please, I hope so." There's the faintest shine to her eyes, a rheumy glow, as she explains that she's looking for a book she's already read.

"These days, I can't remember what I've read, and what I haven't," she explains, shaking her head. "Everything sounds familiar. All the covers look the same. Why do they do that? Why do they make everything like everything else?"

Henry assumes it has to do with marketing and trends, but he knows that's probably not helpful to say. Instead he asks if she remembers anything about it.

"Oh, let's see. It was a big book. It was about life and death, and history."

That doesn't exactly narrow it down, but Henry is used to the lack of details. The number of people who've come in, looking for something they've seen, able to supply nothing beyond "The cover was red," or "I think it had the word *girl* in the title."

"It was sad, and lovely," explains the old woman. "I'm sure it was set in England. Oh dear. My mind. I think it had a rose on the cover."

She looks around at the shelves, wrings her papery hands together. And she's clearly not going to decide, so he does. Desperately uncomfortable, he tugs a thick historical from the nearest fiction shelf.

"Was it this?" he asks, offering *Wolf Hall*. But he knows the moment it's in his hand that it's not the one. There's a poppy on the cover, not a rose, and there's nothing particularly sad or lovely about the life of Thomas Cromwell, even if the writing is beautiful, poignant. "Never mind," he says, already reaching to put it back when the old woman's face lights up with pleasure.

"That's it!" She grabs his arm with bony fingers. "That's *exactly* what I was looking for." Henry has a hard time believing it, but the woman's joy is so clear that he begins to doubt himself.

He is about to ring her up when he remembers. Atkinson. *Life After Life.* A book about life and death and history, sad and lovely, set in England, with a twinned rose on the cover.

"Wait," he says, ducking around the corner and down the recent fiction aisle to retrieve the book.

"Is *this* it?"

The woman's face brightens, exactly as it did before. "Yes! You clever thing, that's just the one," she says, with the same conviction.

"Happy I could help," he says, unsure if he did.

She decides to take both books, says she's sure that she will love them.

The rest of the morning is just as strange.

A middle-aged man comes in searching for a thriller, and leaves with all five titles that Henry recommends. A college student comes looking for a book on Japanese mythology, and when Henry apologizes for not having it, she practically trips over herself to say it's not his fault, and insists on letting him order it in for her, even though she isn't sure about the class. A guy with a model's build and a jaw sharper than a penknife comes to peruse their fantasy section, and he writes his e-mail on the receipt beneath his signature when he pays.

Henry feels off-balance, the way he did when Muriel told him he looked good. It's like *déjà vu,* and not like *déjà vu* at all, because the feeling is entirely new. It's like April Fool's, when the rules change, and everything's a game, and everyone else is in on it, and he's still marveling over the last encounter, face a little flushed, when Robbie bursts in through the door, chime ringing in his wake.

"Oh my god," he says, throwing his arms around Henry, and for a moment, he thinks something awful must have happened, before realizing that it already happened to *him.*

"It's okay," says Henry, and of course it's not, but today has been so weird that everything before it feels a little like a dream. Or maybe this is the dream? If it is, he's not all that eager to wake up. "It's okay," he says again.

"It doesn't have to be okay," says Robbie. "I just want you to know I'm here, I would have been there last night, too—I wanted to come over when you didn't answer your phone, but Bea said we should give you space, and I don't know why I listened, I'm sorry."

It comes out in a single stream of words.

Robbie's grip tightens as he talks, and Henry savors the embrace. They fit together with the familiar comfort of a well-worn coat. The hug lingers a little too long. Henry clears his throat and pulls back, and Robbie gives an awkward laugh and turns away, his face catching the light, and Henry notices a fine streak of purple along Robbie's temple, right where it meets his sandy hairline.

"You're glittering."

Robbie scrubs halfheartedly at the makeup. "Oh, rehearsal."

There's an odd shine in Robbie's eyes, a glassiness Henry knows too well, and he wonders if Robbie's on something, or if it's simply been awhile since he slept. Back in college, Robbie would get so high on drugs or dreams or big ideas that he'd have to burn all the energy out of his system, and then he'd crash.

The door chimes.

"Son of a bitch," announces Bea, slamming her satchel down on the counter. "Ostrich-minded motherfucker."

"Customers," warns Henry, even though the only one currently nearby is a deaf older man, a regular named Michael who frequents the horror section.

"To what do we owe this tantrum?" asks Robbie cheerfully. Drama always puts him in a good mood.

"My asshole adviser," she says, storming past them toward the art and art history section. They share a look, and trail after her.

"He didn't like the proposal?" asks Henry.

Bea has been trying to get a dissertation topic approved for the better part of a year.

"He turned it down!" She whips down an aisle, nearly toppling a pile of magazines. Henry follows behind her, doing his best to right the destruction in her wake.

"He said it was too *esoteric*. As if he'd know the meaning of the word if it blew him."

"Use it in a sentence?" asks Robbie, but she ignores him, reaching up to pull down a book.

"That closed-minded—"

And another.

"—stale-brained—"

And another.

"—*corpse*."

"This isn't a library," says Henry as she carries the pile to the low leather chair in the corner and slumps into it, startling the orange lump of fur from between a pair of worn pillows.

"Sorry, Book," she mutters, lifting the cat gingerly onto the back of the old chair, where he does his best impression of an inconvenienced bread loaf. Bea continues to emit a low stream of curses as she turns the pages.

"I know just what we need," says Robbie, turning toward the storeroom. "Doesn't Meredith keep a stash of whisky in the back?"

And even though it's only 3 P.M., Henry doesn't protest. He sinks onto the floor, sits with his back to the nearest shelf, legs stretched long, feeling suddenly, unbearably tired.

Bea looks up at him, sighs. "I'm sorry," she starts, but Henry waves her away.

"Please, continue trashing your advisor and my art history section. *Some-one* has to behave normally."

But she closes the book, adds it back to the pile, and joins Henry on the floor.

"Can I tell you something?" Her voice goes up at the end, but he knows it's not a question. "I'm glad you broke it off with Tabitha."

A lance of pain, like the cut across his palm. "She broke it off with me."

Bea waves her hand as if that small detail doesn't matter. "You deserve someone who loves you as you are. The good and the bad and the mad-dening."

You want to be loved. You want to be enough.

Henry swallows. "Yeah, well, being me hasn't worked out so well."

Bea leans toward him. "But that's the thing, Henry, you haven't *been* you. You waste so much time on people who don't deserve you. People who don't know you, because you don't let them know you." Bea cups his face, that strange shimmer in her eyes. "Henry, you're smart, and kind, and infuriat-ing. You hate olives and people who talk during movies. You love milkshakes and people who can laugh until they cry. You think it's a crime to turn ahead to the end of a book. When you're angry you get quiet, and when you're sad you get loud, and you hum when you're happy."

"And?"

"And I haven't heard you hum in *years*." Her hands fall away. "But I've seen you eat a shit ton of olives."

Robbie comes back, holding the bottle and three mugs. The Last Word's only customer toddles out, and then Robbie shuts the door behind him, turning the sign to CLOSED. He comes and sits between Henry and Bea on the floor and uncorks the bottle with his teeth.

"What are we drinking to?" asks Henry.

"To new beginnings," says Robbie, eyes still shining as he fills the cups.

The bell chimes and Bea strides in.

"Robbie wants to know if you're avoiding him," she says, in lieu of hello. Henry's heart sinks. The answer is yes, of course, and no. He cannot shake the look of hurt in Robbie's eyes, but it doesn't excuse the way he acted, or maybe it does.

"I'll take that as a yes," says Bea. "And where have you been hiding?"

Henry wants to say, *I saw you at the dinner party,* but wonders if she has forgotten the entire night, or just the parts that Addie touched.

Speaking of. "Bea, this is Addie."

Beatrice turns toward her, and for a second, and only a second, Henry thinks that she remembers. It's the way she's looking at Addie, as if she is a piece of art, but one that Bea has encountered before. Despite everything, Henry expects her to nod, to say, "Oh, good to see you again"—instead, Bea smiles. She says, "You know, there's something timeless about your face," and he's rocked by the strangeness of the echo, the force of the *déjà vu.*

But Addie only smiles, and says, "I've heard that before."

As Bea continues to study Addie, Henry studies her.

She has always been ruthlessly polished, but today there's neon paint on her fingers, a kiss of gold at her temple, what looks like powdered sugar on her sleeve.

"What have you been *doing*?" he asks.

She looks down. "Oh, I was at the Artifact!" she says, as if that's supposed to mean something. Seeing his confusion, she explains. The Artifact is, according to Beatrice, part carnival and part art exhibit, an interactive medley of installations on the High Line.

As Bea talks about mirrored chambers and glass domes full of stars, sugar clouds, the plume from pillow fights, and murals made of a thousand strangers' notes, Addie brightens, and Henry thinks it must be hard to surprise a girl who's lived three hundred years.

So when she turns to him, eyes bright, and says, "We have to go," there's nothing he'd rather do. There is, of course, the matter of the store, the fact he is the sole employee, and there are still four hours until closing. But he has an idea.

Henry grabs a bookmark, the store's only piece of merchandise, and begins writing on the back side. "Hey Bea," he says, pushing the makeshift card across the counter. "Can you close up?"

"I have a life," she says, but then she looks down at Henry's tight and slanting script.

The Library of The Last Word.

Bea smiles, and pockets the card.

"Have fun," she says, waving them out.

Sometimes Henry wishes he had a cat.

He supposes he could just adopt Book, but the tabby feels indivisible from The Last Word, and he can't shake the superstitious belief that if he tried to extricate the ancient cat from the secondhand shop, it would turn to dust before he got it home.

Which is, he knows, a morbid way of thinking about people and places, or in this case pets and places, but it's dusk, and he drank a little too much whisky, and Bea had to go teach a class and Robbie had a friend's show, so he's alone again, heading back to an empty apartment, wishing he had a cat or something waiting for him to come home.

He tests out the phrase as he walks in.

"Hi, kitty, I'm home," he says, before realizing that it makes him a twenty-eight-year-old bachelor talking to an imaginary pet, and that feels infinitely worse.

He grabs a beer from the fridge, stares down at the bottle opener, and realizes it belongs to Tabitha. A pink and green thing in the shape of a *lucha libre* from a trip she took to Mexico City last month. He tosses it aside, opens a kitchen drawer looking for another, and finds a wooden spoon, a dance company magnet, a handful of ridiculous bendy straws, looks around, then, sees a dozen more things strewn around the apartment, all of them hers. He digs up a box of books and turns them out, begins filling it again with photographs, notecards, paperbacks, a pair of ballet flats, a mug, a bracelet, a hairbrush, a photograph.

He finishes the first beer, opens a second on the edge of the counter, and keeps going, moving from room to room, less a methodic procession than a lost wander. An hour later, the box is only half-full, but Henry's losing steam. He doesn't want to do this anymore, doesn't even want to *be* there, in an apartment that somehow feels both empty and cluttered. There's too much space to think. There's not enough to breathe.

Henry sits between the empty beer bottles and the half-filled box for several minutes, knee bouncing, and then surges to his feet, and goes out.

* * *

The Merchant is busy.

It always is—one of those neighborhood bars whose success owes more to its sheer proximity than to the quality of its drinks. A local institution. Most of the people who frequent the Merchant refer to it simply as "the bar."

Henry weaves through the crowd, grabs a stool at the edge of the counter, hoping the ambient noise of the place will make him feel a little less alone.

Mark's on shift tonight, a fifty-something with gray sideburns and a catalog smile. It normally takes a good ten minutes to flag him down, but tonight, the bartender comes straight to him, ignoring the queue. Henry orders tequila, and Mark comes back with a bottle and a pair of shots.

"On the house," he says, pouring himself a matching glass.

Henry manages a wan smile. "Do I look that rough?"

But there's no pity in Mark's gaze, only a strange and subtle light.

"You look great," he says, just like Muriel, and it's the first time he's said more than a single line, his answers usually limited to drink orders and nods.

Their glasses knock together, and Henry orders a second, and a third. He knows he is drinking too much too fast, piling liquor on top of the beers from home, the whisky he'd poured at work.

A girl comes up to the bar, and glances at Henry.

She looks away, and then back again, as if seeing him for the first time. And there it is again, that shine, a film of light over her eyes as she leans in, and he can't seem to catch her name, but it doesn't matter.

They do their best to talk over the noise, her hand resting at first on his forearm, then his shoulder, before sliding through his hair.

"Come home with me," she says, and he's so caught by the longing in her voice, the open want. But then her friends come along and peel her away, their own eyes shining as they say *Sorry*, say *You're such a good guy*, say *Have a great night*.

Henry slides off the stool and heads for the bathroom, and this time, he can feel the ripple, the heads turning toward him.

A guy catches his arm and says something about a photography project, how he'd be a perfect fit, before sliding him his card.

Two women try to draw him into the circle of their conversation.

"I wish I had a son like you," says one.

"*Son?*" says the other with a raucous laugh as he twists free, escapes down the hall and into the toilets.

Braces himself against the counter.

He has no idea what's happening.

He thinks back to the coffee shop that morning, Vanessa's number on the bottom of the cup. To the customers in the store, all so eager for his help. To

Muriel, who told him he looked well. To the pale fog, like candle smoke, in all of their eyes.

He looks down at the watch on his wrist, glinting in the bathroom light, and for the first time, he's certain that it's real.

That the man in the rain was real.

The deal was real.

"Hey."

He looks up and sees a guy, glassy eyed and smiling at Henry like they are the best of friends.

"You look like you could use a bump."

He holds out a little glass jar, and Henry stares at the tiny column of powder inside.

He was twelve the first time he got high.

Someone handed him a joint behind the bleachers, and the smoke burned his lungs, and he almost threw up, but then everything went a little . . . soft. Weed made space in his skull, eased the nervous terror in his heart. But he couldn't control the places it took his head. Valium and Xanax were better, dulling everything at once, but he's always stayed away from the harder stuff, out of fear—not the fear that something would go wrong. Just the opposite: the fear it would feel right. The fear of the slip, the slide, of knowing he wouldn't be strong enough to stop.

It's never been the high he craved, anyway, not exactly.

It's just the quiet.

That happy side effect.

He tried to be better, for Tabitha.

But Tabitha's gone, and it doesn't matter, anyway.

Not anymore.

Now Henry just wants to feel good.

He taps the powder onto his thumb, has no idea if he's doing it right, but he inhales, and it hits like a sudden, jolting cold, and then—the world opens. The details clear, the colors brighten, and somehow everything gets sharp and fuzzy at the same time.

Henry must have said something, because the guy laughs. And then he reaches out, and wipes a fleck from Henry's cheek, and the contact is like static shock, a spark of energy where skin meets skin.

"You're perfect," says the stranger, fingers drifting down his jaw, and Henry flushes with a dizzy heat that makes him need to move.

"Sorry," he says, backing out into the hall.

He slumps against the darkened wall, waits for the world to steady.

"Hey."

He looks up and sees a guy with his arm slung around a girl's shoulders, both of them long and lean and feline.

"What's your name?" asks the guy.

"Henry."

"Henry," echoes the girl with a catlike smile.

She looks at him with such obvious desire, he actually rocks back on his heels. No one has ever looked at him that way. Not Tabitha. Not Robbie. No one—not on the first date, or in the middle of sex, or when he got down on one knee . . .

"I'm Lucia," she says. "This is Benji. And we've been looking for you."

"What did I do?" he asks.

Her smile tilts. "Nothing yet."

She bites her lip, and the guy looks at Henry, his face slack with longing, and at first he doesn't realize what they're talking about.

And then he does.

Laughter rolls through him, a strange, unbridled thing.

He's never been in a threesome, unless you count that one time in school when he and Robbie and one of their friends got incredibly drunk and he's still not entirely sure how far things went.

"Come with us," she says, holding out her hand.

And a dozen excuses spill through his mind and then out again as Henry follows them home.

God, it feels good to be wanted.

Everywhere he goes, he can feel the ripple, the attention shifting toward him. Henry leans into the attention, the smiles, the warmth, the light. For the first time he truly understands the concept of being drunk with power.

It's like setting down a heavy weight long after your arms have gotten tired. There's this sudden, sweeping lightness, like air in your chest, like sunlight after rain.

It feels good to be the user instead of the used.

To be the one who gets instead of the one who loses.

It feels good. It shouldn't, he knows, but it does.

He stands in line at the Roast, desperately needing coffee.

The last few days have been a blur, late nights giving way to strange mornings, every moment fueled by the heady pleasure of being wanted, of knowing that whatever they see, it's good, it's great, it's perfect.

He's perfect.

And it's not just the straightforward gravity of lust, not always. People drift toward him now, every one of them pulled into his orbit, but the *why* is always different. Sometimes it's just simple desire, but other times it's more nuanced. Sometimes it's an obvious need, and other times, he can't guess what they see when they look at him.

That's the only unsettling part, really—their eyes. The fog that winds through them, thickening to frost, to ice. A constant reminder that this new life isn't exactly normal, isn't entirely real.

But it's *enough*.

"Next!"

He steps forward, and looks up, and sees Vanessa.

"Oh, hi," he says.

"You didn't call."

But she doesn't sound angry, or annoyed. If anything, she sounds too bright, teasing, but it's the kind of teasing used to cover up embarrassment. He should know—he's used that tone a dozen times to hide his own hurt.

"I'm sorry," he says, blushing. "I wasn't sure if I should."

Vanessa smiles slyly. "Was the whole name and number thing too subtle?"

Henry laughs, and hands his cell across the counter. "Call me," he says, and she taps her number in, and hits Call. "There," says Henry, taking back the phone, "now I have no excuse."

He feels like an idiot, even as he says it, like a kid reciting movie lines, but Vanessa only blushes, and bites her bottom lip, and he wonders what would happen if he told her to go out with him, right then, if she would take off her apron and duck beneath the counter, but he doesn't try it, just says, "I'll call."

And she says, "You better."

Henry smiles, turns to go. He's almost to the door when he hears his name.

"Mr. Strauss."

Henry's stomach drops. He knows the voice, can picture the older man's tweed jacket, his salt-and-pepper hair, the look of disappointment on his face as he advised Henry to step away from the department, the school, and try to figure out where his passion was, because it clearly wasn't there.

Henry tries to muster a smile, feels himself falling short.

"Dean Melrose," he says, turning to face the man who pushed him off the road.

And there he is, flesh and bone and tweed. But instead of the contempt Henry got so used to seeing, the dean looks pleased. A smile splits his trim gray beard.

"What a lucky turn," he says. "You're just the man I wanted to see."

Henry has a hard time believing that, until he notices the pale smoke twisting through the man's eyes. And he knows he should be polite, but what he wants to do is tell the dean to go fuck himself, so he splits the difference and simply asks, "Why?"

"There's a position opening in the theology school, and I think you'd be perfect for it."

Henry almost laughs. "You've got to be kidding."

"Not at all."

"I never finished my PhD. You failed me."

The dean holds up a finger. "I didn't fail you."

Henry bristles. "You threatened to, if I didn't leave."

"I know," he says, looking genuinely sorry. "I was wrong."

Three words he's sure this man has never said. Henry wants to savor them, but he can't.

"No," he says, "you were right. It wasn't a good fit. I wasn't happy there. And I have no desire to go back."

It's a lie. He misses the structure, misses the path, misses the purpose. And maybe it wasn't a perfect fit, but nothing is.

"Come in for an interview," says Dean Melrose, holding out his card. "Let me change your mind."

"You're late."

Bea's waiting on the bookstore steps.

"Sorry," he says, unlocking the door. "Still not a library," he adds as she slaps a five-dollar bill on the counter and disappears into the art section. She makes a noncommittal *uh-huh*, and he can hear her pulling books from the shelves.

Bea is the only one who hasn't changed, the only one who doesn't seem to treat him differently.

"Hey," he says, following her down the aisle. "Do I look strange to you?"

"No," she says, scanning the shelves.

"Bea, *look* at me."

She turns, gives him a long up-and-down appraisal.

"You mean besides the lipstick on your neck?"

Henry blushes, wiping at his skin. "Yeah," he says, "besides that."

She shrugs. "Not really."

But it's there, in her eyes, that unmistakable shimmer, a faint and irides-cent film that seems to spread as she studies him. "Really? Nothing?"

She pulls a book from the shelf. "Henry, what do you want me to say?" she asks, searching for a second. "You look like *you*."

"So you don't . . ." He doesn't know how to ask. "You don't *want* me, then?"

Bea turns, and looks at him for a long moment, and then bursts out laugh-ing.

"Sorry, hon," she says when she catches her breath. "Don't get me wrong. You're cute. But I'm still a lesbian."

And the moment she says it, he feels absurd, and absurdly relieved.

"What's this about?" she asks.

I made a deal with the devil and now whenever anyone looks at me, they see only what they want. He shakes his head. "Nothing. Never mind."

"*Well*," she says, adding another book to her stack, "I think I found a new thesis."

She carries the books back up to the counter, and spreads them out on top of the ledgers and receipts. Henry watches her turn through the pages until she finds what she's looking for in each, then steps back, so he can see what she's found.

Three portraits, all of them renditions of a young woman, though they clearly come from different times and different schools. "What am I looking at?" he asks.

"I call her the ghost in the frame."

One is a pencil sketch, the edges rough, unfinished. In it, the woman lies on her stomach, tangled in sheets. Hair pools around her, and her face is little more than panes of shadow, a faint scattering of freckles across her cheeks. The title of the piece is written in Italian.

Ho Portato le Stelle a Letto

The English translation sits beneath.

I Took the Stars to Bed.

The second piece is French, a more abstract portrait, done in the vivid blues and greens of Impressionism. The woman sits on a beach, a book face-down on the sand beside her. She looks over her shoulder at the artist, only the edge of her face visible, her freckles little more than smudges of light, absences of color.

La Sirène, this one is called.

The Siren.

The last piece is a shallow carving, a silhouette sculpture shot through with light, pinpoint tunnels burrowed through a pane of cherry wood.

Constellation.

"Do you see it?" asks Bea.

"They're portraits."

"No," she says, "they're portraits of *the same woman*."

Henry lifts a brow. "That's a stretch."

"Look at the angle of her jaw, the line of her nose, and the freckles. Count them."

Henry does. In every image, there are exactly seven.

Bea touches the first and second. "The Italian one's from the turn of the nineteenth century. The French one is fifty years later. And this one," she says, tapping the photo of the sculpture, "this one's from the sixties."

"So maybe one was inspired by the other," says Henry. "Wasn't there a tradition of—I forget what it was called, but basically visual telephone? One artist favored something, and then another artist favored that artist, and so on? Like a template."

But Bea is already waving him away. "Sure, in lexicons and bestiaries, but not in formal schools of art. This is like putting a girl with a pearl earring in a Warhol, *and* a Degas, without ever seeing the Rembrandt. And even if she became a template, the fact is, this 'template' influenced *centuries* of art. She's a piece of connective tissue between eras. So . . ."

"So . . ." echoes Henry.

"So, who was she?" Bea's eyes are bright, the way Robbie's sometimes are when he's just nailed a performance, or done a bump of coke, and Henry doesn't want to bring her down, but she's clearly waiting for him to say something.

"Okay," he starts, gently. "But Bea, what if she was no one? Even if these are based on the same woman, what if the first artist simply made her up?" Bea frowns, already shaking her head. "Look," he says, "no one wants you to find your thesis topic more than I do. For the sake of this store, as much as your sanity. And this all sounds cool. But didn't your last proposal get nixed for being too whimsical?"

"Esoteric."

"Right," says Henry. "And if a topic like 'Postmodernism and its Effects on New York Architecture' was too esoteric, how do you think Dean Parrish will feel about *this*?"

He gestures to the open texts, the freckled faces staring up from every page.

Bea looks at him in silence for a long moment, and then at the books.

"Fuck!" she shouts, taking up one of the giant books and storming out of the shop.

Henry watches her go and sighs. "Not a library," he calls after her, returning the rest to their shelves.

Henry trails off, as the realization dawns.

He'd forgotten about Bea's attempt at finding a new thesis, one quiet detail mixed into a very loud season, but now, it's obvious.

The girl in the sketch, the painting, the sculpture, is leaning on the rail beside him, her face open in delight.

They are walking through Chelsea on the way to the High Line, and he stops, halfway through a crosswalk, realizing the obvious truth, the gleam of light, like a tear, in his story.

"It was you," he says.

Addie flashes a dazzling smile. "It was."

A car honks, the flashing sign gone solid in warning, and they run to the other side.

"It's funny, though," she says as they climb the iron steps. "I didn't know about the second one. I remember sitting on that beach, remember the man with his easel, up on the pier, but I never found the finished piece."

Henry shakes his head. "I thought you couldn't leave a mark."

"I can't," she says, looking up. "I can't hold a pen. I can't tell a story. I can't wield a weapon, or make someone remember. But art," she says with a quieter smile, "art is about ideas. And ideas are wilder than memories. They're like weeds, always finding their way up."

"But no photographs. No film."

Her expression falters, just a fraction. "No," she says, the word a shape on her lips. And he feels bad for asking, for drawing her back to the bars of her curse, instead of the gaps she's found between them. But then Addie straightens, lifts her chin, smiles with an almost defiant kind of joy.

"But isn't it wonderful," she says, "to be an idea?"

They reach the High Line just as a gust of wind blows through, the air still edged with winter, but instead of folding in against him, sheltering from the breeze, Addie leans into the wild gust, cheeks blushing with the cold, hair whipping around her face, and in that moment, he can see what every artist saw, what drew them to their pencils and their paint, this impossible, uncatchable girl.

And even though he's safe, both feet firmly on the ground, Henry feels himself begin to fall.

People talk a lot about home.

Home is where the heart is, they say. There's no place like home. Too long away and you get homesick.

Homesick—Henry knows that one is supposed to mean sick *for* home, not from it, but it still feels right. He loves his family, he does. He just doesn't always like them. Doesn't like who he is around them.

And yet, here he is, driving ninety minutes north, the city sinking behind him as a rented car hums under his hands. Henry knows he could take the train, it's certainly cheaper, but the truth is, he likes driving. Or rather, he likes the white noise that comes with driving, the steady concreteness of going from here to there, the directions, the control. Most of all, he likes the inability to do anything else but drive, hands on the wheel, eyes on the road, music blaring through the speakers.

He offered to give Muriel a ride, was secretly relieved when she said she was taking the train already, that David had gotten in that morning and would pick her up from the station, which means Henry will be the last one there.

Henry is always somehow the last one there.

The closer he gets to Newburgh, the more the weather changes in his head, a warning rumble on the horizon, a storm rolling in. He takes a deep breath, bracing himself for a Strauss family dinner.

He can picture it, the five of them sitting around the linen-covered table like an awkward Ashkenazi imitation of a Rockwell painting, a stiff tableau, his mother on one end, his father on the other, his siblings seated side by side across the table.

David, the pillar, with his stern eyes and stiff posture.

Muriel, the tornado, with her wild dark curls and constant energy.

And Henry, the ghost (even his name doesn't fit—not Jewish at all, but a nod to one of his father's oldest friends).

At least they *look* the part of a family—a quick survey of the table, and one can easily pick out the echo of a cheek, a jaw, a brow. David wears his glasses just like Dad, perched at the end of his nose so the top line of the frames cuts across his gaze. Muriel smiles like Mom, open and easy, laughs like her, too, head thrown back, the sound bright and full.

Henry has his father's loose black curls, his mother's gray-green eyes, but something has been lost in the arrangement. He lacks one's steadiness, and the other's joy. The set of his shoulders, the line of his mouth—these subtle things that always make him seem more like a guest in someone else's house.

This is how the dinner will pass: his father and brother talking medicine, his mother and sister talking art, and Henry dreading the moment when the questions turn toward him. When his mother worries aloud about everything, and his father finds an excuse to use the word *unmoored*, and David reminds him he's almost thirty, and Muriel advises him to commit, really commit—as if their parents aren't still paying her cell phone bills.

Henry turns off the freeway and feels the wind pick up in his ears.

Passes through the center of town, and hears thunder in his skull.

The static energy of tension.

He knows he's late.

He is always late.

It has been the start of many quarrels, and there was a time when he thought it was carelessness on his part, before he realized it was some strange attempt at self-preservation, an intentional, albeit subconscious dawdling, a delay of the inevitable, uncomfortable necessity of showing up. Being seated at that table, boxed in by his siblings, positioned across from his parents like a criminal before a firing squad.

So Henry is late, and when his father answers the door, he braces for the mention of timing, the chastising frown, the cutting remark on how his brother and sister always manage to arrive five minutes early—

But his father only smiles.

"There you are!" he says, eyes bright and warm.

And threaded with fog.

Maybe this won't be like any other Strauss family dinner.

"Look who's here!" calls his father, leading Henry into the study.

"Long time no see," says David, shaking his hand, because even though they live in the same city—hell, on the same subway line—the last time Henry saw his brother was here, on the first night of Hanukkah.

"Henry!" A blur of dark curls, and then Muriel has thrown her arms around his neck. She kisses his cheek, leaving a smudge of coral lipstick he will later scrub off in the hall mirror.

And nowhere between the study and the dining room does anyone comment on the length of his hair, which is always somehow too long, or the state of the sweater he's wearing, which is frayed, but also the most comfortable thing he owns.

Not once does anyone tell him that he's too thin, or that he needs more sun, or that he looks tired, even though all of those usually precede the pointed remarks of how it can't be that hard to run a bookshop in Brooklyn.

His mother comes out of the kitchen, tugging off a pair of oven mitts. She cups his face, and smiles, and tells him she's so happy he's there.

Henry believes her.

"To the family," toasts his father when they sit down to eat. "Together again."

He feels like he's stepped into another version of his life—not ahead, or behind, but sideways. One where his sister looks up to him and his brother doesn't look down, where his parents are proud, and all the judgment has been sucked out of the air like smoke vented from a fire. He didn't realize how much connective tissue was made up of guilt. Without the weight of it, he feels dizzy and light.

Euphoric.

There is no mention of Tabitha, or the failed proposal, though of course the knowledge of their breakup has circulated, the outcome made obvious by the empty chair no one even tries to play off as a household tradition.

Last month on the phone, when Henry told David about the ring, his brother wondered, almost absently, if he thought she would actually agree. Muriel never liked her, but Muriel never liked any of Henry's partners. Not because they were all too good for him, though she would have said that too—but simply because she found them *boring*, an extension of the way she felt about Henry himself.

Cable TV, that's what she sometimes called them. Better than watching paint dry, sure, but little more than reruns. The only one she even vaguely approved of was Robbie, and even then, Henry was sure it was mostly for the scandal it would cause if he ever brought him home. Only Muriel knows about Robbie, that he was ever more than a friend. It's the one secret that she's managed to keep.

The whole dinner is so unnerving.

David is warm, curious.

Muriel is attentive and kind.

His father listens to everything he says, and seems genuinely interested.

His mother tells him she's proud.

"Of what?" he asks, genuinely confused, and she laughs as if it's a ridiculous question.

"Of you."

The absence of judgment is jarring, a kind of existential vertigo.

He tells them about running into Dean Melrose, waits for David to point out the obvious, that he's not qualified, waits for his father to ask him about the catch. His mother will go silent while his sister will go loud, exclaiming that he changed directions for a reason, and demanding to know the point of it all if he just crawls back.

But none of that happens.

"Good," says his father.

"They'd be lucky to have you," says his mother.

"You'd make a good teacher," says David.

Only Muriel offers a shadow of dissent. "You were never happy there . . ."

But there's no judgment in the words, only a fierce protectiveness.

After dinner, everyone retreats to their respective corners, his mother to the kitchen, his father and brother to the study, his sister out into the night to look at stars and feel grounded, which is usually code for getting stoned.

Henry goes into the kitchen to help his mother with the dishes.

"I'll wash, you dry," she says, handing him a towel. They find a pleasant rhythm, and then his mother clears her throat.

"I'm sorry about Tabitha," she says, her voice low, as if she knows the subject is taboo. "I'm sorry you wasted so much time on her."

"It wasn't a waste," he says, even though it does kind of feel that way.

She rinses a plate. "I just want you to be happy. You deserve to be happy." Her eyes shine, and he's not sure if it's the strange frost, or simply maternal tears. "You're strong, and smart, and successful."

"I don't know about that," Henry says, drying a plate. "I still feel like a disappointment."

"Don't talk like that," says his mother, looking genuinely hurt. She cups his cheek. "I love you, Henry, just as you are." Her hand drops to the plate. "Let me finish up," she says. "Go find your sister."

Henry knows exactly where she is.

He steps out onto the back porch, sees Muriel sitting on the porch swing, smoking a joint and looking out at the trees, striking a pensive pose. She always sits like that, as if waiting for someone to snap a photo. He has, once or twice, but it always looked too stiff, too framed. Trust Muriel to make a candid look staged.

The boards creak a little under his feet now, and she smiles without looking up. "Hey, Hen."

"How did you know it was me?" he asks, sinking down beside her.

"You have the lightest step," she says, passing him the joint.

Henry takes a long drag, holds the smoke in his chest until he feels it in his head. A soft, buzzing blur. They pass the joint back and forth, studying their parents through the glass. Well, their parents and David, who trails behind their father, striking the exact same poses.

"So creepy," mutters Muriel.

"Uncanny, really."

She chuckles. "Why don't we hang out more?"

"You're busy," he says, because it's kinder than reminding her they aren't really friends.

She leans her head against his shoulder. "I always have time for you."

They smoke in silence until there's nothing left to smoke, and their mother calls out that it's time for dessert. Henry stands, his head swimming in a pleasant way.

"Mint?" she asks, holding out a tin, but when he opens it, he sees the pile of little pink pills. Umbrellas. He thinks of the rain pelting down, the stranger beside him, perfectly dry, and snaps the tin shut.

"No thanks."

They go back inside for dessert, spend the next hour talking about everything and nothing, and all of it is so nice, so aggressively pleasant, so mercifully free of snide remarks, petty squabbles, passive disapproval, that Henry feels like he's still holding his breath, still holding on to the high, his lungs aching but his heart happy.

He rises, setting his coffee aside. "I should get going."

"You could stay," offers his mom, and for the first time in ten years, he's actually tempted, wonders what it would be like to wake up to this, the warmth, the ease, the feeling of family, but the truth is, the evening's been too perfect. He feels like he's walking that narrow line between a good buzz and a night on the bathroom floor, and he doesn't want anything to tip the balance.

"I have to get back," he says, "the shop opens at ten."

"You work so hard" is a thing his mother has never said. A thing she apparently says now.

David grips his shoulder and looks at him with those mercifully clouded eyes and says, "I love you, Henry. I'm glad you're doing so well."

Muriel wraps her arms around his waist. "Don't be such a stranger."

His father follows him out to the car, and when Henry holds out his hand, his father pulls him in for a hug, and says, "I'm proud of you, son."

And part of him wants to ask why, to bait, to test the limits of this spell, to press his father into faltering, but he can't bring himself to do it. He knows it's not real, not in the strictest sense, but he doesn't care.

It still feels good.

Laughter spills down from the High Line.

Built along a defunct rail, the raised park runs down the western edge of Manhattan from Thirtieth to Twelfth. It's normally a pleasant place, with food carts and gardens, tunnels and benches, winding paths and city views.

Today, it is something else entirely.

The Artifact has consumed a stretch of the elevated rail, transformed it into a dreamlike jungle gym of color and light. A three-dimensional landscape of whimsy and wonder.

At the entrance, a volunteer gives them colored rubber bands to wear around their wrists. A rainbow against their skin, each one providing access to a different piece of the exhibit.

"This will get you into the Sky," she says, as if the works of art are rides at an amusement park.

"This will get you into Voice."

"This will get you into Memory."

She smiles at Henry as she talks, her eyes a milky blue. But as they move through the carnival of free exhibits, the artists all turn to look at *Addie*. He may be a sun, but she is a shining comet, dragging their focus like burning meteors in her wake.

Nearby, a guy sculpts pieces of cotton candy as if they were balloons, then hands out the edible works of art. Some of them are recognizable shapes—here is a dog, here is a giraffe, here is a dragon—while others are abstract—here is a sunset, here is a dream, here is nostalgia.

To Henry, they all taste like sugar.

Addie kisses him, and she tastes like sugar too.

The green band gets them into Memory, which turns out to be a sort of three-dimensional kaleidoscope, made of colored glass—a sculpture that rises to every side, and turns with every step.

They hold on to each other as the world bends and rights and bends again around them, and neither says it, but both, he thinks, are happy to get out.

The art spills into the space between the exhibits. A field of metal sunflowers. A pool of melted crayons. A curtain of water, as thin as paper, that leaves nothing but mist on his glasses, an iridescent shine on Addie's skin.

The Sky, it turns out, lives inside a tunnel.

Made by a light artist, it's a series of interlocking rooms. From the outside, they don't look like much, the wood frames shells of bare construction, little more than nail and stud, but inside—inside is everything.

They move hand in hand so they won't lose each other. One space is glaringly bright, the next so dark the world seems to plunge away, and Addie shivers beside him, fingers tightening on Henry's arm. The next is pale with fog, like the inside of a cloud, and in the next, filaments as thin as rain rise and fall to every side. Henry runs his fingers through the field of silver drops, and they ring like chimes.

The last room is filled with stars.

It is a black chamber, identical to the one before it, only this time, a thousand pinprick lights break through the obscurity, carving a Milky Way close enough to touch—a majesty of constellations. And even in the almost dark, Henry can see Addie's upturned face, the edges of her smile.

"Three hundred years," she whispers. "And you can still find something new."

When they step out the other side, blinking in the afternoon light, she is already pulling him on, out of the Sky and on to the next archway, the next set of doors, eager to discover whatever waits beyond.

For once, Henry is early.

Which, he figures, is better than being late, but he doesn't want to be *too* early because that's even worse, even weirder and—he needs to stop overthinking it.

He smooths his shirt, checks his hair in the side of a parked car, and goes inside.

The taqueria is bright and bustling, a concrete cavern of a place, with garage door windows and a food truck parked in the corner of the room, and it doesn't matter if he's early, because Vanessa is already inside.

She's traded the barista apron for leggings and a print dress, and her blond hair, which he's only seen pulled up, hangs in loose waves around her face, and when she sees him, she breaks into a smile.

"I'm glad you called," she says.

And Henry smiles back. "So am I."

They order using slips of paper and those little pencils Henry hasn't seen since he played mini-golf one time when he was ten, fingers brushing as she points to tacos and he fills them in. Their hands touch again over the chips, legs skimming beneath the metal table, and each time it's like a tiny burst of light inside his chest.

And for once, he isn't talking himself in and out of every single line, isn't chiding himself for each and every move, isn't convincing himself that he has to say the right thing—there's no need to find the right words when there are no wrong ones. He doesn't have to lie, doesn't have to try, doesn't have to be anyone but himself, because he is enough.

The food is great, but the place is noisy, voices echoing off high ceilings, and Henry cringes when someone scrapes their chair back over the concrete floor. "Sorry," he says. "I know it's not fancy."

He picked the place, knows they probably should have just gone for drinks, but it's New York, and cocktails cost twice as much as food, and he can barely afford even this on a bookseller's wages.

"Dude," she says, stirring an agua fresca, "I work in a coffee shop."

"At least you get tips."

Vanessa feigns shock. "What, they don't tip booksellers?"

"Nope."

"Not even when you recommend a good book?"

He shakes his head.

"That's a crime," she says. "You should put a jar on the counter."

"What would I say?" He raps his fingers on the table. *"Books feed hungry minds. Tips feed the cat?"*

Vanessa laughs, sudden and bright. "You're so funny."

"Am I?"

She sticks out her tongue. "Fishing for compliments, are we?"

"No," he says. "Just curious. What do you see in me?"

Vanessa smiles, suddenly shy. "You're . . . well, it sounds cheesy, but you're exactly what I've been looking for."

"And what's that?" he asks.

If she said *real, sensitive, thoughtful,* he might have bought it.

But she doesn't.

She uses words like *outgoing, funny, ambitious,* and the more she talks about him, the thicker the frost in her eyes, the more it spreads, until he can barely make out the color beneath. And Henry wonders how she can see, but of course, she can't.

That's the point.

They're at the Merchant a week later, he and Bea and Robbie, three beers and a basket of fries between them.

"How's Vanessa?" she asks, while Robbie looks pointedly into his drink.

"She's fine," says Henry.

And she is. He is. They are.

"Been seeing a lot of her."

Henry frowns. "You're the one who told me to get Tabitha out of my system."

Bea holds up her hands. "I know, I know."

"It's new. You know how things are. She's—"

"A carbon copy," mumbles Robbie.

Henry turns on him. "What was that?" he asks, annoyed. "Speak up. I know they taught you how to project."

Robbie takes a long swig of beer, looking miserable. "I'm just saying, she's a carbon copy of Tabby. Waifish, blond—"

"Female?"

It's a long-running sore point between them, the fact that Henry isn't *gay,* that he's attracted to a person first and their gender second. Robbie cringes, but doesn't apologize.

"Besides," says Henry. "I didn't go after Vanessa. She picked *me*. She likes *me*."

"Do you like *her*?" asks Bea.

"Of course," he says, a little too fast. He likes her. And sure, he also likes that she likes him (the *him* that she sees) and there's a Venn diagram between those two, a place where they overlap. He's pretty sure he's safely in the shaded zone. He's not really using her, is he? At least, he's not the only one being shallow—she's using him, too, painting someone else onto the canvas of her life. And if it's mutual, well then, it's not his fault . . . is it?

"We just want you to be happy," Bea's saying. "After all that's happened, just . . . don't go too fast."

But for once, he's not the one who needs to slow down.

Henry woke up that morning to chocolate-chip pancakes and a glass of OJ, a little handwritten note on the counter beside the plate with a heart and a *V*. She's slept over the last three nights, and each time, she left something behind. A blouse. A pair of shoes. A toothbrush in the holder by the sink.

His friends stare at him, pale fog still swirling through their eyes, and he knows that they care, knows they love him, knows they only want the best for him. They have to now, thanks to the deal.

"Don't worry," he says, sipping his beer. "I'll take it slow."

"Henry . . ."

He's half-asleep when he feels her run a painted nail down his back.

Weak gray light spills through the windows.

"Hm?" he says, rolling over.

Vanessa's got her head on one hand, blond hair spilling down over the pillow, and he wonders how long she was leaning like that, waiting for him to wake up, before she finally intervened.

"I need to tell you something." She gazes at him, eyes frosted with that milky light. He is beginning to dread that shine, the pale smoke that follows him from face to face.

"What is it?" he asks, rising onto one elbow. "What's wrong?"

"Nothing. I just . . ." She breaks into a smile. "I love you."

And the scary thing is, she sounds like she means it.

"You don't have to say it back. I know it's soon. I just wanted you to know." She nuzzles against him.

"Are you sure?" he asks. "I mean, it's only been a week."

"So what?" she says. "When you know, you know. And I know."

Henry swallows, kisses her temple. "I'm going to take a shower."

He stands under the hot water as long as he can, wondering what he's supposed to say to that, if and how he can convince Vanessa that it isn't love, it's just obsession, but of course, that isn't really true, either. He made the deal. He made the terms. This is what he wanted.

Isn't it?

He cuts the water off, wraps the towel around his waist, and smells smoke.

Not the scent of a match lighting a candle, or something boiling over on the stove, but the char-black smell of things that aren't supposed to be on fire, and are now burning.

Henry surges out into the hall, and sees Vanessa in the kitchen, standing at the counter, a box of matches in one hand, and the cardboard box of Tabitha's things burning in the sink.

"What are you doing?" he demands.

"You're holding on to the past," she says, striking another match and tossing it into the box. "Like, literally holding on. You've had this box as long as we've been together."

"I've only known you a week!" he shouts, but she presses on.

"And you deserve better. You deserve to be happy. You deserve to live in the present. This is a good thing. This is closure. This is—"

He knocks the matches from her hand and pushes her aside, reaching for the tap.

The water hits the box in a sizzle, sending up a plume of smoke as it douses the flames.

"Vanessa," he says, gritting his teeth, "I need you to go."

"Like, home?"

"Like, *go*."

"Henry," she says, touching his arm. "What did I do wrong?"

And he could point to the smoldering remains in his kitchen sink, or the fact it's all going way too fast, or the fact that when she looks at him, she sees someone else entirely. But instead, he just says, "It's not you. It's me."

"No, it's not," she says, tears sliding down her face.

"I need some space, okay?"

"I'm sorry," she sobs, clinging to him. "I'm sorry. I love you."

Her limbs are wrapped around his waist, head buried in his side, and for a second, he thinks he might have to physically pry her off.

"Vanessa, let go."

He guides her away, and she looks devastated, ruined. She looks the way he felt the night he made the deal, and it breaks his heart at the thought that she will walk out feeling that lost, that alone.

"I care about you," he says, gripping her shoulders. "I care about you, I do."

She brightens, just a little. A wilting plant fed water. "So you're not mad?"

Of course he's mad.

"No, I'm not mad."

She buries her face in his front, and he strokes her hair.

"You care about me."

"I do." He untangles himself. "I'll call you. I promise."

"You promise," she echoes as he helps her gather her things.

"I promise," he says as he leads her down the hall, and out.

The door shuts between them, and Henry sags back against it as the smoke alarm finally begins to ring.

"Movie night!"

Robbie flings himself across Henry's sofa like a starfish, long limbs hanging off the back and sides. Bea rolls her eyes and shoves him over. "Make room."

Henry plucks the bag from the microwave, bouncing it from hand to hand to avoid the steam. He dumps the popcorn into the bowl.

"What's the movie?" he asks, rounding the counter.

"*The Shining.*"

Henry groans. He's never been a fan of scary movies, but Robbie loves a reason to scream, treats the whole thing like another kind of performance, and it's his week to choose.

"It's Halloween!" defends Robbie.

"It's the twenty-third," says Henry, but Robbie treats holidays the way he treats birthdays, stretching them from days into weeks, and sometimes into seasons.

"Costume roll call," says Bea.

Dressing up, he thinks, is just like watching cartoons, something you enjoyed as a kid, before it passes through the no man's land of teen angst, the ironic age of early twenties. And then somehow, miraculously, it crosses back into the realm of the genuine, the nostalgic. A place reserved for wonder.

Robbie strikes a pose from the sofa. "Ziggy Stardust," he says, which makes sense. He's spent the last several years working through Bowie's various incarnations. Last year it was the Thin White Duke.

Bea announces she's going as the Dread Pirate Roberts, pun intended, and Robbie reaches out and picks up a camera from Henry's coffee table, a vintage Nikon currently playing the part of paperweight. He cranes his head back, and peers at Henry through the viewfinder upside down.

"What about you?"

Henry's always loved Halloween—not the scary part, just the excuse to change, be someone else. Robbie says he should have just become an actor, that they get to play dress-up all year round, but the thought of living life onstage makes him queasy. He's been Freddie Mercury, and the Mad Hatter, Tuxedo Mask, and the Joker.

But right now, he already feels like somebody else.

"I'm already in costume," he says, gesturing at his usual black jeans, his narrow shirt. "Can't you tell who I am?"

"Peter Parker?" ventures Bea.

"A bookseller?"

"Harry Potter having a quarter-life crisis?"

Henry laughs and shakes his head.

Bea narrows her eyes. "You haven't picked anything yet, have you?"

"No," he admits, "but I will."

Robbie is still fiddling with the camera. He turns it around, purses his lips, and snaps a photo. The camera gives a hollow click. There's no film. Bea plucks it from his hands.

"Why don't you take more photos?" she asks. "You're really good."

Henry shrugs, unsure if she means it. "Maybe in another life," he says, handing each of them a beer.

"You still could, you know," she says. "It's not too late."

Maybe, but if he started now, would the photos stand on their own, judged good or bad on their own merits? Or would each and every picture carry his wish forward? Would every person see the picture they wanted to see, instead of the one he made? Would he ever trust them if they did?

The movie starts, and Robbie insists on turning out all the lights, the three of them crammed together on the couch. They force Robbie to leave the bowl of popcorn *on the table* so he can't throw it at the first scary moment, so Henry doesn't have to pick up kernels after they're gone, and he spends the next hour averting his eyes every time the score whines in warning.

When the boy rolls his tricycle down the hall, Bea mutters, "Nope, nope, nope," and Robbie sits forward, leaning into the scare, and Henry buries his face in his shoulder. The twin girls appear, hand in hand, and Robbie grabs Henry's leg.

And when the moment passes, a lull in the fear, Robbie's hand is still resting on his thigh. And it's like a broken cup coming back together, the shattered edges lining up just right—which is, of course, wrong.

Henry gets up, taking the empty popcorn bowl and heading for the kitchen.

Robbie swings his leg up over the back of the sofa. "I'll help."

"It's popcorn," Henry says over his shoulder as he rounds the corner. He tears the plastic wrapper off, shakes the pouch. "I'm pretty sure I just put the bag in the microwave and press the button."

"You always let it go too long," says Robbie, right behind him.

Henry tosses the pouch into the microwave and swings the door shut.

He presses Start, turns back toward the door. "So now you're the popcorn poli—"

He doesn't get a chance to finish before Robbie's mouth is on his. Henry sucks in a breath, surprised by the sudden kiss, but Robbie doesn't break away. He presses him back into the counter, hips into hips, fingers sliding along his jaw as the kiss deepens.

And this, this is better than all the other nights.

This is better than the attention of a hundred strangers.

This is the difference between a hotel bed and home.

Robbie is hard against him, and Henry's chest aches with want, and it would be so easy, to fall back into this, to return to the familiar warmth of his kiss, his body, the simple comfort of something real.

But that's the problem.

It was real. They were real. But like everything in Henry's life, it ended. Failed.

He breaks the kiss as the first kernels begin to pop.

"I've been waiting weeks to do that," whispers Robbie, his cheeks flushed, his eyes fever bright. But they're not clear. Fog winds through them, clouding the vivid blue.

Henry lets out a shuddering breath, rubs his own eyes beneath his glasses.

The popcorn rattles and pops, and Henry pulls Robbie into the hall, away from Bea and the horror movie score, and Robbie starts toward him again, thinking it's an invitation, but Henry puts his hand out, holding him back. "This is a mistake."

"No, it's not," says Robbie. "I love you. I always have."

And it sounds so honest, so real, Henry has to squeeze his eyes shut to focus. "Then why did you break up with me?"

"What? I don't know. You were different, we weren't a fit."

"How?" presses Henry.

"You didn't know what you wanted."

"I wanted you. I wanted you to be happy."

Robbie shakes his head. "It can't just be about the other person. You have to be someone, too. You have to know who you are. Back then, you didn't." He smiles. "But now you do."

But that's just it.

He doesn't.

Henry has no idea who he is, and now, neither does anyone else.

He just feels lost. But this is the one road he won't take.

He and Robbie were friends before they were more, friends again for years after *Robbie* called it off, when Henry was still in love with him, and now it's reversed, and Robbie's going to have to find a way to move on, or at least, find a way to smooth *in love* into *love,* the way Henry had done when it was him.

"How long does it take to make popcorn?" shouts Bea.

A singed smell wafts from microwave, and Henry pushes past Robbie into the kitchen, hits the Stop button, pulls the bag out.

But he's too late.

The popcorn is irretrievably burned.

Thank god Brooklyn has so many coffee shops.

Henry hasn't been back into Roast, not since the Great Fire of 2013, as Robbie calls the whole Vanessa incident (with a little too much glee). He gets to the front of the line and orders a latte from a very nice guy named Patrick who is mercifully straight, who looks at him with cloudy eyes but only seems to see a perfect customer, someone friendly, and brief, and—

"Henry?"

His stomach drops. Because he knows that voice, high and sweet, knows the way it bends around his name, and it is that night again, and he is down on one knee like a fool as she says no.

You're great. You really are. But you're not . . .

He turns around, and there she is.

"Tabitha."

Her hair has gotten a little longer, the bangs grown out into a sweep of blond across her forehead, a curl against her cheek, and she stands with the easy grace of a dancer between poses. Henry hasn't seen her since that night, has managed, until now, to avoid her, to avoid this. And he wants to back away, to put as much distance between them as possible. But his legs refuse to move.

She smiles at him, bright and warm. He remembers being in love with that smile, back when it felt like a victory every time he earned a glimpse. Now she simply hands it to him, brown eyes shrouded in fog.

"I've missed you," she says. "I've missed you so much."

"I've missed you, too," he says, because it is the truth. Two years of a life together, replaced by a life apart, and there will always be an empty space in the shape of her. "I had a box of your things," he says, "but there was a fire."

"Oh god." She touches his arm. "Are you okay? Was anyone hurt?"

"No, no." He shakes his head, thinking of Vanessa standing over the sink. "It was . . . contained."

Tabitha sways into him. "Oh, good."

Up close, she smells like lilacs. It took a week for that scent to fade from his sheets, another for it to vanish from the sofa cushions, the shower towels. She leans into him, and it would be so easy to lean back, to give in to the same dangerous gravity that drew him to Robbie, the familiar pull of something loved, and lost, and then returned.

But it isn't real.

It isn't real.

"Tabitha," he says, guiding her back. "You ended things."

"No." She shakes her head. "I wasn't ready to take the next step. But I never wanted it to *end*. I love you, Henry."

And despite it all, he falters. Because he believes her. Or at least, he believes that she believes herself, and that is worse, because it still doesn't make it real.

"Can't we try again?" she asks.

Henry swallows, and shakes his head.

He wants to ask her what she sees, to understand the chasm between who he was and what she wanted. But he doesn't ask.

Because in the end, it doesn't matter.

The fog twists across her vision. And he knows that, whoever she sees, it isn't him.

It never was.

It never will be.

So he lets her go.

Henry and Addie offer up their rubber bands to the Artifact, sacrificing one color at a time.

For the purple band, they walk through puddles, inch-thick pools that ripple around their feet. Beneath the water, the ground is made of mirrors, shimmering, reflecting everyone and everything. Addie stares down at the ribbons of motion, the ripples fading, and if hers end a moment sooner than his, it is hard to say.

For the yellow, they are guided into soundproof cubes the size of closets, ones that amplify the noise, and others that seem to swallow every breath. It is a hall of mirrors, if the bending surfaces warped a voice instead of a reflection.

The first message tells them to WHISPER, the word stenciled on the wall in small, black type, and when Addie whispers "I have a secret," the words bend and loop and wrap around them.

The next tells them to SHOUT, this stenciled word as large as the wall it's written on. Henry can't bring himself to go above a small, self-conscious holler, but Addie draws a breath and roars, the way you would beneath a bridge if a train was going by, and something in the fearless freedom of it gives him air, and suddenly he is emptying his lungs, the sound guttural and broken, as wild as a scream.

And Addie doesn't shrink away. She simply raises her voice, and together they shout themselves breathless, they scream themselves hoarse, they leave the cubes feeling dizzy and light. His lungs will hurt tomorrow, and it will be worth it.

By the time they stumble out, sound rushing back into their ears, the sun is going down, and the clouds are on fire, one of those strange spring nights that casts an orange light on everything.

They walk over to the nearest rail and look out at the city, the light reflecting on the buildings, streaking sunset across steel, and Henry pulls her back against him, kisses the crook of her neck, smiling into her collar.

He is sugar-high and a little drunk, and happier than he has ever been.

Addie is better than any little pink umbrella.

She is better than strong whisky on a cold night.

Better than anything he's felt in ages.

When Henry is with her, time speeds up, and it doesn't scare him.

When he is with Addie, he feels alive, and it doesn't hurt.

She leans back against him, as if he is the umbrella, and she the one in need of shelter. And Henry holds his breath, as if that will keep the sky aloft. As if that will keep the days from passing.

As if that will keep it all from falling down.

Bea always says returning to campus is like coming home.

But it doesn't feel that way to Henry. Then again, he never felt at home at *home,* only a vague sense of dread, the eggshell-laden walk of someone constantly in danger of disappointing. And that's pretty much what he feels now, so maybe she's right, after all.

"Mr. Strauss," says the dean, reaching across the desk. "I'm so glad you could make it."

They shake hands, and Henry lowers himself into the office chair. The same chair he sat in three years ago when Dean Melrose threatened to fail him if he didn't have the sense to leave. And now—

You want to be enough.

"Sorry it took me so long," he says, but the dean waves away the apology.

"You're a busy man, I'm sure."

"Right," says Henry, shifting in his seat. His suit chafes; too many months spent among mothballs in the back of the closet. He doesn't know what to do with his hands.

"So," he says awkwardly, "you said there was a position open, in the theology school, but you didn't say if it was adjunct or an aide."

"It's tenure."

Henry stares at the salt-and-pepper man across the table, and has to resist the urge to laugh in his face. A tenure track isn't just coveted, it's cutthroat. People spend years vying for those positions.

"And you thought of me."

"The moment I saw you in that café," says the dean with a fundraising smile.

You want to be whatever they want.

The dean sits forward in his chair. "The question, Mr. Strauss, is simple. What do you want for yourself?"

The words echo through his head, a terrible, reverberating symmetry.

It's the same question Melrose asked that autumn day when he called Henry into his office, three years into his PhD, and told him it was over. On some level, Henry knew it was coming. He'd already transferred from the theological seminary into the broader religious studies program, focus sliding over and between themes that a hundred people had already explored, unable to find new ground, unable to believe.

"What do you want for yourself?" he'd asked, and Henry considered saying *my parents' pride*, but that didn't seem like a good answer, so he'd said the next truest thing—that he honestly wasn't sure. That he'd blinked and somehow years had gone by, and everyone else had carved their trenches, paved their paths, and he was still standing in a field, uncertain where to dig.

The dean had listened, and leaned his elbows on the table and told him that he was good.

But good wasn't enough.

Which meant, of course, *he* wasn't enough.

"What do you want for yourself?" the dean asks now. And Henry still doesn't have any other answer.

"I don't know."

And this is the part where the dean shakes his head, where he realizes that Henry Strauss is still as lost as ever. Only he doesn't, of course. He smiles and says, "That's okay. It's good to be open. But you *do* want to come back, don't you?"

Henry is silent. He sits with the question.

He always liked learning. Loved it, really. If he could have spent his whole life sitting in a lecture hall, taking notes, could have drifted from department to department, haunting different studies, soaking up language and history and art, maybe he would have felt full, happy.

That's how he spent the first two years.

And those first two years, he *was* happy. He had Bea, and Robbie, and all he had to do was learn. Build a foundation. It was the house, the one that he was supposed to build on top of that smooth surface, that was the problem.

It was just so . . . permanent.

Choosing a class became choosing a discipline, and choosing a discipline became choosing a career, and choosing a career became choosing a life, and how was anyone supposed to do that, when you only had one?

But teaching, teaching might be a way to have what he wanted.

Teaching is an extension of learning, a way to be a perpetual student.

And yet. "I'm not qualified, sir."

"You're an unconventional choice," the dean admits, "but that doesn't mean you're the wrong one."

Except in this case, that's exactly what it means.

"I don't have my doctorate."

The frost spreads into a sheen of ice across the dean's vision. "You have a fresh perspective."

"Aren't there requirements?"

"There are, but there's a measure of latitude, to account for different backgrounds."

"I don't believe in God."

The words tumble out like stones, landing heavy on the desk between them.

And Henry realizes, now that they're out, that they aren't entirely true. He doesn't know what he believes, hasn't for a long time, but it's hard to entirely discount the presence of a higher power when he recently sold his soul to a lower one.

Henry realizes the room is still quiet.

The dean looks at him for a long moment, and he thinks he's done it, he's broken through.

But then Melrose leans forward, and says, in a measured tone, "I don't either." He sits back. "Mr. Strauss, we are an academic institution, not a church. Dissent is at the heart of dissemination."

But that's the problem. No one will *dissent*. Henry looks at Dean Melrose, and imagines seeing that same blind acceptance on the face of every faculty member, every teacher, every student, and feels ill. They'll look at him, and see exactly what they want. Who they want. And even if he comes across someone who *wants* to argue, who relishes conflict or debate, it won't be real.

None of it will ever be real again.

Across the table, the dean's eyes are a milky gray. "You can have anything you want, Mr. Strauss. Be anyone you want. And we'd like to have you here." He stands, holds out his hand. "Think about it."

Henry says, "I will."

And he does.

He thinks about it on the way across campus, and on the subway, every station carrying him farther away from that life. The one that was, and the one that wasn't. Thinks about it as he unlocks the store, shrugs out of the ill-fitting coat and flings it onto the nearest shelf, undoes the tie at his throat. Thinks about it as he feeds the cat, and unpacks the latest box of books, gripping them until his fingers ache, but at least they're solid, they're real, and he can feel the storm clouds forming in his head, so he goes into the back room, finds the bottle of Meredith's whisky, a few fingers' worth leftover from the day after his deal, and carries it back to the front of the store.

It's not even noon, but Henry doesn't care.

He pulls out the cork and fills a coffee cup as the customers filter in, waiting for someone to shoot him a dirty look, to shake their head in disapproval, or mutter something, or even leave. But they all just keep shopping, keep smiling, keep looking at Henry as if he can't do anything wrong.

Finally, an off-duty cop comes in, and Henry doesn't even try to hide the bottle by the till. Instead, he looks straight at the man and takes a long drink from his cup, certain that he's breaking some law, either because of the open container, or the public intoxication.

But the cop only smiles, and raises an imaginary glass.

"Cheers," he says, eyes frosting over as he speaks.

Take a drink every time you hear a lie.

You're a great cook.

(They say as you burn toast.)

You're *so* funny.

(You've never told a joke.)

You're so . . .

. . . handsome.

. . . ambitious.

. . . successful.

. . . strong.

(Are you drinking yet?)

You're so . . .

. . . charming.

. . . clever.

. . . sexy.

(Drink.)

So confident.

So shy.

So mysterious.

So open.

You are impossible, a paradox, a collection at odds.

You are everything to everyone.

The son they never had.

The friend they always wanted.

A generous stranger.

A successful son.

A perfect gentleman.

A perfect partner.

A perfect . . .
Perfect . . .
(Drink.)
They love your body.
Your abs.
Your laugh.
The way you smell.
The sound of your voice.
They want you.
(Not you.)
They need you.
(Not you.)
They love you.
(Not you.)
You are whoever they want you to be.
You are more than enough, because you are not real.
You are perfect, because *you* don't exist.
(Not you.)
(Never you.)
They look at you and see whatever they want . . .
Because they don't see *you* at all.

The clock is ticking down, the last minutes of the year dropping away. Everyone says to live in the now, to savor the moment, but it's hard when the moment involves a hundred people crammed into a rent-controlled apartment in Bed-Stuy that Robbie is sharing with two other actors. Henry is trapped in a hall corner, where the coatrack meets a closet. He has a beer hanging from one hand and the other tangled in the shirt of the guy kissing him, a guy who's definitely out of Henry's league, or who would be, if Henry still had one.

He thinks the guy's name is Mark, but it was hard to hear over all the noise. It could be Max, or Malcolm. Henry doesn't know. And he wants to say this is the first person he's kissed tonight, even the first guy, but the truth is, he isn't sure about that either. Isn't sure how many drinks he's had, or if the taste melting on his tongue right now is sugar, or something else.

Henry has been drinking too much, too fast, trying to wash away, and there are too many people in the Castle.

The Castle, that's what they call Robbie's place, though Henry can't remember exactly when they christened it that, or why. He searches for Bea, hasn't seen her since he waded through the crowd into the kitchen an hour before, saw her perched on the counter, playing bartender and holding court for a group of women and—

Suddenly the guy is fumbling with Henry's belt.

"Wait," he says, but the music is loud enough he has to shout, has to pull Mark/Max/Malcolm's ear against his mouth, which Mark/Max/Malcolm takes as a sign to keep kissing him.

"Wait," he shouts, pushing back. "Do you even want this?"

Which is a stupid question. Or at least, the wrong one.

The pale smoke swirls in the stranger's eyes. "Why wouldn't I?" he asks, sinking to his knees. But Henry catches his elbow.

"Stop. Just stop." He pulls him up. "What do you see in me?"

A question he has come to ask of everyone, hoping to hear something like the truth. But the guy looks at him, eyes clouded with frost, and rattles off the words, "You're gorgeous. Sexy. Smart."

"How do you know?" Henry shouts over the music.

"What?" the other guy shouts back.

"How do you know I'm smart? We barely spoke."

But Mark/Max/Malcolm only smiles a sloppy, heavy-lidded grin, his mouth red from kissing, and says, "I just know," and it's not enough anymore, it's not okay, and Henry's in the process of untangling himself when Robbie rounds the corner, and sees Mark/Max/Malcolm practically mounting Henry in the hall. Robbie looks at him as if he's flung a beer in his face.

He turns, and leaves, and Henry groans, and the guy grinding against him seems to think the sound is for him, and it's too hot in here for Henry to think, to breathe.

The room is starting to spin, and Henry murmurs something about having to pee, but walks straight past the toilet and into Robbie's room, shutting the door behind him. He goes to the window, shoves up the glass, and is hit full in the face with a blast of icy cold. It bites at his skin as he climbs out onto the fire escape.

He sucks in a breath of cold air, lets it burn his lungs, has to lean on the window to get it shut again, but the moment the glass comes down, the world hushes.

It's not *quiet*—New York is never quiet—and New Year's has sent a current rippling through the city, but at least he can breathe, can think, can wash away the night—the year—in relative peace.

He goes to take a swig of beer, but the bottle's empty.

"Fuck," he mutters to no one but himself.

He's freezing, his coat buried somewhere in the pile on Robbie's bed, but he can't bring himself to go back inside for a jacket or a drink. Can't bear the tide of turning heads, the smoke filling their eyes, doesn't want the weight of their attention. And he can see the irony in that, he really can. Right now he'd give anything for one of Muriel's little pink umbrellas, but he's run out, so he sinks down onto the freezing metal steps, tells himself he's happy, tells himself that this is what he wanted.

He sets the empty bottle beside a pot that used to be home to a plant. Right now it holds only a small mountain of cigarette stubs.

Sometimes Henry wishes he smoked, just for the excuse to get some air.

He tried once or twice, but he couldn't get over the taste of tar, the stale smell it left on his clothes. He had this one aunt growing up who smoked until her nails went yellow and her skin cracked like old leather, until every cough sounded like she had loose change rattling in her chest. Every time he took a drag, he thought of her, and felt ill, and he didn't know if it was the memory or the taste, only knew it wasn't worth it.

There was pot, of course, but pot was something you were supposed to share with other people, not sneak away to smoke alone, and anyway, it always made him hungry and sad. Or really, sadder. It didn't iron out any of the wrinkles in his brain, after too many hits just made them into spirals, thoughts turning in and in and in on themselves forever.

He has this vivid memory of getting stoned senior year, he and Bea and Robbie lying in a tangle of limbs on the Columbia quad at three in the morning, high as kites and staring up at the sky. And even though they had to squint to make out any stars, and it might have just been their eyes struggling for purchase on the black expanse, Bea and Robbie went on and on about how big it all was, how wonderful, how calm it made them feel to be so small, and Henry didn't say anything because he was too busy holding his breath to keep from screaming.

"What the hell are you doing out here?"

Bea is leaning out the window. She swings her leg over the sill, and joins him out on the step, hissing when her leggings meet the cold metal. They sit in silence for a few moments. Henry stares out over the buildings. The clouds are low, the lights of Times Square shining up against them.

"Robbie's in love with me," he says.

"Robbie's always been in love with you," says Bea.

"But that's the thing," he says, shaking his head. "He wasn't in love with who I was, not really. He was in love with who I could have been. He wanted me to change, and I didn't, and—"

"Why should you change?" She turns to look at him, the frost swirling across her vision. "You're perfect, just the way you are."

Henry swallows.

"And what is that?" he asks. "What am I?"

He's been afraid to ask, afraid to know the meaning of the shine in her eyes, what she sees when she looks at him. Even now, he wishes he could take it back. But Bea just smiles and says, "You're my best friend, Henry."

His chest loosens, just a little. Because that's real.

It's true.

But then she keeps going.

"You're sweet, and sensitive, and an amazing listener."

And that last part makes his stomach drop, because Henry's never been a good listener. He's lost count of the number of fights they've gotten in because he wasn't paying attention.

"You're always there when I need you," she goes on, and his chest aches, because he knows he hasn't been, and this isn't like all the other lies, this isn't washboard abs, or a chiseled jaw or a deep voice, this isn't witty charm, or the son you've always wanted, or the brother you miss, this isn't any of the thousand things other people see when they look at him, things out of his control.

"I wish you saw yourself the way I see you."

What Bea sees is a good friend.

And Henry has no excuse for not already being one.

He puts his head in his hands, presses his palms against his eyes until he sees stars, and wonders if he can fix this, just this, if he can become the version of Henry that Bea sees, if it will make the frost in her eyes go away again, if she, at least, will see him clearly.

"I'm sorry," he whispers into the space between his knees and chest.

He feels her run her fingers through his hair. "For what?"

And what is he supposed to say?

Henry lets out a shuddering breath, and looks up. "If you could have anything," he says, "what would you ask for?"

"That depends," she says. "What's the cost?"

"How do you know there's a cost?"

"There's always give and take."

"Okay," says Henry, "if you sold your soul for one thing, what would it be?"

Bea chews her lip. "Happiness."

"What is that?" he asks. "I mean, is it just feeling happy for no reason? Or is it making other people happy? Is it being happy with your job, or your life, or—"

Bea laughs. "You always overthink things, Henry." She looks out over the fire escape. "I don't know, I guess I just mean I'd want to be happy with myself. Satisfied. What about you?"

He thinks of lying, doesn't. "I think I'd want to be loved."

Bea looks at him, then, eyes swirling with frost, and even through the mist, she looks suddenly, immeasurably sad. "You can't *make* people love you, Hen. If it's not a choice, it isn't real."

Henry's mouth goes dry.

She's right. Of course she's right.

And he's an idiot, trapped in a world where nothing's real.

Bea knocks her shoulder against his. "Come back in," she says. "Find someone to kiss before midnight. It's good luck."

She rises, waiting, but Henry can't bring himself to stand.

"It's okay," he says. "You go."

And he knows it's the deal he's made, knows it's what she sees and not what he is—but he's still relieved when Bea sits back down, and leans against him, a best friend staying with him in the dark. And soon the music dims, and the voices rise, and Henry can hear the countdown at their back.

Ten, nine, eight.

Oh god.

Seven, six, five.

What has he done?

Four, three, two.

It's going too fast.

One.

The air fills with whistles and cheers and wishes and Bea presses her lips against his, a moment of warmth against the cold. Just like that, the year is gone, the clocks reset, a three replaced by a four, and Henry knows that he has made a terrible mistake.

He has asked the wrong god for the wrong thing, and now he is enough because he is nothing. He is perfect, because he isn't there.

"It's going to be a good year," says Bea. "I can feel it." She sighs a plume of fog into the air between them. "Fuck, it's freezing." She stands, rubbing her hands. "Let's go in."

"You go ahead," he says, "I'll be there soon."

And she believes him, her steps clanking as she crosses the fire escape and slips back through the window, leaving it open for him to follow.

Henry sits there, alone in the dark, until he cannot stand the cold.

Henry gives up.

Resigns himself to the prism of his deal, which he has come to think of as a curse. He tries—to be a better friend, a better brother, a better son, tries to forget the meaning of the fog in people's eyes, tries to pretend that it is real, that he is real.

And then, one day, he meets a girl.

She walks into the store and steals a book, and when he catches her in the street, and she turns to look at him, there is no frost, no film, no wall of ice. Just clear brown eyes in a heart-shaped face, seven freckles scattered across her cheeks like stars.

And Henry thinks it must be a trick of the light, but she comes back the next day, and there it is again. The absence. Not just an absence, either, but something in its place.

A presence, a solid weight, the first steady pull he's felt in months. The strength of someone else's gravity.

Another orbit.

And when the girl looks at him, she doesn't see perfect. She sees someone who cares too much, who feels too much, who is lost, and hungry, and wasting inside his curse.

She sees the truth, and he doesn't know how, or why, only knows that he doesn't want it to end.

Because for the first time in months, in years, in his whole life, perhaps, Henry doesn't feel cursed at all.

For the first time, he feels seen.

There is only one exhibit left.

As the light thins, Henry and Addie hand over their blue rubber bands and step into a space composed only of plexiglass. The clear walls rise in rows. They remind him of the stacks in a library, or at the store, but there are no books, only a sign mounted in the air overhead that reads:

YOU ARE THE ART

Bowls of neon paint sit out in every aisle, and sure enough the walls are covered in markings. Signatures and scribbles, handprints and patterns.

Some run the length of the wall, and others are nested, like secrets, inside the larger marks. Addie dips a finger in green paint, and brings it to the wall. She draws a spiral, a single expanding mark. But by the time she reaches the fourth loop, the first has already faded, dropping away like a pebble in deep water.

Impossible, erased.

Her face doesn't falter, doesn't fall, but he can see the sadness before it drops as well, sinking out of sight.

How do you hold on? he wants to ask. Instead, he dips his hand into the green paint, reaches past her, but he doesn't draw anything. Instead, he waits, hovering above the glass.

"Put your hand over mine," he says, and she hesitates only a moment before pressing her palm to the back of his hand, ghosting her fingers over his own. "There," he says, "now we can draw."

She folds her hand over his, guides his index finger to the glass, and leaves a single mark, a line of green. He can feel the air lodge in her chest, can feel the sudden stiffness in her limbs, as she waits for it to disappear.

But it doesn't.

It stays, staring back at them in that fearless shade.

Something breaks inside her, then.

She makes a second mark, and a third, lets out a breathless laugh, and then, her hand on his, and his on the glass, Addie begins to draw. For the first time in three hundred years, she draws birds, and trees, draws a garden, draws a workshop, draws a city, draws a pair of eyes. The images spill out of her, and through him, and onto the wall with a clumsy, frenzied need. And she is laughing, tears streaming down her cheeks, and he wants to wipe them away, but his hands are her hands, and she is drawing.

And then she dips his finger in the paint, and brings it to the pane of glass, and this time, she writes in halting cursive, one letter at a time.

Her name.

It sits, nested among the many drawings.

Addie LaRue

Ten letters, two words. It is no different, he thinks, from the hundred other marks they've made—but it is. He knows it is.

Her hand drops away from his, and she reaches out, runs her fingers through the letters, and for a moment, the name is ruined, streaks of green against the glass. But by the time her fingers fall away, it is back, unmarred, unchanged.

Something changes in her, then. It rolls over her, the way storms roll over him, but this is different, this is not dark, but dazzling, a sudden, piercing sharpness.

And then she is pulling him away. Away from the maze, away from the people stretched beneath the starless night, away from the carnival of art, and the island, and he realizes she is not pulling him away at all, but toward something.

Toward the ferry.

Toward the subway.

Toward Brooklyn.

Toward home.

The whole way, she holds tightly to Henry, their fingers intertwined, the green paint staining both their hands, as they climb the stairs, as he opens the door, and then, she lets go, surging past him, through the apartment. He finds her in the bedroom, pulling a blue notebook from the shelf, scrounging a pen from the table. She presses them both into his hands, and Henry sinks onto the edge of the bed, folds back the cover of the notebook, one of a dozen he's never used, and she kneels, breathless, beside him.

"Do it again," she says.

And he brings the ballpoint to the blank page and writes her name, in tight but careful script.

Addie LaRue.

It doesn't dissolve, it doesn't fade, it sits there, alone in the center of the page. And Henry looks up at her, waiting for her to go on, to dictate what comes next, and she looks down past him, at the words.

Addie clears her throat.

"This is how it starts," she says.

And he begins to write.

PART FIVE

THE SHADOW WHO SMILED AND THE GIRL WHO SMILED BACK

Title: *Ho Portato le Stelle a Letto*
Artist: Matteo Renatti
Date: c. 1806–08
Medium: 20cm x 35cm pencil sketch on parchment
Location: On loan from the Gallerie dell'Accademia
Description: An illustration of a woman, the lines of her body imitated by the twisting bedsheets. Her face is little more than angles, framed by messy hair, but the artist has given her one very specific feature: seven small freckles in a band across her cheeks.
Background: This drawing, found in Renatti's 1806–8 notebook, is thought by some to be the inspiration for his later masterpiece *The Muse*. While the model's pose and the work's medium are different, the number and placement of the freckles is conspicuous enough for many to speculate on the model's enduring importance in Renatti's work.
Estimated Value: $267,000

Addie makes her way to the church.

It sits, near the center of Villon, squat and gray and unchanged, the field beside it bordered by a low stone wall.

It does not take her long to find her father's grave.

Jean LaRue.

Her father's grave is spare—a name, and dates, a Bible verse—*Everyone who calls on the name of the Lord will be saved.* No mention of the man her father was, no mention of his craft, or even his kindness.

A life reduced to a block of stone, a patch of grass.

Along the way Addie had picked a handful of flowers, wild things that grow at the edge of the path, weedy blossoms, yellow and white. She kneels to set them on the ground, stops when she sees the dates below her father's name.

1670–1714.

The year she left.

She searches her memory, tries to remember any signs of sickness. The cough that lingered in his chest, the shadow of weakness in his limbs. The memories from her second life are trapped in amber, perfectly preserved. But the ones from *before,* when she was Adeline LaRue—memories of kneading bread on a stool beside her mother, of watching her father carve faces into blocks of wood, of trailing Estele through the shallows of the Sarthe—those are fading. The twenty-three years she lived before the woods, before the deal, worn to little more than edges.

Later, Addie will be able to recall almost three hundred years in perfect detail, every moment of every day, preserved.

But she is already losing the sound of her father's laugh.

She cannot remember the exact color of her mother's eyes.

Cannot recall the set of Estele's jaw.

For years, she will lie awake and tell herself stories of the girl she'd been, in hopes of holding fast to every fleeting fragment, but it will have the opposite effect—the memories like talismans, too often touched; like saint's coins, the etching worn down to silver plate and faint impressions.

As for her father's sickness, it must have stolen in between one season and the next, and for the first time, Addie is grateful for the cleansing nature of her curse, for having made the deal at all—not for her own sake, but for her mother's. That Marthe LaRue had only to grieve one loss, instead of two.

Jean is buried among the other members of their family. An infant sister who only saw two years. A mother and father, both gone before Addie herself was ten. One row over, their own parents and unmarried siblings. The plot beside him, empty, and waiting for his wife.

There is no place for her, of course. But this string of graves, like a timeline, charting from the past into the future, this is what drove her to the woods that night, the fear of a life like this, leading to the same small patch of grass.

Staring down at her father's grave, Addie feels the heavy sadness of finality, the weight of an object coming to rest. The grief has come and gone—she lost this man fifty years ago, she has already mourned, and though it hurts, the pain isn't fresh. It has long dulled to an ache, the wound given way to scar.

She lays the flowers on her father's grave, and rises, moving deeper between the plots, drawn back in time with every step, until she is no longer Addie, but Adeline; no longer a ghost but flesh and blood and mortal. Still bound to this place, roots aching like phantom limbs.

She studies the names on the gravestones, knows each and every one, but the difference is that once upon a time, the names knew her, too.

Here is Roger, buried beside his first and only wife, Pauline.

Here is Isabelle, and her youngest, Sara, taken in the same year.

And here, almost in the center of the yard, is the name that matters most. The one that held her hand so many times, showed her there was more to life.

Estele Magritte, reads her tombstone. *1642–1719.*

The dates are carved over a simple cross, and Addie can almost hear the old woman hissing through her teeth.

Estele, buried in the shadow of a house she did not worship.

Estele, who would say that a soul is just the seed returned to soil, who wanted nothing but a tree over her bones. She should have been laid to rest at the edge of the woods, or amid the vegetables in her garden. She should have at least been buried in a corner plot, where the branches of an old yew reach over the low wall to shade the graves.

Addie crosses to the small shed at the edge of the churchyard, and finds a trowel amid the tools, and sets off for the woods.

It is the height of summer, but the air is cool beneath the cover of the trees. Midday, but still the smell of night lingers on the leaves. The scent of this place, so universal, and specific. With every breath the taste of soil on her tongue, the memory of desperation, a girl, sinking her hands into the dirt as she prayed.

Now, she sinks the trowel instead, coaxes a sapling from the soil. It is a fragile thing, likely to fall over with the next strong storm, but she carries it back to the churchyard, cradled like an infant in her hands, and if anyone finds it strange, they will forget about the sight long before they think to tell anyone. And if they notice the tree growing over the old woman's grave, perhaps they will stop and think of older gods again.

And as Addie leaves the church behind, the bells begin to chime, calling the villagers to Mass.

She walks down the road as they pour from their homes, children clinging to their mother's hands, and men and women side by side. Some faces new to her, and others, she knows.

There is George Therault, and Roger's oldest daughter, and Isabelle's two sons, and the next time Addie comes, they will all be dead, the last of her old life—her first life—buried in the same ten-meter plot.

The hut sits abandoned at the edge of the woods.

The low fence has fallen in, and Estele's garden is long overgrown, the house itself slowly giving way, sagging with age and neglect. The door is shut fast, but the shutters hang on broken joints, exposing the glass of a single window, cracked open like a tired eye.

The next time Addie comes, the frame of the house will be lost beneath the green, and the time after that, the woods will have crept forward and swallowed it all.

But today, it still stands, and she makes her way up the weedy path, the stolen lantern in one hand. She keeps expecting the old woman to step out of the woods, wrinkled arms filled with cuttings, but the only rustle comes from magpies and the sound of her own feet.

Inside, the hut is damp, and empty, the dark space littered with debris— the clay shards of a broken cup, a crumbling table—but gone are the bowls in which she mixed her salves, and the cane she used when the weather was wet, and the bundles of herbs that hung from the rafters, and the iron pot that sat in the hearth.

Addie is sure that Estele's things were taken up after her death, parceled out through the village, just as her life was, deemed public property simply because she did not wed. Villon, her ward, because Estele had no child.

She goes into the garden, and harvests what she can from the wild plot, carries the ragged bounty of carrots and long beans inside and sets it on the table. She throws the shutters open and finds herself face-to-face with the woods.

The trees stand in a dark line, tangled branches clawing at the sky. Their roots are inching forward, crawling into the garden and across the lawn. A slow and patient advance.

The sun is sinking now, and even though it's summer, a damp has crawled in through the gaps in the thatched roof, between the stones and under the door, and a chill hangs over the bones of the little hut.

Addie carries a stolen lantern to the hearth. It has been a rainy month, and the wood is damp, but she is patient, coaxing the flame from the lamp until it catches on the kindling.

Fifty years, and she is still learning the shape of her curse.

She cannot make a thing, but she can use it.

She cannot break a thing, but she can steal it.

She cannot start a fire, but she can keep it going.

She does not know if it's some kind of mercy, or simply a crack in the mortar of her curse, one of the few fissures she's found in the walls of this new life. Perhaps Luc hasn't noticed. Or perhaps he has put them there on purpose, to draw her out, to make her hope.

Addie draws a smoldering twig from the fireplace and brings it idly to the threadbare rug. It is dry enough that it should catch, and burn, but it does not. It gutters, and cools too quickly, just outside the safety of its hearth.

She sits on the floor, humming softly as she feeds stick after stick into the blaze until it burns the chill off the place like a breath scattering dust.

She feels him like a draft.

He does not knock.

He never knocks.

One moment she is alone, and the next, she is not.

"Adeline."

She *hates* the way it makes her feel to hear him say her name, hates the way she leans into the word like a body seeking shelter from a storm.

"Luc."

She turns, expecting to see him as he was in Paris, dressed in the fine salon fashion, but instead he is exactly as he was the night they met, wind-blown and shadow-edged, in a simple dark tunic, the laces open at the collar. The firelight dances across his face, shades the edges of his jaw and cheek and brow like charcoal.

His eyes slide over the meager bounty on the sill before returning to her. "Back where you started . . ."

Addie rises to her feet, so he can't look down on her.

"Fifty years," he says. "How quickly they go by."

They have not gone quickly at all, not for her, and he knows it. He is looking for bare skin, soft places to slide the knife, but she will not give him such an easy target. "No time at all," she echoes coolly. "To think one life would ever be enough."

Luc flashes only the edge of a smile.

"What a picture you make, tending that fire. You could almost be Estele."

It is the first time she has heard that name on his lips, and there is something in the way he says it, almost wistful. Luc crosses to the window, and looks out at the line of trees. "How many nights she stood here, and whispered out into the woods."

He glances over his shoulder, a coy grin playing over his lips. "For all her talk of freedom, she was so lonely in the end."

Addie shakes her head. "No."

"You should have been here with her," he says. "Should have eased her pain when she was ill. Should have laid her down to rest. You owed her that."

Addie draws back as if struck.

"You were so selfish, Adeline. And because of you, she died alone."

We all die alone. That is what Estele would say—at least, she thinks. She hopes. Once, she would have been certain, but the confidence has faded with the memory of the woman's voice.

Across the room, the darkness moves. One moment he is at the window, the next, he is behind her, his voice threading through her hair.

"She was so ready to die," Luc says. "So desperate for that spot in the shade. She stood at that window and begged, and begged. I could have given it to her."

A memory, old fingers tight around her wrist.

Never pray to the gods that answer after dark.

Addie turns on him. "She would never have prayed to *you*."

A flickering smile. "No." A sneer. "But think of how sad she'd be to know *you* did."

Addie's temper flares. Her hand flies out before she thinks to stop it, and even then, she half expects to find no purchase, only air and smoke. But Luc is caught off guard, and so her palm strikes skin, or something like it. His head turns a fraction with the force of the blow. There is no blood on those perfect lips, of course, no heat on that cool skin, but she has at least wiped the smile from his face.

Or so she thinks.

Until he begins to laugh.

The sound is eerie, unreal, and when he turns his face back toward her, she stills. There is nothing human in it now. The bones are too sharp, the shadows too deep, the eyes too bright.

"You forget yourself," he says, his voice dissolving into woodsmoke. "You forget *me*."

Pain lances up through Addie's feet, sudden and sharp. She looks down, searching for a wound, but the pain lights her from within. A deep, internal ache, the force of every step she's ever walked.

"Perhaps I have been too merciful."

The pain climbs through her limbs, infecting knee and hip, wrist and shoulder. Her legs buckle beneath her, and it is all she can do not to scream.

The darkness looks down with a smile.

"I have made this too easy."

Addie watches in horror as her hands begin to wrinkle and thin, blue veins standing out beneath papery skin.

"You asked only for life. I gave you your health, and youth, as well."

Her hair comes loose from its bun and hangs lank before her eyes, the strands going dry and brittle and gray.

"It has made you arrogant."

Her sight weakens, vision blurring until the room is only smudges and vague shapes.

"Perhaps you need to suffer."

Addie squeezes her eyes shut, heart fluttering with panic.

"No," she says, and it is the closest she has ever come to pleading.

She can feel him, moving closer. Can feel the shadow of him looming over her.

"I will take away these pains. I will let you rest. I will even raise a tree over your bones. And all you have to do"—the voice seeps through the dark—"is surrender."

That word, like a tear in the veil. And for all the pain, and terror, of this moment, Addie knows she will not give in.

She has survived worse. She will survive worse. This is nothing but a god's foul temper.

When she finds the breath to speak, the words come out in a ragged whisper. "Go to Hell."

She braces herself, wonders if he will rot her all the way through, bend her body into a corpse, and leave her there, a broken husk on the old woman's floor. But there is only more laughter, low and rumbling, and then nothing, the night stretching into stillness.

Addie is afraid to open her eyes, but when she does, she finds herself alone.

The ache has faded from her bones. Her loose hair has regained its chestnut shade. Her hands, once ruined, are again young, smooth, and strong.

She rises, shaking, and turns toward the hearth.

But the fire, so carefully tended, has gone out.

That night, Addie curls up on the moldering pallet, beneath a threadbare blanket left unclaimed, and thinks of Estele.

She closes her eyes and inhales until she can *almost* smell the herbs that clung to the old woman's hair, the garden and sap on her skin. She holds fast to the memory of Estele's crooked smile, her crow-like laugh, the voice she used when she spoke to gods, and the one she used with Addie. Back when she was young, when Estele taught her not to be afraid of storms, of shadows, of sounds in the night.

II

Addie leans against the window, watching the sun rise over Brooklyn.

She wraps her fingers around a cup of tea, savoring the heat against her palms. The glass fogs with cold, the dregs of winter clinging to the edges of the day. She is wearing one of Henry's sweatshirts, cotton branded with the Columbia logo. It smells like him. Like old books and fresh coffee.

She pads barefoot back into the bedroom, where Henry lies facedown, arms folded beneath the pillow, his cheek turned away. And in that moment, he looks so much like Luc, and yet nothing like Luc at all. The resemblance between them wavers, like double vision. His curls, spread like black feathers on the white pillow, fading to downy fluff at the nape of his neck. His back rises and falls, steady with the smooth, shallow tread of sleep.

Addie sets the cup down on the bedside table, between Henry's glasses and a leather watch. She traces her finger along the dark metal rim, the gold numerals set into the black ground. It rocks under her touch, reveals the small inscription on the back.

Live well.

A small shiver runs through her, and she's about to pick it up when Henry groans into his pillow, a soft protest to morning.

Addie abandons the watch, and climbs back into bed beside him. "Hello."

He gropes for his glasses, puts them on, and looks at her, and smiles, and this is the part that will never get old. The knowing. The present folding on top of the past instead of erasing it, replacing it. He pulls her back against him.

"Hello," he whispers into her hair. "What time is it?"

"Almost eight."

Henry groans, and tightens his grip around her. He is warm, and Addie wishes aloud they could stay there all day. But he is awake now, that restless energy winding around him like rope. She can feel it in the tension of his arms, the subtle shifting of his weight.

"I should go," she says, because she assumes that is what you are supposed to say when you are in someone else's bed. When they remember how you got there. But she doesn't say "I should go *home*" and Henry senses the dropped word.

"Where do you live?" he asks.

Nowhere, she thinks. Everywhere.

"I manage. The city is full of beds."

"But you don't have a place of your own."

Addie looks down at the borrowed sweatshirt, the sum total of her current possessions flung over the nearest chair. "No."

"Then you can stay here."

"Three dates, and you're asking me to move in?"

Henry laughs, because of course it is absurd. But it is hardly the strangest thing in either of their lives.

"How about I ask you to stay—for now."

Addie doesn't know what to say. And before she can think of something, he is out of bed, pulling open the bottom drawer. He pushes the contents to one side, carving out space. "You can put your stuff here."

He looks at her, suddenly uncertain. "Do you have things?"

She will explain, eventually, the details of her curse, the way it twists and curls around her. But he doesn't know them yet—doesn't need to. For him, her story has just started.

"There's no point really, in having more than you can hold, when you have no place to put things down."

"Well, if you get things—if you want them—you can put them there."

With that, he heads sleepily for the shower, and she stares at the space he's made for her, and wonders what would happen if she had things to put inside. Would they disappear immediately? Go slowly, carelessly missing, like socks stolen by a dryer? She has never been able to hang on to anything for long. Only the leather jacket, and the wooden ring, and she's always known it is because Luc wanted her to have both—had bound them to her under the guise of gifts.

She turns and studies the clothes flung over the chair.

They are streaked with paint from the High Line. There's green on her shirt, a purple smear on the knee of her jeans. Her boots, too, are flecked with yellow and blue. She knows the paint will fade, rinsed off by a puddle, or simply wiped away by time, but that's how memories are *supposed* to work.

There—and then, little by little, gone.

She gets dressed in yesterday's outfit, takes up the leather jacket, but instead of shrugging it on, she folds it carefully, places it in the empty drawer. It sits there, surrounded by open space, waiting to be filled.

Addie rounds the bed, and nearly steps on the notebook.

It lies open on the floor—it must have slipped off the bed during the night— and she lifts it gingerly, as if it's bound with ash and spider silk instead of paper and glue. She half expects it to crumble at her touch, but it holds, and when she chances to pull back the cover, she finds the first few pages filled. Addie takes another chance, runs her fingers lightly over the words, feels the indent of the pen, the years hidden behind each word.

This is how it starts, he wrote under her name.

The first thing she still remembers is the ride to market. Her father in the seat beside her, cart filled with his work . . .

She holds her breath as she reads, the shower filling the room with a quiet hush.

Her father tells her stories. She doesn't remember the words but she remembers the way he said them . . .

Addie perches there, reading until she runs out of words, the script giving way to page after page of empty space, waiting to be filled.

When she hears Henry turn the water off, she forces herself to close the book, and sets it gently, almost reverently, back on the bed.

To think, she could have lived and died and never seen the sea.

No matter, though. Addie is here now, pale cliffs rising to her right, stone sentinels at the edge of the beach where she sits, skirts pooling on the sand. She stares out at the expanse, the coastline giving way to water, and water giving way to sky. She has seen maps of course, but ink and paper hold nothing to this. To the salt smell, the murmur of waves, the hypnotic draw of the tide. To the scope and scale of the sea, and the knowledge that somewhere, beyond the horizon, there is more.

It will be a century before she crosses the Atlantic, and when she does, she'll wonder if the maps are wrong, will begin to doubt the existence of land at all—but here and now, Addie is simply enchanted.

Once upon a time, her world was only as large as a small village in the middle of France. But it keeps getting bigger. The map of her life unfurls, revealing hills and valleys, towns and cities and seas. Revealing Le Mans. Revealing Paris. Revealing this.

She has been in Fécamp for nearly a week, spending her days between the pier and the tide, and if anyone takes notice of the strange woman alone on the sand, they have not seen fit to bother her about it. Addie watches boats come and go, and wonders where they are going; wonders, too, what would happen if she boarded one, where it would take her. Back in Paris, the food shortages are getting worse, the penalties, worse, everything steadily worse. The tension has spilled out of the city, too, the nervous energy reaching all the way here, to the coast. All the more reason, Addie tells herself, to sail away.

And yet.

Something always holds her back.

Today, it is the storm that's rolling in. It hovers out over the sea, bruising the sky. Here and there the sun splits through, a line of burned light falling toward the slate gray water. She retrieves the book, lying in the sand beside her, begins to read again.

> *Our revels now are ended. These our actors,*
> *As I foretold you, were all spirits and*
> *Are melted into air, into thin air:*

It is Shakespeare's *Tempest*. Now and then she trips over the playwright's cadence, the style strange, English rhyme and meter still foreign to her mind. But she is learning, and here and there she finds herself falling into the flow.

> *And, like the baseless fabric of this vision,*
> *The cloud-capp'd towers, the gorgeous palaces,*
> *The solemn temples, the great globe itself . . .*

Her eyes begin to strain against the failing light.

> *Yea, all which it inherit, shall dissolve*
> *And, like this insubstantial pageant faded,*
> *Leave not a rack behind—*

"'We are such stuff as dreams are made on,'" comes a now familiar voice behind her. "'And our little life is rounded with a sleep.'" A soft sound, like breathless laughter. "Well, not all lives."

Luc looms over her like a shadow.

She has not forgiven him for the violence of that night back in Villon. Braces for it even now, though they have seen each other several times in the intervening years, forged a wary kind of truce.

But she knows better than to trust it as he sinks onto the sand beside her, one arm draped lazily over his knee, the picture of languid grace, even here. "I was there, you know, when he wrote that verse."

"Shakespeare?" She cannot hide her surprise.

"Who do you think he called on in the dead of night, when the words would not come?"

"You lie."

"I boast," he says. "They are not the same. Our William sought a patron, and I obliged."

The storm is rolling in, a curtain of rain sliding toward the coast. "Is that really how you see yourself?" she asks, tapping sand from her book. "As some splendid benefactor?"

"Do not sulk, simply because you chose poorly."

"Did I though?" she counters. "After all, I am free."

"And forgotten."

But she is ready for the barb. "Most things are." Addie looks out to sea.

"Adeline," he scolds, "what a stubborn thing you are. And yet, it has not even been a hundred years. I wonder, then, how you will feel after a hundred more."

"I don't know," she says blandly. "I suppose you'll have to ask me then."

The storm reaches the coast. The first drops begin to fall, and Addie presses the book to her chest, shielding the pages from the damp.

Luc rises. "Walk with me," he says, holding out his hand. It is not an invitation so much as a command, but the rain is quickly turning from a promise to a steady pour, and she has only the one dress. She rises without his help, brushing the sand from her skirts.

"This way."

He leads her through town, toward the silhouette of a building, its vaulted steeple piercing the low clouds. It is, of all things, a church.

"You're joking."

"I am not the one getting wet," he says. And indeed, he's not. She is soaked through by the time they reach the shelter of the stone awning, but Luc is dry. The rain has not even touched him.

He smiles, reaching for the door.

It does not matter that the church is locked. Were it draped in chains, it would still open for him. Such boundaries, she has learned, mean nothing to the dark.

Inside, the air is stuffy, the stone walls holding in the summer heat. It is too dark to see more than the outlines of the pews, the figure on its cross.

Luc spreads his arms. "Behold, the house of God."

His voice echoes through the chamber, soft and sinister.

Addie has always wondered if Luc could set foot on sacred ground, but the sound of his shoes on the church floor is answer to that question.

She makes her way down the aisle, but she cannot shake the strangeness of this place. Without the bells, the organ, the bodies crowding in for services, the church feels abandoned. Less a house of worship and more a tomb.

"Care to confess your sins?"

Luc has moved with all the ease of shadows in the dark. He is no longer behind her, but sitting in the first row now, his arms spread along the back of the pew, his legs thrown out, ankles crossed in lazy repose.

Addie was raised to kneel in the little stone chapel in the center of Villon, spent days folded into Paris pews. She has listened to the bells, and the organ, and the calls to prayer. And yet, despite it all, she has never understood the appeal. How does a ceiling bring you closer to heaven? If God is so large, why build walls to hold Him in?

"My parents were believers," she muses, her fingers trailing over the pews. "They always spoke of God. Of His strength, His mercy, His light. They said He was everywhere, in everything." Addie stops before the altar. "They believed in everything so easily."

"And you?"

Addie looks up at the panels of stained glass, the images little more than ghosts without the sun to light them. She wanted to believe. She listened, and waited to hear His voice, to feel His presence, the way she might feel sun on her shoulders, or wheat beneath her hands. The way she felt the presence of the old gods Estele so favored. But there, in the cold stone house, she never felt anything.

She shakes her head, and says aloud, "I never understood why I should believe in something I could not feel, or hear, or see."

Luc raises a brow. "I think," he says, "they call that faith."

"Says the devil in the house of God." Addie glances his way as she says it, and catches a brief flash of yellow across the steady green.

"A house is a house," he says, annoyed. "This one belongs to all, or none. And you think me the devil, now? You weren't so certain in the woods."

"Perhaps," she says, "you have made me a believer."

Luc tips his head back, a wicked smile tugging at his mouth. "And you think if I am real, then so is he. The light to my shadow, the day to my dark? And you are convinced, if only you had prayed to him instead of me, he would have shown you such kindness and such mercy."

She has wondered as much a hundred times, though of course she does not say it.

Luc's hands slide off the pew as he leans forward.

"And now," he adds, "you will never know. But as for me," he says, rising, "well—the *devil* is simply a new word for a very old idea. And as for *God*, well, if all it takes is a flair for drama and a bit of golden trim . . ."

He flicks his fingers, and suddenly the buttons on his coat, the buckles on his shoes, the stitching on his waistcoat are no longer black, but gilded. Burnished stars against a moonless night.

He smiles, then brushes the filigree away like dust.

She watches it fall, looks up again to find him there, inches from her face.

"But this is the difference between us, Adeline," he whispers, fingers grazing her chin. "*I* will always answer."

She shivers, despite herself. At the too-familiar touch against her skin, at the lurid green of his eyes, at the wolfish, wild grin.

"Besides," he says, fingers falling from her face, "all gods have a price. I'm hardly the only one who trades in souls." Luc holds his hand, open, to one side, and light blooms in the air just above his palm. "*He* lets souls wither on shelves. I water them."

The light warps and coils.

"He makes promises. I pay up front."

It flares once, sudden and brilliant, and then draws close, taking on a solid shape.

Addie has always wondered what a soul would look like.

It is such a grand word, *soul*. Like *god*, like *time*, like *space*, and when she's tried to picture it, she's conjured images of lightning, or sunbeams through dust, of storms in the shapes of human forms, of vast and edgeless white.

The truth is so much smaller.

The light in Luc's hand is a marble, glassy and glowing with a faint internal light.

"Is that all?"

And yet, Addie cannot tear her gaze from the fragile orb. She feels herself reaching for it, but he draws it back, out of her reach.

"Do not be deceived by its appearance." He turns the glowing bead between his fingers. "You look at me and see a man, though you know I am nothing of the sort. This shape is only an aspect, designed for the beholder."

The light twists, and shifts, the orb flattening into a disk. And then a ring. Her ring. The ash wood glows, and her heart aches to see it, to hold it, to feel the worn surface against her skin. But she clenches her hands into fists to keep from reaching out again.

"What does it really look like?"

"I can show you," he purrs, letting the light settle in his palm. "Say the word, and I will lay your own soul bare before you. Surrender, and I promise, the last thing you see will be the truth."

There it is again.

One time salt, and the next honey, and each designed to cover poison.

Addie looks at the ring, lets herself linger on it one last time, and then forces her gaze up past the light to meet the dark.

"You know," she says, "I think I'd rather live and wonder."

Luc's mouth twitches, and she cannot tell if it is anger or amusement.

"Suit yourself, my dear," he says, dousing the light between his fingers.

IV

Addie sits folded in a leather chair in the corner of The Last Word, the soft purr of the cat emanating from the shelves somewhere behind her head, as she watches customers lean toward Henry like flowers toward the sun.

Once you know about a thing, you start to see it everywhere.

Someone says the words *purple elephant,* and all of a sudden, you catch sight of them in shop windows and on T-shirts, stuffed animals and bill-boards, and you wonder how you never noticed.

It is the same with Henry, and the deal he made.

A man, laughing at everything he says.

A woman beams, radiant with joy.

A teenage girl steals chances to touch his shoulder, his arm, blushing with blatant attraction.

Despite it all, Addie is not jealous.

She has lived too long and lost too much, and what little she's had has been borrowed or stolen, never kept to herself. She has learned to share—and yet, every time Henry steals a glance her way, she feels a pleasant flush of warmth, as welcome as the sudden appearance of sunlight between clouds.

Addie draws her legs up into the chair, a book of poems open in her lap.

She's swapped the paint-spattered clothes for a new pair of black jeans, and an oversized sweater, lifted from a thrift store while Henry was work-ing. But she kept the boots, the little flecks of yellow and blue a reminder of the night before, the closest thing she has to a photo, a material memory. "Ready?"

She looks up, sees the shop sign already turned outwardly to closed, and Henry standing near the door, his jacket slung over his arm. He holds out his hand, helps her from the leather chair, which, he explains, has a way of eating people.

They step outside, climb the four steps back to the street.

"Where to?" asks Addie.

It is early, and Henry's buzzing with a restless energy. It seems to worsen around dusk, sunset a steady marker of one day gone, time passing with the loss of light.

"Have you been to the Ice Cream Factory?"

"That sounds like fun."

His face falls. "You've already been."

"I don't mind going again."

But Henry shakes his head, and says, "I want to show you something new. Is there anywhere you *haven't* been?" he asks, and after a long moment, Addie shrugs.

"I'm sure there is," she says. "But I haven't found it yet."

She meant it to be funny, light, but Henry frowns, deep in thought, and looks around.

"Okay," he says, grabbing her hand. "Come with me."

An hour later, they are standing in Grand Central.

"I hate to break it to you," she says, looking around at the bustling station, "but I've been here before. Most people have."

But Henry shoots her a grin that's pure mischief. "This way."

She follows him down the escalator to the station's lower level. They weave, hand in hand, through a steady sea of evening travelers, toward the bustling food hall, but Henry stops short, beneath an intersection of tile arches, corridors branching every direction. He draws her into one of the pillared corners, where the arches split, curving overhead and across, turns her toward the tiled wall.

"Stay here," he says, and starts to walk away.

"Where are you going?" she asks, already turning to follow.

But Henry returns, squaring her shoulders to the arch. "Stay here, like this," he says. "And listen."

Addie turns her ear to the tile wall, but she can't hear anything over the shuffle of foot traffic, the clatter and rattle of the evening crowd. She glances over her shoulder.

"Henry, I don't—"

But Henry isn't there. He's jogging across the hall to the opposite side of the arch, maybe thirty feet away. He looks back at her, and then turns away and buries his face in the corner, looking for all the world like a kid playing hide-and-seek, counting to ten.

Addie feels ridiculous, but she leans in close to the tiled wall, and waits, and listens.

And then, impossibly, she hears his voice.

"Addie."

She startles. The word is soft but clear, as if he's standing right beside her.

"How are you doing this?" she asks the arch. And she can hear the smile in his voice when he answers.

"The sound follows the curve of the arch. A phenomenon that happens when spaces bend just right. It's called a whispering gallery."

Addie marvels. Three hundred years, and there are still new things to learn.

"Talk to me," comes the voice against the tile.

"What should I say?" she whispers to the wall.

"Well," says Henry, softly, in her ear. "Why don't you tell me a story?"

Paris is burning.

Outside, the air reeks of gunpowder and smoke, and while the city has never been truly quiet, for the last fortnight the noise has been ceaseless. It is musket rounds, and cannon fire, it is soldiers shouting orders, and the retort carried from mouth to mouth.

Vive la France. Vive la France. Vive la France.

Two weeks since the taking of the Bastille, and the city seems determined to tear itself in two. And yet, it must go on, it must survive, and all those in it, left to find a way through the daily storm.

Addie has chosen to move at night instead.

She weaves through the dark, a saber jostling at her hip and a tricorne low over her brow. The clothes she peeled from a man who had been shot in the street, the torn cloth and dark stain on the stomach hidden beneath a vest that she salvaged from another corpse. Beggars can't be choosers, and it is too dangerous to travel as a woman alone. Worse still these days to play the part of noble—better to blend in in other ways.

A current has swept through the city, at once triumphant and intoxicating, and in time, Addie will learn to taste the changes in the air, to sense the line between vigor and violence. But tonight, the rebellion is still new, the energy strange and unreadable.

As for the city itself, the avenues of Paris have all become a maze, the sudden erection of barriers and barricades turning any path into a series of dead ends. It is no surprise then when she rounds another corner and finds a pile of crates and debris burning up ahead.

Addie swears under her breath, is about to double back, when boots sound on the road behind her and a gun goes off, cracking against the barricade above her head.

She turns to find half a dozen men barring her retreat, dressed in the mottled garb of the rebellion. Their muskets and sabers glint dully in the evening light. She is grateful, then, that her clothes belonged once to a commoner.

Addie clears her throat, careful to force her voice deep, gruff as she calls out, *"Vive la France!"*

The men return the cheer, but to her dismay, they don't retreat. Instead, they continue toward her, hands resting on their weapons. In the light of the blaze, their eyes are glassy with wine, and the nameless energy of the night.

"What are you doing here?" demands one.

"Could be a spy," says another. "Plenty of soldiers parading about in common dress. Robbing the bodies of the valiant dead."

"I want no trouble," she calls out. "I am simply lost. Let me pass, and I will be gone."

"And return with a dozen more," mutters the second.

"I am not a spy, nor a soldier, nor a corpse," she calls back. "I was only looking—"

"—to sabotage," cuts in a third.

"Or raid our stores," suggests another.

They are no longer shouting. There is no need. They have drawn close enough to speak in level tones, pressing her back against the burning barricade. If she can only get past them, get away, out of sight and out of mind— but there is nowhere to run. The side streets have all been barred. The crates burn hot behind her.

"If you are a friend, then prove it."

"Lay down your sword."

"Take off your hat. Let us see your face."

Addie swallows, and casts the hat aside, hoping the dark will be enough to hide the softness of her features. But just then, the barricade crackles behind her, some beam giving way to flame, and for an instant, the fire brightens, and she knows the light is strong enough to see by. Knows it by the way their faces change.

"Let me pass," she says again, hand going to the sword at her hip. She knows how to wield it, knows too that there are five of them and only one of her, and if she draws steel, there will be no way out of this but through. The promise of survival is small comfort against the prospect of what might happen first.

They close in, and Addie draws the sword.

"Stay *back*," she growls.

And to her surprise, the men stop walking. Their steps drag to a halt, and a shadow falls across their faces, the expressions going slack. Hands slip from weapons, and heads loll on shoulders, and the night goes still, save for the crackle of the burning crates and the breezy arrival of a voice at her back.

"Humans are so ill-equipped for peace."

She turns, her sword still raised, and finds Luc, his edges black against the blaze. He doesn't retreat from the sword, simply reaches up and runs his hand along the steel with all the grace of a lover touching skin, a musician fondling an instrument. She half expects the blade to sing beneath his fingers.

"My Adeline," says the darkness, "you do have a way of finding trouble." That vivid green gaze drifts to the motionless men. "How lucky I was here."

"You are the night itself," she parrots. "Shouldn't you be everywhere?"

A smile flickers across his face. "What a good memory you have." His fingers curl around her blade, and it begins to rust. "How tiresome that must be."

"Not at all," she says dryly. "It is a gift. Think of all there is to learn. And I, with all the time to learn i—"

She is interrupted by a volley of gunfire in the distance, the answer of a cannon, heavy as thunder. Luc frowns in distaste, and it amuses her to see him unsettled. The cannon sounds again, and he takes her by the wrist.

"Come," he says, "I cannot hear myself think."

He turns swiftly on his heel, and draws her in his wake. But instead of stepping forward, he steps sideways, into the deep shadow of the nearest wall. Addie flinches back, expecting to strike stone, but the wall opens, and the world gives way, and before she can draw breath, draw back, Paris is gone, and so is Luc.

As she is plunged into absolute darkness.

It is not as still as death, not as empty, or calm. There is a violence to this blind black void. It is birds' wings beating against her skin. It is the rush of the wind in her hair. It is a thousand whispering voices. It is fear, and falling, and it is a feral, wild feeling, and by the time she thinks to scream, the darkness has peeled away again, the night has re-formed, and Luc is once again beside her.

Addie sways, braces herself against a doorway, feeling ill, and empty, and confused.

"What was that?" she asks, but Luc does not answer. He is now standing several feet away, hands splayed on the railing of a bridge as he looks out over the river.

But it is not the Seine.

There are no burning barricades. There is no cannon fire. No men waiting, weapons at their sides. Only a foreign river running beneath a foreign bridge, and foreign buildings rising along foreign banks, their rooftops capped in red tiles.

"That's better," he says, adjusting his cuffs. Somehow, in the moment of nothing, he has changed clothes, the collar higher now, the cut and trim a looser silk, while Addie wears the same ill-fitted tunic, salvaged from a Paris street.

A couple passes arm in arm, and she catches only the highs and lows of a foreign tongue.

"Where are we?" she demands.

Luc glances over his shoulder, and says something in the same choppy flow before repeating himself in French. "We are in Florence."

Florence. She has heard the name before, but knows little of it, besides the obvious—that it is not in France but *Italy*.

"What have you done?" she demands. "How have you— No, never mind. Just take me back."

He arches a brow. "Adeline, for someone with nothing *but* time, you are always in a hurry." And with that, he ambles away, and Addie is left to follow in his wake.

She takes in the strangeness of the new city. Florence is all odd shapes and sharp edges, domes and spires, white stone walls and copper-slated roofs. It is a place painted in a different palette, music played in a different chord. Her heart flutters at the beauty of it, and Luc smiles as if he can sense her pleasure.

"You would rather the burning streets of Paris?"

"I assumed you would be fond of war."

"That isn't war," he says curtly. "It's only a skirmish."

She follows him into an open courtyard, a plaza scattered with stone benches, the air heavy with the scent of summer blossoms. He walks ahead, the picture of a gentleman taking the night air, slowing only when he sees a man, a bottle of wine beneath one arm. He curls his fingers, and the man changes course, coming like a dog to heel. Luc slides into that other tongue, a language she will come to know as Florentine, and though she does not yet know the words, she knows the lure in his voice, that gauzy sheen that takes shape in the air around them. Knows, too, the dreamy look in the Italian's eyes as he hands over the wine with a placid smile, and strolls absently away.

Luc sinks onto a bench, and draws two glasses out of nothing.

Addie does not sit. She stands, and watches as he uncorks the bottle and pours the wine, and says, "Why would I be fond of war?"

It is the first time, she thinks, he has asked an honest question, one not meant to goad, demand, coerce. "Are you not a god of chaos?"

His expression sours. "I am a god of promise, Adeline, and wars make terrible patrons." He offers her a glass, and when she does not reach to take it, he lifts, as if to toast her. "To long life."

Addie cannot help herself. She shakes her head, bemused. "Some nights, you love to see me suffer, so that I will yield. Others, you seem intent to spare me from it. I do wish you'd make up your mind."

A shadow sweeps across his face. "Trust me, my dear, you don't." A small shiver runs through her as he lifts the wineglass to his lips. "Do not mistake this—any of it—for kindness, Adeline." His eyes go bright with mischief. "I simply want to be the one who breaks you."

She looks around at the tree-lined plaza, lit by lanterns, the moonlight shining on the red-capped roofs. "Well, you'll have to try harder than . . ."

But she trails off as her attention returns to the stone bench.

"Oh, hell," she mutters, looking around the empty square.

Because Luc, of course, is gone.

VI

✦ ✦ ✦ ✦ ✦

"He just left you there?" says Henry, aghast.

Addie takes a fry, turning it between her fingers. "There are worse places to be left."

They're sitting at a high-top table in a so-called pub—what passes for a pub outside of Britain—sharing an order of vinegary fish-and-chips and a pint of warm beer.

A waiter passes by, and smiles at Henry.

A pair of girls heading for the bathroom slow as they come into his orbit, and stare as they leave again.

A stream of words drifts over from a nearby table, the low, rapid staccato of German, and Addie's mouth twitches in a smile.

"What is it?" asks Henry.

She leans in. "The couple over there." She tilts her head in their direction. "They're having a fight. Apparently the guy slept with his secretary. And his assistant. And his Pilates instructor. The woman knew about the first two, but she's mad about the third, because they both take Pilates at the same studio."

Henry stares at her, marveling. "How many languages do you know?"

"Enough," she says, but he clearly wants to know, so she ticks them off on her fingers. "French, of course. And English. Greek and Latin. German, Italian, Spanish, Swiss, some Portuguese, though it's not perfect."

"You would have made an amazing spy."

She raises a brow behind her pint. "Who says I haven't been one?"

The plates are empty when she looks around, sees the waiter duck into the kitchen. "Come on," she says, grabbing his hand.

Henry frowns. "We haven't paid."

"I know," she says, hopping down from the stool, "but if we go now, he'll think he just forgot to clear the table. He won't remember."

This is the problem with a life like Addie's.

She has gone so long without roots, she doesn't know how to grow them anymore.

So used to losing things, she isn't sure how to hold them.

How to make space in a world the size of herself.

"No," says Henry. "He won't remember *you*. But he'll remember me. I'm not invisible, Addie. I'm the exact opposite of invisible."

Invisible. The word scrapes over her skin.

"I'm not invisible either," she says.

"You know what I mean. I can't just come and go. And even if I could," he says, reaching for his wallet, "it would still be *wrong*."

The word hits like a blow, and she is back in Paris, doubled over with hunger. She is at the marquis's house, dining in stolen clothes, stomach twisting as Luc points out that someone will pay for every bite she takes.

Her face burns with shame.

"Fine," she says, pulling a handful of twenties from her pocket. She drops two on the table. "Better?" But when she looks at Henry, his frown has only deepened.

"Where did you get that money?"

She doesn't want to tell him that she walked out of a designer store and into a pawn shop, moving pieces from one hand to the other. Doesn't want to explain that everything she has—everything besides *him*—is stolen. And that in some ways, so is he. Addie doesn't want to see the judgment on his face, doesn't want to think about how merited it might be.

"Does it matter?" she asks.

And Henry says, *"Yes,"* with so much conviction, she flushes crimson.

"Do you think I want to live like this?" Addie grits her teeth. "No job, no ties, no way to hold on to anyone or anything? Do you think I like being so alone?"

Henry looks pained. "You aren't alone," he says. "You have me."

"I know, but you shouldn't have to do everything—be everything."

"I don't mind—"

"But *I* do!" she snaps, thrown by the anger in her own voice. "I'm a person, not a pet, Henry, and I don't need you looking down at me, or coddling me either. I do what I have to, and it's not always nice, and it's not always fair, but it's how I survive. I'm sorry you disapprove. But this is who I am. This is what works for me."

Henry shakes his head. "But it won't work for *us*."

Addie pulls back as if struck. Suddenly the pub is too loud, too full, and she can't stand there, can't stand still, so she turns, and storms out.

The moment the night air hits her, she feels ill.

The world rocks, re-steadies . . . and somewhere between one step and the next, the anger evaporates, and she just feels tired, and sad.

She doesn't understand how the night went sideways.

Doesn't understand the sudden weight on her chest until she realizes what it is—fear. Fear that she's messed up, thrown away the one thing she's always wanted. Fear that it was that fragile, that it came apart so easily.

But then she hears footsteps, feels Henry coming up beside her.

He doesn't say anything, only walks, half a step behind, and this is a new kind of silence. The silent aftermath of storms, the damage not yet tallied.

Addie swipes a tear from her cheek. "Did I ruin it?"

"Ruin what?" he asks.

"Us."

"Addie." He grabs her shoulder. She turns, expecting to see his face streaked with anger, but it's steady, smooth. "It was just a fight. It's not the end of the world. It's certainly not the end of us."

Three hundred years she's dreamed of this.

She always thought it would be easy.

The opposite of Luc.

"I don't know how to be with someone," she whispers. "I don't know how to be a normal person."

His mouth quirks into a crooked grin. "You're incredible, and strong, and stubborn, and brilliant. But I think it's safe to say you're never going to be normal."

They walk, arm in arm, through the cool night air.

"Did you go back to Paris?" asks Henry.

It is an olive branch, a bridge built, and she is grateful for it.

"Eventually," she says.

It had taken far longer to get back there, without Luc's help, or her naïve drive to reach the city, and she's embarrassed to say she did not hurry back. That even if Luc meant to abandon her, stranding her there in Florence, in doing so he broke a kind of seal. In yet another, maddening way, he forced her free.

Until that moment, Addie had never conceived of leaving France. It's absurd to think of now, but the world felt so much smaller then. And then, suddenly, it was not.

Perhaps he meant to cast her into chaos.

Perhaps he thought she was getting too comfortable, growing too stubborn.

Perhaps he wanted her to call for him again. To beg him to come back.

Perhaps perhaps perhaps—but she will never know.

VII

Addie wakes to sunlight and silk sheets.

Her limbs feel leaden, her head full of muslin. The kind of heaviness that comes with too much sun, and too much sleep.

It is ungodly hot in Venice, hotter than it ever was in Paris.

The window is open, but neither the faint breeze nor the silk bedding are enough to dissipate the stifling heat. It is only morning, and sweat already beads on her bare skin. She is dreading the thought of midday as she drags herself awake, and sees Matteo perched at the foot of the bed.

He is just as beautiful in daylight, sun-kissed and strong, but she is struck less by his lovely features, and more by the strange calm of the moment.

Mornings are usually muddled with apologies, confusion, the aftermath of forgetting. They are sometimes painful, and always awkward.

But Matteo seems utterly unfazed.

He doesn't remember her, of course, that much is obvious—but her presence there, this stranger in his bed, seems neither to startle nor to bother him. His attention is focused solely on the sketchpad balanced on his knee, the charcoal skating gracefully across the paper. It is only when his gaze flicks up to her, and then down again, that she realizes he is drawing *her*.

She makes no move to cover herself, to reach for the slip cast off on the chair, or the thin robe at the foot of the bed. Addie hasn't been shy about her body in a long time. Indeed, she has come to enjoy being admired. Perhaps it is the natural abandon that comes with time, or perhaps it is the constancy of her shape, or perhaps it is the liberation that comes with knowing her spectators won't remember.

There *is* a freedom, after all, in being forgotten.

And yet, Matteo is still drawing, the motions swift and easy.

"What are you doing?" she asks gently, and he tears his gaze from the parchment.

"I'm sorry," he says. "The way you looked. I had to capture it."

Addie frowns, begins to rise, but he lets out a stifled sound and says, "Not yet," and it takes all her strength to stay there, on the bed, hands tangled in the sheets until he sighs and sets the work aside, eyes glazed with the afterglow unique to artists.

"Can I see?" she asks in the melodic Italian she has learned.

"It is not finished," he says, even as he offers her the pad.

Addie stares at the drawing. The marks are easy, imprecise, a quick study by a talented hand. Her face is barely drawn, almost abstract in the gestures of light and shadow.

It is her—and it is not her.

An image, distorted by the filter of someone else's style. But she can see herself in it. From the curve of her cheek to the shape of her shoulders, the sleep-mussed hair and the charcoal dots scattered across her face. Seven freckles charted out like stars.

She brushes the charcoal toward the bottom edge of the page, where her limbs dissolve into the linens of the bed, feels it smudge against her skin.

But when she lifts her hand away, her thumb is stained, and the line is clean. She has not left a mark. And yet, she *has*. She has impressed herself upon Matteo, and he has impressed her upon the page.

"Do you like it?" he asks.

"Yes," she murmurs, resisting the urge to tear the drawing from the pad, to take it with her. Every inch of her wants to have it, to keep it, to stare at the image like Narcissus in the pond. But if she takes it now, then it will find a way to disappear, or it will belong to her, and her alone, and then it will be as good as lost, forgotten.

If Matteo keeps the picture, he will forget the source, but not the sketch itself. Perhaps he will turn to it when she is gone, and wonder at the woman sprawled across his sheets, and even if he thinks it the product of some drunken revel, some fever dream, her image will still be there, charcoal on parchment, a palimpsest beneath a finished work.

It will be real, and so will she.

So Addie studies the drawing, grateful for the prism of her memory, and hands it back to her artist. She rises, reaching for her clothes.

"Did we have a good time?" Matteo asks. "I confess, I cannot remember."

"Neither can I," she lies.

"Well then," he says with a rakish grin. "It must have been a *very* good time."

He kisses her bare shoulder, and her pulse flutters, body warming with the memory of the night before. She is a stranger to him now, but Matteo has the easy passion of an artist enamored with his newest subject. It would be simple enough to stay, to start again, enjoy his company another day—but her thoughts are still on the drawing, the meaning of those lines, the weight of them.

"I must go," she says, leaning in to kiss him one last time. "Try to remember me."

He laughs, the sound breezy and light as he pulls her close, leaves ghosts of charcoal fingers on her skin. "How could I possibly forget?"

That night, the sunset turns the canals to gold.

Addie stands on a bridge over the water, and rubs at the charcoal still on her thumb, and thinks of the drawing, an artist's rendition, like an echo of the truth, thinks of Luc's own words so long ago, when he cast her from Geoffrin's salon.

Ideas are wilder than memories.

He meant it as a barb, no doubt, but she should have seen it as a clue, a key.

Memories are stiff, but thoughts are freer things. They throw out roots, they spread and tangle, and come untethered from their source. They are clever, and stubborn, and perhaps—perhaps—they are in reach.

Because two blocks away, in that small studio over the café, there is an artist, and on one of his pages, there is a drawing, and it is of her. And now Addie closes her eyes, and tips her head back, and smiles, hope swelling in her chest. A crack in the walls of this unyielding curse. She thought she'd studied every inch, but here, a door, ajar onto a new and undiscovered room.

The air changes at her back, the crisp scent of trees, impossible and out of place in the rank Venetian heat.

Her eyes drift open. "Good evening, Luc."

"Adeline."

She turns to face him, this man she made real, this darkness, this devil brought to life. And when he asks if she has had enough, if she is tired yet, if she will yield to him tonight, she smiles, and says, "Not tonight."

Rubs her finger anew against her thumb, and feels the charcoal there, and thinks of telling him about her discovery, just to savor his surprise.

I have found a way to leave a mark, she wants to say to him. *You thought you could erase me from this world, but you cannot. I am still here. I will always be here.*

The taste of the words—that triumph—is sweet as sugar on her tongue. But there is a warning tint to his gaze tonight, and knowing Luc, he would find a way to turn it against her, to take this small solace from her before she's found a way to use it.

So she says nothing.

A wave of applause rolls across the grass.

It's a gorgeous spring day, one of the first where the warmth lingers as the sun goes down, and they're sitting on a blanket at the edge of Prospect Park as performers file on and off a pop-up stage across the green.

"I can't believe you remember it all," he says as a new singer climbs the steps.

"It's like living with *déjà vu*," she says, "only you know exactly where you've seen or heard or felt a thing before. You know every time, and place, and they sit stacked on top of each other like pages in a very long and complicated book."

Henry shakes his head. "I would have lost my mind."

"Oh, I did," she says blithely. "But when you live long enough, even madness ends."

The new singer is . . . not good.

A teenage boy whose voice is equal parts growl and screech. Addie hasn't been able to catch more than a word or two of the lyrics, let alone detect a melody. But the lawn is full, the audience brimming with enthusiasm, less for the performance than the chance to wave their numbered cards.

It's Brooklyn's answer to an open mic: a charity concert where people pay to perform, and others pay to judge them.

"Seems kind of cruel," she pointed out when Henry handed her the cards.

"It's for a good cause," he said, cringing at the final notes of a flat saxophone.

The song ends to a wave of weak applause.

The field is a sea of *2*s and *3*s. Henry holds up a *9*.

"You can't give them all nines and tens," she says.

Henry shrugs. "I feel bad for them. It takes a lot of guts to get up there and perform. What about you?"

She looks down at the cards. "I don't know."

"You told me you were a talent scout."

"Yes, well, it was easier than telling you I was a three-hundred-and-twenty-three-year-old ghost whose only hobby is inspiring artists."

Henry reaches out and runs his finger down her cheek. "You're not a ghost."

The next song starts, and ends, and scattered applause falls like rain across the lawn.

Henry gives it a 7.

Addie holds up a 3.

Henry looks at her, aghast.

"What?" she says. "It wasn't very good."

"We were rating on *talent*? Well, shit."

Addie laughs, and there's a lull between acts, some dispute about who is supposed to go up next. Canned music spills from the speakers, and they lie back in the grass, Addie's head resting against his stomach, the soft in and out of his breath like a shallow wave beneath her.

Here is a new kind of silence, rarer than the rest. The easy quiet of familiar spaces, of places that fill simply because you are not alone within them. A notebook sits beside them on the blanket. Not the blue one; that is already full. This new one is an emerald green, nearly the same shade as Luc's eyes when he is showing off.

A pen juts up between the pages, holding Henry's place.

Every day, Addie has told him stories.

Over eggs and coffee, she recounted the torturous walk to Le Mans. In the bookstore one morning, as they unpacked new releases, she relived that first year in Paris. Tangled in the sheets last night, she told him of Remy. Henry has asked for the truth, her truth, and so she is telling it. In pieces, fragments tucked like bookmarks between the movement of their days.

Henry is like bottled lightning, unable to sit still for long, full of nervous energy, but every moment there's a lull, a sliver of peace and quiet, he grabs the latest notebook, and a pen, and even though she always thrills at the sight of the words—her words—spilling across the page, she teases him for the urgency with which he writes them.

"We have time," she reminds him, smoothing his hair.

Addie stretches out against him, and looks up at the dying light, the sky streaked purple and blue. It is almost night, and she knows that a roof would do nothing if the darkness looked her way, but lying here, beneath the open sky, she still feels exposed.

They've been lucky, so lucky, but the trouble with luck is that it always ends.

And perhaps it is just the nervous tapping of Henry's fingers on the journal.

And perhaps it is just the moonless sky.

And perhaps it is just that happiness is frightening.

The next band takes the stage.

But as the music rings out across the lawn, she can't take her eyes from the dark.

She could *live* in the National Gallery.

Indeed, she has spent a season here, wandering from room to room, feasting on the paintings and the portraits, the sculptures and the tapestries. A life spent among friends, among echoes.

She moves through marble halls, and counts the pieces she has touched, the marks left by other hands, but guided by her own.

At last count, there were six in this particular collection.

Six pillars, holding her aloft.

Six voices, carrying her through.

Six mirrors, reflecting pieces of her back into the world.

There is no sign of Matteo's sketch, not among these finished works, but she sees those early lines reflected in his masterpiece, *The Muse*, sees them again in the sculpture of a face resting on a hand, the painting of a woman sitting by the sea.

She is a ghost, a gossamer, laid like film across the work.

But she is there.

She is there.

An attendant informs her they will be closing soon, and Addie thanks him, and continues on her round. She could stay, but the vast halls are not as cozy as the flat in Kensington, a gem left unattended in the winter months.

Addie pauses in front of her favorite piece, a portrait of a girl before a looking glass. Her back is to the artist, the room and girl rendered in high detail, but her reflection little more than streaks. Her face rendered only in the silver smudges of the mirror. And yet, up close, anyone would see the scattering of freckles, like floating stars against the warped grey sky.

"How clever you are," says a voice behind her.

Addie was alone in the gallery, and now she is not.

She glances left, and sees Luc staring past her at the painting, his head inclined as if admiring the work, and for a moment, Addie feels like a cabinet, the doors flung open. She is not coiled, not wound tight with waiting, because there are still months until their anniversary.

"What are you doing here?" she asks.

His mouth twitches once, relishing her surprise. "I am everywhere."

It has never occurred to her that he could come as he pleased, that he is not bound in some way by the dates of their deal. That his visits, just like the absence of them, have always been by design—by *choice*.

"I see you've been busy," he says, those green eyes trailing over the portrait.

She has. She has scattered herself like breadcrumbs, dusted across a hundred works of art. It would not be a simple thing for him to erase them all. And yet, there is a darkness to his gaze, a mood she distrusts.

He reaches out, trails a finger along the frame.

"Destroy it," she says, "and I will make more."

"It does not matter," he says, hand falling. "*You* do not matter, Adeline."

The words bite, even now.

"Take your echoes and pretend they are a voice."

She is no stranger to Luc's foul moods, his streaks of ill temper, brief and bright as lightning. But there is a violence to his tone tonight. An edge, and she does not think it is her cunning that's upset him, this glimpse of her folded between the layers of the art.

No, this dark mood is one that he's brought with him.

A shadow dragging in his wake.

But it's been almost a century since she struck him, that night in Villon, when he struck back, reduced her to a gnarled corpse on the floor of Estele's house. And so instead of retreating at the sight of teeth, she rises to the bait.

"You said it yourself, Luc. Ideas are wilder than memories. And I can be wild. I can be stubborn as the weeds, and you will not root me out. And I think you are glad of it. I think that's why you've come, because you are lonely, too."

Luc's eyes flash a sickly, stormy green. "Don't be absurd," he sneers. "Gods are known to *everyone*."

"But remembered by so few," she counters. "How many mortals have met you more than twice—once to make a deal and once to pay the price? How many have been a part of your life as long as I have?" Addie flashes a triumphant smile. "Perhaps that's why you cursed me as you did. So you would have some company. So someone would remember *you*."

He is on her in an instant, pressing her back against the museum wall. "I cursed you for being a fool."

And Addie laughs.

"You know, when I imagined the old gods, as a child, I thought of you as grand immortals, above the petty worries that plagued your worshipers. I thought that you were bigger than us. But you're not. You're just as fickle and wanting as the humans you disdain." His hands tighten on her, but she does not quiver, does not cower, simply holds his gaze. "We are not so different, are we?"

Luc's anger hardens, cools, the green of his eyes plunging into black. "You claim to know me so well now. Let us see . . ." His hand drops from her shoulder to her wrist, and too late, she realizes what he means to do.

It has been forty years since he last dragged her through the dark, but she hasn't forgotten the feeling, the primal fear and the wild hope and the reckless freedom of doors thrown open onto night.

It is infinite—

And then it is over, and she is on her hands and knees on a wooden floor, limbs trembling from the strangeness of the journey.

A bed lies, disheveled and empty, the curtains have been flung wide, and the floor is covered in sheets of music, and there is a stale air of sickness to the space.

"What a waste," murmurs Luc.

Addie rises unsteadily to her feet. "Where are we?"

"You mistake me for some lonesome mortal," he says. "Some heartsick human in search of company. I am neither."

Movement, across the room, and she realizes they are not alone. A ghost of a man, white-haired and wild-eyed, sits on a piano bench, his back to the keys.

He is pleading in German.

"Not yet," he says, clutching a handful of music to his chest. "Not yet. I need more time."

His voice is strange, too loud, as if he cannot hear. But Luc's, when he answers, is a smooth hard tone, a low bell, a sound felt as much as heard.

"The vexing thing about time," he says, "is that it's never enough. Perhaps a decade too short, perhaps a moment. But a life always ends too soon."

"Please," begs the man, sinking to his hands and knees before the darkness, and Addie flinches for him, knows his pleas won't work.

"Let me make another deal!"

Luc forces the man to his feet. "The time for deals is done, Herr Beethoven. Now, you must say the words."

The man shakes his head. "No."

And Addie cannot see Luc's eyes, but she can feel his temper changing. The air ripples in the room around them, a wind, and something stronger.

"Surrender your soul," says Luc. "Or I will take it by force."

"No!" shouts the man, hysterical now. "Begone, Devil. Begone, and—"

It is the last thing he says, before Luc *unfolds*.

That is the only way to think of it.

The black hair rises from his face, climbing through the air like weeds, and his skin ripples and splits, and what spills out is not a man. It is a monster. It is a god. It is the night itself, and something else, something she has never seen, something she cannot bear to look at. Something older than the dark.

"Surrender."

And now the voice is not a voice at all, but a medley of snapping branches and summer wind, a wolf's low growl, and the sudden shifting of rocks underfoot.

The man burbles and pleads. "Help!" he cries out, but it is no use. If there is anyone beyond the door, they will not hear.

"Help!" he cries again, uselessly.

And then the monster plunges its hand into his chest.

The man staggers, pale and gray, as the darkness plucks his soul like a piece of fruit. It comes loose with a tearing sound, and the composer stumbles, and falls to the floor. But Addie's eyes are locked on the bloom of light in the shadow's hand, jagged and unsteady. And before she can study the ribbons of color curling on its surface, before she can wonder at the images coiling inside, the darkness closes its fingers around the soul, and it crackles through him like lightning, and plunges out of sight.

The composer sits slumped against his piano bench, head back, and eyes empty.

Luc's hand, she will learn, is always subtle. They will see his work and call it sickness, call it heart failure, call it madness, suicide, overdose, accident.

But tonight, she only knows that the man on the floor is dead.

The darkness turns on Addie, then, and there is no vestige of Luc in the roiling smoke. There are no green eyes. No playful smirk. Nothing but a menacing void, a shadow filled with teeth.

It has been a long time since Addie felt true fear. Sadness, she knows; loneliness and grief. But fear belongs to those with more to lose.

And yet.

Staring into that dark, Addie is afraid.

She wills her legs to stay, wills herself to hold her ground, and she does, as it takes its first step, and its second, but by the third, she finds herself retreating. Away from the writhing dark, the monstrous night, until her back comes to rest against the wall.

But the darkness keeps coming.

With every forward step it draws itself together, the edges firming until it is less a storm than smoke bottled into glass. The face finds form, shadows twisting into loose black curls, and the eyes—there are eyes again now—

lighten like a drying stone, and the cavernous maw narrows to a cupid's bow, the lips curving into sly content.

And he is Luc again, wrapped in the guise of flesh and bone, close enough that she can feel the cool night air wafting off him like a breeze.

And this time, when he speaks, it is with the voice she knows so well.

"Well, my darling . . ." he says, one hand rising to her cheek. "Are we so different now?"

She does not have the chance to answer.

He gives the barest push, and the wall opens up behind her, and she is not sure if she falls, or if the shadows reach out and pull her down, only that Luc is gone, and the composer's room is gone, and for an instant, the dark is everywhere, and then she is standing outside, on the cobblestone banks, and the night is full of laughter and lights shining on the water, and the soft, melodic strain of a man singing somewhere along the Thames.

It is Addie's idea to bring the cat home.

Perhaps she has always longed for a pet.

Perhaps she simply thinks he must be lonely.

Perhaps she thinks it will do Henry good.

She does not know. It does not matter. All that does is that one day, as he is closing up the store, she appears next to him on the stoop, a novel under one arm and the ancient tabby in the other, and that is that.

They carry Book back to Henry's place, and introduce him to the blue door, and go up to the narrow Brooklyn apartment, and despite Henry's superstition, he does not turn to dust, severed from his store. He simply toddles around for an hour before leaning up against a philosophy stack, and he is home.

And so is she.

They are curled together on the couch when she hears the click of the Polaroid, catches the sudden flash, and there's a moment when she wonders if it will work, if Henry will be able to take her photo, the way he wrote her name.

But even the writing in his journals isn't entirely hers. It's her story in his pen, her life in their words.

And sure enough, when the film exposes, and the Polaroid appears, it's not of her, not really. The girl in the frame has her wavy brown hair. The girl in the frame wears her white shirt. But the girl in the frame has no face. If she does, it's turned from the camera, as if caught in the process of spinning away.

And she knew it wouldn't work, but her heart still sinks.

"I don't get it," says Henry, turning the camera in his hands.

"Can I try again?" he asks, and she understands the urge. It is harder to manage, when the impossible is so obvious. Your mind can't make sense of it, so you try again and again and again, convinced that this time, it will be different.

This, she knows, is how you go mad.

But Addie indulges Henry as he tries a second time, and a third. Watches as the camera jams, spits out a blank card, comes back overexposed, underexposed, blurred, until her head is swimming with flashes of white.

She lets him try different angles, different light, until photos litter the floor between them. She's there, and not there, real, and a ghost.

He must see her fraying a little more with every flash, the sadness rising through the cracks, and forces himself to put the camera down.

Addie stares at the photos, and thinks of the painting in London, of Luc's voice in her head.

It does not matter.

You do not matter.

She picks up the latest attempt, studies the shape of the girl in the frame, her features blurred beyond recognition. She closes her eyes, reminds herself there are many ways to leave a mark, reminds herself that pictures lie.

And then she feels the solid body of the camera being placed into her hands, and she is drawing in the breath to tell him it will not work, it will not, but then Henry is there, behind her, folding her fingers over his, lifting the viewfinder to her eye. Letting her guide the pressure of his hands the way she did the paint on the glass wall. And her heart quickens as she lines up a shot of the photos littering the floor, her own bare feet at the bottom of the frame.

She holds her breath, and hopes.

A click. A flash.

This time, the picture comes out.

Here is a life in still frames.

Moments like Polaroids. Like paintings. Like flowers pressed between the pages of a book. Perfectly preserved.

The three of them, napping in the sun.

Addie, stroking Henry's hair while she tells him stories, and he writes, and writes, and writes.

Henry, pressing her down into the bed, their fingers tangled, their breath quick, her name an echo in her hair.

Here they are, together in his galley kitchen, his arms threaded through hers, her hands over his as they stir béchamel, as they knead bread dough.

When it is in the oven, he cups her face with floury hands, leaves trails everywhere he touches.

They make a mess, as the room fills with the scent of freshly baking bread.

And in the morning it looks like ghosts have danced across the kitchen, and they pretend there were two instead of one.

XI

Villon was not supposed to change.

When she was growing up, it was always so painfully still, like summer air before a storm. A village carved in stone. And yet, what was it Luc said?

Even rocks wear away to nothing.

Villon has not worn away. Instead, it has shifted, grown, new roots thrown out, and others cut. The woods have been forced back, trees on the forest edge all felled to feed hearth fires and make way for fields and crops. There are more walls now than there were before. More buildings. More roads.

As Addie makes her way through town, hair tucked beneath a well-trimmed bonnet, she marks a name, a face, a ghost of a ghost of a family she once knew. But the Villon of her youth has finally faded, and she wonders if this is what memory feels like for others, this slow erasure of details.

For the first time, she does not recognize every path.

For the first time, she is not sure she knows her way.

She takes a turn, expecting to find one house, but instead finds two, divided by a low stone wall. She goes left, but instead of an open field, she finds a stable, surrounded by a fence. At last, she recognizes the road home, holds her breath as she makes her way down the path, feels something inside her loosen at the sight of the old yew tree, still bent and knotted at the edge of the property.

But beyond the tree, the place is changed. New clothes laid over old bones.

Her father's workshop has been cleared away, the footprint of the shed marked only by a shadow on the ground, the weedy grass long filled in, a slightly different shade. And though Addie braced herself for the stale stillness of abandoned places, she is met instead by motion, voices, laughter.

Someone else has moved into her family home, one of the new arrivals in the growing town. A family, with a mother who smiles more, and a father who doesn't, and a pair of boys running in the yard, their hair the color of straw. The older one chases a dog who has absconded with a sock, and the younger one climbs the old yew tree, his bare feet finding the same knots and crooks as hers, back when she was a girl, the drawing pad tucked under her arm. She must have been his age . . . or was she older?

She closes her eyes, tries to catch hold of the image, but it slips and slides between her fingers. Those early memories, not trapped within the prism. Those years before, lost to that other life. Her eyes are only closed a moment, but when she opens them, the tree is empty. The boy is gone.

"Hello," says a voice, somewhere behind her.

It is the younger one, his face open and upturned.

"Hello," she says.

"Are you lost?"

She hesitates, torn between yes and no, unsure which is closer to the truth.

"I am a ghost," she says. The boy's eyes widen in surprise, delight, and he asks her to prove it. She tells him to close his eyes, and when he does, she slips away.

In the cemetery, the tree Addie transplanted has taken root.

It looms over Estele's grave, bathing her bones in a pool of shade.

Addie runs her hand over the bark, marvels at how the sapling has grown into a wide-trunked tree, its roots and branches escaping to every side. A hundred years since it was planted—a span of time once too long to fathom, and now, too hard to measure. So far, she has counted time in seconds, and in seasons, in cold snaps and in thaws, in uprisings and in aftermaths. She has seen buildings fall and rise, cities burn and be remade, the past and present blurred together into a fluid, ephemeral thing.

But this, this is tangible.

The years marked in wood and bark, root and soil.

Addie sits back against the woman's grave and rests her own aged bones in the dappled shade, and recounts the time since her last visit. She tells Estele stories of England, and Italy, and Spain, of Matteo, and the gallery, of Luc, and her art, and all the ways the world has changed. And even though there is no answer, save the rustle of leaves, she knows what the old woman would say.

Everything changes, foolish girl. It is the nature of the world. Nothing stays the same.

Except for me, she thinks, but Estele answers, dry as kindling.

Not even you.

She has missed the old woman's counsel, even in her head. The voice has gone brittle, worn away in the intervening years, smudged like all those mortal memories.

But here, at least, it returns to her.

The sun has crossed the sky by the time she rises and walks to the edge of the village, to the edge of the woods, to the place the old woman once called home. But time has claimed this place as well. The garden, once overgrown, has been swallowed up by the encroaching woods, and the wild has won its war against the hut, dragged it down, saplings jutting up among the bones. The wood has rotted, the stones have slipped, the roof is gone, and weed and vine are in the slow process of dismantling the rest.

The next time she comes, there will be no trace, the remains swallowed by the advancing woods. But for now, there is still the skeleton, being slowly buried by the moss.

Addie is halfway to the decaying hut when she realizes it is not entirely deserted.

A shiver of motion in the ruined mound, and she squints, expecting to find a rabbit, or perhaps a young deer. Instead, she finds a boy. He is playing amid the ruins, climbing the remains of the old stone walls, swatting at weeds with a switch pulled from the woods.

She knows him. It is the older son, the boy she first saw chasing a dog through her yard. He is maybe nine, or ten. Old enough for his eyes to narrow in suspicion when he sees her.

He holds out his switch as if it were a sword.

"Who are you?" he demands.

And this time she is not content to be a ghost. "I am a witch."

She doesn't know why she says it. Perhaps simply to humor herself. Perhaps because when truth is not an option, fiction takes on a mind of its own. Or perhaps because it is what Estele would say, if she were here.

A shadow crosses the boy's face. "No such thing as witches," he says, but his voice is unsteady as he says it, and when she steps forward, shoes cracking over sun-dried branches, he begins to back away.

"Those are my bones you're playing on," she warns. "I suggest you get down before you fall."

The boy stumbles in surprise, nearly slips on a patch of moss.

"Unless you'd rather stay," she muses. "I'm sure there's room for yours as well."

The boy makes it back to the ground, and takes off running. Addie watches him go, Estele's crow-like laughter cawing in her ears.

She doesn't feel bad for scaring the child; she does not expect him to remember. And yet, tomorrow, he will come again, and she will stand hidden at the edge of the woods and watch him begin to climb the ruins, only to hesitate, a nervous shadow in his eyes. She will watch him back away, and wonder if he is thinking of witches and half-buried bones. If the idea has grown like a weed in his head.

But today, Addie is alone, and her mind is only on Estele.

She runs her hands along a half-fallen wall, and thinks of staying, of becoming the witch by the woods, the figment of someone else's dream. She imagines rebuilding the old woman's house, even kneels to stack a few small stones. But by the fourth, the pile crumbles, the rocks landing in the weedy grass exactly as they were before she lifted them.

The ink unwrites.

The wound uncuts.

The house unbuilds.

Addie sighs as a handful of birds take flight from the nearby woods, croaking laughter. She turns toward the trees. There is still light left, an hour maybe until night, and yet, staring into the forest, she can feel the darkness staring back. She wades between the half-buried stones and steps into the shade beneath the trees.

A shiver slides through her.

It is like stepping through a veil.

She weaves between the trees. Once, she would have been afraid of getting lost. Now, the steps are carved into her memory. She could not lose her way even if she tried.

The air is cooler here, the night closer beneath the canopy. It is easy to see, now, how she lost track of time that day. How the line between dusk and dark became so blurred. And she wonders, would she have called out, had she known the hour?

Would she have prayed, knowing which god would answer?

She does not answer herself.

She does not need to.

She doesn't know how long he's been there, at her back, if he followed her some time in quiet. Only knows the moment she hears branches crack behind her.

"What a strange pilgrimage you insist on making."

Addie smiles to herself. "Is it?"

She turns to see Luc leaning back against a tree.

It is not the first time she's seen him since the night he reaped Beethoven's soul. But she still hasn't forgotten what she saw. Nor has she forgotten that he wanted her to see it, to look at him, and know the truth of his power. But it was a foolish thing to do. Like tipping a hand of cards when the highest bets are on the table.

I see you, she thinks as he straightens from the tree. *I have seen your truest form. You cannot scare me now.*

He steps into a shallow pool of light.

"What drives you back here?" he asks.

Addie shrugs. "Call it nostalgia."

He lifts his chin. "I call it weakness. To only walk in circles when you could make new roads."

Addie frowns. "How am I supposed to make a road when I cannot even raise a pile of stones? Set me free, and see then how well I fare."

He sighs, and dissolves into the dark.

When he speaks again, he is behind her, his voice a breeze through her hair. "Adeline, Adeline," he chides, and she knows that if she turns again, he will not be there, and so she holds her ground, keeps her eyes on the forest. Does not flinch when his hands slide over her skin. When his arm snakes around her shoulders.

Up close, he smells of oak, and leaf, and rain-soaked field.

"Aren't you tired?" he whispers.

And she flinches at the words.

She braced for his attack, his verbal barbs, but she was not braced for that question, not braced for the almost gentle way he asks.

It has been *a hundred and forty years*. A century and a half, living as an echo, as a ghost. Of course she is tired.

"Wouldn't you like to rest, my dear?"

The words drag like gossamer against her skin.

"I could bury you here, beside Estele. Plant a tree, make it grow over your bones."

Addie closes her eyes.

Yes, she is tired.

She may not feel the years weakening her bones, her body going brittle with age, but the weariness is a physical thing, like rot, inside her soul. There are days when she mourns the prospect of another year, another decade, another century. There are nights when she cannot sleep, moments when she lies awake and dreams of dying.

But then she wakes, and sees the pink and orange dawn against the clouds, or hears the lament of a lone fiddle, the music and the melody, and remembers there is such beauty in the world.

And she does not want to miss it—any of it.

Addie turns in the circle of Luc's arms, and looks up into his face.

She doesn't know if it's the creeping night, or the nature of the woods themselves, but he looks different. These last few years, she has seen him bound in velvet and lace, done up in the latest fashion. And she has seen him as the void, unbridled and violent. But here, he is neither.

Here, he is the darkness she met that night. Feral magic in a lover's form.

His edges blur into shadow, his skin the color of moonlight, his eyes the exact shade of the moss behind him. He is wild.

But so is she.

"Tired?" she says, summoning a smile. "I am just waking up."

She braces for his displeasure, the feral shadow, the flash of teeth.

But there is no trace of yellow in his eyes.

In fact, they are a new and lurid shade of green.

It will take years for her to learn the meaning of that color, to understand it as *amusement*.

Tonight, there is only that brief glimpse, and then the brush of his lips against her cheek.

"Even rocks," he murmurs, and then he's gone.

A boy and a girl walk arm in arm.

They're heading to the Knitting Factory, and like most things in Williamsburg, it isn't what it sounds like, not a craft store or a place for yarn, but a concert venue on the northern edge of Brooklyn.

It is Henry's birthday.

Earlier, when he asked her when *her* birthday was, and when she told him it was back in March, a shadow crossed his face.

"I'm sorry I missed it."

"That's the great thing about birthdays," she said, leaning against him. "They happen every year."

She'd laughed a little then, and so had he, but there was something hollow in his voice, a sadness she mistook for mere distraction.

Henry's friends have already staked out a table near the stage, small boxes stacked on the table between them.

"Henry!" shouts Robbie, a pair of bottles already empty in front of him.

Bea ruffles his hair. "Our literal sweet summer child."

Their attention slides past him, and lands on her.

"Hi guys," he says, "this is Addie."

"Finally!" says Bea. "We've been dying to meet you."

Of course, they already have.

They've been asking for weeks to meet the new girl in Henry's life. They keep accusing him of hiding her, but Addie has met them over beers at the Merchant, been for movie nights at Bea's, crossed paths with them at galleries and parks. And every time, Bea talks of *déjà vu,* and then again of artistic movements, and every time Robbie sulks, despite Addie's best efforts to placate him.

It seems to bother Henry more than it does her. He must think she has made peace with it, but the truth is, there is none to be found. The endless cycle of *hello, who is this, nice to meet you, hello* wears at her like water against stone—the damage slow, but inevitable. She has simply learned to live with it.

"You know," says Bea, studying her, "you look so familiar."

Robbie rises from the table to get a round of drinks, and Addie's chest tightens at the thought of him resetting, of having to start it all again, but Henry steps in, touches Robbie's arm. "I've got it," he says.

"Birthday doesn't pay!" protests Bea, but Henry waves her off and wades away through the growing crowd.

And Addie is left alone with his friends. "It's really great to meet you both," she says. "Henry talks about you all the time."

Robbie's eyes narrow in suspicion.

She can feel the wall rising up between them, again, but she's no stranger to Robbie's moods, not anymore, and so she presses on. "You're an actor, right? I'd love to come to one of your performances. Henry says you're amazing."

He picks at the label on his beer. "Yeah, sure . . ." he mumbles, but she catches the edge of a smile when he says it.

And then Bea cuts in. "Henry seems happy. Really happy."

"I am," says Henry, setting down a round of beers.

"To twenty-nine," says Bea, raising her glass.

They proceed to debate the merits of the age, and agree it is a fairly useless year, as far as birthdays go, falling just shy of the monumental thirty.

Bea collars Henry. "But next year, you'll officially be an adult."

"I'm pretty sure that was eighteen," he says.

"Don't be ridiculous. Eighteen is old enough to vote, twenty-one is old enough to drink, but thirty is old enough to make decisions."

"Closer to a midlife crisis than a quarter-life one," teases Robbie.

The microphone flares, whining slightly as a man takes the stage and announces a special opening act.

"He's a rising star, I'm sure you've heard his name, but if you haven't you will soon. Give it up for Toby Marsh!"

Addie's heart lurches.

The crowd whoops and cheers, and Robbie whistles, and Toby steps onto the stage, that same beautiful, blushing boy, but as he waves to the crowd, his chin lifts, his smile is steady, proud. The difference between the first questing lines of a sketch and the finished drawing.

He sits down at the piano and begins to play, and the first notes hit her like longing. And then he begins to sing.

"I'm in love with a girl I've never met."

Time slips, and she is in his living room, perched on the piano bench, tea steaming on the windowsill as her absent fingers pick out the notes.

"But I see her every night, it seems . . ."

She is in his bed, his broad hands playing out the melody on skin. Her face flares hot at the memory as he sings.

"And I'm so afraid, afraid that I'll forget her, even though I've only met her in my dreams."

She never gave him the words, but he found them anyway.

His voice is clearer, stronger, his tone more confident. He just needed the right song. Something to make the crowd lean in and listen.

Addie squeezes her eyes shut, the past and present tangling together in her head.

All those nights at the Alloway, watching him play.

All the times he found her at the bar, and smiled.

All those firsts that were not firsts for her.

The palimpsest bleeding up through the paper.

Toby looks up from the piano, and there's no way he can see her in a place this big, but she is sure his eyes meet hers, and the room tilts a little, and she doesn't know if it's the beers she drank too fast or the vertigo of memory, but then the song ends, replaced by a warm wave of applause, and she is on her feet, moving toward the door.

"Addie, wait," says Henry, but she can't, even though she knows what it means to walk away, knows that Robbie and Bea will forget her, and she will have to start again, and so will Henry—but in that moment, she doesn't care.

She cannot breathe.

The door swings open and the night rushes in, and Addie gasps, forcing air into her lungs.

And it should feel good to hear her music, it should feel right.

After all, she has gone to visit pieces of her art so many times.

But they were only pieces, stripped of context. Sculptured birds on marble plinths, and paintings behind ropes. Didactic boxes taped to whitewashed walls and glass boxes that keep the present from the past.

It is a different thing when the glass breaks.

It is her mother in the doorway, withered to bone.

It is Remy in the Paris salon.

It is Sam, inviting her to stay, every time.

It is Toby Marsh, playing their song.

The only way Addie knows how to keep going is to keep going forward. They are Orpheus, she is Eurydice, and every time they turn back, she is ruined.

"Addie?" Henry is right behind her. "What's wrong?"

"I'm sorry," she says. She wipes the tears away and shakes her head because the story is too long, and too short. "I can't go back in there, not now."

Henry looks over his shoulder, and he must have seen the color drop from her face during the show because he says, "Do you know him? That Toby Marsh guy?"

She hasn't told him that story—they haven't gotten there yet.

"I did," she says, which isn't strictly true, because it makes it sound like something in the past, when the past is the one thing Addie's not entitled to, and Henry must hear the lie buried in the words, because he frowns. He laces his hands behind his head.

"Do you still have feelings for him?"

And she wants to be honest, to say that of course she does. She never gets closure, never gets to say good-bye—no periods, or exclamations, just a lifetime of ellipses. Everyone else starts over, they get a blank page, but hers are full of text. People talk about carrying torches for old flames, and it's not a full fire, but Addie's hands are full of candles. How is she supposed to set them down, or put them out? She has long run out of air.

But it is not love.

It is not love, and that is what he's asking.

"No," she says. "He just—it caught me off guard. I'm sorry."

Henry asks if she wants to go home, and Addie doesn't know if he means both of them, or only her, doesn't want to find out, so she shakes her head, and they go back in, and the lights have changed, and the stage is empty, the house music filling the air until the main act, and Bea and Robbie are chatting, heads bent just the way they were when they walked in. And Addie does her best to smile as they reach the table.

"There you are!" says Robbie.

"Where did you run off to?" asks Bea, eyes flicking from Henry to her. "And who's this?"

He slides his arm around her waist. "Guys, this is Addie."

Robbie looks her up and down, but Bea only beams.

"Finally!" she says. "We've been dying to meet you . . ."

XIII

The glasses rattle faintly on the table as the train rolls through the German countryside. Addie sits in the dining car, sipping her coffee and staring out the window, marveling at the speed with which the world goes past.

Humans are capable of such wondrous things. Of cruelty, and war, but also art and invention. She will think this again and again over the years, when bombs are dropped, and buildings felled, when terror consumes whole countries. But also when the first images are impressed on film, when planes rise into the air, when movies go from black-and-white to color.

She is amazed.

She will always be amazed.

Lost in her thoughts, she doesn't hear the conductor until he is beside her, one hand coming to rest lightly on her shoulder.

"Fräulein," he says, "your ticket, please."

Addie smiles. "Of course."

She looks down at the table, pretends to shuffle through her purse.

"I'm sorry," she says, rising, "I must have left it in my room."

It is not the first time they have done this dance, but it is the first time the porter has decided to follow her, trailing like a shadow as she makes her way toward a car she does not have, for a ticket that she never bought.

Addie quickens her pace, hoping to put a door between them, but it is no use, the conductor is with her every step, and so she slows, and stops before a door that leads to a room that is certainly not hers, hoping that at least it will be empty.

It is not.

As she reaches for the handle, it escapes, sliding open onto a dim compartment, an elegant man leaning in the doorway, black curls drawn like ink against his temples.

Relief rolls through her.

"Herr Wald," says the conductor, straightening, as if the man in the door were a duke, and not the darkness.

Luc smiles. "There you are, Adeline," he says in a voice as smooth and rich as summer honey. His green eyes slide from her to the conductor. "She has a way of running off, my wife. Now," he says, a sly smile on his lips, "what's brought you back to me?"

Addie manages a smile of her own, cloyingly sweet.

"My love," she says. "I forgot my ticket."

He chuckles, drawing a slip of paper from the pocket of his coat. Luc draws Addie close. "What a forgetful thing you are, my dear."

She bristles, but holds her tongue, leans instead into the weight of him.

The conductor surveys the slip, and wishes them a pleasant night, and the moment he is gone she pulls away from Luc.

"My Adeline." He clicks his tongue. "That is no way to treat a husband."

"I am not yours," she says. "And I did not need your help."

"Of course not," he answers dryly. "Come, let's not quarrel in the hall."

Luc draws her into the compartment, or at least, that is what she thinks he is doing, but instead of stepping into the familiar confines of the cabin, she finds only the darkness, vast and deep. Her heart catches on the missed step, the sudden drop, as the train falls away, the world falls away, and they are back in the nothing, the hollow space between, and she knows she will never fully know it, never be able to wrap her mind around the nature of the dark. Because she realizes now, what it is, this place.

It is *him*.

It is the truth of him, the vast and savage night, the darkness, full of promise, and violence, fear, and freedom.

And when the night shudders back into shape around them, they are no longer on the German train, but on a street, in the center of a city she does not yet know is Munich.

And she should be mad at the abduction, the sudden change in the direction of her night, but she cannot stifle the curiosity blossoming in the wake of her confusion. The sudden flush of something new. The thrill of adventure.

Her heart quickens, but she resolves not to let him see her marvel.

She suspects he does anyway.

There is a pleased glint in those eyes, a thread of darker green.

They are standing on the steps of a pillared opera house, her traveling clothes gone, replaced by a far finer dress, and Addie wonders if the gown is real, as far as anything is real, or simply the conjurings of smoke and shadow. Luc stands beside her, a gray scarf around his collar, green eyes dancing beneath the brim of a silk top hat.

The evening bustles with movement, men and women climbing the steps arm in arm to see the show. She learns that it is Wagner, it is *Tristan und Isolde*, though these things mean nothing to her yet. She does not know it is the height of his career. She does not know it has become his masterpiece.

But she can taste the promise, like sugar in the air, as they pass through a lobby of marble columns and painted arches, and into a concert hall of velvet and gold.

Luc rests a hand on the small of her back, guiding her forward to the front of a balcony, a low box with a perfect view of the stage. Her heart quickens with excitement, before she remembers Florence.

Do not mistake this for kindness, he said. *I simply want to be the one who breaks you.*

But there is no mischief in his eyes as they take their seats. No cruel twist to his smile. Only the languid pleasure of a cat in the sun.

Two glasses arrive, brimming with Champagne, and he holds one out to her.

"Happy anniversary," he says as the lights dim, and the curtain rises.

It begins with music.

The rising tension of a symphony, notes like waves: rolling through the hall, crashing against the walls. The inversion of a storm against a ship.

And then, the arrival of Tristan. Of Isolde.

Their voices larger than the stage.

She has heard musicals, of course, heard symphonies and plays, voices so pure they bring her to tears. But she has never heard anything like this.

The way they sing. The scope and scale of their emotions.

The desperate passion in their movements. The raw power of their joy, and pain.

She wants to bottle this feeling, to carry it with her through the dark.

It will be years before she hears a record of this symphony and turns the volume up until it hurts, surrounds herself with sound, though it will never be the same as this.

Once, Addie tears her gaze from the players on the stage, only to see that Luc is watching her instead of them. And there it is again, that peculiar shade of green. Not coy, or chiding, not cruel, but *pleased.*

She will realize later that this is the first night he does not ask for her surrender.

The first time he makes no mention of her soul.

But right now, she is thinking only of the music, the symphony, the story. She is drawn back to the stage by the anguish in a note. By the tangle of limbs in an embrace, by the look of lovers on the stage.

She leans forward, breathes the opera in until it aches inside her chest.

The curtain falls on the first act, and Addie is on her feet, ringing with applause.

Luc laughs, soft as silk, as she sinks back into her seat. "You are enjoying it."

And she doesn't lie, even to spite him. "It is wonderful."

A smile plays across his face. "Can you guess which ones are mine?"

At first, she does not understand, and then, of course, she does.

Her spirits sink. "Are you here to claim them?" she asks, relieved when Luc shakes his head.

"No," he says, "not tonight. But soon."

Addie shakes her head. "I don't understand. Why end their lives as they're reaching their peak?"

He looks at her. "They made their deal. They knew the cost."

"Why would anyone trade a lifetime of talent for a few years of glory?"

Luc's smile darkens. "Because time is cruel to all, and crueler still to artists. Because vision weakens, and voices wither, and talent fades." He leans close, twists a lock of her hair around one finger. "Because happiness is brief, and history is lasting, and in the end," he says, "*everyone* wants to be remembered."

The words are a knife, cutting swift and deep.

Addie knocks his hand away, and turns her attention back to the stage as the opera resumes.

It is a long play, and yet, it is over too soon.

Hours, gone in moments. Addie wishes she could stay, tucked in this seat, and start the opera again, fold herself between the lovers and their tragedy, lose herself in the beauty of their voices.

And yet, she cannot help but wonder. If all the things that Addie has loved, she loved because of them—or *him*.

Luc stands, offering his arm.

She does not take it.

They walk, side by side, through the Munich night, and Addie still feels buoyant in the wake of the opera, the voices ringing through her like a bell.

But Luc's question echoes, too.

Which of them are mine?

She looks at him, the elegant shape beside her in the dark.

"What is the strangest deal you've ever done?"

Luc tips his head back, and considers. "Joan of Arc," he says. "A soul for a blessed sword, so that she could not be struck down."

Addie frowns. "But she was."

"Ah, but not in *battle*." Luc's smile goes sly. "Semantics may seem small, Adeline, but the power of a deal is in its wording. She asked for the protection of a god while it was in her hands. She did not ask for the ability to keep hold of it."

Addie shakes her head, bemused.

"I refuse to believe that Joan of Arc made a deal with the dark."

The smile splits, showing teeth. "Well, perhaps I let her believe I was a little more . . . angelic? But deep down, I think she knew. Greatness requires sacrifice. Who you sacrifice *to* matters less than what you sacrifice *for*. And in the end, she became what she wanted to be."

"A martyr?"

"A legend."

Addie shakes her head. "But the *artists*. Think of all they could have done. Don't you mourn their loss?"

Luc's face darkens. And she remembers his mood the night he met her in the National, remembers his first words, in Beethoven's room.

What a waste.

"Of course I do," he says. "But all great art comes with a cost." He looks away. "You should know that. After all, we are both patrons, in our way."

"I am nothing like you," she says, but there is not much venom in the words. "I am a muse, and you are a thief."

He shrugs. "Give and take," he says, and nothing more.

But when it's late, and he is gone, and she is left to wander, the opera plays on, perfectly preserved inside the prism of her memory, and Addie wonders, softly, silently, if their souls were a fair price for such fine art.

XIV

Lights explode over the city.

They've gathered on the roof of Robbie's building along with twenty other people to watch the fireworks go off, paint the Manhattan skyline pink and green and gold.

Addie and Henry stand together, of course, but it's too hot to touch. His glasses keep fogging, and he seems less interested in drinking his beer than holding the can against his neck.

A breeze trickles through the air, carrying as much relief as a dryer vent, and everyone on the roof make exaggerated noises, letting out *ooh*s and *ahh*s that might be for the fireworks, or simply the limp gust of air.

A kiddie pool sits in the center of the roof surrounded by lawn chairs, a huddle of people sloshing their feet in the tepid water.

The fireworks finish, and Addie looks around for Henry, but he's wandered off.

He's been in a strange mood all day, but she assumes it's the heat, sitting like a weight on everything. The bookstore was closed, and they spent most of the day stretched together on the sofa in front of a box fan, Book pawing at an ice cube as they watched TV, the heat enough to temper even Henry's manic energy.

She was too tired to tell him stories.

He was too tired to write them down.

The rooftop doors burst open and Robbie appears, looking as if he's raided an ice-cream truck, his arms full of melting ice pops. People whoop and cheer, and he makes his rounds of the roof, doling out once-frozen treats.

Twelfth time's the charm, she thinks as he hands her a fruit bar, but even though he doesn't remember her, Henry's obviously said enough, or perhaps Robbie simply recognizes everyone else, and makes the deduction.

One of these things is not like the others.

Addie doesn't lose a second. She breaks into a sudden grin. "Oh my god, you must be Robbie." She throws her arms around his neck. "Henry's told me all about you."

Robbie pulls free. "Did he?"

"You're the actor. He said you're *amazing*. That it's only a matter of time before you're on Broadway." Robbie blushes a little, looks away. "I'd love to come to one of your shows. What are you performing in right now?"

Robbie hesitates, but she can feel him faltering, torn between shunning her and sharing his news. "We're doing a spin on *Faust*," he says. "You know, man makes a deal with the devil . . ."

Addie bites into the ice pop, sending a wave of shock through her teeth. It is enough to mask the grimace as Robbie goes on.

"But it's going to be set against a stage that's more *Labyrinth*. Think Mephistopheles but by way of the Goblin King." He gestures at himself when he says it. "It's a really cool spin. The costumes are amazing. Anyway, it doesn't open until September."

"It sounds wonderful," she says. "I can't wait to see."

At that, Robbie *almost* smiles. "I think it will be pretty cool."

"To Faust," she says, lifting her ice pop.

"And the devil," answers Robbie.

Her hands have gone sticky, and she dunks them in the kiddie pool and goes in search of Henry. She finally finds him alone in a corner of the roof, a stretch where the lights don't reach. He's staring out—not up, but down over the edge.

"I think I finally cracked Robbie," she says, wiping her hands on her shorts.

"Hm?" he says, not really listening. A bead of sweat runs down his cheek, and he closes his eyes into the faint summer breeze and sways a little on his feet.

Addie pulls him away from the edge. "What's wrong?"

His eyes are dark, and for a moment, he looks haunted, lost.

"Nothing," he says softly. "Just thinking."

Addie has lived long enough to recognize a lie. Lying is its own language, like the language of seasons, or gestures, or the shade of Luc's eyes.

So she knows that Henry is lying to her now.

Or at least, he's not telling her the truth.

And maybe it is just one of his storms, she thinks. Maybe it is the summer heat.

It is not, of course, and later, she will know the truth, and she will wish she'd asked, wish she'd pressed, wish she'd known.

Later—but tonight, he pulls her close. Tonight, he kisses her, deeply, hungrily, as if he can make her forget what she saw.

And Addie lets him try.

* * *

That night, when they get home, it is too hot to think, to sleep, so they fill the bathtub with cold water, turn off the lights, and climb inside, shivering at the sudden, merciful relief.

They lie there in the dark, bare legs intertwined beneath the water. Henry's fingers play a melody across her knee.

"When we first met," he muses, "why didn't you tell me your real name?"

Addie looks up at the darkened ceiling tiles, and sees Isabelle as she was, that last day, sitting at the table, her eyes gone empty. She sees Remy in the café, staring dreamily past her words, unable to hear them.

"Because I didn't think I could," she says, running her fingers through the water. "When I try to tell people the truth, their faces just go blank. When I try to say my name, it always gets stuck in my throat." She smiles. "Except with you."

"But why?" he asks. "If you're going to be forgotten, what does it matter if you tell the truth?"

Addie closes her eyes. It's a good question, one she's asked herself a hundred times. "I think he wanted to erase me. To make sure I felt unseen, unheard, unreal. You don't really realize the power of a name until it's gone. Before you, he was the only one who could say it."

The voice curls like smoke inside her head.

Oh Adeline.

Adeline, Adeline.

My Adeline.

"What an asshole," says Henry, and she chuckles, remembering the nights she screamed up at the sky, called the darkness so much worse.

And then he asks, "When's the last time you saw him?" and Addie falters.

For an instant, she is in a bed, black silk sheets twisted around her limbs, the New Orleans heat oppressive even in the dark. But Luc is a cool weight, wrapped around her limbs, his teeth skating along her shoulder as he whispers the word against her skin.

Surrender.

Addie swallows, pushes the memory down like bile in her throat.

"Almost thirty years ago," she says, as if she doesn't count the days. As if the anniversary isn't rushing up to meet them.

She glances sideways at the clothes piled on the bathroom floor, the indent of the wooden ring in the pocket of her shorts. "We had a falling-out," she says, and it is the barest version of the truth.

Henry looks at her, clearly curious, but he doesn't ask what happened, and for that, she is grateful.

There is an order to the story.

She will tell him when she gets there.

For now Addie reaches up, and turns the shower on, and it falls down on them like rain, soothing and steady. And this is the perfect kind of silence. Easy, and empty. They sit across from each other beneath the icy stream, and Addie closes her eyes and tips her head back against the tub, and listens to the makeshift storm.

It is snowing.

Not a patina of frost, or a few wayward flakes, but a dousing of white.

Addie sits curled in the window of the little cottage, a fire at her back, and a book open on her knee, as she watches the sky fall.

She has ushered in the change of years so many ways.

Perched on London rooftops holding bottles of Champagne, and torch in hand through the cobbled roads of Edinburgh. She has danced in the halls of Paris, and watched the sky go white with fireworks in Amsterdam. She has kissed strangers, and sung of friends she'll never meet. Gone out with bangs and with whispers.

But tonight she is content to sit, and watch the world go white beyond the window, every line and curve erased by snow.

The cottage is not hers, of course. Not in the strictest sense.

She found it more or less intact, a place abandoned, or simply forgotten. The furniture was threadbare, the cupboards almost empty. But she has had a season to make it hers, to gather wood from the copse of trees across the field. To tend the wild garden, and steal what she could not grow.

It is simply a place to rest her bones.

Outside, the storm has stopped.

The snow lies quiet on the ground. As smooth and clean as unmarked paper.

Perhaps that is what drives her to her feet.

She pulls the cloak tight around her shoulders and surges out, boots sinking instantly into the snow. It is light, whipped into a sugar film, the taste of winter on her tongue.

Once, when she was five, or six, it snowed back in Villon. A rare sight, a film of white several inches deep that coated everything. In hours, it was ruined by horses and carts, and people trudging to and fro, but Addie found a small expanse of untouched white. She rushed out into it, leaving a trail of shoes. She ran bare hands over the frozen sheets, left fingers in her wake. She ruined every inch of the canvas.

And when she was done, she looked around at the field, now covered in tracks, and mourned that it was over. The next day, the frost broke, and the ice melted, and it was the last time she played in snow.

Until now.

Now, her steps crunch the perfect snow, and it rises in her wake.

Now, she runs her fingers through the gentle hills, and they smooth behind her touch.

Now she plays in the field, and does not leave a mark.

The world remains unblemished, and for once she is grateful.

She spins and twirls, and dances partner-less across the snow, laughing at the strange and simple magic of the moment, before stepping wrong, a patch deeper than she thought.

She loses her balance, and crashes down into the pile of white, gasping at the sudden cold along her collar, the snow that creeps inside her hood. She looks up. It has begun to snow again, lightly now, flakes falling like stars. The world goes muffled, a cotton kind of quiet. And if it were not for the icy damp leaching through her clothes, she thinks she could stay here forever.

She decides she will at least stay here for now.

She sinks into the snow, lets it swallow the edges of her sight, until there is nothing but a frame around the open sky, the night cold and clear and full of stars. And she is ten again, stretched in the tall grass behind her father's workshop, dreaming she is anywhere but home.

How strange, the winding way a dream comes true.

But now, gazing up into the endless dark, she does not think of freedom, but of him.

And then, he's there.

Standing over her, haloed by the dark, and she thinks perhaps she is going mad again. It would not be the first time.

"Two hundred years," Luc says, kneeling beside her, "and still behaving like a child."

"What are you doing here?"

"I could ask the same of you."

He holds out his hand, and she takes it, lets him draw her up out of the cold, and together they walk back to the little house, leaving only his steps in the snow.

Inside, the fire has gone out, and she groans a little herself, reaching for the lantern, hoping it will be enough to coax the fire back to life.

But Luc only looks at the smoking ruins and flicks his fingers in an absent way, and the flames surge up inside the hearth, a bloom of heat, casting shadows over everything.

How easily he moves through the world, she thinks.

How hard he's made it for her.

Luc considers the little cottage, the borrowed life. "My Adeline," he says, "still longing to grow up and become Estele."

"I am not yours," she says, though by now the words have lost their venom.

"All the world, and you pass your time playing the part of a witch in the wild, a crone praying to old gods."

"I did not pray to you. And yet you're here."

She takes him in, dressed in a wool coat and cashmere scarf, the collar high against his cheeks, and realizes this is the first she has seen Luc in winter. It suits him, as well as summer did. The fair skin of his cheeks gone marble white, the black curls the color of the moonless sky. Those green eyes, as cold and bright as stars. And the way he looks, standing before the fire, she wishes she could draw him. Even after all this time, her fingers itch for charcoal.

He runs a hand over the mantel.

"I saw an elephant, in Paris."

Her words to him, so many years before. It is such a strange answer now, filled with unspoken things. I saw an elephant, and thought of you. I was in Paris, and you were not.

"And you thought of me," she says.

It is a question. He does not answer. Instead, he looks around and says, "This is a pitiful way to usher out a year. We can do better. Come with me."

And she is curious—she is always curious—but tonight, she shakes her head. "No."

That proud chin lifts. Those dark brows draw together. "Why not?"

Addie shrugs. "Because I'm happy here. And I do not trust you to bring me back."

His smile flickers, like firelight. And she expects that to be the end of that.

To turn and find him gone, stolen back into the dark.

But he's still there, this shadow in her borrowed home.

He lowers himself into the second chair.

He conjures cups of wine from nothing, and they sit before the fire like friends, or at least, like foes at rest, and he tells her of Paris at the close of a decade—the turn of the century. Of the writers, blooming like flowers, of the art, and the music, and the beauty. He has always known how to tempt her. He says it is a golden age, a time of light.

"You would enjoy it," he says.

"I'm sure I would."

She will go, in the spring, and see the World's Fair, witness the Eiffel Tower, the iron sculpture climbing toward the sky. She will walk through buildings made of glass, ephemeral installations, and everyone will talk of the old century and the new one, as if there is a line in the sand between present and past. As if it does not all exist together.

History is a thing designed in retrospect.

For now, she listens to him talk, and it is enough.

She does not remember drifting off, but when she wakes, it is early in the morning, and the cottage is empty, the fire little more than embers. A blanket has been cast over her shoulders, and beyond the window, the world is white again.

And Addie will wonder if he was ever there.

PART SIX

DO NOT PRETEND
THAT THIS IS LOVE

Title: "Dream Girl"

Artist: Toby Marsh

Date: 2014

Medium: sheet music

Location: on loan from the Pershing family

Description: This piece of original sheet music, signed by singer/song-writer Toby Marsh, captures the beginnings of the song "Dream Girl" and was auctioned off as part of the Music Notes annual gala to fund public school arts programs in New York City. While some of the lyrics differ from the final song, the most famous lines—"I'm so afraid, afraid that I'll forget/Her, even though I've only met her in my dreams"—are clearly legible in the center of the page.

Background: This is largely considered to be the song that launched Marsh's career. The musician has only added to the mythology surrounding the subject by claiming the song came to him over the course of several dreams. "I would wake up with bars of music in my head," he said in a 2016 interview with *Paper Magazine*. "I'd find lyrics scribbled on notepads and receipts, but I had no memory of writing them. It was like sleepwalking. Sleep-making. The whole thing was a dream."

Marsh denies being under the influence of any drugs at the time.

Estimated Value: $15,000

It is pouring in Villon.

The Sarthe swells against its banks, and the rain turns footpaths into muddy rivers. It spills over doorways, fills her ears with the steady white noise of rushing water, and when Addie closes her eyes, the years dissolve, and she is ten again, she is fifteen, she is twenty, her skirts wet and hair flying behind her as she races barefoot through a countryside washed clean.

But then she opens her eyes again, and it has been two hundred years, and she cannot deny that the little village of Villon has changed. She recognizes less and less, finds more and more strange. Here and there she can still make out the place that she once knew, but her memories are threadbare, those years before her deal left to weather and fade.

And yet, some things are constant.

The stretch of road that runs through the town.

The small church sitting in the center.

The low wall of the graveyard, immune to the slow procession of change.

Addie lingers in the chapel doorway, watching the storm. She had an umbrella when she started out, but a sharp gust of wind bent the frame, and she knows she should wait for the rain to ease, that she has only the one dress. But as she stands there, one hand held out to cup the falling water, she thinks of Estele, who used to stand beneath the storms, arms wide and welcoming.

Addie abandons her shelter and heads for the cemetery gate.

In moments, she is soaked, but the rain is warm, and she will hardly melt. She passes a few new headstones, and many old, sets a wild rose on each of her parents' graves, and goes to find Estele.

She has missed the old woman these many years, missed her comfort, and her counsel, missed the strength of her grip, and her woody laugh, and the way she believed in Addie when she was Adeline, when she was still here, still human. And even though she holds on to what she can, Estele's voice has all but vanished with the passing years. This is the only place she can still conjure it, her presence felt in the old stones, the weedy earth, the weathered tree over her head.

But the tree is not there.

The grave slumps, weary, in its plot, the stone moldering and cracked, but the beautiful tree, with its wide limbs and its deep roots, is gone.

Nothing but a jagged stump remains.

Addie lets out an audible gasp, sinking to her knees, runs her hands over the dead and splintered wood. No. No, not this. She has lost so much, and mourned it all before, but for the first time in years, she is struck with a loss so sharp it steals her breath, her strength, her will.

Grief, deep as a well, opens inside her.

What is the point in planting seeds?

Why tend them? Why help them grow?

Everything crumbles in the end.

Everything dies.

And she is all that's left, a solitary ghost hosting a vigil for forgotten things. She squeezes her eyes shut and tries to conjure Estele, tries to summon the old woman's voice, so she can tell her it will be all right, that it's just wood—but the voice is gone, lost beneath the raging storm.

Addie is still sitting there at dusk.

The rain has slowed to a drizzle, the occasional tap of water against stone. She is soaked through, but she cannot feel it anymore, cannot feel much of anything—until she feels the shifting air, and the arrival of the shadow at her back.

"I'm sorry," he says, and it is the first time she has ever heard those words in that silken voice, the only time they will ever sound honest.

"Did you do this?" she whispers without looking up.

And to her surprise, Luc kneels beside her on the sodden earth. His own clothes do not seem to dampen.

"You cannot blame me for every loss," he says.

She doesn't realize she is shivering until his arm folds around her shoulders, until she feels her limbs trembling against the steady weight of his.

"I know I can be cruel," he says. "But nature can be crueler."

It is obvious, now, the charred line along the center of the stump. The swift, hot shear of lightning. It doesn't ease the loss.

She cannot stand to look upon the tree.

She cannot bear to linger here any longer.

"Come," he says, drawing her to her feet, and she does not know where they are going, and she does not care, so long as it is somewhere else. Addie turns her back on the ruined stump, the tombstone worn to nothing. Even rocks, she thinks as she follows Luc away from the graveyard, and the village, and the past.

She will never go back.

*　*　*

Paris, of course, has changed far more than Villon.

Over the years, she has seen it polished to a shine, white stone buildings capped with charcoal roofs. Long windows and iron balconies and wide avenues lined with flower shops and cafés beneath red awnings.

They sit on a patio, her dress drying in the summer breeze, a bottle of port open between them. Addie drinks deeply, trying to wash away the image of the tree, knowing no amount of wine will cleanse her memories.

It doesn't stop her from trying.

Somewhere along the Seine, a violin begins to play. Under the high notes, she hears the tremor of a car's engine. The stubborn clop of a horse. The strange music of Paris.

Luc lifts his glass. "Happy anniversary, my Adeline."

She looks at him, lips parting with their usual retort, but then stops short. If she is his—then by now he must be hers as well.

"Happy anniversary, my Luc," she answers, just to see the face he'll make.

She is rewarded with a raised brow, the crooked upturn of his mouth, the green of his eyes shifting in surprise.

Then Luc looks down, turns the glass of port between his fingers.

"You told me once that we were alike," he says, almost to himself. "Both of us . . . lonely. I loathed you for saying it. But I suppose in some ways you were right. I suppose," he goes on slowly, "there is something to the idea of company."

It is the closest he has ever come to sounding *human*.

"Do you miss me," she asks, "when you are not here?"

Those green eyes drift up, the emerald even in the dark. "I am here, with you, more often than you think."

"Of course," she says, "*you* come and go whenever you want. I have no choice but to wait."

His eyes darken with pleasure. "Do you wait for me?"

And now it is Addie who looks away. "You said it yourself. We all crave company."

"And if you could call on me, as I call on you?"

Her heart quickens a little.

She does not look up, and that is why she sees it, rolling toward her on the table. A slim band, carved of pale ash wood.

It is a ring.

It is *her* ring.

The gift she made to the dark that night.

The gift he scorned, and turned to smoke.

The image conjured in a seaside church.

But if it is an illusion now, it is an exceptional one. Here, the notch where her father's chisel bit a fraction too deep. There, the curve rubbed smooth as stone by years of worrying.

It is real. It must be real. And yet—

"You destroyed it."

"I took it," says Luc, looking over his glass. "That is not the same thing."

Anger flares in her. "You said it was nothing."

"I said it was not *enough*. But I do not ruin beauty without reason. It was mine, for a time, but it was always yours."

Addie marvels at the ring. "What must I do?"

"You know how to summon gods."

Estele's voice, faint as a breeze.

You must humble yourself before them.

"Put it on, and I will come." Luc leans back in his chair, the night breeze blowing through those raven curls. "There," he says. "Now we are even."

"We will never be even," she says as she turns the ring over between finger and thumb, and decides she will not use it.

It is a challenge. A game, parading as a gift. Not a war so much as a wager. A battle of wills. For her to don the ring, to call on Luc, would be to fold, to admit defeat.

To surrender.

She slips the token into the pocket of her skirts, forces her fingers to let go of the talisman.

Only then does she notice the tension in the air that night. It is an energy she's felt before, but cannot place, until Luc says, "There is about to be a war."

She had not heard. He tells her of the archduke's assassination, his face a mask of grim displeasure.

"I hate war," he says darkly.

"I would have thought you fond of conflict."

"The aftermath breeds art," he says. "But war makes believers out of cynics. Sycophants desperate for salvation, everyone suddenly clinging to their souls, clutching them close like a matron with her finest pearls." Luc shakes his head. "Give me back the Belle Epoque."

"Who knew gods were so nostalgic?"

Luc finishes his drink, and rises. "You should leave, before it starts." Addie laughs. It sounds almost as if he cares. The ring sits, a sudden weight in her pocket. He holds out his hand. "I can take you."

She should have accepted, should have said yes. Should have let him lead her through the horrible dark and out again, and saved herself an ocean, a miserable week stowing away in the belly of a ship at sea, the beauty of the water tarnished by the unending nature of it.

But she has learned too well to hold her ground.

Luc shakes his head. "You are still a stubborn fool."

She toys with staying, but after he is gone, she cannot help but conjure the shadows in his gaze, the grim way he spoke of the coming strife. It is a sign, when even gods and devils dread a fight.

A week later, Addie caves, and boards a ship for New York.

By the time she docks, the world is already at war.

It is just another day.

That is what Addie tells herself.

It is just a day—like all the others—but of course, it is not.

It is three hundred years since she was meant to be married—a future given against her will.

Three hundred years since she knelt in the woods, and summoned the darkness, and lost everything but freedom.

Three hundred years.

There should be a storm, an eclipse. Some way to mark the monument of it.

But the day dawns perfect, and cloudless, and blue.

The bed is empty beside her, but she can hear the soft shuffle of Henry moving through the kitchen, and she must have been gripping the blankets, because her fingers ache, a knot of pain in the center of her left palm.

When she opens her hand, the wooden ring falls out.

She brushes it off the bed as if it were a spider, an ill omen, listens to it land, and bounce, and roll away across the hardwood floor. Addie draws up her knees, and lets her head fall forward on them, and breathes into the space between her ribs, and reminds herself it is just a ring, and it is just a day. But there is a rope inside her chest, a dull dread winding tighter, telling her to go, to put as much distance between her and Henry as possible, in case he comes.

He won't, she tells herself.

It's been so long, she tells herself.

But she doesn't want to take the chance.

Henry's knuckles rap on the open door, and she looks up to see him holding a plate with a donut, three candles stuck into the top.

And despite everything, she laughs. "What's this?"

"Hey, it's not every day that your girlfriend turns three hundred."

"It's not my birthday."

"I know, but I didn't exactly know what to call it."

And just like that, the voice rises like smoke inside her head.

Happy anniversary, my love.

"Make a wish," says Henry.

Addie swallows, and blows the candles out.

He sinks onto the bed beside her. "I've got the whole day," he says. "Bea's covering at the store, and I thought we could take the train out to . . ." But he trails off when he sees her face. "What?"

Dread claws at her stomach, deeper than hunger. "I don't think we should be together," she says. "Not today."

His face falls. "Oh."

Addie cups his cheek, and lies. "It's just a day, Henry."

"You're right," he says. "It's a day. But how many of them has *he* ruined? Don't let him take it from you." He kisses her. "From us."

If Luc finds them together, he will take more than that.

"Come on," insists Henry, "I'll have you back long before you turn into a pumpkin. And then, if you want to spend the night apart, I understand. Worry about him in the dark, but it's hours until then, and you deserve a good day. A good memory."

And he's right. She does.

The dread loosens a little in her chest.

"Okay," she says, one little word, and Henry's whole face lights with pleasure. "What do you have in mind?"

He disappears into the bathroom, reemerges in a pair of yellow swim trunks, a towel cast over one shoulder. He tosses her a blue-and-white bikini.

"Let's go."

Rockaway Beach is a sea of colored towels, and flags planted in the sand.

Laughter rolls in with the tide as kids make castle mounds and people lounge beneath the glaring sun. Henry stretches their towels out on a narrow patch of unclaimed sand, weights them down with shoes, and then Addie grabs his hand and they run down the beach, the soles of their feet stinging until they hit the damp line of the tide and plunge into the water.

Addie gasps at the welcome brush of the waves, cool even in the heat of summer, and wades out until the ocean wraps around her waist. Henry ducks his head beside her, and comes back up, water dripping from his glasses. He pulls her to him, kisses the salt from her fingers. She slicks the hair from his face. They linger there, tangled together in the surf.

"See," he says, "isn't this better?"

And it is.

It is.

They swim until their limbs ache, and their skin begins to prune, and then retreat to the towels waiting on the beach, and stretch out to dry beneath the sun. It's too hot to stay there long, and soon the scent of food wafting from the boardwalk is enough to draw them up again.

Henry gathers his stuff and starts up the beach, and Addie rises to follow, shaking the sand from her towel.

And out falls the wooden ring.

It lies there, a fraction darker than the beach, like a drop of rain on a dry sidewalk. A reminder. Addie crouches down before it, and sweeps a handful of sand over the top, before jogging after Henry.

They head for the stretch of bars overlooking the beach, order tacos and a pitcher of frozen margaritas, savoring the tang and the sweet-salted chill. Henry wipes the water from his glasses, and Addie looks out at the ocean, and feels the past fold over the present, like the tides.

Déjà vu. Déjà su. Déjà vecu.

"What is it?" asks Henry.

Addie glances toward him. "Hm?"

"You get this look on your face," he says, "when you're remembering."

Addie looks back out at the Atlantic, the infinite hem of the beach, the memories spooling out along the horizon. And as they eat, she tells him of all the coasts she's seen, of the time she ferried across the English Channel, the White Cliffs of Dover rising from the fog. Of the time she sailed the coast of Spain, a stowaway in the bowels of a stolen boat, and how, when she crossed to America, the whole ship fell ill, and she had to feign sickness so they wouldn't think she was a witch.

And when she gets tired of talking, and they have both run out of drinks, they spend the next few hours bouncing between the shade of the concession stands and the cool kiss of the surf, lingering on the sand only long enough to dry.

The day goes by too fast, as good days do.

And when it's time to go, they make their way to the subway, and sink onto the bench, sun-drunk and sleepy, as the train pulls away.

Henry takes out a book, but Addie's eyes are stinging, and she leans against him, savoring his sun-and-paper scent, and the seat is plastic and the air is stale, and she has never been so comfortable. She feels herself sinking into Henry, head lolling on his shoulder.

And then he whispers three words into her hair.

"I love you," he says, and Addie wonders if this is love, this gentle thing.

If it is meant to be this soft, this kind.

The difference between heat, and warmth.

Passion, and contentment.

"I love you too," she says.

She wants it to be true.

There is an angel over the bar.

A stained-glass panel, lit from behind, with a single figure, chalice raised and hand outstretched, as if calling you to prayer.

But this is no church.

Speakeasies are like weeds these days, springing up between the stones of Prohibition. This one has no name, save the angel with its cup, the number *XII* over the door—twelve, the hour of midday, and of midnight—the velvet curtains and chaises that lounge like sleepers round the wooden floor, the masks given to the patrons at the door.

It is, like most of them, only a rumor, a secret passed from mouth to liquored mouth.

And Addie *loves* it.

There is a wild fervor to this place.

She dances—sometimes alone, and sometimes in the company of strangers. Loses herself in the jazz that rocks against the walls, rebounds, filling the crowded space with music. She dances, until the feathers of her mask cling to her cheeks, and Addie is breathless, and flushed, and only then does she retreat, falling into a leather chair.

It is almost midnight, and her fingers drift like the hands of a clock up to her throat, where the ring hangs on a silver cord, the wooden band warm against her skin.

It is always within reach.

Once, when the cord snapped, she thought it lost, only to find it safe within the pocket of her blouse. Another time, she left it on a windowsill, and found it hours later at her neck again.

The only thing she doesn't lose.

She toys with it, a lazy habit now, like curling a lock of hair around one finger. She skims the edge of the band with her nail, twirls it, careful to never let the ring slide over her knuckle.

She has reached for it a hundred times: when she was lonely, when she was bored, when she saw a thing of beauty and thought of him. But she is too stubborn, and he is too proud, and she is determined to win this round.

Fourteen years she has resisted the urge to put it on.

And fourteen years he has not come.

So she was right—it is a game. Another kind of forfeit, a lesser version of surrender.

Fourteen years.

And she is lonely, and a little drunk, and she wonders if tonight will be the night she breaks. It would be a fall, but it is not so great a height. Perhaps— perhaps— To occupy her hands, she decides to get another drink.

She goes to the bar and orders a gin fizz, but the white-masked man sets instead a Champagne glass before her. A single candied rose petal floats among the bubbles, and when she asks, he nods at a shadow in a velvet booth. His mask is made to look like branches, the leaves a perfect frame for perfect eyes.

And Addie smiles at the sight of him.

She would be lying if she said it was nothing but relief. A weight set down. A breath set free.

"I win," she says, sinking into his booth.

And even though he folded first, his eyes are bright with triumph. "How so?"

"I didn't call, and yet you came."

His chin lifts, a study in disdain. "You assume I'm here for you."

"I forget," she says, sliding into his smooth, low cadence. "There are so many maddening humans around to swindle out of their souls."

A wry smile tugs at perfect lips. "I promise, Adeline, few are as maddening as you."

"Few?" she teases. "I'll have to try harder."

He lifts a glass, and tips it toward the bar. "The fact remains, you have come to me. This place is mine."

Addie looks around, and suddenly, it is obvious.

She sees the markings everywhere.

Realizes, for the first time, that the angel above the bar has no wings. That the curls rising around his face are black. That the band she took for a halo might as well be moonlight.

And she wonders what it was that drew her here the first time.

Wonders if they are like magnets, she and Luc.

If they have circled each other for so long that now they share an orbit.

It will become a hobby of his, these kinds of clubs. He will plant them in a dozen cities, tend them like gardens, and grow them wild.

As plentiful as churches, he will say, *and twice as popular.*

And long after the days of Prohibition, they will still flourish, catering to many tastes, and she will wonder if it is the energy that stokes him, or if they are a grooming ground for souls. A place to ply, and pry, and promise. And in a way, a place to pray, albeit a different kind of worship.

"So you see," says Luc, "perhaps *I* win."

Addie shakes her head. "It is only chance," she says. "I did not call."

He smiles, gaze falling to the ring against her skin. "I know your heart. I felt it falter."

"But I didn't."

"No," he says, the word nothing but a breath. "But I was tired of waiting."

"So *you* missed *me*," she says with a smile, and there is the briefest glimpse in those green eyes. A fracture of light.

"Life is long, and humans boring. You are better company."

"You forget that *I* am human."

"Adeline," he says, a shade of pity in his voice. "You have not been human since the night we met. You will never be human again."

Heat flushes through her at the words. No longer pleasant warmth, but anger.

"I am still human," she says, voice tightening around the words as if they were her name.

"You move among them like a ghost," he says, his forehead bowing against hers, "because you are not one of them. You cannot live like them. You cannot love like them. You cannot belong with them."

His mouth hovers over her own, his voice dropping to nothing but a breeze. "You belong to me."

There is a sound like thunder in the back of his throat.

"With me."

And when she looks up into his eyes, she sees a new shade of green, and knows exactly what it is. The color of a man off-balance. His chest rises and falls as if it were a human thing.

Here is a place to put the knife.

"I would rather be a ghost."

And for the first time, the darkness flinches. Draws back like shadows in the face of light. His eyes go pale with anger, and there is the god she knows, the monster she has learned to face.

"Suit yourself," mutters Luc, and she waits for him to bleed into the dark, braces for the sudden, reaching void, expects to be swallowed up and spit out on the other side of the world.

But Luc does not vanish, and neither does she.

He nods at the club. "Go on, then," he says, "go back to them."

And she would rather he had banished her. Instead, she rises, even though she's lost her taste for drinks, for dancing, for any kind of company.

It is like stepping out of sunlight, the humid room gone cold against her skin, as he sits there in his velvet booth, and she goes through the motions of her night, and for the first time she feels the space between the humans and herself, and fears that he is right.

In the end, she is the one to leave.

And the next day, the speakeasy is boarded up, and Luc is gone. And just like that, new lines are drawn, the pieces set, the battle started.

She will not see him again until the war.

The A train jostles Addie out of sleep.

She opens her eyes just as the lights overhead flicker and go out, plunging the car into darkness. Panic surges like a current through her chest, the world beyond the windows dark, but Henry's hand squeezes hers.

"It's just the line," he says, as the lights come on again, and the train settles back into its easy motion, and she realizes when the voice comes on the intercom that they're back in Brooklyn, the last stretch of subway underground again, and when they get off, the sun is still safely in the sky.

They walk back to Henry's, heat-logged and drowsy, shower off the salt and sand, and collapse on top of the sheets, wet hair cooling on their skin. Book curls around her feet. Henry pulls her against him, and the bed is cool, and he is warm, and if it is not love, it is enough.

"Five minutes," he mumbles in her hair.

"Five minutes," she answers, the words half plea, half promise as she curls into him.

Outside, the sun hovers over the buildings.

They still have time.

Addie wakes in the dark.

When she closed her eyes, the sun was still high. Now, the room is full of shadows, the sky a deep indigo bruise beyond the window.

Henry is still asleep, but the room is too quiet, too still, and dread rolls through Addie as she sits up.

She doesn't say his name, doesn't even think it as she climbs to her feet, holding her breath as she steps out into the darkened hall. She scans the living room, braced to see him sitting on the sofa, long arms stretched along the cushioned back.

Adeline.

But he's not there.

Of course he's not there.

It has been almost forty years.

He is not coming. And Addie is so tired of waiting for him.

She returns to the bedroom, sees Henry on his feet, his hair a mess of loose black curls as he searches under the pillows for his glasses.

"I'm sorry," he says. "I should have set an alarm." He unzips a bag, puts a change of clothes inside. "I can stay at Bea's. I'll—"

But Addie catches his hand. "Don't go."

Henry hesitates. "Are you sure?"

She isn't sure of anything, but she has had such a good day, she doesn't want to waste her night, doesn't want to give it to *him*.

He has taken enough.

There's no food in the apartment, so they get dressed and head over to the Merchant, and there's a sleepy ease to all of it, the disorientation of waking after dark added to the effects of so long in the sun. It lends everything a dreamy air, the perfect end to a perfect day.

They tell the waitress they're celebrating, and when she asks if it's a birthday, or an engagement, Addie lifts her beer and says, "Anniversary."

"Congrats," says the waitress. "How many years?"

"Three hundred," she says.

Henry chokes on his drink, and the waitress laughs, assuming it's an inside joke. Addie simply smiles.

A song comes on, the kind that rises above the noise, and she drags him to his feet.

"Dance with me," she says, and Henry tries to tell her that he doesn't dance, even though she was there, at the Fourth Rail, when they flung themselves into the beat, and he says that is different, but she doesn't believe him, because times change, but everyone dances, she has seen them do the waltz and the quadrille, the fox-trot and the jive, and a dozen others, and she is sure that he can manage at least one of them.

And so she draws him between the tables, and Henry didn't even know that the Merchant had a dance floor, but there it is, and they are the only ones on it. Addie shows him how to lift his hand, to move with her in mirror motions. She shows him how to lead, how to twirl her, how to dip. She shows him where to put his hands, and how to feel the rhythm in her hips, and for a little while, everything is perfect, and easy, and right.

They stumble, laughing, up to the bar for another drink.

"Two beers," says Henry, and the bartender nods, and steps away, comes back a minute later, and sets down their drinks.

But only one is a beer.

The other is Champagne, a candied rose petal floating in the center.

Addie feels the world tip, the darkness tunnel.

There is a note beneath the glass, written in elegant, sloping French.

For my Adeline.

"Hey," Henry is saying, "we didn't order this."

The bartender points to the end of the bar. "Compliments of the gentleman over . . ." he starts, trailing off. "Huh," he says. "He was just there."

Addie's heart tumbles in her chest. She grabs Henry's hand. "You have to go."

"What? Wait—"

But there is no time. She pulls him toward the door.

"Addie."

Luc cannot see them together, he cannot know that they have found—

"Addie." She finally looks back. And feels the world drop out beneath her.

The bar is perfectly still.

Not *empty*, no; it is still brimming with people.

But none of them are moving.

They have all stopped mid-stride, mid-speech, mid-sip. Not frozen, exactly, but forcibly stilled. Puppets, hovering on strings. The music is still playing; softly, now, but it is the only sound in the place besides Henry's unsteady breath, and the pounding of her heart.

And a voice, rising from the dark.

"Adeline."

The whole world holds its breath, reduces to the soft echo of footfalls on the wooden floor, the figure stepping out of the shadows.

Forty years, and there he is, unchanged in the ways she is unchanged, the same raven curls, the same emerald eyes, the same coy twist to his cupid's bow mouth. He's dressed in a black button-down, the sleeves of his shirt rolled to the elbows, a suit jacket flung over one shoulder, his other hand hooked loosely in the pocket of his slacks.

The picture of ease.

"My love," he says, "you're looking well."

Something in her loosens at the sound of his voice, the way it always has. Something at the center of her unwinds, release without relief. Because she has waited, of course she has waited, held her breath in dread as much as hope. Now it rushes from her lungs.

"What are you doing here?"

Luc has the nerve to look affronted. "It's our anniversary. Surely you haven't forgotten."

"It's been forty years."

"Whose fault is that?"

"Yours, entirely."

A smile tugs at the edge of his mouth. And then his green gaze slides toward Henry. "I suppose I should be flattered by the resemblance."

Addie doesn't rise to the bait. "He has nothing to do with this. Send him away. He'll forget."

Luc's smile drops away. "Please. You embarrass us both." He carves a slow circle around them, a tiger rounding on its prey. "As if I don't keep track of all my deals. Henry Strauss, so desperate to be wanted. Sell your soul just to be loved. What a fine pair you two must make."

"Then let us have it."

A dark brow rises. "You think I mean to pull you apart? Not at all. Time will do that soon enough." He looks to Henry. "Tick tock. Tell me, are you still counting your life in days, or have you begun to measure it in hours? Or does that only make it harder?"

Addie looks between them, reading the triumphant green in Luc's eyes, the color bleeding out of Henry's face.

She does not understand.

"Oh, Adeline."

The name draws her back.

"Humans live such short lives, don't they? Some *far* shorter than others. Savor the time you have left. And know, it was *his* choice."

With that, Luc turns on his heel and dissolves into the dark.

In his wake, the bar shudders back into motion. Noise surges through the space, and Addie stares at the shadows until she's sure they are empty.

Humans live such short lives.

She turns toward Henry, who's no longer standing behind her, but slumped in a chair.

Some far shorter than others.

His head is bowed, one hand clutching his wrist where the watch would be. Where it is, somehow, again. She is sure he didn't put it on. Sure he wasn't wearing it.

But there it is, shining like a cuff around his wrist.

It was his choice.

"Henry," she says, kneeling before him.

"I wanted to tell you," he murmurs.

She pulls the watch toward herself, and studies the face. Four months she's been with Henry, and in that time, the hour hand has crept from half past six to half past ten. Four months, and four hours closer to midnight, and she always assumed it would go around again.

A lifetime, he said, and she *knew* it was a lie.

It had to be.

Luc would never give another human so much time—not after *her.*

She knew, she must have known. But she thought, perhaps he'd sold his soul for fifty, or thirty, or even ten—that would have been enough.

But there are only twelve hours on a watch, only twelve months in a year, and he wouldn't, he *couldn't* be so foolish.

"Henry," she says, "how long did you ask for?"

"Addie," he pleads, and for the first time, her name sounds wrong on his lips. It is cracked. It is breaking.

"How long?" she demands.

He is silent for a long time.

And then, at last, he tells her the truth.

A boy is sick of his broken heart.

Tired of his storm-filled brain.

So he drinks until he cannot feel the pieces scraping together in his chest, until he cannot hear the thunder rolling through his head. He drinks when his friends tell him it will be all right. He drinks when they tell him it will pass. He drinks until the bottle is empty and the world gets fuzzy at the edges. It is not enough to ease the pain, so he leaves, and they let him go.

And at some point, on the walk home, it begins to rain.

At some point, his phone goes off, and he doesn't answer.

At some point, the bottle slips, and he cuts his hand.

At some point, he is outside his building, and he sinks onto the stoop, and presses his palms against his eyes, and tells himself it is just another storm.

But this time, it shows no signs of passing. This time, there is no break in the clouds, no light on the horizon, and the thunder in his head is so damn loud. So he takes a few of his sister's pills, those little pink umbrellas, but they are still no match for the storm, and so he takes some of his own, as well.

He leans back on the rain-slicked stairs, and looks up at the place where the rooftop meets the sky, and wonders, not for the first time, how many steps from here to the edge.

He isn't sure when he decides to jump.

Perhaps he never does.

Perhaps he decides to go inside, and then he decides to go upstairs, and when he reaches his door he decides to keep going, and when he gets to the last door he decides to step out onto the roof—and at some point, standing there in the pouring rain, he decides he doesn't want to decide anymore.

Here is a straight path. A tarred stretch of empty asphalt, nothing but steps between him and the edge. The pills are catching up, dulling the pain and leaving behind a cotton quiet that's somehow even worse. His eyes drift shut, his limbs are so heavy.

It is just a storm, he tells himself, but he is tired of looking for shelter.

It is just a storm, but there is always another waiting in its wake.

It is just a storm, just a storm—but tonight it is too much, and he is not enough, and so he crosses the roof, doesn't slow until he can see over the side, doesn't stop until the tips of his shoes graze empty air.

And that is where the stranger finds him.

That is where the darkness makes an offer.

Not for a lifetime—for a single year.

It will be easy to look back and wonder how he could have done it, how he could have given away so much for so little. But in the moment, shoes already skimming night, the simple truth is that he would have sold his soul for less, would have traded an entire life of this for just a day—an hour, a minute, a moment—of peace.

Just to numb the pain inside his chest.

Just to quiet the storm inside his head.

He is so tired of hurting, so tired of being hurt. And that is why, when the stranger holds out his hand, and offers to pull Henry back from the edge, there is no hesitation.

He simply says yes.

Now it all makes sense.

He makes sense.

This boy, who could never sit still, never waste time, never put off a single thing. This boy, who writes down every word she says, so she'll have something when he's gone, who doesn't want to lose even a single day, because he doesn't have that many more.

This boy she's falling in love with.

This boy, who will soon be gone.

"How?" she asks. "How could you give up so much for so little?"

Henry looks up at her, his face hollow.

"In that moment," he says, "I would have given it for less."

A year. It seemed like so long, once.

Now it is no time at all.

A year, and it is almost up, and all she can see is the curve of Luc's smile, the triumphant color of his eyes. They were not clever, they were not lucky, they were not slipping past his notice. He knew, of course he knew, and he let it come to this.

He let her fall.

"Addie, please," says Henry, but she is already up, already moving across the bar.

He tries to grab her hand, but he is too late.

She is already out of reach.

Already gone.

Three hundred years.

She has survived three hundred years, and in those centuries, there have been so many times when the ground gave way, moments when she could not catch her balance or her breath. When the world left her feeling lost, broken, hopeless.

Standing outside her parents' house, that night after the deal.

On the docks in Paris, where she learned what a body was worth.

Remy, pressing the coins into her palm.

Soaked through, at the ruined stump of Estele's oak tree.

But in this moment, Addie isn't lost, or broken, or hopeless.

She is *furious*.

She shoves her hand into her pocket, and of course the ring is there. It is always there. Grains of sand flake from the smooth wooden surface as Addie slides the band over her knuckle.

It's been forty years since she last wore it, but the ring slips effortlessly on.

She feels the wind, like a cool breath at her back, and turns, expecting to find Luc.

But the street is empty—empty, at least, of shadows and promises and gods.

She twists the ring around her finger.

Nothing.

"Show yourself!" she shouts down the block.

Heads turn, but Addie doesn't care. They'll forget her soon enough, and even if she weren't a ghost, this is New York, a place immune to the actions of a stranger in the street.

"Dammit," she swears. She wrenches the ring from her finger, and hurls it down the road, hears it bounce, and roll. And then the sound suddenly drops away. The nearest streetlight flickers out, and a voice comes from the dark.

"All these years, and you still have such a temper."

Something brushes her neck, and then a silver thread, thin as dew shine, the same one snapped so long ago, shimmers on her collar.

Luc's fingers trail along her skin. "Have you missed me?"

She turns to shove him away, but her hands pass straight through, and then he is behind her. When she tries a second time, he is as solid and un-yielding as rock.

"Undo it," she snaps, striking his chest, but her fist barely grazes the front of his shirt before he takes her wrist.

"Who are you to give me orders, Adeline?"

She tries to pull free, but his grip is stone.

"You know," he says, almost casually, "there was a time when you groveled, pressed yourself against the damp forest soil and pleaded for my intercession."

"You want me to beg? Then fine. I beg you. Please. Undo it."

He steps forward, forcing her to step back. "Henry made his deal."

"He didn't know—"

"They always know," says Luc. "They just don't want to accept the cost. The soul is the easiest thing to trade. It's the *time* no one considers."

"Luc, please."

His green eyes gleam, not with mischief, or triumph, but power. The shade of someone who knows they're in control.

"Why should I?" he asks. "Why *would* I?"

Addie has a dozen answers, but she scrambles to find the right words, the ones that might appease the dark, but before she can find them, Luc reaches out, and lifts her chin, and she expects him to play out their old, tired lines, to mock her, or ask for her soul, but he does neither.

"Spend the night with me," he says. "Tomorrow. Let us have a *proper* anniversary. Give me that, and I'll consider freeing Mr. Strauss from his obligations." His mouth twitches. "If, that is, you can persuade me."

It is a lie, of course.

It is a trap, but Addie has no other choice.

"I accept," she says, and the darkness smiles, and then dissolves around her.

She stands on the sidewalk, alone, until her heart steadies, and then walks back into the Merchant.

But Henry is gone.

She finds him at home, sitting in the dark.

He's on the edge of the bed, the blankets still tangled from their afternoon nap. He stares ahead, into the distance, the way he did that summer night on the rooftop, after the fireworks.

And Addie realizes that she is going to lose him, the way she has lost everyone.

And she doesn't know if she can do it, not again, not this time.

Hasn't she lost enough?

"I'm sorry," he whispers as she crosses to him.

"I'm so sorry," he says, as she runs her fingers through his hair.

"Why didn't you tell me?" she pleads.

Henry is quiet for a moment, and then he says, "How do you walk to the end of the world?" He looks up at her. "I wanted to hold on to every step."

A soft, shuddering sigh.

"My uncle had cancer, when I was still in college. It was terminal. The doctors gave him a few months, and he told everyone, and do you know what they did? They couldn't handle it. They were so caught up in their grief, they mourned him before he was even dead. There's no way to un-know the fact that someone is dying. It eats away all the normal, and leaves something wrong and rotten in its place. I'm sorry, Addie. I didn't want you to look at me that way."

She climbs into bed, and pulls him down beside her.

"I'm sorry," he's saying, soft and steady as a prayer.

They lie there, face-to-face, their fingers intertwined.

"I'm sorry."

And Addie forces herself to ask, "How long do you have left?"

Henry swallows. "A month."

The words land like a blow on tender skin.

"A little more," he says. "Thirty-six days."

"It's after midnight," Addie whispers.

Henry exhales. "Then thirty-five."

Her grip tightens around his, and his tightens back, and they hold on until it hurts, as if any minute someone might try to pull them apart, as if the other might slip free, and disappear.

VII

Her back hits the rough stone wall.

The cell grinds shut, and German soldiers laugh beyond the bars as Addie slumps to the floor, coughing blood.

A handful of men huddle in one corner of the cell, slouched and murmuring. At least they don't seem to care that she's a woman. The Germans have noticed. Though they caught her dressed in nondescript trousers and coat, though she kept her hair pulled back, she knew by the way they scowled and leered that they could tell her sex. She told them in a dozen different tongues what she would do if they came near, and they laughed, and satisfied themselves with beating her senseless.

Get up, she wills her weary body.

Get up, she wills her tired bones.

Addie forces herself to her feet, stumbles to the front of the cell. She wraps her hands around the frozen steel, pulls at it until her muscles scream, until the bars groan, but they do not move. She pries at the bolts until her fingers bleed, and a soldier slams his hand against the bars and threatens to use her body as kindling.

She is such a fool.

She is a fool for thinking it would work. For thinking that forgettable was the same as invisible, that it would protect her here.

She should have stayed in Boston, where the worst she had to worry about was wartime rations and winter cold. She should never have come back. It was foolish honor, and stubborn pride. It was the last war, and the fact she ran away, fled across the Atlantic instead of facing the danger at home. Because somehow, despite it all, that's what France will always be.

Home.

And somewhere along the way, she decided she could help. Not in an official sense, of course, but secrets have no owner. They could be touched, and traded, by anyone, even a ghost.

The only thing she had to do was not get caught.

Three years of ferrying secrets through Occupied France.

Three years, only to end up here.

In a prison outside Orleans.

And it does not matter that they will forget her face. It does not matter, because these soldiers do not care about remembering. Here, all the faces are strange, and foreign, and nameless, and if she doesn't get out, she is going to disappear.

Addie sags back against the icy wall and pulls her ragged jacket close. She closes her eyes. She does not pray, not exactly, but she does think of him. She does, perhaps, even wish that it were summer—a July night when he might find her on his own.

The soldiers have searched her, roughly, taken anything she might use to hurt them, or escape. They have taken the ring, too, snapped the leather cord it hung on, cast the wooden band away.

And yet, when she rifles through her ragged clothing, it is still there, waiting like a coin in the crease of her pocket. She is grateful, then, that she cannot seem to lose it. Grateful, as she lifts it to her finger.

For a moment, she falters—twenty-nine years she has had the ring, with all its strings attached.

Twenty-nine years, and she hasn't used it.

But right now, even Luc's smug satisfaction would be better than the eternity in a prison cell, or worse.

If he comes.

Those words, a whisper in the back of her mind. A fear she cannot shake. Chicago rising like bile in her throat.

The anger in her chest. The venom in his eyes.

I would rather be a ghost.

She had been wrong.

She does not want to be this kind of ghost.

And so, for the first time in centuries, Addie prays.

She slides the wooden band over her finger, and holds her breath, expects to feel something, a stirring of magic, a rush of wind.

But there is nothing.

Nothing, and she wonders if, after all this time, it was just another trick, a way to lift her hopes, only to drop them, in the chance they might shatter.

She has a curse ready on her tongue, when she feels the breeze—not biting, but warm, cutting through the prison cell, carrying the far-off scent of summer.

The men across the cell stop talking.

They slouch in their corner, awake but inert, staring off into space, as if caught in the throes of some idea. Beyond the cell, the soldiers' boots stop sounding on the stones, and the German voices drop away like a pebble down a well.

The world goes strangely, impossibly quiet.

Until the only sound is the soft, almost rhythmic tap of fingers trailing along bars.

She has not seen him since Chicago.

"Oh Adeline," he says, hand drifting down the icy bars. "What a state you're in."

She manages a small, pained laugh. "Immortality breeds a high tolerance for risk."

"There *are* things worse than death," he says, as if she does not already know.

He looks around at the prison, brow furrowed in disdain.

"Wars," he mutters.

"Tell me you are not helping them."

Luc almost looks offended. "Even *I* have limits."

"You bragged to me once about the successes of Napoleon."

He shrugs. "There is ambition, and there is evil. And as much as I'd like to create a roster of my past exploits, your life is the important one right now." He leans his elbows on the bars. "How do you plan to get out of this?"

She knows what he wants her to do. He wants her to *beg*. As if donning the ring were not enough. As if he has not already won this hand, this game. Her stomach knots, and her bruised ribs ache, and she is so thirsty she could cry just to have something to drink. But Addie cannot bring herself to fold.

"You know me," she says, with a tired smile. "I always find a way."

Luc sighs. "Suit yourself," he says, turning his back, and it is too much; she cannot bear the thought of him leaving her here, alone.

"Wait," she calls desperately, pushing into the bars—only to find the lock undone, the cell door swinging open beneath her weight.

Luc looks back over his shoulder, and he almost smiles, turning toward her just enough to offer up his hand.

She stumbles forward, out of the cell and into freedom, into him. And for a moment, the embrace is only that, and he is solid, and warm, folded around her in the dark, and it would be easy to believe that he is real, that he is human, that he is home.

But then the world cracks wide, and the shadows swallow them whole.

The prison gives way to nothingness, to blackness, to the wild dark. And when it parts, she is back in Boston, the sun just beginning to set, and she could kiss the ground in sheer relief. Addie pulls the jacket close around her, and sinks onto the curb, legs shaking, the wooden band still wrapped around her finger. She called, and he came. She asked, and he answered. And she knows he will hold it over her, and but right now, she does not care.

She does not want to be alone.

But by the time Addie looks up to thank him, he is gone.

Henry trails her through the apartment as she gets ready.

"Why would you agree to this?" he asks.

Because she knows the darkness better than anyone, knows his mind if not his heart.

"Because I don't want to lose you," says Addie, pulling up her hair.

Henry looks tired, hollowed out. "It's too late," he says.

But it's not too late.

Not yet.

Addie reaches into her pocket and feels the ring where it always is, waiting, the wood warm from being pressed against her body. She draws it out, but Henry catches her hand.

"Don't do this," he pleads.

"Do you want to die?" she asks, the words cutting through the room.

He pulls back a little at the words. "No. But I made a choice, Addie."

"You made a mistake."

"I made a *deal*," he says. "And I'm sorry. I'm sorry I didn't ask for more time. I'm sorry I didn't tell you the truth sooner. But it is what it is."

Addie shakes her head. "You may have made peace with this, Henry, but I haven't."

"This won't work," he warns. "You can't reason with him."

Addie tugs free of his grip. "I'm willing to try," she says, slipping the ring over her finger.

There is no flood of darkness.

Only a stillness, a vacant quiet, and then—

A knock.

And she is grateful that at least he didn't invite himself in. But Henry stands between her and the door, his hands braced across the narrow hall. He doesn't move, his eyes pleading. Addie reaches up and cups his face.

"I need you to trust me," she says.

Something cracks in him. One hand drops from the frame.

She kisses him, and then she slides by, and opens the door for the dark.

"Adeline."

Luc should look out of place in the building's hall, but he never does.

The lights on the walls have dimmed a little, softened to a yellow haze that haloes the black curls around his face, and catches slivers of gold in his green eyes.

He is dressed in all black, tailored slacks and a button-down shirt, the sleeves rolled to the elbows, an emerald pin driven through the silk tie at his throat.

It is far too hot for such an outfit, but Luc doesn't seem to mind. The heat, like the rain, like the world itself, seems to have no hold on him.

He does not tell her she looks beautiful.

He does not tell her anything.

He simply turns, expecting her to follow.

And as she steps into the hall, he looks to Henry. And winks.

Addie should have stopped right there.

She should have turned around, let Henry pull her back inside. They should have shut the door, and bolted it against the dark.

But they didn't.

They don't.

Addie glances back over her shoulder at Henry, who lingers in the doorway, a cloud shadowing his face. She wills him to close the door, but he doesn't, and she has no choice but to step away, and follow Luc as Henry watches.

Downstairs, he holds open the building's door, but Addie stops. Looks down at the threshold. Darkness coils in the frame, shimmers between them and the steps down to the street.

She doesn't trust the shadows, she can't see where they lead, and the last thing she needs is for Luc to strand her in some far-off land if and when the night goes bad.

"There are rules tonight," she says.

"Oh?"

"I won't leave the city," she says, nodding at the door. "And I won't go that way."

"Through a door?"

"Through the dark."

Luc's brows draw up. "Don't you trust me?"

"I never have," she says. "There's no use starting now."

Luc laughs, soft and soundless, and steps outside to hail a car. Seconds later, a sleek black sedan pulls up to the curb. He holds out his hand to help her in. She doesn't take it.

He does not give the driver an address.

The driver does not ask for one.

And when Addie asks where they are going, Luc does not answer.

Soon they are on the Manhattan Bridge.

The silence between them should be awkward. The halting conversation of exes too long apart, and still not long enough to have forgiven anything.

What is forty years against three hundred?

But this is a silence born of strategy.

This is the silence of a chess game being played.

And this time, Addie has to win.

IX

"God, you're beautiful," says Max, lifting his glass.

Addie blushes, eyes dropping to her martini.

They met on the street outside the Wilshire that morning, the creases from his bedsheets still pressed into her skin. She was lingering on the curb in his favorite wine-colored dress, and when he came out for his morning stroll, he stopped and asked if he could be so bold as to walk with her, wherever she was going, and when they got there, to a pretty building picked at random, he kissed her hand, and said good-bye, but he didn't leave, and neither did she. They spent the whole day together, strolling from a tea shop to a park to the art museum, finding excuses to continue in each other's company.

And when she told him that it was the best birthday she'd had in years, he blinked at her in horror, shocked at the idea a girl like her would find herself alone, and here they are, drinking martinis at the Roosevelt.

(It is not her birthday, of course, and she's not sure why she told him it was. Perhaps to see what he would do. Perhaps because even she is getting bored of living the same night over again.)

"Have you ever met someone," he says, "and felt like you've known them for ages?"

Addie smiles.

He always says the same things, but he means them every time. She toys with the silver thread at her throat, the wooden ring tucked into the neckline of her dress. A habit she cannot seem to break.

A server appears at her elbow with a bottle of Champagne.

"What's this?" she asks.

"For the birthday girl on this special evening," says Max brightly. "And the lucky gentleman who gets to spend it with her."

She admires the tiny bubbles rising through the flute, knows even before she takes a sip that it's the real thing; old, expensive. Knows, too, that Max can easily afford the luxury.

He is a sculptor—Addie has always had a weakness for the fine arts—and talented, yes, but far from starving. Unlike so many of the artists Addie has been with, he comes from money, the family funds sturdy enough to weather the wars, and the lean years between them.

He raises his glass, just as a shadow falls across the table.

She assumes it's their server, but then Max looks up, and frowns a little. "Can I help you?"

And Addie hears a voice like silk and smoke. "I do believe you can."

There is Luc, dressed in an elegant black suit. He is beautiful. He is always beautiful. "Hello, my dear."

Max's frown deepens. "Do you two know each other?"

"No," she says at the same time Luc says, "Yes," and it's not fair, the way his voice carries and hers does not.

"He's an old friend," she says, a biting edge in her tone. "But—"

Again, he cuts her off. "But we haven't seen each other in a while, so if you'd be so kind . . ."

Max bristles. "That's quite impertinent—"

"*Go.*"

It is just one word, but the air ripples with the force of it, the syllable wrapping like gauze around her date. The fight drops out of Max's face. The annoyance smooths, and his eyes go glassy as he rises from the table, and walks away. He never even looks back.

"Dammit," she swears, sinking in her seat. "Why must you be such an ass?"

Luc lowers himself into the vacant chair, and lifts the bottle of Champagne, refilling their glasses. "Your birthday is in March."

"When you get to be my age," she says, "you celebrate as often as you like."

"How long have you been with him?"

"Two months. It's not so bad," she says, sipping her drink. "He falls for me every day."

"And forgets you every night."

The words bite, but not as deeply as they used to.

"At least he keeps me company."

Those emerald eyes trail over her skin. "So would I," he says, "if you wanted it."

A flush of warmth sweeps across her cheeks.

He cannot know that she has missed him. Thought of him, the way she used to think of her stranger, alone in bed at night. Thought of him every time she toyed with the ring at her throat, and every time she didn't.

"Well," she says, finishing her drink. "You've stripped me of my date. The least you can do is try and fill the space."

And just like that, the green in Luc's eyes is back, brighter.

"Come," he says, drawing her up from her chair. "The night is young, and we can do far better."

* * *

The Cicada Club buzzes with life.

Art deco chandeliers hang low, shining up against a burnished ceiling. It is crushed red carpet and stairs sweeping up to balcony seats. It is linen-covered tables and a polished dance floor set before a low stage.

They arrive as a brass band finishes its set, trumpets and sax spilling through the club. The place is packed, and yet, when Luc draws her through the crowd, there is a table sitting empty at the front. The best in the house.

They take their seats, and moments later a waiter appears, two martinis balanced on his tray. She thinks of that first dinner they shared in the marquis's house, centuries ago, the meal ready before she even agreed to have it, and wonders if Luc planned this in advance, or if the world simply bends to meet his wish.

The crowd erupts in cheers as a new performer takes the stage.

A narrow man with a wan face, narrow brows arching beneath a gray fedora.

Luc stares at him with the sharp pride of something owned.

"What's his name?" she asks.

"Sinatra," he answers as the band lifts, and the man begins to sing. A crooner's melody, smooth and sweet, spills into the room. Addie listens, mesmerized, and then men and women begin to rise from their chairs and step out onto the dance floor.

Addie stands, holding out her hand. "Dance with me," she says.

Luc looks up at her, but doesn't rise.

"Max would have danced with me," she says.

She expects him to refuse her, but Luc rises to his feet, and takes her hand, leading her onto the floor.

She expects him to be stiff, unyielding, but Luc moves with the fluid grace of wind rushing through fields of wheat, of storms rolling through the summer skies.

She tries to remember a time they were this close, and can't.

They have always kept their distance.

Now, the space collapses.

His body wraps around hers like a blanket, like a breeze, like the night itself. But tonight, he does not feel like a thing of shadow and smoke. Tonight, his arms are solid against her skin. His voice slides through her hair.

"Even if everyone you met remembered," Luc says, "I would still know you best."

She searches his face. "Do I know *you?*"

He bows his head over hers. "You are the only one who does."

Their bodies press together, one shaped to fit the other perfectly.

His shoulder, molded to her cheek.

His hands, molded to her waist.

His voice, molded to the hollow places in her as he says, "I want you." And then, again, "I have always wanted you."

Luc looks down at her, those green eyes dark with pleasure, and Addie fights to hold her ground.

"You want me as a prize," she says. "You want me as a meal, or a glass of wine. Just another thing to be consumed."

He dips his head, presses his lips to her collarbone. "Is that so wrong?"

She fights back a shiver as he kisses her throat. "Is it such a bad thing . . ." His mouth trails along her jaw. ". . . to be savored?" His breath brushes her ear. "To be relished?"

His mouth hovers over hers, and his lips, too, are molded to her own.

She will never be quite sure which happened first—if she kissed him, or he kissed her, who began the gesture, and who rose to meet it. She will only know that there was space between them, and it has vanished. She has thought of kissing Luc before, of course, when he was just a figment of her mind, and then, when he was more. But in all her conjurings, he'd taken her mouth as if it is a prize. After all, that is how he kissed her the night they met, when he sealed the deal with the blood on her lips. That is how she assumed he would always kiss.

But now, he kisses her like someone tasting poison.

Cautious, questing, almost afraid.

And only when she answers, returns the kiss in kind, does he deepen his advance, his teeth skating along her bottom lip, the weight and heat of his body pressing against hers.

He tastes like the air at night, heady with the weight of summer storms. He tastes like the faint traces of far-off woodsmoke, a fire dying in the dark. He tastes like the forest, and somehow, impossibly, like home.

And then darkness reaches up around her, around them, and the Cicada Club vanishes; the low music and the crooner's melody swallowed up by the pressing void, by rushing wind, and racing hearts, and Addie is falling, forever and a single backward step—and then her feet find the smooth marble floor of a hotel room, and Luc is there, pressing her forward, and she is there, drawing him back against the nearest wall.

His arms lift around her, forming a loose and open cage.

She could break it, if she tried.

She doesn't try.

He kisses her again, and this time, he is not tasting poison. This time, there is no caution, no pulling back; the kiss is sudden, sharp, and deep, stealing air and thought and leaving only hunger, and for a moment, Addie can feel the yawning dark, feel it opening around her, even though the ground is still there.

She has kissed a lot of people. But none of them will ever kiss like him. The difference doesn't lie in the technicalities. His mouth is no better shaped to the task. It is just in the way he uses it.

It is the difference between tasting a peach out of season, and that first bite into sun-ripened fruit.

The difference between seeing only in black-and-white, and a life in full-color film.

That first time, it is a kind of fight, neither letting down their guard, each watching for the telltale glint of some hidden blade seeking flesh.

When they finally collide, it is with all the force of bodies kept too long apart.

It is a battle waged on bedsheets.

And in the morning, the whole room shows the signs of their war.

"It's been so long," he says, "since I haven't wanted to leave."

She looks at the window, the first thin edge of light. "Then don't."

"I must," he says. "I am a thing of darkness."

She props her head up on one hand. "Will you vanish with the sun?"

"I will simply go where it is dark again."

Addie rises, goes to the window, and draws the curtains closed, plunging the room back into lightless black.

"There," she says, feeling her way back to him. "Now it is dark again."

Luc laughs, a soft, beautiful sound, and pulls her down into the bed.

It is only sex.

At least, it starts that way.

He is a thing to be gotten out of her system.

She is a novelty to be enjoyed.

Addie half expects them to burn out in a single night, to waste whatever energy they've gathered in their years of spinning.

But two months later, he comes to find her again, steps out of nothing and back into her life, and she thinks about how strange it is, to see him against the reds and golds of autumn, the changing leaves, a charcoal scarf looped loose around his throat.

It is weeks until his next visit.

And then, only days.

So many years of solitary nights, hours of waiting, and hating, and hoping. Now he is there.

Still, Addie makes herself small promises in the space between his visits.

She will not linger in his arms.

She will not fall asleep beside him.

She will not feel anything but his lips on her skin, his hands tangled in hers, the weight of him against her.

Small promises, but ones she does not keep.

It is only sex.

And then it is not.

"Dine with me," Luc says as winter gives way to spring.

"Dance with me," he says as a new year begins.

"Be with me," he says, at last, as one decade slips into the next.

And one night Addie wakes in the dark to the soft pressure of his fingertips drawing patterns on her skin, and she is struck by the look in his eyes. No, not the look. The *knowing*.

It is the first time that she has woken up in bed with someone who hasn't already forgotten her. The first time she's heard her name again after the pause of sleep. The first time she hasn't felt alone.

And something in her splinters.

Addie does not hate him anymore. Has not for a long time.

She does not know when the shift started, if it was a specific point in time, or, as Luc once warned her, the slow erosion of a coast.

All she knows is that she is tired, and he is the place she wants to rest.

And that, somehow, she is happy.

But it is not love.

Whenever Addie feels herself forgetting, she presses her ear to his bare chest and listens for the drum of life, the drawing of breath, and hears only the woods at night, the quiet hush of summer. A reminder that he is a lie, that his face and his flesh are simply a disguise.

That he is not human, and this is not love.

The city slides past beyond the window, but Addie doesn't turn her head, doesn't admire the skyline of Manhattan, the buildings soaring to every side. Instead, she studies Luc, reflected in the darkened glass, the line of his jaw, the arc of his brow, angles drawn by her hand so many, many years ago. She is watching him, the way one watches a wolf at the edge of the woods, waiting to see what it will do.

He is the first to break the silence.

The first to move a piece.

"Do you remember the opera in Munich?"

"I remember everything, Luc."

"The way you looked at the players on that stage, as if you'd never seen theater before."

"I'd never seen theater like *that*."

"The wonder in your eyes, at the sight of something new. I knew then I'd never win."

She wants to savor the words like a sip of good wine, but the grapes turn sour in her mouth. She does not trust them.

The car pulls to a stop outside Le Coucou, a beautiful French restaurant on the lower side of SoHo, ivy climbing the outer walls. She has been there before, two of the best meals she's had in New York, and she wonders if Luc knows how much she likes it, or if he simply shares her taste.

Again, he offers his hand.

Again, she does not take it.

Addie watches a couple as they approach the doors of the restaurant, only to find them locked, watches them walk away, murmuring something about reservations. But when Luc takes the handle, the door swings open easily.

Inside, massive chandeliers hang from the high ceilings, and the large glass windows shine black. The place feels cavernous, large enough to seat a hundred, but tonight it is empty, save for two chefs visible in the open kitchen, a pair of servers, and the maître d', who drops into a low bow as Luc approaches.

"Monsieur Dubois," he says in a dreamy voice. "Mademoiselle."

He leads them to their table, a red rose set before each place. The maître d' pulls back her chair, and Luc waits for her to take her seat before taking his own. The man opens a bottle of merlot, and pours, and Luc lifts his glass to her and says, "To you, Adeline."

There is no menu. No order to be taken. The plates simply arrive.

Foie gras with cherries, and rabbit terrine. Halibut in beurre blanc, and fresh-baked bread, and half a dozen kinds of cheese.

The food is, of course, exquisite.

But as they eat, the host and servers stand against the walls, eyes open, empty, a bland expression on their faces. She has always hated this aspect of his power, and the careless way he wields it.

She tips her glass in the direction of the puppets.

"Send them away," she says, and he does. A silent gesture, and the servers disappear, and they are alone in the empty restaurant.

"Would you do that to me?" she asks when they are gone.

Luc shakes his head. "I could not," he says, and she thinks he means because he cared for her too much, but then he says, "I have no power over promised souls. Their will is their own."

It is cold comfort, she thinks, but it is something.

Luc looks down into his wine. He turns the stem between his fingers, and there in the darkened glass, she sees the two of them, tangled in silk sheets, sees her fingers in his hair, his hands playing songs against her skin.

"Tell me, Adeline," he says. "Have you missed me?"

Of course she has missed him.

She can tell herself, as she has told him, that she only missed being seen, or missed the force of his attention, the intoxication of his presence—but it is more than that. She missed him the way someone might miss the sun in winter, though they still dread its heat. She missed the sound of his voice, the knowing in his touch, the flint-on-stone friction of their conversations, the way they fit together.

He is *gravity*.

He is three hundred years of history.

He is the only constant in her life, the only one who will always, always remember.

Luc is the man she dreamed of when she was young, and then the one she hated most, and the one she loved, and Addie missed him every night that he was gone from her, and he deserved none of her pain because it was his fault, it was his fault no one else remembered, it was his fault that she lost and lost and lost, and she does not say any of that because it will change nothing, and because there is still one thing she hasn't lost. One piece of her story that she can save.

Henry.

So Addie makes her gambit.

She reaches across the table and takes Luc's hand, tells him the truth.

"I missed you."

His green eyes shimmer and shift at the words. He brushes the ring on her finger, traces the whorls in the wood.

"How many times did you almost put it on?" he asks. "How often did you think of me?" And she assumes he is baiting her—until his voice softens to a whisper, the faintest roll of thunder in the air between them. "Because I thought of you. Always."

"You didn't come."

"You didn't call."

She looks down at their tangled hands. "Tell me, Luc," she says. "Was any of it real?"

"What is real to you, Adeline? Since my love counts for nothing?"

"You are not capable of love."

He scowls, his eyes flashing emerald. "Because I am not human? Because I do not wither and die?"

"No," she says, drawing back her hand. "You are not capable of love because you cannot understand what it is to care for someone else more than yourself. If you loved me, you would have let me go by now."

Luc flicks his fingers. "What nonsense," he says. "It is because I love you that I won't. Love is hungry. Love is selfish."

"You are thinking of possession."

He shrugs. "Are they so different? I have seen what humans do to things they love."

"People are not things," she says. "And you will never understand them."

"I understand you, Adeline. I know you, better than anyone in this world."

"Because you let me have no one else." She takes a steadying breath. "I know you won't spare me, Luc, and perhaps you are right, we do belong together. So if you love me, spare Henry Strauss. If you love me, let *him* go."

His temper flashes through his face. "This is our night, Adeline. Do not ruin it with talk of someone else."

"But you *said*—"

"Come," he says, pushing back from the table. "This place no longer suits my taste."

The server has just set a pear tart on the table, but it turns to ash as Luc speaks, and Addie marvels, the way she always has, at the moodiness of gods.

"Luc," she starts, but he is already on his feet, casting the napkin off onto the ruined food.

"I love you."

They are in New Orleans when he says it, dining in a hidden bar in the French Quarter, one of his many installations.

Addie shakes her head, amazed the words do not turn to ash in his mouth. "Do not pretend that this is love."

Annoyance flashes across Luc's face. "What is love, then? Tell me. Tell me your heart doesn't flutter when you hear my voice. That it doesn't ache when you hear your name on my lips."

"It's my own name I ache for, not your lips."

The edge of his mouth curls up, his eyes now emerald. A brightness born of pleasure. "Once, perhaps," he says. "But now it's more."

She is afraid that he is right.

And then, he sets a box before her.

It is simple, and black, and if Addie were to reach for it, it would be small enough to fit within her palm.

But she doesn't, not at first.

"What is it?" she asks.

"A gift."

Still she does not take it.

"Honestly, Adeline," he says, sweeping the box from the table. "It will not bite."

He opens it, and sets it back before her.

Inside, there is a simple brass key, and when she asks him where it leads, he says, "Home."

Addie stiffens.

She has not had a home, not since Villon. Has never, in fact, had a place of her own, and she is almost grateful, before she remembers, of course, that he is the reason why.

"Do not mock me, Luc."

"I am not mocking you," he says.

He takes her hand and leads her through the Quarter, to a place at the end of Bourbon Street, a yellow house with a balcony, and windows as tall as doors. She slides the key into the lock, and listens to the heavy sound of the turn, and realizes, if it belonged to Luc instead of her, the door would simply open. And suddenly, the brass key feels real and solid in her hand, a treasured thing.

The door swings open onto a house with high ceilings, and wooden floors, with furniture, and closets, and spaces to be filled. She steps out onto the balcony, the layered sounds of the Quarter rising to meet her on the humid air. Jazz spills through the streets, crashing, overlapping, a chaotic melody, changing and alive.

"It is yours," says Luc, "a home," and the old warning sounds, deep in the marrow of her bones.

But these days, it is a shrinking beacon, a lighthouse viewed too far from port.

He pulls her back against him, and Addie notices again the perfect way they fit together.

As if he was made for her.

Which, of course, he was. This body, this face, these features, made to make her feel at ease.

"Let's go out," he says.

Addie wants to stay in, to christen the house, but he says there will be time, there will always be time. And for once, she doesn't dread the idea of forever. For once, the days and nights don't drag, but race ahead.

She knows that, whatever this is, it will not last.

It cannot last.

Nothing ever does.

But in the moment, she is happy.

They make their way through the Quarter, arm in arm, and Luc lights a cigarette, and when she tells him it's bad for his health, he lets out a breathy, noiseless laugh, smoke pouring between his lips.

Her steps slow before a shop window.

The store is closed, of course, but even through the darkened glass, she can see the leather jacket, black with silver buckles, draped over a mannequin.

Luc's reflection shimmers behind her as he follows her gaze.

"It is summer," he says.

"It won't always be."

Luc smooths his hands over her shoulders and she feels the soft leather settling against her skin, the mannequin in the window now bare, and tries not to think of all the years she went without, forced to suffer through the cold, of all the times she had to hide, and fight, and steal. She tries not to think of them, but she does.

They are halfway back to the yellow house when Luc peels away.

"I have work to do," he says. "Go on home."

Home—the word rattles through her chest as he walks away.

But she does not go.

She watches Luc round the corner, and cross the street, and then she lingers in the shadow as he approaches a shop with a luminescent palm painted on the door.

An older woman stands on the sidewalk, closing up, her frame bent over a ring of keys, a large bag drooping from one elbow.

She must hear him coming, because she murmurs something to the dark, something about closing, something about another day. And then she turns, and sees him.

In the glass of the shop window, Addie sees Luc, too, not as he is to her, but as he must appear to the woman in the doorway. He has kept those dark curls, but his face is leaner, sharper in a wolfish way, his eyes deep-set, his limbs too thin to be human.

"A deal is a deal," he says, the words bending on the air. "And it is done."

Addie watches, expecting the woman to beg, to run.

But she sets her bag down on the ground, and lifts her chin.

"A deal is a deal," she says. "And I am tired."

And somehow, this is worse.

Because Addie understands.

Because she is tired, too.

And as she watches, the darkness comes undone again.

It has been more than a hundred years since Addie last saw the truth of him, the roiling night, with all its teeth. Only this time, there is no rending, no tearing, no horror.

The darkness simply folds around the old woman like a storm, blotting out the light.

Addie turns away.

She goes back to the yellow house on Bourbon Street, and pours herself a glass of wine, crisp and cold and white. It is blisteringly hot; the balcony doors are flung open to ease the summer night. She is leaning on the iron rail when she hears him arrive, not on the street below, as a courting lover might, but in the room behind her.

And when his arms drift around her shoulders, Addie remembers the way he held the woman in the doorway, the way he folded around her, swallowing her whole.

Luc's mood lifts a little as they walk.

The night is warm, the moon barely a crescent overhead. His head falls back, and he inhales, breathing in the air as if it were not ripe with summer heat, too many people in too little space.

"How long have you been here?" she asks.

"I come and go," he says, but she has learned to read the space between his words, and guesses he has been in New York almost as long as she has, lurking like a shadow at her back.

She doesn't know where they are going, and for the first time, she wonders if Luc does either, or if he is simply walking, trying to put space between them and the end of their meal.

But as they make their way uptown, she feels time folding around them, and she does not know if it's his magic or her memory, but with each passing block, she is storming from him down the Seine. He is leading her away from the sea. She is following him in Florence. They are side by side in Boston, and arm in arm on Bourbon Street.

They are here, together, in New York. And she wonders what would have happened if he hadn't said the word. If he hadn't tipped his hand. If he hadn't ruined everything.

"The night is ours," he says, turning toward her, and his eyes are bright again. "Where shall we go?"

Home, she thinks, though she cannot say it.

She looks up at the skyscrapers, surging to either side.

"Which one," she wonders, "has the best view?"

After a moment, Luc smiles, flashing teeth, and says, "Follow me."

Over the years, Addie has learned many of the city's secrets.

But here is one she did not know.

It resides not underground, but on a roof.

Eighty-four stories up, reached by a pair of elevators, the first one nondescript and rising only to the eighty-first floor. The second, a direct replica of Rodin's *Gates of Hell*, with its writhing bodies, clawing to escape, takes you the rest of the way.

If you have a key.

Luc draws the black card from his shirt pocket and slides it into a yawning mouth along the elevator's frame.

"Is this one of yours?" she asks as the doors slide open.

"Nothing is really mine," he says by way of answer as they step inside.

It is a short ascent, three brief floors, and when it stops, the doors open onto an uninterrupted view of the city.

The bar's name winds in black letters at her feet.

THE LOW ROAD.

Addie rolls her eyes. "Was *Perdition* taken?"

"Perdition," he says, eyes sparkling with mischief, "is a different kind of club."

The floors are bronze, the railings glass, and the ceiling open to the sky, and people mill on velvet sofas and dip their feet in shallow pools, and linger along the balconies that ring the roof, admiring the city.

"Mr. Green," says the hostess. "Welcome back."

"Thank you, Renee," he says smoothly. "This is Adeline. Give her anything she wants."

The hostess looks to her, but there is no compulsion in her eyes, no sense that she has been enchanted, only the cooperation of an employee, one very good at her job. Addie asks for the most expensive drink, and Renee grins at Luc. "You've found yourself a match."

"I have," he says, resting his hand on the small of Addie's back as he guides her forward. She quickens her step until it falls away, and weaves through the milling crowd to the glass rail, looking out over Manhattan. There are no stars visible, of course, but New York rolls away to every side, its own galaxy of light.

Up here, at least, she can breathe.

It is the easy laughter of the crowd. The ambient noise of people enjoying themselves, so much nicer than the stifled quiet of the empty restaurant, the cloistered silence of the car. It is the sky opening above her. The beauty of the city to every side, and the fact they are not alone.

Renee returns with a bottle of Champagne, a visible film of dust coating the glass.

"Dom Perignon, 1959," she explains, holding the bottle out for inspection. "From your private case, Mr. Green."

Luc waves his hand, and she opens the bottle, pouring two flutes, the bubbles so small they look like flecks of diamond in the glass.

Addie sips, savors the way it sparkles on her tongue.

She scans the crowd, filled with the kinds of faces you would recognize, even though you're not sure where you've seen them. Luc points them out to her, those senators, and actors, authors and critics, and she wonders if any of them have sold their soul. If any of them are about to.

Addie looks down into her glass, the bubbles still rising smoothly to the surface, and when she speaks, the words are barely more than a whisper, the sound stolen by the chattering crowd. But she knows he is listening, knows he can hear her.

"Let him go, Luc."

His mouth tightens a fraction. "Adeline," he warns.

"You told me you would listen."

"Fine." He leans back against the rail and spreads his arms. "Tell me. What do you see in him, this latest human lover?"

Henry Strauss is thoughtful, and kind, she wants to say. *He is clever, and bright, gentle, and warm.*

He is everything you're not,

But Addie knows she must tread lightly.

"What do I see in him?" she says. "I see myself. Not who I am now, perhaps, but who I was, the night you came to rescue me."

Luc scowls. "Henry Strauss wanted to die. You wanted to live. You are nothing alike."

"It's not that simple."

"Isn't it?"

Addie shakes her head. "You see only flaws and faults, weaknesses to be exploited. But humans are messy, Luc. That is the wonder of them. They live and love and make mistakes, and they *feel* so much. And maybe—maybe I am no longer one of them."

The words tear through her as she says them, because she knows this much is true. For better or worse.

"But I remember," she presses on. "I remember what it's like, and Henry is—"

"Lost."

"He is searching," she counters. "And he will find his way, if you let him."

"If I let him," says Luc, "he would have leapt off a roof."

"You don't know that," she says. "You never will, because you intervened."

"I am in the business of souls, Adeline, not second chances."

"And I am begging you to let him go. You will not give me mine, so give me his, instead."

Luc exhales, and sweeps his hand across the roof. "Choose someone," he says.

"What?"

He turns her to face the crowd. "Choose a soul to take his place. Pick a stranger. Damn one of them instead." His voice is low and smooth and certain. "There is always a cost," he says gently. "A price must be paid. Henry Strauss bartered his own soul. Would you sell someone else's to have it back?"

Addie stares out at the crowded roof, the faces she recognizes and the ones she doesn't. Young and old, together and alone.

Are any innocent?

Are any cruel?

Addie does not know if she can do it—until her hand drifts up. Until she points to a man in the crowd, heart plunging through her stomach as she waits for Luc to let go of her, to step forward, and claim his price.

But Luc doesn't move.

He only laughs.

"My Adeline," he says, kissing her hair. "You have changed more than you think."

She feels dizzy and ill as she twists to face him.

"No more games," she says.

"All right," he says, just before he pulls her into the dark.

The roof drops away, and the void surges up around her, swallowing everything but a starless sky, an infinite, violent black. And when it withdraws again an instant later, the world is silent, and the city is gone, and she is alone in the woods.

XIV

This is how it ends.

With candles burning on the sill, unsteady light casting long shadows across the bed. With the blackest part of night stretching beyond the open window, and the first blush of summer on the air, and Addie in Luc's arms, the darkness draped around her like a sheet.

And this, she thinks, is home.

This, perhaps, is love.

And that is the worst part. She has finally forgotten something. Only it is the wrong thing. It is the one thing she was supposed to remember. That the man in the bed is not a man. That the life is not a life. That there are games, and battles, but in the end, it is all a kind of war.

A touch like teeth along her jaw.

The darkness whispering against her skin. "My Adeline."

"I am not yours," she says, but his mouth only smiles against her throat.

"And yet," he says, "we are together. We belong together."

You belong to me.

"Do you love me?" she asks.

His fingers trail along her hips. "You know I do."

"Then let me go."

"I am not holding you here."

"That isn't what I mean," she says, rising on one arm. "Set me free."

He draws back, just enough to meet her gaze. "I cannot break the deal." His head falls, black curls brushing her cheek. "But perhaps," he whispers against her collar, "I could bend it."

Addie's heart thuds inside her chest.

"Perhaps I could change the terms."

She holds her breath as Luc's words play along her skin.

"I can make it better," he murmurs. "All you have to do is surrender."

The word is a cold shock.

A curtain falling on a play: the lovely sets, the stagings, the trained actors all vanish behind the darkened cloth.

Surrender.

An order whispered in the dark.

A warning given to a broken man.

A demand made over and over and over for years—until it stopped. How long ago did he stop asking? But of course, she knows—it was when his method changed, when his temper toward her softened.

And she is a fool. She is a fool for thinking it meant peace instead of war.

Surrender.

"What is it?" he asks, feigning confusion, until she throws the word back in his face.

"Surrender?" she snarls.

"It is just a word," he says. But he taught her the power of a word. A word is everything, and his word is a serpent, a coiled trick, a curse.

"It is the nature of things," he says.

"In order to change the deal," he says.

But Addie pulls back, pulls away, pulls free. "And I am meant to *trust you?* To give in, and believe that you will give me back?"

So many years, so many different ways of asking the same thing.

Do you yield?

"You must think me an idiot, Luc." Her face burns with anger. "I'm amazed you had the patience. But then, you've always been fond of the chase."

His green eyes narrow in the dark. "Adeline."

"Don't you dare say my name." She is on her feet now, singing with rage. "I knew you were a monster, Luc. I saw it often enough. And yet, I still thought—somehow I thought—after all this time—but of course, it wasn't love, was it? It wasn't even kindness. It was just another *game.*"

There is an instant when she thinks she might be wrong.

A fraction of a moment when Luc looks wounded and confused, and she wonders if he meant only what he said, if, if—

But then, it is over.

The hurt falls from his face and it passes into shadow, the effect as smooth as a cloud across the sun. A grim smile plays across his lips.

"And what a tiresome game it's been."

She knows she drew it out, but the truth still crashes through her.

If she was cracked before, now she is breaking.

"You cannot fault me for trying a different hand."

"I fault you for *everything.*"

Luc rises, the darkness drawing into silk around him. "I have given you everything."

"None of it was real!"

She will not cry.

She will not give him the satisfaction of seeing her suffer.

She will not give him anything, ever again.

This is how the fight begins.

Or rather, this is how it ends.

Most fights, after all, are not the work of an instant. They build over days, or weeks, each side gathering their kindling, stoking their flames.

But this is a fight forged over centuries.

As old and inevitable as the turning of the world, the passing of an era, the collision of a girl and the dark.

She should have known it would happen.

Perhaps she did.

But to this day, Addie doesn't know how the fire started. If it was the candles she swept from the table, or the lamp she tore from the wall, if it was the lights Luc shattered, or if it was simply a last act of spite.

She knows she doesn't have the strength to ruin anything, and yet she did. They did. Perhaps he let her start the fire. Perhaps he simply let it burn.

It does not matter, in the end.

Addie stands on Bourbon Street and watches the house go up in flames, and by the time the firefighters come, there is nothing left to save. It is only ashes.

Another life gone up in smoke.

Addie has nothing, not even the key in her pocket. It was there, but when she reaches for it, it is gone. Her hand goes to the wooden ring still at her throat.

She tears it free, hurls the band into the smoking ruins of her home, and walks away.

✦ ✦ ✦ ✦ ✦ ✦ ✦ ✦

Addie is surrounded by trees.

The mossy scent of summer in the woods.

Fear winds through her, the sudden, horrible certainty that Luc has broken both rules instead of one, that he has dragged her through the dark, stolen her away from New York, abandoned her somewhere far, far from home.

But then her eyes adjust, and she turns, and sees the skyline rising above the trees, and realizes she must be in Central Park.

Relief sweeps through her.

And then Luc's voice drifts through the dark.

"Adeline, Adeline . . ." he says, and she cannot tell what is an echo, and what is simply him, unbound by flesh and bone and mortal shapes.

"You promised," she calls.

"Did I?"

Luc steps out of the dark, the way he did that night, drawing together from smoke and shadow. A storm, bottled into skin.

Am I the devil or the darkness? he asked her once. *Am I a monster or a god?*

He is no longer dressed in the sleek black suit, but as he was when she first summoned him, a stranger in trousers, a pale tunic open at his throat, his black hair curling against his temples.

The dream conjured so many years ago.

But one thing has changed. There is no triumph in his eyes. The color has gone out of them, so pale they're almost gray. And though she's never seen the shade before, she guesses it is sadness.

"I will give you what you want," he says. "If you will do one thing."

"What?" she asks.

Luc holds out his hand.

"Dance with me," he says.

There is longing in his voice, and loss, and she thinks, perhaps, it is the end, of this, of them. A game finally played out. A war with no winners.

And so she agrees to dance.

There is no music, but it does not matter.

When she takes his hand, she hears the melody, soft and soothing in her head. Not a song, exactly, but the sound of the woods in summer, the steady hush of the wind through the fields. And as he pulls her close, she hears a violin, low and mournful, along the Seine. His hand slides through hers, and there is the steady murmur of the seaside. The symphony soaring through Munich. Addie leans her head against his shoulder, and hears the rain falling in Villon, the brass band ringing in an L.A. lounge, and the ripple of a saxophone through the open windows on Bourbon.

The dancing stops.

The music fades.

A tear slides down her cheek. "All you had to do was set me free."

Luc sighs, and lifts her chin. "I could not."

"Because of the deal."

"Because you are *mine*."

Addie twists free. "I was never yours, Luc," she says, turning away. "Not in the woods that night. And not when you took me to bed. You were the one who said it was just a game."

"I lied." The words, a knife. "You loved me," he says. "And I loved you."

"And yet," she says, "you didn't come to find me until I'd found someone else."

She turns back toward him, expecting to see those eyes yellowing with envy. But instead, they have gone a weedy, arrogant green, mirrored by the expression on his face, the faint lift of a single brow, the corner of his mouth.

"Oh, Adeline," he says. "You think you *found* each other?"

The words are a missed step.

A sudden drop.

"Do you truly think that I would let that happen?"

The ground tilts beneath her feet.

"That for all the deals I do, such a thing would *ever* pass beneath my notice?"

Addie squeezes her eyes shut, and she is lying beside Henry, their fingers laced together in the grass. She is looking up at the night sky. She is laughing at the idea that Luc finally made a mistake.

"You must have thought yourselves so clever," he is saying now. "Starcrossed lovers, brought together by chance. What are the odds that you would meet, that you would both be bound to me, both have sold your souls for something only the other could provide? When the truth is so much easier than that—I put Henry in your path. I gave him to you, wrapped and ribboned like a gift."

"Why?" she asks, throat closing around the word. "Why would you do that?"

"Because it's what you *wanted*. You were so set upon your need for love, you could not see beyond it. I gave you this, I gave you *him*, so you could see that love was not worth the space you held for it. The space you kept from *me*."

"But it was worth it. It *is*."

He reaches out to brush her cheek. "It won't be, when he's gone."

Addie pulls away. From his words, his touch. "This is cruel, Luc. Even for you."

"No," he snarls. "Cruelty would be ten years instead of one. Cruelty would be to let you have a lifetime with him, and have to suffer more for losing."

"I would choose it anyway!" She shakes her head. "You never intended to let him live, did you?"

Luc inclines his head. "A deal is a deal, Adeline. And deals are binding."

"That you would do all this to torment me—"

"No," he snaps. "I did it to *show* you. To make you understand. You put them on such a pedestal, but humans are brief and pale and so is their love. It is shallow, it does not last. You long for human love, but you are not human, Adeline. You haven't been for centuries. You have no place with them. You belong with *me*."

Addie recoils, anger hardening to ice inside her.

"What a hard lesson it must be for you," she says. "That you can't have everything you want."

"Want?" he sneers. "Want is for children. If this were want, I would be rid of you by now. I would have forgotten you centuries ago," he says, a bitter loathing in his voice. "This is need. And need is painful but patient. Do you hear me, Adeline? I need you. As you need me. I love you, as you love me."

She hears the pain in his voice.

Perhaps that is why she wants to hurt him worse.

He taught her well, to find the weakness in the armor.

"But that's the thing, Luc," she says, "I don't love you at all."

The words are soft, steady, and yet they rumble through the dark. The trees rustle, and the shadows thicken, and Luc's eyes burn a shade she's never seen before. A venomous color. And for the first time in centuries, she is afraid.

"Does he mean so much to you?" he asks, voice flat and hard as river stones. "Then go. Spend time with your human love. Bury him, and mourn him, and plant a tree over his grave." His edges begin to blur into the dark. "I will still be here," he says. "And so will you."

Luc turns away, and is gone.

Addie sinks to her knees in the grass.

She stays there until the first threads of light seep into the sky, and then, at last, she forces herself up again, walks to the subway in a fog, Luc's words looping through her head.

You are not human, Adeline.

You thought you found each other?

You must have thought yourselves so clever.

Spend time with your love.

I will still be here.

And so will you.

The sun is rising by the time she gets to Brooklyn.

She stops to pick up breakfast, a concession, an apology, for staying away all night. And that is when she sees the paper stacked against the newsstand. That is when she sees the date stamped in the upper corner.

August 6, 2014.

She left the apartment on the 30th of July.

Spend time with your love, he said.

But Luc has taken it. He didn't just steal a night. He took an entire week. Seven precious days, erased from her life . . . and Henry's.

Addie runs.

She stumbles through the door, and up the stairs, turns out her purse, but the key is gone, and she pounds on the door, terror surging through her that the world has changed, that Luc has somehow rewritten more than time, somehow taken more, taken everything.

But then the lock slides, and the door falls open, and there is Henry, exhausted, disheveled, and she knows, by the look in his eyes, that he did not expect her to come back. That at some point, between the first morning and the next, and the next, and the next, he thought she was gone.

Addie throws her arms around him now.

"I'm so sorry," she says, and it is not just for the stolen week.

It is for the deal, the curse, the fact it is her fault.

"I'm sorry," she says, over and over, and Henry doesn't shout, doesn't rage, doesn't even say *I told you so.* He simply holds her tight, and says, "Enough," says, "Promise me," says, "Stay."

And none of them are questions, but she knows he is asking, pleading with her to let it go, to stop fighting, stop trying to change their fates, and just be with him until the end.

And Addie cannot bear the thought of giving up, of giving in, of going down without a fight.

But Henry is breaking, and it is her fault, and so, in the end, she agrees.

XVI

These are the happiest days of Henry's life.

It is an odd thing to say, he knows.

But there is a strange freedom to it, a peculiar comfort in the knowing. The end is rushing up to meet him, and yet, he does not feel like he is falling toward it.

He knows he should be scared.

Every day he braces for the restless terror, waits for the storm clouds to roll in, expects the inevitable panic to climb inside his chest, pry him apart.

But for the first time in months, in years, in as long as he can remember, he is not afraid. He is worried about his friends, of course, about the bookstore, and the cat. But beyond the low hum of concern is only a strange calm, a steadiness, and the incredible relief that he found Addie, that he got to know her, to love her, to have her here beside him.

He is happy.

He is ready.

He is not afraid.

That is what he tells himself.

He is not afraid.

They decide to go upstate.

To get out of the city, away from the stagnant summer heat.

To see the stars.

He rents a car, and they drive north, and he realizes, halfway up the Hudson, that Addie has never met his family, and then he realizes, with a sudden, sinking weight, that he is not supposed to go home until Rosh Hashanah, and that he will be gone by then. That if he does not take this exit, he will never get a chance to say good-bye.

And then, the clouds begin to roll in, and fear tries to climb inside his chest, because he doesn't know what he would say, he doesn't know what good it would do.

And then he is past the exit, then it is too late, and he can breathe again, and Addie is pointing to a sign for fresh fruit, and they pull off the freeway and buy peaches from the stand, and sandwiches from the market, and drive an hour north to a state park, where the sun is hot but the shade beneath the trees is cool, and they spend the day wandering the woodland paths, and when night falls they make a picnic on the roof of the rented car, and stretch out between the wild, weedy grass and the stars.

So many, the night doesn't seem that dark.

And he is still happy.

And he can still breathe.

They have no tent, but it is too hot for covers anyway.

They lie on a blanket in the grass, and look up at the ghost of the Milky Way, and he thinks of the Artifact on the High Line, the exhibit of the sky, how close the stars felt then, and now, how far away.

"If you could do it again," he says, "would you still make the deal?"

And Addie says *yes*.

It has been a hard and lonely life, she says, and a wonderful one, too. She has lived through wars, and fought in them, witnessed revolution and rebirth. She has left her mark on a thousand works of art, like a thumbprint in the bottom of a drying bowl. She has seen marvels, and gone mad, has danced in snowbanks and frozen to death along the Seine. She fell in love with the darkness many times, fell in love with a human once.

And she is tired. Unspeakably tired.

But there is no question she has lived.

"Nothing is all good or all bad," she says. "Life is so much messier than that."

And there in the dark, he asks if it was really worth it.

Were the instants of joy worth the stretches of sorrow?

Were the moments of beauty worth the years of pain?

And she turns her head, and looks at him, and says, "Always."

They fall asleep beneath the stars, and when they wake up in the morning, the heat has leaked away, the air is cool, the first whispers of another season, the first one he won't see, waiting in the distance.

And still, he tells himself, he is not afraid.

And then the weeks turn into days.

There are some good-byes he has to make.

He meets Bea and Robbie at the Merchant one night. Addie sits across the bar, sipping a soda and giving him space. He wants her there, he needs her there, a silent anchor in the storm. But they both know that if she were at the table with him, Bea and Robbie might forget, and he needs them to remember.

And for a little while, everything is wonderfully, painfully normal.

Bea talks about her latest thesis proposal, and apparently ninth time's the charm, because it's been approved, and Robbie talks about the show's premiere next week, and Henry does not tell him that he snuck into a dress rehearsal yesterday, that he and Addie lurked in the last row of seats, slouched low so he could watch Robbie on the stage, brilliant, and beautiful, and in his element, lounging on his throne with Bowie's flare, and a devil's grin, and a magic all his own.

And at last, Henry lies, and tells them he is going out of town.

Upstate, to see his parents. No, it is not time, he says, but he has cousins visiting, his mother asked. Just for the weekend, he says.

He asks Bea if she can work the store.

Asks Robbie if he will feed the cat.

And they say yes, as simple as that, because they do not know it is goodbye. Henry pays the tab, and Robbie jokes, and Bea complains about her undergrads, and Henry tells them he'll call when he gets back.

And when he gets up to go, Bea kisses his cheek, and he pulls Robbie in for a hug, and Robbie says he better not miss his show, and Henry promises he won't, and then they are going, they are gone.

And this, he decides, is what a good-bye should be.

Not a period, but an ellipsis, a statement trailing off, until someone is there to pick it up.

It is a door left open.

It is drifting off to sleep.

And he tells himself he is not afraid.

Tells himself it is okay, he is okay.

And just when he begins to doubt, Addie's hand is there, soft and steady on his arm, leading him back home. And they climb into bed, and curl into each other against the storm.

And sometime in the middle of the night, he feels her get up, hears her padding down the hall.

But it is late, and he thinks nothing of it.

He rolls over, and goes back to sleep, and when he wakes again it is still dark, and she is back beside him in the bed.

And the watch on the table twitches one step closer to midnight.

XVII

It is such an ordinary day.

They stay in bed, curled together in the nest of sheets, head to head and hands trailing over arms, along cheeks, fingers memorizing skin. He whispers her name, over and over, as if she can save the sound, bottle it up to use when he is gone.

Addie, Addie, Addie.

And despite it all, Henry is happy.

Or at least, he tells himself he is happy, tells himself he is ready, tells himself he isn't afraid. And he tells himself that if they just stay here, in the bed, the day will last. If he holds his breath, he can keep the seconds from moving forward, pin the minutes between their tangled fingers.

It is an unspoken plea but Addie seems to sense it, because she makes no motion to get up. Instead, she stays with him in bed, and tells him stories.

Not of anniversaries—they have run out of July 29ths—but of Septembers and Mays, of quiet days, the kind no one else would remember. She tells him of fairy pools on the Isle of Skye, and the Northern Lights in Iceland, of swimming in a lake so clear she could see the bottom ten meters down, in Portugal—or was it Spain?

These are the only stories he will never write down.

It is his own failing; he cannot bring himself to unfold, to let go of Addie's hands and climb out of the bed, and grab the latest notebook from the shelf—there are six of them now, the last only half-filled, and he realizes it will stay that way, those last blank pages, his cramped cursive like a wall, a false end to an ongoing story, and his heart skips a little, a tiny stutter of panic, but he can't let it start, knows it will tear through him, the way a shiver turns a momentary chill into teeth-chattering cold, and he cannot lose his hold, not yet, not yet.

Not yet.

So Addie talks, and he listens, letting the stories slide like fingers through his hair. And every time the panic tries to fight its way to the surface, he fights it back, holds his breath and tells himself he is fine, but he doesn't move, doesn't get up. He cannot, because if he does, it will break the spell, and time will race forward and it will be over too fast.

It is a silly thing, he knows, a strange surge of superstition, but the fear is there now, real now, and the bed is safe, and Addie is steady, and he is so glad she is here, so glad for every minute since they met.

Sometime in the afternoon, he is suddenly hungry. Famished.

He shouldn't be. It feels frivolous, and wrong, inconsequential now, but the hunger is swift and deep, and with its arrival, the clock begins to tick.

He can't hold time at bay.

It is racing forward now, rushing away.

And Addie looks at him as if she can read his mind, see the storm building in his head. But she is sunshine. She is clear skies.

She draws him out of bed, and into the kitchen, and Henry sits on a stool and listens as she makes an omelet and tells him about the first time she flew a plane, heard a song on the radio, saw a moving picture.

This is the last gift she can give him, these moments he will never have.

And this is the last gift he can give her, the listening.

And he wishes they could climb back into bed with Book, but they both know there's no going back. And now that he's up, he cannot bear the stillness. He is all restless energy, and urgent need, and there isn't enough time, and he knows of course that there will never be.

That time always ends a second before you're ready.

That life is the minutes you want minus one.

And so they get dressed, and they go out, and walk, wearing circles into the block as the panic begins to win. It is a hand pressing against weakened glass, a steady pressure on spreading cracks, but Addie is there, her fingers laced through his.

"Do you know how you live three hundred years?" she says.

And when he asks how, she smiles. "The same way you live one. A second at a time."

And eventually his legs are tired, and the restlessness recedes, doesn't vanish but dulls to a manageable degree, and they go to the Merchant, and order food they do not eat, and order beers they do not drink because he cannot bear to dull these last few hours, as frightening as it is to face them sober.

And he makes some comment about his last meal, laughs at the morbid thought of it, and Addie's smile falters, for just a second, and then he is apologizing, he is sorry, and she is folding herself around him, and the panic has its claws in him.

The storm is brewing in his head, churning the sky on the horizon, but he doesn't fight it.

He lets it come.

Only when it starts raining does he realize the storm is real.

He tips his head back, and feels the drip of rain on his cheeks, and thinks of the night they went to the Fourth Rail, the downpour that caught them breathless when they reached the street. He thinks of that before he thinks of the rooftop, and that is something.

He feels so far from the Henry who climbed up there a year ago—or perhaps he's not that far at all. It is only a matter of steps, after all, from the street to the edge.

But what he would give to go back down.

God, what he would give for just another day.

The sun is gone now, the light going thin, and he will never see it again, and the fear crashes into him, sudden and traitorous. It is a gust of wind, cutting through a too-still scene. He fights it back, not yet, not yet, not yet, and Addie squeezes his hand, so he won't blow away.

"Stay with me," she says, and he answers, "I'm here."

His fingers tighten on hers.

He doesn't have to ask, she doesn't have to answer.

There is an unspoken agreement that she will be there, with him, until the very end.

That this time, he won't be alone.

And he is okay.

It is okay.

It will be okay.

XVIII

It is almost time, and they are on the roof.

The same roof he nearly stepped off a year before, the same one where he stood with the devil and made his deal. It is a full-circle moment, and he doesn't know if it has to be here, if *he* has to be here, but it feels right.

Addie's hand is linked in his, and that feels right, too.

A grounding force against a rising storm.

There is still a little time, the hand on the watch a fraction of a fraction of a fraction from midnight, and he can hear Bea's voice in his head.

Only you would arrive early to your own death.

And Henry smiles, despite himself, and wishes he had said more to Bea, and Robbie, but the simple fact is he didn't trust himself. He has made his good-byes, though they will not know it until he's gone, and he is sorry for that, for them, for whatever pain he might cause. He is glad they have each other.

Addie's hand tightens in his.

It is almost time, and he wonders what it will feel like, to lose a soul.

If it will be like a heart attack, sudden and violent, or as easy as falling asleep. Death takes so many forms. Perhaps this does, too. Will the darkness appear and reach a hand into his chest, and pull his soul out between his ribs like a magic trick? Or will some force compel him to finish what he started? To walk to the edge of the roof, and step off? Will he be found on the street below, as if he'd jumped?

Or will they find him up here, on the roof?

He does not know.

He does not need to know.

He is ready.

He is not ready.

He wasn't ready last year on the roof, when the stranger held out his hand. He wasn't ready then, and he isn't ready now, and he is beginning to suspect no one is ever ready, not when the moment comes, not when the darkness reaches out to claim its prize.

Music streams, thin and tinny, through a neighbor's open window, and

Henry pulls his thoughts back from death, and the edge of the roof, to the girl with her hand in his, the one telling him to dance with her.

He pulls her close, and she smells of summer, she smells of time, she smells of home.

"I'm here," she says.

Addie has promised to stay with him until the end.

The end. The end. The end.

It echoes through his head like the striking of a clock, but it's not time, he still has time, though it is vanishing so fast.

They teach you growing up that you are only one thing at a time—angry, lonely, content—but he's never found that to be true. He is a dozen things at once. He is lost and scared and grateful, he is sorry and happy and afraid.

But he is not alone.

It is beginning to rain again, the air gone damp with the metallic scent of storms in the city, and Henry doesn't care, thinks there is something to be said for symmetry.

They turn in a slow circle on the roof.

He has not slept well in days, and it has made his legs heavy, his mind too slow, the minutes speeding up around him, and he wishes the music were louder, wishes the sky were lighter, wishes he had just a little more time.

No one is ever ready to die.

Even when they think they want to.

No one is ready.

He isn't ready.

But it is time.

It is time.

Addie is saying something, but the watch has stopped moving, it hangs weightless on him now, and it is time, and he can feel himself slipping, can feel the edges of his mind going soft, the night heavy, and any moment the stranger will step out of the dark.

Addie is guiding his face to hers, she is saying something, and he doesn't want to listen, he's afraid it's a good-bye, he just wants to hold on to this moment, to make it last, to will it still, turn the film into a freeze frame, let that be the end, not darkness, not nothing, just a permanent moment. A memory, trapped in amber, in glass, in time.

But she is still speaking.

"You promised you would listen," she says, "you promised you would write it down."

He doesn't understand. The journals are on the shelf. He has written her story—every part.

"I did," he says. "I did."

But Addie is shaking her head.

"Henry," she says. "I haven't told you how it ends."

Some decisions happen all at once.

And others build up over time.

A girl makes a deal with the darkness, after years of dreaming.

A girl falls in love with a boy in a moment, and resolves to set him free.

Addie doesn't know exactly when she decided.

Perhaps she has known since the night Luc walked back into their lives.

Or perhaps she has known since the night he wrote her name.

Or perhaps she has known since he said those words:

I remember you.

She isn't sure.

It doesn't matter.

What matters is that, three nights before the end, Addie slips out of bed. Henry rolls over in his sleep, wakes enough to hear her padding down the hall, but not enough to hear her put on her shoes, or slip out into the dark.

It is almost two—that time between very late, and very early—and even Brooklyn has quieted to a murmur as she walks the two blocks to the Merchant bar. It is an hour until closing, the crowd thinned to a few determined drinkers.

Addie takes a stool at the bar, and orders a shot of tequila. She's never been one for hard liquor, but she downs the drink in one, feels the warmth settle in her chest as she reaches into her pocket and finds the ring.

Her fingers curl around the wooden band.

She draws it out, balances the ring upright on the counter.

She spins it like a coin, but there are no heads or tails, no yes or no, no choice beyond the one she's already made. She decides that when it settles, she will put it on. When it falls—but as it begins to wobble and tip, a hand comes down on top of it, pressing it flat against the bar.

The hand is smooth and strong, the fingers long, the details just as she once drew them. "Shouldn't you be with your love?"

There is no humor in Luc's eyes. They are flat, and dark.

"He's sleeping," she says, "and I cannot." Luc's hand has withdrawn, and Addie looks at the pale circle of the ring still on the counter.

"Adeline," he says, stroking her hair. "It will hurt. And it will pass. All things do."

"Except for us," she murmurs. And then she adds, as if to herself, "I am glad it was only a year."

Luc sinks onto the stool beside her. "And how was it, your human love? Was it everything you dreamed of?"

"No," she says, and it is the truth.

It was messy. It was hard. It was wonderful, and strange, and frightening, and fragile—so fragile it hurt—and it was worth every single moment. She does not tell him any of that. Instead, she lets the "no" hang in the air between them, heavy with the weight of Luc's assumption. His eyes, such a smug shade of green.

"But Henry doesn't deserve to die to prove your point."

The arrogance flickers, cut through with anger.

"A deal is a deal," he says. "It cannot be broken."

"And yet, you told me once that a deal could be bent, the terms rewritten. Did you mean it? Or was it just part of the ploy to get me to surrender?"

Luc's expression darkens. "There was no ploy, Adeline. But if you think I'll change the terms of his—"

Addie shakes her head. "I'm not talking about Henry's deal," she says. "I'm talking about mine." She has practiced the words, but they still tumble awkwardly off her tongue. "I'm not asking for your mercy, and I know you have no charity. So I'm offering a trade. Let Henry go. Let him live. Let him *remember me,* and—"

"You would surrender your soul?" There is a shadow in his gaze when he says it, a hesitation in the words, less want than worry, and she knows then, she has him.

"No," she says. "But only because you do not want it." And before he can protest, she continues, "You want *me.*"

Luc says nothing, but his eyes brighten, his interest piqued.

"You were right," she says. "I am not one of them. Not anymore. And I am tired of losing. Tired of mourning everything I ever try to love." She reaches out to touch Luc's cheek. "But I won't lose you. And you won't lose me. So yes." She looks straight into his eyes. "Do this, and I will be yours, as long as you want me by your side."

He seems to hold his breath, but she's the one who cannot breathe. The world tips, falters, threatening to fall.

And then, at last, Luc smiles, his green eyes emerald with victory.

"I accept."

She lets herself fold, bows her head against his chest in relief. And then his fingers come up beneath her chin, tipping her face to his, and he kisses her the way he did the night they met, swift, and deep, and hungry, and Addie feels his teeth skate across her bottom lip, the taste of copper blossom on her tongue.

And she knows that it is done.

"No," says Henry, the word half-swallowed by the storm.

The rain falls hard and fast on the roof. On them.

The clock has stopped, the hand thrown up in surrender. But he is still there.

"You can't do this," he says, head spinning. "I won't let you."

Addie flashes him a pitying look, because of course, he cannot stop her.

No one has ever been able to.

Estele used to say she was stubborn as a stone.

But even stones wear away to nothing.

And she has not.

"You can't do this," he says again, and she says, "It is already done," and Henry feels dizzy, feels sick, feels the ground sway beneath him.

"Why?" he pleads. "Why would you do it?"

"Think of it as a thank-you," she says, "for seeing me. For showing me what it's like to be seen. To be loved. Now you get a second chance. But you have to let them see you as you are. You have to find people who see you."

It is wrong.

It is all wrong.

"You don't love him."

A sad smile crosses her face.

"I've had my share of love," she says, and it is time, it must be time, because his vision is blurring, the edges going black.

"Listen to me." Her voice is urgent now. "Life can feel very long sometimes, but in the end, it goes so fast." Her eyes are glassy with tears, but she is smiling. "You better live a good life, Henry Strauss."

She begins to pull away, but his grip tightens. "No."

She sighs, fingers threading through his hair. "You've given me so much, Henry. But I need you to do one more thing." Her forehead presses against his. "I need you to remember."

And he can feel his hold slipping as darkness washes across his vision, blotting out the skyline and the roof and the girl folding herself against him.

"Promise me," she says, and her face is beginning to smudge, the swipe of her lips, brown curls in a heart-shaped face, two wide eyes, seven freckles like stars.

"Promise," she whispers, and he is just lifting his hands, to hold her against him, to promise, but by the time his arms close around her, she is gone.

And he is falling.

PART SEVEN

I REMEMBER YOU

Title of Piece: *The Girl Who Got Away*

Artist: Unknown

Date: 2014

Medium: Polaroid

Location: On loan from the personal archives of Henry Strauss

Description: Collection of six (6) photographs depicting a girl in motion, her features erased, obscured, or otherwise unreadable. The final photo is different. It features a living room floor, the edge of a table, a pile of books, only a pair of feet visible at the bottom.

Background: The subject of the photos remains a topic of intense speculation, given the author's relationship to the source material. The flash has erased all meaningful details, but the medium is what makes the pieces remarkable. In standard photography, long exposure would make it possible to achieve the desired effect of motion, but the Polaroid's fixed shutter speed makes the illusion of movement all the more impressive.

Estimated Value: Not for sale

All works currently on display at the Modern Museum of Art exhibit In Search of the Real Addie LaRue *curated by Beatrice Caldwell, PhD, Columbia.*

This is how it ends.

A boy wakes up alone in bed.

Sunlight spills through the gap in the curtains, the buildings beyond slick with the aftermath of rain.

He feels sluggish, hungover, still caught within the dregs of sleep. He knows he was dreaming, but he can't for the life of him remember the details of the dream, and it must not have been very pleasant, because he feels only a deep relief at waking.

Book looks over the mound of the comforter, orange eyes wide and waiting.

It's late, the boy can tell by the angle of the light, the sounds of traffic on the street.

He didn't mean to sleep so long.

The girl he loves is always the first to wake. Shuffling beneath the sheets, the weight of her attention, the soft touch of her fingers on his skin—they are always enough to rouse him out of sleep. Only once did he wake first, and then he had the strange pleasure of seeing her, knees curled up and face tucked against the pillows, still beneath the surface of sleep.

But that was a rainy morning just after dawn, when the world was gray, and today the sun is so bright he doesn't know how either of them slept through it.

He rolls over to wake her.

But the other side of the bed is empty.

He splays his hand over the place where she should be, but the sheets are cold and smooth.

"Addie?" he calls, rising to his feet.

He moves through the apartment, checks the kitchen, the bathroom, the fire escape, even though he knows, he knows, he knows, that she is not there.

"Addie?"

And then, of course, he remembers.

Not the dream, there was no dream, only the night before.

The last night of his life.

The damp concrete smell of the rooftop, the last tick of the watch as its hand found twelve, her smile as she looked up into his face, and made him promise to remember.

And now he's here, and she's gone, and there's no trace of her left behind except the stuff in his head and—

The journals.

He's up, crossing the room to the narrow set of shelves where he kept them: red, blue, silver, black, white, green; six notebooks, all of them still there. He pulls them from the shelf, spreads them on the bed, and as he does, the Polaroids tumble out.

The one he took that day of Addie, her face a blur, her back to the camera, a ghost at the edges of the frame, and he stares at them a long time, convinced that if he squints, she will come into focus. But no matter how long he looks, all he can see are the shapes, the shadows. The only thing he can make out are the seven freckles, and those are so faint he can't tell if they're really visible, or his memory is simply filling them in where they should be.

He sets the photograph aside and reaches for the first journal, then stops, so convinced that if and when he opens it, he will find the pages blank, the ink erased like every other mark she tried to make.

But he has to look, and so he does, and there they are, page after page written in his slanting script, shielded from the curse by the fact the words themselves are his, though the story is hers.

She wants to be a tree.

There is nothing wrong with Roger.

She simply wants to live before she dies.

It will take her years to learn the language of those eyes.

She claws her way up, and out, hands splayed across the bony mound of a dead man's back.

This is her first. How it should have been.

She feels him press three coins into her hand.

Soul is such a grand word. The truth is so much smaller.

It does not take her long to find her father's grave.

He picks up the next journal.

Paris is burning.

The darkness comes undone.

And the next.

There is an angel above the bar.

Henry sits there for hours against the side of the bed, turning through every page of every book, every story she ever told, and when he's done, he closes his eyes, and puts his head in his hands amid the open books.

Because the girl he loved is gone.

And he's still here.

He remembers everything.

"Henry Samuel Strauss, this is *bullshit*."

Bea slams the last page down on the coffee counter, startling the cat, who'd drifted off on a nearby tower of books. "You can't end it there." She's clutching the rest of the manuscript to her chest, as if to shield it from him. The title page stares back at him.

The Invisible Life of Addie LaRue.

"What happened to her? Did she really go with Luc? After all that?"

Henry shrugs. "I assume so."

"You *assume* so?"

The truth is, he doesn't know.

He's spent the last six months trying to transcribe the stories in the note-books, to compile them into this draft. And every night, after his hands had cramped and his head had begun to ache from staring at the computer screen, he'd collapse into bed—it does not smell like her, not anymore—and wonder how it ends.

If it ends.

He wrote a dozen different endings for the book, ones where she was happy, and ones where she was not, ones where she and Luc were madly in love, and ones where he clung to her like a dragon with its treasure, but those endings all belonged to him, and not to her. Those are his story, and this is hers. And anything he wrote beyond those last shared seconds, that final kiss, would be fiction.

He tried.

But this is real—though no one else will ever know it.

He does not know what happened to Addie, where she went, how she is, but he can hope. He *hopes* she is happy. He hopes she is still brimming with defiant joy, and stubborn hope. He hopes she did not do it just for him. He hopes, somehow, one day, he'll see her again.

"You're really going to method actor this shit, aren't you?" says Bea.

Henry looks up.

He wants to tell her it's all true.

That she met Addie, just like he wrote, that she said the same thing every time. He wants to tell her that they would have been friends. That they *were*, in that first-night-of-the-rest-of-our-lives kind of way. Which was, of course, as much as Addie ever got.

But she wouldn't believe him, so he lets it live for her as fiction.

"Did you like it?" he asks.

And Bea breaks into a grin. There is no fog in her eyes now, no shine, and he has never been more grateful to have the truth.

"It's good, Henry," she says. "It's really, really good." She taps the title page. "Just make sure you thank me in the acknowledgments."

"What?"

"My thesis. Remember? I wanted to do it on the girl in those pieces. The ghost in the frame. That's her, isn't it?"

And of course, it is.

Henry runs his hand over the manuscript, relieved and sad that it is done. He wishes he could have lived with it a little longer, wishes he could have lived with her.

But now, he is glad to have it.

Because the truth is, he is already beginning to forget.

It's not that he's fallen victim to her curse. She has not been erased in any way. The details are simply fading, as all things do, glossing over by degrees, the mind loosening its hold on the past to make way for the future.

But he doesn't want to let go.

He is trying not to let go.

He lies in bed at night, and closes his eyes, and tries to conjure her face. The exact curve of her mouth, the specific shade of her hair, the way the bedside lamp lit against her left cheekbone, her temple, her chin. The sound of her laughter late at night, her voice when she was on the edge of sleep.

He knows these details are not as important as the ones in the book, but he still can't bear to lose them yet.

Belief is a bit like gravity. Enough people believe a thing, and it becomes as solid and real as the ground beneath your feet. But when you're the only one holding on to an idea, a memory, a girl, it's hard to keep it from floating away.

"I knew you were going to be a writer," Bea is saying. "All the trappings, you've just been living in denial."

"I'm not a writer," he says absently.

"Tell that to the book. You're going to sell it, right? You have to—it's too good."

"Oh. Yeah," he says thoughtfully. "I think I'd like to try."

And he will.

He will get an agent, and the book will go to auction, and in the end he'll sell the work on one condition—that there is only one name on the cover, and it is not his—and in the end, they will agree. They'll think it some clever marketing trick, no doubt, but his heart will thrill at the thought of other people reading these words—not his, but hers, of *her* name carried from lips to lips, from mind to memory.

Addie, Addie, Addie.

The advance will be enough to pay off his student loans, enough to let him breathe a little while he figures out what he's going to do next. He doesn't know yet what that is, but for the first time, it doesn't scare him.

The world is wide, and he's seen so little of it with his own eyes. He wants to travel, to take photos, listen to other people's stories, maybe make some of his own. After all, life seems very long sometimes, but he knows it will go so fast, and he doesn't want to miss a moment.

The bookstore is about to close.

It gets dark early this time of year, and there's snow in the forecast, which is rare for London. The various clerks bustle about, dismantling old displays and putting up new ones, trying to finish their work before the mist outside turns to frost.

She lingers nearby, thumb skating along the ring at her throat as a pair of teenage girls restock a wall in New Fiction.

"Have you read it yet?" asks one.

"Yeah, this weekend," says the other.

"I can't believe the author didn't put their name on it," says the first. "Must be some kind of PR stunt."

"I don't know," says the second. "I think it's charming. Makes the whole thing feel real. Like it's really Henry, telling her story."

The first girl laughs. "You're such a romantic."

"Excuse me," cuts in an older man. "Could I grab a copy of *Addie LaRue?*"

Her skin prickles. He says the name with so much ease. Sounds tripping off a foreign tongue.

She waits until the three of them have moved off to the till, and then, at last, she approaches the display. It is not just a table, but a full shelf, thirty copies of the book, faced out, the pattern repeating down the wall. The covers are simple, most of the space given over to the title, which is long and large enough to fill the jacket. It's written in cursive, just like the notes in the journals by the bed, a more legible version of her words in Henry's hand.

The Invisible Life of Addie LaRue.

She runs her fingers over the name, feels the embossed letters arc and curve beneath her touch, as though she had written them herself.

The shop girls are right. There is no author's name. No photo on the back. No sign of Henry Strauss, beyond the simple, beautiful fact that the book is in her hands, the story real.

She peels back the cover, turns past the title to the dedication.

Three small words rest in the center of the page.

I remember you.

She closes her eyes, and sees him as he was that first day in the store, elbows leaning on the counter as he looked up, and frowned at her behind his glasses.

I remember you.

Sees him at Artifact, in the mirrors and then in the field of stars, sees his fingers tracing her name on the glass wall, and peering over a Polaroid, whispering across Grand Central and head bowed over the journal, black curls falling into his face. Sees him lying next to her in bed, in the grass upstate, on the beach, their fingers hooked like links in a chain.

Feels the warm circle of his arms as he pulled her back beneath the covers, the clean scent of him, the ease in his voice when she said, *Don't forget,* and he said, *Never.*

She smiles, brushing away tears, as she sees him on the roof that final night.

Addie has said so many hellos, but that was the first and only time she got to say good-bye. That kiss, like a piece of long-awaited punctuation. Not the em dash of an interrupted line, or the ellipsis of a quiet escape, but a period, a closed parenthesis, an end.

An end.

That is the thing about living in the present, and only the present, it is a run-on sentence. And Henry was a perfect pause in the story. A chance to catch her breath. She does not know if it was love, or simply a reprieve. If contentment can compete with passion, if warmth will ever be as strong as heat.

But it was a gift.

Not a game, or a war, not a battle of wills.

Just a gift.

Time, and memory, like lovers in a fable.

She thumbs through the chapters of the book, *her* book, and marvels at the sight of her name on every page. Her life, waiting to be read. It is bigger than her now. Bigger than either of them, humans, or gods, or things without names. A story is an idea, wild as a weed, springing up wherever it is planted.

She begins to read, makes it as far her first winter in Paris when she feels the air change at her back.

Hears the name, like a kiss, at the nape of her neck.

"Adeline."

And then Luc is there. His arms fold around her shoulders, and she leans back against his chest. They do fit together. They always have, though she wonders, even now, if it's simply the nature of what he is, smoke expanding to fill whatever space it is given.

His eyes drop to the book in her hands. Her name splashed across the cover.

"How clever you are," he says, murmuring the words into her skin. But he does not seem angry.

"They can have the story," he says. "So long as I have you."

She twists in his arms to look at him.

Luc is beautiful when he is gloating.

He shouldn't be, of course. Arrogance is an unattractive trait, but Luc wears it with all the comfort of a tailored suit. He glows with the light of his own work. He is so used to being right. To being in control.

His eyes are a bright, triumphant green.

Three hundred years she's had to learn the color of his moods. She knows them all by now, the meaning of every shade, knows his temper, wants, and thoughts, just by studying those eyes.

She marvels, that in the same amount of time, he never learned to read her own.

Or perhaps he saw only what he expected: a woman's anger, and her need, her fear and hope and lust, all the simpler, more transparent things.

But he never learned to read her cunning, or her cleverness, never learned to read the nuances of her actions, the subtle rhythms of her speech.

And as she looks at him, she thinks of all the things her eyes would say.

That he has made a grand mistake.

That the devil is in the details, and he has overlooked a crucial one.

That semantics may seem small, but he taught her once that words were everything. And when she carved the terms of her new deal, when she traded her soul for herself, she did not say *forever*, but *as long as you want me by your side.*

And those are not the same at all.

If her eyes could speak, they would laugh.

They would say that he is a fickle god, and long before he loved her, he hated her, he drove her mad, and with her flawless memory, she became a student of his machinations, a scholar of his cruelty. She has had three hundred years to study, and she will make a masterpiece of his regret.

Perhaps it will take twenty years.

Perhaps it will take a hundred.

But he is not capable of love, and she will prove it.

She will ruin him. Ruin his idea of them.

She will break his heart, and he will come to hate her once again.

She will drive him mad, drive him away.

And then, he will cast her off.

And she will finally be free.

Addie dreams of telling Luc these things, just to see the shade it turns his eyes, the green of being bested. The green of forfeit, and of losing.

But if he's taught her anything, it's patience.

So Addie says nothing of the new game, the new rules, the new battle that's begun.

She only smiles, and sets the book back on its shelf.

And follows him out into the dark.

ACKNOWLEDGMENTS

Anyone who follows me online knows I have a rather fraught relationship with stories.

Or rather, with bringing them to life. With holding up the whole messy beast until my arms shake and my head hurts and I know if I drop it now, before it's ready, it will shatter, and I'll have to sweep it up, and I'll lose at least a few of the pieces along the way.

And so, while I held up Addie's story, so many people held up *me*.

Without them, there would be no book.

This is where I'm supposed to acknowledge them all.

(I hate acknowledgments.)

(Or rather, I hate Acknowledgments. I have a terrible memory. My mind, I think, has been burrowed full of holes by all these books, so when it comes to thanking the people who helped *this* book come into being, I freeze up, certain that I'll forget.)

(I know I'll forget.)

(I am always forgetting.)

(I think that's why I write, to try and catch the ideas before they slip away and leave me staring off into space wondering why I walked into this room, or why I opened that browser tab, or what I was looking for in the fridge.)

(It's ironic, of course, given the theme of this book.)

(This book, which lived in my head for so long, and took up so much space, it's responsible for at least some of the forgetting.)

So, this will serve as an incomplete list.

This book is for my dad, who walked the streets of our East Nashville neighborhood and listened while I first spelled out the idea growing in my head.

For my mum, who followed me down every winding road, and never let me get lost.

For my sister, Jenna, who knew exactly when I needed to write, and when I needed to stop writing and go get a fancy cocktail instead.

For my agent, Holly, who has dragged me through so many fire swamps, and never once let me get singed or drowned or eaten by ROUSes.

For my editor, Miriam, who was with me every step of the long and winding way.

For my publicist, Kristin, who's become my knight, my champion, and my friend.

For Lucille, Sarah, Eileen, and the rest of my incredible team at Tor, who believed in this story when it was an idea, cheered me on when it was a draft, championed it when it was a finished book, and made me feel, at every step, like I could let go, and you would catch me.

For my friends—you know who you are—who dragged me through the dark, and ran away with me in search of words (and roast chicken).

For Al Mare, and Red Kite, for giving me a place to think, and write, and supplying me with ample pots of tea.

For Danielle, Ilda, Britt, and Dan, for your passion, and for sliding pizza under the door.

For every bookseller who has kept me on shelves this long.

For every reader who told me they couldn't wait, while promising they would.

A GHOST IN THE FRAME:
THE MYSTERIOUS APPEARANCES
THAT INSPIRED ADDIE LaRUE

Beatrice Reynolds

Before she became the titular character of the author's novel, Addie LaRue was my ghost.

I first saw her in my junior year, staring out from a sketch in the textbook. *Ho Portado le Stelle a Letto (I Took the Stars to Bed).* A lithe, naked body, edges disappearing into sheets. Her sleeping face, half-hidden by hair, lips parted faintly, caught between a smile and a dream. Her freckles—I did not count them, then—little more than smudges, the artist's pencil gestures quick, imperfect.

At the time, the piece struck me as beautiful, simple, but forgettable. (You come across so many works in your time as a student, then a graduate. A thousand faces portrayed a thousand ways. You cannot hold them all. You see, and file, and let go.)

Then, in my first year of graduate school, I saw her again, rendered in oil paint instead of pencil, as *The Siren.* She sat, skirts pooling, in the sand, and looked back, almost coyly, over her shoulder. I remember running a finger lightly over her face, the brown flecks across her cheeks so small and faint, they might have been shadows on the paint. I stared at her for some time, struck by a sense of familiarity, but unable to place its source. I wrote it off— good art, I've found, can make you long for lives you never lived, and people you've never met.

Over the next three years I would see her again and again, the images separated by time, and medium, and so, kept apart in my mind, until I came across a work with no apparent connection, a modern sculpture called *Constellation,* a wooden silhouette, a carving of a woman's face, upturned, with seven holes carefully drilled across the cheek to let through light. Ironic, that in the more abstract interpretation, I found her, staring back.

And I remembered.

I began retracing my steps through each year of school, scouring notebooks for marginalia, those wondrous thoughts scribbled to one's self in the middle of a lecture, waymarks for things that interest you, attraction in the form of distraction. And I found her. Again and again, like bread crumbs cast back down the trail of my academic career. I became a time traveler, a treasure hunter, scouring art history for signs of this girl as if she were a part of my own past, a friend I'd lost along the way. The truth, of course, is that I don't know if she was ever real.

Perhaps she is the stuff of time, and truth. A young woman, with a kind of timeless beauty, captured and carried on. Or perhaps she is an idea (as the author says, ideas are so much wilder than memories).

Here is what I know.

Zeitgeists (literally "time ghosts") occur in any field. They are the product of cultural trends, artistic movements, the culmination of myriad aesthetic or idealistic threads, converging at the same point. They're like flowers—we notice the bloom, without paying much attention to the roots. In art, such zeitgeists often reflect the aesthetic preferences at the time. Even a cursory glance at English portraiture or Roman sculpture reveals what was in the moment considered beautiful.

But the girl I found was something else.

She wasn't a template, in the classical sense, a blank model on which artists could build. She wasn't raw clay, to be molded to suit a movement or school. She wasn't stock. If anything, she was *specific*. A collection of details that, piecemeal, might have read as universal, but in their combination, read only as her. A real person. My ghost. I never saw her face on a different form, never saw those fair brown waves without the curve of her cheek, the point of her chin. In no piece did I find her long limbs without the slope of her narrow hips. And not once did I see her wide brown eyes without those freckles.

The freckles—always seven, always arranged in roughly the same order. Those marks became a clue, the first thing I looked for as I searched, but also, I began to suspect, an artistic wink, a creative nod. I began to feel as if I'd stumbled across a conversation, a series of artists playing a game of "visual telephone" as Strauss once called it. What is a person but a collection of traits? A particular curve of the cheek, a posture of the limbs, the weight of a bosom, the arrangement of curls, the color of eyes, and hair, and skin. Unless an artist is attempting to re-create a real person, they borrow and combine, creating their own subjects. But that is not what they've done to my ghost. They've carried her forward across time, transported her from period to period and school to school and medium to medium, myriad artists reusing the same model, and in so doing, creating the illusion of continuity, of artists rendering the same woman.

Making her seem immortal.

It is no surprise then, that these images would go on to inspire—or at least plant the seed for—Strauss's protagonist, a young woman who moves through history without leaving a mark, except in other's art. He has made her the carrier of a powerful message: that art persists. It survives. Despite the nature of my own studies, I firmly believe that art is not history. It is not a thing of the past. It is immortal, a narrative that stretches back, and reaches forward.

And what of my ghost?

Either she was real, or she was not. I want to believe she was, that there was an inspiration for the girl I've seen in paint and pen, wood and ink, a real woman made immortal through art. I want her to be real. But perhaps it does not matter if she was. Addie LaRue is real now. In writing, the author has taken the ghost in the frame and given her life. He has become the latest artist to carry her forward. He has changed the medium, and finally added something new to the image of my ghost, my mysterious girl.

She has always had a face.

Now she has a story.